Praise for

*Reunion*

"Reunion by P.W. Walters is one of the most gripping and poignant books centered on bullying and sexual abuse, especially of males. I'm sure writing this story was a challenge, one which P.W. Walters conquered masterfully. Prepare yourself to also be challenged, not just by the content of Reunion, but by its thought-provoking truths."

**— Viga Bloand for *Readers' Favorite***

"From paradoxes to life purposes, *Reunion* is no light read, but toes the line between Stephen King's *Carrie* and a novel of psychological suspense as Owen confronts the kinds of decisions that build, warp, and direct his character towards an almost inevitable (yet unpredictable, in many ways) outcome."

"*Reunion* is about finding love, facing loss, and ultimately learning how to view life on different terms. Owen's character is nicely drawn, and his dilemmas and their ultimate resolution will keep readers thinking long after the final, passionate moments which press together broken hearts in an outstanding, surprise conclusion to Owen's intense, gritty life journey."

**— D. Donovan, Senior Reviewer, *Midwest Book Review***

"The visceral abuse, bullying, and degradation Owen Crowley endures in this coming-of-age story make for painful reading. This revenge fantasy centers on a paragon of perfection whose tumultuous life story will evoke readers' sympathies."

**— *Publishers Weekly/BookLife Review***

"In P. W. Walters's harrowing novel *Reunion*, a young man tries to recover from his childhood traumas. *Reunion* is a tragic novel about a young man marked by abuse who, in his adulthood, is still trying to learn to live for himself."

**— *Foreword/Clarion Reviews***

"A Utah boy who survives horrific child sexual abuse fails to put it behind him as he matures into a brilliant, caustic, verbose teenager in this debut coming-of-age novel."

"He's a complex, magnetic character, and the author skillfully dissects Owen's inner turmoil as he deploys his arrogant intellect to cover up his insecurities and ward off the emotional connections he fears and craves."

— *Kirkus Review*

# REUNION

Abuse has no limits . . .
but neither does love.

# P. W. WALTERS

IZZARD INK
PUBLISHING

IZZARD INK PUBLISHING
PO Box 522251
Salt Lake City, Utah 84152
www.izzardink.com

LIBRARY OF CONGRESS CONTROL NUMBER: 2019941610

*Designed by Alissa Rose Theodor*
*Cover Design by Andrea Ho*
*Cover Images: Lilawa/Shutterstock*

First Edition December 3, 2019

Contact the author at info@izzardink.com

Hardback ISBN: 978-1-64228-032-6
Paperback ISBN: 978-1-64228-031-9
eBook ISBN: 978-1-64228-030-2

*For Dennis Jurgens*
*1961-1965*


*And for all those children who have survived abuse,*
*and for those who have not, this story is written.*

*As every student should have skillful educators, every writer should have a skillful editor. I was blessed to have had three—Margaret Diehl, Kathy Cadigan, and Aimee Elliott. A heartfelt thank you to each of them for their counsel, candor, and keen eyes.*

# *Author's Note:*

This is a story about child abuse and the permanent and ineradicable effects it creates. It is based on true events. For legal, moral, and personal reasons, all character names and names of certain establishments are fictitious. Certain characters are composites of actual individuals, and certain incidents are constructions for thematic purposes. However, all content bridged to and centered around child abuse, be it clinical or personal, is not fictitious. It is true and real.

# *Prologue*

Every minute of every day child abuse occurs. It has many faces; it goes by many names: physical abuse, verbal abuse, psychological abuse, and sexual abuse. Abuse is a blind bird of prey: it sees neither rank nor race, gender nor age. It cares not if a child sleeps in a canopied crib or on a soiled carpet. Its talons can reach any child, at any time, in any place.

Most abused children survive their abuse. They grow beyond it. But they never grow beyond the memories of the abuse. They never forget. They may try to push the memories away, pack them away, or even throw them away, but the memories never truly go away. They are there, waiting. It is these permanent memories, these iron manacles of the mind, that will shape them into the adults they will become. Some will be consumed with insecurities, others with fears, others with compulsions, others with addictions, and others with rage. Of them all, the adult consumed with rage is the one to watch, the one to fear....

*"Truth is stranger than fiction, because fiction is obligated to stick to possibilities. Truth isn't."*

MARK TWAIN

# Part 1

# CHAPTER 1

## *A Bad Seed*

*"When sorrows come, they come not single spies, but in battalions."*

WILLIAM SHAKESPEARE

I have always possessed the faculty of exceptional recall. I did not deserve this faculty, yet I was given it all the same. Events of which I was a part I have particularly excellent recollection. These recollections are not fragmentary images of the events; rather, they are vivid and detailed canvases of the experiences.

My name is Owen. Owen Nicholas Langley. My first and middle name came from film stars. This, my mother told me while sitting on a wide smear of my father's blood on our living room couch. Who those stars were she did not say.

My parents were poor. My father was a custodian for a local high school, my mother a charwoman for a bargain motel.

The first memories of my life were not terrible; they certainly weren't good, but they weren't terrible. It was later—not much later—that my memories took on the color of night. Those memories were of pain, beatings, torture, and blood. My blood. Sometimes the blood came from my face, other times from my chest, other times from my back, and then others from my legs and feet.

I had one sibling, a sister. Her name was Susan. She was eleven and a half when she died. I was almost five. She drowned while trying to save my life.

The year was 1965. It was Saturday, May 22.

My parents took Susan and me to Millcreek Canyon, a popular place of escape for those who lived in the city. The streams in the eastern canyons were running unusually high and heavy that year. Parents were warned not to let their children play in them, as the fast runoff could easily take a child away.

After my father parked the car, Susan and I raced for the stream. More for Susan's safety than mine, my parents warned us to be careful around the water. At first, I stood back and simply watched the stream dive, tumble, and roll. Then I moved closer to its edge. It was a hot day, so the white, rushing current looked cooling and inviting. I pulled off my Keds and gingerly dipped my feet into the water. The fast-moving stream was so frigid my heart nearly stopped. But my feet quickly adjusted to the temperature, which gave me the confidence to venture farther in. As soon as I started walking, I lost my footing and went down. My head went under, and my left ear slammed against a jagged streambed rock. I knew instantly my ear had been cut. My fingers tried to grasp anything to prevent me from being pulled away, yet everything below the waterline was slimy and slippery, so my fingers easily slid away. My left kneecap made contact with a massive, granite promontory jutting into the freezing water from the south bank of the creek. The pain of the impact made me scream. Then I swallowed water—too much water. I choked, then gagged.

The terror of dying temporarily attenuated the solar flares of pain jetting from my knee.

I was being thrown around like a toy in a dog's mouth. Then, abruptly, something took hold of my shirt collar. This time it wasn't something from the creek. It was a hand. My head came out of the water, and I caught sight of my sister. Panic was carved into her gentle, young face. A smile took the place of fright when she saw my open eyes. I was alive. Battered—but alive. She pulled me onto dry ground and hugged me. Then panic suddenly seized her face again. The earth on which she was kneeling gave way like a sinkhole, and she fell into the water. I was safe; but now she was the one in peril. The freezing, charging snowmelt kidnapped her without mercy. She was gone.

Though bleeding and badly injured, I ran after her, but the current was swifter than my legs. I knew, even at age four, that trying to rescue her on my own would be futile, so I ran back to my parents. Since the stream ran parallel to the road, we could quickly get to her by car.

When my mother and father saw me, they screamed in anguish and shouted, "Where's your sister!"

"I fell in and Susan pulled me out. But then she fell in. The water took her away."

Without another word, my parents bolted for the car and sped down the twisting canyon road, leaving me alone by the picnic table.

Minutes turned into hours as I waited for my parents to return. The setting sun was beginning to paint the sky scarlet, and the hour was turning the air cold. I had neither a coat nor sweater to warm me. When we had arrived at the spot where my parents wanted to picnic, it was only one in the afternoon and far too warm for any clothing other than a short-sleeved shirt.

I was beside myself with guilt and worry over my sister. But after the sun had surrendered itself to the evening, my worry turned from my sister to me. The clothes I was wearing, though no longer soaked, were damp. The polar-like air had made them colder than they would have been had they been dry. My body was shaking from the falling temperature. I knew if I didn't get warm soon, the cold would most likely take my life. There were several trees lining the stream, so I chose the largest I could see and sat up against it. At least my back would have some shelter from the cold. I then elbowed my legs up to my chin and wrapped my arms around my bare legs to give them some cover. I didn't want to, but I started to cry. I was alone, frightened, and cold.

Like an advancing fog, nighttime quickly rolled into the narrow, winding canyon. Soon I was surrounded by inky blackness. The darkness frightened me even more, and the fear intensified the pain from the biting air.

Headlights from a passing car shined on my face. I shielded my eyes from the blinding beams. My heart leapt—my parents had returned! Then my heart fell again as I saw the car vanish into the night.

I laid my forehead on my knees, and again I began to cry.

Moments later, I heard footfalls.

"Little boy, what are you doing out here all alone?"

I lifted my head. Standing in front of me was a tall woman. She was pointing a long, silver-ribbed flashlight at me whose beam was so bright I had to turn away. Immediately, the woman pointed the flashlight to the ground.

A short, heavyset man was standing next to the woman.

"My sister fell in the water, and my parents went to look for her," I answered, my voice trembling.

Looking down at me in fright, the woman asked, "What happened to you?"

"I fell in the water too."

"Go get that extra blanket out of the back of the car," the woman told the man.

The man rushed over to a long station wagon parked off the side of the road. He came back quickly with a thick, dark blanket. The woman took it from the man, and she wrapped it around me. The warmth instantly made my tears stop.

"Thank you," I said to the woman, looking up at her.

"What's your name, little boy?" she asked.

"Owen."

"How old are you?"

"Four."

"What kind of parents abandons their kid out in the cold woods at night?" the man asked. "What do you think we should do?"

"We can't just leave him out here in the cold. Let's get him in the car and get the heater going. We'll wait for his parents to come back."

"What if they don't?" the man speculated.

"I guess we'll have to take him to the police. They'll know what to do."

The woman knelt down in front of me. "Owen, we'd like to take you over to our car and put you in the front seat so you can get warm. Is that okay?"

I nodded. I could sense they weren't going to harm me.

The woman stood and extended her hand. I took it without hesitation, and the three of us walked over to the station wagon. The man opened the rear passenger door and slid into the car. The woman opened the front passenger door for me, and I crawled onto a supple-soft bench seat. She gently shut my door and walked around to the driver's side. As soon as she situated herself behind the wheel, she started the engine. In seconds, warm, comforting air enfolded me. I became very sleepy.

"May I go to sleep?" I asked the lady.

"Of course you may," she replied.

I laid my head on the middle section of the seat, and my eyes closed instantly.

The woman stroked my hair as I lay there.

My mother never did this. Neither did my father. Neither of them liked to touch me. They probably thought I never took notice of it, but I did. Susan, on the other hand, was always receiving their touch. They would kiss her and hug her and tell her how much they loved her. But I didn't hold this against her, for she didn't want to be the chosen child. She wanted them to treat us equally.

I sensed early on that Susan was the apple of my parents' eye. Some parents think children haven't the intelligence or perception to pick up on favoritism. But they do. There was always pride and joy in my parents' eyes when they looked at Susan. They always smiled adoringly at her. Never once did they smile at me. The portions she received at the dinner table were always more than mine. Her food was always arranged neatly on her plate, almost symmetrically, whereas my food looked as if it had been thrown on the plate from across the room. But when my parents weren't looking, Susan would slip me extras from her plate. When my sister was younger and brought home clay figurines she had molded in art class or drawings she had made during recess, my parents would fawn and gush effusively over her creations. But when I drew pictures, my parents said nothing. They didn't even glance at them. My parents read to Susan every night before she went to sleep. They didn't even say *"good night"* to me. When my tummy was upset or when I had a fever, it was Susan who made me feel better. Yes, Susan clearly was the apple of my parents' eye. I was the worm who slithered out of it.

A banging sound awakened me. I sat straight up. I was still in the front seat of the station wagon. The overhead light came on. The woman next to me rolled down her window. I could tell it was very late.

"Have you seen a dirty, little kid around here?" my mother asked hatefully. Then she saw me sitting on the front seat. "There you are, you little bastard! Get out of there and get over here!"

The woman looked over at me and swallowed. "We found him sitting all alone in the dark, shivering," she said to my mother.

"Pity you didn't find him dead! He could give his sister some company. *I said*, get out of the car, you little puke!"

Fearfully, I opened the door and walked around to the driver's side of the car.

I didn't even see it coming. My mother hit me in the face so hard my body left the ground and flew back. My face made contact with the ground first. I tasted blood, and my left cheek was on fire.

In unison, the couple shouted, "What are you doing!" They leapt out of the car and raced for me.

"Your sister's dead, you piece of crap!" my mother screamed at me.

My father came over to me and pulled me up off the ground by my hair. The other man, whose name I didn't even know, punched my father in the stomach. My father collapsed to the ground.

Like lightning, my mother kicked the man between his legs. With a deep scream, he buckled and fell to his knees. She then kicked him in the forehead. His body recoiled, and he landed on his side. He lay there, motionless. I thought he was dead. The woman—presumably the man's wife—dashed over to her fallen husband and started screaming at my parents. My mother, being the loyal wife she was, went to my father and helped him to his feet. He held his gaunt stomach with both hands.

Glaring at me, my mother ordered, "Get in the car!"

Dutifully, I entered the back seat of our rusty, drafty, and noisy 1951 Plymouth Cranbrook. I was both hurting and numb—hurting from my mother's slap and numb from her words: "*Your sister's dead.*"

How could Susan be dead? How? Where was she? Her body was not in the car. Was she in the trunk? Did they just leave her where they had found her? Surely, they wouldn't have done that.

After my parents were back in the car, I timidly asked, "Where's Susan?"

"*Were you not listening!*" my mother spat. "She's dead! Thanks to you!"

"I'm sorry," I said, crying. "I didn't mean to kill her."

Her arm flew over the seat, and she gave the side of my face the back of her hand. "Shut up!"

The strike almost made me lose consciousness.

My parents wept all the way home. More than once my father had to pull over. He was so overcome with grief his body convulsed in my mother's arms.

I did not want to be hit again, so I kept completely silent, even though on the inside I was dissolving. My sister was really gone.

When we arrived home, I sprang from the car and dashed to our front door. I wanted to get to my room and hide from my parents. Our apartment was on the ground level, and it was the only one in the building that exited directly outside. The other apartments were accessed through a long hallway.

My father slowly walked to our front door and pushed me aside when he got there. He unlocked the door and told my mother to go in. When I took a step forward to follow her, he stopped me with his hand. "You're stayin' outside tonight," he said. "Your sister's in a refrigerator right now—stone-cold and alone. Just like you're gonna be tonight. You're gonna feel exactly what she's feeling. If I find you dead in the morning, that'll be okay by me. I'll throw your worthless carcass in the garbage can—right where it belongs. If you run away, that'll be even better. Either way, you won't be missed." With those words, he closed the door and locked it.

When I awoke the next morning, the sun was peeking through a cluster of leafy, nutant willow branches. I should have passed away during the night, but I didn't. Sometimes it takes very little to kill the human body; other times it takes everything. The night before, I had taken refuge under a breezeway of a nearby house. Remembering what I had done in the canyon, I wrapped my arms tightly around my chest, curled my body into a tight ball and got as close to the side of the house as I could. I didn't think I would sleep, but soon my eyes became heavy, and they closed. Before sleep took over, I thought of Susan and all that had happened that afternoon. I so hoped I would never have to go through another day like that one. That was my hope. But hope is as evanescent as a mist…it hovers, and then disappears.

Susan was gifted with both beauty and brilliance. She was the brightest star in her class, and her report cards were always cornucopias of A's and praise. Glowing comments from her teachers always decorated the tops of the papers she wrote. Easily, she would have been chosen homecoming queen and valedictorian had she lived to those ages. Where her dazzling beauty came from was a mystery to me, for both of my parents were head-to-heel homely. My father was angular and hunchbacked, with a face so lined it made a sheet of wadded paper look like a sheet of glass. My mother was diminutive in both height and frame, with a visage so bland it made a stick of chalk look like a stick of gold. It was a wonder she ever got a man to notice her, let alone impregnate her. Maybe the glamour gene skipped a generation in my family; maybe it was my grandparents whom Susan mirrored. But I would never know this for certain, for I never knew my grandparents or saw any photographs of them.

Susan had radiant, golden-brown hair; her teeth were stunningly white; her complexion was flawless, and her heart was without hate in any measure. She was truly perfect. Why my parents loved her so was not a question that demanded operose rumination: she was everything they were not. She was the only thing of value in their empty and insignificant lives.

But why wasn't I? What was it about me—before Susan's death—that prevented them from loving me?

My parents did not let me attend Susan's funeral. They locked me in my room for the day. After her death, I was forbidden to speak her name in front of them, and they refused to speak her name in front of me, but I knew her face was all they could see.

Before Susan's death, I knew my parents didn't want me. I didn't know why—I just knew. After Susan's death, their unconcealed apathy morphed into uninhibited antipathy. They hated every cell in my being, and they had no unease about letting me know this. Oddly, they didn't show this contempt until after I was asleep. Before then, I was left alone; they didn't even speak to me. But after I went to sleep, this was when I would feel their teeth, their hate. They both would slip into my room, not turning on the naked bulb hanging from the ceiling, and close the door. One would stand by the push-button light switch while the other would tiptoe through the dirty blackness over to my bed and awaken me. The one standing by the door would turn on the light, and the night would begin. They seemed to take delight in what they did to my body, for they always smiled, even laughed, while they made its nerves catch fire and its flesh bleed. Their nocturnal visits were always random, never routine. Two or three nights would pass with never a sound from them. Then, for three or four nights in tandem, they would sneak in, with their toys in hand, and make me their playmate.

My face, chest, torso, and abdomen were never without contusions; some were so dark they almost looked black. Breathing was never easy. Neither was walking. I wondered, even as a small boy, if I had any ribs that were *not* broken.

A bat was my parents' toy of choice, but they appreciated other playthings as well. Sometimes my father would have my mother sit on my stomach while he dropped a hammer onto my kneecaps and shins and chest. Sometimes they would lash my chest and back with a notched extension cord. They had cut the PVC insulation every few inches and then pulled out some of the wiring. When the cord struck me, the shard-sharp fangs of copper wiring would slice my skin like pieces of glass. Other times, they would make me stand naked in front of them while they would whip my torso with a long strand of fishing line plaited with thin, lead sinkers. (Years later, I would wonder why they hadn't just gone all the way and made a cat-o'-nine-tails—they would have had nine times the pleasure.) Each time the line and sinkers would strike my body, I would scream as my flesh tore open. So that my screams would never be heard by our neighbors, they would place duct tape over my mouth and then wrap it twice around my head. In the mornings, I would scream into my sheetless and bloodstained mattress as I pulled the tape from the back of my head. Tufts of bloodied, brown hair would be bound to the viscous side of the tape.

Though not their favorite, another toy my parents found gratifying was a mousetrap. Despite my tears and muffled pleadings, they would set my feet in the mousetrap and tease it until the kill bar snapped down on my toes.

When my parents entered my room with beer and honey, I knew blood would not flow, but agony would. My parents would tell me to get off my bed, undress and stand next to the window. They would take my place on the bed, tell me to extend my arms and not move. For hours, in front of a blanket-covered window, I would stand—like a man nailed to a crucifix—and watch them down bottle after bottle of Pabst. Exhaustion and pain would eventually send me to the floor. After I collapsed, my father would walk over to me, and, as I lay on my soiled and pungent carpet, drip honey over my nude body. "It's time to feed your friends," he would say. Too weakened to rise, I would remain on the floor and quickly fall asleep. The next morning, I would still be on the floor, but I wouldn't be alone: moving over the sequins of honey dotting my body would be hundreds of small, black ants.

After each visit from my parents, they would turn off the light, depart from my room, close the door and hook it from the outside. The hook, or so they believed, would not come off until they needed me for work...or play. (Fortuitously, the doorframe was out of plumb, which made it possible for me to slip the end of a wire hanger through the breach and flip up the hook.)

I was given neither food nor water, and I wasn't permitted to use the bathroom. When my parents were home, I would slip out my window and do what I needed to do. When they weren't home, I would make use of the bathroom in the apartment. During the warm months, I would drink from a mineral-caked garden spigot in the back of the apartment house. In the cold months, I would get my water from the cleanest snow I could find. I never took water from the kitchen or bathroom, for fear I might accidentally leave some trace of my presence. If my parents discovered I had been letting myself out of my room, I knew I would face a punishment without equal.

Neighbors' table-trash and pantry toss-outs were my meals. People were thoughtlessly (and thankfully) wasteful with their food. They threw away bread, cereal, peanut butter, jam, cheese, cookies, apples, bananas, and all sorts of fruits and vegetables simply because they had mold or a bruise or two. Other men's trash was this little boy's treasure.

Endless questions traveled through my head during those months after Susan's death. But there were two that kept coming back. Did it ever transit through the disfigured minds of my parents why I didn't die? And how would they explain the many scars and cuts on my body once I started school? They couldn't keep me locked away forever. Or maybe they could. Adults, I was learning, were capable of anything.

The Christmas before Susan's death was unnaturally nice. My parents—for some unfathomable reason—were generous, even magnanimous, to me. From them, not Santa (for there is no Santa, they told me), I was given Tinkertoys, Lincoln Logs, Legos, and a G.I. Joe. However, all of these gifts were placed not under the tree, but against the wall next to it. The ring of space under the tree was reserved for Susan's presents, which voyaged well beyond its tartan skirt. How my parents afforded this sea of largesse for my sister and me I hadn't a clue. Maybe he had taken from the cafeteria register at the school and she from the guests at the motel. Anything was possible…especially with them.

The Christmas after Susan's death was the polar opposite of the one before it. That year, there was no tree in our apartment, no presents, no decorations, no holiday music, and no crayoned Santa Clauses taped to the living room window for passersby to see. But more noticeably, there were no smiles in our tiny home. Only pain.

*Friday, December 17, 1965.*
*A day of lasts.*

I heard crying coming from beyond my door. Both of my parents were weeping. For a brief moment, I felt sorry for them. Why were they crying? Then I remembered there was something unique about this day…but I couldn't remember what it was, which was odd for me, for I never forgot anything. I heard the front door close. As they did every morning, my parents left for work at precisely seven-fifteen. (They might have been anthropoid dragons, but they were punctual and committed anthropoid dragons.)

If my parents were home for the day, I would hunt for food while they were still asleep. If they had to go to work, I would start right after they left. But on this day, I was sick to my stomach, so I decided to start my search later. Around noon, I left my room and made my way to the garbage cans. (It was a messy job searching for food, even dangerous. The day after Thanksgiving, while combing through a can glutted with holiday throwaways, I accidentally slid my left arm over a broken mayonnaise jar. The long cut bled unceasingly. I wasn't worried about my parents finding out—for the cut would simply look a close copy to all the others—I was worried about not being able to stop the bleeding. But after a lengthy compression, the cut clotted. My parents never saw the laceration, or, if they did, never commented on it. After the day with the mayonnaise jar, I was constantly tempted to take food from our kitchen, but each time I stopped myself. I couldn't risk getting caught. And yet, robbing garbage cans carried its own risk. If a neighbor saw me going through the cans, they would ask me who I was, and I would tell them, for what else could I say? They would then tell the police, who, in turn, would tell my parents. If that happened, I would be in for the longest—and possibly last—night of my life.) The air was ruthlessly cold that mid-December morning, but the sky above was cloudless and magically blue. I cautiously searched through the badly dented metal cans for anything edible. I didn't want to be too eager in my scout for food, lest I come across another broken jar. While sifting through the rancid castoffs, I heard something. Something whimpering. Because it was daylight, it would be easy to discover what was causing the pitiful sound. I began looking around the cans. Cowering next to the last can was the tiniest dog I had ever seen. It had adorably large ears, with alert but very sad eyes. Its cream-colored coat was darkened with dirt, and small pieces of ice were cemented to two very delicate and frail legs. It was shivering uncontrollably. I felt my heart break for the tiny creature. It crouched in fear and turned its small face away as I bent down to pick it up.

"I'm not going to hurt you, little one," I said softly. "I promise."

It slowly turned its face to me as I lifted it into my arms. It was homeless, friendless, and dangerously thin.

Frantically, I searched the trash for some food for the little dog, not caring if I got cut again. Finally, I found some edible items: three half-eaten hot dogs, an unopened can of yams, and a large cube of cheddar cheese. Small freckles of mold dotted one end.

With dog and food in hand, I ran back to the apartment and locked the door. Quickly, I washed off the hot dogs and removed the mold from the cheese. I tore the hot dogs and cheese into small pieces and placed them on a plate. The little dog, a male, was up on his hind legs and barking happily at the sight of his meal. When I put the plate down on the floor, the little dog, without hesitation, ate and ate and ate. While he enjoyed his lunch, I opened the can of yams, smelled them to make sure they weren't spoiled, and spooned a couple onto his plate. These, too, he eagerly swallowed.

After he had finished, I cleaned the plate and erased all signs of the food I had given him. I couldn't let my parents know I had him: they would surely kill him, or, at the very least, throw him back outside.

I picked him up, put him in my arms and placed him in the kitchen sink. Carefully, I ran lukewarm water over his back and slowly removed the dirt embedded in his hair. It took some time, but I was finally able to make him clean again. He didn't fuss or squirm while I bathed him. After drying him and the sink and the plate from which he had eaten, I took him into the living room and played with him on the couch. Over and over, he lay on his side and held out his legs so I could kiss his tummy, chest, and the side of his face. I wondered if all dogs did this. He was so affectionate. Often, he would leap up and lick my face or take my finger into his mouth and playfully chew on it.

I picked him up, and the two of us went over to the closet. On the closet floor was a set of encyclopedias stored in a box. I wanted to find out what kind of dog this was. Without much searching, I found his breed. He was a Chihuahua.

"What name would you like, little guy?" I asked him.

He tilted his head in bewilderment.

"How about...Yogidog?"

He barked excitedly and licked my chin. There was my answer. Yogi Bear was my favorite cartoon, so Yogidog would be his name.

"Yogidog it is," I said and kissed the top of his head, which felt like silk. "I sure do love you, little one."

I looked at the clock: it was 2:55. My father arrived home at three o'clock every day! I needed to hide my Yogidog somewhere in my room, and fast!

I ran into my room, replaced the hook on the door with the hanger I kept under my bed, and put my new, little friend in the closet. "Now don't make a sound, okay? I won't be gone long. I love you." I slowly and quietly closed the door, but not all the way. I didn't want him to leave him in the dark. I knew what it was like to be alone and surrounded by blackness.

Sitting on my bed, I waited for my father to unhook my door. Every afternoon, immediately after he arrived home, he would let me out of my room to get him his beers. I would go out into the kitchen, open the refrigerator, take out five beers, open them, set them on an aluminum TV tray in front of our threadbare couch and wait to see if he wanted anything else. If he didn't, I would return to my room.

Shortly after three that afternoon, my father opened my door. Without a word, he went into the living room, sat down on the far end of the couch and waited for his beers. When he got them, he downed them feverishly. This was most peculiar, even for him. Normally, he would turn on our black-and-white Zenith and drink his beers slowly. This day, he didn't turn on the TV and, while he drank, stared straight ahead. Something had happened, though I didn't dare ask.

In less than five minutes, he had finished all five beers. He went to our cracked and yellowing Frigidaire and took out four more beers. Again, he walked straight past me, sat down on the couch and began drinking.

Just then, a piercing bark came from my bedroom.

"What the hell was that!" my father thundered.

My mouth went dry and my heart quickened.

*No, please! Please don't let this happen!*

My bedroom door inched open, and Yogidog ran over to me and stood on his back legs for me to pick him up. I did so.

"Who the hell do you think you are bringing an animal into this house!" my father roared.

"Please, Daddy. Please let me keep him. Please." I started to cry. I was holding Yogidog tightly against my face. He was licking the tears off of my face. "He won't get in the way, I promise. Please don't hurt him. I love him. Please don't hurt him."

My father arose from the couch and staggered over to me. He looked down at me with glassy eyes. "What have I told you? Don't *ever* call me *Daddy*! It's *Mr. Langley*!"

"I'm sorry, Mr. Langley. Please don't hurt him. Please."

"I'm not going to hurt him," my father said with a reassuring tone.

I wiped the remaining tears off of my face and smiled up at my father with gratitude.

"I'm not going to hurt him," my father said again. "I'm going to kill him." In the wink of an eye, my father thrust his hand at my face, grabbed Yogidog by his scruff and, with one swift torque of his hands, broke his neck. Yogidog yelped loudly, then fell limp. My father dropped him on the floor in front of me and then stumbled back to the couch.

I looked down at my little one. His once-happy eyes were now still and inanimate, his little tongue was hanging out of his mouth, and his tiny chest was no longer moving.

I fell to my knees and buried my face in his side. I couldn't move. I couldn't breathe. Every part of me felt like it was dying.

*I'm so sorry, Yogidog. I'm so sorry.*

"It hurts when someone kills something you love, doesn't it?" I heard my father say.

"Look at me, you little rodent!" my father demanded.

I looked up at my father, my body so heavy with pain I wished he would kill me as he had killed my Yogidog.

"Get over here, boy!" he ordered.

I no longer cared what he did to me. I wanted him to kill me too. For the first time in my life, I went to him without fear. I wanted him to end my life.

"Do you know what today is, you little piece of filth?" he asked me. "It's your sister's birthday. Did you know that? No, I guess not—you were too busy with your ugly, little rat over there. Do you have any idea how much I *hate* you? Do you?"

I nodded.

"And acourse, bein' the dummy you are, you prob'ly don't even know why. Well, I'm gonna tell you why. Before I check out, I'm gonna tell you."

I knew why he hated me: I had caused my sister's death. Both he and my mother made it clear why they hated me each time they came into my room.

"You're not mine, boy," he began. "Not one bit a you. Round about six years ago, me and your mother wasn't gettin' along too good, *especially in the bedroom*—if you know what I mean," he said with a misshapen smile. "Seems your mom needed more attention than I was givin' her at the time. So she paid lots of visits to the bars here in town. Met some men all too willin' to give her some attention.

She didn't sleep with them, though. She just teased them...like most women do. Seems one man she teased, she teased a little too far. He raped her in the basement of one of them bars. *Hello, Owen.* We didn't want you, but we couldn't afford to have you cut out, so, nine months later, out you popped, alive and well. We was gonna give you away, but Susan fell madly in love with you while you was still in your mother's belly. What Susan wanted, Susan got. I'm proud of that. We gave her anything she wanted...including *you*. We couldn't give to ourselves, but by Jupiter, we was gonna give to her. Do you know that if you never came along, she'd be alive today? You wouldn't be here, and she would. You know what you are, boy? You're a rape-child. A sin-child. A bad seed. A bastard. A bastard if there ever was one. You killed my daughter, you lousy, good-for-nothin' pissant! You ruined our lives!"

He moved forward on the couch and slipped his right hand under the wafer-thin, dusty-rose cushion on which he was sitting. His hand quickly emerged, and in it was a long-nosed revolver.

I looked at the gun calmly, without fright. I knew the gun was for me. I was glad. I wanted to die. I was only five years of age...yet I felt so old, so worn-out. I closed my eyes in acceptance and capitulation, waiting for the bullet to enter me.

A moment later, a deafening explosion stabbed my ears. The sound was so intense it pushed me back like a punch from a giant fist. From the floor, I opened my eyes and saw that my father was no longer sitting. Half of his body was lying on the couch, and the other half was hanging over it. Suddenly, his flaccid body fell to the floor, leaving a wide swath of blood on the center cushion of the couch.

Seconds later, another booming sound assaulted me. But this sound came from the front door: someone was pounding on it. Then the door flew open and a young woman whom I had never seen before stormed into the room. She gasped when she saw my father. She cupped her hands over her mouth and turned away. A moment later, she turned back to my father. Then to me.

Blankly, I stared at her.

"Little boy, are you all right?"

I didn't answer.

"What happened here?"

"He didn't love me," I said mechanically. "He loved my sister. He killed my Yogidog. I wanted him to kill me, but he didn't. He killed himself, but he wouldn't kill me. Why wouldn't he kill me?"

The woman stared at me in disbelief. It was obvious what she was thinking: *What five-year-old talks like this?*

*This* five-year-old.

"You stay right here, you understand?" she said. "I'm going for some help." She ran out of the apartment.

On my knees, I went over to my Yogidog. I picked him up and held him against my face.

"What are you doing out of your room!" my mother bellowed from the open front door. "And why is the door wide open in the dead of winter!" She paused, and her eyebrows dipped. "What is that you're holding?" she asked with a scowl. She turned and saw my father on the floor. Her scream should have made me shrink in fright, but it didn't. I didn't care anymore. She ran over to my father and tried to sit him up. His bloody head fell limp in her hands.

"What have you done!" she shrieked. She bolted up from the floor and charged at me. She hit my face with her fist and then kicked my ribs. I felt the blasts of pain...but I didn't care. She then kicked me again...and again...and again.

"Stop it! Stop it!" shouted the woman who had come in earlier. "You're going to kill him!" The woman was trying desperately to pull my mother away from me. Then, two men appeared out of nowhere. My mother, though small, could be a frightening force. The two men discovered this as they tried to hold her back from me.

"He killed my husband! He killed my husband!" my mother yelled, still straining madly to get at me.

"He didn't kill him!" the woman shouted at my mother. "Your husband killed himself!"

My mother went still. "What?" Her voice was barely audible.

"He killed himself."

"He wouldn't do that. Why would he do that? Why would he do this to me?"

"I don't know. But the boy didn't do it. Look at him—he's just a little boy."

Though my mother was now quiescent, the men kept their hold on her.

The woman knelt next to me. She looked with sadness at my lifeless Yogidog. She kissed my forehead and said, "Everything is going to be okay. My name is Karen. I live upstairs. I'm going to stay right here with you until the police come. I'm not going to let your mother hurt you anymore." She was a young woman with silky, red hair and the softest skin I had ever seen…even softer than Susan's.

The apartment became as quiet as a forest in winter. It seemed everyone on Earth had vanished, except those in our bloody and dirty apartment.

The sound of sirens broke the thick silence.

Multiple vehicles with revolving red beacons affixed to their tops stopped on the street outside our front door. Soon, people dressed in all types of uniforms were entering our foul-smelling apartment.

After my father was removed, a middle-aged woman under a white, pillbox hat and warmed by a pale-green serge coat with huge, round buttons entered the apartment. She came over to where I was sitting and knelt down next to me.

"Hello there," she said evenly. "My name is Donna. Can you tell me yours?"

"Owen. This is Yogidog."

She looked at my dog and tried to smile. She turned her attention to the other woman next to me. "I'm Donna Mills. Are you a relative?"

"No, I live upstairs. My name is Karen Tozzoli. I'm the one who called the police."

"Did he see it happen?"

"I think so."

"Terrible," she said, shaking her head. She then at looked at me intently, oddly. "Owen, may I lift up your shirt for a moment?"

I nodded.

She carefully lifted up my frayed pullover. Both women winced when they saw my chest, stomach, and sides. Both women shot their eyes to my mother, who was staring at the place where my father's body had been. The woman named Donna shook her head and tightened her lips.

"Have you or anyone else in the building heard or noticed anything suspicious going on in this apartment?" Donna asked Karen.

"No, but then I've only been living here a few weeks," Karen replied. "I didn't even know this boy was living here. The parents are really standoffish. What are you going to do with him?" Karen asked, dropping her eyes to me.

"First, we'll get him in for a complete physical," Donna answered. "Then some food. He's seriously malnourished. Then we'll place him in an orphanage until we locate any relatives, assuming there are any. Failing that, we'll try to foster him out."

"What about *her*?" Karen asked contemptuously, nodding to my mother.

"If I had my way, she'd be shot."

"I need to sit down," said my mother, looking at the uniformed officer standing next to her. "Please."

The officer looked at Donna for permission.

After pausing, Donna nodded.

My mother walked over to the couch and sat down on the middle cushion, in my father's blood.

I had seen some strange things in my short life, but that was one of the strangest. Why would anyone sit in another's blood? It wasn't like she couldn't see it. Everyone in the room saw it. Why would she do such a thing?

My mother looked at me. "What was your doggy's name?" she asked dulcetly.

I couldn't believe my ears. It was the first time my mother had ever used a tender tone with me.

"Yogidog," I answered.

"I'm sorry he died. He looks like he was a nice doggy."

Why? Why was she being so sweet when she had never been before? Was it an act for the other people in the room? Theater to convince them she wasn't a monster? Or was she, for the first time ever, actually seeing *me* rather than Susan?

"I think Susan would have liked him," she said with a brittle smile. "I don't think I'll ever see you again, Owen. After you was born, we—me and your dad—wanted to take to you, for Susan's sake, but we couldn't. We even named you after two of our favorite movie stars, just like we did with Susan. We kept you because of her. We tried to love you. We did. But we couldn't. It just wasn't there. There wasn't anything about you to love. When I look at you, all I feel is hate. You never should have been born."

*"Get her out of here!"* Donna snapped at the officer who had been standing next to my mother.

Karen placed her hand on my back. "Owen, would it be okay if I took Yogidog?" she asked softly, her eyes brimming with tears, her face like a mirror, reflecting my own emptiness. "I think he would like to be in a place where he can sleep...and be happy."

I kissed Yogidog's small, angel-soft forehead. I stroked his gentle face and porcelain paws. "Good-bye, Yogidog. Sleep good, okay? Have lots of happy dreams. I love you, little one. I'm sorry I let you die. Please don't ever forget me."

I handed him to Karen. Her face was wet with tears.

So was Donna's.

I was removed from the apartment shortly after my mother was taken away. I would never see it again. I so hoped life would treat me kindly in the future. But hope, like smoke, disappears as quickly as it appears. The days and years ahead of me, I knew, would be anything but kind.

Three weeks after my father's death, my mother hanged herself.

# CHAPTER 2

# *The Devil Never Dies*

*"There is a thing worse than death. That thing is life."*

RACHAEL ERBIN

The term *orphanage* is much nicer than the actual institution… at least it was in generations past. In former years, an orphanage could be a place of loneliness, isolation, torment, and even physical asperity. In some ways, it could be far worse than the place from which a child had come.

I was placed in Greenwood Children's Home—an imposing and shadowy two-story structure clad in dismal red brick. Built in 1928, it was originally Johnson-Mead Elementary School.

Most of my time at the children's home was spent on a sagging twin bed. All I wanted to do was sleep. My closest companion was a stuffed animal I had spirited away from the home's toy collection. Though I took the toy without permission, I was not told to put it back. The stuffed animal was a little, white dog. I called him Yogidog.

Most children in such a situation would have longed for a family: brothers, sisters, parents, and grandparents. I didn't. All I wanted was my first Yogidog. But he was dead, gone forever. His memory haunted me; his end tortured me. One moment he was happy because of me, the next he was dead because of me.

The children at Greenwood did not have individual bedrooms. We slept in large, cavernous rooms on the second floor; the girls slept in one room, the boys in another. We were of different ages, histories, and ethnicities.

We ate our meals in a sizable room on the main floor. It must have been the lunchroom of the original school, for it had long tables, numerous chairs, and an immense kitchen. Most of the children complained about the lack of variety in the meals. I shared their view, but only partly: the meals *were* unvaried, but after what I had had—or *hadn't* had—anything, no matter how monotonous, was manna from above to me.

Our bodies were fed well...but our spirits and emotions were not. The staff, all women, except for the janitor—a frightening-looking man who always kept to himself—were aloof and cold. Perhaps this was their way of protecting themselves from getting too close to the children, for a child might be there one day and gone the next, never to be seen again. Or perhaps the orphanage was just a place to work, a place that handed them a paycheck every two weeks. I would not last long enough to find out.

The older children, seven and above, were put in structured classes during the daytime hours. The younger children, six and below, were put in less-structured settings during that time. Although they would be in classrooms like the older children, they could do whatever they pleased: color, finger-paint, put together puzzles, or play with the many toys provided by the home.

Some children, I came to find out, stay in orphanages for months, even years. My stay at Greenwood Children's Home lasted only five weeks. Why mine was so brief I learned only minutes after I was taken away from it. The foster parents who selected me did not pick me because I was special: they chose me because I was easy money. Foster parents were given a monthly stipend from the State to care for a child. If a child had perceptible damage, physical and/or emotional, he or she might not be selected by foster parents because the parents might not have the background or ability to deal with such a child. But if a child appeared emotionally stable—if he or she did not act up or act out—this child would be placed in foster care sooner than the other children. Since I appeared to fit within the brackets of the latter, I was quickly chosen. All my foster parents had to do was feed me and clothe me, and the remainder of the stipend would be theirs. I was easy money.

But I was also something else...something a child doesn't know exists until he is in the eye of it.

I made no friends at Greenwood; not with any of the other children and not with any of the staff. Not that I didn't want friends—I did; I just didn't know how to nurture friendships, or even initiate them. I didn't know how to relate to other children...on any level.

The children's home was staffed with a collection of women whose skin was as hard as timber. There was one woman who didn't even have skin—she had an exoskeleton. She was a towering arthropod who was as wide as she was tall. She always wore midnight-blue, matchstick-straight dresses. Glued to those dresses was the horrid stench of cigarette smoke. Her face was pasty and tight. She never smiled; or if she did, it must have been in private. If she had any children of her own, they must have run off as soon as their legs could carry them. Her name was Mrs. Constance. How she carried the prefix of *Mrs.* was beyond me. She was the headmistress of the facility. No one liked her, not even the employees who worked directly with her. Had the rubric *CEO* been in vogue at that time, she would have been called the "*Chief Executive Orifice.*"

I was sitting on the edge of my bed, holding my Yogidog for the last time. I knew I wouldn't be allowed to take him with me. I was waiting for my foster parents to arrive. Herman and Janice Wilson were their names. That's all I was told. On the main floor below, all of the children were in their classrooms. Beside me on my bed was a brown grocery sack. In it were the few pieces of clothing I owned. I was terribly cold.

I heard loud footsteps. I looked over. Mrs. Constance was walking toward me. Her heavy, black shoes sounded like thunderclaps as they made contact with the old hardwood floor.

Terror made me look away.

"*Get up*," she said coldly after her legs came to a stop.

I stood without looking at her face. All I could see was her massive, black-as-night Oxfords. And, of course, the odor of cigarettes filled the air like toxic fumes.

She grabbed my chin and forced my face upward so I would look at her.

"You're pathetic, you know that!" she hissed, her plosives intentionally accentuated. "It's no wonder your mother put a belt around her neck. I would have done the same had I a son like you! Look at you—you never talk, you never play with the other children, you never do anything except stay in this stupid bed, holding that stupid dog!" She grabbed my Yogidog out of my hands and threw him across the room. "You're just like him, that meritless son of mine. You'll probably end up marrying some black trailer trash too! It should have been *you* your father shot. I pity the Wilsons. I doubt you'll be with them very long. When they kick you out, don't you dare come back here! Understand!"

It was difficult to move my head with her hand clamping my face, but I managed to make a nod.

"Very good," she said, smiling proudly. Then she turned and left.

I was fearful she would return, so I didn't rescue my Yogidog. I sat back down on the bed and slid my hands under my legs to keep them warm. I closed my eyes and wished I could crawl back into bed and escape into the safety of dreams.

The paper bag next to me rustled. My eyes flashed open. Standing next to me was the school's janitor. He was gently burying my Yogidog deep inside the brown paper bag. Then he sat down next to me. "It'll be our little secret," he said. "I think he'll be happier with you than with us."

The custodian's name was Larry. He was a tall man and horrifyingly thin. He wasn't old, and he wasn't young; he was in the middle of his life. Dense, jet-black hair covered the tops of his arms. Like overgrown grass huddling next to a neglected berm, a thick tuffet of soot-colored hair was always crawling out from where his shirt buttons ended and his collar began. And he always looked like he needed a shave. Behind his back, the other children called him *"Hairy Larry."* Heavy, silver-framed glasses were always perched on a bony and bristly face. A small, navy-blue tattoo had been inscribed on the top of his left hand, near the wrist. The tattoo was three capital letters: *VCA*. I wanted to ask him what the letters meant, but I didn't dare. I feared he would take offense at my curiosity.

"Pay Mrs. Constance no mind," he said to me with a voice that had seen better days. "We all do what we do for a reason. She acts like she does prob'ly 'cause a somethin' done ta her long ago. So don't take it personal. I ain't excusin' her—I'm just explainin' her." He tried to smile. "Owen is it?"

I nodded.

"Yer gonna have a tough road ahead, Owen. But ya gotta be tough back…or ya won't survive. Just shy a my thirteenth birthday, my mom kicked me out. My dad was dead, and my mom said she didn't want me around no more. I had ta get some hard skin on me real quick. If I didn't, I'd die. Yer gonna meet lots a people in this world who'll tell ya what ta think, what ta do and how ya should do it. But ya gotta hold firm ta what ya are. Be yer own man. Be what yer heart tells ya ta be. Ya won't go wrong if ya do. Yer a good kid, Owen, I can see that. Ya ain't like the other scofflaws around here, but ya got a problem—ya got weakness. That'll kill ya quicker than anything. And ya got prettiness ta boot—that's gonna work against ya too. Just remember, if people think yer an easy mark, they'll take the hide right off ya—so you make 'em think twice."

He stood and extended his hand. I took it and we shook. He left the room as quietly as he had entered it.

Only a few of the younger children waved good-bye to me as I walked out of Greenwood Children's Home.

Children, like animals, can sense a person's feelings about them. Like an animal, I had grown invisible antennae to people: I could read them well. Very well. The moment I met the Wilsons, I sensed something was...not right.

The couple had no children of their own, so they took in foster children. Before meeting the Wilsons, I was told that they had had three foster children prior to me. I wondered why the three were no longer living with them. Had the children been bad?

At first sight, the Wilsons were an unremarkable couple: old, overweight, and graying. And their demeanor was as colorless as a corpse in a casket.

The Wilsons owned a 1966, tea-green Chrysler 300. We weren't two blocks from the children's home when Mr. Wilson pulled the car over to the side of the road. I saw a yellow arch out the windshield. It was a McDonald's. Mrs. Wilson turned around to face me; I was in the back seat, she was in the front. Even before she opened her mouth, she burrowed her eyes into mine.

"Here are the rules, little man," she laid out. "You do what we say and what we want, and we'll all get along like franks and beans. If you don't, you'll know hurt. *Or worse.* You do for us, and we'll do for you. You'll get bread for belly and a bed for your body—if you obey. If you don't, you'll cry like you've never cried before. Tit for tat, so to speak," she winked, and then she gave me a chilling smile that made me draw back into the seat. "The State's gonna take care of us for takin' care of you, so don't you dare cause us any trouble—or we'll cause trouble for you. We're not your mommy and your daddy. From here on out, you'll call us sir and ma'am. You'll call *everyone* sir and ma'am. You got that?"

I nodded.

"When the social worker asks you how you're being treated, you tell them you're being treated fine. If you tell them anything but that, we'll kill you. The last thing you'll know in this life will be tears. That's a promise. We've already killed one kid—one more won't make any difference."

I couldn't help it—I started to cry.

"Stop that! You need to grow up! You're a boy, not a baby!" Again, she threw me a chilling smile. "Speaking of *boys*...Mr. Wilson here likes them. He needs them. Personally, I don't need that bedroom stuff anymore, but Mr. Wilson does. He wants you to know he likes you. *A lot.* He's liked you from the start. He thinks you're terribly cute."

I didn't understand what she was talking about. Why was she one minute threatening to kill me and the next telling me how cute her husband thought I was?

Not once did Mr. Wilson turn around or say a word.

"When Mr. Wilson tells you to lower your pants, you do it," she said flatly. "If you don't...well, then, I'll have to make you cry. I don't think you'll want that. You ever been stuck with a lit cigarette?"

I wiped my eyes with my hands and shook my head.

"It hurts...real bad," she said tonelessly.

"On a similar topic," she went on, "it'll hurt and bleed the first few times he enters you, but your...*private place* will get used to it. You might even come to enjoy it," she said with a grin. "If you tell anyone—*anyone*—you'll wish you'd never been born." With those words, she threw her fist into my face.

I passed out.

I woke up in a basement. I knew it was a basement because its windows were small and high up. The basement was unfinished. Rust-coated pipes and knob-and-tube wiring were running through the exposed ceiling joists like slithering snakes.

I was lying on my side on a bare, twin mattress. Warm air was caressing the left side of my body. I sat up and instinctively turned toward the heat: next to me was a tall gas furnace.

The left side of my face hurt intensely, especially around my eyebrow. Mrs. Wilson made Mrs. Constance look like a dove.

The basement was unnaturally clean, almost sanitary, and it was devoid of anything normally kept in a basement. There were no storage boxes, or old clothing, or paint cans, or tools, or used furniture, or holiday decorations. Except for the mattress on which I sat, the room was completely empty.

The room was lit only by fading sunlight. There were no lamps or ceiling bulbs to light the room after the sun went down. Soon I would be in darkness.

My lower insides were throbbing with pain. And my underwear felt wet. I slipped my hand into the back of my shorts. My fingers came out dark red. Blood!

I screamed. I was bleeding!

My screams soon gave way to sobs as I feared for my life. I shut my eyes tightly, and I curled into a ball. I didn't want to look at the blood on my hand again.

The door leading down into the basement opened with a violent crash.

"Shut up!" Mr. Wilson roared from above. "I can't eat with all that damn racket you're making down there!"

I continued to cry. I was so afraid—afraid of the coming darkness, afraid of being alone, afraid of the blood, afraid of Mr. Wilson.

"I'm bleeding," I said, looking up at him.

"Of course you're bleeding, you idiot! We told you you would. But you'll heal."

"Why am I bleeding? Am I going to die?"

"You ain't going to die. But you will if you resist and don't cooperate. I'll use Vaseline next time. You'll like that."

Fearfully I asked, "Can I have my Yogidog?"

He stared down at me. "Sure…you can have him. But you got to do something for me first," he said with a smirk.

He moved forward, closed the door behind him and descended the stairs.

If God calls sodomy between two men an abomination, what does He call it when it's between a man and a boy?

I knew nothing about sex. I didn't even know what it was. I knew about *Gilligan's Island* and *Batman* and *Lost in Space* and *Bugs Bunny*, but not about sex. I didn't understand why Mr. Wilson had to do something so filthy and disgusting to me. I only knew that it hurt, and I felt shameful and dirty because of it.

In the beginning, when Mr. Wilson would come for me, I would remember what Larry the janitor said: "*We all do what we do for a reason. She acts like she does prob'ly 'cause a somethin' done ta her long ago.*" Perhaps when Mr. Wilson was little, he had these acts done to him, so now he felt he had to do them to me. But as the weeks passed, my thinking changed. I began to think I was getting exactly what I deserved. My first father once called me a "*little piece of filth…a rape child.*" Maybe he was right. If I truly was filth, then I was only getting what I had coming.

Wayne Elementary was the name of my first school; it was given that name in honor of John Wayne. (I learned at the orphanage I should have been in school since September, but no one knew I was even alive to compel my first parents to send me.) It was a single-story structure that seemed to stretch on forever. The kindergarten room—my room— was the first to greet people after they passed through the front doors.

I didn't enter the classroom for the first few days. I couldn't. I stood by the open door. I feared my teacher would close the door with me in there. But my teacher, Ms. Chipman, was very kind: she didn't force me to come into the classroom until I was ready. When I finally did enter the room, she let me have the desk closest to the door; she even left the door open whenever I was in the room.

Ms. Chipman, though average in height and appearance, had a sweetness loftier than the clouds. Quite often, I would catch her looking at me with deep concern, almost sympathy. Then she would smile at me lovingly. My heart longed to have a parent who looked at me the way she did.

The other children loved kindergarten. They colored and played and learned the letters of the alphabet with zeal and zest. I stayed to myself. I learned my letters quickly and picked up reading just as rapidly. I spent my recess periods in the school library. Books were my rescuers. They let me escape. I could open a book and be drawn into a world where children were protected and not rejected, a place where pets were loved and not killed.

The school librarian and Ms. Chipman were in awe that I was reading so much and so quickly at such a young age. Both encouraged me to keep reading and to challenge myself to read beyond my grade level. It was a challenge I gladly accepted.

I had been with the Wilsons for many weeks. I was never allowed upstairs, except to leave to go to school and to use the bathroom. The mattress on which I slept was never sheeted, and the pillow on which I laid my head was never cased. A scratchy, woolen blanket kept the chill off of my body when I slept. For some odd reason, the Wilsons did not take my Yogidog away from me. It was their only act of kindness. Mrs. Wilson would put my dinner on the top step of the basement stairs every evening at six and then close the door. The dinner was always the same: a lukewarm, Swanson turkey TV dinner still in its foil tray.

My lunches were far worse. Because children only stayed half days in kindergarten, Mrs. Wilson didn't have to make me a nice lunch to give the appearance she was feeding me well, so for my afternoon meal, she gave me a margarine sandwich and a half Dixie cup of milk.

My clothes, all discount store purchases, were kept in an old and marred, avocado-green chest of drawers. It stood next to my mattress in the basement. The bureau was unnecessary, for I only used the bottom drawer. In it were three shirts, three pairs of pants, three pairs of underwear, and three pairs of socks. Next to the dresser I kept my shoes: a pair of black Keds.

Though unneeded, the dresser soon proved to be a blessing. I frequently brought home books from the school library, and I kept them underneath it. Its bottom front molding was scalloped, which left a two-inch opening, and through this gap I slid my books. I didn't want the Wilsons to know I was reading, for then they would have— simply to hurt me—taken the books away. Later, when I read her diary, I understood the fear and thankfulness Anne Frank must have the felt toward the walls that separated her from arrest and death.

The furnishings in my basement bedroom were the dark side of the moon compared to the appointments in my off-limits, make-believe bedroom upstairs. That room was a fiction, an illusion for visitors. When friends would call or when my social worker would visit to check on me, the Wilsons would show them this room. It was furnished with a thick-blanketed double bed, a lustrous cherry wood highboy, and a child-sized mahogany desk. New paint, new wall décor, and a closet dense with name-brand boy's clothing also filled the eyes of the guests. The Wilsons were the perfect, idyllic foster parents. Any child would be holding aces to have them as his guardians.

A man does what he has to do in order to survive. So does a little boy.

In the beginning, Mr. Wilson would come down into the basement only a few times a week. But as the year grew on, he would come down every day. In the beginning, he would lubricate himself, empty himself, and then return upstairs. But later, he added to his routine. He would come downstairs, make me sit next to him on my bare mattress and show me his magazines, each one filled with black-and-white pictures of naked, teenage boys. After this, he would take me upstairs to the shower. While the hot water was stinging my flesh, he would make me touch him. By relaxing my body and giving my mind to the pages of one of the many books that secretly lay under my chest of drawers, I was able to make Mr. Wilson, and all his acts, disappear.

With me through it all was my Yogidog, even in the shower. I would clutch him in my hands as Mr. Wilson poured out his savage lust on my young and frangible body. My Yogidog was the only one who saw my tears and heard my cries.

I used to wonder what my Yogidog would think of me if he were real. Would he feel about me as I felt about myself? Would he run away from me? Would he stop loving me?

He wasn't the only one I wondered about. What if Ms. Chipman knew about me? What would she do? Would she demand that I leave her class? What would the principal do? Would he demand that I leave his school?

I would soon find out.

It was now springtime. While all the other children were outdoors enjoying the warm sunshine, I stayed in, content to be being warmed by the imaginings and recollections of the authors whose books lined the many shelves of my school's library.

It was a Friday in early May. All of the children were outside at morning recess; I was sitting at a reading table in the library by the door. Directly outside the library was the school's office. I suddenly heard a familiar voice. I turned my head toward the door. I saw a woman standing in front of the office desk, talking to the secretary. It was Mrs. Clawson, my social worker! What was she doing at my school? Fear grabbed my stomach. Had she somehow discovered what I had been doing with Mr. Wilson? Mrs. Wilson told me she would kill me if anyone found out about her husband and me.

"…I have an appointment to see Ms. Chipman at ten," Mrs. Clawson said. "What room is she in?"

"Her classroom is one-o-three," the secretary told her.

Mrs. Clawson thanked her and walked in the direction of the hallway.

I got up from my seat and stealthily followed her to room 103.

A young woman with a Jacqueline Kennedy hairstyle, Mrs. Clawson had a fragile frame and spoke very gracefully. I liked her tremendously. She always took a sincere interest in me, though I rarely spoke during her visits. My reticence came not from choice, but fear. If I spoke too much, I might say something that would accidentally expose my *secret life*…a life I knew no one else in my class—my whole school—was living. Mrs. Clawson was reserved herself, but I suspected that was due more to her job than her personality: working with discarded and abandoned children must have been more sad than satisfying.

Mrs. Clawson knocked on Ms. Chipman's door.

"Ms. Chipman?" Mrs. Clawson asked. "I'm Jan Clawson. We spoke on the telephone yesterday."

"Oh, yes," Ms. Chipman answered cordially. "You're Owen's social worker, is that correct?"

Mrs. Clawson nodded. "I am, yes," she replied.

"Please, come in."

After Mrs. Clawson passed through the door, I tiptoed toward the room.

"I didn't want to discuss this over the phone," Mrs. Clawson began. "I wanted to talk with you in person about Owen."

"He's a very unique little boy. He has an amazing precocity. I've never run across it. He really should be in a school for gifted children—not in a public school like this."

"Have you ever noticed anything odd about his behavior?"

"Odd? No. He's shy and introverted, but I wouldn't call that odd. He does seem very troubled, though," Ms. Chipman offered in a melancholy voice.

"Yes, he is troubled—that's why I'm here. Has he ever intimated that something might be wrong at home?"

"No. Never. He rarely talks. And yet, as I said, he's *very* bright. He reads constantly."

"Has he ever drawn disturbing or unsettling pictures?"

"No, but then he doesn't like to draw. He only likes to read. What is this all about?"

"Have you ever caught him secretly performing sex acts on any of the stuffed animals you have here? Or maybe making two of the animals—"

"Of course not! Why would you ask such a thing!"

"As you and I both know, Ms. Chipman, children are natural imitators. They reproduce what they see and what they experience. If a child is going through something traumatic, something out of his control, he replicates it. It's his way of coping with it; it's his way of controlling a situation he *can't* control. I think Owen is being abused, physically and sexually, but I can't confirm it. He has no markings on his body, and he won't say he's being hurt. But that's to be expected if abuse is occurring. The child is afraid of discovery and retaliation from his abuser."

Ms. Chipman was quiet for many moments. "You really think he's being abused?"

"Yes."

"Why haven't you removed him from the Wilsons' home then?"

"Because if nothing is found, and he is returned, the parents could harm him—possibly fatally. This has to be investigated very carefully. Besides, you just can't accuse people of neglect and abuse without substantiation."

"I've met the Wilsons—they seem like very nice people."

"Yes, too nice. Too perfect. They showed me Owen's bedroom. It looks like something out of a magazine. They made sure I saw the inside of his closet, and they opened each drawer of his dresser. Very peculiar behavior. Parents don't do that, at least not the parents I've met. Most parents are embarrassed by their children's bedrooms because they're always so messy. But that's to be expected—kids have messy bedrooms. But not Owen's. His is pristine, immaculate, nearly untouched. All of his clothes are brand-new. Nothing has been worn. Everything is laid out and lined up like it's on display."

"That's very strange, because he comes to school in paper-thin clothes that look like hand-me-downs. I don't think he's got more than two or three pairs of anything."

"Something is wrong in that home. I know it."

"How does Owen act when he's with the Wilsons?"

"Distant...detached. Whenever I go to their home, Owen stands far away from them, sometimes on the opposite side of the room, like he's afraid of them. But he doesn't say he's afraid. He says nothing, and he won't make eye contact with anyone."

"I've noticed that myself."

"That's an indicator of shame, especially in a child."

"Why would *he* be ashamed? I'm sure *he's* not doing anything wrong. He's such a sweet boy. And so polite. Calls everyone sir and ma'am. He gives the impression of apathy, but he's far from that. He notices everything. I think he's starved for attention...and love. Sometimes the poor dear breaks my heart."

"If Owen is being harmed or molested, he probably feels like he deserves it. That's the way a child's mind works."

"Maybe you should look into the Wilsons' history—see if they've had previous foster children. Ask them if they ever had any trouble with the Wilsons."

"I did that. The Wilsons had three foster children before Owen: two girls and one boy. The two girls are over eighteen now. I located them; both are still living here. I asked one of them if they were ever harmed by the Wilsons."

"And?"

"She hung up on me."

"What about the boy? Did you ask him?"

"He died. Accidental poisoning. Rat poison." Mrs. Clawson paused for a long moment.

"What is it?"

*"Rat poison."*

"Is that significant?"

"If you'd seen the Wilsons' home, you'd think it was very significant. That house is cleaner than an operating room. A house like that doesn't have rats. It doesn't even have germs. What are they doing with rat poison?"

"I think you need to get Owen out of that house as soon as possible," Ms. Chipman said quickly.

"The basement," Mrs. Clawson said offhandedly.

"What about it?"

"I'm allowed to go into any part of a foster home. When I asked the Wilsons if I could see their basement, they said the steps were broken. They said they had to lock the door so Owen wouldn't go down the stairs and hurt himself. Something is happening down in that basement. I'm sure of it."

The bell rang overhead.

"The children will be coming back any moment," Ms. Chipman said.

"I know. I'll be in touch. I'll let you and the principal know of any new developments."

"Is there anything I can do in the meantime?"

"Not specifically. Just try to make Owen feel like he's not alone. If he's going through what I think he's going through, he's carrying an incredible burden."

I heard the stampede of children heading to classrooms. I hurried away from the room so Mrs. Clawson wouldn't catch me by the door.

I slipped into the boys' lavatory. I went into one of the stalls, locked the door and crouched next to the toilet. My body was trembling with fear. It was only a matter of time before Mrs. Clawson talked to the Wilsons about her suspicions. When that happened, Mr. and Mrs. Wilson would end my life. Mrs. Clawson said the first foster boy was dead, and Mrs. Wilson openly admitted to me that she and her husband had killed him. She said she would have no reservations about killing me too. She said the last thing I would know in this life would be tears.

Mrs. Clawson was right about me being alone. I was. Completely. There was no one to whom I could turn. I had only myself. And there was only one way I could save myself. Leave. Run away. I was small, so I could hide in garages and sheds and inside bushes and never be seen. I had eaten out of garbage cans before—I could do it again. I could survive. And I would finally be away from the Wilsons.

I slowly rose to my feet and went to the door. It opened quietly. No one was in the hallway. The nearest exit was just down the hall.

I escaped without one person seeing me.

Mrs. Wilson never drove me to school in the morning, nor did she pick me up at noon when my school day was done. She always slept until one in the afternoon, at which time she arose to watch TV. I could sneak into the house, get my clothes and my Yogidog and be long gone before she awoke. Every afternoon at two, she would put my margarine sandwich and milk on the top step of the basement stairs, never looking down to see if I were there. It wouldn't be until much later in the day when Mr. Wilson arrived home that they would discover my absence. By then, I would be long gone.

Somehow, someway, I would survive.

I noticed a 1961, forest-green Plymouth Fury parked in front of the school. In it were two young women. I wondered why they were there so early—the kindergartners wouldn't be dismissed for another two hours and the other grades for another five.

I started to walk in the direction of the Wilsons' home. The Fury's engine started, and the car began to follow me. My heart quickened. I began walking faster. I heard the car stop and one of its doors open.

"Little boy, don't run away. Please don't run away. We aren't going to hurt you, I promise."

I could spot sincerity and insincerity immediately. There was deep earnestness in this woman's voice, so I halted my steps.

"May I come over to you?" she asked softly.

I nodded.

She walked over to me slowly, carefully. She was a pretty woman, very young with troubled eyes. She knelt in front of me. "My name is Elizabeth. You're Owen, aren't you?"

"How do you know my name, ma'am?"

"Your social worker and I talked briefly the other day."

I backed away from her: if they had talked, that meant they discussed Mr. Wilson and me.

"Please don't run away. I'm not going to hurt you. I want to help you."

I should have run away, for I didn't have much time before Mrs. Wilson woke up, but there was a melodic, almost hypnotic quality in her voice that compelled me to stay.

"Owen, I need to ask you something. If I do, will you tell me the truth?"

"I don't know, ma'am."

"Before I ask you the question, could you tell me something first? Are you running away? Is that why you're leaving school so early?"

I had always been afraid of lying and its repercussions, so I never did it. I had enough to deal with—I didn't need punishment as well.

"I can't tell you, ma'am," I answered. "It's my secret."

"Okay, that's fair. Can I ask you this then? If you are running away, would you be running away from the Wilsons?"

"Why would I run away from them, ma'am?"

"Because they're bad people. *Very* bad people. Aren't they?"

"I don't want to talk about this anymore, ma'am."

"Owen, I'm going to ask you something, all right?"

"What is that, ma'am?"

She looked at me with amazement. "You're awfully mature for your age. But then, I guess you've been forced to grow up very quickly."

"I don't know what you mean, ma'am."

"Owen, just for right now, would you not call me ma'am?"

"Yes, ma'—okay."

She smiled. "Thank you. Being taught to use words like sir and ma'am is a good thing, but if they're taught by the wrong teacher, it's a bad thing. Mrs. Wilson is a bad teacher. Owen, I'm going to ask you that question now. Has Mr. Wilson...done things to you? Bad things? Things to your...private parts?"

I felt my face burn. Why was it doing that? I lowered my eyes in shame. I wanted to leave...but I wanted this woman's kindness even more.

The woman tenderly touched my face. "Oh, sweetheart. It's all right. He's not going to hurt you ever again. *Ever.* I give you my word."

I looked into her topaz-blue eyes. They were shimmering with tears.

"They killed my little brother," she unveiled. "His name was Oliver. He was about your age. He was such a sweet little boy. But he could be feisty too. That's what got him killed. They poisoned him because he said he was going to tell his teacher what Mr. Wilson was doing to all of us. They forced him to eat rat poison. He suffered terribly before he died. They vowed to kill me and my sister too if we ever told. And we believed them. Once we turned eighteen, we left that house with nothing but the clothes on our bodies, and we never looked back. Then, the other day, your Mrs. Clawson called about you and the Wilsons. I'm ashamed to say it, but I hung up on her. I was...scared. Very scared. Scared they would come after my sister and me. Then it hit me—we're grown women now; they can't hurt us anymore. But they can continue to hurt *you*. But we're not going to let that happen. We won't let them hurt you ever again. We're going to face them together."

"No! She said she'd kill me if anyone found out!"

"I know. She said the same thing to my sister and me. But there's a difference now: people know about the Wilsons today; back then they didn't. I won't let them hurt you, Owen. I promise. This is what we're going to do—we're going to go over to that house, we're going to get your things, and we're—"

"No! She'll grab me and she'll—"

"No, she won't. I won't let her. Owen, I know you're very young and you're scared, but you need to listen to me. If you don't face her now, you may not like yourself later on. She needs to see that she didn't win. A big part of life is standing up to bad people. If you run away from them, you run away from yourself, and that's no way to live. Believe me, I know."

"They'll come after me."

"No, they won't. I won't let them. Once we get your things, we're going to call Mrs. Clawson, and then we're going to call the police. The sun is about to set on the Wilsons' life, and a long, dark night is heading their way."

Elizabeth's sister was named Rebecca. Like her sister, Rebecca had cascading, sunny-brown hair. She was a lovely young woman in face and form, but she was intensely reserved, worse than I. She was nearly catatonic. She was alive…but dead. She said hello to me when I crawled into the backseat of the car, but that was all. She kept her head forward… like a ship's sail at sea, guided by the winds of revenge.

The Wilsons' single-story, clapboard home was six blocks from my school. The two girls sat motionless when the car came to a stop in front of the house. They stared out the passenger's window for the longest time, saying nothing.

"We have to do this, Rebecca," Elizabeth reminded her sister.

"I know. But planning to do it and *actually* doing it are two different creatures."

"We have to do it for Owen, Rebecca. We have to do it for us. And for Oliver. If we don't speak for him, who will? We have a responsibility to—"

"Don't lecture me! I'm more than aware of our responsibility."

"They can't be allowed to get away with what they did! With what they're still doing! It's evil, and it's wrong! If we do nothing, we're just as guilty as they are! I know you're scared, but so is Owen, and *he's* here."

Rebecca regarded her sister. Then she turned to me. Her face carried only one expression: determination. "Give me your keys, Owen," she said unemotionally.

I did as she requested. Rebecca gently took them from my hand and exited her side of the car. She then opened my door, took my hand, waited for her sister, and the three of us started walking toward the front door of the house.

I noticed the watch on Rebecca's wrist, which was unusually large; it said 10:30.

The Wilsons' home was as quiet as a church…although this was no house of God. The two sisters stopped in their steps as soon as their feet touched carpet. Their breathing became heavy and was noticeably loud in the soundless, dustless, Queen Anne-styled living room. Mrs. Wilson might have had no fondness for sex, but she was an unabashed, unashamed, unblushing sybarite.

The two sisters locked hands. Both girls were trembling.

"How can such a filthy-minded woman keep such an immaculate home?" Rebecca asked.

"Hasn't changed at all, has it?" Elizabeth observed.

"Hell never does," Rebecca came back.

"Still smells like lavender. I *hate* lavender."

"Smells like sh—" Rebecca stopped herself and dropped her eyes to me. "Let's get this over with."

Rebecca let go of her sister's hand and walked me to the cellar door. She opened it, and we all descended into the basement.

How did she know this was where my bedroom was?

Elizabeth covered her face with her hand. She began to weep when she saw the bare mattress on the floor. "They're making him live the same way they made Oliver live."

Rebecca did not weep. Nor did she speak. She simply opened her clutch purse, pulled out a black plastic bag, walked over to my dresser, removed the few pieces of clothing kept inside it and dropped them into the bag.

I ran to my Yogidog, who was sitting on my pillow.

"This is Yogidog. Can he come with me?"

Rebecca gave me a forlorn smile. "Of course he can."

"Now for the *coup de grace*," Rebecca said, looking up. She clasped my hand again and led me up the stairs.

Elizabeth was not with us when we reached the top. Rebecca pivoted and peered down into the shadowy basement. "Beth, what are you doing?" Rebecca asked impatiently.

"I was just thinking of Oliver," Elizabeth answered back.

"You can do that another time. We came here to do a job—so let's get it done."

Compliantly, Elizabeth climbed the stairs and joined her sister.

With my hand still interlocked with hers, Rebecca walked me deeper into the house. The three of us stopped in front of the master bedroom. Its door was closed, as always.

I should have been frightened at what we were doing, but Rebecca's boldness and confidence fended off my fears. It was an unexpected turn of events: in the beginning, it was Elizabeth who was in command; now it was Rebecca who was in the center seat. The most unlikely people will do the most unlikely things.

Rebecca wrapped her hand around the brass doorknob and turned it.

The bedroom, like the living room, was large and elegantly appointed. All of its pieces—the headboard, the nightstands, the vanity, the chifforobe, the armoire, even the bed bench—was high-gloss cherry wood. Mrs. Wilson was sleeping supine on a king-sized bed. She looked more deceased than asleep: her skin was sallow and synthetic; her cheeks were bloated and stretched, and her lips were flat and lifeless. We all stared at her in silence, hoping she *was* dead, but knowing all too well she wasn't.

Suddenly and without any warning, her eyes opened. Both Elizabeth and I jumped back; Rebecca stayed where she was, still as a stone. Mrs. Wilson's head jerked in our direction. For a second, there was genuine terror on her face. Then her eyes turned as cold as glacial ice. She sat up in bed, revealing a daffodil-yellow, flannel nightgown.

Again, Elizabeth and I drew back.

Not a hair on Rebecca's head moved.

"Well, look at what the cat dragged in—a couple a whores," Mrs. Wilson uttered contemptuously. "Couldn't stay away, huh? I can call Mr. Wilson, and he can be here in a flash...if you're interested." She smiled wickedly.

"You disgust me!" Rebecca hissed.

"Oh, come on, you liked it and you know it. Whores always like it. That's why they're whores. If you didn't like it, Rebecca, you would have run away. Why didn't you run away?" Her tone was dripping with scorn.

"You have a very short memory, Mrs. Wilson. You said if we ran away, you'd find us and kill us? *All of us.* Remember saying that?"

"But I didn't kill all of you, did I? Only one of you died, so you're ahead. Look at it that way." She smiled perniciously.

"I *hate* you!" Rebecca said.

"Well, you know what they say, you can't be loved by everybody." She laughed.

"You think you're pretty cute, don't you?"

"No, not really. But I'll tell you who *was* cute—your kid brother. Too bad about him—I would have liked having a time or two with him myself." Again, she laughed.

Faster than a synaptic transmission, Rebecca clamped her fingers around Mrs. Wilson's wrinkled throat. Mrs. Wilson grabbed Rebecca's hand and tried to free it from her windpipe. It was like watching a hornet struggling to lift an elephant. Mrs. Wilson's senescent hand was no match for Rebecca's youthful one.

"Rebecca, don't!" Elizabeth screamed.

"Shut up!" Rebecca screamed back.

"We agreed to let the police handle this," Elizabeth countered.

"And we will. But there are a few things she's going to know first."

Terror had returned to Mrs. Wilson's face.

"Do you have any idea what kind of damage you've done!" Rebecca screamed at Mrs. Wilson. "Do you!"

Mrs. Wilson didn't respond; either because she wasn't able to—due to Rebecca's choke hold—or because she didn't care. Still, she gave Rebecca a hard stare. Though there was gravid fear in Mrs. Wilson's face, there was also defiance and hate in her spavined eyes. An immovable object meeting an unstoppable force.

"First you kill my little brother," Rebecca leveled, "and now you all but kill this little boy. You've maimed him for life! You maimed my sister and me for life! You're not human. How God allows you and that thing you call a husband to live is beyond me. But I guess if He can allow plagues to exist, He can allow the two of you to exist too.

"You know, when animals and insects hurt and kill, they do it to survive. When you and your husband hurt and kill, you do it for kicks. It's funny, we exterminate natural insects who *do* belong, but we don't exterminate fecal insects like you and your husband who *don't* belong. How is that?

"I'm not afraid of you anymore, Mrs. Wilson. Here's what's going to happen. After we leave here, we're going to take Owen to the hospital, and then we're going to call the police. They're going to come here, and they're going to throw you and that pig of a husband of yours in with all the other sick perverts. You know what happens to men in prison who've gone after little children, especially little boys? First they beat 'em…then they rape 'em…then they kill 'em. You be sure to tell Herman the hermaphrodite that." Rebecca laughed at her own wit. "If I were you, I'd end it before the police get here. Why don't you take some of that rat poison you gave my little brother? Works real good." With those words, Rebecca released her grip on Mrs. Wilson.

Mrs. Wilson quickly grabbed and massaged her throat. "No one's going to believe a couple a whores like you," she scoffed in a raspy voice.

"Oh, I think they will," Rebecca mocked in a whisper. "Besides, once Owen is examined and it's been discovered that he's been raped, you and your husband can count on never seeing freedom again."

"Dream on, girl. I'll just tell 'em he did it to himself. Boys are always sticking things up themselves. That's what boys do. They like it. They *all* like it."

"You *are* sick. Little boys *don't* do that. It's only the twisted, demented growths like your husband who do that. And then they turn around and do it to little boys. And malignancies like you who allow it are just as vile as they are." Rebecca turned to leave. Then she eddied back in Mrs. Wilson's direction. "Enjoy your stay in prison, Mrs. Wilson. I'd keep one eye open while I slept if I were you. Men aren't the only ones who kill pedophiles." Rebecca let loose a happy laugh. "I'll be looking for you and your husband in the obituaries. Be sure to tell him hello from us."

"You go to Hell!" Mrs. Wilson flared at Rebecca.

"Oh, by all means, *you first.*" She smiled victoriously and then shot her middle fingers up in the air.

I wondered why she did that.

Before Mrs. Wilson could utter another virulent syllable, the three of us left her bedroom, and then the house.

I was given a complete examination later that day, just as Rebecca said I would. The physician and nurse who conducted it were very kind. They spoke softly to me while they evaluated my body for trauma. They let me hold my Yogidog during their audit. Having him there eased my nervousness. After they finished, they gave me a cherry Popsicle, and they both hugged me.

Mrs. Clawson and a child psychologist came into examination room after the doctor and nurse had left. Mrs. Clawson apologized repeatedly for what I went through and for not acting on her suspicions sooner. I told her it was all right. And it was all right: how could she possibly have known what I was going through? Only I knew that.

I slept soundly and peacefully that night. I would learn the next morning that Mr. and Mrs. Wilson fled their home before the authorities arrived. They were free to harm and kill children once again.

# CHAPTER 3

# *Angels Die,*
# *Demons Don't*

*"Each of us is born hungry. Not for food. For significance."*

KELLY E. DAVIDSON

A week later, Rebecca drove herself up into the mountains, parked next to a meandering stream, left her car, walked over to a picnic table, pressed a revolver against her right temple, and sent a bullet into her brain. She died instantly. She died alone. She died in the rain. She left no letter, no note. And none was needed. Everyone knew, even me, why she did what she did: Oliver. She felt she had failed him, and herself. If she hadn't made the Wilsons aware of her intent to involve the police, they would not have fled and escaped their punishment. But she did tell them, and they did flee. Rebecca must have thought that the punishment should then fall on her. But amercement is not transferred like a deed; it belongs to the guilty man forever, and someday, someway it rises up and tramples the man without mercy and without pity.

I was not allowed to attend Rebecca's funeral. I was told I was too young for something so grim. It would be too traumatic for my young mind. Little did people know that my young mind had witnessed things they could not even imagine.

Shortly after Rebecca's funeral, Elizabeth left the state. Where she moved to I was not told. I hoped I would meet her again someday, for I wanted to thank her for her courage and bravery. Few, if any, would have done what she and her sister did.

I was summarily returned to Greenwood Children's Home after my rescue from the Wilsons' home. No one asked me if I wanted to go back, or if I was treated well while I was there. Had I been asked, my answer would have been *no* to both queries. Why was I not asked where I wanted to live? After all, was it not my life? Shouldn't I have had a say? Apparently not. Apparently, obviously, children were never to be heard and barely seen. While the children's home was not the house of horrors I was removed from, it certainly had its own brand of terror. The isolation and coldness from the staff were enough to make me feel like I was in a prison.

To make a dismal situation darker, I learned that Larry the janitor was no longer employed at the children's home. He had been terminated for stealing a sandwich. Greenwood Children's Home was heavy on rules and light on compassion.

Mrs. Constance was out of the building the day I returned. I was told she was on vacation. It was hard to imagine her wanting a normal pleasure like a vacation when she obviously found so much delight in being the queen of mean at the orphanage. I knew she would seek me out as soon as she discovered I had been returned. It would not be a pleasant reunion.

I did not reenter my old life of sleeping my days and nights away. As in kindergarten, I took refuge in books. Greenwood's library was nowhere near as global as the library at Wayne Elementary. Still, it was ample for my needs. And my need was simple: escape. There would soon come a time when I would read to learn, but for now, I read to retreat.

It was summertime again. I felt trapped inside, so I took to the outdoors. I also took my books and made my place under the sun.

Though I was not far from the doors of the orphanage, I was still outside.

But being outside made reading difficult. It was hard to concentrate on the written beauty in my books when so much physical beauty was all around me. The fluttering leaves, the lustrous green grass, the dancing butterflies, the searching honey bees, the rainbow-colored pansies made me happy to be alive. There was something safe and non-threatening about the outdoors: it didn't expect performance; it didn't make demands; it didn't criticize; it didn't judge; it didn't condemn, and it didn't rape. It only provided pleasure and peace.

I had been back a week and a half, and there was still no sign of Mrs. Constance. I hoped she would find vacationing more gratifying than governing and never return.

I was outside on the front steps, watching a bumble bee survey a white rose, when the secretary to Mrs. Constance brusquely opened her office window and summoned me over.

"Mrs. Constance is back from her vacation," the gray-haired assistant informed me, a thick film of brine canvassing her words. "She would like to see you—*immediately*." She closed the window as abruptly as she had opened it.

The sound of the frame smacking its sill made me flinch.

My heart began to race. I had known this day would come sooner or later.

On my way to Mrs. Constance's office, I began making plans for my life on the streets. Mrs. Constance told me I dare not come back—which meant that I would not be allowed to stay. I cursed myself for letting this day arrive. I should have saved myself the acrimony that would most assuredly spew from Mrs. Constance when she saw me and simply left the day I was returned. But I didn't leave that day. Part of me didn't want to leave, for I was afraid to be out on my own. Living hand-to-mouth was a hard and frightening existence, especially for a child. My birthday was July 4th, Independence Day. If Mrs. Constance stayed true to form, I would be out on my own long before then. *Truly independent.*

I entered Greenwood's main office and went up to the counter.

The stone-faced, albescent-haired assistant saw me and, without a word, pointed to Mrs. Constance's office door.

Nervously, I walked over to the door, opened it and walked into her office.

Mrs. Constance's back was to me; she was looking out her corner window.

"Would you close the door, please?" she asked in an uncharacteristically mild voice.

I did as she requested.

Still facing the window, she said, "Please, sit down."

Again, I obeyed.

I sat and waited for her to spin around and launch invective-tipped arrows at me.

More silence.

As the seconds passed, I grew more nervous. Why didn't she just lay me out and be done with it?

"If memory serves, the last time we spoke, I told you never to come back here," she said finally, her voice strangely meek.

"I'm sorry, Mrs. Constance," I said, my voice shaking. "They brought me back here. I didn't want to come back. I know you don't want me here. I know you don't like me. I'll leave if you want me to."

She turned around.

Her eyes were red; her face was flushed, and her cheeks were streaked with tears.

Had it been anyone else, I would have thought she had been crying. But this was Mrs. Constance. Granite doesn't cry.

She looked at me for the longest time. But she wasn't staring. She was...*feeling.*

She went over to her desk, sat down, folded her hands and rested them on a leather-edged blotter.

"Owen," she began hesitantly, "the things I said to you the last day you were here were...reprehensible. I was wrong and unbelievably cruel. I am sorry, and I hope you will forgive me."

I didn't know how to respond. What do you say to Satan when he apologizes?

"Owen, I would like to explain myself to you. Call it a confession or a catharsis. Or call it something else. Whatever it is, I feel an explanation is in order. I know you are very young, and you may not understand what I am about to tell you, but I truly hope that someday you will.

"Last week, I was made aware of what you went through while living with the Wilsons. I cannot believe people would do such things. But sin has no boundaries; it has no limits, no fences, no perimeter it isn't permitted to cross. Man is capable of amazing goodness. But he is also capable of unbelievable darkness. I myself have unthinkable darkness...as you have seen. As everyone in this building has seen. I take full responsibility for what happened to you, Owen. It is my duty to make sure that all of the children here are placed with parents who will love them and care for them—not use them and hurt them. Had I done my job appropriately and checked the backgrounds of Mr. and Mrs. Wilson, they never would have entered this building. In fact, I would have seen to it that they and the police would have had a very close relationship. But I didn't do that, and that is something I have to live with, forever. I am so sorry that it happened to you. It is a harm and a violation that you will never forget, and possibly never forgive.

"I am told you are a very gifted child. Very intelligent and sensitive. And extremely brave. My loss that I never got to know you.

"I am due to retire soon, within six weeks, actually. Before I end my tenure here, I am going to do all I can to make sure that you are placed with foster parents who will give you the love and nurturing that you have yet to know in your young life. That is my promise to you, Owen."

She paused for a long patch of time.

"I know what the children and staff think of me," she said wistfully. "They think I am the Devil in a dowdy dress. *Mrs. Martinet.* Truly, I wish they thought differently. It's just that age makes you coarse, and life makes you jaded. Most people don't know this, but I have a son—" she stopped. "No, I *had* a son. He lives still, but he is long dead to me. We named him David. A good, Biblical name. I bore him late in life. He was our only child. We gave him a fine home. A fine education. We taught him right from wrong, good from bad. We wanted him to find a nice woman, have children, and live near us so that we might enjoy our grandchildren. Six years ago, he met a woman, a much older woman... and also black. They fell in love—at least that's what they called it. She moved him away from me, and I am not even in his memory now. I am told—and that goes back two years—that they are somewhere in Uganda, of all places. We are all alone now, my husband and I. I am not a racist, mind you, but I do believe that interracial amalgams are not good. They are unnatural and divisive. They bring nothing but conflict and heartache. Some would call my estrangement from my son poetic justice, and they would be right in their judgment, for I confess that I possess unforgivable darkness, and yet I still oppose the conjoining of Caucasians and Negroes. I suppose then it is only fitting that my son is now wed to one." She smiled ruefully.

Again, I didn't know what to say. What is a small boy supposed to say to such adult revelations?

"You remind me of my own son when he was your age," she revealed. "He, too, adored the written word. He had your hair color and your shyness. He loved being beneath the trees, as you do. I loved him so when he was a boy. I don't want you to leave this place, Owen, believing that all adults—myself included—are like the Wilsons, because they are not. I don't want you to fear me as you feared them. I want you to think well of me and not ill. I do not want you to forget me, Owen."

She smiled and looked at the clock on the wall behind me. "It's nearly lunchtime. Why don't you run along and get something to eat? Feel free to take your meal outside."

I arose from my chair and walked to the door. As I opened it, I turned back to Mrs. Constance.

"Yes, Owen?" she asked affectionately.

I hesitated. Nervously, I said, "Was Larry the janitor pretty sad when he was told he had to go?"

She regarded me for a few moments. "Yes, he was sad. But rules are rules. Did you like Larry?"

"Yes, ma'am. He was the only one here who was ever nice to me. I've been hungry lots of times, Mrs. Constance. Many times, I had to eat out of garbage cans. When you're hungry, you don't think about it—you just eat."

She looked at me with astonishment. "What a remarkable boy you are. So much like my David when he was your age. So sensitive to others. Though I do hope you take a different path than he when you are older." She sighed heavily. "Would it make you feel better if I were able to bring Larry back?" she asked.

I smiled and nodded.

"Consider it done."

I left Mrs. Constance's office feeling pleased…but also dismayed. It was nice that Mrs. Constance was now benevolent toward me rather than malevolent, but it really wasn't *me* that caused her to reform: it was my likeness to her son. In the beginning, she despised me because I reminded her of her son, and in the end, she prized me for the same reason. Why couldn't she have valued me for me and not who I reminded her of?

Larry the janitor was so right when he said, "*We all do what we do for a reason.*" Monsters are not born monsters…they are fashioned into them.

Less than two weeks later, I met my new foster parents. I liked them immediately. His name was James, hers Jean. Their last name was Crowley. Beginning in their youth, their friends called them "*JJ,*" for they were nearly inseparable. They found one another their first year of high school…and their dance never stopped. I was told they were in their fifties, yet, unlike the Wilsons, they were dashingly fit. He had the frame of a redwood: towering, thick, erect. Above his barrel chest was a face strongly reminiscent of Thomas E. Dewey. There was a crescent-moon scar on the cusp of his left lower jaw. Rather than diminishing the artistry of his face, the scar only added to it, like the signature at the bottom of a painting. I was told he was an architect. Mrs. Crowley was a foot shorter than her husband. She was demure, though openly sweet-natured. She beamed a radiant smile at me whenever our eyes met. Her chestnut hair was beginning to gray.

Something was strange about my new foster mother: she was a watery reflection of my natural mother, especially in her nose and eyes.

But how could that be? If the two were related, I would have known about it, or, at the very least, been told.

The Crowleys had had one child, a son. Leukemia took him two years earlier. He was six when he passed away. His name was Eben.

Mrs. Constance told me that she had had several meetings with Mr. and Mrs. Crowley, and she had no reservations about them as suitable parents for me. She said I couldn't ask for better guardians. I believed her.

Mrs. Constance walked with me out to the Crowleys' car.

I was hoping to say good-bye to Larry, but he was not due to start working at the home again for another week. With great determination, Mrs. Constance had finally located him. She told me she had apologized to him for his termination. He said he was sorry too and promised never to steal from them again. She told him he needn't worry about going without food from then on: he would be fed without charge for as long as he was employed there.

Mrs. Constance hugged me and gave me a kiss on my forehead before I got into the Crowleys' car. She waved good-bye as I was driven away. I felt my eyes fill with tears as I watched her become smaller and smaller in the rear window. The last time I cried over a loss was when my father killed my Yogidog. I never thought I would cry because I was leaving Mrs. Constance. But mine was a life filled with eccentric events.

The Crowleys owned a 1965, lemon-yellow Cadillac Eldorado. The three of us weren't two blocks from the children's home when Mr. Crowley pulled the car over to the side of the road. I saw a yellow arch out the windshield. It was a McDonald's. Mrs. Crowley turned around to face me; I was in the back seat, she was in the front.

She looked at me...and smiled.

"Are you hungry?" she asked. "Mr. Crowley and I love McDonald's. They have the best humbugs around." She laughed.

*Humbugs?* I was tempted to point out her mispronunciation, but I quickly put away the temptation. I was taught that a child never corrects an adult.

It struck me odd that a woman of her position—the wife of an architect—would mispronounce a common word like *hamburger.* But perhaps she heard her mistake and that was why she laughed.

"Yes, me and the missus like to indulge ourselves every now and then," Mr. Crowley said, "so we head out to the nearest McDonald's and load up on humbugs, French ties, and chocolate shacks."

He laughed ebulliently.

Mrs. Crowley joined him.

Evidently, the errors were intentional, but I didn't understand what was so amusing about them. Perhaps they were just trying to lighten the mood in the car. I tried to smile, but it was halfhearted at best. It is difficult to enjoy a joke when its meaning is concealed.

"The poor boy doesn't understand us, dear," Mrs. Crowley said to her husband.

She returned her eyes to me. "You see, our little Eben, God rest his precious soul, loved McDonald's. But he had a little trouble with some of the words. Hamburgers were '*humbugs*,' French fries were '*French ties*,' and shakes were '*shacks*.' Do you like McDonald's, Owen?"

"I've never had it, ma'am," I replied.

Mrs. Crowley smiled thoughtfully. "Well, it's time you did."

Mr. Crowley parked the car, and the three of us walked over to one of the takeout windows. Mr. Crowley ordered for all of us. He then drove us to a park so we could eat under the shade of a tree.

It was all like a dream. How could I go from despair to delight in such a short space of time? I had come to learn that each person does what he does for a reason, and that reason is rooted in his past—which is why some humans are saints and others sadists. But is not being a sadist a choice? Does a horrible past constrain someone to become a horrible person? Cannot a victim choose to be like these two people who were now my new parents? Is it not more taxing and wearing to be brutish and beastish than charitable and honorable? Do not most people take the path of least resistance in life? And for those who choose to tread the challenging roads instead, are not the smoother streets, at least in the domain of human behavior, more satisfying in the end?

My first meal with the Crowleys was pleasant, though awkward. They were talkers; I was not. They would ask me benign questions, and I would answer them with benign replies. What was my favorite color? *Red.*

What was my favorite cartoon? *Yogi Bear.* What was my favorite time of year? *Summer.* What was my favorite thing to eat? *Spaghetti* (or as some of the younger children at the home used to say, *"Busgetti.")* Had I ever been to the zoo? *No.* Did I like animals? *Yes—little dogs.* Did I like music? *Yes* (what little I had heard). What did I want to be when I grew up? *I didn't know.* What made me feel happy? *Being there with them.* What made me feel sad? *Everything else.*

I'm sure I came across as an unnaturally quiet and unsociable little boy. But I had had a life in which I was not asked, I was ordered. Conversation was not part of my daily bread.

There was a cool, aromatic breeze that caressed our faces that day in the park; it made that first memory with the Crowleys even more fragrant. They both kept eyeing me with esteem, almost reverence, as if I were somebody else, somebody they had known for a very long time. But how could that be? Beyond knowing my favorite color and if I had ever been to the zoo, they knew very little about me, so where was this veneration coming from? How could I be so special so soon?

After we finished our cheeseburgers and fries and soft drinks (mine was a clear, cryptically labeled drink called 7UP), Mrs. Crowley and I swung on some nearby swings. Mr. Crowley remained in the shade of the tree by which we had just eaten. He was sitting on the blanket Mrs. Crowley had spread out for us earlier and casually smoking a cigarette. Sometimes he exhaled the smoke upward like Barbara Eden coming out of her Jeannie bottle, other times he released the smoke sideways like he was exhaling breath on a winter's day, and still other times he respired the smoke in perfect rings from his perfectly masculine lips. It was obvious he loved smoking, but it was also obvious that it did not love him: after each performance, he would cough furiously. Mrs. Crowley didn't seem too concerned when she heard his coughs. It wasn't that she didn't care—she did. But she, like most people of the time, was unaware of the lethality of cigarettes. The coughs were warnings, but neither she nor her husband knew that.

Mr. Crowley loved Winstons. Like most cigarettes, Winston pushed an absurd and inane slogan. Later, when I was a teenager, I came up with one that wasn't: *A Winston will kill like a cyanide pill.* A bit callow...but more than a bit true.

We left the park late in the afternoon. We weren't five minutes on the road before I was asleep in the backseat. When I awoke, my head was on Mrs. Crowley's lap. Apparently, they had stopped somewhere, and Mrs. Crowley climbed in the back with me. Mr. Crowley picked me up, carried me into their house and put me to bed. As in the car, I quickly fell asleep.

When I awoke the next morning, I found out, very abruptly, why I was so special to the Crowleys.

The sun was shining brightly on the wall opposite the bed. Against it was a small pine dresser, the size a child would use. On the wall around the dresser, like a sacred nimbus, were hand-drawn pictures on white construction paper. Some of the drawings were in chalk, some in watercolor, some in finger paint, some in crayon, and some in colored pencil. It was clear that they came from the hand of a very young child. Not a prodigy, just an ordinary youngster who loved to color and draw. The illustrations were of houses, apple trees, flowers, stick people, cats, dogs, horses, butterflies, and Mommy and Daddy.

On top of the dresser was an assortment of framed photographs. A few of the pictures were in black and white, but most were in color. Behind the photos, on the rear right corner, sat a Kodak Brownie. Evidently, this was the camera that took most, if not all, of the pictures. The subject in each photograph was a young boy, no more than four years of age. The boy looked strangely familiar. I slowly climbed out of the bed and went over to the dresser. The photographs took my eyes captive, then my breath.

The pictures were of...*me!*

But it wasn't me. It was Eben, Mr. and Mrs. Crowley's son. Their dead son. But he could easily have been my twin.

So this was why Mr. and Mrs. Crowley took such a liking to me: I reminded them of Eben. It wasn't *me* they felt affection for or wanted a relationship with—it was my resemblance to their deceased child to which they were drawn.

I turned and looked around the spacious room. Sprightly hued pennants of the Boston Red Sox, the Chicago Cubs, the San Francisco Giants, and many others were thumb-tacked to the south wall. The north wall was sheeted with hundreds of baseball cards. Long metal shelves painted Crayola gold were also affixed to the wall. Placed on the shelves, like diamonds on display, were autographed baseballs, scuffed baseballs, unblemished baseballs, baseball mitts, baseball bats, and baseball jerseys. Had Eben really been that much of a baseball enthusiast, or was Mr. Crowley the real baseball admirer of the family? If it were him, was this his way of making sure Eben was a baseball devotee as well? But what if Eben had come to ensky *danseurs* rather than double plays? Would Mr. Crowley have accepted it? Sadly, it was something neither son nor father would ever find out.

My eyes came back to the photographs on the dresser. They made me remember my own mother and father. They didn't love me—they only loved Susan. They only kept me around because of her. Mrs. Constance treated me kindly because I reminded her of her son. And now the Crowleys: I was a mirror image of their apotheosized son, their lost cynosure. They could have him back through me. Why couldn't people have loved me for me...like Susan did? To her, I was important, relevant, someone who had worth for who he was and not for who he was like. Was I destined to live my entire life in the shadows of others?

The Crowleys were upright and moral people; of that I was certain. And I knew they were just two people who desperately wanted their son back. But how could they want me to replace him? I looked like him...but I was *not* him; I was me. Didn't they know this?

I had a decision to make.

If I let the Crowleys know I knew why I was so important to them, it might upset them, and they might return me to the children's home. While the children's home was not as unfriendly as it had been when I first entered it, it was not a place I wanted to revisit. The new superintendent would assuredly not be as generous and openhanded with me as Mrs. Constance had been. And the staff, save for Larry the janitor, was less than a delight.

On the opposite hand, the Crowleys were kind, moral, and ethical people. Irrespective of why I was meaningful to them, the life I would have with them would be immeasurably better than the life I would have at the children's home...or with other foster parents. Would it be so terrible being the Crowleys' resurrected son? Would it be so unendurable to be unloved for who I really was? There certainly were far worse burdens to bear.

There was a soft knock on the bedroom door. Mr. and Mrs. Crowley came into the room. Cheerful smiles greeted me. Although devoid of sincerity, I returned the gesture.

Polonius in Shakespeare's *Hamlet* said: *"This above all: to thine ownself be true. And it must follow, as the night the day, thou canst not be false to any man..."*

Larry the janitor said: *"Be what yer heart tells ya ta be. Ya won't go wrong if ya do."*

Polonius spoke the truth, but Larry spoke reality. A man must follow his own heart. My heart told me to be false, delusive. When a man's life orbits around the sun of survival, he cares only about getting through each day, not getting through the gates of honesty and self-respect.

Mr. and Mrs. Crowley spent nearly every waking moment with me. I wondered if Mr. Crowley was nettling his employer and jeopardizing his job by staying at home so much. He didn't seem to care, though. His focus was on his wife and his new son and spending as much time with them as he could.

The three of us lived a fairy-tale life that summer: every morning we would have breakfast on their glass-enclosed veranda; every afternoon we would have lunch in the park, and every evening we would have dinner by candlelight. We would fish in the nearby mountains; we would roller-skate around their neighborhood; we would take evening walks; we would read books before bedtime (actually, it was I who read to them, for they loved the sound of my voice), and on Sundays, after Mass, we would play croquet or badminton or baseball in their immense backyard. Regrettably, I was abjectly inept at all of these games. Still, the Crowleys were unsparingly kind and patient with me. The rare times I would strike the ball correctly, Mr. Crowley would clap and praise me: *"Attaboy, sport!"* or *"Now you're cookin' with gas, champ!"* or *"You're the cat's meow, my boy!"* Maybe the Crowleys were so long-suffering with me because Eben had been like me: a little boy who couldn't hit a ball, throw a ball, or catch a ball to save his life.

My existence became a series of Norman Rockwell paintings—literally. Norman Rockwell did not paint real life; rather, he painted life the way he wanted it to be. That was my journey with the Crowleys. It wasn't real, because *I* wasn't real. I was someone else. I was *Eben.* I never brought it to their attention, but on occasion, the Crowleys would call me Eben instead of Owen. Perchance the mistake was made because the two names were in part homophonic, but, more than likely, it was no mistake at all.

Going from privation to plenitude was a gift not lost on me. Yet, there is always a fare to ride on the gift carriage. That price is unspoken conditions and unvoiced expectations. Nothing is free. *Nothing.* The price I had to pay to maintain my storybook life was to keep a spirited smile and cheerful stride. I had been given a wonderful new life—jouissance was in order. From a distance, the delight seemed authentic, yet if one were to spade down, they would find in me impenetrable strata of fear, distrust, and self-hatred. It was exhausting pretending to be happy and content all the time, but it was either maintain the pretense or face the orphanage again. Not quite the lesser of two evils, but certainly the lesser of two undesirable situations.

My new foster parents were not aware of what I was going through—not during the hours when the sun was in the sky and not during the hours when the stars were in its place. Never was there a night I didn't wake up from a dream about Mr. and Mrs. Wilson. My eyelids would snap open, and I would kick the blankets off of my legs. With Yogidog firmly gripped in my hands, I would dash over to the double-doored clothes closet to see if the Wilsons were crouching in there, waiting to steal me away. The closet was always empty, yet the dreams continued, as did my fear that my closet was concealing them and somehow abetting them so they could one day drag me away to their new basement, lock the door, end the light, and laugh while I cried in the darkness below.

If I had told my new parents about my nightmares and fears, I knew they would have sent me back to the children's home. They didn't want a child under their roof who was not a duplicate of their firstborn, and if they found out he wasn't, he would be gone.

The day after Labor Day would be my first day of first grade. For the first time, I would be in real school. Kindergarten was not real school—it was play school. First grade is the first step into the real world—a world not friendly to abnormal and heteromorphic people like me.

I awoke that Tuesday morning neither excited nor apprehensive about going to school. I knew that first grade would be more formal and structured than its younger cousin kindergarten. I assumed I would again be sitting by the door during class, and if I had to go outside during recess, I would be sitting alone there too.

Mrs. Crowley drove me to school. She parked on the street and then walked me inside the building. She held my hand as we made our way to my classroom. When we reached the entrance to my room, I froze with terror. I couldn't go into that room. I couldn't. The teacher would close the door, and I would be trapped—trapped like I was with Mr. Wilson and his hirsute body and his sweaty hands and his garlic-thick breath; like I was with my real parents and their tape and their toys and their never-ending hatred.

I started to cry.

Mrs. Crowley knelt in front of me. "Sweetheart, what's the matter?" she asked, confusion and deep worry painted on her face.

"You'll make me go back if I tell you," I said through my tears.

"Go back where, honey?"

"The children's home."

"Why would we make you go back there?"

I glanced into the room. Three boys sitting next to one another in the front row were staring at me. Their faces were contorted into caricatures of sadness. They were mocking me. The boys then looked at one another and laughed.

"I'm not him," I finally answered her.

"Not who, darling?"

"Eben."

She looked startled. "Of course you're not Eben," she said quietly. "Eben's dead."

"Then why do you call me Eben sometimes?"

Mrs. Crowley blanched and looked away from me.

"I've known from the very beginning I remind you of him," I said, "and that's why you want me around."

She returned her eyes to me; they were brimming with tears. "Is that really what we've made you feel?"

I nodded. "I know you only want him. You don't want me. I get scared at everything. Nothing ever scared Eben. You won't want me around now because I'm not like him. I try to be, but I'm not. Could you maybe ask Mr. Crowley if he has some friends he works with who would want me?"

Mrs. Crowley swallowed; she looked visibly shaken. "I can't believe we've done this to you. We didn't mean—"

"The first day of school can be hard for some children." A woman's voice.

Both Mrs. Crowley and I looked up. Standing next to us was a tall lady with straight, blond hair and a plain vanilla face.

"My name is Mrs. Dobson," the woman introduced herself. "I'm going to be your teacher." She knelt next to me. "And what's your name?"

"This is Owen, my son," Mrs. Crowley answered.

"Please don't make me go in there," I pleaded with Mrs. Crowley. "Can't we just go to the park like we used to?"

"I'm sorry, honey, but you have to stay here," she answered tenderly. "You're of an age when you have to be in school. But I'll be right here at three o'clock to pick you up. And I tell you what— right after school today we'll go straight home, and we'll have warm brownies and cold milk. Okay?"

The woman named Mrs. Dobson softly touched my face. "I promise you, Owen, it won't be as bad as you think."

"Do I have to go in the room?" I asked the woman.

"Not if you don't want to. You can stay right here by the door if you would like. You can come in when you're ready."

"You're very gracious," Mrs. Crowley commented.

"This is a critical period for children. How they're treated now is how they'll think of themselves later."

"Very true," Mrs. Crowley concurred. She smiled at me. "Owen, tonight your father and I will sit down with you, and we'll have a long talk about your feelings. We want to know them. We love you, Owen. We truly do." She kissed me on the forehead and then turned to Mrs. Dobson. "Please take good care of him."

"I will," Mrs. Dobson assured, smiling warmly. "You have my word."

Mrs. Crowley stroked my hair with her hand. "I will be here at three o'clock to pick you up, sweetheart," she promised and kissed my forehead. She left my side and then my sight.

I had been by myself many times in my nearly six and a half years, but at that moment, I felt more alone and vulnerable than at any other time before.

Mrs. Dobson smiled at me. "I'll bring you out a chair. Today is going to be very easy. We're just going to get to know one another and then play some games. If you feel like joining in, you can. If you don't feel like it, that's okay too." She smiled again, patted my arm and vanished into the room.

One of the boys who had mocked me earlier was eyeing me. Revulsion and contempt were pasted on his young face. He was a stout boy with tanned skin and thick, black hair.

True to her word, Mrs. Dobson brought me a folding chair from the back of the room. She left me with a smile and walked to the front of the classroom.

"Good morning, everyone," she began. "Welcome to first grade. My name is Mrs. Dobson, your teacher. Today, we're going to start by getting to know one another. We'll begin by going around the room. I want each of you to stand, tell us your name and a little bit about yourself. Why don't we begin with you," she said, pointing to the student on her far right who was seated in the front row.

Mrs. Dobson's posture changed when the black-haired boy who had sneered at me earlier stood to speak. Her face tightened, her body stiffened, and her frame seemed to thin before my eyes.

"Is the *crybaby* gonna stand by the door all day?" asked the boy.

"If he stands there *all year*, it's none of your business—is it, Mr. Farnsworth?" Mrs. Dobson countered.

"Look at him—he's a *baby*. He belongs in a crib."

She stared at him. "And you belong in a cage!" Mrs. Dobson fired back. "This is a classroom, Mr. Farnsworth, not your bedroom. You'll not voice whatever you please! Do you understand me?"

The boy's face turned scarlet.

I couldn't be sure if he was red from embarrassment or anger.

"*Do you understand me?*" she repeated.

"Yeah, I understand ya," he came back nastily.

"That's *you*, not *ya!*" she admonished him.

He said nothing in return.

She stared at him again. "So tell us about yourself, William," she asked him. "Tell us what you like to do when you are not at school. Tell us what you do when you are, say, in your backyard."

How did she know his name before he had given it?

Did this woman dislike this boy because of what he said to me or because of something else? I had a feeling it was something else. Something personal.

I also had a feeling her curiosity was intended more to punish him than acquaint herself with him.

"What I do away from school is my own business, lady!" he flamed.

"Today it is everyone's business," she returned. "It will be their fortune to know what kind of boy you are and what kind of pastimes you enjoy when you're away from these grounds."

"You can't make me say anything I don't want to."

"Since when don't you want to wag that trashy tongue of yours, *Billy*? *Billy*—isn't that what your father—"

"Don't call me that!" he snapped back caustically. "It's William! Not *Will*, not *Bill*, not *Willy*, not *Billy*—just *William*!"

"Don't you raise your voice or dictate to me, Mr. Farnsworth!" Mrs. Dobson raised her own voice. "You're forgetting yourself, boy! You're not at home now—you're in *my* classroom. You won't speak to me like you speak to your—" she stopped suddenly. She closed her eyes as if to compose herself and gather strength.

There *was* something personal between them. A history...a *bad* history.

Thin-lipped, she said, "Sit down."

Apparently, she had lost her desire to continue his punishment.

"You *like* the crybaby, don't you, Mrs. Dobson?" he asked with a smirk, looking at her, then at me. "We all saw you talking to him and treating him so special. If a grownup gives special attention to a little kid, it's 'cause they want to get in the little kid's underwear. Do you want to get in the crybaby's underwear, Mrs. Dobson?"

What would possess a child to say such a thing? Unless...he was only doing what he was asked to do: to tell us about himself. Could he have unconsciously tried to sneak us all into his bedroom and let us see what went on in there at night when his father knocked on the door?

The normal pigment of Mrs. Dobson's face was pale pink, but now it was the color of a blood-soaked sheet. More prominent than the color of her face were her lips: they were as taut as a length of nautical rope.

Unlike when William was red-faced, there was no guessing why Mrs. Dobson was red-faced—rage.

She walked over to William and slapped him hard across the mouth. The sound was as jarring as shattering glass. It thrust me back in my chair.

A slap like that would have made most children wail like a siren, but William didn't make a sound. I could tell he wanted to cry, but he didn't. Instead, he tightened his face to control the pain. On his lower lip, by the left corner, there was a small sliver of blood.

Mrs. Dobson grabbed his chin and locked her eyes on his.

"Don't you *ever* talk to me like that again! *Ever!* You want to say filth like that you do it somewhere else! Do you understand me!"

He nodded with glaring, molten eyes.

"Choices have consequences, Mr. Farnsworth," Mrs. Dobson informed him. "If you choose to behave like a degenerate, you will be treated like one!"

She brusquely let go of his chin and looked out at the class. "And that goes for the rest of you too! This is not your home—this is *my* classroom, and before you enter it, you leave your gutter talk outside!"

I looked at William. He was licking his lower lip and staring down at his desktop. There was pure, primordial hatred in his eyes. He was a boy of vengeance and wrath. I knew it. I also knew that both Mrs. Dobson and I would someday feel that wrath.

Seconds later, the morning recess bell rang. All the children sprang out of their seats and ran past me like leaves in a gust. I wasn't sure if they were running to get outside or running to get away from Mrs. Dobson. Probably both.

After all of the children had left, Mrs. Dobson rested her elbows on her desk and put her face in her hands.

I walked over to her and gingerly put my hand on her arm.

Her hands flew away from her face, and she abruptly turned to me. "Oh, Owen, what are you doing here? Why aren't you outside?"

"Mrs. Dobson, are you okay?" I asked.

The inanity of my question instantly hit me. If she were okay, she wouldn't have looked so distressed. I felt foolish for asking her.

Mrs. Dobson stared at me for a moment. "You're an unusual little boy, aren't you? Usually kids only ask me when's lunch, or can I go to the bathroom." She dropped her head back and sighed heavily. "Not the best way to start first grade, is it?"

"William started it, ma'am," I said. "He kind of asked for it."

She looked at me softly. "I'm sorry you had to see all of that. I knew he was going to be in my class. I promised myself I was going to keep myself in check. So much for keeping my promise." She sighed again.

"Do you and William know each other?"

She didn't answer right away. "Yes, I know him. He and his family live next door to my husband and me. He's not a normal child, Owen. He's not right. He's dangerous. Last year, my little dog went missing. Animals disappear all the time. But I found my dog's collar in his back yard. I asked him about it, and he said to me, '*Koreans eat dogs—go ask them.*' Then he walked away. I couldn't prove he had done something to my dog, but I knew he had. He runs around in his back yard wearing only his underwear. He even goes to the bathroom back there. He pulls apart little birds and insects. He pushes around his little sister and screams at her. I've wanted to call someone, but my husband insists that I stay out of it. He says it's William's parents' problem, not ours.

"Owen, I'm telling you all of this because I want you to be careful. I was going to talk to you about it later today. William could hurt you— badly—and he wouldn't care. He seems to favor hurting things weaker than he. I'm not saying you're not strong, but William is stronger."

"Maybe he's going through something, ma'am," I said. "Maybe that's why he acts the way he does."

"What do you mean?"

"It's just that sometimes mean people are mean because the people they know are mean to them. Some people do bad stuff because bad stuff is all they know."

She canted her head to one side. "You *are* a unique little boy. Maybe William *is* going through something. If he is, I don't know how to help him. I'm not trained for it. I'm just a woman who teaches first grade." She shook her head. "I can't believe I'm having this kind of conversation with you."

"Just because I'm little doesn't mean I don't know what's going on, ma'am."

"I'm sorry, Owen, I didn't mean it like that. I've just never had such an adult conversation with a child before."

"Some kids know more about adult stuff than kid stuff. Some kids go home and all they know is adult stuff. Maybe William is one of those kids."

"You're quite the little thinker, aren't you?" she asked.

*That's what happens when you spend most of your life inside your head*, I thought.

The bell rang again. Recess was over.

Time to get back to the door.

I didn't like William, but I understood him. If he was going through what I guessed he was going through—rape and abuse at the hands of his father—then I knew why he didn't like me. I was allowed to cry; he wasn't. I didn't have to do things children shouldn't do; he did. But he didn't know that I had been where he was. If his father was anything like Mr. Wilson, William was raped more viciously and beaten more severely for crying, so he had trained himself not to cry and to take the pain to avoid receiving more pain.

William was an abuser, for he himself was abused. Those he mistreated were those who were at his mercy...just as he was at his father's mercy. To feel less helpless and less scared, William hurt others because he himself was scared. Only in this way did he find relief and a measure of control in his life. He could not overpower his father, but he could overpower others; he needed to dominate in order to mask the acidic and rancid taste of being dominated.

William was at the hands of a monster—his father. The longer the abuse went on, the more of a monster William himself would become. Just like his father.

Mr. and Mrs. Crowley and I sat down that evening and, as Mrs. Crowley promised, we discussed my feelings. They also told me theirs. They told me how deeply sorry they were if they had made me feel like they wanted me to replace the son they lost. It had never entered their minds to take me in simply to fill Eben's empty chair.

In the two months I had been living with the Crowleys, they hadn't asked me much about my former years, for they didn't want to upset me by excavating painful memories. But that early September evening, they asked me about those years, and I willingly told them, for it was a weight I needed to share. They listened, and they cried.

*Mensch*: a Yiddish word meaning *upstanding, worthy, honorable*. The Crowleys were the embodiment of that word. They were the quintessence of integrity and decency.

I didn't understand it. These two people were the apogee of kindness, and yet my first parents were the nadir of it. Why did some children, like William, have beasts for fathers, and yet others, like me, have saints? Why do some children only know scarcity and inequity, while other others only know bounty and plenty? Why do some children have to suffer the wake of the wrong choices of the ones who are supposed to care for them?

My bedtime was eight o'clock. The Crowleys let me stay up beyond it so we could talk.

There are certain colloquialisms that time will never exsanguinate. One such antique is: *They saved the best for last.* That night, the Crowleys did just that—*they saved the best for last.*

They told me they wanted to adopt me.

That is, if I wanted to be.

Of course I did!

Adoption meant permanency, stability, safety. It would mean no more foster parents, no more Greenwood Children's Home, no more unknown future. It would also mean a new name. A new start. Owen Nicholas Langley would soon become Owen Nicholas Crowley.

I was finally going to be someone's son; I was finally going to belong; I was finally going to be loved.

I crawled into bed that night feeling lighthearted and delivered. Life was actually good.

Good, though, is like sweetness on the tongue—it is fleeting and evanescent. And sometimes it is like an aircraft—it crashes.

While drifting off to sleep that night, I heard Mr. Crowley coughing in his bedroom. It was a hard cough, harder than usual. I felt so bad for him. He was such a good man. Good people shouldn't be the ones to suffer; that should be reserved for the bad people in the world...and there were plenty of those.

At the advice of his doctor, Mr. Crowley tried to quit smoking, yet he found it impossible. He even changed brands; he went from Winston to Viceroy because he had heard it was a safer cigarette. How did he not know that there was no such thing as a *safe* cigarette?

I was awakened the next morning by my alarm clock. I set Yogidog aside and enthusiastically scrambled out of bed. I was looking forward to going to school. I liked my teacher. I knew she would keep William and his arachnid compatriots in line, and because of that, I felt I wouldn't be bullied. I might even venture into the classroom.

Mrs. Crowley drove me to school, but she did not walk me inside this time: she knew I wasn't an infant who needed protecting and coddling. I couldn't grow up and develop normally if I was continually handled like a newborn.

I expected Mrs. Dobson to greet me with her comforting smile when I arrived at my classroom door. What greeted me instead was a grizzled, six-axe-handles-wide woman with a face like a prune, a frown like a scythe, and a jaw like a shovel. She had seen seventy summers if she had seen a day. It was plain to see this relic abided no backtalk or ill manners from anyone, especially children.

"Why are you just standing there?" the crepe-skinned crone asked me curtly. "Get yourself in here and take a seat."

"I want to stay by the door," I said fearfully.

"I don't care what you want! Get in here and sit down!"

William and his marionettes were smiling victoriously as the shrew ordered me into the room.

Had I the nerve, I would have destroyed William and his arrogance with a tidy, little revelation to the class: "*Willyboy is daddy's feelyboy!*" But I wouldn't have said it even if I possessed the nerve, for saying it would have hurt him, and that would have made me just like him. He didn't ask for what was happening to him, so, to a large degree, his behavior was out of his control. Chances are, had he different parents, he would have been a different child.

I saw three empty desks in the back row. Nervously, I passed under the transom window above the door. Trembling, I made my way to the aft part of the room. My left arm was pressed hard against the chalkboard during my walk. When I reached the seats, I immediately sat in the one closest to the door and fixed my eyes on the desktop.

I knew all the children in the room were staring at me. I felt the pigment in my face change from pale white to deep rubicund.

"You better clap yourself when you go outside," a girl in front of me said. Her name was Susan. She didn't deserve to bear that name.

All the children laughed.

I raised my eyes to her.

She was staring at my left arm.

I looked at it. The outermost surface of my shirtsleeve was covered with white chalk dust. I looked over at the chalkboard. Cutting through the middle of newly written letters and words was a wide spear of blurred chalk, like the wake of a snowplow after a blizzard.

I blushed again. But this time, the erythema was so intense my skin stung. I wanted to die.

The children laughed again.

"Next time, would you wait until I have finished with the blackboard *before* you erase it?" the prune-faced ironclad said to me.

"I'm sorry," I said.

"What's your name?" she asked almost toxically.

"We call him '*crybaby*,'" William injected.

"How about *sissybaby*?" one of William's puppets sitting next to him said.

"How about talking only when you're *asked* to talk," the prune recommended.

A girl sitting next to the outside window raised her hand.

For a brief second, the prune looked pleased: *Finally, a child with some propriety.*

"Yes?" asked the prune.

The girl stood. "Where's the teacher we had yesterday—Mrs. Dobson?"

"She has been dismissed. She won't be returning."

"How come?" asked the girl.

Shifting her eyes downward toward William, the elephantine pedagogue said, "Because, while this school believes in disciplining unruly children, it does not believe in disciplining them severely. And it *certainly* will not tolerate, nor does it understand, indecency with them."

*What did she mean by that?* I asked myself.

"How did—" the girl ventured further.

"Enough questions about Mrs. Dobson," the prune cut the girl off. "She is gone, and I am her replacement. My name is Mrs. Wilson."

Fear seized my entire body!

I knew this was not the same Mrs. Wilson who had fostered me, but the name alone was enough to fill me with terror.

Recess couldn't arrive soon enough. I needed to escape that room and be outside where I felt unconfined and unburdened. The day certainly wasn't turning into the bouquet of roses I had hoped for.

Under a red maple, I sat. I closed my eyes and took in the sounds and scents of the late-summer morning. In the background, the squeals of children at play added to the music of the moment. I both adored and abhorred the sound. I was jealous that I couldn't be so happy, and yet it was comforting to know that there were children who were simply children, and nothing else.

"Crybaby, crybaby, sittin' by a tree, all alone 'cause he ain't me."

My eyes shot up.

Standing next to me was William.

I swallowed in fear. *"William could hurt you—badly—and he wouldn't care,"* Mrs. Dobson had warned me.

"Got no friends, huh?" William asked mockingly. *"Poor crybaby.* If you was more like me, you would. If you wasn't such a baby, you would. Everybody likes me 'cause I ain't no runnin' rabbit like you. I stick up for myself. I ain't like you—a yellow-backed chicken. *Bwuuck, bwuuck, bwuuck, bwuuck, bwuuck."*

Amir Kammerer, bard and balladist, wrote: *If I hate me, I hate those who mirror me. If I hate my reflection at home, I will hate it when I am away from home.* William hated me more than he hated himself, for I was a reminder of the weakness and timidity he showed his father. Yet away from his father, he elevated himself: it was his only way of living with his cowardice. Yet he wasn't a coward: he was only a boy, not a man. How does a boy fight off a man? He can't. Why didn't he see that? I saw it when Mr. Wilson was forcing himself on me. Why didn't William see it when his father was forcing himself on him?

"Please leave me alone," I said, my voice quavering.

"*You wish*," he said. "I got that dog-face Dobson—and now I'm gonna get *you*!" he vowed. "Just you wait. You won't see it comin'. That bitch didn't see it comin' neither. You shoulda seen the principal's face when I told him she tried to put her hand down my pants in the boys' pee-room."

William laughed, and then his eyes narrowed, and his lips tightened. "You wanna put your hand down my pants, faggot? Do ya? Just try it and I'll *kill ya*!"

Such words would have shocked others, but they didn't me, for I knew William was not a natural child. He was a mutation, a monstrosity, a creation of abnormal lust and brutal care. Perhaps couched in William's threat was the desire not to kill me but his father. If this were so, I could understand, for so many times I wished Mr. Wilson dead.

Or, perhaps, William was actually daring me to reach for his private place so that he could kill me and finally become the strong and untouchable boy he desired to be and not the shrinking and recreant whey-face he was with his father.

Whichever the case, I wasn't about to stay and find out.

I stood up to leave.

"Where do ya think yer goin'?" he challenged.

"Away from you."

"Yer not goin' anywhere."

He stepped in front of me and stared at my eyes.

"Get away from me," I said. My fear was dissolving; anger was taking its place.

"You know, you *are* kinda cute. I can see why that dog-face Dobson went for you. My *daddy* would too."

"What do you want, William?"

He leaned toward me. "I want to hurt you," he whispered.

His eyes shifted to the playground behind us and paid it a quick glance. Then, with the speed of a spark, he slammed his fist into my stomach.

I yelled and collapsed in agony.

He bent over and grabbed my hair. "You tell and I'll kill ya."

He let go of my hair, stood up, and quickly stepped away from me.

I heard hard-soled shoes running in my direction. My yell must have been heard.

"What happened here?" a woman asked frantically.

"I dunno. He just screamed and fell down," William said flatly.

"Little boy, are you all right?" the woman asked. "What's wrong? Are you sick?"

Dozens of children were gathering around me.

The punch went to my stomach, but my whole body felt it. I had read that a bullet to the stomach produces the worst kind of pain. I felt like I had just been shot.

"Is it your middle—are you sick to your tummy?" she repeated.

It wouldn't have been a lie if I had told her that, yes, I was sick to my stomach. Very sick.

"I want to go home," I managed to say.

"Yes, of course," the woman agreed. "Let me help you to the office, and we'll call your mother so she can come and get you."

The woman, whose name I did not know, helped me to my feet.

I happened to catch a glimpse of William as I was rising. He was standing off in the distance. His hands were tucked in his back pockets...and he was smiling.

The plane crashed.

The day was October 31, 1966.

Halloween. The day of black. The day of death.

The good in my life, like an airplane in distress, came down and burst into flames.

My Zenith radio/alarm clock said it was 4:15 P.M. I was lying on my bed, dressed in my *Batman* costume. *David Copperfield* by Charles

Dickens was perched in my hands. I was waiting for nightfall to arrive so I could go trick-or-treating.

There was a soft tap on my door. It was Mom! She was home!

She didn't pick me up from school that day. Mrs. Kleen, our neighbor, brought me home. Mrs. Kleen didn't explain why she was picking me up; she just said that my mother had asked her to make sure I was brought home. Mrs. Kleen wasn't her usual festal and mirthful self during the ride. Rather, she was almost funereal. I asked her if there was something wrong, but she didn't answer.

"Come in, Mom," I said happily.

Right after my adoption, I began calling Mrs. Crowley *"Mom."* It seemed perfectly natural. She seemed to enjoy hearing me call her *"Mom,"* and I enjoyed saying it. There was a part of me—deep down—that felt I was betraying my natural mother by calling Mrs. Crowley *"Mom,"* but my natural mother didn't want me and didn't love me, so why shouldn't I call Mrs. Crowley *"Mom"*?

Mom opened the door and came into my room. Her face was ashen. I had never seen her look like that. It frightened me.

She came over to my bed, gently took hold of my book, and placed it next to the alarm clock on my night table.

She kissed my forehead.

"What's wrong, Mom?" I asked.

"Oh, sweetheart…" She started to weep.

"Mom, what's wrong?"

"You are such a mature little boy. We were so blessed to have you come into our lives. Your father loved you so."

*Loved? Doesn't he love me anymore?*

"When we lost Eben, our whole world came to an end. Your father's especially. There's a bond between a father and son that goes beyond words. Just as there's an inexplicable bond between a mother and daughter. Your father couldn't go to work after Eben's death. All he could do was cry. He just stayed in bed. No one could reach him. Not even me."

Her eyes drifted away from mine. They drifted away through the window behind my bed.

"Your father and I never made it to our senior prom," she said numbly. "We were dressed to the nines and ready to trip the light the whole night. Instead, we spent the evening in the emergency room. We were walking out to his car when he tripped on something on the lawn. He fell and landed on the handlebar of my little brother's tricycle. It got him right on the lower jaw. The handlebar didn't have one of those rubber grips, so he got a pretty nasty cut. He got twelve stitches and a permanent scar from that fall. But he didn't get upset. Not at my little brother for leaving his bike out, not at his ruined tuxedo, not even about missing the dance. In all the years we were together, he never once lost his temper. Never once raised his voice. He was such a kind man. He wanted to be an architect; I wanted to be a nurse. Not many people know that. I never did become a nurse, but that was all right. I wanted to start a family with your father. We had three miscarriages, your father and I. Then we had Eben. We weren't expecting him. We were in our forties. It's almost unheard-of to have a baby in your forties... but I did. But then we lost him too. Hard times. But I never wished for another life. I've never regretted a single moment I had with your father." She took a labored breath.

"Your father died this morning, Owen," she said, still looking out the window.

# CHAPTER 4

# *Seeds of Columbine*

*"For every action, there is always an equal and opposite reaction."*

ISAAC NEWTON

On April 20th, in the year 1999, Eric Harris and Dylan Klebold entered Columbine High School in Jefferson County, Colorado, and killed twelve students and one teacher, and injured twenty-four others with two sawed-off shotguns, one carbine rifle, and a semi-automatic handgun. After the killings, the two boys turned the firearms on themselves. Eric put the muzzle of one of the sawed-off shotguns against the roof of his mouth and engaged the trigger. Dylan put the semi-automatic against his left temple and did the same.

In total, thirty-seven people suffered injuries—some minor, some serious, some fatal. The number of those injured emotionally and mentally, however, is unknowable. The massacre—like the blast waves at Hiroshima and Nagasaki—was felt far beyond the city in which it happened.

It was said at the time that the number of deceased victims was not thirteen, but fifteen: the two other victims being Eric and Dylan. They were thought to be victims as well, for they were bullied, demeaned, traduced, and excluded by the other students at Columbine, and their rampage was simply a response to that treatment.

Thousands of children are bullied daily by their classmates. Why do they not strike back? Why do they not seek reprisal and demand indemnification? Why is it that some children can suffer torment and never show a crack, but others break apart completely? Why is it that some children, after being bullied and persecuted, can move on, while others must seek revenge for their mistreatment?

Some said that Eric Harris was a narcissist who was led by a corrosive psychopathology; and that Dylan was led by Eric. But why did Eric possess that pathology? Was its genesis in gestation, or in life? Were the seeds of Columbine planted after Eric and Dylan entered high school, or were they planted before...when they were in grade school? Was it there that they were first teased and maligned?

It was in grade school that I was first teased and berated.

In the year 1851, a renowned piece of American literature was published: *Moby-Dick*. The protagonist, Captain Ahab, pursues his antagonist, a great white sperm whale named Moby Dick. On a previous voyage, the great whale maimed Captain Ahab by taking off his leg, and now the captain is consumed with revenge and hatred.

I read this novel when I was very young. After reading the book, I considered myself. I knew that I had a retaliatory nature, and I wondered if, when I reached adulthood, I would act on that nature and become like Captain Ahab: vengeful and unrelentingly vindictive. I had also read about the beauty of karma and the ugliness of an eye for an eye and blood for blood. The misdeeds and wrongs a person does are always revisited upon him, so seeking retribution is unnecessary. Still, was it in my nature to someday have my revenge on those who mistreated me? Or would I forgive and forget and let karma be my retaliator? Something deep inside told me that if anyone were to make my tormentors accountable, it would be me.

*What do you call a pig who knows karate? A pork chop.*

*Why did the student study in an airplane? He wanted a higher education.*

*What did one eye say to the other? Between you and me something smells.*

*Waiter, waiter, there's a fly in my soup! It's okay, sir, there's no extra charge.*

*Doctor, Doctor, I feel like a spoon. Well, sit still and don't stir.*

*How do you make a hot dog stand? Take away its chair.*

*What did the chicken say when she laid a square egg? Ouch!*

*What do you call a bee that's always complaining? A grumble-bee.*

*What word is always pronounced wrong? Wrong.*

*What happened when the egg laughed? It cracked up.*

*What did the handsome chewing gum say to the pretty shoe? I'm stuck on you.*

*What did the banana say to the doctor? I'm not peeling very well.*

*What do you get when you cross a baby with a UFO? An unidentified crying object.*

*What did the sick elevator say to the other? I think I'm coming down with something.*

*What do you call a dentist in the army? A drill sergeant.*

*What kind of key opens a banana? A mon-key.*

*Why do bees have sticky hair? Because they use a honey comb.*

*What did the tie say to the hat? You go on ahead and I'll hang around.*

*Why don't you play cards in Africa? Because it has too many cheetahs.*

*Why wouldn't the chicken cross the road? Because he was a chicken.*

These were some of the jokes Mr. Crowley told me. He loved to see me laugh.

I missed Mr. Crowley. I missed my father. I missed my daddy. I didn't even get the chance to say good-bye to him.

My father awoke the day of his death with an unusually painful headache. He also awoke very confused and disoriented, not even knowing who my mother was. He could not stand and had no coordination of his arms and legs. My mother immediately called an ambulance. At 12:36 that afternoon, he passed away. Cause of death: acute hemorrhagic stroke resulting from advanced metastatic lung cancer. I knew my father was not well, but I did not know the gravity of his illness. At the time, I had no idea he had cancer. Neither he nor my mother would discuss the nature of his sickness with me. All I knew was what I saw.

Around the end of September, I noticed changes in him; first slight, then drastic. He lacked the energy he used to have, and he was starting to lose weight. He tried to be happy when he and I were together, but I could tell his smiles were forced. Sometimes he would wince suddenly and then close his eyes as if to gather strength. He slept more, and he stopped going to work.

Friends, neighbors, colleagues, and family (close and distant) attended his viewing. I stood next to my mother as they all came up to her and gave their sympathies. My mother kept a tight composure, but I knew that deep down she, too, was dying.

Strangely, no one asked me how I was feeling. They must have thought that since I was adopted, I had no real connection with my father and therefore could not feel any pain from his death.

After my father's internment, hundreds guested our home. On the dining room table, casseroles, meats, salads, soups, breads, fruits, sandwiches, desserts, and beverages of every color and kind were there to greet them.

I stood back and watched the crowd, perplexed. It made no sense. It was illogical to me. There they were eating, laughing, drinking, and enjoying themselves, and yet only a few hours earlier they were weeping and disconsolate. How could people go from downhearted to happy-hearted so quickly?

I put on my coat and went out into the backyard. I sat on one of the U-shaped swings on my Swing-and-Slide playset. I remember when my father assembled it. He and one of his office friends put it together one Saturday. It took them nearly the entire day.

Each night, if the weather allowed, my father and I would play on the set. Sometimes, he would get behind me and push me. He knew I was afraid of heights, so he never pushed too hard.

On Sunday evenings, he and I would sit on the front porch and play Go Fish or Old Maid or Crazy Eights and count the cars that drove by.

Sometimes we would sleep out in the backyard. If there were passing clouds before we went to sleep, we would tell each other what we thought the clouds looked like. My father usually saw animals and insects and sea creatures; I usually saw mountains and trees and flowers.

He so wanted to buy me a dog, a Chihuahua, but my mother was allergic to animals, so instead, he bought me the biggest picture book he could find on puppies and dogs.

That kind of love and closeness I would never find again.

Sitting there on the swing, I began to cry. Everyone who had been good to me was gone: Susan, Yogidog, Larry, Mrs. Chipman, Rebecca, Elizabeth, Mrs. Constance, Mrs. Dobson, and now my father. My mother would soon be gone as well—not bodily, but mentally. I was important to her, yet I was more so to my father. I knew she would turn into herself, and after that, she would be gone, forever.

There was no wind that cold November day; there wasn't even a breeze, but as I sat on the swing, it began to move, ever so slightly.

There was a faint aroma of Right Guard deodorant in the air. Morning and night my father wore it.

"I love you, Daddy," I said through my tears. I called Mrs. Crowley *"Mom,"* but I called Mr. Crowley *"Daddy."*

Minutes later, my swing came to a slow stop. And the masculine scent of Right Guard faded away.

"Good-bye, Daddy," I said.

As I imagined—and feared—my mother turned inward. She still spoke, but her intonations were flat and lifeless. She cleaned the house, drove me to school, made me breakfast, made me dinner, and tucked me into bed at night. But the days of happy smiles and sweet kisses and lovely laughter were gone. On weekends, she made my meals and washed the dishes, but in between these tasks, she stayed in her bedroom with the door closed.

Thanksgiving was my mother's first holiday alone. It was a long and lonely day. My mother stayed in her room, not once venturing out, not even to check on me. I poured myself a bowl of cereal for breakfast, made myself a peanut butter sandwich for lunch, and heated a can of Campbell's tomato soup for dinner. I stayed on the living room couch most of the day and read. I didn't mind being there, for the couch was bigger and more comfortable than my bed. Neither did I mind that I didn't have a traditional Thanksgiving dinner: I was unaccustomed to celebrating the day, so I didn't feel any kinship with it.

The days slowly crawled into December. They became routine again, like the days before I entered the Crowleys' life. But routine had once been my only companion, so it was not an unbearable one. Routine is like nighttime: it always returns.

My mother hired a house overseer in mid-December to manage the affairs of our home; she no longer had the mental desire or physical ability to carry out these responsibilities.

The house overseer my mother hired was a widow and a Torrance, California transplant whose signature spelled Hilda Windom. She was a grim, elderly, ponderous boilerplate with henna-colored hair. She had been a CPA in her younger years. My mother insisted that she reside in our home. Since our two-story Colonial had six bedrooms, there was plenty of space to accommodate her.

I could tell immediately Ms. Windom didn't like me. I sensed she thought me some silver-spooned teacup; a dainty, babied brat who had never known want, who had never felt discomfort, and who had never heard the word *no*.

Her husband was deceased, so she insisted that she be addressed as *Ms.* and not *Mrs.* She laid down a litany of house rules almost immediately: "*You are to leave your shoes outside before entering the house. You are to walk about the house only in clean socks* (what if I came home with dirty socks?). *You are to be ready for dinner at precisely 5:30 P.M.* (no, I would be ready at 5:30 A.M.). *You are to come straight home from school* (where else would I go?). *You are to either be in the backyard or in your room when not in school. You are to sit, not stand, when using the toilet* (was she going to watch me every time to make sure?). *You are never to bathe but always shower, as bathing is unhygienic. You are to shower and brush your teeth twice a day—once after rising and once before retiring. You are never to answer the telephone. You are never to speak without first asking permission* (did I not have to speak to ask for permission?). *You are allowed only one hour of television per week. You are never to come into the kitchen. You are never to open the refrigerator* (if I wasn't allowed in the kitchen, how could I open the refrigerator?). *You are never to ask or inform your mother of anything. You are never to have friends over* (what friends?). *You will work for your allowance—it will no longer be given to you without effort. And you are to bring home nothing but A's on your report cards—if you don't, you will feel the burn of a branch."*

It was Mrs. Wilson (my first foster mother) all over again—just in a different body. Both despised me, but there was one difference between them: Ms. Windom didn't threaten to kill me if I got out of line. But that could change within time. Unintentionally, but invariably, I brought out the worst in people.

*There is an end to everything, to good things as well.* Chaucer wrote those words in the thirteenth century; it seemed they applied just as aptly in the twentieth. My short life had come full circle: under dark clouds, I was born; then, for a short time, the sun came out, and then, once more, the clouds reappeared.

To keep the peace with Ms. Windom, I stayed away from her as much as possible. I stayed in my room most of the time. Being in the backyard reminded me of my father, so I only left the house to go to school. I ate my meals as expeditiously as I could so I would not have to be near Ms. Windom any longer than necessary. She made me eat all of my meals on my knees over the downstairs toilet. She would stand by the sink and watch me eat to make sure my head was always directly over the bowl. She said she knew I would spill, and she was not about to clean up after me.

As with Thanksgiving, the Christmas season was invisible in our home. Not a single Santa was unboxed and not a single colored light was strung. The holidays were a painful reminder of my father, so my mother did not want any decorations put up.

I awoke Christmas morning to a soundless house. The house was always hushed, yet this morning it was disturbingly quiet; it was as if the house itself had died. Something was wrong. I hurried downstairs. No one was around. I dashed back upstairs and ran into my mother's bedroom. Ms. Windom prohibited me from entering my mother's room, but that day I didn't care.

Clothes and shoes and jewelry were littered about. Fearing my mother had fallen in the bathroom, I ran into it. It was empty.

She was gone.

Soon after Thanksgiving, my mother had stopped coming downstairs. She never left her room. But this day, she was nowhere.

I heard the front door close.

I bolted from the room and raced down our crescent–shaped staircase.

Ms. Windom was hanging her red, Mackinaw jacket on our mirrored coat rack when I reached the bottom of the stairs.

"Did I not tell you never to run in the house!" she growled.

"Yes, ma'am. It's just that I couldn't find my mother. I didn't know where she was at. I thought you were her."

She sighed with irritation. "That's *she*, not *her*. Don't they teach you English in that school of yours?"

"Yes, ma'am."

"And you *never, ever* end a sentence with a preposition. Do you want to be thought of as some unschooled rube?"

"No, ma'am." I wanted to protest and tell her that I had seen many a sentence capped with a preposition, but I held my tongue. It would profit me nothing to cross swords with her.

Instead, I asked, "Do you know where my mother is?"

"Your mother is not well. Your father's passing has put her in a bad place. She is very ill. She is in hospital at present."

*She is in hospital.* Why did she omit the definite article? Such syntax was British, not American. Very strange. But then, Ms. Windom was a *very* strange woman.

"When will she be coming home?" I asked.

"That I do not know. She may never come home. On the other hand, she may return within the month, although I should think that is highly unlikely. Were I you, I would not expect her back any time soon. Of course, whether she returns or not, you are still under my supervision. Understood?"

"Yes, ma'am."

"Go to your room and shower, and then I will feed you."

I began ascending the stairs.

"And, Owen," she called to me.

I turned around. "Yes, ma'am?"

"Remember, *sit—do not stand*—when you make use of the commode."

"Yes, ma'am," I responded politely.

While going up the stairs, I thought, *I'd like to stand and make use of her face as a commode! Stupid, neurotic cow!*

"I heard your mom's in the crazy house," William said to me. "What happened—did looking at you finally make her go nuts?"

We were at morning recess. It was the first Monday after Christmas vacation. I was sitting on one of the swings, wishing I were somewhere else.

Some of William's friends were flanking him. They were all laughing and smiling as William was having his daily fun with me.

So I wouldn't have to listen to William's constant sniping, I had asked Mrs. Wilson if I could take recess and lunch in the classroom instead of going outside. She said no. She said it isn't healthy for children to be indoors all of the time—they need to be outside under the sun and surrounded by fresh air.

She didn't care about her students needing fresh air and sun—she just wanted to be rid of them. It made me wonder why she went into teaching in the first place.

William was a paradox. After my father died, he left me completely alone. He didn't say one taunting word. Before that, he was forever shadowing me, calling me *"baby"* or *"sissy-boy"* or *"mama's boy"* or *"retard"* or *"dumb-ass."* What he lacked in imagination, he made up for in persistence.

I came to dread recesses and lunch periods. I tried to ignore William, yet he kept at me, like a fly on a mound of offal.

"You know what else I heard?" William advanced. "I heard you come from a whole clan of crazies. I heard the mom you got now ain't even your real mom—she's a parking-meter mom. You put money in her and she'll take care of you. Your real old lady offed herself. She tied a belt around her neck and flew off a table like a bird. And your real dad turned off his own lights too. He blew his brains out. Was that 'cause he was a weak freak like you?"

How did he know all of this? Whose door did he have his snooping little ear pressed against? He must have overheard our mentally challenged principal talking to someone about me. Good old Mr. Shorr—he couldn't keep his mouth shut if it were sewn shut.

I hadn't any compassion for William anymore. It had disappeared weeks ago. In the beginning, I knew his actions were reactions, but now they were just actions: actions of a foul-mouthed flannelmouth, a pompous, prepubescent demon. I wanted to feel bad for him, for no one else did, but it wasn't in me anymore. My empathy had become apathy.

"You come from a long line of losers, don't you, sissy-boy?" Steve Rafferty asked. Steve was William's best friend. "We heard your real parents were losers just like you. Your real mom was a fifty-cent slut and your real dad was a pissing-in-his-pants drunk. Maybe he wasn't even your real dad. That would make you a bastard. A sissy-boy bastard. Just a squirt of dick milk from some horny pervert."

With disgust and disbelief, I stared at them. What made them talk like that? The other children in my class didn't. Many found pleasure in deriding me, but vulgarity was never part of that derision. How could such raunch come from children so young? It made me wonder what kind of parents they both had.

"I think you should go home and put a gun to your head like your real dad did," William resumed. "Hey, maybe your rent-a-dad did the same thing. I bet they made that whole story up about him croaking from cancer. I bet he was a drunk too. And I bet your parking-meter mom opened her legs for all the guys in the neighborhood like your real mom."

"Shut up, William!" I demanded. "Don't talk about my parents like that!"

"I'll say whatever I want to about your deadbeat parents."

"No, you won't."

"*Yes*, I will."

"I won't let you soil my parents' good name."

"You know what, sissy-boy? You talk as weird as you look."

I always swallowed it when someone commented on the way I spoke or looked or carried myself, but now the memory of my father was being debased and the character of my mother defiled, and that I could not abide. I didn't care what people said about my biological parents—they deserved it all—but I refused to let that toilet-mouthed pathogen cast stones at my adoptive parents.

William stepped near me. "Your crazy moms and deadbeat dads were all a bunch of boozers and losers."

I was not going to listen to any more.

I drew my fist back to silence him. William saw this and drew his back as well. But before I could launch mine, William missiled his into my face.

I went down hard and fast. Before I could get back on my feet, William began hammering my midsection with his large winter boots. The metal fasteners on the front of the boots sounded like tambourine zills each time the boots struck me.

Children from the playground had assembled around us; they were cheering William on. I tried to coil my body into a ball to protect my torso, but the maneuver was crowding the impossible because I was in so much pain.

"Stop that!" a woman yelled. "Stop that!"

William kept kicking me.

"What do you think you're doing!" the woman screamed at William.

"That freak started it!" Steve declared, pointing at me. "He took a swing at William! William was just defending himself."

The woman grabbed me by my coat collar and pulled me off the ground. I recognized the woman immediately: it was Mrs. Ladd, the seventh-grade teacher. She occasionally monitored the playground during recess.

As if directed by a choirmaster, the gathering of children around me echoed Steve's lie: I had started the fight.

Looking at me, she asked belligerently, "What's your name!"

"*Owen Crowley!*" Steve shouted disdainfully.

"But we call him '*Creepy Crowley*,'" Roland Mason said proudly. Roland was a boy from my class and a close confidant of William.

"*Creepy Crowley*" was a recent addition to a swelling list of colorful cognomens my classmates gave me. A few other favorites were: "*Owen is a no one*"…"*Owen is a dull one*"…"*Owen is a slow one*." The first two were true, but the third was pure invention. Slow I was not. Socially and physically inept, yes—but not slow.

I understood why William hated me, but I didn't understand why many of the other children shared that hatred. I knew I was odd: I stayed to myself; I was studious; I ate alone at lunch; I read constantly, and I spoke to no one—but was that call for such enmity? Did I have to be their clone in order to win their acceptance, to be their friend? Why didn't any of the children in my kindergarten class—or even those at the children's home—make fun of me? Why were some groups so accepting of me and others not?

"Well, young man, we're going to see what Mr. Shorr has to say about this!" Mrs. Ladd said to me hotly, dragging me toward the school building, her hand clasped tightly around my wrist.

The laughter from William and the children next to him was as thick as the cold morning air.

Mrs. Ladd didn't even knock on Mr. Shorr's door—she threw it open and dragged me over to his desk.

Mr. Shorr, a lanky primate with a small, pallid face, slowly raised his bantam eyes from his desk and regarded us without expression.

"Mr. Shorr," Mrs. Ladd began, "this boy incited a fight on the playground. I saw the entire incident. The other boy had no choice but to fight back. He's a troublemaker. Suspension is mandatory. Shall I call his home?"

The principal's yellow, rheumy eyes stared at Mrs. Ladd with something close to contempt; then he locked them onto mine. "Is this true, Owen? Did you start the fight?"

I said nothing. Mr. Shorr did not like me—I didn't know why; I just knew he didn't. He would shoot down and flense apart whatever I said in my own defense, no matter how logical that defense might be. He would plow through any argumentative rampart I put up. I had already taken one beating that day—I wasn't about to invite another.

"Your silence tells me that Mrs. Ladd is right."

Again, I said nothing.

"Mrs. Ladd is also right about suspension. I know you have suffered a great loss, Owen, and I'm sure that has made you angry, but that does not give you license to be aggressive and truculent. Accordingly, you will not be allowed on this school's campus for two weeks. Your class assignments will be sent to you during that time. We will call Ms. Windom and have her pick you up."

"May I gather my books and supplies from my desk first?" I asked matter-of-factly.

"You may," he replied, almost angrily. He probably thought I would cry and beg for mercy, which would have made him feel powerful and mighty. Instead, I made him feel powerless and insignificant.

I departed his office before he could utter another word and walked to my classroom. Mrs. Ladd trailed me to make sure I returned to the office with my belongings.

Recess was over, and all students were back in their seats.

When I entered my classroom, all eyes shifted to me. Many in the room leered at me. A few didn't, and I wondered why. They were the same ones who never joined William in his crusade against me. They were not outcasts like me—they were just ordinary children who, distinct from William, had no desire to put me down in order to raise themselves up.

I should have foreseen it, but my mind was not on smart navigation but swift expedition: getting in and getting out of that room as quickly as possible. I passed William's desk and I instantly went down. My face hit the hard, tiled floor. The room ignited with laughter. I got to my feet and stared at William. He smirked at me in return.

I looked over at Mrs. Wilson. She was seated in a bland, metal armchair...not unlike her own personality. Her left hand was propped up against the side of her face, her thumb reposing under her jaw, and her index finger resting against her temple. She took note of my circumstance with disinterested eyes.

Why did she hate me so?

Why did the first Mrs. Wilson hate me so?

What was it about me that elicited such spleen and disgust?

Hastily, I went to my desk, lifted its scratched-and-doodled top and collected my books, folders, and pens.

*Fool me once, shame on you, fool me twice, shame on me*: I did not take the same route to the door as I took to my desk. If I fell again, it would be by mistake, not by William's foot.

"Don't hurry back," William said as I was exiting the room.

Calmly, I turned and faced him. As always, he was wearing a haughty, smug grin. Many others in the room had donned the same smile.

*Someday, my friends*, I thought, *someday I'm going to wipe those smug smiles from your faces, and then we shall see who smiles last.*

She cuffed me across the face with a force that should have bloodied my nose and loosened my teeth. It did neither.

"How dare you bring more heartache into this family by getting into a fight!" Ms. Windom shrilled at me after we had entered her car.

She had been restrained inside the school. She listened to the principal without expression, and then, like Mrs. Ladd, led me out of the building by the wrist.

My face was on fire from her slap. My eyes were tearing from the pain, but I refused to let her see me cry. Something told me she would hit me again if she saw tears. Tears, to her, meant weakness, and weakness meant unworthiness to live.

"Only felons and malefactors fight!" she scolded. "Is that what you want to grow up to be—a felon!"

"No, ma'am," I answered as firmly as I could so she would not know how afraid I was. I hated showing fear, although I had the feeling that was exactly what everybody saw.

"I think you do. Why else would you have started that fight today!"

"William was—"

"I don't want to hear it!" she instantly shut me down.

Then she stared at me. "What kind of boy are you anyway? What kind of boy just lies on the ground and lets himself be kicked over and over? I can't believe you let yourself be bested like that! You know what they call boys like you who bend at the first sign of confrontation? A flower. No—a *yellow* flower."

Where was this coming from? How could she reprove me for fighting and then turn around and call me a coward for *not* fighting? What did she want from me? I didn't understand.

"Why are you getting so angry with me?" I asked. "Just a minute ago you told me that only felons and malefactors fight."

Her face turned red with rage. In less than a millisecond, her arm was in flight and her fist slammed into the side of my face. "Don't you *ever* talk back to me again!"

The force of the blow sent my body into the side of the door. The right side of my head smacked hard against the window. The glass should have shattered, but it held.

My entire head was searing with pain: first from William's punch and now from the two blows Ms. Windom had given me. I cupped my hands over the left side of my face. It felt hot and swollen.

Something unnaturally warm and metallic-tasting was starting to coat the inside of my mouth. I knew instantly what it was—blood.

I wanted to cry. I wanted my mother back. I wanted my daddy back.

"Your mother told me you have a fear of basements," Ms. Windom said. "Is this true?"

It was true. But why did she ask about it?

"Yes," I answered apprehensively, swallowing the blood that had pooled in my mouth.

"Do you know where felons and malefactors go?"

I hesitated. "Jail?"

"Correct. And that is where *you* will be going—jail. *My* jail. In the basement. For two weeks. Maybe a little confinement will cause you to think twice about raising your fist to another. Call it a foretaste of your future if your ways go unmended."

"*But—*"

She raised her hand again to strike me.

I quailed against the door.

I did not pursue the matter, though I was desperate to. The urge to cry was overwhelming. The thought of being locked in the basement terrified me.

"Save your tears!" she remarked disdainfully. "You should have thought of the consequences of your actions before you took them."

"Please don't make me—"

I couldn't help it, I began to cry.

She grabbed me by the throat. "You know what your problem is, boy? You're as weak as sodden bread. You're nothing but a rich kid who's had everything handed to him his whole life! All you've ever known is luxury and comfort and ease! You've never known hardship or pain or loneliness! You don't know what it's like to feel hunger and cold and misery. I do. Hear this, *rich boy*—your life of silk and mahogany has *ended*! Your days and wine and roses are over."

She released her hand from my throat and started the car.

On our way home, I contemplated running away. But the thought of finding food and shelter in the winter frightened me more than spending two weeks in the basement. If I could only hold out for the two weeks, I would be all right.

Ms. Windom took me by the wrist again once we reached my home and she led me straight to the basement door. Before she opened it, she spun me around so that I was facing her.

"Here's how your life will play out for the next two weeks, rich boy. Any deviation from that course and you will feel the burn of one of your father's belts. Understood?"

I nodded.

"Very good. You will do your school assignments as soon as they arrive. I will check them thoroughly before they are returned to the school. If I find any errors, you will stand in the snow without shoes for a period I decide is commensurate with those errors. If your feet turn necrotic from the cold and have to be cut off, so be it. You will be fed once a day. You will consume everything I bring you—no matter *what* it is. You will shower each morning and each evening. While in the bathroom, make sure you make use of the commode, for you will not have access to it until your next shower. When not engaged in your school work, you may read or sleep, but that is all. You will make no noise whatsoever. This is no vacation, rich boy. Remember that."

She took hold of my coat and yanked it from my body. Then she took hold of the brass knob on the basement door. Before she opened it, she grabbed my shirt collar. "One last item, rich boy," she supplemented. "Everything that happens under this roof *stays* under this roof. If I get wind that you have acquainted anyone with how I handle the affairs of this household—which includes how I handle you—you will wish you had died inside that pusillanimous mother of yours."

Too late...I had wished that long before I met her.

Her words were all too familiar. I had heard them before—from Mrs. Wilson, the first Mrs. Wilson. I had no doubt that Ms. Windom and Mrs. Wilson were cut from the same dirty cloth.

After opening the door, she commanded, "Go on—get downstairs."

I hesitated. Like the Wilsons' basement, it was lit only by sunlight, which was minimal because the room was underground.

"Don't be such a little girl!" she snorted.

My body was trembling. "Please don't make me go down there," I pleaded. "Please let me stay in my room. I won't make any noise—I promise. I'll do anything you want. Please let me stay upstairs."

"You're just like your mother—*weak*! Now get down those stairs!"

She pushed my arm. I lost my footing, and my body tipped sideways, then backward. Panic and terror filled my chest—like water gushing into a ship whose hull has been ruptured. My back hit the edge of a step, then my head slammed against the tread of a step. Then it hit another, and another. It seemed like forever before I came to a stop. Only a moment ago, I was upright—now my body was supine on the cement floor at the base of the carpeted stairs, my legs resting limply on the last two, pointing up toward the door. I had slid down the stairs on my back like a sled on snow. Had the steps not been carpeted, and had I fallen at a different angle, I most surely would have been killed.

Ms. Windom eyed me without concern. "Maybe next time you will listen to me. Maybe next time you will not be so lucky. *Maybe*...I should have said *hopefully* you will not be so lucky. You are extra work I do not need. You are inconsequential."

I looked at her in disbelief. She actually tried to kill me.

"Do you know what an inconsequential human is?" she asked flatly. She did not wait for a response.

"An inconsequential human has no value," she explained. "He is worthless. Do you know what a worthless human does...or *should* do? He extinguishes himself. He considers the greater good and guarantees that he will no longer be an expense or an offense to anyone by performing the simple act of killing himself." She gave me that hateful stare again, turned, closed the door and locked it.

Uneasily, I rose to my feet. The back of my head pulsated with pain. Carefully, I touched it. It was knotted and, even through my hair, was calescent.

The air around me was bitterly cold. I couldn't understand why. Even the Wilsons' basement was not this frigid.

Then I heard a strange sound in the room, like metal tapping against metal. I looked around. I instantly saw the cause of the noise and the source of the cold. At the far end of the basement was an open window, and above it, suspended from the ceiling, were two wire hangers tapping against one another. Wind coming in from the open window was causing them to mate. I wondered why the window would be open during the winter. It wasn't until I got close to the window that the answer was revealed. The window had been broken. Deliberately. Glass was scattered on the snow in the window well outside. Nothing, except the hangers, was close enough to the window to have broken it, so it had to have been broken on purpose. Had someone tried to force their way in, the shards would have been on the floor of the basement. Instead, they were on the outside, so the window had to have been shattered from the inside. And had someone breached the glass by accident from the inside, which could only have been done by my parents, for they were the only ones who would have gone into the basement, there would have been a build-up of snow and debris on the floor under the window. There was no snow and no debris, so the glass had been broken recently...and deliberately.

There was only one person who would have done it.

And she was right upstairs.

I had to cover the window somehow. I saw a pillar of five velvet throw pillows on the floor. They should have been coated with dust from lying on the bare cement, but they were as pristine as if they had been sitting on a department-store shelf. I estimated that two would adequately seal the window.

They did.

This reparatory rose stowed a hidden thorn, however. The covered window made the room darker and more menacing. Dark basements can be unfriendly places...especially to children.

I looked up to see where the light bulbs were, so when night came, I could stay under one of them. The bulbs had been removed from their sockets. Another of Ms. Windom's affable reminders of her bile for me.

Unlike the Wilsons' basement, this one was well-occupied. Boxes, books, rugs, pictures, lamps, storage trunks, suitcases, knickknacks, and dusty pieces of furniture were lying all about. There was no order or organization to any of it. It was a bold contrast to the rooms above, which were tidy and uncluttered. My parents were such clean people— why would they let this area be so unclean? It didn't make sense.

No matter. There was a more pressing matter at hand: survival. I had to find a blanket or coat or something heavy to wrap around me. If I didn't, I would surely freeze.

The chill in the basement proved to be an unexpected blessing. Because my focus was on finding warmth, my mind was no longer drawn to the dusky room or the memories it elicited.

I wasn't going to worry if I made a mess trying to find something to warm me, for Ms. Windom would never be able to differentiate the mess I made from the one already there.

I suspected that the suitcases would be empty, for they are typically used for traveling, not storing, but the storage trunks should have something in them I could use as a wrap.

There were three trunks in all. Each was very large, about the size of a cedar chest. All but one was padlocked. What could they contain that needed securing?

The metal fasteners and corner guards on all of the trunks were tarnished and dulled, and the skins of the trunks were cracked and black. The locked trunks were dusty and dirty, as if human hands hadn't touched them in years. The unlocked trunk, however, was not as dusty and had visible finger marks along its top and front. Maybe it held a few pieces of heavy clothing.

The trunk opened easily. The smell of my mother's perfume quickly rolled over me. It was like a strong and reassuring embrace.

As I had hoped, the chest was full of all types of protective raiment. Hats, sweaters, coats, gloves, mufflers, even a rain slicker lay in the trunk. All of the vesture was feminine, but I didn't care—I just needed to get warm.

All of the clothing was neatly folded. I carefully lifted out one of the coats and slipped it on. It was a candy-pink, double-breasted, gabardine jacket with a white collar. To the eye, it looked rough and scratchy, but to the skin, it felt smooth and soft. I put on a pair of white, embroidered evening gloves. They were terribly large, yet they immediately took the chill from my fingers. If the children at school could have seen me, they would have laughed themselves into unconsciousness. But again, I didn't care. One does what one has to do to survive.

With my mother's coat and gloves now covering me, my body temperature climbed quickly.

Going through part of the trunk made me want to go through all of it. There is something about an old chest that seduces curiosity.

James Allan Mair had a unique optique about curiosity—*it kills the cat.*

It also has a way of killing people too...or at least a part of them.

Three-quarters of the chest was occupied with clothing. The remaining fourth, at the bottom, was tenanted by thick layers of documents, photographs, and files. These items, unlike the clothes that had been laid over them, were in disarray and confusion, almost as if they had been thrown in the trunk in haste. Lying with the photographs was an open padlock. It had to have been for the trunk, and my parents had forgotten to lock the trunk the last time they closed it.

I picked up a large dune of photographs. The top layer was of Eben.   ·
One of the photographs had a Glad sandwich bag stapled to it. In it was a curly lock of fine, brown hair. It must have been Eben's. Another photograph also had a sandwich bag stapled to it. Snug in its bottom corners were two baby teeth. These, too, must have been Eben's.

The photographs at the bottom of the mound were of Christmas parties and outdoor barbecues and fishing trips. Still others were of birthday celebrations and Easter-egg hunts and Halloween nights. It truly was a perfect life Eben and my parents had had.

Respectfully, I set the mound of square Kodaks back into the chest. I had always been drawn to photographs. When I held a photograph, I felt I was actually holding the past, touching time itself. A moment is gone in an instant, yet a photograph takes hold of that moment and never lets it go. A smile may be replaced with tears the second after a photograph is taken, but that moment of happiness lives forever in the ink on that small piece of paper.

I was about to take hold of another knoll of photographs when I noticed something odd. The tops of two small, yellow sacks were sprouting up against the back side of the chest. They were out of place, for they were the only sacks in the trunk.

I lifted out the first sack and opened it. A triple-folded piece of paper rested inside. I pulled out the paper and unfolded it. Pale-green water spots stained the top and bottom of the ruled piece of paper. In between the stains was a poem.

*—My Children—*
*My children are down and so is the riot,*
  *our home seems a haven to have it so quiet.*
*The day has been all but a tranquil one,*
  *but my children professed they were only having fun.*
*They sounded like a challenge to a sonic boom,*
  *I wouldn't care if we weren't crowded for room.*
*My efforts to curb it fail to compete,*
  *experience has taught me when to acknowledge defeat.*
*I'm sometimes forced to a drastic course,*
  *but when I do,*
    *their sadness shows through.*
*"Don't you want us to play?" they invariably say.*
*If I'm quick to be shy,*
  *they're fast to ply, "If not, pray tell us why."*
*They usually smile with me giving in,*
  *I've found it easier that way than trying to win.*
*But now as I tiptoe to the sides of their beds,*
  *they're a darling sight to see as I tenderly kiss them on their heads,*
  *and softly whisper, "I love you."*
*Although my day was trying,*
  *a vigil we must keep,*
    *for they need a watchful eye even when they are asleep.*
*They are far more precious than a priceless gem!*

*So, when I turn out my light,*
  *for the rest of the night,*
    *I'll turn over my duties to Him.*

                                                            *P. C. S.*

Who in the world was P. C. S.? It wasn't Mr. and Mrs. Crowley—the initials didn't match. And they only had had the one child. Eben. Why were they holding on to a poem about someone else's children? A mystery for another day.

I lifted out the second sack. I was about to open it when I saw that it was stapled shut, as if it were a vault and only the owner was permitted access.

From the feel of the bag, I could tell there were only a few items inside it. Whatever those items were, it was clear they were very important. Crowley family treasures? Crowley family secrets? I instantly felt a sting of guilt. I shouldn't be looking through my parents' belongings. I was trespassing into their privacy. But then it occurred to me: was I not a member of the Crowley family?

*Yes.*

After carefully prying out the staples, I opened the bag and peered into it. A small piece of folded paper and two unframed, palm-sized photographs lay inside.

I pulled all three out.

The first photograph was a cracked and stained black-and-white of a small boy, a year or two younger than me, lying in a white casket. His face looked bloated and unnatural. He looked as if he had suffered horribly before he passed away. I didn't know who the little boy was. It wasn't Eben—that much I knew. I looked on the back of the photograph for a name, but none had been written. All I knew was that the picture was old and had been taken years—possibly decades—before.

The second photo, also a black-and-white—but in better condition than the boy's—was of two young women standing next to a new but old car—new for the time, but old for the photograph. It was a mid-1930s Buick. I remember seeing this model in a picture book of period automobiles. One woman, with an hourglass figure, was wearing a long, dark dress and a white, wide-brimmed hat. The second woman, also flashing a wasp waist, was wearing dark pants, a white, collarless shirt and a dark, feathered, Robin Hood hat. Both women were captivatingly pretty.

I couldn't believe my eyes. I didn't want to believe them.

Both women were a part of me.

Both women were…*my mother*!

One was my Mrs. Crowley—my true mother. And the other was Susan Langley—my biological mother!

A barrage of questions bombarded my mind.

Perhaps the folded piece of paper would answer those questions.

I unfolded the piece of paper. On it was a brief letter in lacy cursive.

*August 5, 1948*

*Dear Jean,*

*I can't tell you how much I miss you! I think of you daily, and I hope that someday you will forgive me for Andrew's death. You must believe me when I say I didn't mean for it to happen. It simply got out of hand. I'm not a bad person. You know that. Please don't shut me out forever.*

*Your loving sister,*
*Susan*

The letter answered my questions…but then created more.

Who was Andrew? Was he my uncle, my nephew, my brother? What part did my natural mother play in his death? Did she want him dead like me? Whatever the details and whoever he was, I would never find out.

I was all clear to me now: the Crowleys took me into their home because Mrs. Crowley was my aunt. She felt it was her duty. I was blood—diseased blood, but blood nonetheless. If I hadn't been, and if I hadn't looked like her dead son, she and her husband wouldn't have given me a second glance.

I tossed the missive and photographs back into the chest. Without concern, I tore off the gloves and the coat I had been wearing and threw them on top of the letter. I then grabbed the clothes that I had carefully put on the floor and flung them back into the trunk as well. I slammed down the lid, took the padlock that had been in the chest and looped it through the hasp of the trunk and pressed it shut. I wanted no part of my adoptive parents anymore. They deliberately kept the truth from me. Withholding the truth is the same as lying. Mrs. Crowley deliberately didn't tell me she was my aunt. She and Mr. Crowley kept her identity a secret because they were ashamed of me; they didn't want anyone to know I was part of the Crowley family tree. The broken branch. The rape child.

The Crowleys said they loved me for me and not for my resemblance to Eben. Another lie. Who can feel love for someone and be ashamed of them at the same time? Is not true love expressed through true acceptance? Sadly, but not unexpectedly, I was right about the Crowleys: it was my similitude to Eben they were drawn to, not me.

What kind of family was I born into? Certainly not an honest and forthright one. And certainly not a genuine and sincere one either. Mrs. Constance must have searched all over the map for my relatives, and that search must have led her to my mother's sister. No wonder I looked so much like Eben, and no wonder my adoptive mother looked so much like my natural mother. We were all one big, defective family.

I wish I had never found that sack and opened it. Spying only begets regrets.

The only other means of warmth in the room were the remaining throw pillows in the corner by the broken window. I went over to the corner, sat down, pressed my back firmly against the concrete wall, elbowed my knees up to my rib cage and compressed the pillows tightly against my chest to keep it warm. I tucked my arms and hands in between my chest and the pillows to heat them. While I was not as warm as I had been while wearing the coat and gloves, my improvisatory solution made me warm enough that I would not freeze.

Larry the janitor said I was weak; William said I was weak; Ms. Windom said I was weak. Was this the reason I was hated so? What was it about weakness that brought out contempt and ire in people? Or was it weakness plus something else in me that people found so detestable?

Crying was not as much a part of my behavioral diet as it used to be. But while sitting there on that cold, cement floor, the tears came easily. All I wanted was to be loved and not hated. Was that so much to ask? I felt so empty and worthless. Maybe I should end my life, as Ms. Windom suggested. Children die every day, and the world goes on. Who would mourn my passing? Who would care if I was no more? Not a soul. But to end one's own life, one must have strength, and that was something I sadly lacked. I *was* weak. So I would have to go on...even though I had no reason to.

Ms. Windom, I'm sure, was expecting, if not hoping, that I would find my sentence in the basement distressing. As it turned out, it was my salvation. She restricted my non-sleeping activities to reading and sleeping. She should have known, but obviously didn't, that reading was my escape, my sanctuary, my savior. The memory of Mr. Wilson and his basement soon dissipated, and I became quite comfortable in my underground jail. The basement actually became my friend. In trying to terrify me, Ms. Windom saved me.

There was no bed of any kind in the Crowleys' unfinished basement, so Ms. Windom put her meager mind to work and divined an idea I knew she thought would vex me: she brought down a thin and crusty foam mattress, a thin and tatty blanket, and a thin, caseless pillow for me to sleep on at night. Though she didn't know it, this was far from a pebble in my shoe or a thorn in my paw. She assumed I had been born into wealth and abundance and would not be able to bear up against any discomfort. She assumed I had been ushered into this world with a silver spoon in my mouth. It wasn't a silver spoon I was born with—it was a dirty one. My natural parents were not affluent—they were effluent. I had slept on far worse things than a spotted and crispy sponge Ms. Windom called a bed.

My meals were another form of punishment...or so Ms. Windom thought. Once a day, for two weeks, I was given a bowl of dry Shredded Wheat and a glass of warm water. As always, I ate this banquet under Ms. Windom's watchful eye over the downstairs toilet. My natural parents didn't give me much, but they did give me one thing: the ability to survive and adapt. Dry Shredded Wheat and warm water were not punitions—they were simply part of life. Hardship and repetition, I had learned, were simply the ways of the world.

It is said that a child would rather have negative attention than no attention at all. Not this child. I was actually sad when my two-week imprisonment came to an end. I easily could have lived in my basement barracoon forever and never complained. I was left alone, and the stress of interacting with other people was as nonexistent as snow in the Everglades. I never saw any of my classmates, and I rarely saw Ms. Windom—to me, this societal indigence was far from punishment...it was perfection.

I found something while down in my dusty cocoon. It wasn't the kind of thing one finds in an old trunk, but the kind one finds in one's own soul. It was a satori not expected. And yet it was. The discovery was just a matter of time, for it was, I believe, inside of me all along—it simply needed the right impetus to bring it to the surface.

The impetus was my forced stay in the basement, and the discovery was the realization that I was my own worst enemy. I found out that all of the basilisks inside my head were alive only because I allowed them to live. My classmates, my teachers, Ms. Windom, everyone who made me afraid and insecure had that power over me because I allowed it. The basement initially held terror for me, but after living in it, I realized that the terror was not in the room, but in my mind. The more I feared it, the more frightening it became. I gave it power, so it had power. I gave it importance, so it had importance. I cared about it, so it bothered me. Thus, I learned, the less I cared about something—or someone—the more success and control I would have over it.

In the latter half of the 1960s, there ran an unusually intelligent television series. Its badge was science fiction, but I saw it as more of an ongoing morality tale; a series on the three C's: compassion, conduct, and character. The show's heroes and anti-heroes were multiracial, multiplanetary and multidimensional. Its creator called it *Star Trek*. There was one in its ensemble who, like Sirius in a night sky, stood out from all the others. The character was a chartreuse-skinned, tightly-controlled, quietly esteemed alien named Mr. Spock. Female viewers were drawn to him because he was someone they wanted to reach; male viewers were drawn to him because he couldn't be reached. Around himself he had built a wall of logic and detachment; a wall that forfended all hurt and pain. Ms. Windom allowed me one hour a week of television. I spent that hour with *Star Trek*. The visuals were unequaled and the stories unparalleled, but the magnet that pulled me back every week was Mr. Spock—the infrangible, untouchable, impenetrable Mr. Spock. That's who I needed to be. He permitted no one into his world. That's what I needed to do. While in my basement prison, I decided that if I were to survive, I had to become like him. I had to be unaffected, unmoved, and unresponsive to every person and every feeling. I had to destroy my heart and my soul. They had to become as cold and as still as death. Like the chest that held my family's secrets, everything beneath my flesh had to be shut and locked, never to be reopened again.

After I returned to school, William and his friends found me changed. I, however, found them the same. Once they saw me again, they resumed their shellings. Only now, the bombs didn't hurt. I didn't even feel them. Sometimes I didn't even hear them. At lunch, at recess, even during class they would launch their munitions at me, and I would simply stare beyond them, to a time when they and their insults would no longer be in my life. My impassivity seemed to make them more militant and vitriolic. Still, I didn't care. They might have thought they had a tight collar around me, but in actuality, it was I who had *them* on a leash. The tail was wagging the dog. It was such a freeing feeling to be insensate, numb to what others thought of me.

Those adults who were my sovereigns also seemed to be maddened by my newfound insouciance. I knew that as long as I did what they asked and expected, they were powerless to harm me.

Yes...Mr. Spock had become me, and I had become him.

Nothing ever stays on plan. But that is a good thing—for one of life's best teachers, though one of its most brutal, is the unexpected.

It was now the month of hearts, candy, and sugar notes. February.

Mrs. Wilson gave everyone in my class two assignments for Valentine's Day. First: decorate a small box and bring it to school February 14th. We could color the box, paper it, paint it, anything we wanted. In it would go the Valentine cards we received from our classmates and friends. It could be any type of box we liked, but a shoebox was the most accommodating. We should cut a large slit in the lid of the box so the cards could be easily inserted. And second: give each student in our class a Valentine's Day card. The cards could be hand-drawn or store-bought.

Not wanting to bring any trouble on myself, I brought an undecorated shoebox to school on Valentine's Day. Mrs. Wilson said we could do anything we wanted with the box, and that's what I wanted to do with it: nothing. Resentfully, Ms. Windom purchased a box of children's Valentine's cards for me, the kind that were small and emblazoned with big, red hearts and rosy-cheeked boys and girls inviting the recipient to be their Valentine. Like I really wanted to ask anyone in my class to be my Valentine. That had about as much chance of happening as them asking me to be theirs. But Mrs. Wilson demanded that the tradition be upheld. I wanted to tell her it was a deplorable tradition. To compel children to give cards of affection to people for whom they felt no affection at all was arrant hypocrisy.

Including me, there were forty-three students in my class. I brought forty-two Valentine's cards to school. On each, I wrote the name of one of my classmates. Of course, not one was penned with affection or sincerity.

With Valentine box in hand, I took my seat in the back of the room Valentine's Day morning. The first bell of the day had not yet rung, so the room was alive with activity. Everyone was milling about, giving and receiving tiny enveloped cards. I could see that many of the envelopes were not flat but slightly protuberant. Obviously, those cards held a Sweetheart or two—the miniature heart candies that read *Be Mine* or *Cutie Pie* or *Kiss Me* or some similar tripe. If a boy had a deep pash for a certain girl, she might get a red sucker in the shape of a heart or a diminutive box of Russell Stover chocolates. If a girl had a deep crush on a certain boy, he might get a small lock of her hair or a sugar note written on his card. Love knows no bounds.

I waited for my classmates to come over and drop their Valentines into my box. In return, I would drop one into theirs.

The first bell of the day sang out. Everyone in my class took their seats.

Not one of my classmates had come over to my desk.

After a few brief announcements from Mr. Shorr via the overhead speaker, Mrs. Wilson began the first class of the day: History. That day's topical study: the origin of Valentine's Day.

I didn't hear any of Mrs. Wilson's lecture. I was in another place. A place of pain. I brought the cards because I was told to, because I wanted to keep myself from conflict. I should have stood my ground; my class certainly did. They didn't care about me and showed it by shunning me and the box on my desk. They were strong; I was weak. *"This above all: to thine ownself be true. And it must follow, as the night the day, thou canst not be false to any man..."* I knew that Shakespearean tuition all too well—why did I not follow it? Could it be that at my core I wanted my classmates to like me, even if they only expressed it through a silly, vapid Valentine? I had always been on the outside looking in. Was it possible that, deep down, I wanted to be inside with everyone else? Was I hurting so much right then because my unfilled Valentine's box was the affirmation that I was truly unlovable and worthless?

Mrs. Crowley had instructed Ms. Windom to drive me to and from school. When Mrs. Crowley left to be hospitalized, that luxury came to an end. It was only a mile or so to my school, but on wintry days, it seemed like ten. That Valentine's Day was cold and snowy. On my walk home that day, I saw a metal garbage can in front of a red-brick house. I went over to the can, brushed the fluffy, cold powder off its lid and dropped my Valentine's box, full of cards I had made for my classmates, into the empty can. I replaced the lid and continued home. The tears on my face quickly froze.

The tears had stopped by the time I reached my house. I had been taught a priceless lesson that day: regardless of the consequences, I must hold tight to my commitment to veer from any course whose final destination was emotion. The only way I would survive was if I stayed true to myself. I would not permit myself to feel anything ever again.

There was one thing I failed to calculate into my plan.

Girls.

# Part 2

# CHAPTER 5

# *New Beginnings, New Enemies*

*"If a child is handed acceptance, he returns acceptance.*
*If he is handed condemnation, he returns condemnation."*

MICHAEL TURSHON, PH.D.

Her name was Robin. She had just turned fourteen. She and I had shared the same classroom since the first grade. When she was seven, she was unexceptional; when she was twice that age, she was unbelievable! She had become as beautiful as the bird after which she was named. She had long and lustrous red hair, a china-doll complexion, and a dimpled smile. A few faint freckles resided below emerald-green eyes. Her body was tall and thin and willowy, and when she walked, it was like watching a spring flower swaying in a cool breeze. Like many girls of the time, she lived in body shirts. Hers were always pastel-hued cotton pullovers that never failed to accentuate her blossoming hills and valleys. Perhaps this was the reason they were called body shirts.

Robin was the kind of girl every boy in our school longed to touch and to kiss and to hold, the kind of girl every boy fantasized over while lying in his bed late at night. But she had a flaw: she wasn't her own person. She belonged to the praise of others. She needed the approval and approbation of her peers. On the outside, she was a masterpiece, but on the inside, where it mattered, she was ugly.

She was walking toward me.

My heart did not quicken at the sight of her approach, for I knew why she was coming.

I had been spying her all through lunch period. I was sitting by myself in the uncool section of the cafeteria: the north side of the room, the side not easily seen by the world. If a student wanted to be noticed and envied, he sat at one of the tables in the center of the room; this was where the pretty people congregated, where the *bon viveurs* rendezvoused to gossip and gasconade. This was the gathering place of the *haves*; the *have-nots* sat on the outer fringes of the room. The *haves* were the blessed children: the children with the perfect homes, the perfect faces, the perfect bodies, the perfect lives.

And yet...there was one among them who was far from perfect. His name was Tim. Covering his neck, chest, arms, and lower face were post-burn hypertrophic scars. He was unblushingly open about how he received the scars. When he was a small boy, he and a friend were frying bugs with a magnifying glass. They would capture insects—grasshoppers, worms, beetles, potato bugs, any unfortunate crawling thing they could find—and put the magnifying glass between the creatures and the sun. Instant bug barbecue. Tim and his friend thought it would be more spectacular if they could actually incinerate some bugs instead of just toasting them. They came across a colony of sugar ants and dowsed them with gasoline. The petrol came from a gas can in Tim's garage. Tim aimed the magnifying glass at the mound of ants, and the gasoline instantly ignited and flashed upward. Tim and his clothing also ignited. His feet and legs took no burns—owed to Tim's friend, who ran for the garden hose and quickly killed the fire—but seventy percent of Tim's upper body and arms were attacked by the fire.

Any other child—or adult, for that matter—would have spun into a bottomless depression. But not this boy. Tim was always positive, always happy. He even made fun of his accident and his appearance: *"Now I'm the one who looks like a fried bug,"* he once said with a laugh. *"Just call me 'Timmy the Timex': he takes a lickin' and keeps on tickin',"* I also heard him say. Never once did I hear him judge, or gossip, or vilify another. He accepted everyone as they were. It was such an unlikely marriage, he and the cutesy crowd. I couldn't understand it. They should have rejected him because he wasn't pretty, and he should have rejected them because they were. The humble usually hate the haughty, and the haughty usually hate the humble. In appearance, he was fathoms beneath them, and yet, there they were, together, thick as thieves.

Robin came over to my table. She stopped in back of the seat next to mine. I didn't want to, but I glanced up at her breasts. I jerked my head back down and pretended to be studying the equations in my algebra book. I felt my face burn with embarrassment.

"Is this seat taken?" she asked.

Reality quickly returned, and I remembered why she was there. I felt my face cool, and when I knew the red had dissipated, I looked up. This time, my eyes ignored her young swells and found her eyes.

"Does it look taken?" I answered with deliberate asperity. Were she there out of kindness, my tone would have been polite, but she was there out of meanness and greed.

She sat down.

I gave my algebra book my attention again, hoping she would get the hint and leave.

"Whatcha doin'?" she chirped.

"What does it look like I'm *doin'*?" I replied, still not making eye contact with her.

"Looks like you're reading your math book."

Shocked at her brilliance, I glanced over at her. "Figured that out, huh?"

"I've never been very good at math."

*No, but I'll bet you're good at counting money,* I thought.

"I got something I want to ask you," she said.

*Hmm, I wonder what that could be.*

"Might I ask you something first?" I said.

She hesitated. "Sure, go ahead."

"Why is Tim in your...*group*?"

"We like him."

"Why is that?"

"He's fun. He makes us laugh. He's really a cool guy."

"Hmm. So I take it if someone makes your group giggle, that person is automatically invited into it? Is that the idea?"

She looked at me with tepid irritation. Getting what she came for was not going to be as easy as she had been told.

"Who wants to be around someone who can't even crack a smile?" she said more to make a point than to answer my question.

"Indeed. Do remember that."

Her irritation was building.

"Tell me, Robin, do you not see Tim's scars?"

"Sure, I see 'em."

"And they don't bother you?"

"No."

"Why not?"

"I don't know. Maybe because they don't bother *him*."

"I see. So because he makes you giggle, and because he is cool and self-confident, you have welcomed him into your...*clique*?"

"Tim's a terrific guy. And we're not a *clique*. We're just kids who like each other."

"I, too, am *just a kid*. Why then am I not in your...*clique*?"

She folded her arms across her chest. A defensive posture. "You wouldn't fit in."

"Is that right? Then why are you sitting here talking with me?"

"I came to ask you something."

I knew exactly what she was going to ask me. But first I would lure her...then snare her...then eviscerate her.

I gave her my complete attention. "*I'm all ears*," I breathed. The lure.

"The Sadie Hawkins dance is coming up. I was wondering if you'd like to go with me."

She asked me exactly what I thought she would ask. Before I gave her my answer, I would have a little fun with her. I would watch her squirm.

"Tell me, Robin, why, out of all the boys in this school, are you asking me?" The snare.

"Because."

"Because why?"

"I don't know. You seem like you'd be fun to be with."

"Like Tim? Why not ask him? According to you, he is the *King of Cool*. Why would you want to be in the company of an *Untermensch* like me? Or, more to the point, why would you want to be with someone who can't even *crack a smile*?"

"Tim already has a date," she answered stiffly.

"Is that a fact? And who might she be?"

"Jennifer."

"Ah, yes, Jennifer. *I am queen and the world is my footstool.*"

"She doesn't think she's a queen."

"Ah, but she does. But no matter. Tell me, Robin, this dance, this girl's choice dance, would I pick *you* up, or would you do the honors?"

Her face brightened.

"I'd pick you up, of course."

"How might you do that? You're too young to drive."

She moved in her seat. "Um, I mean, I'd have my mom drive us to the dance." She looked over at the table where her fellow pretty people were sitting. Her profile told me she was growing nervous. Her fish was proving to be harder to reel in than they had promised.

I shifted my eyes to the group. Tim was sitting with them. Our eyes met. I canted my head and smiled darkly at him so that he would know I was on to him and the scheme of which he was a part. I had thought he had more character and depth than that. But obviously, for Tim, fitting in and being liked was more important than making sure someone else was not being made sport of.

Tim lowered his eyes to the ground. He knew he was caught.

The others in the group were smiling, hoping for victory.

*Sorry, boys and girls, no victory today.*

Robin turned her face to me again. "So do you want to go?"

"That depends."

"On what?" Her tone was now impatient.

"On your willingness."

She squinted. "My willingness?"

"Allow me to elucidate. If, while we are dancing, I become amorous, would you let me kiss you and touch you and press my maleness against you?"

Her face turned angry. "I'm just asking if you want to go to the dance—I'm not asking if you want to—" she stopped herself. "Look, do you want to go or not!"

I smiled. "Just *one* last question, Robin." The evisceration.

She sighed and shook her head. "No wonder nobody likes you. What is it!"

"What is smaller than five dollars?"

"*What?*"

"What is smaller than five dollars? It's a simple question."

She stared at me, confounded.

"*What is smaller than five dollars?*" I repeated a third time.

"I don't know—*four dollars?*"

"No...your IQ."

The confusion on her face turned into fury. Her color was now crimson.

I leaned into her. "You are a fool, Robin, and thus you are on a fool's errand. I'm not stupid like you and your pretty pals over there! Nothing escapes my notice! I know the Sadie Hawkins dance is coming up. I also know that no one would ever dream of asking me, and if they did, it would be as a joke. I have excellent vision, Robin. I saw your *clique of cuties* over there slip you five dollars to get you to come over here and ask me to the dance. Confident I would jump at the invitation, you took the five dollars. But you could only keep it if I said yes. But after I said yes, you'd say, '*Sorry—just a joke.*' Then you'd walk away, laughing, five dollars richer. But the joke is on you, Robin. *You* are the fool...not I.

"*Have you learned the lessons only of those who admired you, and were tender with you, and stood aside for you? Have you not learned the great lessons from those who rejected you, and braced themselves against you, or who treated you with contempt, or disputed passage with you?* Walt Whitman's words. You would extract so much more from life, Robin, if you would stop trying to make everyone love you. Obstructions harden us, better us. No obstructions weaken us, bind us. You're spineless, Robin. You're not your own person. You never have been. You don't stand for anything. You're a follower. You conform so that people will think well of you. You don't think for yourself. You've always let others do your thinking for you so that they will like and applaud you. You derive your worth from their praise. You're their puppet. The thing about puppets is, they're never respected, only used."

The color on Robin's face had been red from rage; now it was red from humiliation. Tears had pooled in her eyes. She slowly rose from her seat and left my table, defeated.

Mangling her made me feel good. I didn't like Robin, but I was very attracted to her. I desired her with the heat of melted ore. But I knew I could never have her, so I lashed out in retaliation. My vindictive side was shining through. I watched her as she walked away from my table. I couldn't help but look down at her Levi's; they were pressed tightly into her valley of delight. The sight of her body made me ache. I hungered for her, though it was not a hunger in my stomach…it was a hunger in a different place, a lower place. I forced myself to look away from her.

I hated wanting Robin, or any other girl, and yet I wanted them all…desperately. My pubescent body was betraying me. It had become my enemy. Since first grade, I had held a tight rein on every thought and emotion. I had become impermeable and impenetrable. I heard what I chose to hear; all else I shut out. When people demanded, I complied; when they scoffed, I hardened. I had assumed I would live the rest of my life unaffected, unmoved, and undeterred. I had decided never to let anyone in. *When you get close, you get hurt* was my personal anthem. I, along with every other teenager in the world, knew about puberty, but I, unlike every other teenager in the world, knew it would not affect me. Just as I controlled everything else in my life, I would control it. I would simply ignore my sexual longings.

After all, what is sex but a release of hormones and compounds: norepinephrine, dopamine, cortisol, vasopressin, prolactin, oxytocin, serotonin, endorphins, and semen? Biochemicals all, not Goliaths. My pubescent brain would begin to find females attractive, yet I would not act on that attraction. Mr. Spock didn't act on it, and neither would I. But there I was, sitting in the cafeteria, craving Robin as if she were food.

I was surprised I had any sexual thirst at all. After what Mr. Wilson did to me, I should have been repulsed by sex, and yet I wasn't. My carnal appetency for Robin was certainly proof of that.

"Do you know what you are?" A girl's voice.

Startled, I shot my eyes upward.

Robin was standing next to me again, her cheeks stained with ribbons of wetness.

I sensed we were the object of attention. I looked beyond her. People were staring at us. Except for the noise of dishes being stacked and pots being moved in the kitchen nearby, the room was quiet.

The attention didn't faze me. My years of forced stoicism had made me impregnable to people's view of me.

Looking back at her, I asked condescendingly, "No, Robin, what am I?"

"You're a nothing," she said flatly. "You're right, I've always been a follower—but you've always been a nothing. Even in grade school. I'm not very smart; I know it; I never have been. You're really smart—but that's *all* you are."

"That is a contradiction, Robin. It falls into the file of oxymorons. I cannot be smart and a *nothing* at the same time."

"I meant you're nothing as a person. You think using big words makes you better than the rest of us. It doesn't make you better—it just makes you weird. Do you know why you don't have any friends? Because you never make any effort to be a friend. Remember in first grade when Mrs. Wilson had us make those stupid Valentine's Day boxes? Remember what you did? You sat at your desk and waited for everyone to come over to you. It doesn't work that way, Owen. Friendship's a two-way street, and you think all roads should lead to you. You're a self-centered, self-important, conceited, arrogant smart-ass who thinks only of himself, and that makes you a nothing.

"Do you want to know the main reason we like Tim? It's not just because he likes himself. It's because he makes us want to be better than we are, because we know we aren't all that great. He makes us want to be like him. No one will *ever* want to be like *you*. Tim has scars, but so what. You look far worse than Tim ever will. You're ugly on the inside, and that's where it counts."

She turned and walked away from me.

How ironic. I considered *her* the ugly one below the skin, and there she was, thinking the same of me.

The noise in the room returned as everyone went back to their conversations.

I arose from my chair and walked out of the cafeteria. I rounded a couple of corners and stopped. I fell back against a wall, closed my eyes tightly and rolled my hands into fists. I felt tears collect in my eyes, but I would not let them fall—I would not let my emotions win. I detested this side of me: this side that still felt hurt and sorry for what I was. I hated feeling anything, be it lust or pity or sympathy or regret or anger or even happiness. Emotion, any emotion, weakened the barrier around me. Like a pile driver, it broke through my wall, creating wide fissures, and through those fissures, people could slip through and do me harm.

A secret part of me longed to be liked and included, and yet I knew that would never happen, so I had to steel myself and drive my longings back into the bedrock of my mind, back into their prison where they belonged.

Graduation: a time of final endings and new beginnings. For one in my class, however, there would be no new beginnings, just a final ending.

My graduation from junior high school was slated for Sunday, June 2nd, 1974. But I would not be attending. Neither would Mrs. Crowley or Ms. Windom. I hadn't seen Mrs. Crowley in years; I didn't even know if she was still alive, but I assumed she was, for surely Mr. Pulsifer, the

Crowleys' family attorney, would have told me if she were not. Ms. Windom never offered to take me to visit her, and I certainly never asked. While I rarely spoke to Ms. Windom, she routinely spoke to me. Her words, however, were never affectionate or complimentary. Continually, she pelted me with put-downs and insults. I had learned to be self-sustaining and self-sufficient so I would not fan the flames of her antipathy by inconveniencing her with requests. I was nothing but an antigen to Ms. Windom, and she to me. I wasn't about to ask her to be present at my graduation.

All year I had been looking forward to leaving eighth grade. It meant I would finally be free of my classmates. But I found out that April I wouldn't be free from them at all. The tassels on their mortarboards would turn toward the same high school I was going to: Moran High.

During lunchtime, two days before the break for summer vacation, I had an unexpected visitor. I was sitting under one of the maples in front of the school, reading. The air outside was warm, and the sky was a swimming-pool blue.

"Mind if I share your shade?"

Normally, an unexpected voice would have startled me, but this time I had no reaction at all. Although, when I saw the owner of the voice, I did—contempt.

"I don't own the school grounds, Tim—you can sit wherever you please," I remarked.

"You don't even have to try to be offensive—it just comes out, doesn't it?" Tim asked evenly and sat down.

I stared at him with disgust. "It comes out only if there is a reason. I'm looking at a reason right now."

Then I noticed something about Tim that I hadn't noticed before: he looked thin and pale, and his eyes looked smaller, as if over time they had reduced in size.

"Is it life you hate, or just people?" he inquired.

"*People*," I answered. "People like *you*."

"You do enjoy being hostile, don't you?"

"I *enjoy* being left alone."

A look of pity came over Tim. "You know, when I was in the hospital, I knew a couple kids like you. They were bitter, and they hated everyone too. They said all they wanted was to be left alone. But you know what I noticed?"

"No, nor do I want to know."

Ignoring me, he went on, "I noticed that the more they were left alone, the more bitter they became. I think what they really wanted was *not* to be left alone. I think they needed people as much as anyone else does, more perhaps; they just didn't want to get hurt so they pushed everyone away. We all need people in our lives, Owen. If we shut them out, we grow into something we don't want to be, something hateful. It doesn't take a genius to know that you've been hurt pretty bad, and you shut people out to keep from getting hurt again. I think that's why you're so sarcastic too—it's a defense, a way of beating people to the punch…or, in your case, the insult. You think everyone's out to put you down, so you put them down first. I think you use it to push people away before they have the opportunity to push you away."

I stared at him. "Are you a standard contributor to *Psychology Today*, or is it just every now and then?"

He rolled his eyes and shook his head. "I'm just saying you're not all that hard to figure out. You've been walked on, stepped on, and trampled on—and now you're just doing the same to everyone else. I think you had a bad childhood. And I think it's *still* bad. Am I right?"

"My childhood, then or now, good or bad, is no affair of yours. Besides, what's it to you anyway?"

"Like I said, I don't think you really want to be alone. I think you feel very deeply. What's more, I think you really want to share those feelings."

"And why would I share my feelings with you? So you can run and repeat them to those carrion-eating Viet Cong you call friends? No, thank you."

"Most people aren't bad, Owen—they just make bad choices."

"You talking about your friends—or *you*?"

"*Everyone*. Jesus is the only one who never made a bad choice. Kids say and do cruel things. Have *you* never said anything mean or cruel?"

"No."

"*Really?* What about last December with Robin?"

To what he was referring, I did not know. "You will have to resuscitate my memory."

"What?" he asked shortly.

"*Refresh* my memory then."

"Why didn't you just say that?"

"I just did."

He shook his head again in irritation. "Last December, in the cafeteria, you made Robin cry. Remember?"

"Ah, yes, Robin. How could I forget? So I made the dear doe cry—so what?"

"You don't think that was cruel?"

"I simply told her the truth. And the truth, as everyone knows, is like a wasp—it packs a nasty sting."

"You know, if you would lay down your sword just once, you might find yourself actually liking people."

"Now why would I want to like them when hating them is so much more satisfying? But I do suppose anything is possible. Try me next year."

"I don't think so," he remarked wistfully.

"I take it that means you're not moving on to Moron High with all the other *dullards* in our class?"

"That's *Moran* High."

"Same difference. Wherever you'll be going, you'll be better off than there."

"Yes, I will be better off. I'll be dead."

For a brief moment, I felt shock, then intense sadness. Most illogical—how could I feel sadness for Tim when I disliked him so?

"You're a curious one, Owen, you know that?"

His use of the word *curious* struck me as an insult and it instantly put me on the defensive. "And how am I *curious*, Tim?"

"You come across as a kid who cares about no one except himself. Cold as a January morning. But I've been watching you over the months, and I don't think you're nearly as cold as you let on. I think you feel very deeply about everything...*and* everyone."

"I feel for *no one*."

"You don't make a good liar, Owen. Remember last February when Jill lost her sister? Someone left a book of poetry on her desk one morning. She told me she read that book over and over. She showed it to me once. It was filled with poems about loss and healing. To this day, she has no idea who gave it to her. There's only one person in our class who would have left such a gift. It wasn't me, it wasn't Mrs. Vance, and it certainly wasn't any of my *carrion-eating* friends. That only leaves one other person. Care to take a guess who it was?"

"I found it in my basement is all," I defended. "It was just an old book lying around collecting dust. I thought she could use it. Nothing more."

"Again, you make a lousy liar. That book was brand-new. You bought it especially for Jill.

"And what about the little fourth-grader who always sat alone during morning and afternoon recess? That is, until a certain eighth-grader started sitting with her. He, too, is always alone. Any idea who that eighth-grader might be?"

I knew he wasn't making fun of me, but it certainly had the markings of it.

"And then there's Robin," he continued. "You look at her with such desire. And not just sexual desire, but longing, as if you desperately want to love her...and be loved *by* her.

"And then a minute ago, when I told you about my death, for a moment, you looked sad."

I felt like I was under a microscope, and I didn't like it. "Why do I warrant this secret scrutiny, Tim? Why are you sharing these observations with me?"

"Because I won't see you again after graduation. You've got so much to give, Owen, but so often you stop yourself. You act like a machine, but in reality, you're just the opposite. Beneath your cement-hard skin, you're a very softhearted boy. A boy who desperately wants to get close but who refuses to."

"When you get close, you get hurt."

"So you get hurt? So what? You think you're the only one who's ever been injured? Everyone has pain. Even the advantaged kids I hang around with have pain."

"Oh, please! Their biggest upset is finding a scratch on their favorite forty-five or missing a sale at their favorite store. Those conceited carcinomas wouldn't know pain if it fell on them."

"You're smart, Owen, but you're not as smart as you think you are. I'm going to let you in on a few things. Dawn, one of the girls in our *'clique,'* as you call it, often times sleeps in her dad's car at night so she doesn't have to listen to her parents fighting. Sometimes she steals money from her dad's wallet, walks to a motel and sleeps there. Stephen, another of the exalted ones, is invisible to his parents. Two years ago, his brother killed himself after coming back from Nam. Now his mom and dad can only see their own pain, and they can't, or won't, see their other son who is still alive. Sheresa Jennings, who could easily be a model, will not look at herself in the mirror with the light on. She thinks she's fat and hideous. Rick Winstead, jock of jocks, is gay. He hates himself for it. William Farnsworth, boy beautiful, used to be molested by his father. Everybody has pain, even the proud and pretentious."

"Why then do they all act so superior if their lives are so *inferior*?" I counterpointed confidently.

"Why do *you* act superior?" Tim answered.

"I don't."

"But you do. You know you're intelligent, and you hide behind it so no one will see the real you: a scared, lonely, insecure, deep-feeling teenager. They do the same thing, only not with intelligence but arrogance."

"And is maliciousness part of the act too?"

"Of course. If they can beat someone else down, they won't feel so trampled on themselves."

"My, my, my. You got it all figured out, don't you?"

"It's not that hard to see."

"And how did you come by all this tragic trivia on our classmates?"

"They told me."

"They told you?"

"Yes."

"Well, if they're hiding, like me, like you say, why did they expose their underbelly to you?"

"I'm not a threat. In their eyes, no one could be worse off than me. And everyone needs someone to talk to, so who better to vent their misery to than someone who is in no position to judge and won't think less of them?"

I hesitated to ask my next question.

"If you don't mind me asking..."

"I have cancer," he answered quickly and matter-of-factly. "They think it's got something to do with my burns. But they don't know for sure. I got a couple of months yet."

"I'm sorry."

"Don't be. I know where I'm going. Many don't."

"You're not afraid?"

"Not at all. I know the end will be painful, but God said that in this life we will have trouble. He also said that the momentary afflictions we experience in this life cannot compare to the glory we will experience in the next."

Tim, though sure and confident of his future, looked forlorn.

"Something tells me you'd rather live, though, wouldn't you?" I said.

He smiled dolefully. "You're smart *and* perceptive." He remained quiet for a few moments. "I'll never know what it's like to kiss a girl. Even if I wasn't dying, I'd still never know. What girl would want to kiss this face?"

His words hit my chest like a hammer...and I knew what that was like.

"You're not the only one in love with Robin," he revealed. "Would you do me a favor, Owen?"

"If I can."

"Next year, when you see Robin again, would you tell her how I feel?"

"Wouldn't it mean more if you told her yourself?"

"My words would scare her, and I don't want to leave this life with the memory of fear on her face. I want to leave with the memory of her smiling and glad that we were friends."

"I will see to it that she knows."

"There's more light in you than you know, Owen. Stop hiding it. Don't waste your life inside yourself. You have too much to give." He arose. "If you don't mind, may I give you one more suggestion?"

"What's that?"

"I have no room to be giving advice on appearance, for obvious reasons, but I think you should know this. I think you would benefit from dressing a little more...your age."

"Yes, I know," I agreed. It was Ms. Windom who bought my clothes, and it was Ms. Windom who made me wear them.

"Your clothes..." he inched, "...are what a little boy would wear. You might not get teased as much if you would dress...more like a teenager. If you go into high school looking like you do, the kids will roast you alive. Just something to consider." He smiled at me and walked back toward the school.

I was wrong about Tim. He *was* a boy of character. He did care about others; he wasn't just out for popularity. I now knew why he went along with Robin that day in December. He was in love with her. Love makes a person do contrary things; it makes him turn a blind eye to the misdemeanors of the one who holds his heart.

I wanted to cry for Tim; I wanted to cry for his death. I wanted to cry for the friend I would never have. I wanted to cry...but I didn't. I had trained myself to fight my feelings, to stomp them down. It was the first time I wished I had chosen a different path.

### Father's Day Night, 1974.

I sensed I was being watched. I had been sensing it for months. Yet it occurred only while I was showering in the downstairs bathroom. I never sensed it in any other place or at any other time. Earlier in the year, Ms. Windom asked me to start using this shower. She said its glass door was easier to clean than the plastic curtain hanging in the upstairs shower. Her request immediately struck me as peculiar. For three reasons. First, Ms. Windom never *requested*—she *demanded*. Second, I had been using the upstairs shower since I was a boy—why was its curtain suddenly so difficult to clean? And third, if the curtain was so burdensome to clean, why didn't she just tell me to wipe it off after each use?

I didn't see how anyone could be watching me. The windows in all the bathrooms in the house were frosted so no deviant eyes on the outside could sample the occupants. The only other person in the house was Ms. Windom, and she certainly wouldn't have been secretly observing me; she couldn't even stand being in the same room with me. Although, she might have seen me by accident, for she demanded that I keep the bathroom door ajar while I was showering so the steam would not collect on the wallpaper and make its edges peel away. No, it wasn't her. It was as if a stranger were consciously, deliberately, and continually watching me. Like a voyeur.

On this particular night, I felt the invisible eyes again. Only this time, they weren't distant as before; it felt as if they were only inches from my body. The texture of the glass door was wavy and rippled, like raindrops on still water, so I had to slide it open to see who was in the room with me. No one was there. Anxiously, I slid the door closed. I quickly finished my shower and stepped out of the tub to dry off. The pink bath towel that had been hanging on the towel bar when I entered the shower was gone. So was the pink shag bathmat.

*Where did they go?* I asked myself in a panic.

Though it had been a warm day, the bathroom was punishingly cold. As was the rest of the house. Ms. Windom always kept every room in the house near freezing, even in the winter months. She said the low temperatures would keep me thin because my body would have to burn its fat stores to keep me warm. I wondered why it didn't work on her. Personally, I thought she kept it cold so she could pocket the money she would have sent to the gas company.

The papillae on my skin rose quickly, first on my arms, then elsewhere. I started to shiver. I had nothing to put around me. The bathroom had a tall closet for storing towels, but Ms. Windom kept it empty. Mold, she insisted, would form on the towels because there is always moisture in a bathroom. The clothes I had on before my shower were in the washer. (Ms. Windom insisted I always deposit my worn clothes into the washing machine before showering and set the washer for thirty minutes exactly.) I had no choice but to run to my room naked. If Ms. Windom saw me...

From the bathroom doorway, I surveyed the hallway and adjacent rooms to see if Ms. Windom was nearby. She wasn't. I dashed up the stairs to my bedroom. I quickly shut the door after entering it. My heart was hammering in my chest.

"You have the acuity of an apricot," said a familiar voice, "but the body of Apollo."

I shot my head to the southwest corner of my room. Sitting on a wooden step stool just inside my closet was Ms. Windom. She stood, and her immense body came into full view.

My hands flew to my middle.

"You lose a couple of points for the scars, though. Who put them there? Could it be your *mommy* was not as saintly as she appears? Well, no matter, you are nevertheless...*mouthwatering.*"

I felt like a trapped animal.

"If you wished to cover your young manhood," she said, "why didn't you just make haste to the linen clothespress and retrieve a fresh towel?"

My face, I could tell, was nearly purple from embarrassment. I couldn't talk.

"I'll tell you why you didn't," she answered for me. "Because you are stupid. You excel scholastically, but beyond that, you are a chowderheaded muttonhead. Now drop your hands."

I swallowed in fear.

"Drop your hands...or I'll cut it off."

Terrified, I lowered my hands.

She moored her eyes to my private place. "You *are* beautiful," she uttered, her tongue wetting her cracked, bulbous lips. "What you lack in circumspection, you make up for in perfect circumcision." She grinned at her wordplay. "I like boys who are cut." A glassy sheen of lust formed over her eyes as she gazed at my male pudenda. "Your pubic hair has come in very nicely. *Very nicely*. I could make it out only slightly through the shower glass."

So I was right: someone *had* been spying on me, and it was her, this behemoth Mephistopheles. Now I knew why she had me use the downstairs shower: it was the only one in the house with a glass shower door through which she could watch me; the others had printed curtains through which she could not.

She began moving toward me. Fearfully, I inched back. I was stopped abruptly by the closed door.

"This is going to happen, Owen," she informed me. "You're going to let me do to you whatever I want, or else I will make your life so wretched you will wish you were in the ground with your father. And if you disclose to anyone the secret union we are about to share, I will kill you in your sleep. Understood?"

Trembling, I nodded.

She approached me confidently. Her body smelled sickly sweet, like the flowers that picket a casket.

She put her fingers on my chest and let them drift down my body.

My hands were clenched into fists; my face was turned away from her, and my eyes were shut tightly. My stomach was roiling with disgust and rage. I knew it was only a matter of minutes before I threw up.

Why did I have to intersect with adults like this? Why couldn't I have just been born into a normal home with normal parents, far away from perverted roadkill like her?

"I must admit," Ms. Windom said breathily, her wattled throat now close to my ear, "when you were young, I found you quite foul, but now that you are courting adolescence, I find you *quite fetching*."

Looking at her again, I asked, "Why are you doing this?"

"Because I want to. Because you owe me. You owe me for taking care of your sorry soul all these years."

"I took care of myself!" I fired back.

She clamped her fingers around my scrotum. I let loose a guttural yell. I had never felt such agony.

"You watch your mouth, boy! Were I not here, you would be living in a foster home or an orphanage! Or worse—the streets! That's where unwanted waifs like yourself go! That unhinged, invertebrate mother of yours took me into her employ to prevent that very thing from happening! So you mind your tongue!"

I didn't know if it was because I was in physical pain or because I was afraid of being raped again, but I began to cry. I hadn't cried in years. And I hated myself for it! I had yielded to my emotions, and I had vowed that I would never do that again.

"What is this—tears?" Ms. Windom gibed. "Since when does the stolid, phlegmatic Owen display emotion?"

"Please let me go," I supplicated through my tears. I was a little boy again, once more in the hands of a monster.

"When I am satisfied, you may go. But until then, you may not. But do not conclude that just because I am through means that I am done. On the contrary, I shall make use of you often. Who knows, my lovely lad, you may even come to enjoy it as much as I."

Where had I heard those words before?

My terror, coupled with the crushing pain below, made my stomach give way. The vomit hit her neck and the front of her blouse.

Her eyes widened with fury; her lips thinned to mere streaks of pink, and the pigment in her face mutated into pomegranate red.

She grabbed me by the neck and threw me to the ground. Her high-heeled shoes struck my stomach, chest, and kidneys repeatedly. This made me vomit again. I knew many of my middle ribs were fractured.

"You little excretion!" she screamed. "Look at me! Look what you've done! You've ruined my shirt! Now I stink like puke!"

She tore off her blouse, making some of the buttons detach and fly into the air. She sank to her knees, grabbed my hair and forced my face into that part of her shirt soaked with regurgitated acid and food.

The smell made me retch.

She got to her feet again, chucked her shirt onto my face and threw open the door. Its lower corner hit my forehead. I felt like I had been hit with a bat.

I thought I had known pain when I was a small boy, but this was worse. Far worse.

I crawled over to my bed and tried to sit up. I couldn't. The pain kept me on the floor. My head, chest, and back were throbbing. I needed to see to my injuries, but I couldn't. All I wanted was sleep. I closed my eyes. Instantly, I was unconscious.

Lamplight greeted me when I awoke. Looking over at the window, I saw that it was still pressing against darkness. I glanced at the clock on my bedside table: it said 1:47.

Fierce pain was surging through my upper body. Trembling, I touched my forehead. As I expected, there was a hard mass where the door had hit me. Around the mass was a texture of crust. I knew instantly what it was: dried blood. I gingerly lifted my shirt to see how badly I was bruised. Though I had been the beneficiary of many contusions over the years, what I saw that morning frightened me. My chest was a tumescent land of ghastly blues and purples and reds. Breathing was torturous. Moving wasn't much easier. But I couldn't remain on the floor until I healed. The sooner I began moving, the stronger I would become. Grabbing the side of the bed, I raised myself to my feet. I almost screamed from the pain. Yet I kept silent, lest I awaken Ms. Windom. Rested, she was a thunderstorm; tired, she was a tornado. I had had enough battering for one day.

Soundlessly, I made my way downstairs. I entered the bathroom, closed the door and locked it. After stepping into the shower, I slid the door shut and turned the knobs. Warm water coated my throbbing and discolored body. I sat down in the tub, closed my eyes and tried to concentrate on the gentleness of the water instead of what had occurred the night before. It didn't work. All I could think about was what had happened. What Ms. Windom wanted to do, tried to do and did do filled every corner of my mind. Why did I let her get away with it? Though not her breadth, I was her height. I could have fought back. Why didn't I? What was I afraid of? Getting hit...getting kicked…getting bloody? I had been hit, kicked, and bloodied many times in my life…and I survived each time. Was it because she threatened to kill me? Empty wind. If I died, so would she. My death would mean *her* death: prison—the end of her freedom. Was it the fear of being raped again? I surmised it was all of it. But my fear belonged to the past. I was not a little boy anymore. I was nearly fourteen years of age. It was time I stopped being afraid. It was time everyone knew this. I decided that Ms. Windom would be the first to learn. And she would learn it at first light.

Her body hit the tile below the staircase with a sickening thud. I had hoped she would hit facedown to bloody her nose or crack a tooth or two, but instead, she landed on her back.

My simple, Hollywood-like trap worked flawlessly. Her foot caught the taut fishing line I had tied across the last step of the staircase just as it was supposed to. I could have surprised her in bed, but I wanted her fully awake, fully aware. I wanted her to know what was happening and who was in control.

Ms. Windom lay dazed on the floor for many seconds. Slowly, she started to rise. My leg crossed over her massive body, and I straddled her chest. Looking up at me, her countenance turned fearful, then wrathful. Not wanting her to complete her ascension, I lowered myself onto her rotund stomach. The pain from my broken ribs was searing, but I was not going to let that stop me from doing what needed to be done.

"Get off of me, you lab animal!" she ordered, now clearheaded.

From my right back pocket, I produced a foot-long Phillips screwdriver. I quickly inserted it into her ear canal. I made sure not to go in too far: I didn't want to rupture the eardrum…not yet anyway. But the tool was in deep enough to make her afraid. All movement from her ceased. She knew she was in a serious situation.

"Now is that any way to talk to someone whom you find…*fetching*?" I asked her. "It's time we had a talk, you and I. *Check that*—it's time that *I* talk and *you* listen. So let's begin. Let's begin with last April.

April twenty-second to be exact. Remember that day? It was an awful day. A bloody day. A day of death and suffering. Five people were tortured in the basement of the Hi-Fi Shop up in Ogden. Remember that? Three of the five victims were killed. Orren Walker and Cortney Naisbitt survived. You remember Orren Walker, don't you? He had a pen stomped into his ear and was forced to drink liquid Drano...as were all the victims."

The kraken's face was sweating now. She had actually lost her hubris, probably for the first time in her life. I was about to make her sweat even more.

Reaching into my other back pocket with my left hand, I retrieved an uncapped, clear glass liquor flask. It was filled halfway with aqua-blue pellets.

Crystal Drano.

Ms. Windom's face tightened with fear. She squirmed to get free. In response, I pushed the screwdriver deeper into her ear and tipped the bottle slightly over her face. She instantly became still.

"You made me cry last night, Ms. Windom," I told her. "You made me break my promise to myself. You made me look weak, pathetic, infantile. You made me hate myself even more than I already do. You know what you are, Ms. Windom? You are a parasite. You give nothing—all you do is take. You feed off of others. I don't love Mrs. Crowley anymore, but I know you are stealing from her, and I detest that. You stole from me last night so you could satisfy that perverted and depraved and degenerate appetite of yours. Adults like you who lust after children are worms who should be cut in half and left to bleed out under a blistering sun. The only reason I don't report you is because you were right: I would be taken away and put in some place far worse than this. I've already been there, and I'm not going back. But make no mistake, Ms. Windom, if you ever touch me again, in any way, I will kill you. That is one promise I *will* keep. I will empty this bottle of Drano into your putrid mouth, and I will shove this screwdriver right into your putrid brain."

"I should have killed you years ago like your mother's sister killed Andrew!" she shot through clenched, nearly slate-colored teeth.

How did Ms. Windom know about Andrew? And if she had knowledge going back that far, how did she not know that I was adopted? I was only prepared for resistance that morning, not revelations.

Evidently, my surprise showed, for she said, "Kinda caught you off guard, didn't I?" She smiled. "You didn't know your aunt was a murderess, did you? Her name was Susan, I believe. And her victim was your uncle—Andrew."

"How?" was all I could manage.

"Asphyxiation," she replied coolly, still smiling. "She smothered him...with a pillow."

"Why?"

"That you will have to ask your mother. Alas, she departed before she could press in that last piece of the puzzle. Seems you come from a long line of mad Mabels, pretty boy."

"Don't call me that!"

"Pretty boy...or mad? Both suit you, you know. I mean, you *are* profoundly pretty, and as for the latter, well, who's holding a screwdriver in one hand and a bottle of Drano in the other? If that's not crazy, I don't know what is. I guess the apple doesn't roll too far from the tree, does it, *pretty boy*?" She smirked cavalierly.

"I *said*, don't call me that! I'm not your *pretty boy*! What's more, don't call my family crazy! Just because my mother and her sister had mental deficits doesn't mean my whole family does!" Her broad-stroke indictment of my family meant she was including my sister in her charge. Susan was anything but crazy. She had not been the chipped piece of china like her aunt, and she certainly hadn't been the jagged piece of glass like her mother.

"Ah, but how many of you crazy Crowleys have been hiding in the grass over the years, not seen, but still there?" she aspersed.

Her hauteur had returned.

"Better to be hiding in the grass than be a snake in it like you!" I whipped at her.

"Your petty insults faze me not. *You* faze me not. You're a runt. You're a bug that should be squashed! I don't fear you. I *laugh* at you. Your threats amuse me," she fleered. "Speaking of things amusing, this brings to mind an epigram by Aristotle. Are you at all conversant with the writings of Aristotle?"

"What do you think?"

She knew I read everything, including Aristotle. Where was she going with this?

"I'll wager you're not conversant with his words on humor, though, are you?" Her tone carried a subtle though ominous threat.

I didn't answer her.

"I thought not," she said. "Humor has never been your *métier*, has it, *pretty boy*?"

"Nor yours."

"Very true. At any rate, Aristotle had this to say regarding comedy: *The secret to humor is...surprise.*" She stared at me, then began to laugh.

Her laugh was almost demonic: its pitch both high and low, its essence both male and female. I had never heard anything like it before. It chilled me.

"Surprise!" she blurted out while still in her spasm of glee.

Her arms, situated at her sides, flew up. Her left arm made contact with my right arm, causing my hand and the screwdriver to jerk away from her body. My hand, upon reaching its maximum vertex, whiplashed and released the tool. Flying like shrapnel, the screwdriver hit the front door with a loud crack. I saw that it made an ugly gouge in the ornate carving on the door. Ms. Windom would be furious when she discovered it.

The flask of Drano suffered the same fate. It landed and shattered on the oak steps of the staircase behind us. If not removed quickly, the lye would eat through the wood. Another mutilation that would boil Ms. Windom's blood.

One weapon was now useless to me, but the other was not. Springing off of her body, I leapt for the door. Before the wen of cellulite lying on the floor could stand and gain the advantage, I grabbed the screwdriver and bounded back to her. I crashed down onto her stomach, pinning her to the floor again. She let out a painful yell as my weight compressed and displaced her organs. With my legs, I quickly restrained her arms against the sides of her body. This time, I chose a different point of entry for the screwdriver.

"Open your mouth!" I screamed at her, the screwdriver pressed hard against her tightly shut lips, my other hand clasped savagely around her throat.

She refused.

"Open your mouth, or I'll knock out your teeth and drive it in!"

Fearfully and reluctantly, she obeyed.

The screwdriver entered her and didn't stop until it reached the posterior wall of her oropharynx. She gagged violently.

"If you struggle, you gag—so *don't* struggle," I advised.

She took my advice and relaxed. Her gagging ceased.

"Not quite the pablum-brained *apricot* after all, am I, Ms. Windom?" I said. "Your dim-bulbed attempt at escape failed because of what you are: *old, fat, and slow.* Whereas I am *young, thin, and quick*—just what you wanted last night...*remember*? You know what they say: be careful what you wish for.

"Now then, let's return to what I was saying before you breathed your regret for having not killed me when I was younger. I am going to quote a phrase used on me when I was but a boy by a certain well-padded maidservant. This maidservant—a boorish, bawdy, overcooked, profligate wretch, chuff in both size and pride, whose face (I hadn't noticed until now) is amazingly similar to a coffin-countenance, and whose name I think you know—said to me, '*Here's how your life will play out.*' So now I say to you, Ms. Windom, *here's how your life will play out.* From this moment on, you will keep your roaming eyes, your perverted hands, and your diseased thoughts to yourself. The only time you will talk to me is when I talk to you. If I need money, you will give it. If I need something signed, you will sign it. If I need something cleaned, you will clean it. If I want something to eat, you will fix it. Your days of demands are over. You will begin doing what you were originally brought here to do: *serve.* That is, after all, what a maidservant is supposed to do, yes, Ms. Windom? Or would you prefer Ms. *Wanton*?"

Her eyes narrowed at the insult.

"I like that—*Ms. Wanton*," I said. "Or how about *Hilda the Horny Harpy*? They both suit you, don't you agree? What do you think— which should be your new tag? A new tag for an old rag. A new tag for an old hag. The slams just keep getting better and better, don't they?" I laughed.

Withdrawing the screwdriver, I stood and stepped over her. "Jocular affronts aside, Ms. Roan—forgive me, I couldn't resist; it's just that your face reminds me of a horse—stay out of my way, and you will live. If you don't, you won't. Don't make me raise my hand against you again, Ms. Windom, because believe me, the next time you will not live long enough to regret it. And in case your randy, mangy mind thinks the legal repercussions from extinguishing your existence would dissuade me, think again. That's a good word, by the way: *extinguish*. Wonder where I got it from? Oops, I ended that question with a preposition. *Sorry*.

"My apologies, I keep digressing. As I was saying, the legal repercussions would in no way deter me. And do you know why? Because there wouldn't be any. And how do I know this? Because I am adopted, Ms. Windom. Before I came here, I was in a foster home whose possessors were not unlike yourself. You see, they, too, were dung flies. The man, if you could call him that, did just about everything he could to me. When the authorities found out, the flies flew away, as flies always do. So when I tell the police I had no choice but to kill you because you were molesting me, they will believe me. They will simply think you got what you deserved. And, yes, I will be taken away and fostered out once more. I am a minor, so I won't see the walls of any prison. Once I reach my eighteenth birthday, I will reunite with this house and take control of it. *All* of it.

"Of course, if that drawing is never sketched, this one certainly will be: the day of my eighteenth birthday, that very day, Ms. Windom, your service here will be ended, terminated. The management of Mrs. Crowley's estate will pass to me, and I will make all of the decisions regarding it from then on."

"That's not how it works, *boy!*" she declaimed. "I am the legal guardian of this estate until Mrs. Crowley is able to resume that duty, at which time she may choose to pass it to you. But I doubt that will ever occur since she has never shown any signs of improvement since she took her leave of it many years ago. If you doubt me, feel free to contact her attorney, Mr. Pulsifer. I will be glad to give you his number." She smiled triumphantly...much the same way William used to when he thought he had me.

"No need," I replied calmly. "But I think *you* should call him. Because *I* already have. Since I am Mrs. Crowley's adopted son, I am legally entitled dominion over her monies, investments, possessions, and properties when I turn eighteen. When she dies, it all transfers to *me, not you, not one penny.*"

"I don't believe you!"

"It matters not if you believe me. What matters are the facts."

"We'll see about that!"

"You're not grasping this, lady. In four years, you are gone! If, at that time, you contest my position as guardian of Mrs. Crowley's estate, you will lose. And not only financially, for you will have to retain your own attorney, but you will also lose your freedom. I will gladly bring to light your handling of me last night: the kicking, the screaming, the threatening, and let's not forget the *jewel in the crown*—the fondling. And then I will share with the police how you secretly watched me in the shower; how you made me eat over an open toilet; how you once locked me in the basement for two weeks—not that I minded, but the police certainly will; how you made me walk to school in the cold and snow when there was a car just inside the garage; how, for seven years, without intermission, you willingly, generously, and gleefully gave me the rough side of your tongue; how you gave me only water for a week after each report card because I always brought home D's in Physical Education, never mind that I brought home A's in everything else; how you always made me wear little-boy shirts and little-boys pants—pants so short that those lobotomized asshats at my school couldn't help but laugh at me in my *floods*, and how you made me shovel the snow with no boots on, only socks. The fondling alone will put you in jail. So go ahead, take issue with my rights—but you will lose.

"This is a knot *you* tied, Ms. Windom, not me. It is a noose you put around your own neck. You'll not use me as your personal *plaything* anymore. I will not be your little *boy-toy* any longer."

I turned and started up the stairs. Without facing her, I spoke as I climbed, "I know you are thinking retribution as I leave you. If I were you, I'd let those thoughts die; let them drown in the waters of impossibility. Your revenge will not succeed. Early this morning, I composed and mailed a letter to Mr. Pulsifer. I informed him of your animosity and irrational ill will toward me. I told him that should an accident bechance me, fatal or otherwise, he is to look no further than *you* for the cause of it. Consider yourself warned, Ms. Windom: if you harm me or *try* to harm me one more time, it will be the last thing you *ever* do."

I entered my bedroom, closed the door and slowly lay my body down on the olive-green carpet. The pain from my fractured ribs was overwhelming. My battle with Ms. Windom had distracted me from it. Now that the confrontation was over, I was fully aware of the severe damage within my chest.

Larry the janitor would have been proud of me. I had stood up to Ms. Windom; I had stood up for myself. Still, it angered me. Why did I have to have such strife with everyone? Why couldn't people simply let me be? I wasn't asking for them to love me, only to leave me alone. Was that so much to want?

While part of me took pride in my grit at finally putting Ms. Windom in her place, another part of me was disgusted by it. She had forced me to become what she was: violent and base. I had become just like her. No—I was *worse*. I knew that dispensing violence was wrong; she didn't. A snake bites because that's what it does; it knows no better.

The story about the letter to Mr. Pulsifer had been a lie. But I felt Ms. Windom needed to be made afraid. If I had actually sent the letter, I would have run the risk of Mr. Pulsifer letting Child Protective Services know of the things Ms. Windom had done to me. That would have led to an investigation and ultimately my removal from the Crowleys' home. Leaving was not in the blueprint; it was not an option. I would not go into another foster home or be sent to another orphanage. Only through the door of Ms. Windom's demise would I leave my home.

Throughout that summer, Ms. Windom was as silent as a Trappist. She neither spoke to me nor looked in my direction. Both behaviors were fine by me. She was right where I wanted her.

The doors to my high school were due to open soon, and I wasn't about to pass through them clad in high-water pants and toddler T-shirts. Tim was right: I would be roasted alive if I entered high school looking like I did. I left a note on Ms. Windom's bedroom door one evening telling her to leave me three hundred dollars on the kitchen counter for new school clothes. Twelve hours later, six fifty-dollar bills were lying next to the Osterizer on our marble kitchen counter. I had demanded her obedience and that's exactly what I was getting. I should have threatened to kill her years before.

Jack David, Auerbach's, The Paris, Arthur Frank, Hibbs, Pullman's, English Tailor—these were the stores that took Ms. Windom's money that day. My days of looking like a penurious six-year-old were over.

By bus, I went downtown to shop, and by bus, I returned home. I refused to ask Ms. Windom to take me anywhere. The thought of being in the same room with her, let alone the same car, sickened me.

The Ridgeway longcase in the living room was chiming its fifth toll as I walked through the front door. Bags of various sizes and colors were snug in my hands. In those bags was the new me. In them were Oxford long-sleeves, pastel polos, pleated slacks, V-neck sweaters, sweater vests, contoured turtlenecks, tasseled hard-soles, dark argyles, low-rise briefs, and leather belts. (Save for the socks, everything was solid colors.) I even purchased something I didn't think I would use until I was older: cologne. There were two that I liked: Elsha and Pierre Cardin. The first was sweet and spicy, the second athletic and lemony. I couldn't decide which was better, so I bought both. Most of the men's fashions in the clothiers I visited, though expensive, were loud and garish. It took me hours to find apparel that was fashionable but not flagrant, traditional but not tasteless. The last thing I wanted was to wrap myself in brash colors and risible patterns. I had spent years looking pitiful; I wasn't about to go in the other direction and look comical.

Something plagued me that long summer of my fourteenth year. I tried to outdistance it by venturing deep into multiple books, but it clung to me like chewing gum on a shoe. It was the secret Ms. Windom had let slip that cold June morning: the secret about my mother and her little brother Andrew. Why did my mother kill him? Why had she not been prosecuted and imprisoned? Was my father involved? Did Mrs. Crowley play a part? Had my mother killed other children? I believed Ms. Windom when she told me she had no knowledge beyond the bare facts she related that morning. I needed to uncover the rest of the story. Though my biological mother was long dead and was never meaningful or significant to me, she nevertheless was my mother, and that alone, made me want to know the details. Collateral to that, though just as substantial, was the fact that Andrew was my uncle. He very well might have been someone in my family with whom I could have been close. Mrs. Crowley was the only link to my mother, so if I wanted to know what had occurred, I would have to speak with her once again. But not by phone. I needed to see her face, to see if she were lying when I asked her why my mother had murdered an innocent little boy.

Mrs. Crowley was presently living in Hill Haven Care Center. Mr. Pulsifer told me this when I spoke with him over the phone concerning Mrs. Crowley's will. He told me she had been a resident there since she left our home in 1966.

I awoke Labor Day morning and decided that would be the day I would get my answers. Consulting the phone book, I found the address of Hill Haven Care Center. It was some distance from my home. The buses didn't run on holidays, so I would have to take a taxi. Money for a cab would not be an issue, for I had told Ms. Windom to start giving me an allowance the day after our *consensus ad idem* on the foyer floor.

I called the care center, identified myself and asked if I could visit Mrs. Crowley. They gave me their visiting hours and the minimum age for all visitors: fourteen.

I had just turned fourteen, so all was in place for me to see Mrs. Crowley once again.

Hill Haven Care Center, at first sight, was as drab as dishwater. Formerly named Bonneville Care Center, it sat on the side of a hill facing west. It was a bland and blemished, five-story International Style piece of architecture. It earnestly and zealously embraced the axiom: *Form follows function.*

Mr. Crowley had loved the International Style. He loved its quietness, its natural lack of complexity, and its intentional lack of embellishment. It didn't embrace symmetry, as he did, but he adored the style nevertheless.

Long before the Twin Towers of the World Trade Center became immediate landmarks, Mr. Crowley was an ardent admirer of them. He had seen models and concept drawings of them years before their core columns started to rise. The towers were International Style II architecture. Though the towers had some exterior embroidery, they were nevertheless artless, white-bread boxes. Very *tall*, artless, white-bread boxes. "*Twin Monoliths of Mediocrity*," a deprecator once called them. Yet Mr. Crowley loved them for their mediocrity. He told me that once the towers were completed, the public and critics would lambaste them for their sterile, industrial appearance. He also said that the negative opinions would someday tide toward positive, and the very things that people hated about them—their deliberate restraint and crisp simplicity—is what they would come to appreciate and enjoy.

Strangely, as I got closer to the care center, I found myself liking its rectilinear design; its modesty and abstention greatly appealed to me. The building's lines were clean and simple. Though all of its glass and stainless-steel cladding was dirt-streaked and rain-stained, it still reflected the blue sky magnificently. Perhaps that was another reason why Mr. Crowley liked the staid style so fervently: it brought down to the ground the blue sky he loved so much.

Right inside the main floor was a half-moon metal desk. Behind it sat an elderly man in a jejune, white uniform. I told him my name, my age and who I wanted to visit.

"Through there," he mumbled and pointed to two glass doors that opened like the bellows of an accordion when a visitor stepped onto a black, rubber pad in front of them. "Fifth floor."

In my walk to the elevator, I couldn't help but think what laughable security the facility had. An apathetic, nearly comatose, long-in-the-tooth graybeard at a desk was all that stood between confinement and escape.

The elevator smelled of new materials: new flooring, new walls, and new opaque ceiling panels covered stingingly bright fluorescents. Taped to the simulated wood walls were numerous memos and reminders to the staff.

Two pieces of paper, one steno-sized, the other letter-sized, were taped to the elevator door. Apparently, they were more important than those on the walls since they were on the door where everyone was sure to see them.

Written in longhand on the steno paper were but a few words:

> *Quote of the Week—*
> *"Age is an issue of mind over matter. If you don't mind, it*
> *doesn't matter."*
>
> MARK TWAIN

On the letter-sized paper was a typed poem, a very lengthy poem:

*What do you see, nurse, what do you see?*
*What are you thinking when you're looking at me?*
*A crabby old woman, not very wise,*
*uncertain of habit with faraway eyes.*
*Who dribbles her food and makes no reply,*
*when you say in a loud voice, "I do wish you'd try."*

*Who seems not to notice the things that you do,*
 *and forever is losing a stocking or shoe.*
*Who, resisting or not, lets you do as you will,*
 *with bathing and feeding, the long day to fill.*
*Is that what you're thinking, is that what you see?*
 *Then open your eyes, nurse, you're not looking at me.*

*I'll tell you who I am as I sit here so still,*
 *as I move at your bidding, as I eat at your will.*
*I'm a small child of ten with a father and mother,*
 *brothers and sisters who love one another.*
*A young girl of sixteen with wings on her feet,*
 *dreaming that soon a love she will meet.*
*A bride at twenty, my heart gives a leap,*
 *remembering the vows that I promised to keep.*
*At twenty-five now I have young of my own,*
 *who need me to build a secure, happy home.*

*A woman of thirty, my young now grown fast,*
 *bound together with ties that should last.*
*At forty, my young sons have grown up and gone,*
 *but my man's beside me to see I don't mourn.*
*At fifty, once more babies play at my knee,*
 *again we know children, my loved one and me.*
*Dark days are upon me, my husband is dead,*
 *I look at the future, I shudder with dread.*
*For my young are all rearing young of their own,*
 *and I think of the years and the love that I've known.*

*I'm an old woman now and nature is cruel,*
 *'tis her jest to make old age look like a fool.*
*The body it crumbles, grace and vigor depart,*
 *there now is a stone where once I had a heart.*
*But inside this old carcass a young girl still dwells,*
 *and now and again my battered heart swells.*

*I remember the joys, I remember the pain,*
 *and I'm loving and living life over again.*
*I think of the years, all too few, gone too fast,*
 *and accept the stark fact that nothing can last.*
*So open your eyes, nurse, open and see,*
 *not a crabby old woman,*
 *look closer...see me!*

Written on the very bottom of the paper, in very small print, were these words:

*This poem was written by a woman who died in the geriatric ward of Ashludie Hospital near Dundee, England. It was found among her possessions and so impressed the staff that copies were made and distributed to every nurse in the hospital. It was addressed to the nurses who surrounded the woman in her last days. But because it cries for recognition of a common humanity, it could have been written to all of us.*

After the elevator door opened, I found myself staring at the open space where the poem had been. The inside of my chest felt heavy and tight. The few elderly people I had known were venomous, callous, and weary. It never occurred to me that maybe they acted that way because they were in pain. I, too, had acted petulantly because I had been in pain. The poem made me look at how I treated older people and how I would treat them in the future.

The elevator connected to a long, wainscoted hallway. There were many open doors along the corridor. Tentatively, I started to walk. I was nervous about seeing Mrs. Crowley again. Part of me didn't want to hear about my natural mother. Part of me didn't want to feel pity for Mrs. Crowley. Part of me didn't want to be reminded of a time when I felt love for her and when I was loved by her. These were tributaries that fed into a parent river, and the parent was issuing me an order: *don't feel*. But I had to know about Andrew...and Mrs. Crowley was the only one left who knew the answers.

Glancing briefly in the open rooms, I saw people whose youth, strength, and endurance had left them decades ago. Lying in bed, sitting on the edge of a bed, curled over in a wheelchair next to a bed, staring out a window, sitting on the floor or in a recliner, they seemed barely alive. Blankness and emptiness resided in their eyes. Slumped in a wooden armchair out in the hallway, one elderly woman, frail as an eyelash, had her eyes cast downward. She had one arm draped over the side of the chair, and the other elbowed up to her face. Her hand was lightly scratching her upper forehead as if she were burdened with unbearable grief. These were forgotten people, discarded people. These were people who, in the beginning, met the world with strong bodies and healthy limbs, but who now could hardly move. These were people who, in the beginning, showed the mirror supple faces and flawless skin, but who now were accursed with lines and creases and lentigines. These were people who, in the beginning, were loved but who now were abandoned. None of these people started out life with nullity and vacuity holding their hands. They were infants once, squirmy one minute, peacefully asleep the next. Then they were children, crying one moment, giggling the next. Then they were teenagers, hopelessly in love one week, completely out of love the next. In their twenties, they were confident in the future in the morning, then terrified of it at night. In middle-age, they admired their vitality one year, then noticing its decline the next. Then they were gray-haired, slow moving, slow thinking, but knowing all too well that they were neither wanted nor needed by a world that once was their friend. Now all they did was stare away their lives, alone with regrets they couldn't shed and memories they couldn't share. My eyes moistened at the sight. I wanted to run from that place and never come back. I didn't know how to handle it; I didn't want to see this incurable rejection and hopeless dejection.

But I couldn't run. I was there for answers...and answers I would get.

Directing my eyes forward, I headed for the nurses' station, which I assumed was close by.

At the end of the hallway and around the corner was the station where the staff did their charting and reporting and calling.

"Excuse me, ma'am," I said to the first nurse I saw at the station. "My name is Owen Crowley. I'm here to see Jean Crowley."

The nurse, a stone-faced, gray-haired, aircraft-sized woman, looked at me suspiciously. "*Who are you?*" she asked coldly.

"I'm her—" I bit my answer in half. I couldn't bring myself to say it, for I no longer saw myself as Mrs. Crowley's son. "She adopted me."

The old nurse eyed me contemptuously. "Well, where have *you* been hiding?"

Stunned at her effrontery, I asked, "*Pardon me?*"

"Mrs. Crowley's a wonderful woman," the nurse exclaimed. "The kindest woman here. She rarely gets visitors. Occasionally a friend, never family. And now you show up. What do you want with her?"

I looked down at the nurse's name badge, then into her eyes. "Ms. Madill—"

"That's *Mrs.* Madill!"

I rolled my eyes. "Whatever."

"It's not *whatever*! I'm proud to be married! Been so for thirty-two years!"

"*Who cares!*"

"I care!"

"Look, lady, I didn't come here to talk to you! I came here to see Mrs. Crowley! Why I'm here now and why I *haven't* been here is none of your damn business!" For as angry as I was, I was surprised I didn't say more. "Just tell me what room she's in!"

Minus the silver hair, the nurse looked the twin of Ms. Windom the morning I had the screwdriver flagpoled in her mouth. "You know, in my day, if a kid talked to an adult like you just did to me, that kid would have been smacked into the next century!"

"This is *not* your day," I reminded her. "That day is gone. As will you if you don't tell me what room she's in!"

She flushed deeply. "Five-sixty!" she snarled.

"Thank you," I replied and walked away.

"That's one boy *I* never would have adopted!" *Mrs.* Madill announced to another nurse as I was leaving. "I would have left him in the orphanage to rot with all the other brats!"

Inclined as I was to go back and tell her what she could do with her orphanage, I restrained myself. My mission was not to have a verbal shootout with some antediluvian dishrag, I was there to learn about my uncle.

Room 560 was at the end of the hallway, by the stairwell. Locked, I hoped.

Before appearing in the doorway of Mrs. Crowley's room, I stopped, closed my eyes and inhaled deeply.

Then I stepped forward.

Mrs. Crowley was just exiting the bathroom.

I couldn't believe my eyes.

The woman in the room was a fraction of what she used to be. I saw a diminutive creature with hunched shoulders and hair the color of winter clouds. Her gait was guarded and cautious. The woman I once knew had vanished. In the span of just a few years, she had gone from firm to infirm, tall to small, vigorous to vulnerable. My throat constricted with an invisible ache. I felt tears fill my eyes again. I so missed the love I once felt from her. Yet hers was not true love—it was duty.

I willed my feelings away.

I knocked on the door. Mrs. Crowley turned slowly and looked at me blankly.

"Is it pill-time already?" she asked feebly.

She didn't recognize me. Out of sight, out of mind. I had vanished too.

Then her face changed. "You...you look familiar," she said to me. "Do I know you?"

"Yes," I answered firmly. "I'm Owen."

"Owen?" she asked searchingly. "Owen? *Owen? My* Owen?"

"Yes, I'm the boy you adopted some years ago." I wanted to rush into her arms. But I didn't. I couldn't.

"Look at you!" she crooned. "Look how you've grown! What a handsome young man you are! Oh, the girls will be buzzing around you, if they aren't already."

"They aren't, I assure you," I remarked stiffly. "Nor are they ever likely to."

Her joyous smile faded. "Why have you never come to see me, or even called? In all these years, not once. Why?"

I had to steel my heart. I wanted to go back in time and be her little boy again. I so wanted to feel what I used to feel when I was with her: the comfort from her touch, the warmth from her concern, the calm from her protection. But I was my own protection now. And I wasn't a little boy anymore. And she wasn't my mother—a true mother doesn't keep the truth from her child. Nor does she pretend to love him or care for him out of obligation.

"Please, sit down," I requested coolly, "and I'll tell you why I've come."

On a cushioned chair next to a round, secondhand, Formica-topped table by the window, she sat.

Her room was as spartan as the ascetic table next to her. Above her bed was a painting of Jesus on His cross. Below the painting was an oval, pink-and-red sampler. The sampler had but five words: *Man Proposes, But God Disposes*. Under a crocheted, snowflake-shaped doily on a cheap chest of drawers beside her bed was a sepia-toned photo of her and Mr. Crowley when they were teenagers. Next to the photograph was a lone bottle of perfume. On her bureau at home, there was always a colonnade of perfume bottles, each ethereal but richly fragrant. Not one had been a dime-store purchase. This solitary bottle of perfume she had now probably was. Against the wall opposite her bed was a rolling TV cart, on top of which sat a vintage, 19-inch RCA; I couldn't tell if it was black and white or color, but given the parsimony of the room, I assumed it was black and white. Why was she brooking this kind of life? It had to have been by her own election, for I knew she had ample funds to live very comfortably. She had gone from Swarovski finery to Gandhian austerity. Why?

Mrs. Crowley gave me her attention without further word.

"I'm here for one reason, and one reason only," I commenced. "I want to know about Andrew. I want to know why your sister killed him."

Mrs. Crowley instantly looked shaken. Her eyes left mine, and she sighed painfully. "I knew this would come to light someday, although I hoped it wouldn't. This is why you haven't come to see me, isn't it?"

"Answer me."

She paused. "May I ask you something first before I tell you?"

I gave a slight nod.

"How did you find out?"

"It's a very long story. Besides, it doesn't matter. All that matters is that I know about him."

"You're so mature for your age, so well-spoken. And yet so grim. I'm guessing the past few years have not been very kind to you...have they?"

Was she stalling or trying to change the subject? I wouldn't let her do either.

"*I want to know about Andrew,*" I pushed.

"Okay, I'll tell you. Andrew was your uncle, my brother. He was six when he passed away."

"He didn't *pass away*—he was murdered!" I corrected.

"Yes, I'm sorry, he was...murdered."

"And you had a hand in it?"

"Yes, I did."

"*Why?*"

"How much do you know?"

"Not enough, obviously. That's why I'm here. Why did you and my mother kill him?" My emotional temperature was starting to rise. But I had to turn down the fire, lest I cause her to draw back and tell me nothing. I had to keep in mind that she was not only a geriatric patient but a psychiatric one.

She winced at my words. "So then you know about your mother?"

"Of course—" I blocked myself from saying what I was going to say. My anger was surging again. "Yes, I know about her."

"May I start from a different place, before Andrew's death?"

"I don't care where you start—I just want to know why you and my mother killed him."

She gestured to the edge of her bed. "Please, sit down. Standing people make me nervous."

I obliged her and sat on the end of her twin bed.

She began slowly. "I'd first like to tell you a few things about your mother—things you probably don't know. Maybe after I tell you, you might understand why we did what we did."

"I wouldn't count on it but go ahead."

"Your mother was once a beautiful woman. She was so kind and thoughtful to everyone. She adored small animals; all small animals. She loved marine life, especially jellyfish; she was fascinated by them. She wanted to be a film actress. She did lots of school plays. Her directors were enthralled with her. Everyone thought she had the talent to make it in Hollywood. The stage was just one of her loves. Another was art. She could draw and sketch nearly anything: dogs, cats, flowers, churches, houses, even people. There wasn't much your mother couldn't do. She was the plum on our family tree. My parents loved me, but they loved her more. She was their favorite. Yes, parents have their favorite child. Any parent who tells you otherwise is lying."

"Yes, I'm all too aware of that."

"Your mother's given name was not Susan. It was Judith, after her grandmother. Your mother loved the actress Susan Hayward. She thought she was the most beautiful woman she had ever seen. Susan Hayward was a New York model before she became a Hollywood actress, you know. Your mother begged us to call her Susan instead of Judith, a name she loathed. So to please your mother, my parents told everyone to start calling her Susan. The name stuck, and that's what everyone knew her as.

"Then she met Floyd. After that, all the good in her vanished like so much cigarette smoke. Floyd was your father. He was—"

"He was *not* my father and you know it! You know perfectly well my mother was raped—and I'm the diseased offspring from that rape!"

Mrs. Crowley whitened. "Owen...I had no idea. I promise you I didn't. How would I have known? Owen, darling, I truly—"

"Don't call me that! I'm not your darling anymore!"

She looked as if she had just been slapped.

"Look, I didn't come here to talk about me," I said. "I came here to find out why you and my mother killed an innocent little boy."

She paused. "Andrew was born...very sick. He was born with spina bifida—a terrible thing. Our mother had him late in life. He was an accidental baby, you might say. One afternoon, my mother asked Susan to take care of him while she went to the doctor. She would have asked me, but I was at work. She didn't want to bother me, so she called Susan. If she had only called me, our family history would have been written differently. Grudgingly, Susan came over…with Floyd. Susan didn't like Andrew. Neither did Floyd. Andrew was not what you would call an attractive child, and Susan came to like only attractive people. What's more, Andrew didn't have bowel and bladder control, which made him more odious to her. Andrew needed special care, but Susan only cared about herself…and Floyd. Andrew was a tragic case, to be sure, but Susan, at that point, was beyond tragic: she was death without dying. When she was young, she had such a compassionate heart. If there was a hurt cat or sick dog in the neighborhood, she'd be right there tending to it. It was that Floyd who changed her. I believe that. He was trouble from the very beginning. He was a welder—a good one too. There was only one other thing he did better: tossing back. There were days he never ate, only drank. The saints as my witness, there wasn't a night he wasn't potted. What she saw in him, no one knew. *Bad company corrupts good character*, the New Testament says. It's true. He was in a pit, and he pulled your mother right in there with him."

I was becoming bored with her reminiscences.

"Why did she smother him?" I redirected her to the issue at hand. "And why did you help her? He was disabled and defenseless! How could you do such a thing?"

She hesitated, contemplating her answer. "Andrew was in terrible discomfort that day. He was crying, and he wouldn't stop. Susan never admitted to it, but it's my guess that your mother and Floyd were…" she cleared her throat, "…probably having relations when Andrew's crying became too much for them. Your mother and Floyd had no inhibitions or restraint when it came to their love making. They were always ravenous for each other. They didn't care where or when.

"Anyway…Floyd told Susan to shut Andrew up, or he would walk out." Tears were forming in her eyes. "I loved my brother, Owen, I really did. In spite of his burden, he was such a sweet little boy. His smile could melt your heart. My mother and father loved him too. Susan didn't. He wouldn't stop crying that day…so she put a pillow over his face and kept it there until he stopped."

She wiped her eyes. "She called me at work that day, hysterical. She told me she had killed Andrew accidentally. She said she didn't mean for it to happen. Her temper just got the better of her. She was sobbing uncontrollably. I went straight over to my mother's home. Susan was—"

"Why did she tell you at all? Why didn't she just keep it to herself? No one would have known except her and Floyd. She could have said he died in his sleep." I wasn't sure if my questions were true curiosity, or if I were trying to catch her in a lie.

"I don't know. I asked myself those same questions at the time. I think it was the last good part of her to come out. She could have kept it to herself, but she didn't."

"Why wasn't she prosecuted?"

"Because we never told anyone."

"*Why?*"

"It was an awful time, Owen. When you go through something like that, you have so many conflicting thoughts and emotions. My parents' world came apart when Andrew died. They had already lost one child—they didn't want to lose another to prison. They told Susan to say nothing. They told everyone that Andrew had passed away as a result of his condition. Children at that time didn't live many years if they were born with what Andrew had, so no one questioned his death. My mother told everyone he died peacefully while she was away."

"And you just kept silent. Didn't say a word. This brother you loved so much is murdered, and you just *tick-a-lock*."

"Yes," she affirmed, almost inaudibly.

"*Why?* He was your brother!"

"I hated Susan for what she did. But I loved her too. She was my sister. I didn't want anything more to do with her, but I didn't want to see her go to jail either. So I kept quiet. An unpardonable sin of omission, I know."

"Was your silence at the behest of your parents...or was it of your own volition?"

"Both." Again, her voice was quiet.

"I see. Andrew was going to die soon anyway, so what the hell, right? My mother simply expedited his death. No harm, no foul."

"Please don't swear around me." Her voice was no longer subdued. "And please do me the courtesy of not being flippant about the death of my brother. It was a horrible time. You weren't there. You can't know what it's like to be faced with a decision like we had. I understand you had a sister. I don't know if you were close to her, but if you were, and if she were alive today and she committed a terrible crime, would you rush to call the police and just hand her over?"

I didn't respond. She was right.

"Owen, my sister did not walk away without punishment. My parents disowned her. They didn't want to see her in jail, but they didn't want to see her in their home anymore either. After Andrew's funeral, as far as I know, they never saw her again. As for me, I cut her off too. She'd write, but I wouldn't write back. I decided she was a poisonous human being, and I couldn't have that kind of person in my life.

"Your mother made some reckless choices, Owen, and she paid for those choices for the rest of her life. She could have had and been so much. But she aligned herself with a man who pulled her under. She lived and died in a sea of alcoholism, destitution, and shame.

"I heard from a friend that she stayed married to Floyd even after he cheated on her and lost his welding job to drinking. In the end, he was nothing but a juiced-up janitor. She herself ended up cleaning toilets too. Choices have consequences, Owen."

"Yes, they do, Mrs. Crowley. Your choice to keep all this from me cost you our relationship. You should have told me. But you didn't. Why was that? I'll tell you why. You think I don't know, but I do. You didn't want any of your precious friends to find out who I was—the rape-child of your penniless, white-trash sister. You were ashamed of me."

"That's not true, Owen!"

"I also know why you took me in after Mrs. Constance contacted you. You felt obligated, duty-bound. I was bad blood, but blood nonetheless. Conscience, responsibility, and duty took me to your home, not love. That and the fact that I resembled Eben."

"How can you say such things! We loved you for you. If we didn't, we never would have adopted you."

"Save it! I'm not stupid. I'm good with book math...*and* people math. I know why people do what they do."

"Owen, the reason we never told you who I was is that we, your father and I, wanted you to have a fresh start. We didn't want you to have any reminders of your mother or Floyd or what they did to you. We felt that if you knew who I was, I would remind you of your mother. We felt you would fear me. We didn't even know your mother had died until Mrs. Constance found us and told us. If we had known, we would have taken you in the day she died. And, Owen, I honestly did not know you were not Floyd's son. Think about it—how *could* I have known? I had absolutely no contact with your mother. All I knew about her was a few bits and pieces told to me over the years."

What she said was logical. But there was one part of her story—my mother's reason for hating Andrew—that did not square with logic. I saw the flaw instantly. How could Mrs. Crowley have missed it? It was so obvious. Even more obvious was the reason that *did* square with logic.

"You say my mother hated Andrew because he was *uneasy on the eyes.* Yes?"

"That's what she told me. She said he was ugly, grotesque, and deformed, and she hated the sight of him."

"Doesn't her reason strike you as a tad untenable?"

"I'm sorry, I don't know what that word means."

"Illogical."

"No, it's not illogical. Sometimes what a person does makes sense only to them."

"Very true. But think now, why would my mother, even as shallow and inconsiderable as she was, hate a child simply because he was unattractive? That's inane."

"That's what she said."

"And you believed her?"

"I had no reason not to."

"How could you have lived so long and not know that when people attack the surface of someone, it's because they hate what's *beneath* the surface. My mother attacked Andrew's plague when deep down she wanted to attack his *place.*"

"I'm sorry, I'm not following you."

"You honestly don't know what I'm talking about?"

"No, Owen, I don't."

"Andrew held a very special place in your parents' heart, yes?"

She nodded.

"A very special place that *my mother* once occupied. Getting the picture now? I'll wager that my mother's slide into dissipation and bad company coincided with Andrew's coming onto the scene, yes?"

Mrs. Crowley swallowed. "Yes."

"The princess lost her throne in your parents' palace. And on that throne went Andrew."

"I never even considered that. Why didn't I think of it?"

"Yes, why didn't you think of it?"

Suddenly, unexpectedly, my interest in Andrew vanished. In its place came a question that hit me like a bolt from the blue. In all the years, it had never entered my mind until that moment. My true surname: what was it? Floyd Langley was not my biological father, nor did he adopt me, so was my surname my mother's maiden name or her married name? Legally, I was a Crowley, but who was I actually?

"What is your maiden name?" I asked.

Mrs. Crowley drew her head back in bewilderment. "Where did *that* come from?"

"Just answer me—what is your maiden name?"

"Hamill. You didn't know that?"

"No, I didn't."

"Why is it you want to know?"

"No reason...just curious."

So what was my true name: Hamill, Langley, or Crowley? The Hamills never knew me, the Langleys didn't want me, and the Crowleys didn't create me. I felt like I didn't belong, anywhere. It was as though I wasn't meant to be at all. Maybe Robin was right: maybe I was a nothing.

"Owen, may I say something to you?"

"What is it?" I said absently.

"I know your life has been challenging and hard, and I'm sorry for that. Mine, too, has been heavy-laden. Maybe if our paths were joined together again, life wouldn't be so difficult for us. Can't you find it in your heart to come back to me?"

Her sudden lane change into the reestablishment of our relationship threw me off. I hadn't planned on even talking about it. I only wanted to confront her about Andrew and then leave her feeling exposed and found out. She had steered me onto the road of delicate emotion, and I didn't want to travel there.

I rose from the bed and started for the door.

"Owen, will you visit me again?" she petitioned almost pleadingly.

"I don't know," I replied and continued walking.

From out of nowhere, the epiphany broadsided me like a drunk driver. It made me stop in my steps.

I turned back toward Mrs. Crowley. "I need to know one last thing," I said. "Andrew—did I look like him?"

She appeared confused again.

*"Did I look like him?"* I restated angrily.

"A little," she answered, still looking addled. "Is that surprising? You *were* related."

I nodded. "I guess if a person lives long enough, he'll get his answers."

"What do you mean?"

"You don't see it?"

"I'm sorry, I don't. I don't have the agile mind I used to have."

"She didn't even try to see me—she only saw *him.*"

"Who?"

*"My mother and Andrew!"* I snapped impatiently. "Who else? I wasn't her son—I was her brother!"

Mrs. Crowley regarded me thoughtfully. "Are you saying you think your mother disfavored you because you looked like Andrew?"

"It adds up to that, doesn't it? My mother hated her brother, and she hated me because I looked like her brother. One plus one. Simple math. Occam's Razor: the simplest explanation is usually the correct one."

"You don't know what was going through your mother's mind at that time. Whatever the reason was, she took it to her grave."

"It was the resemblance—I know it."

"If you honestly believe that, Owen, then let that be your comfort. If your mother was truly seeing Andrew in you, then it wasn't *you* she rejected."

"Why couldn't she have tried to love me? Why couldn't she have tried to look past the resemblance and just see me?"

"The world is full of whys, Owen. You can spend your life asking why. And even if you do get an answer, it very often doesn't help."

"My father was nothing more than foul afterbirth, but at least he was honest with me: he told me he hated me because I was a weed that sprang from a barroom rape. Why couldn't my mother have been that honest?"

"Maybe she didn't know herself. Then again, it might have been your resemblance to Andrew. And it might not have. You don't know for certain. You'd be acting as judge if you said that was the reason, and you can't do that. It would be wrong. Only God can be judge. For all we know, she might have even been on drugs. I hear they can make a person do terrible things.

"Owen, forgive me for being this direct, but you need to let this go. You're almost a man now. A good man does not hold grudges, and he doesn't obsess about the past. A good man doesn't look back. He forgets the wrongs done to him and forgives the people who did those wrongs. Marcus Aurelius once said: *The best revenge is not to be like your enemy*. Revenge is always, thirsty, Owen. It's time you took away its water.

"It would seem, by all appearances, that your mother did not love you. Why, I don't know. But I do know that *I* love you. I have since the first time I saw you. I haven't many years left, and I want you in those years. Would you at least think about it?"

"I'll consider it. I have to go. I don't want to stay anymore." Without any further words, I quit her room and returned to the elevator. Once inside, I fought with my tears over my mother and Mrs. Crowley. But I would not let the tears win. I didn't like the way they made me feel: vulnerable, weak, unmanly.

Mrs. Crowley wouldn't commit herself to the idea that my mother rejected me because I looked like her brother, but *I* was committed to it. She said it would be wrong of me to act as judge of my mother. If that's what I was doing, so be it, for I knew I was right. And one cannot be in the wrong if he knows he is in the right.

As for Mrs. Crowley and the explanations she gave regarding the past, I believed her. Logic and the voice of reason, gelled with intuition, told me she had given me a true account of everything: the murder of her brother, why she kept her identity from me, not knowing I was not Floyd's child, all of it. I wanted her back in my life…but I didn't want the emotions that would accompany the relationship. I favored no emotion at all, but negative emotions were at least on my side, whereas positive ones were not. Positive emotions lie in the hands of the one to whom they are given. A man gives his heart to someone, and then that someone leaves him, for whatever reason, and that vacancy destroys his world. *When you get close, you get hurt.* But negative emotions lie in the man's hands. A hard heart never allows someone to leave, for a hard heart never allows anyone to enter; it refuses to let itself be injured. *When you don't get close, you don't get hurt.*

Necessity, not desire, demanded that I think about Mrs. Crowley at a later time. I had a more pressing matter at hand: high school. It was only hours away. Within me were equal measures of excitement and dread. I wanted—and needed—new learning, new knowledge, new challenges, new mathematics. Conversely, I neither wanted nor needed the interaction with the blathering, jabbering, prattling teenagers Moron High would be infested with.

Yet…yet, there was a private, very private part of me that desperately wanted to see and be near the girls in my high school. I knew this craving to be my enemy, and I tried to force it from my mind, but it remained obdurate. This new enemy of mine, I knew, would one day be my undoing.

# CHAPTER 6

# *Who Would Have Thought?*

*"Sometimes spring comes in the fall, when you open the door and expect to find the sad leaves of autumn frosted to the earth; but instead you find the flowers and blossoms of love and acceptance reaching up to embrace you."*

BRUCE BALSAM

Raised in 1965, Moran High School (*aka Moron High*), my home away from home for the next four years, was a sprawling, bracket-shaped edifice on the east side of the city. Affixed to its street facade, just beneath the top floor windows, was its name lettered out in gleaming, polished steel. The building stood four stories high and was shelled in stately ecru brick. In the center of a manicured front lawn stood a soaring flagstaff embedded in an elliptical cement foundation. Below the ground-level windows were ruler-straight rows of yellow chrysanthemums. Its grandness and stateliness brought to my mind the aphorism by J. J. Ryan about the beautiful woman: *What lies beneath that comely skin are thoughts afoot of unspeakable sin.* The building was the skin, the students the sin.

The average population of this imposing institution of secondary education: 1200.

If grade school had been a train wreck, then high school would most assuredly be a plane crash. The freshman class alone was triple the size of my eighth-grade class, which meant triple my adversaries. In spite of this, I was not worried, nor did I care, and I had Ms. Windom to thank for it. Her libertine advances and subsequent explosion Father's Day night had killed the coward in me. No longer would I be a slave to people's petulant words or their arrogant conduct.

The first sight to greet all who entered Moran High was a foyer walled in cream travertine marble and floored in beige mosaic tiles. A circled M was in the middle of the floor. All I could think of was not how handsome this anteroom was, but how difficult the floor must be to keep clean during the winter.

The main hallway, carpeted in seaweed green, was teeming with students. Their bodies were filling the transitway and their mindless chatter was filling the air. I found the senseless noise grating and irritating. For three months, I had had absolute quiet, and suddenly I was in the center of a garrulous, strepitous, teenage cattle drive.

The first day of school for all freshmen would be orientation, which was to begin in the auditorium. We would be served a canned greeting from the principal and be told that high school was the first step onto the vast terra firma of adulthood. After this purple prose, we would meet with guidance counselors who would assist us in creating our class schedules. Following that, we would be given a tour of the school and then dismissed for the day. The next morning, each of us would go to his homeroom before going to any classes and then begin his glorious (or inglorious if he did not adapt well) journey through the colorful and prismatic world of high school.

I happened to notice a small cluster of students gathered in front of a display case far down the main hallway. The entire group was facing the glass. What would cause this small cabal to be so transfixed? I had to find out. I turned and headed for the display case.

I was only a few steps into my journey when a spare, almost fragile-looking boy stepped in front of me.

"E-E-E-Excuse me, sir, d-d-do you know wh-wh-wh-wh-where the au-au-au-auditorium is?" the boy stuttered nervously, almost frantically.

"How should I know?" I snapped. "I'm new here myself!"

The boy recoiled in fear. "I-I-I'm sorry," he swallowed, "I th-th-th-thought you were a t-t-teacher," he stammered and dashed away.

Suddenly, I was overcome with guilt. There had been no need for curtness, and yet I had been curt. I wanted to find the boy and apologize. But I had no idea where to look for him. Still, I needed to tell him I was sorry for my rudeness. Surely, I would see him again, and then I would tell him.

I had been taught many lessons during my fourteenth summer: the most profound had been about habit. If one behaves in a certain manner long enough, it becomes the only behavior he knows. It becomes habit. Ms. Windom was a miserable, hateful, spiteful woman who scalded everyone she met, and it was due to one driving force: habit. I had become just like her—dour and sour—and I didn't like it. I didn't want to be anything like her. I had to change, or else I would live out the remainder of my life hurting people like she did, and I didn't want that as my legacy. I didn't like it when someone hurt me, so I had no right to hurt someone else. I didn't want my life to be guided by emotion, yet I didn't want it guided by meanness either.

As I drew closer to the display case, I recognized its congregants. They were all students from my eighth-grade class. Making up this fetid, adolescent stew were Sheresa Jennings, Rick Winstead, Amy Shields, Dawn Morrison, Wayne Redding, Jeremy Lamb, and Aasha Arapaho. All had been confreres of the pretty-people club—the exalted ones.

I wanted to turn around and head in the opposite direction—as I would have done in years past—but I was not going to give way to that pull any longer. No student, no matter his rank, would drive me away from what I chose to do.

As if I had just shouted their names—though I hadn't said a word—they all turned in my direction. Their mouths opened when they saw what was in front of them.

"*Whoa!*" Dawn exclaimed. "Owen, is that *you*?" Her tone was not inquisitive but pejorative.

I felt my body tense. Calmly, I slipped my left hand into my pants pocket and contracted it into a fist. I was hoping that if I rerouted my anger into my fist, it would vent there and not from my mouth.

This was my first opportunity to break my mold, to sever my habit of being like Ms. Windom. I had to remind myself that just because people were primitive with me did not give me permission to be that way with them. By being like them, I *was* them. And that I did not want. At the same time, I didn't want to be a valet of people's insolence either. There had to be an acceptable middle ground between rude retaliation and pigeon-hearted submission.

"He must be Owen's doppelganger," Wayne remarked with a smirk. "Owen couldn't look that good if he tried," he chuckled.

My fist was now as hard as frozen meat. It is true what they say: *It is harder to keep quiet when assaulted than to return an assault.*

"Oh, I don't know," Jeremy said, "you've heard of Cinderella? Maybe what we got here is Cinder*fella*." The two boys laughed. Strangely, the girls did not.

"Lay off, you guys," Dawn broke in, eyeing me oddly.

Taking the high road is one thing—being run over on it is another.

I drilled my eyes into Wayne's. "I see that you have not changed any over the summer, Wayne," I noted. "Rather like a tedious ostinato, aren't you? Or a birth defect—tiresome, monotonous, ineradicable.

"Let's idle on the subject of birth defects for a moment, shall we? Do you know what they are, Wayne? Of course you do—your sister has a birth defect, I believe. A malformed ear, if I overheard correctly."

Wayne, a red-headed boy with a football-player physique, didn't answer, but instead gave me an algid, gimlet-eyed stare.

"You're even more knowledgeable about birth defects when you look in the mirror, aren't you, Wayne?" I asked. "What defect do you see when you look at your reflection? I'll enlighten you, if you'll permit me. You see a birth defect *en masse*. You are deformed *head to heels, soil to sky*.

"And you, Jeremy, are the reason the word *filicide* is in our vocabulary. Do you know why some parents kill their young? Because some of the young deserve it. Why didn't your parents kill *you*?"

"Shut up, Owen!" Aasha threw at me.

I stepped closer to all of them. "*You* lifted the cover off this sewer, not me. Let me tell all of you something. The daunted doormat you schooled with last year is gone. I don't scare like I used to. I'll not lay down for any of you anymore. I'll cut you in half, and I'll smile while I do it. You are no match for me, so don't even try. Do yourselves a favor—keep your *vacuous* remarks inside your *vacuous* heads! Do you know what you all remind me of? A swamp—stagnant, stale, stenchful. Each of you is a locked cellar—nothing old gets out, and nothing new gets in. You are all rusting cars disintegrating in an abandoned scrapyard—no longer moving, no longer beneficial, no longer useful. But why am I expending my breath on the likes of you? You're nothing but a changeless legion of witless morons. I suppose that explains why you are occupiers of *Moron High*."

They all stared at me.

Wayne rolled his eyes. "Let's get outta here."

"*Ciao*," I said mockingly to them.

I watched them leave. The others trooped behind Wayne like ducklings following their mother. Dawn and Amy looked back at me. During my life, I had seen it directed at others many times, but never at me, so I wasn't sure if what I was seeing on the girls' faces was for real, but I couldn't help but think it looked like…admiration.

Before making my way to the auditorium, I needed to see what the class of 1978 had been eyeing so intently.

In the center of the school's trophy case—resting on a small, metal easel—was his photograph. It was an exceptional picture of him. Sidling the photograph was a written tribute that was equally superb. It read:

*Timothy Gilbert, or simply "Tim," as he liked to be called, passed away over the summer. Tim went to Jackson Junior High. Had Tim lived, he would have graced the halls of Moran High School with his wonderful presence. Tim had a rare form of cancer. But even more rare than his illness was the boy himself. Positive always, negative never, Tim was the kind of boy people were drawn to. Let us all try to keep his memory alive by trying to emulate his gentle spirit and loving nature.*

A wave of intense sadness washed over me. I truly wished we had become friends. I know I would have benefited from him, and, I think, he might have benefited from me.

"Owen, is that *you*?" A familiar—*and irritating*—female voice.

I had indeed changed over the summer. Before, I would have flinched or even jumped had someone uttered my name unexpectedly like that.

Calmly, I turned my head toward the girl.

"Hello, Robin," I said tonelessly.

*"You goin' to church or somethin'?"* she asked, eyeing my clothes.

"No, I'm not going to *church or something*," I replied tightly.

"Boy, you fell right out of the ugly tree and right into the pretty patch, didn't you?"

I stared at her. How could such an empty head be attached to such an extraordinary body?

I so wanted to tear her apart, but out of respect for Tim's affection for her—and in obedience to my commitment to acting less arctic—I reined in my tongue.

Inhaling deeply, I said, "Did you know that Tim passed away over the summer?"

The perfect skin on Robin's perfect face turned white. *"What? How?"*

"Cancer. You didn't know?"

"No. None of us knew. We knew he wasn't quite himself, but we had no idea he was—"

"Maybe if you had bothered—" I stopped myself. Tim would not want me to censure her; he would want me to be kind to her. "His picture is in the display case here." I nodded to the glass.

Tears left her eyes as she read Tim's memorial.

"Robin, I am obligated to tell you something."

She wiped her eyes and gave me her attention.

"Tim asked me to give you a message. I gave him my word that I would deliver that message. Tim wanted you to know that he was in love with you."

She swallowed. "Why didn't he tell me?"

"He was afraid."

"Of *me*?"

"Of frightening you. He thought you would be frightened of him if he laid bare his feelings, and he didn't want to leave this life with that memory. He didn't think any girl would ever love him because of the way he looked."

Her face turned reflective. "He was wrong."

"Then you should have told him that, shouldn't you? Chances are not limitless, Robin—once they are gone, they are gone forever."

"Yes, they are. I'll see you around, Owen." She glanced back at Tim's picture and then went on her way.

It was time that I, too, went on my way. Life goes on. It has to.

The architecture of the auditorium appeared older than the rest of the school, which led me to think it predated the school. Its ceiling was concave and buttressed with massive steel trusses. Weak tungsten lamps within pendants the shape of overturned bowls were suspended from the trusses. Bland-white, cinder-block walls supported the entire structure. It was all very utilitarian and cold. The interior of the school, however, was clothed in newly painted drywall and bright fluorescents. That the auditorium was obviously older meant that the school itself had a predecessor. It made me wonder what the original school had looked like.

The more years of life I acquired, the fonder I became of older architecture. Modern buildings appealed to me visually, but those of former eras appealed to me emotionally. In my eyes, buildings of yesterday were more thoughtful and respectful than their modern counterparts; they seemed to copy the character of the people who designed and built them. To me, senior structures reflected integrity; neoteric constructions reflected audacity.

Though the auditorium had hundreds of seats, only a few were occupied. Most of my fellow freshmen were standing or milling around. And, of course, only a few were quiet. They were the ones who were sitting.

I took a seat in the center of the room. Ardently, I tried to ignore them...but I couldn't. I couldn't help but gaze at the girls in the room. I drank them in as one would marvel at a crimson sunset or a kaleidoscopic painting. The sight of them stirred me feverishly. They were such magnificent creatures; what a tragedy they weren't as exquisite internally as they were externally. I didn't want to desire them...yet I did. I so wanted to have command over my venereal hunger, but I could not resist it. Its strength was pythonic and its roots fathomless. And it seemed the older I got, the more intense my appetite became.

Already my class had segregated itself into little hives. The gentry girls, the future cheerleaders, the double-X-chromosome plums, with their glossy lips and skintight pants, were banded together by the stage and were chinning heedlessly and smiling arrogantly; the jocks, with their orotund, haughty laughter, were flaunting their lithe and sinewy bodies in clothes that were as close-fitting as those worn by the succubi at the front of the room; the intellectuals and the brains, with their bland, *I-don't-care* togs, were being very animated and gesticular; and the hippies and the potheads, with their stringy hair and drapes for clothes, were looking at each other with insensible eyes. All of this bloat I found obnoxious. It was only the diffident children—those sitting alone but wishing to belong—who I found digestible. Tim would say I would find the others digestible as well if I only knew them. He said that everyone has pain, even the proud and pretentious. It was difficult to imagine that any of these self-orbiting, self-crowning, self-glorifying adolescents had any knowledge of—let alone experience with—pain. But perhaps they did, and that was the reason for their demeanor and dress. And perhaps I would have found them likable if I truly knew them, as Tim said, but it was doubtful the reverse would be true.

Then I saw something, something I almost couldn't process. In the society of pompous princesses by the stage was a girl I had not seen before. She must have been in the nucleus of the group, concealed. Now she was on its perimeter. She had long, flowing, blond hair and was beyond even *my* ability to describe. I had never seen such a thing of beauty! She was eyeing a girl sitting by herself. The blond girl was looking at the solitary girl with compassion and sympathy. She left the group and walked over to the sitting girl. The blond girl sat down next to the solitary girl and began to talk to her. The solitary girl, previously downcast, was now smiling and radiant.

What did the blond girl say to her?

The two rose and headed for the stage.

*Fascinating.*

My eyes were fixed on the blond girl. She must have sensed she was being watched, for she looked around to see who was paying her such rapt attention. When our eyes met, I did not look away...nor did she. What she did next, I had never before witnessed: she smiled at me. What I did next, I had never before imagined: I smiled back.

She smiled once more and continued walking with the shy girl to the girls by the stage.

Glancing back at me, she gave me a slight wave with her fingers.

I gave her a reciprocal wave with mine.

She turned away and joined her group.

My face felt unusually hot, and my heart was beating unusually fast. My breathing was quick and heavy. I didn't want to entertain such longings, for they made me feel controlled and out-of-control. And yet...yet these longings were euphoric. They were almost like cocaine... and, in a way, they were. When the blond girl smiled and waved at me, I felt a rush of dopamine in my head. When it enters the brain, cocaine causes a significant accretion of dopamine, which creates a state of euphoria.

*Fascinating.*

This blond girl, whoever she was, was not only hypnotically beautiful, she was...angelic.

An extrinsic, rhythmic sound broke me out of my delirium.

My head turned toward the sound. It was coming from my left, from the south side of the room.

A janitor was pushing a mop bucket, and its wheels were making a continuous clicking sound, much like the ticking sound made by a playing card pinned to the spokes of a child's bicycle.

The janitor, a hunched but refined-looking man in his mid-forties, appeared distraught. I wanted to go over to him and ask what was wrong, but of course, I couldn't do that, for it was none of my business.

Still, he looked terribly sad and in need of a friend. I hoped there was someone in his life he could lean on and share with.

Someone tested the microphone on the stage. A corpulent, gray-haired man with jowls like pancakes was tapping the head of the microphone with his finger.

The man introduced himself as Mr. Heald, the principal. He then asked that everyone take a seat. Noisily, but obediently, the chaparral of self-important teenagers, whose thinking sat them next to Zeus on Mount Olympus, dispersed and sat down.

With a smile, Mr. Heald gave us all a heartfelt welcome to his school, now *our* school. Following this friendly salutation, his smile gave way to a frown. Departing from the speech I thought he would give, he gave my class stern warnings about conduct and deportment; what he would and would not tolerate in his school. (It was now *his* school again.) Of course, every student listened, but teenagers have selective hearing: they take in what they want and discard the rest. My classmates, like all teens, would do what they wanted, regardless of the boundaries and the consequences of crossing them. *Devil-may-care* would be their yardstick and *go to the devil* would be their song.

While Mr. Heald was cautioning us, I caught sight of the janitor again. He was just inside a door to the left of the stage. He was standing and looking out at the class of 1978. His face, sad still, had an added emotion now...regret.

The janitor turned and left.

I wondered if anyone in the auditorium had seen the janitor. If so, had they been curious about him? I hoped that at least a few had wondered.

Like the lovely, blond girl sensing she was being watched, I now felt that *I* was being observed. In the row in front of me, far to my right, was an ebony-haired girl smiling at me. Before turning to face the principal again, she winked.

The dark-haired girl was pruriently pretty, but she wasn't the blond girl. And although I didn't even know the blond girl's name, she was the only girl I wanted looking at me, and the only girl I wanted to look at in return. In my short but long life, I had developed a keen feel for people: I could sense who was good and who was not. The blond girl, I knew, was good. Purity was in her heart, virtuousness in her spirit, and love in her soul.

I saw many from my eighth-grade class that day, and they saw me. For the first time in our long history together, there was no distaste or disinclination in their eyes; rather, there was almost warmth. Some even said hello to me. Of course, in every crowd, there is always one salmon who fights to swim upstream, who fights against the current, who resists moving forward. In that crowd of freshmen at Moran High, that salmon was William. He began as my nemesis, and he would end as that. When he saw me that first day of high school, his eyes did not convey warmth, like the others, but, as on my first day at elementary school, he anchored his cold, gray eyes into mine. The vessel attached to that anchor was a warship. If William could have his way, he would be the author of my end.

By the time we all had created our class schedules, it was time for lunch. The cafeteria was a typical lunchroom: hundreds of hard-plastic chairs were grouped around numerous circular and oblong tables that sat on an olive-green, terrazzo floor. This lunchroom, however, was many times larger than the one in my grade school. The menu items that day were meatloaf with mashed potatoes and hamburgers with fries. I just bought a bottle of Pepsi from the vending machine. I expected to eat (or rather, *drink*) alone, as I did in grade school, but minutes after I sat down, I had company.

"Hi, I'm Mark," a lean, maize-haired boy introduced himself to me. "Mark Sorrell."

Shocked, though pleased, I returned, "Hello, I'm Owen."

"What's your last name?"

"Crowley."

"What school did you come from?" he asked as he sat down. "I bet you came from a private school. No one dresses like you unless they have money."

His comment was off-putting, but I knew he was just making conversation, so I dismissed it. "No, I went to Jackson Junior High. As for my clothes, I simply want to look nice."

"Got a girlfriend?"

I looked at him with surprise. Was he always this forward…or was I that backward? I concluded that it was the latter. Since I had never had any friends, I was unaccustomed to the blunt manner in which young people conversed with one another.

"I do not," I answered. "You?"

"Naw. Wish I did, though. Hey, do you want to go to the first stomp together? Maybe a couple a girls will want to dance with us, and we can cop a few feels!" He smiled roguishly.

Appalled at his crassness, I said, "You don't believe in preliminaries, do you?"

"If you don't put your line in the water, you ain't gonna catch no fish—know what I mean?"

*Charming double negative*, I mused. *Maybe having no friends all this time wasn't such a bad thing after all.*

"Apart from…*fishing for feels*, what other interests do you have?" I inquired half-heartedly. He was boring me, but I hadn't the nerve or the heart to ask him to leave.

"Lots of stuff. I'm really good at making model cars, and I throw a mean softball! And I love comic books! Got loads of *Fantastic Four* and *Spider-Man* and *Captain America* and *Captain Marvel*! Hey, do you know what?"

"Hmm?"

"This Saturday morning *Captain Marvel* is going to be on TV! It's going to be called *Shazam!* It's not going to be animated, though. It's supposed to be what they call live action. The real deal! I can't wait! You know what else I like?"

"What's that?"

"TV. I love TV! Especially science fiction. I love *Lost in Space*. My favorite episode is *Space Creature*. It's the one where Will wishes everyone away. You ever see it?"

"That particular episode? Or the series itself?"

"Any of it."

"I've seen a few episodes. Unfortunately."

"You didn't like 'em?"

"If one is into stupid, the series is top drawer. Now if it's exceptional science fiction you're after, *Star Trek* is the only bread to buy. Sharp scripts, marvelous special effects, a natural blend of comedy and drama, and stories that deal with real human problems. *Lost in Space*, on the other hand, just deals with absurdity."

"Hey, I love *Star Trek* too! I know everything about it. I never miss it! My favorite episode is *Obsession*. But you got to admit, the Jupiter Two on *Lost in Space* is one cool spaceship!"

"And too small for all that it is supposed to accommodate. The Tardis Effect in spades. You cannot suspend disbelief in a fictional program if the basic imperatives in that program are disregarded. *Lost in Space* broke through the fourth wall because of bad scripts and bad design. It would have been a blue-chip series had Irwin Allen done two simple things: retained serious science fiction writers and made the ship bigger. Simple as that."

"You talk really cool! You must be really smart."

"I just read a lot."

"Hey, speaking of reading, I read in *TV Guide* that pretty soon everyone will have to pay for TV. Everyone will get TV through a cable and not an antenna on the roof like we do now."

"Nothing in the universe remains constant, Mark...even television."

"My friend says that everyone will have a box installed in their home and will have to put a quarter or fifty cents in it to watch an hour of TV."

"I doubt that's the way it will work, Mark."

"Even if it's another way, what if you can't afford to pay for TV? Why should we have to pay for it anyway? We never had to pay for it before. Sometimes..." he blushed, "my mom can't even afford to buy dinner." He looked away from me.

I hadn't noticed it until that moment: he didn't have a lunch tray in front of him. He hadn't even a lunch sack.

A choking ache formed in my throat. I knew what it was like to be hungry. Mark knew it too. He was just a simple kid trying to survive his reality and trying to escape that reality through television.

"I wouldn't worry about pay TV just yet, Mark," I said, surreptitiously slipping my hand into my right front pocket. "You know, a residential cable system would have to be in place before we lose the TV service we now have, and such a cable service does not yet exist. Besides, I'm certain by the time it's in place, you will be able to afford it." I cast my eyes downward. "Hey, look at that."

Mark lowered his eyes.

Lying on the floor between our chairs was a wrinkled five-dollar bill.

Mark leaned over and picked it up. "Wow! What do you think we should do with it?" He gazed at the crumpled currency as if it were solid gold.

"Finders keepers," I ruled.

"You don't think we should turn it in?"

"Naw. Some rich kid probably dropped it. They don't need it. You keep it. Go buy yourself some lunch."

He hesitated. "You saw it first."

"I'm not hungry. You use it."

"You sure?"

"Positive. You better go before they stop serving."

He leapt up and hurried over to the tray line.

I cleared my throat and balled my hand into a fist to force away the hurt I was feeling for Mark. I didn't want the hurt inside me. I didn't know how to handle it. It was too overwhelming. Too frightening. I had had enough hurt in my life; I didn't want anymore. Anger was the only emotion I knew how to handle. And yet, there was a growing part of me that desperately wanted to feel emotions other than anger, but I was afraid to give them life, lest they crush me. For years, I desired to be like Mr. Spock, unwilling to feel, and there I was, doing exactly that, and desperately wishing I wasn't. Mr. Spock once counseled that attaining something was never as satisfying as desiring it. His counsel was right. And ironic: I wanted what Mr. Spock had, and I got it...and now all I wanted was to get rid of it.

Maybe if I stopped fighting my emotions and flew with them, I wouldn't fear them. I once read a disquisition on the madness of the Vietnam War. Evil, the author opined at the conclusion of the essay, doesn't flourish when good men do nothing, as Edmund Burke believed; evil flourishes when good men think that the only answer is war. Fighting, he said, ends only in failure. True victory lies in harmony, not hate. If two opponents embrace, they are no longer opponents. Two swords will bring blood, but two hammers can build a city. Maybe it was time I stopped doing battle with my emotions and started building a life with them.

While waiting for Mark to return, my eyes browsed the cafeteria. They came to an abrupt halt at the tray line in which the students were standing, waiting to be served. My heart leapt and my face grew hot again. Standing one person away from the cashier was the beautiful blond girl who had smiled at me in the auditorium. I couldn't help it—I found myself mesmerized by her body. Like water running over stones, her body flowed easily, effortlessly; and like wax dripping from a candle, it formed into perfect curves and swells. A stinger of guilt stabbed me: I was objectifying the girl. I had to look away, for she was not an object but a person. Mr. Wilson had objectified me, and there I was objectifying her.

Just as I was turning my eyes away, I happened to see something that pulled my eyes back. The boy who had stopped me earlier that morning and asked for directions to the auditorium was at the cashier. He was standing next to the blond girl. He was frantically feeling his pockets. Either he hadn't enough money to pay for his lunch or he couldn't find his money.

I felt that familiar ache form in my throat again. I couldn't stand by and let him go through the humiliation he was experiencing. As I was giving weight to my feet, I saw the blond girl gesturing: she was pointing to the boy's tray and hers and speaking to the cashier. It was clear what she was doing: she was paying for *both* their lunches.

Incredible!

"Hi, Owen," someone called. The voice came from behind me.

I was surprised. No one ever said hello to *me*. Turning around, I saw Luann Searle smiling at me.

*Since when!* I thought.

Luann had been in my eighth-grade class. She was in the *elite* herd.

Woodenly, I smiled at her and turned back around.

It wasn't right. Only three months before, I was the class pariah, the misfit who sat below the salt, the school's *bête noire*. And only three months later, I was an equal, a member of the *troupe*. Tim had been correct about my clothes: they *had* brought out people's ire. But it wasn't just my clothing that had brought out their virulence. It was more than that. People will react to what they see, but they will also react to what they sense. All of my life, people sensed my deficit of self-confidence, and they reacted negatively to it. Now that I was self-assured and nicely attired, they were responding positively. But why did I have to have a bronze self-image and a well-accoutered body to be liked? It was all so wrong.

"May I sit down here?" A girl's voice.

The voice broke me out of my introspection.

I looked up.

I froze in my chair.

Standing, with a lunch tray in hand, was the beautiful blond girl.

I stood.

"You aren't going to leave, are you?" she asked, her voice like a silken wrap.

I held her eyes with mine. Brilliant azure was the color of the windows to her soul. They acted like a sedating and soothing breeze. And her face was so sweet and disarming that I instantly felt relaxed.

"No, ma'am. I am standing out of respect."

Her face went blank. "What?"

"Albeit antiquated, it is still proper and appropriate for a man to rise when a woman graces his presence, especially a woman of refinement and beauty."

"*Okay...*" she said, slightly shaking her head. "Can I still sit down?"

"Please."

"*You like a teacher's aide or something?*" she asked almost suspiciously.

"No, ma'am. Student, like yourself."

"You don't act like a student," she pointed out as she was lowering herself into a chair. "You don't even look like one."

"I hope not. Conformity is so *banal*, wouldn't you say?"

"I guess so. Anyway, my name is Roxanne. What's yours?"

"Owen. Yours, *Roxanne*...a name with a fine pedigree, a deep and intricate history. Are you wise to that? Are you keen to learn that history?"

The girl stared at me. I knew what was going through her mind: *What kind of a flake have I sat down next to?* But I also knew she wouldn't leave, for she was attracted to me, in spite of my unusual and unconventional essentia. I was a curious zephyr stroking her delicate cheek; a still, small voice wafting in her graceful ear. A shout will repel...but a whisper will attract.

"The first wife of Alexander the Great was named Roxana," I illuminated. "She was said to be the most beautiful woman in all Asia. Your name means '*dawn.*' It also means '*little star.*' It is from the Greek, Roxane, with one *n* only. The Greek appellation is a derivative of the Persian Roschana, which means '*dawn of day.*' That is you."

The girl wetted her lips and cleared her throat. "How do you...how do you know all that stuff? I don't know you, and you don't know me." There was a splinter of fear in her voice.

"Fear not, Roxanne. Put to bed your anxiety. It is your name I know, not you. Your name—or rather, the Greek orthography of it— figures prominently in the book *Cyrano de Bergerac*. Dynamically, magnetically tragic story, which led me to query the substance of your name. I do that. I read a book, the topsoil, and then I dig beneath that topsoil to learn more. That is how I gain knowledge."

Mark came back to the table and sat down with meatloaf and potatoes and pudding and milk. "Mark," I said, "this is Roxanne. Roxanne, this is Mark."

"Hey, you know who you look like?" Mark asked galvanically.

She shook her head again, appearing addled.

"You look like that actress, Farrah Fawcett. Man, is she hot! She's married to the *Six Million Dollar Man*—Lee Majors. My brother calls him '*Lucky Lee*'! We got a lady in our apartment house that's named Roxanne. She's really stacked, like you. She's got a license plate cover on her Fiat that says *Roxy Is Foxy*. Do you want me to ask her where she got it from so you can get one too?"

She stared at him with disbelief and restrained indignation. "No, thank you."

She turned to me again.

"The price of pulchritude," I consoled her.

She stood up. "I think I'm going to sit somewhere else. A little too much weirdness at this table. It was...*interesting* meeting you both."

"*Enchanté*," I requited.

She stared at me in mystification, then left.

"Did I say something wrong?" Mark asked.

"No, I think she was expecting something other than what she got."

"What did she expect?"

"Something a little less *avant-garde*."

"What's that?"

"Weirdness."

In no time, Mark's and my small round table was filled with other students.

Mark was sitting at my left, and at my right was the dark-haired girl who had winked at me in the auditorium that morning. "Hi, I'm Cristal, with an *i*," the girl said, holding out her hand.

Out of courtesy, not attraction, I took her hand and tentatively shook it.

Withdrawing her hand, the girl began to chat about herself. As she rambled, I thought about Roxanne. What a delight she was. Mark was correct: she was eerily similar to Farrah Fawcett. But it wasn't just her beauty that mesmerized me; it was her kindness—the kindness she showed to the shy girl earlier in the day and the generosity she showed to the shy boy in the lunch line. Her somatic artistry was merely cream from the milk.

I did not regret the way I came across to her, or what I had said. Neither was offensive. They had been merely atypical. I was not the average boy, and I never would be. I was what I was.

While Roxanne was chilled by her first encounter with me, she was not deflated by it. Her interest was still there. I sensed it. I knew it.

As if an invisible finger tapped me on the shoulder, I glanced to my right. Sitting far away, at a long table with a coterie of future cheerleaders, was Roxanne. This was where she had lighted after she left me. She was looking at me.

She smiled and gave me a little wave with her fingers, just as she had done earlier that morning in the auditorium.

I smiled…and waved back.

Yes, she was still very much interested.

I dreamt of Roxanne that night. It was a dream sent from the purse of Eros; a dream very charged, very intimate. In all ways but one, I was an uncommon and unusual young man. But in the land of lust, I was an ordinary citizen, a full resident, very much a normal teenage boy.

My first class of my first day (after homeroom—a positively pointless function of high school) was English; or more specifically, Classic Literature and Plays. This would occupy the first half of the year; the second half would be Speech Presentation. I entered room 130 neither nervous nor excited. I was curious, however, to see what material we would be given to read and discuss. I hoped it wouldn't be the juvenile selections Jackson Junior High had given us.

All entering room 130 were met with a large circle of chairs; there were maybe forty. Only half were occupied. The new freshmen, though given a tour of the school the day before, were no doubt still searching for this room.

I brought with me Theodore Dreiser's *An American Tragedy* to keep me company until class began.

Something interrupted my concentration while I was reading: it was the feeling I should give the door my attention. I gave heed to the feeling.

Roxanne was entering the room with a friend. They took the seats parallel to the door. She didn't notice that I was one of her classmates. She made the breath flee from my lungs. She was so incredibly lovely that she made my entire body ache. I wanted to take her in my arms and jail her behind molten bars of passion.

Unexpectedly, she turned her face toward the door. Under its lintel was the boy whose lunch she had purchased the day before. He looked scared, almost terrified.

"Hi, Christopher," she called to him.

The bantam boy flinched at the sound of Roxanne's voice. His face reddened. It betrayed his enchantment with her. And clearly, he was unaccustomed to being acknowledged by someone of her beauty and class.

"Come over here," she invited. "Sit next to me."

The boy timidly walked over to where Roxanne was sitting. He took the seat to her right and cowered down into it, as though he wanted to avoid being seen. I was many seats away, also to her right. She patted his leg to encourage him.

I looked on in amazement.

Then she saw me.

Her face kindled with delight.

"Good morning," I silently mouthed to her.

She did the same to me. Then she did something I couldn't believe: she winked.

"Good morning, everyone," a spindly, drab voice said from the direction of the door.

The classroom, now full, turned toward the voice.

A very short, very thin man clad in a dry-washed seersucker suit, who was clearly past the age of retirement, was entering the room.

"My name is Karl Wheatley," he introduced himself lifelessly. "I'm going to be teaching you English for the next year." His voice was so frail I thought him ill. "Before we begin, I want to get to know each of you, if that's all right with everyone. Please stand, give me your name and a brief synopsis of yourself."

*Synopsis? What are we, books?*

I had a suspicious feeling that this class was going to be another Ford Pinto: a total disaster.

"Do you mind if we begin with you?" he asked the student in front of him.

Since when does a teacher ask permission from his pupils?

Then I noticed that William was also in the room. This class was *definitely* going to go up in flames.

William and one of his cerebrally deficient friends talked as the other students gave their names and *synopses*.

Mr. Wheatley (or, more accurately, *Mr. Weakling*) did not silence William or his friend. He let their rudeness reign.

*What kind of a teacher is this?*

Roxanne stood. Before she could breathe out a syllable, William whistled at her. "Forget your name, girl—I just want to hear you *moan*!" William and his friend broke out in loud laughter.

Again, Mr. Weakling said nothing. Was he so at home with the bawdy behavior of teenagers that he simply didn't hear what they said anymore, or was it that he didn't care?

It was obvious he was not going to intervene, so I did.

"William—will you shut the hell up!" I shouted. "If you don't want to be here, leave! No one will stop you, and believe me, no one will care! How would you like it if we asked you to *moan*? I don't think you would—even though you lack all sensibility. Just because *you* love the sewage that gushes from that mouth of yours doesn't mean the rest of us do! For once in your abysmal life, grant someone your silence! Let her talk!"

Roxanne stared at me, her eyes unblinking, her lips parted. She swallowed.

"You're horny for her, aren't you, Owen?" William gibed. "You're probably jizzing your jeans right now."

"I don't wear jeans, William. But you do."

"Shut up, you two!" the girl sitting next to Roxanne threw up a verbal dam between William and me.

"Yes, I agree," Mr. Weakling tonelessly subscribed and returned his eyes to Roxanne. "Go ahead, Ms...." he stopped. "Sorry, I forgot your name."

"She hasn't given it yet," I interrupted. "Don't you even listen! She has already been disrespected once—don't supplement the incivility with rudeness."

How was this man allowed in the classroom!

Mr. Weakling said nothing.

Roxanne stared at me.

"Please, Roxanne, continue," I said. "You will not be ambushed again. I promise."

She paused before going forward, still staring at me. Then she angled her head toward Mr. Weakling. "My name is Roxanne Solleveld. I moved here from New Mexico. I want to go into teaching. I like skiing and volleyball and running. I have two brothers and a dog. Is that good enough?"

"I suppose so," he answered indifferently.

Roxanne rolled her eyes and sat down.

What planet did this paltry nebbish come from? If he didn't care who we were or what we enjoyed, why did he even ask?

The class then focused its attention on the diminutive boy slumped next to Roxanne.

"You're next, go ahead," Mr. Weakling prodded.

The boy stood. His body was shaking, his face was the color of blood, and his lips were trembling.

"M-M-M-M-My n-n-n-n-name i-i-is Chr-Chr-Chr—"

"Here, let me give you a hand, stupid—my name is *cr-cr-crap*," William laughed.

"His name is *Christopher*!" Roxanne interceded angrily.

"His name is *retard*," William jeered. "He can't he even t-t-t-talk."

The boy began to cry. Without collecting his books or uttering another word, he ran from the room.

"What a fag!" William sniggered.

Roxanne's face turned harder than an iron. "That was a terrible thing to do! Who do you think you are!"

"I'll tell you what he is," I answered for William. "He is a dung heap, and he loves it. He is foul; he is corrupt; he is immoral; he is lewd; he is vulgar, and he is unprincipled. In short, he is a pig!" I stood and walked over to William.

"Go back to your seat," ordered Mr. Weakling.

"Shut up!" I shot at him. "If you had had more balls, it wouldn't have come to this."

"Whoa!" the class rumbled.

Mr. Weakling crawfished into silence.

"Leave—*now*!" I demanded, boring my eyes into William.

"Make me!" he postured, grinning.

"I shan't tell you again."

"*Shan't.* Man, you're weird! And you get more weirder by the year."

"And you more *feral*! And incidentally, William, it is either *more weird* or simply *weirder—not more weirder,*" I disabused him with delight.

He gave me scissors for eyes.

"You know, I used to feel sorry for you," I said.

For a brief instant, his face softened.

"I don't need your pity!" he fumed.

"No, what you need is a hard kick in the ass!"

The class laughed.

"And are you goin' to give it to me?" he dared. "You couldn't kick a beach ball across the street!"

"You know, when I was little, William, I was afraid of you. I was even afraid of you last year. But as I was telling some of the synapse-challenged, half-brained troglodytes you call friends, I don't scare anymore. You haven't changed at all...have you? In all these years—still a thug. Still a punk! Still doing to others what has been done to you and thinking you have the right to do it. If evolution were true, you would be the evidence against it. You are, like someone else I know, a parasite. Did you know that in some cultures human feces is used productively? No culture could ever make use of *you*. You are profitless, pointless, worthless, and valueless! As someone asked me, a long time ago, do you know what a worthless human does...or *should* do? He *extinguishes* himself. He considers the greater good and guarantees that he will no longer be an expense or an offense to anyone by performing the simple act of killing himself. Do the world a favor, William, go somewhere and *extinguish* yourself."

I turned and headed back for my chair. I knew what his next move would be. I heard the legs of his chair screech as he bolted up. I darted to my right just as he ran past me. He couldn't slow himself in time and crashed into my empty chair. Both he and it became one and tumbled hard onto the floor. He sprang up and came at me like the animal he was. Just before we made contact, I ducked and rammed my fist into his stomach. He collapsed onto the ground, instantly forming into a ball. His arms were now folded across his stomach, and his throat released moans of pain.

"Jerome, go get Mr. Heald!" yelled Mr. Weakling.

A flaxen-haired boy sitting by the door ran out of the room.

I crouched down next to William and grabbed his hair and pulled his head back so he could see me. "Well, it looks like you got your *moaning* after all, didn't you, *Willyboy*? I told you—I don't scare anymore. I'm going to tell you this once, and only once—don't you *ever* talk to Roxanne like that again! *Ever!* And keep your toilet-tongued mouth shut when Christopher is around! He doesn't need your vomit-smelling voice in his life! Nobody does!"

I released his hair, returned to my chair, set it back on its legs and sat down.

The room was deathly quiet.

Most of the girls had their hands clasped over their mouths. Roxanne was one of them. I hoped she didn't think I was a carbon of William because of what I did to him. What I said needed to be said, and what I did needed to be done.

Mr. Heald charged into the room. "What in the hell is going on in here!"

No one said a word, not even Mr. Weakling.

I stood. "I hit him—that's what's going on in here. He needed it; I did it. If you wish to expel me, then do so."

"No!" Roxanne objected loudly. "William came at Owen!"

"I don't care who came at who," Mr. Heald ejected.

*That's* who *came at* whom, *Mr. Principal!*

"There will be no fighting in my school!" Mr. Heald mandated. "Both boys are suspended for two days, effective immediately." He grimaced at the sight of William lying on the floor. "And don't just stand there, Mr. Wheatley, get that boy off the floor!" He exited as abruptly as he had entered.

I gathered my books, stepped over William and left the room.

When I was a few doors down, someone called to me from behind, "Owen, wait a minute. Don't leave yet."

I turned around.

Roxanne was hurrying toward me. "I'm sorry about what happened in there."

"Don't be. It was wonderful! I've wanted to give him my thoughts—*and my fist*—for years."

"You sure did," she laughed. "Where'd you learn to fight like that? No offense, but you don't seem like the fist-fighting type."

"Correct—I am not. My mind did not craft the move. I abstracted it from a book. One of the many benefits of the printed word."

"Owen…" She paused. "Thank you. Really."

"For?"

"For what you said in class. For defending me. No one's ever defended me like that."

"Again, Roxanne, the pleasure was mine. A *grand* pleasure. Yet I find it strenuous to believe that you need defending at all. Who but that awful William would ever descend so low as to cast darkness on someone as luminescent and as lovely as you?"

She fastened her eyes to mine. "Where'd you learn to talk like that?"

"Books."

She smiled. "It's sexy."

The compliment colored my face.

"I'm sorry," she said. "I didn't mean to embarrass you."

"Quite all right. Laurels are not something I am accustomed to receiving."

"You know, when you were talking to me yesterday, I'd never had anyone talk to me like you did. I mean, I'd never come across anyone so…"

"*Weird?*"

"At first, that's what I thought. And then I started to think about it, and I thought: he's not weird at all. He's just the opposite. He's unique. No one could say what you did and not be. I mean, you could have been crude like your friend, but you weren't. You were respectful. That means a lot to a girl."

"My words are not perishable, Roxanne, so I will gladly, over time, lay them at your feet, like camellias, if you will permit me."

"I could listen to you forever." She looked behind her back to see if anyone was around. "Can I tell you something kind of personal?"

"As the poet Rochia Kalma declared to her intended the morning of their marriage: *My soul finds sustenance at the very sound of your voice*. Please, tell me."

"I don't talk as good as you, but I got to tell you—you are the hottest-looking boy I've ever seen! Man, when I first saw you yesterday, I was blown away! I wanted to—" She stopped, and her face reddened. "I can't believe I'm talking like this. I never do this. I'm so sorry, Owen. I'm embarrassed now. I'm going to go back to class now before I make a bigger fool of myself."

As she was starting to move, I touched her arm.

"Roxanne, please do not feel foolish. I, too, say what I feel. As you have seen. Words are everything to me. They're all I have. They're all I've ever had. Without words, people cannot connect. I have come to learn that people need people. I never thought I would need anyone... until I met you. You make me feel...everything that is good. I look at you, and for the first time in my very long life, I feel...*happy*. I have such...longing for you." I stopped and cleared my throat, my face mantled with crimson once more. "Now *who* looks foolish?" I smiled awkwardly.

"How can I be this attracted to you?" she asked. "I mean, I don't even know you. I...I feel...I have never felt this way before. I didn't know I could, at least not so soon in my life, and so suddenly. Who feels this way at fourteen? Man, this is crazy!"

"Indeed. But, as the humorist Simon Bailey once penned: *On the playing field of fondness, there are no rules—anything goes. The heart is the football, and Cupid is the quarterback*. In aviation parlance, we are in *free fall*. We are no longer being thrust by the engines of reason and logic; instead, we have been taken over by the gravity of our own feelings. The heart writes the rules for romance, Roxanne, not the head."

"You are one amazing boy, Owen Crowley, do you know that?" she said, smiling again.

"As are you. How did you know my last name? I don't recall telling you."

"I asked around." She leaned in and kissed my cheek. "Hurry back. I'll be waiting for you." She sprinted back to room 130.

I leaned against the wall. I laid my palms over my eyes and rubbed them. My hands were trembling. The school halls were still and quiet, yet inside my head questions and thoughts collided and shouted. I was both delirious and terrified. I wanted to wrap myself around Roxanne, and yet I wanted to run from her. I was troubled by my behavior with William, and yet I was proud of it. I had been violent and mean with him, and I enjoyed it. How could I possess so many contradictions? How could I have been committed to sexual nephalism for so long, and in a matter of hours discard it for blatant carnalism? When I first entered puberty, I cinched a bridle around my sensual longings—now *they* had one around *me*. I had let both Roxanne and I off the hook for being confused—so was I now hanging myself back on that hook? Was it normal to be this conflicted, uncertain, and unknowing? Perhaps it was. Perhaps having inner conflicts was what was normal, and what was abnormal was running from them. I truly needed to stop fighting my feelings; I needed to face them, fly with them—if I didn't, I would always be in turmoil, and I would end in failure. But more important than any of that was Roxanne. If I kept up the fight, I would lose her. Even the thought of that terrified me.

It wasn't even nine in the morning, and I was already going home. Had I the relationship with Ms. Windom I once did, she would have beat me, kicked me, and screamed herself into a stroke for being suspended, and on the second day of school no less! But she was afraid of me now, so I could have been expelled, and there would have been no repercussions. Father's Day of that year had been a critical turning point for me. The day had been horrendous, but it had been the most beneficial of my life.

On my way to my locker, I passed the boys' restroom. I heard crying coming from inside it. I knew it was Christopher. I couldn't simply go home and leave him in pain.

I entered the lavatory. He was crouched next to the heat register with his face in his hands. He was weeping. But it wasn't Christopher. It was the janitor I saw the day before.

He darted his face in my direction and sprang to his feet. "What do *you* want?"

"Nothing," I answered.

"Then will you please get outta here?"

A small voice inside my head told me to do as he petitioned, but there was a louder voice that told me to do just the opposite. He was alone, in pain, and desperate. We weren't friends, for we didn't even know each other's names, yet I could still listen. Many times in my life I had longed to have someone's ear, and *only* their ear; not their advice, not their counsel, not even their own tragedy, just their hushed attention. So often a good listener is the best and only prescription for sorrow.

"I'm sorry," he apologized. "I shouldn't be in here." He wiped his eyes and walked past me and out the door.

He wouldn't like me intruding; he probably would even become angry, but it was a storm I had to chance. I had been alone and in pain many times in my life, so I knew what he was going through. I also I knew the last thing he needed was the aloneness he requested. Tim had taught me that.

I followed him.

He made his way to a stairwell and descended to the basement. There were classrooms on that level as well. He entered one of the rooms and let the door close after him. It was either a maintenance closet or classroom not in use.

I slowly opened the door. No lights were on; only the light from a long, narrow strip of windows illuminated the room. It was a storage room, a very large one. Dusty desks, portable blackboards, metal folding chairs, metal trashcans, dirty Venetian blinds, and boxes of all sizes were scattered around the room.

"What are you doing in here!" he barked. "What do you want!"

"Nothing," I answered calmly, evenly. I had to gain his trust, and trust is first established through tone. Tone, like timing, is everything.

"Then get out!"

"You didn't happen to see a small boy walking around crying, did you?"

The man's face softened. "No, I didn't."

"Oh, that's too bad. I was hoping I could find him."

"Why…why was he crying?"

"Oh, some crawling crustacean was teasing him because he stuttered, so he ran from the classroom, crying."

"What a lousy thing to do. The kid who did that must be some piece of work."

"Yeah, he's a regular Rosemary's baby."

The man laughed for a second.

If it hadn't been so true, I would have laughed with him.

"There are a lot of terrible people in the world, aren't there?" I said, trying to draw him out.

"There sure are," he agreed pensively.

"And tears are still tears…regardless of age."

"Yeah."

"I've done my share of crying. I've met some pretty lousy people in my life. You've lived longer, so I'll bet you've met even more."

"Yes, I have. People who I didn't think would ever treat me badly ended up doing just that."

"I know what you mean. My own mother, who should have been my first ally, was my first enemy." I shared this only to show him that I, too, had scars. I hoped that by exposing myself I would make him comfortable doing the same.

"Yeah?"

"Seems I was not the fruit of love—but the weed of domination. Academics say that rape is not about sex, but about control and power."

"That's a bad trip, kid."

"Yes, it was. What's *your* trip? We all have at least one."

"You couldn't understand. You're too young."

"You'd be surprised at what young people can understand."

He regarded me. Then his eyes floated away.

"You ever wish you were dead?" he asked. "I do…all the time. I should be dead, you know. I should never have been born. It's funny, you know, because I was really quite spruce when I was young—but I was never quite normal. I was weird from the start. I was a weird little boy, a weird teenager, a weird young man, a weird middle-aged man, and now soon I'll be a weird old man. You know what I would do if I could go back in time? I'd stay alone. Totally alone. I wouldn't talk to anyone, except when I had to. No open doors for people to slam in my face. I look at all these young kids around here and wish I were one of them. I'd do it right. You have that chance, kid, you know that? You can pull back before it's too late. When you're young, you think pain will be the property of others—never you. It's so aslant: we're lonely when we don't have people in our lives, but then when we do, we're still lonely.

"I'm so contrary. I say I hate who I am, but when I look back on my days as a teenager, I long for them...the days when everything was ahead of me, when there was still a chance for love, a chance to be important to someone. I miss having that chance in front of me. I have nothing in front of me now. Only emptiness and deafening quiet. If I died tonight, no one would weep...no one would care...no one would notice. They'd get another janitor to take my place, and I would slip into the dark closets of the minds of the few people who know me."

"You honestly think no one would care if you died?"

"I don't think it—I know it. The only time I'm given a smile is when someone wants something. Then they're sweeter than cereal. After I've seen to their needs, I'm invisible again.

"I wish I could go back to the time when I was a boy. I took the coldness and disregard of people much better then than I do now. You wouldn't know it to look at me, but when I was your age, I was quite happy. *Weird*, but happy. I swear, I was in love with every girl I saw. They never saw me, but I certainly saw them. I look back and wonder how I could have been so happy when I was so invisible. But I was. I'd see a pretty girl walk by and know I would never have her, and I'd say, *'Scratch another one.'*

"I was a writer at one time, believe it or not. Never published, but I still wrote. My first story was called *The Day*. It was about a plane that hits the Hoover Dam. I kind of stole the idea from the Johnstown dam failure in 1899. Pretty good yarn, though, for a thirteen-year-old. And then there was *Tsunami*. Another tale that reached, but was still remarkable for a boy of fifteen. Seems I excel at imagination, but not reality. I've never been able to connect with people. Especially women. I tried, though. I really did. I'm Ernest Borgnine's *Marty* all the way: the stuff the opposite sex wants, I don't got."

"May I ask you something?" I intruded.

"What?"

"Why is love so important to you?"

"It's important to everyone, isn't it? We measure our worth by it. If we're loved, we have worth; if we're hated, we don't."

"Are you hated?"

"I am by her."

"Who's her?"

He paused. "Sharla. That's her name. She's three years older than me, but she always had the maturity of somebody twice that. She was such an amazing woman. We met when I was twenty-four, and she left when I was twenty-four. From September to December, 1954, I had worth. She gave me love. She gave me value. I'm not a professional, obviously. Never have been. But she was. She was a pharmacist. I was a janitor...even then. But she didn't care; she just saw *me*, not what I did. She didn't have to talk to me, but she did. She didn't even have to acknowledge me, but she did. She could have ignored me like everyone else, but she didn't. She didn't care that I didn't have a degree. We had such deep and vulnerable talks. They would last for hours, sometimes into the early morning. We would take long walks in the late afternoon and at night and just talk—no rivalry, no competition, no attacking, just listening and sharing. She would have me up to her parents' home on Sunday nights for dinner. On Thanksgiving night, she brought me dinner to my apartment because I had worked that day. She was the only woman—the only person—I ever cried in front of. She was the only person I ever trusted. Never once did she make fun of me or expect me to be someone I wasn't. She loved the way I kissed. She used to look at me with such fascination. She used to say, '*You are so handsome.*' I always used to ask myself what she saw in me. She could have had any man she wanted, but she chose to be with me for those four months."

"Why did she leave?"

"I knew she was going to. She told me so in the beginning. She had been planning to leave long before she met me. New York…that's where she needed to go, and that's where she went."

"Why there? Why didn't she stay here?"

"She needed to test herself. She was a restless spirit, very driven, always pushing herself to be better, to go farther, higher. She was the most intelligent person I had ever known, but she never paraded it. She had this brilliant, copper-toned hair. Still does. Beautiful could have been her first name and dazzling her last. After she moved away, she would write occasionally, and I would do the same. The years passed, and our letters stopped. It hurt, but that happens. People move on; they find others to take your place. Life moves forward, and if you're smart, you move forward with it. I guess I wasn't very smart."

"I take it she came back to Salt Lake and back into your life?"

He scrutinized me distrustfully. "Who are you anyway? New staff? I've never seen you before."

"No, sir, I'm not staff."

"Who are you then?"

"Suspended student at present."

"What kind of student gets suspended on the second day of school?"

"This one. I was in a fight."

"*You?* You don't look like a fighter. Model maybe, but not a fighter."

"So I've been told. But appearances are often deceiving, aren't they? Violent waters often run below calm ones. Our outside and inside don't often match, do they? Yours don't match. You are highly intelligent, but your carriage and your line of work mask that. People think you are a simple, basement-dwelling custodian, yet you are much more. You are very intuitive, sensitive, perceptive, creative. Very acute and well-informed. But you lack the self-confidence to raise yourself above your situation. And you think you are too old to even begin to try. You condemn yourself for never having attained a degree. In spite of your natural insight, you do not believe you possess the ability to learn. You came from poverty, and that is all you know. You think you don't deserve to have more than you do, because you loathe yourself. You are astonished when someone even says hello to you. You desperately want love, but you believe love is for others, not for you, for you are not worthy of it."

His face was frozen with alarm and amazement. "How do you know those things? How *could* you know them? You're just a kid."

"Like I said, you would be surprised at what young people can understand."

"Maybe you're right. I understood a lot too when I was your age."

We were veering away from the subject at hand. "Sharla came back... but she wasn't the same woman this time, was she? Before, she was the color of springtime...now she is the color of winter. Tell me why."

"Why do *you* care? Why do you even care at all? You don't even know me. You don't even know my name."

"Then let's introduce ourselves. My name is Owen. And yours?"

He studied me for a moment. "Austin."

"Now we know each other."

"I've met thousands of kids in my day, but I've never, ever met one like you. You're very...odd."

"I've been called worse."

"I didn't mean it as a slam. I've just never run across someone so mature who is also so young."

"Life will make us that way, won't it? The people we meet make us into the people we are, and the people we will become. You, too, were unusual when you were young. Gifted but misunderstood. Teased, hated, envied. Often, the flower of malice comes from the barbed seed of jealousy, wouldn't you agree?"

"Why don't you just answer my question? Why do you care about me or what I'm feeling?"

"Call it...a reflection. I know what it's like to be you...where self-hatred is your shadow, and loneliness is your spouse. What happened with Sharla this time?"

Redness formed on his cheeks, and his eyes teared. "I loved her so much. I truly did. She was the only woman I ever truly wanted. I had my crushes in high school—who doesn't?—but they weren't love, and they certainly weren't reciprocated. But Sharla, she was what all men secretly want but never attain. I think most men will say they want a woman who is good in bed—because that's what they're expected to say—but what they really want is someone who is pure in heart, a woman whom they don't have to act around. The world demands that a man be a warrior, a conqueror, but deep down he gets afraid. He wants to come home and be able to strip off the armor and the shield and the facade and just be who he is. That's what I could be with Sharla. Stripped but not assailable. She was every man's dream. That's what she was back then. But all of that changed. A couple of years ago she came back here to live. About a month ago, our paths crossed in the same hospital in which we both had worked years earlier. It was like time had stopped for us. We saw each other, and it was 1954 again; we picked up right where we left off. For a few days anyway. And then, as if overnight, she changed. She became this...this inhuman human. I'm a quiet man by nature; she knew that. We had dinner with some of her friends one night, and, of course, I was quiet. Later, when we were alone, she angrily asked why I didn't speak up. I'd reach out to kiss her, and she'd become like stone. I'd try to take her hand, and she'd pull it away. We flew down to San Diego one weekend to see her brother. During the flight, she made fun of me because I was afraid of flying. We rented a car, and she became angry at me for driving slowly. We sat on the beach, and she ignored me—wouldn't say a word, just drank her wine and went somewhere else in her mind. We ate at an outdoor café, and she criticized me for my lack of ambition. In our hotel room, she'd stay on the phone with her friends and leave me to watch TV alone. On the way home, she said I needed to dye my hair. Gray is not at all becoming.

"Last week...she finally said good-bye. But not before telling me what she truly thought of me. She said I was a man without a place or a purpose; I was a failure. She said I had done nothing with my life, that I was as dead as a fallen tree. She said I was an embarrassment to her, and she was sorry she had reconnected with me. She told me to stop living in the past and get on with the future. She said if a man doesn't move forward, he should move out of the way to make room for those who will. I don't know which was worse—her words or the look of hate and disgust on her face as she spoke them."

He started to cry. He took a folded piece of tissue from his shirt pocket and wiped his eyes. Then he tossed the tissue onto the floor in front of him.

My throat was swollen with sorrow. It was hard to breathe. My eyes leaked stinging tears.

He arose from the classroom chair. Through a cracked and shattered voice, he said, "Thank you, Owen, for listening. You're a good kid. Be careful who you give your heart to. Just remember, most things begin in gladness, but all things end in sadness."

Walking over the tissue that held his tears, he left the room.

Per Mr. Heald's directive, I did not go back to school until Friday. Not Roxanne, not school, not my lost class time, none of this occupied my mind (or even mattered) during the two days I had been gone. Only one concern filled my mind: Austin. I was him, and he was me. He had been destroyed, and there wasn't a soul who cared. He was completely alone and thoroughly empty. This Sharla...would that I could meet her. I would take her in my teeth...and shred her into sweepings.

When my name was called in homeroom, I didn't hear it. It wasn't until the second calling that I heard it; my mind was with a man I hoped was better than he had been three days before. I would look for him during lunch and find out how he was feeling.

English was my first class of the day. When Roxanne saw me, she beamed. She discreetly patted the seat of the chair next to hers. I took it and bathed in her warm attention.

Then, without pause, a veil of solemnity fell over her countenance. "Are you going to go to the memorial?" she asked.

Her question took me by surprise. One moment she was joyous, the next she was talking about a memorial.

"I'm sorry, I don't know what you're talking about."

"Oh, that's right—you probably wouldn't have heard. The janitor that worked here during the day committed suicide Wednesday night. He shot himself. I think his name was Austin. The service is going to be this Sunday afternoon in the auditorium. I think I'll go. I kind of felt sorry for him. He always looked so sad and..."

She paused.

"Owen, are you all right? Are you...*crying*? Where are you going?"

I left the room and made my way to the basement, to the storage room where Austin and I had talked earlier in the week.

My chest felt like it was under an avalanche of rocks. My lungs groped for air. My arms encircled my middle as I tried to keep myself together. My body felt as if it were being cut apart. My eyes were shut tightly—they didn't want to see Austin's lifeless face, empty of hope.

"Owen!" Roxanne gasped and came over to me. "What's the matter?" Terror was thick in her voice. Clasping my hand, she said, "Let's get you upstairs to the office."

"No," I refused, squeezing her hand. "Oh, Roxanne. He had no one. Absolutely no one. He was all alone. He died without anyone caring that he was dying." The tears came easily, willingly.

Her arms encircled me.

I wept on her chest, like a child.

Minutes later, I broke away from her, ashamed. I had cried in front of her. I had disgraced myself. I knew what I must have looked like to her in that dark, cluttered room: a tiny infant, a baby who has years to go before he is a man.

I wiped my face and straightened my sweater. "Forgive me, Roxanne, for my release of emotion. It was unmannerly and unmanly. It must have embarrassed you greatly."

Staring at me, she came back, "No, it didn't. Not at all. Not in the least. In fact, it makes me l—" she arrested the rest of her thought.

"I'm going to leave for the day," I told her. "I can't stay. I wish Austin had had someone like you in his world. Life would have turned out differently for him. Thank you for noticing him, Roxanne. Why are there so few angels like you, and so many reptiles like her?"

I left the storage room and went home.

*Austin Montgomery Richardson*
*Born September 4, 1930, in Austin, Texas*
*Died September 4, 1974, in Salt Lake City, Utah*
*After graduating from Moran High School in 1948, Austin*
*entered the military. He served in the Korean War and was*
*decorated with the Silver Star and Purple Heart. He returned*
*to Utah in 1953. In 1960, he joined the staff of Moran High*
*School and quickly became a member of its family. Austin*
*was a dedicated employee and a good friend to all. His*
*absence will be greatly felt, and his presence surely missed.*

*Life and death are but phases of the same thing, the*
*reverse and obverse of the same coin. Death is as necessary*
*for man's growth as life itself.*
*Mahatma Gandhi*

These words were lodged next to a black-and-white photograph of Austin, which was placed at the front of the auditorium. Both were enclosed in 8 x 10 pewter frames and positioned upright on a card table just below the stage. Other, smaller photographs of Austin ringed the 8 x 10 picture and written tribute.

Because Austin made little money, and because he had no family—neither close nor distant—the city would see to his burial. The school wanted to do a memorial of its own since no formal service would be held.

Only teachers and office staff were gathered in the auditorium with me. Naturally. What student would give up his or her Sunday to come to a memorial for a janitor?

I sat near the front of the room, for I wanted to hear the eulogy clearly.

As I sat there, I pondered—as I had done numerous times since I heard about Austin's death—the question of Sharla. So far as I knew, Austin hadn't left any farewell note explaining his suicide. But I knew why. Sharla. *She* was the reason. Did she know of his death? If so, did it even enter her subhuman mind that she was the cause of it? What I would give to see her. She would never be the same again.

"Do you mind if I sit with you?" someone asked me.

I looked up. To my right was a young man, tall and stout, handsome and tanned. Judging from the voluminous thews in his arms and chest, and the abundance of collagen in his face, I figured him to be about seventeen, maybe eighteen, and most definitely a football player or some other athlete. He wore a dark-chocolate, three-piece suit. I had to wonder why he was there. He was going against type: athletic boys are not known for soft and saccharine leanings.

"Please do," I waved to the seat next to mine.

"I'm Paul," he held out his hand.

"I'm Owen."

"I can't believe this has happened," he voiced.

"Yes. Certainly caught me by surprise. I gather you're a student."

"Was a student. I graduated last year. Were you a student too?"

"Just started."

"Really? You look like you're in your twenties."

"Thank you." I was truly flattered. When you're older, you want to look younger, and when you're younger, you want to look older.

"Did you know him outside of school?' he asked.

"No, I only met him a few days ago. I wish I had known him longer."

"Yeah, he was an amazing man. Hardly anyone knows that because they never took the time to get to know him. In their eyes, he was nothing more than a middle-aged toilet-cleaner. But he sure was more than that to me."

"How did you two become acquainted?"

"We became friends last year. I was having trouble in my art class. We all had to be able to draw this miniature statue of Michelangelo's David or else we didn't pass the course. But I just couldn't get it. I couldn't get the arms and legs to look right. One day after school, Austin saw me struggling to draw the statue. He stayed after school for two weeks and showed me how to draw the human body. It's so simple if you're taught correctly. Just start everything out as a swirl, then define the parts and bring them together. *He* should have been my teacher, not the idiot who said she was.

"Austin brought from home some of the sketches he'd done with charcoal. Man, he was good! He had these three Korean landscapes—they should have been in a gallery. He brought in one of a woman he'd done when he was a young man. It was so lifelike it was spooky. He said it was of a woman he once loved.

"And it wasn't just art he was good at. He knew English and literature too. He had a mastery of our language like no one else. He knew Shakespeare up and down, side to side, corner to corner. His favorite was *Richard the Third*. He was probably the most sensitive man I've ever known. He certainly was the most generous. My dad walked out on my mom and me last year. We were having a real hard time making ends meet. Austin paid our rent for many months until we got back on our feet. He didn't want to be repaid; he didn't even want to be thanked. He just wanted to do it. He said that he had lived on the streets when he was a boy, and he knew what it was like to go without.

"None of these people in this room knew the Austin I knew. They're here probably because they're expected to be. Just a dead broom-pusher to them.

"You know, if we all would stop and just get to know one another, we'd discover that there's more to love and admire in people than there is to hate."

"You seem quite mature for someone so young," I commented.

"Life will do that to you."

"Indeed it will."

"I wish—"

"Pardon me, Paul. If you will excuse me, there is someone who just came in who needs my attention."

"Sure."

She stood directly in front of the card table. A short—*very short*—red-striped skirt wrapped her middle, while a white, ruffled blouse cloaked her top. Suntan-hued nylons veneered her legs. The ensemble was engaging, and it complimented her, but it belonged on a younger woman.

"Hello, Sharla," I said. "So nice of you to join us."

She looked at me, perplexed. "Do I know you?" she inquired, brushing ribbons of russet hair out of her eye.

"No, but I know *you*. What are you doing here?"

"*I beg your pardon?*"

"What are you doing here?"

Her face tightened. "Is *that* any of your business?"

"Yes, it is my business. In fact, it is the business of everyone in this room. It is because of *you* that we have all gathered here."

"Me?"

"Yes, *you*. You killed him."

"I don't think so," she argued, smiling.

"You're right—you *don't* think. You just strike—like a snake."

"Why don't you crawl away and go *bug* somebody else!" She smirked at her serrated turn of phrase.

"Because it is *you* who needs *bugging*."

"You got more balls than your underwear can hold, don't you?"

"And you've got more *scales* than you can count. Austin killed himself because of *you*."

"That's not how I see it."

"I'm sure you don't. We are here for Austin, and Austin is dead because of *you*!"

"Austin is dead because of himself."

I stared at her. "Take a walk with me."

"I'm not going anywhere with you!"

"That was not a request."

"Go blow yourself."

"You have *two* choices, Sharla: you can either leave peacefully with me now or leave in humiliation later. Of that you can be certain. Do not worry—I'm not out to harm you, only to talk to you. *Now—walk with me.*"

Without further words, she began moving. I joined her side.

Once outside, I stopped.

She stopped too.

I turned and trained my eyes on her.

She *was* a beauty...but then, so was Lucifer before his fall. I could see why Austin was attracted to her. She was slim and poised and refined.

Her face was showing signs of senescence, yet it still held some of the suppleness of youth.

"All right, talk!" she snapped defensively.

"My name is Owen. I knew Austin, briefly. I am told that you knew Austin longer. And more intimately."

"So?"

"You feel no guilt?"

"No. Why should I? Austin pulled the trigger, not me."

"You say that like you're ordering a pizza at a restaurant. Austin once said you were every man's dream. What made you go from *that* to what you are now?"

"*His* dream—not mine."

"Austin is dead—is that registering with you? He's *never* coming back."

"Oh, well," she tossed out.

I couldn't believe my ears. Who could be that cold?

"Neither ice nor butter melts in your mouth, does it, Sharla?" I asked.

She squinted in confusion.

"*Why are you here?*" I dug.

"Because I want to be."

"Why, so you can dance on his grave?"

She smiled.

I wanted to slap her. "Why do you hate him so?"

Her smile remained.

I stepped closer to her.

She drew back slightly. Her smile dissolved.

"You killed Austin, Sharla. You took his life from him."

"Austin was an empty, barren man who didn't like to hear the truth, and that's what I gave him. He was going nowhere. He was a loser. He did himself a favor. He probably would have died old and homeless. He was halfway there already."

"Who are you to say someone is going nowhere?"

"I call 'em as I see 'em."

My hand tightened into a fist. I stepped back from Sharla; if I hadn't, I would have thrown it into her face.

"Do you know what cancer is, Sharla?"

Her face turned confused. "Of course I know what it is."

"I don't think so. When you get back into your car today, look in the mirror—*that* is cancer. *You!* You destroy life, and you don't care if you do. You exist only to bring pain. It's interesting—you informed Austin that he had no purpose or place, when in fact, it is *you* who has no purpose or place. Just like cancer."

I ran my eyes over her. Then it came to me. It was as clear as water in a glass.

"Accurate metaphors aside," I said, tunneling my eyes into hers, "do you know what you *really* are, Sharla? You are a first-rate, top-of-the-line, name-brand, five-star, Godless, bloodless bitch. You verbalize whatever enters your corrupt, acidic mind because you think it is your right, regardless of the pain it inflicts. Well, here's some truth for *you*: your prime has past, and you hate it—that's why you dress the way you do, and that's why you hated Austin so much. Being with him reminded you of your advancing age, didn't it? You are no longer young; instead, you are a woman on the wrong side of forty who has become a spiteful, judgmental, critical, cynical, hateful, inflexible, unaccountable wretch! You were once kind, but your fixation on being young has made you hard and depthless and one-dimensional. We hate in others what we hate in ourselves, don't we, Sharla? You said Austin was a failure, that he was living in the past. But it is *you* who are dwelling there. You reunited with him hoping to go back to a time when you were young and perfect, but being with him only reminded you that your youth and perfection are but curled-at-the-corners memories now. Austin drove slowly, like an old man; he had gray hair, like an old man; his body was declining, like an old man; and he was not ambitious, like an old man. He represented everything your youth-obsessed mind detests. Austin cared about things beneath the surface—whereas you only care about things *above* it. You are as shallow and superficial and about as meaningful as a page of pornography. Austin wasn't the failure—*you are*. You are a morally bankrupt human being whose life should be removed from her without thought.

"Are you at all familiar with Winston Churchill, Sharla? Of course you are. Who isn't? But what you may not be familiar with is that Mr.

Churchill had a very sulfuric tongue, not unlike yourself. During the thick of World War Two, he said these few ominous words on the matter of Adolf Hitler: *'With God's help, we shall rid the Earth of his shadow.'* Good words, Sharla. Very good words. Do you know why they are so good? Because they can be applied to other bipedal fungi as well. *You, for instance.* Make Christmas come early this year for all the people in your life, Sharla, and give them this gift: go somewhere and *rid the Earth of your shadow. Do* go gentle into that good night. It should be *you* lying in a morgue refrigerator right now—not Austin."

Her eyes became welding torches. She stepped close to me and torpedoed my face with a spray of spit. She pivoted around and walked off.

I lifted my tie and wiped my face. I slowly pulled the tie out from underneath the collar of my shirt and dropped it into the trash can next to the auditorium door.

I sat down on the steps in front of the door. My desire to return to the memorial was gone; I just wanted to go home and go to bed.

"You are indeed a boy of many colors," said a very familiar voice.

I turned.

Roxanne, dressed in a stunning, shimmering, lapis lazuli dress that made her figure even more enrapturing, was standing just outside the door.

I shot up.

"Roxanne?" I asked, shocked. "What are you doing here?"

"Mind if I sit with you?"

Still overwhelmed, I answered, "Yes! I mean, of course not. I mean, please, sit." I felt my face tingle. I was blushing.

She sat down first. Nervously, I sat down next to her.

Her mere presence lifted me to the clouds. That she came to Austin's memorial lifted me even higher. She was probably the only current student who had the decency to come. Her thoughtfulness made her that much more precious to me.

"I have a confession to make," she announced. "I was behind the door there while you were talking to that woman. I was coming through the other entrance when I saw the two of you leave.

"Owen…up until five days ago, I didn't think anyone could ever come close to my dad. He's the bravest, strongest, and purest person I've ever known. Then I met someone last week who stands right next to him. His name is Owen Crowley."

"When a girl deposits a boy into the same account as her father, that is quite an honor."

"There's something else I want to tell you."

"What is it?"

She hesitated. "I'm afraid to say it."

"I'm the last person you should fear."

"I can't believe I want to say this."

"Why don't you just say it."

"It's not that easy. I've never said it to a boy before."

"In which pocket does it lie?—the right being good, the left bad."

"The right…I think. It's just that I don't know if it's real. I mean, I'm only fourteen."

It dawned on me what she was trying to say: she trying to tell me she was attracted to me. It was painful seeing her in distress. It would be ill-fitting and arrogant of me to say it for her, so to help, I recalled a quote: "The father of Shakespeare's Juliet did not want her to marry, for she was, as he declared, '…*yet a stranger in the world. She hath not seen the change of fourteen years.*' Yet Romeo and Juliet thought differently."

I waited for her words.

"That was just a play, Owen. Fiction."

"True. But there's an even greater truth: just as life imitates art, Roxanne, art imitates life."

Her eyes turned glassy, as though she were going to cry. Her lips parted slowly. "I love you, Owen," she said, her eyes not leaving mine.

For the first time in a very long time, I was without words. I was numb with joy and disbelief. I didn't expect her to say that.

Her hands were resting in her lap. It would have been ill-fitting and arrogant of her to take my hand, so to help, she recalled a quote: "The father of Roxanne said this to her mother the night of their first date, '*Forever begins when his hand takes hers.*'"

It was now she who was waiting for me.

Trembling slightly, I took her hands and gazed at them.

"I have never known love, Roxanne," I confided. "At least not love I could trust. When I first saw you, I quaked. You were not of this world. You were a magnificent, iridescent nebula in a cold, unfeeling universe; a calming and comforting rainbow in a frightening storm. You were the sun's warmth on my skin." I rejoined her eyes. "You are torturously beautiful, Roxanne. The loving way you treat people brings me to my knees. I could look upon you for an eternity and still want for more. In countless millennia, I could never tire of the sight of you.

"My world, since I was a boy, has been books, and books alone. I relate to them, and they to me. I parrot them, and I want to be like them because they have never left me; they were my strength, my comfort, and my friend when no one else was. They were my only love. But last Tuesday, in the early hours of the day, I found another love, one greater and deeper. Her eyes have the color of the morning sky, her skin the softness of nursling down, and her heart the glow and delicacy of a rose. She is indeed the brightness and glory of dawn." I took her left hand, raised it to my lips and kissed it. "I love you, Roxanne."

I leaned in and put my lips to hers.

My head swam, my body came alive, and my soul sang as she returned the kiss.

Who would have thought that the boy who was once shunned and excluded, disdained and ridiculed, taunted and reviled would have come this far? Who would have thought that that same boy would now be strong and confident, resolute and determined, embraced and loved?

Who would have thought?

# CHAPTER 7

# *A Life Unexpected*

*"We can't help everyone, but everyone can help someone."*

RONALD REAGAN

*Tuesday, September 10th, 1974.*

I arrived for gym class early. I wanted the locker room to myself so I could dress alone. I didn't want anyone to see the scars. Had my natural parents been alive, they would have been happy and proud that their handiwork was still there for all to see when my shirt came off. The scars on my back and chest had faded and contracted over the years, yet they were profoundly visible under sunlight and fluorescent light. Locker rooms were lit by fluorescents. So were shower rooms. Showering after PE class was mandatory. I didn't know how I was going to get out of it. Perhaps the steam in the shower room would cloud the scars some.

This was my first gym class since leaving junior high school. Before and after gym there, I dressed in the stairwell, and I didn't shower until I got home.

I saw Christopher sitting on the bleachers in the gymnasium when I arrived. He was by himself and already dressed in his gym clothes. PE twice a week was compulsory for all freshmen and sophomores; juniors and seniors were not required to take it. Rank does have its privileges.

I wasn't the only one nervous about the class—so was Christopher. His anxiety was far and near on his face, although what he feared and what I feared were universes apart. Christopher, I suspected, was the kind of boy who wore his heart on his sleeve. A dangerous place to keep it.

His eyes were directed straight ahead, as if he were bracing himself for some type of impact.

I went over to him.

"Hi, Christopher," I initiated.

He looked at me, his eyes flooded with anxiety. "Hi," he returned shakily.

"You look a little nervous."

The fear left his eyes. What took its place was anger. "Does it make you feel superior to people to point out their weaknesses?"

Stung by his answer, I said, "No, it was just an observation."

"Why don't you go shove your observations up your ass and leave me alone!"

"I'm sorry—I didn't mean to hurt your feelings."

"What do you want!" he asked hotly.

"I want to apologize."

"You just did!" he said curtly.

"No, I want to apologize for last week. I was rude to you when you asked me how to get to the auditorium. I behaved badly, and I'm sorry for that."

He surveyed my eyes closely.

I suspected he was searching for disingenuousness or deceit.

His stare hardened. "Since when does one kid apologize to another?" A thick coating of capsaicin lay over his words.

"I was impolite last week, and that was wrong. I'd like to be friends… if you would. Who knows, we may end up liking each other. Anything is possible, Christopher. Let me go get dressed and then we'll go from there. Sound good?"

"It's your time—waste it if you want."

His reply took me by surprise. Was he saying it was a waste of time trying to be his friend or was he saying *he* was a waste of time? I figured it best not to ask. It would be better just to show him that I was sincerely interested in him as a person.

Something else took me by surprise: his phonations had been flawless; he hadn't stuttered once. Why?

I left Christopher and made my way to the locker room. While dressing, I noticed the shower room. Just the sight of it terrified me: not only might my scars be seen, but Mr. Wilson and Ms. Windom might be hiding somewhere in the room, waiting to pin me against the wall and force themselves on me all over again. Water and rape: I would always and forever link the two together. I didn't know if I could go near the shower room after class, let alone enter it.

As I was tying my gym shoes, four other boys entered the room. I quickly finished, closed my locker and left.

Soon, the basketball court of the gymnasium was noisy with talking and laughing and basketballs slapping the floor. Quietly, I sat next to Christopher.

I saw Mark appear from the locker room. He saw me and smiled. He padded over to me and sat down. I introduced him to Christopher.

Mark and Christopher instantly connected. They both knew they were the odd boys out and this bonded them. I let them talk and did not interrupt. I was glad they were creating a friendship, for they needed one another.

"You ever watch *Star Trek*?" Mark asked Christopher.

"Yeah, I l-l-love it! I-I-I never miss it. I l-l-l-like M-M-M-Mr. Sp-Sp-Spock the best. I-I-I wish I was like him."

"Me too."

*Be careful what you wish for, boys*, I thought.

"Know what?" Christopher expanded.

"What?"

"I-I-I m-m-made the c-c-c-communicator and the pistol phaser."

"You mean from scratch?" Mark asked hungrily.

"Yep—I m-m-made 'em out of cardboard. And then I painted 'em with m-m-model-c-c-c-car paint."

"Wow! Do you think maybe you could bring them to school?"

"No, I d-d-don't want to r-risk breaking 'em. But if you want to c-c-c-come over to my house after school sometime, I-I-I'll show 'em to you then. I-I-I'll even l-l-let you hold 'em."

"Really? That would be so cool! How about sometime this week?"

"Sure. I-I-I'll ask my mom t-t-t-tonight if it's okay."

"I can't wait!"

"I wish *Star Trek* was real," Christopher gave away, his voice different, remote, his eyes cemented to the boys on the court. "I'd flip open my communicator and have a full security team beam down right in front of those stuck-up jocks. I'd like to see how stuck-up they'd be then."

"Yeah, that would be great!"

"Then I'd have the security team phaser 'em all down."

"I don't know if I'd go that far."

"I would."

It was as if Christopher were in another dimension, another world. He wasn't stuttering at all. It was as if he were inside himself, playing out a fantasy he had visualized many times before. He struck me as the kind of boy who, if pushed far enough, would shove back with a force that would stun and astound. Beware the quiet man.

I saw the coach enter the gymnasium. He wasn't what I expected. I imagined a lean man in his twenties with bushy hair and long sideburns entering the room. Instead, a tall, brawny man in his fifties came onto the court. He had olive skin that clearly came from the sun rather than heredity. And his hair nearly moved me to laughter. It was a gray, flat-topped, every-strand-in-place pompadour that belonged more on a haberdasher's mannequin than a high school gym coach.

"All right, you turkeys, line up!" the man commanded.

We all formed ourselves into rows.

"My name is Michael Zigich. You can call me Coach, or Coach Z, or Mr. Zigich. We're going to start the hour off with five laps around the court, and then we're going to do some exercises. Then we'll head down to the football field for some baseball. I want to see what you turkeys are made of. All right, let's hit it. I want to hear some shoes hitting the floor! I said, let's move it! No hustle, no muscle!"

Like obedient dogs, we all began to run clockwise around the gymnasium.

Mark, Christopher and I ran side by side. I noticed Mark doing something very peculiar with his right hand each time we turned a corner. Discreetly, but noticeably, he flattened out his hand and made two or three revolutions with it.

After our exercises, I asked him about it.

"Mark, if you don't mind me asking," I said while we were exiting the gym to go down to the football field, "what was that you were doing with your hand while we were running?"

"I was turning the Grand Prix," he responded proudly.

Puzzled, I asked, "What?"

"I was turning the Grand Prix," he repeated, his tone mustardy, as if his answer was abundantly clear.

There were only two things in the known universe with the name *Grand Prix*, so I probed deeper, "You talking about the race, or the car?"

"The car, of course! How could I turn a race?"

Stymied at the strangeness of our conversation, I said, "I haven't the faintest idea. I was just asking what you were doing."

"I told you, I was turning the Grand Prix." His tone was even edgier this time.

"May I ask why?"

"Because it's the Grand Prix. Or as my friend calls it, the *Grawn* Prix. My friend lives on the East Side, where the rich people live. He just turned nineteen. His dad lets him take out their family car every Friday night. Guess what car it is."

"The Grand Prix?"

"Not just *any* Grand Prix. A ' 73 Grand Prix. Brand-new. Man, you should see it! Beige top, brown body, and after it's been hot-waxed, man, does that baby shine! And drive—man, it's like nothin' else! Four-fifty-five-cubic V-eight with two-hundred-fifty horses! That's the SJ model. That's what my friend has. And turning, man, is it a dream! With one finger, you can turn that whole car! That's what my friend does, but I like to palm the wheel when I turn. You should see the way the girls look at me when I pull up next to them!"

"Your friend lets you drive his car?"

"Sure. I always play KRSP when I do. My friend calls me '*The Krisper.*'"

"Do you have a license to drive?"

"No. I don't need one. I'm a great driver. My friend taught me how to drive in parking lots before he let me take it out on the road. I would sit between his legs, and he would let me steer."

"*He what?*" An alarm went off in my head.

"I used to sit between his legs and steer."

"Doesn't that strike you as a tad...*unusual*?"

"I already know what you're thinking: he's gay, and he just wanted me against his crotch." He leaned closer to me and whispered, "You're right—he is gay. I may be poor, Owen, but I'm not stupid."

"Does he do anything else to you?" I asked suspiciously.

"Everything," he answered nonchalantly.

Stunned, I clasped his arm and pulled him aside.

Christopher was walking behind us. He stopped when Mark and I did. I told him to go on without us and we would meet up with him on the field. He shrugged his shoulders and continued walking.

"Mark, this is— What your friend is doing to you is *wrong*—and illegal!" I informed him. "It's rape. It's against the law. You're a minor, he isn't."

"So. He doesn't force himself on me. I let it happen. Nobody's getting hurt."

"*You* are. You *both* are."

"*No*, we aren't. He gets what he wants, and I get what I want. It's no big deal."

"But you're not gay, so what are you getting?"

"The Grand Prix. I give him sex, and he gives me his dad's car. Not only that, he takes me out to eat."

"Is driving a car and going out for hamburgers worth it?"

"When you're hungry all the time, you're damn right it is. And when I'm behind the wheel of that car, I actually feel like something. For a few hours once a week, I don't feel poor and worthless."

"Could it be that what you're doing with your friend is what's making you feel worthless?"

"I felt worthless long before he came along."

"Mark, sex is not something you play around with. It's dangerously powerful. When used for egocentric gain, it maims people— permanently. Right now, you may think that what your friend is doing is okay because you're getting something in return, but later, when you get older, you will feel used and angry. It is that anger you have to watch. It may turn you into an exact duplicate of your friend. And incidentally, Mark, your friend is *no* friend, believe me. If he were, he would feed you for nothing."

"No one is perfect, Owen. Not even you. We do what we gotta do to survive. I'm sure you've done that a time or two in your life. Everyone has. Come on, let's get down to the field."

He left my side and sprinted for the bleachers.

He was right: we all do what we have to do to survive. When Mr. Wilson was raping me, I didn't fight back; if I had, he would have done far worse things to me. I did what I did to survive.

When I first met Mark, I thought him just a simple kid. As it turned out, he was far from simple—he was frighteningly intelligent.

Both Mark and I were the last to arrive on the field. When the coach saw us, his face worked. "This isn't a social club, boys! When I say *down on the field*, I don't mean down on the field when you're damn good and ready—I mean *now*! You pour on the coal and you get your asses down here! Where were you anyway—jacking each other off?"

Some of the boys laughed.

I glanced at Mark. He looked at me with resignation on his face: *People are going to think what they're going to think.*

Casually, I walked over to the coach.

"Let's get one thing straight," I said to him. "We are not your property. You are not—"

"Back off!" he commanded.

"Get this through your head, *Mr. Zigich—you* are a teacher; *we* are your students. *You* are not our master, and *we* are not your subjects. You will not talk to us in any manner that you please. Do you understand that? *Can* you understand that! Maybe you and those anthropophagous groundlings over there think that what you said was witty, but it wasn't. It was disgusting and inflammatory. You ever say anything like that to me again—*or to anyone*—and you'll be out of a job. I don't think the school board will look too favorably on a teacher—or, in your case, a brainless functionary who is trying to pass himself off as a teacher—who pairs a lack of punctuality with homosexuality, and who uses homosexual innuendo as punishment. Just do your job, *Mr. Zigich*, and keep your reprobative thoughts to yourself!"

I left him and took my place next to Christopher and Mark.

The coach's face was tight with anger. He knew he was out of line, but to be exposed, reprimanded, and threatened in front of his class by a teenager who was supposed to tremble at the mere sight of him made him furious.

"I need two captains!" he rasped.

Two muscular boys stepped forward.

"Pick your players!" the coach shouted again.

"Wrong!" I said loudly.

"Hey, why don't you and your two pansy-assed friends go off somewhere and blow each other!" one of the captains squawked.

"I have a better idea," I rejoined, walking over to the boy. "Why don't you hit me? It's what you want to do, isn't it?"

Taken aback, the tall, towheaded dromedary stared at me.

"Go ahead," I teased. "But…before you do, keep in mind that you will be suspended, maybe expelled. I wonder how your parents will feel about that. What will they think of their son hitting a boy who didn't hit first?"

"They'll think you had it coming."

"Well, then, do it. Go for it."

"You'll be expelled too."

"I don't care. I will just go to another school. I can excel anywhere. You, on the other hand, will merely subsist. Where I have brains, you have cardboard."

His face reddened with rage.

I kept my eyes fixed on him.

"All right, that's enough!" the coach broke in. "What's your name, kid?"

Though our eyes were not connected, I knew the coach was talking to me.

"Owen," I answered.

"Step away, Owen," the coach ordered.

I returned to Christopher and Mark. Both were staring at me.

"Steve, pick your team," the coach ordered.

"*Wrong!*" I dissented again.

Many of the boys in the class sighed and folded their arms across their chests.

The coach approached me. "Owen, you told me to get something through my head, now I'm going to tell you the same thing: I'm the teacher of this class, not you. I believe those were your words—right?"

"Unfortunately, yes, you are the teacher."

"And as the teacher, I say how the game is played and what the rules are."

"Not if those rules are unfair. You will let those two junkyard alpha dogs over there choose who they want and who they don't want."

"So?"

"So they will leave the ones they *don't* want standing alone—feeling unessential, unimportant, and unwanted."

"I got a newsflash for you, kid—*that's life.* That's the real world. When you go out looking for a job, the company you apply at will pick the best man they can find—and *only* the best."

"Sometimes who you think will be the best turns out to be the worst, and the worst sometimes turns out to be the best."

"Life's a crapshoot, kid—you never know."

"Then make the captains choose the worst of the class—since you *never know.*"

"I'll go one better: I'll let *you* choose. For both teams."

Many of the boys released groans of disapproval.

"If your choices are good ones," he outlined, "you'll take the praise. If your choices are bad, you'll take the consequences."

"Which are?"

"You'll be very *unpopular.* That's an unfriendly place to be when you're fourteen."

"Your attempt at intimidation is, at best, impotent, and at worst, laughable. It falls on deaf ears. I have *never* been popular. I am well-accustomed to it."

Turning from him, I faced the class and chose the teams: last names A through M was one team, last names N through Z was the other.

To everyone's surprise (except mine), both teams scored equally. Even Christopher and Mark, whom I knew were both terrified, hit the ball and made it back to home plate successfully.

As we all were heading back to the gymnasium, the coach stopped me. "I don't particularly care for you, kid, but—"

"Right back at you."

"*But*—good job today," he said with a nod and continued to the gym.

Once back at the locker room, the boys began to undress immediately and uninhibitedly. In minutes, I was surrounded by boys clad only in white briefs or jock straps or nothing at all. Those who were nude went straight for the showers.

Seeing the boys enter the shower room filled me with dread. It was now my turn to undress and enter it.

Or perhaps not.

The coach wasn't there watching us to make sure we all showered. I could slip out of the locker room and no one would be the wiser. But then, more than likely, I would carry the smell of the class on my body for the rest of the day, and I certainly was not going to permit that.

I felt weak and cowardly for my anxiety and timidity about undressing and showering. Still, the shy boy with the scars and the little boy with the memories were pleading with me to leave.

"No!" I resolved through gritted teeth.

Four boys were near me and they pivoted their heads in my direction.

"*What!*" I snapped at them.

Their eyes moved from my face to my chest. They were fixed intently at the horizontal and diagonal scars on my chest. Apparently, their parents had not taught them not to stare.

Pushing the four ill-mannered boys out of my mind, I hurriedly flipped off my shoes, pulled off my shirt and socks, yanked down my shorts and underwear and headed into the showers. Purposely and deliberately, I scanned the steam-filled room. There was no Mr. Wilson and no Ms. Windom—only well-formed and under-formed teenage boys. I got under one of the shower heads and reached for the handle. I saw that my hand was trembling. I hoped no one saw. The last thing I wanted anyone to see on me was fear.

"Mind if we join you?" a boy said to me.

I flinched.

"What's wrong?" the boy asked.

I turned. Standing next to me was Mark and Christopher.

Staring at my back and chest, Mark asked, "What happened to *you*?"

"I'd rather not talk about it if you don't mind," I said as evenly as I could. I know Mark wasn't prying—he simply was concerned.

"I-I-I hope the c-c-c-coach lets you b-b-be c-c-captain every gym day!" Christopher said, changing the subject.

"You don't look so good," Mark pointed out to me.

"I'm fine. My stomach's just a little upset."

Like a firecracker, a boy whose vocal cords were still in the throes of pubescent maturation burst out laughing.

Again, I flinched. I thought I had outgrown blenching at sudden noises. Obviously not.

Everyone turned in the direction of the shrill report.

All eyes were now nailed to a boy standing next to a shower pole. He was an average boy: blond hair, thin build, nice face, and, at that moment, a garnet face. His hands were desperately trying to cover up his private place. He had an erection.

Nearly everyone was laughing.

"Hey, Lyle, who do you want to do?" some boy quipped.

"Who's your hard-on for, Lyle—all of us...or for *someone special*?" another boy piped.

Fleering, three boys turned around and angled their backsides to the boy.

The only ones in the room not enjoying the spectacle were Mark, Christopher, and me.

I sighed in disgust: not for the boy but for the reaction to the boy's plight. Why was everyone so obsessed with making fun of human sexual responses, human reproduction, and human genitalia? Instead of marveling at the intricate function and design of sex, it seemed all people wanted to do was mock it. If any of these boys had any idea of the complexity of the male erection—the chemical, neurological, vascular, and psychological makeup of penile tumescence—they would not be jesting...they would be in awe.

"Hey, Lyle, here's some soap—lather up and finish the job," a boy sallied, throwing Lyle a bar of soap.

Lyle did not reach out for the soap, but stood frozen where he was, dripping with both water and humiliation.

"Give it a rest!" I shouted.

All laughter stopped, and everyone turned to me. Soon their eyes left mine and rested on my chest. The steam had obviously not clouded the scars as I had hoped. But I didn't care. All I cared about at that moment was getting Lyle out of the room.

I walked over to Lyle, grabbed his arm and pushed him toward the exit. He nearly stumbled.

I turned back around. "Not that any of you unpolished pigs care," I said, "but just for your edification, getting sexually aroused in a public shower is not an indicator or identifier of homosexuality. There are myriad triggers for an erection, or in your vulgar parlance, a *hard-on*. For your further edification, it has been estimated—*conservatively*—that ten percent of the US population is homosexual, which means, statistically, *right now*, in this *very room*, there are at least four gay boys. Chew on that for a while, *boys*."

I left the room.

It was one o'clock in the afternoon. I was sitting by myself in the cafeteria, drinking a Pepsi, thinking about what had happened in gym class. I felt bad for Lyle. What had happened to him would shadow him for the rest of the year...if not the rest of his life.

I saw Roxanne enter the cafeteria. She appeared to be looking for someone. I hoped that someone was me. The only person in the world I enjoyed seeing was her.

She spotted the person she was looking for and ran to him. Without greetings, she took his face in her hands and kissed him deeply.

Her breath was flavored with peppermint, and her neck was scented with Charlie perfume.

Her erotic kiss, her pheromonic perfume, her aromatic breath made me feel dizzy and lightheaded.

Kids at a nearby table whistled and hollered in approval at our passionate exchange.

After her lips left me, she exclaimed, "I love you! I want the whole world to know it!"

Trying to hide my embarrassment, I shifted the subject. "You're in a very good mood."

"That's because of you."

So much for shifting the subject.

"I heard what you did this morning," she expounded. "You were a hero—*twice!*"

"Hardly a hero. I simply wanted to get a couple of points across."

"You're too modest. If you hadn't been in Lyle's class, who knows what would have happened to him. They might have beat him up or something."

"Yes, it could have developed into something very ugly."

"What's wrong? You should be happy—he didn't get hurt. Not only that, you put all those dumb jocks right in their place."

She was such a unique girl, so unlike all the others.

I touched her face. "I am such a hypocrite."

"Why do you say that?"

Apprehensively, I answered, "I want to..."

"What?"

"I want to...be with you."

"You are with me. We're together right now."

"Not that kind of together. I want to...I want to be inside you."

I felt my face redden. It was the first time I said it out loud to her.

Her face stopped all motion.

I couldn't tell if she were offended or pleased.

She locked her eyes into mine. "I want you there too," she whispered.

"I truly am a hypocrite," I iterated. "I criticize everyone for obsessing about sex, and yet I want to have it so badly with you. But I won't let it happen. We're too young. I wouldn't use you like that. I've been on the dark end of sex, Roxanne. People can make it so ugly. It's not supposed to be, you know. It's there to help us. It's supposed to be a place where two people can go where they don't feel alone or threatened or misused. Just once in my life, I don't want to feel alone."

Roxanne took hold of my hands. "Owen, as long as I am alive, you will never be alone."

"Hey, Roxanne!" some girl shrieked from across the room.

Roxanne sighed with dismay and turned to see who was calling her.

Traveling in our direction was a group of six other freshmen. In the troop were four girls and two boys. What their names were, I had no idea. Nor did I care.

Without asking permission, the six sat down at our table.

*Please, join us.*

"Owen, I never see you eat," one of the girls observed. "All you ever have at lunch is a bottle of Pepsi. How come?"

*What are you, the Pepsi police!* I wanted to bark but didn't.

"I'm not really into food," I said instead.

"Well, if you're ever hungry, I'll be happy to share my lunches with you. I always bring mine from home. My dad makes it for me every morning. He's a chef for a country club."

I looked over at Roxanne.

She raised her eyebrows.

"Hey, Roxanne, did you hear what happened to Lyle this morning?" one of the boys asked her, grinning. "He popped a rod in the showers. Everyone's talking about it," the boy informed her with unabashed guffaws. Three of the girls also found it richly humorous. Curiously, the girl who offered me her lunch did not.

"Enough already!" I snapped hotly.

*"Enough of what?"* the boy came back defensively.

"There are *girls* at the table, in case you hadn't noticed! If you are not going to respect what happened to Lyle, then at least respect *them*! They don't need your gossip, and they *certainly* don't need it laced with your vulgar metaphors!"

One of the girls contorted her face. "We don't care! Boys get hard-ons—what's the big deal?"

I inhaled deeply and slipped my hands under the table and grabbed my legs so I wouldn't grab the girl's neck.

"Besides, we think it's funny," the girl added.

I stared at her. "Do you now?" I asked, bringing my hands up and steepling them under my chin. I had heard enough. It was time to take them down.

Roxanne twisted in her seat.

"Yeah, we do," the girl returned. "Lyle's a queer. He couldn't keep it down and now everyone knows. I guess that means he won't be coming to any of the dances." She laughed heartily.

"Oooh, I'll bet your parents are proud to have you as their daughter," I said.

Roxanne let loose a giggle.

"They sure are," the girl defended herself tartly.

"You get your homophobia from them, or did you get it all on your own?"

"Huh?"

"I take it you hate homosexuals."

"You got it."

The quickness of her answer shocked me.

"So you now hate Lyle because you think he's gay," I said.

"I don't *think* he's gay—he *is* gay. He boned up in the showers."

"And that means he's homosexual?"

"*Duh!*"

I wanted to reach up and rip her tongue out. "So let me understand this," I delved. "If a boy remains pendulous while in the company of other boys, he's straight. But if he becomes tumescent, he's not. Is that your calculation?"

"What?"

"If he gets hard, he's gay; if he doesn't, he's not. Correct?"

"Yep, pretty much."

"One could logically extrapolate from your answer that you have an extensive knowledge of boys: what excites them and what doesn't… yes?"

"I know if a guy gets turned on around other guys, he's a fem. If he doesn't, he's normal."

"I see. And tell me, what turns most *normal* boys on?"

"T and A. Getting some trim. Or the hope of getting it anyway." She laughed.

"Anything else?"

"Frenching…petting—"

"You do indeed know a lot about boys, don't you?"

"I know a few things."

Nodding, I said, "So do most whores."

I heard Roxanne gasp.

The girl went rigid and red.

"Oh, my, look at that—you're hurt," I mocked, slightly canting my head. "*Poor baby*. Imagine the hurt that Lyle is feeling at this very moment. How does it feel when someone calls you a name that isn't true? Stings, doesn't it?

"Quick lesson—*whatever your name is*—in male sexual physiology. Girls and boys are not wired the same sexually. Girls, by and large, must be excited emotionally before they can become excited sexually. Boys, on the other hand, can become excited at nearly *anything*, without any emotional link. Simple physical sensations, like wearing new underwear, or riding a bike, or *taking a shower*, can create an erection. Clinically, this is called spontaneous sexual arousal. Hormonal spikes cause instantaneous sexual animation. In short, boys—*all* boys—can and do get aroused without *any* sexual attraction *whatsoever*. This entire school has made—and *still is* making—a normal function into something *ab*normal. Well done."

The girl had not softened. Anger was still embedded in her flawless face.

"Screw you!" she whiplashed and abruptly got up to leave.

"Incidentally, whoever you are," I said to the girl, "your use of '*boned up*,' while accurate visually, is wrong semantically. To '*bone up*' is to refresh one's memory; to learn quickly, as in, '*I boned up for the exam*.' As you can see, as anyone with half a brain can see, it *doesn't* mean to get sexually excited. But don't feel too bad—you get an A for imagery." I winked at her.

Her lips tightened, and she flipped me two short-nailed birds. Then she stormed away.

Slowly, the other five arose to follow her.

"Before you scatter like the rats you are," I said, "might I make a suggestion? In the future, when you feel the urge to smear someone with one of your choice delineations, you might want to research those delineations before you vomit them out. Just so you know—so you won't look like fools again, like your middle-finger friend who just stomped off like a spoiled, I-can't-take-the-truth *enfant terrible*—the expression '*popped a rod*,' at least in the context of today, is a misnomer, another semantic blunder. It is mechanical nomenclature used to describe the popping sound made by a tie rod in an automobile that has lost its integrity; hence the term, '*popped a rod*.'" I smiled at them. "Now you can scatter."

Except for the girl who offered me her lunch, the others glared at me. Then they all walked away.

"You don't let anyone get away with anything, do you?" Roxanne said.

"Not anymore."

Roxanne slipped her hand into mine. "I'm so lucky to have you."

Unexpectedly, the girl who offered me her lunch returned. "For what it's worth, Owen, I think you're amazing!" she said with a smile, turned and went after her friends.

"Well...it looks like someone has a crush on you," Roxanne commented.

"The only one I want liking me is *you*."

She smiled. "Listen, what are you doing this Sunday night?"

"Studying, probably. Why?"

"Would you like to come over to my house for dinner? I know you're not into eating, but I want you to meet my dad, and my dad wants to meet you."

"Your father knows about me?"

"*Oh, yeah.* You're all I talk about."

I felt my face tingle.

"You know, you're adorable when you blush."

Still embarrassed, I replied, "I would love to come. Any chance to be with you. Can I bring anything?"

"Just your gorgeous self. My dad's a terrific cook. Is around four okay?"

"I will be there promptly at four chimes."

Roxanne glanced at the clock on the wall. "I got to get to class. You'll never guess what it is?"

"What?"

"Health—sex education."

I was at a complete loss for words, so I simply replied, "Enjoy."

She smiled mysteriously and started to say something, but immediately stopped herself. Instead, she gave me a tender kiss good-bye.

I lived only a mile from school. As I did in elementary school and junior high, I walked to high school and walked home afterward. I could have made Ms. Windom take me, but I simply could not stand any proximity to her.

There was a small park two blocks from school. Like all parks, it had swings, monkey bars, and a sand square for young children. When I was very young, Mr. and Mrs. Crowley would take me there. In spite of the unpleasant history I had had with Mrs. Crowley, I found the park a wonderful memory. Occasionally, I would stop and sit on the very swing I sat on as a child.

After school that Tuesday, a small, quiet voice told me to visit the park before I went home.

The park was deserted...except for one lone figure. A boy. A blond boy, about my age. He was sitting on one of the swings with his head bowed to his chest. Suddenly, his head raised and now he was looking up at the early September sky.

My heart dropped.

It was Lyle.

I had no idea he lived in the area.

He put his hand over his face and started to cry.

My heart split in two.

I suspected he probably wanted to be left alone, but I couldn't just continue on home.

He didn't look away or order me away when he saw me.

I sat down on the swing next to his.

"Thanks for today," he said.

"I'm sorry it happened. But things like that *do* happen, and sometimes they happen in the worst possible places. One of the misfortunes of being a boy. But you are not the first it has happened to, and you will definitely not be the last."

"I'm not gay," he declared. "It just…happened. I'm going to ask my mom if I can go to another school. I can't go back there."

"I don't blame you. But…if you run now, from this, you will more than likely run later, from something else. Were I you, I would not run. It has a way of catching up with you. In the end, you feel far worse about fleeing than about what made you flee. You only borrow trouble when you choose the path of least resistance. High school is temporary, Lyle. It lasts only four years, but the rest of your life lasts decades. Someday, you might have children, and one them might be a boy. And if he has the same thing happen to him that happened to you today, what are you going to advise him to do? Run away? If it's not an erection in gym class, it'll be something else. In the next few days, you will have many jokes thrown at you. *Don't* react. Weather the storm; it *will* die down. New dramas, new traumas will arise, and the misfortune you experienced today will soon fade into a hazy memory. However, if you leave, it will *not* fade. Just the reverse. You'll be remembered as the queer boy who tucked his tail and ran. People will say that you must have been gay, for why else would you have left?"

"I'm not strong like you, Owen. I won't make it."

"Do this, okay? Try staying for one week. Just one week. Mark my words, by next Tuesday, the mountain you are trapped on right now will be a very small hill. I guarantee it."

"And if it isn't?"

"It will be. Trust me. Just *don't* run and *don't* react."

"How did you get to be so strong?"

"I got tired of being afraid."

"I'm so scared right now I'm sick to my stomach."

"I know you are. You have gym again this week, right?"

"Friday."

"Go to it. Shower like you're supposed to. Show them strength. Don't back down and don't show fear. *Don't* react. If you feed them a response, they will keep coming back, like wolves. If you don't, they will leave you alone. Just remember, Lyle, life is a trade-off: when you let go of something bad, something good will always take its place."

He got up from the swing. "I gotta get home. My mom will be worried. Thanks for stopping and talking with me. No one else would have."

"Think hard on my words."

Instantly, I realized my infelicity. "Sorry…accidental pun," I said remorsefully.

He smiled sadly and walked out of the park.

I took a cab to Roxanne's home. She lived many miles north of our school. Her home was a dusty-rose, clapboard rambler with a small front lawn. Knee-high rosebushes lined the perimeter of the lawn. Hanging above the mailbox next to the front door was a wooden plaque that read *Solleveld Estate*.

Nervously, I rang the doorbell.

Almost immediately, the door opened.

What greeted me abducted my breath.

Roxanne was clothed in a soft-pink, chiffon dress. The top edges of the dress cascaded over her shoulders and dovetailed together just below her neck. It reminded me of the fluid curvature of a wine glass. Below her waist, the dress flared out slightly in willowy, shallow pleats. Her legs were veiled in fawn-hued nylons. Lustrous, pastel-pink slingbacks cradled her feet. Encircling her right wrist was a simple silver bracelet.

Her hair was naturally lovely, but this day it was especially so. She had curled it ever so slightly for the occasion. Her lips were painted with a faint, clear gloss that made them sparkle, like the twinkle of morning dew. Glinting through her silken hair were petite diamond earrings.

In all the universe, there was no creation like her!

I was definitely a hypocrite. At that moment, all I wanted to do was take Roxanne into her bedroom and….

"*You are stunning!*" I said.

"So are *you*! *Wow!* You are *so* handsome! You really know how to fill out a suit!"

From behind me, I brought out some flowers: a single red rose chaperoned by blooms of baby's breath.

She smiled and shook her head, "What did I ever do to deserve you?"

"Roxanne, is that Owen?" a man asked from inside the house.

"Yes, Dad."

"Well, don't you think you should invite him in?"

Her etiquettical misstep pinked her face. "Oh, I'm so sorry," she said. "Where are my manners? Please, come in."

First to come into view was Mr. Solleveld. He was a spiring man, thick-haired and imposingly built. I found myself instantly ill at ease. If the man only knew the longing I had for his daughter, he probably would have—and could have—snapped me in two with one hand. But then, maybe he did know and understand, for he had been a teenage boy himself once. Young people forget that older people were young at one time. I needed to stop thinking that what I was feeling for Roxanne was wrong. What would be wrong would be to act on my feelings and cross the line and take from her what did not belong to me…like what Mr. Wilson and Ms. Windom had taken. It wasn't sexual desire that was wrong—it was what one did with it.

Mr. Solleveld extended his hand. "Hello, Owen, it's nice to meet you."

"Thank you, sir. It is agreeable to meet you as well."

He smiled. "Roxanne was right, you *are* a handsome devil."

"Thank you, sir. But…whatever attractiveness I may possess pales and disappears in the glory of your daughter."

He paused and smiled. "You're a poet."

"Only when inspired, sir. Were the moon able to speak, your daughter would cause it to flood forth sonnets of praise for all eternity. She is that lovely...both in countenance and spirit."

There was silence.

Roxanne's eyes sparkled.

"She is...life to me," I uttered.

Again, there was silence.

"Forgive me, Mr. Solleveld," I broke the quietness, "I often speak more than people want to hear."

Mr. Solleveld regarded me soberly. "Owen, before we go any further with this evening, I need you to be completely honest with me."

"Yes, sir."

"How old *are* you—*truthfully*?" Suspicion was thick in his voice.

"Dad!" Roxanne cried.

"Fourteen, sir."

"I've lived a few years, and I've been around the block a few times, and I have *never, ever* met a fourteen-year-old who talks like you...or even dresses like you."

"Dad, what are you doing!"

"I'm asking a legitimate question."

"Lying is not in my nature, sir," I came back calmly. "But if it is honesty you want, then honesty you shall have. I have seen things you could not even imagine. I know things you will never know. Each of us is the totality of our experiences. Who I am, how I dress, how I speak, what I feel, what I desire is *my* totality. If you distrust me, I'll be on my way. But in my own defense, I must convey to you that there is no one you can trust more. I would never let any harm come to your daughter. *Ever.* I say this without magnification of expression or amplification of emotion...I love her. My heart left me the moment I saw her. I have known some terrible people in my life, Mr. Solleveld, and I have known good. But they are rare. Roxanne is rare. *Surpassingly* rare. All I want is to be near her."

Mr. Solleveld held out his hand. "I apologize. I spoke without thinking. I misjudged you, and I'm sorry."

"Consider it forgotten."

"Would you like something to drink?" he asked warmly.

"I would, thank you. Might I ask if you have any Pepsi?"

"We do. Please, sit down and make yourself comfortable. I'll be right back."

Eyes shimmering, Roxanne shook her head. "You amaze me every time I'm with you." She leaned in and kissed me passionately.

Mr. Solleveld cleared his throat.

Roxanne pulled away from me.

"Pardon me," Mr. Solleveld said, standing under the archway that led into the kitchen. "Roxanne, honey, I forgot to ask you if you wanted something to drink."

"Yes, please. A Pepsi too. Thanks, Dad."

"Two Pepsis coming up," Mr. Solleveld said and left us.

Roxanne stepped close to me again and gently took my hand. She spoke no words; she simply held my hand in hers and gazed at them.

Quiet encircled us for many moments.

"Here you go," Mr. Solleveld said, severing my silent union with Roxanne. He handed a glass tumbler to Roxanne and one to me.

"Thank you, sir," I said, sitting down on the couch.

"Thank you, Dad."

Mr. Solleveld sat down in a black-leather, wingback chair, and Roxanne sat next to me.

I saw something odd on the floor of the kitchen. A small shadow. Both Roxanne and her father saw my notice of it and turned their eyes to the floor as well. A tiny, furry face peeked around the corner. It was a little dog, a black-and-white Boston Terrier.

"Oh, that's Kenny," Mr. Solleveld informed me. "We found him a few years ago. He was abandoned by his owners. They left him tied up in their basement after they moved out. He's very shy, very skittish. He doesn't go to anybody new, so don't be offended. Most times he doesn't even come to us."

I set my glass down on a ceramic coaster on the coffee table, arose slowly from the couch and gently lowered myself onto my knees. I flattened my hands together, as though I were praying.

"Hi there, little one," I crooned to him. "What's your name?" I tapped my hands together. "You're a cutie, aren't you? You're just as cute as can be. Come here, little one." I gave my voice the placid and melodic pitch of a child. I feared a deep voice might scare and intimidate him.

The little dog ran to me.

Both Roxanne and her father gasped.

The little dog started to whine with pleasure as I lightly scratched his ears and neck and sides.

"You are just so cute," I fawned. "Yes, you are."

He let loose more squeals of pleasure.

Speaking very softly, I said, "Can I pick you up? Hmm? Can I? Do you want some kisses on your tummy?"

He stood up on his back legs.

Very gently I lifted him. Returning to the couch, I sat back down with the little dog snuggling against my stomach. I then rested him in the V of my legs. He eased himself over so his paws were facing me.

"You want some kisses now? You want some kisses?"

Very slowly, so as not to make him feel frightened or threatened, I lowered my lips to his chest and tummy. Then I touched my lips to the side of his face. His tongue tried to lick my cheek. I stroked his little lips with the tip of my finger, and he licked it. I then stroked his eyes, and they closed dreamily.

I was a little boy again. I was holding my Yogidog. I was making him feel secure and loved. He was alive again, happy and warm and unharmed.

I began to hum to him softly.

He curled into a peaceful ball.

Tears dripped from my eyes. I saw my Yogidog lying on our kitchen floor, so sweet, and so lifeless. He had trusted me...and I let him die.

I bent over, gently rested my face on his body and gave his soft chest a long kiss.

I suddenly remembered where I was.

I quickly raised my head and looked shyly over at Roxanne and her father.

Roxanne's hands were pressed against her mouth. She was crying.

"I'm sorry," I said. "I must look very foolish."

Not moving, Mr. Solleveld said, "Hardly, son. I've never seen anything like that in my life. Roxanne was right—you are an amazing boy."

A door opened and closed somewhere in the kitchen. Within seconds, a small boy appeared under the archway.

Mr. Solleveld raised himself from his chair, went over to the child and picked him up. The boy looked to be about five or six; it was clear he was Roxanne's little brother. He looked in astonishment at what was lying on my lap.

"How'd he do that?" the youngster inquired, astounded.

"Walter, this is Owen," Mr. Solleveld said to his son. "He's Roxanne's boyfriend."

"Why is Roxanne's eyes all wet?" the child asked.

"She's just happy."

"I want to hold Kenny." The youth squirmed out of his father's arms.

Without hesitation, the boy walked over to me.

I saw a look of awe materialize on Mr. Solleveld's face. It struck me as very odd. What did he find so incredible?

"Can I hold him?" the boy asked eagerly.

I tenderly scooped up the dog and laid him in the boy's outstretched hands.

"He never lets me hold him," the boy revealed. "He never lets anybody hold him. He always runs away."

"Well, I tell you," I said. "Sometimes, Walter, animals are like people—if something is too big, we get afraid. So when you want to play with Kenny or hold him, get down on the ground very slowly and show him that you're not bigger than he is. And don't move fast. Move really slowly. Show him he can trust you. Animals are like you and me—we have to trust someone before we let them get close to us."

"That's a pretty tie," he commented, looking at the front of my shirt.

"Thank you."

"What are those things in it?"

"The one on top is called a collar pin or tie bar, and the one in the middle is called a tie tack. It holds the tie in place so it won't fly around. If I didn't have it, it might do this…" I unpinned the tie tack, slowly raised the end of the tie and gently touched the end of his nose with it.

The boy giggled.

"Can I hold it?" he asked.

"Certainly."

I removed Kenny from the boy's hands and placed him back on my lap. I then gave the jewelry to the boy.

"That's a pretty rock in it."

"That's called a ruby. It's the birthstone for the month of July. That's when I was born."

"I was born in December. That's when Santa Claus comes. Know what he brought me last year?"

"What?"

"I got a stuffed doggy. I named him Hungarian."

"I got a stuffed doggy too when I was about your age. I named him Yogidog."

The boy laughed. "That's a funny name for a doggy."

"I know. I named him after a real doggy I had."

"Is he still around?"

"No, I'm afraid not."

"What happened to him?"

"He died."

"Oh. Want to see my room?" he changed the subject.

I looked at Roxanne for approval. Her hands were still shielding her mouth, as though she were trying to keep herself from crying even more. Why? What was wrong?

I looked at Mr. Solleveld. His eyes were glistening, as though he had also been crying. Very peculiar.

Behind him stood a woman; a tall, middle-aged woman with black-from-a-bottle hair. Presumably, this was Mrs. Solleveld, although Roxanne and Walter had none of her features. She, too, appeared dumbstruck.

"Have I done something wrong?" I asked.

"Oh, sweetie, not at all," Roxanne soothed and put her hand on my arm.

If I hadn't done or said something amiss, why were she and Mr. Solleveld so emotional?

The boy took my hand. "Come on. Let's go to my room."

Returning my attention to Mr. Solleveld, I asked, "May I?" I felt it was proper to get his permission.

Still overcome, he managed, "Of course."

I set Kenny in Roxanne's lap and let the boy guide me to his room.

Roxanne's home was a modest dwelling, plentiful with knickknacks on the tabletops and photographs on the walls. It was also a fragrant home, ample with the scent of fresh flowers.

Walter's room was not what I expected it to be. I assumed it would be populated with children's books, coloring books, crayons, hanging airplanes, toy soldiers, plastic cars, and stuffed animals. Instead, it was a menagerie of plants and photographs. The photographs were of a woman and a little boy; some of the pictures were just of the boy, and some were just of the woman. The boy was older than Walter but similar in appearance. His brother, no doubt. The woman was easily Roxanne, only older. Her mother. So who was the woman I saw standing behind Mr. Solleveld? And where was Mrs. Solleveld?

"You like my room?" Walter asked me. "I picked out all the plants all by myself."

"They're very pretty. You know, you have to have a very kind heart to make plants grow like this."

"You want to sit on my bed?"

I accepted his invitation.

Glancing around the room, I thought: *Something is definitely wrong here. Something bad has happened. The boy is fixating; he is escaping.*

"Walter, is that your older brother in these pictures?"

He nodded.

"And is that your mommy?"

He nodded.

"Where are they?"

He didn't answer right away. "They died."

"I'm sorry. I don't have a mommy either. I had a big sister like you had a big brother. She died too."

"Did you cry?"

"Yes, I did. Sometimes I still do."

"I miss my mommy every day."

"Did your mommy like plants?"

"She grew all kinds of green plants. She grew us vegables and pretty flowers and stuff that stayed in pots in the house. Did your mommy like plants?"

"No, I'm afraid she didn't."

"Was she a good mommy?"

"No, she wasn't."

"Do you get lonely for a mommy?"

"Yes, I do. I get lonely a lot."

"I get lonely too." He started to cry.

"Come here." I held out my arms.

He willingly entered them.

I lifted him on my lap and stroked his hair.

He laid his head on my shoulder and wept.

Then I heard someone else crying.

I turned to the doorway. Roxanne and her father were standing there. Roxanne's head was resting against her father's shoulder and she was crying, this time not withholding her emotions.

Soon the boy stopped crying and looked at me. Then he put his arms around me. He got down and rushed over to the door. "I'll be right back. Don't go nowhere." Then he dashed off.

Mr. Solleveld smiled at me. "Thank you," he said quietly and walked away.

Roxanne wiped her eyes and came over to me. She sat down next to me.

"He hardly talks to anyone," she bared, "except to my dad every now and then. He won't even talk to his counselor. Most of the time he just stays in this room. I've tried to get close to him, but he won't let me. And then you walk in and..." She stared at me. "How do you know so much?"

"I don't. Sometimes I just think with my heart rather than my head. You're not supposed to, but I do."

"I don't deserve you, Owen. I ask myself, why does he love me?"

"You're what I've never known and what I've always wanted. All my life, I've known people who are ugly and mean. You aren't. I feel safe when we're together. I feel at peace. If you only—"

"I'm sorry, you two," Mr. Solleveld cut in, "but dinner is ready."

"We'll be right there, Dad," Roxanne replied.

Mr. Solleveld left us alone.

"I love you so much, Owen," she said, her voice breaking.

Just then, Walter raced back into the room. "These are for you." He handed me some snipped black-eyed Susans. "My mommy grew these."

I leaned forward and kissed him on the forehead. "Thank you, Walter, they're beautiful."

"Will you sit next to me at the table?"

"Of course I will."

He took me by the hand, pulled me from his bed, and we were off.

Roxanne was right—her father was an excellent cook. We had peppered roast pork, steamed carrots, quartered and roasted potatoes, sautéed apples, and made-from-the- cupboard rolls. For dessert, he made *crème brûlée*, even though Roxanne was not a fan of sweets.

The woman who came in the house earlier with Walter had joined us for the meal. She was a neighbor who watched Walter during the day. Her name was Shiloh Stansbury. She was a pleasant woman but dominated the evening. We all heard about her and her husband's trips to India and Greece and Germany and Alaska and Russia. I was certain this non-pictorial travelogue was for my benefit and not for Roxanne and her family. Given Mrs. Stansbury's blind prolixity, they must have heard it all before. There are two types of people in the world, I discovered: listeners and talkers. Mrs. Stansbury was a talker. Listeners learn from talkers, but talkers rarely learn from listeners. Mr. Stansbury, I was sure, knew everything about his wife. I wondered if she knew anything about him.

After dinner, without protest, Walter let Mrs. Stansbury take him for his bath. Before he went away, he hugged me tightly and kissed my cheek.

I arose from the table to clear the dishes.

"No, no, you leave those there," Mr. Solleveld directed. "Company doesn't do dishes in this house."

Respectfully, I set the china back on the table.

"Owen, I must tell you, you are the most polished, well-mannered, well-spoken young man I have ever met," Mr. Solleveld complimented. "You have many amazing gifts. I hope you can see that. I'm glad you and my daughter are together. She couldn't find a finer boy than you."

I felt my face flush. "I thank you...but it is your daughter who is amazing. And I don't think she sees it. She is the sweetest, purest, most compassionate girl our high school has under its wings. A finer daughter, a kinder soul, a prettier girl you will not find."

"Her mother would have adored you," he said.

"If it is not stepping on sacred soil, might I ask how your wife and son passed away?"

Father and daughter glanced at one another. A heavy, silent communication crossed between them.

"Forgive me," I said. "I didn't mean to unearth painful memories."

Mr. Solleveld nodded to his daughter.

"My mother was murdered," Roxanne said with extreme control.

Those four words, and the immediate way they were spoken, hit me like a car.

"I'm very sorry," I offered. "I shouldn't have asked. I should have respected your privacy. Please forgive me."

Unprompted, Roxanne went on. "She was killed by a man down the street. That was a little more than two years ago. He had been, um...molesting my little brother. Not Walter, my other brother. The man's name was Milton. That was his first name. He was maybe in his fifties, I think. We all thought he was a good man. He always took good care of his house and yard and always decorated around Christmas. Lights all around his house, a Santa in the yard, reindeer. He used to give all the neighborhood kids candy and comic books and toys. When the Girl Scouts sold cookies door to door, he always bought. Then my brother, his name was Douglas—we all called him Dougie—started to withdraw. He was nine years old. He wouldn't go outside. He...um... wouldn't go to the bathroom. He would go in his underwear. He didn't want to tell anyone what was wrong, but somehow my mom was able to find out what was happening. She didn't call the police. She went straight to Milton's house and confronted him herself. He shot her, right there on his front porch. He went back inside, went into his bathroom and then shot himself. My mom died without mercy, and he died without punishment."

I remember reading about the event in the newspaper. I remember thinking that child predators are everywhere, in *every* generation. I felt so bad for the family. Who would have imagined I would be having dinner with them two years later?

"After that," she continued, "Douglas completely shut down. He blamed himself for my mom's death. He said that if only he had kept what was happening to himself, she wouldn't have been killed. That's what he wrote in his journal. He put a knife in his throat and...died."

Mr. Solleveld took hold of Roxanne's hand.

A pall of quietness fell over the table.

"When my mother was a young woman, she was raped," I shared. "From that rape came your guest. Neither my father nor my mother wanted me. Who wants a rape child? My sister drowned trying to save me one spring afternoon, and after that, my parents took out their pain on me. There was no one to stop them. I should have died from what they did, but I didn't. Children can be remarkably resilient. I should have killed myself, like Douglas did, but I didn't. There was no point in me going on living. There wasn't a soul who would have cared if I had died.

"A few months after my sister's death, my father shot himself in front of me. I saw his life pour out of his head onto our living room couch. Before he took his own life, he took my dog's life. He broke his neck right in front of me. My mother couldn't take the loss of her daughter and husband both, so soon after that, she hung herself.

"I was put into a children's home, and then into a foster home. The husband in the foster home preferred little boys to his wife. He raped me...many times. They kept me in their basement. They let me out only to go to school and use the bathroom. While the man was ripping and tearing me, I'd fly away. I'd go into the pages of one of my books and disappear. After he'd leave me, I'd clean off the blood and force out the semen.

"About a year later, I went into a second foster home. They adopted me. But they didn't love me. He died of cancer and she, like Douglas and Walter, withdrew into her own mind.

"A man I once knew described himself as a weird little boy, a weird teenager, a weird young man, and a weird old man. That is me. A weird boy on the outside of a house looking in, wanting to be let in, but not wanted in. I put on a good mask, but behind it, I long to be anyone else but me."

Once more, I was lost in my own thoughts and memories.

I forced myself to return to the present.

On the faces of Roxanne and her father were shock and tears.

"I'm sorry, I didn't mean to go on like that," I said. "I only wanted you to feel a little less alone. I cannot take your pain away, nor can you take away mine, but sometimes knowing that someone else is carrying a cross too makes your cross a little less heavy."

Just then, we all heard whimpering. Behind the sliding glass door leading to the back yard was Kenny. He wanted to be let back in. Mr. Solleveld had put him outside while we ate.

I went over and slid the door open. Kenny stood on his hind legs in front of me. I gently picked him up. He nuzzled his face into my shirt, as though he were frightened and wanted me to shelter him. I held him firmly against me so he would feel secure.

"Mr. Solleveld," I said, "is there a park in the area?"

"A couple blocks away."

"Would it be all right with you if Roxanne and I walked over to it? There is still some light left. I thought Kenny might like to run around. I promise, we won't be long."

"Certainly, you can go. Thank you for asking."

I stepped behind Roxanne's chair and eased it out.

It was a magnificent evening. Summer was still in full bloom. Some crickets had started their evening chorus. Intoxicating aromas from outdoor barbecues filled the evening air. Clouds had decided to absent themselves that night. The fading sun was spreading a patina of gold across the Egyptian-blue sky.

Soon, Kenny wanted to be let down. Going for a walk was a new adventure for him, and he wanted to go exploring. While he sniffed and played, Roxanne and I walked, hand in hand, without words.

The park was an expansive retreat, complete with a playground, a baseball diamond, and restrooms. It was treed with old maples, lindens, cottonwoods, and pines.

Roxanne and I sat down on a metal bench while Kenny roamed and ran near us.

"Owen?" Roxanne asked.

"Yes."

"Thank you. Thank you for coming tonight. This has been the best night of my life. After my mom and brother died, I never thought I'd be happy again. You've made me so happy I can't believe it. I know you didn't plan it, but…thank you for coming into my life. I want to make you as happy as you've made me."

She turned to me and joined her lips to mine.

She took my hand and placed it on her breast.

I wanted to remove my hand, for I didn't want to act inappropriately with her. And yet, I didn't want to move it…*ever.*

My body started to tremble.

I pulled my hand away.

"Owen, what is it? Are you okay?" Fright was riveted to her words.

I lifted my hand. It was shaking. I had to set it on my lap to steady it.

"Honey, what is it?" she asked, her voice more frightened than before.

My mouth was dry. "I've never felt this before…this level of passion and desire. I've always been so controlled. My body is not used to it. It scares me. I'm so close to becoming another person. I want it, and yet I don't."

"What do you mean?"

"It's safe being who I am. And yet I don't want to be that person anymore. I want to be free. I want to—" I stopped myself.

"What?"

"You don't understand. All I've ever known is self-control. I've prided myself on it. But since I met you, I don't want it anymore. But I'm afraid to let it go. It's all I know. It's all I can trust. But if I keep embracing it, I can't embrace you. And I *want* to embrace you. I want to smile and laugh and be like other teenagers. I want—" I stopped myself again. I felt ashamed for what I was thinking.

"Don't stop," she encouraged, her voice strong and mature. "Tell me."

"I've already told you." I felt my face start to redden.

"Tell me again."

"Why?"

"Because you can't have a relationship with someone if you don't trust them. You said to Walter earlier, '*We have to trust someone before we let them get close to us.*' The other side of that is equally true: if we *don't* trust someone, we *won't* let them get close to us. You and I have to be open and honest with each other about everything. That includes things that are...embarrassing."

I touched her hands. "I want to make love to you, Roxanne." I felt my face burn hotter with embarrassment. "I'm sorry. I can't seem to stop saying that."

She smiled understandingly. "Owen, it's okay. It's normal to want sex, especially at our age."

"It's more than just sex. It's not just being inside your body I want—I want to be a part of it. I want to be a part of *you*. I want to be on top of you, looking at you, feeling you, caressing you, kissing you, talking to you. I want to see you smile while we both let go."

She smiled compassionately.

"It's too soon," I declared. "I shouldn't want you like that so soon. But I do. I ache to show you how much I love you."

"I want you to show me your love, and I want to show you mine. But...I can't go all the way. I want to, but I can't. Maybe it's old-fashioned and silly, but I want my first time to be on my wedding night. I believe in my Catholic faith, and I want to live it."

"I know you do. I'm sorry if I offended you. I shouldn't have said anything."

"Oh, Owen, you didn't offend me. Remember, it was me who put your hand on my breast. Just because I don't want to go all the way doesn't mean we can't do *other* things." She smiled and winked.

She stood up and took my hand. "Let's get back home."

I took her hand.

Roxanne lowered herself to her knees. "Come on, Kenny, let's go."

The little dog came running to her.

# CHAPTER 8

## *Secrets*

*"It is the best of times, it is the worst of times.*
*What time is that? High school."*

SUE MEYERS

L yle did not feed the wolves.

He was strong and took the remarks and the innuendos and the flouting and the snickering. So the wolves went away for lack of food. Soon his friends returned to him. Personally, I wouldn't have called them *friends*, but when you are an outcast teenager, anyone who talks to you is considered a friend.

Though the incident in the boys' shower room had come and gone for Lyle, I knew, from personal experience, that he would never forget it. Sexual traumas never leave; they remain, just below the surface, and the smallest scrape will cause them to break through. I hoped Lyle would never have another day like that day in the shower; but if he did, I hoped it would be a wound that would heal easily and quickly. Mine never did.

Roxanne and I took Walter trick or treating Halloween afternoon. He didn't want to go in the evening, for the darkness of night scared him. With both hands, he held his bag of candy close to his body, and he stayed close to my side. I wasn't sure if it was because he was afraid to be outside in the dark, or if he simply liked being near me. Because of his measureless loss, I had to conclude that he clung to me out of fear.

Roxanne and I had become inseparable. It was as though we couldn't get enough of one another. She would pass me folded notes in class, and I would pass them to her. She would leave folded notes in my locker, and I would leave them in hers: *Have a beautiful day, Sweetie!...I love you, Baby!...I'll be daydreaming of you!...Can't wait to see you again!... Can't wait to kiss you again!* We would share all of our breaks and lunchtimes together. I even started to eat with her. This was difficult at first, for I didn't enjoy eating, but within time, it became a delight. I even looked forward to it. Before Roxanne entered my life, I ate to survive, and that was all, for eating brought to mind my younger years, when I had to search through garbage cans for anything edible...when my food was laid out on the top step of the Wilsons' basement stairs... when Ms. Windom forced me to eat over an open toilet. After Roxanne came into my world, I associated food with her, and that made me want to eat. At night, every night, she and I would talk on the phone. Every Saturday—if the weather allowed it—we would take Walter and Kenny to the park. Afterward, we would take Walter to McDonald's. If the heavens weren't cooperative, the three of us would stay indoors and play board games. Sometimes, if he wasn't working, Mr. Solleveld would join us. Every Sunday morning, she and her family and I would attend Mass, and then later I would share dinner with them. Sometimes I would even prepare the meal myself. So many couples, I noticed, were together physically, but not emotionally. They had intercourse, but not interaction.

No one at school ever came right out and said it, but I sensed jealousy from many of them. They were not accustomed to seeing two people so twined, and they secretly hated us for it.

Thanksgiving was exactly two weeks away. Warm weather was teasing the city—it was spurring people to think that maybe winter was going to winter elsewhere that year.

I was sitting on the north-entrance steps of the school, bound in a straitjacket of anxiety and worry. Roxanne was not in school that day. She was at home, sick with a cold. Everyone in the world gets sick, this I knew, but this was Roxanne—when she was sick, so was I.

A dark-brown car with an ivory-landau top pulled up in front of the school. It was a prodigious automobile whose sheet metal sported bold and aristocratic lines. Its brightwork winked brilliantly under the late-autumn sun. Someone alighted from the driver's side. It was Mark. He looked in my direction as he was walking toward the south entrance of the building, but he didn't acknowledge me. Evidently, his mind was elsewhere, and he didn't see me. The car, the famous Grand Prix, didn't move. Apparently, Mark was coming back. Sitting in the passenger seat was Mark's friend… or more accurately, the lesion on the skin of Mark's life.

My feet started to move. In seconds, I was standing by the driver's side door of the Grand Prix. I opened the door and slipped into the car.

Mark's friend was looking out the windshield when I entered the car. He jumped when he saw me.

"Who the hell are you!" he boomed.

"Be quiet and listen," I told him evenly. "I know the sickening things you are doing to Mark. Not *with*, but *to*. *With* implies reciprocal desire. Mark does not desire you—he *allows* you."

The boy's face went swan white. Seconds later, it went radish red.

"You are a predator," I accused him. "Worse—you are a *child* predator. How many other boys have you used?" I didn't wait for him to answer. "I should go to the police, but I won't—for Mark's sake. It would come out that he was one of your *toys*, and Mark has enough burdens in his life as it is.

"I'm going to give you a choice: be Mark's friend *only*, or be gone. If you continue to have a sexual relationship with him, I *will* go to the police. Mark needs friends above all else right now. What he doesn't need is a bacterium like you feeding off him to satiate its own deviant, vulturine hungers. Try being a man for a change. Try being a friend. I think you will find it infinitely more satisfying."

I left the car and went back into the building.

I had told Roxanne in September that I was close to becoming another person. In the months since, I had indeed become someone else. I was less vitriolic, less vicious, and less vindictive. I had stopped making every issue a battleground. Being a rattlesnake only scared people away…and, for once in my life, I wanted them near me. And yet, I still spoke up when I had to, especially when I felt no one else would. For the first time in my life, I liked myself.

My short exposure to Mark's friend left me feeling dirty and soiled.

I headed for the lavatory to wash my hands. I knew the Grand Prix was just an object and couldn't be impure, but Mark's friend was, and his diseased hands had touched the very door I had.

"Hey, Owen," someone called to me.

I turned around.

Coming down the hall toward me was Katherine Moore, a tall, carbonated, ginger-haired girl who always spoke very loudly and very rapidly. Some called her *"Katherine the Klaxon"* behind her back.

She had an infuriating habit of using the discourse marker *like* in nearly every sentence.

"Do you, like, have a second?" she asked; her posture, as usual, was unnaturally straight and erect.

Listening to her made my skin tighten.

"What do you want?" My tone was more abrasive than I had intended.

"I, like, need your help."

*"You, like, need my help?"*

Her eyes ping-ponged for a moment. "Isn't that what I just said?"

"What do you want, Katherine?"

"I have a friend who's, like, going through something really bad. You know her. She's in our class. She's, like, really a nice girl."

I was digging my fingernails into my palms. "Okay."

"You have, like, a reputation around the school for, like, being really smart and saying just the right thing. You aren't afraid to, like, speak up about anything."

"The same could be said of you."

"Yeah, but you're, like, totally better at it. And you, like, act more mature. She needs that. You act more like an adult than a kid. You act more grown up than most of the grownups I know. And you're, like, smarter than a lot of them too."

"What is it you need, Katherine?" I couldn't stand it when people served me dessert first so I would feel obligated to eat the main course second.

"I have this friend who needs someone to, like, talk to her. She's really messed up. She's, like—"

My hand went up. "Stop!"

"*What?*"

"If you say *like* one more time, I'm going to throw up! What is it with you and that word?"

"What word? What are you talking about?"

I shook my head in exasperation. "It's like talking to a cement wall."

"Are you calling me dense?"

"*Like, duh!*"

She looked hurt. "Now you're mocking me for the words I use."

"At last you get the picture."

"Not everyone talks perfect like *you*, Owen!"

"Perfect*ly*. Your modifier is wrong. But we aren't talking about your less-than-empyrean grammar—we're talking about your lexical leanings; namely, your incessant use of the adverbial form of *like*. What would you do if that obnoxious, four-letter filler didn't exist? Die, I suspect. I'm surprised you don't include the darling of them all—*dude*."

She stared at me. "Were you born a horse's ass, or did you just wake up one day like that?"

I smiled. "All of the above."

Her eyes narrowed at my answer. "What does it matter if I say *like* a lot? It's not killing anyone."

"No, it's not killing anyone. But there are some things worse than death. Like having to hear *like* every four seconds. Why are you so enamored with it?"

"You're the smart one—you tell me."

"Obviously I'm not, since I'm asking."

"I don't know. Sometimes I say it when I'm nervous. *Like now.*"

"I make you nervous?"

"You make *everybody* nervous. You're always so uptight."

"Any other reasons?"

"I don't know. Sometimes I say it out of habit. Sometimes I say it because I don't know quite how to say something, and it gives me a couple seconds to think about it. And sometimes I say it because I don't want to sound too serious. Is that good enough?"

"It's a crutch, Katherine. Crutches are for cowards. Throw it away. Trust me, you won't miss it. So tell me about this friend of yours— *minus the cane.*"

She glared at me. "She's scared. Really scared."

"Of? Is someone bothering her?"

"Not someone—some*thing.*"

"Some*thing*?"

"A movie."

"A movie?"

"Last March, she went to see *The Exorcist.* It's about this girl who is, like—" she closed her eyes in frustration, "who is possessed by the Devil."

"She is not possessed by the Devil—she is possessed by a demon."

She rolled her eyes. *"Devil, demon, whatever!* My friend is scared to death!"

"Of what?

*"What do you mean of what!* Of being possessed—what else!"

"It was just a movie, Katherine."

"Not to her, it wasn't. Not to a lot of people, it wasn't. If you saw it, you'd know why she's so scared."

"I did see it."

"You did?" She sounded surprised.

"Yes, I did. I went alone."

"How? It's rated R. You're not seventeen."

"It's amazing how far a coat and tie will go. If you look the part, you must be the part."

"You weren't scared?"

"No. But then, I was looking at it from a different perspective than most. I was there to examine the special effects, which, for the most part, were believable. Some looked staged and contrived, but as a whole, they were convincing."

"Well, my friend was *very* convinced. She's terrified she's going to be possessed. She hasn't slept in her own room since last March. She sleeps on her couch in her living room."

"How did she get into the movie in the first place when she's only fourteen?"

"Her grandmother took her. Her mom didn't want her sneaking off to the movie with some of her friends, so she had her grandmother take her."

"Probably not the smartest move by a parent. Has she been to counseling?"

"Yeah, she's been to two psychologists. She's talked to Mr. Taggart too, the school's guidance counselor. She's even talked to a priest. She's convinced if she sleeps in her room or goes in it at night, the door will slam shut on her and the Devil will throw her down on the bed and possess her. She's petrified her eyes are going to roll back in her head, and she'll never see again. Would you talk to her? Tell her what she is feeling is wrong. I know she'll listen to you."

"Feelings are never wrong, Katherine. What is irrational to one is quite rational to another."

"See, you're smart—she'll listen to you."

"She doesn't need argumentation or logic—she needs security."

"See, you already know."

"Who is this friend of yours? What is her name?"

"Corey. I know you've seen her; she's the small girl with the light-brown hair. Really pretty; very shy."

"Yes, I know her. Very timid."

"You would be too if you lived in fear all the time."

"I have."

"Then you know what it's like. So will you talk to her?"

"I'm not sure what I can say. Fear is not an easy safe to crack. It doesn't open with just a few words."

"Will you at least try?"

I hesitated. "I will try. That's the best I can do."

"Thanks."

"Oh…and…two cigars."

"What?"

"Congratulations."

"For what?"

"You got through that whole conversation without once leaning on your little, four-letter friend."

I smiled.

She glared at me again.

Later that day, by happenstance, I saw Corey in the cafeteria sitting with Katherine. Corey appeared deep in thought, far away.

I went to the vending machine, retrieved a bottle of Pepsi and went over to their table.

"May I sit here?" I asked them.

Katherine smiled. Corey didn't.

"Sure," Katherine replied eagerly.

After I took my seat, I motioned with my eyes to Katherine for her to leave. She smiled stealthily and got up from the table.

"Where are you going?" Corey asked nervously.

"I have to go do number two. I'll be back in a little while."

I closed my eyes in disgust and shook my head.

Reopening my eyes, I began, "You're Corey?"

She nodded.

"I'm Owen. I believe we have a few classes together."

"Yeah."

"You have a very pleasant voice. I remember thinking that when you were giving your speech in English."

"So do you."

"What's your favorite thing in school?"

"Nothing, really. I'm not very smart."

"I'll bet you're a lot smarter than you think."

"*You're* the one that's smart. Your name was at the top of the honor roll last quarter. I saw it."

"Due to luck *only*. I simply have the abilities of retention and comprehension. Where I acquired those abilities, I do not know. They couldn't have come from my parents. Flies wouldn't even go near them, let alone intelligence. They were accidents of nature. Well, actually, they were more like *freaks* of nature."

She stared at me. "I never heard anyone talk about their parents like that."

"That's because you didn't know my parents."

"Yeah."

"Do *you* like your parents?"

"They're divorced. I live with my mom."

"Is she good to you?"

"She's okay, I guess."

"My mom did a lot of bad stuff to me when she was alive. Has *your* mom ever done anything bad to you?"

"Not bad things, just things I wish she hadn't done."

"Like what?"

She looked askance at me. "Why are you asking me this stuff?"

She caught me off guard. "I don't know, I just thought...you know, we could talk, one person relating to another."

"Since when do *you* want to relate to *me*? You're so busy swapping spit with Roxanne, I'm surprised you want to relate to anyone but her. Why would you take an interest in a bottom-of-the-barrel girl like me?"

Her questions sounded more like self-indictments than inquiries.

"You're not asking me things, are you? You're *telling* me things. What are they?"

She stayed quiet for a few moments. "If I was beautiful like Roxanne, would you have noticed me?"

Was I reading her correctly? Was she saying she was attracted to me? I didn't dare ask her straight out. If I were wrong, I would come across as conceited and prideful. I would have to proceed carefully.

"Do you think the reason I like Roxanne is because she's attractive?"

"Why else would you like her?"

"Because she's kind and generous."

"So am I. But because I'm not drop-dead gorgeous, no one notices me. And yet, I see these great-looking girls with these ugly guys. I don't understand it."

"Corey, it's not how the mirror sees you that attracts people—it's how you see yourself. People are attracted to confidence. No one wants to be a mother to their mate. As for Roxanne, she came into my world quite unexpectedly. *She* made the first move, not I."

"If *I* had made the first move, would you have asked me out?"

"But you wouldn't have made the first move, so it's all academic, isn't it? Corey, you have your entire life ahead of you, and you will have many suitors during the course of it."

"There won't be *any* suitors. I'm too messed up."

"Why do you—"

"Have you ever heard the song, 'Goodbye to Love'?"

"By the Carpenters?"

"Yes. It's my favorite song. I listen to it every day when I get home from school. It's like it was written just for me."

"There is—"

"I'm never going to find love, Owen."

"There is another Carpenters song I think was written just for you: 'Only Yesterday.' I think you should listen to it. There are over four billion people on the Earth, Corey. I would say the chances of you living the balance of your life as a bachelorette are, unless you die young, minute."

"Even if the world had *ten* billion people, all boys, not one of them would want me. I'm too screwed up."

"Why do you say that about yourself?"

"Because I am."

"Because why?"

"Because I'm afraid of everything."

"Like what?" She didn't answer immediately. "Do you believe in the Devil, Owen?"

"I do. However, I think we give him far too much credit. Too often we lay things at the Devil's door when we should lay them at our own door."

"Do you think the Devil can take over a person's body?"

"You mean the average person?"

"Yeah."

"The mind, yes, the body, no. I think the Devil is everywhere in this world. I think he enters the minds of men and implants destructive thoughts and ideas, but it is ultimately men who make those thoughts a reality. The Devil may say, '*Go kill*,' but it is man who actually does the killing. As for the Devil entering a person and possessing them, I think that can only happen if a person volitionally and consciously invites him in. If a person willfully paws at the occult or endeavors to know darkness, then, yes, I think that person's body can be taken over. But those people are devilishly small in number. Sorry, accidental calembour. Most people don't want anything to do with the Devil, Corey. Most don't even like to *think* about him."

"*I* think about him—all the time."

"Why?"

"Because of that movie."

"What movie?" I already knew which movie.

"*The Exorcist*. I saw it. It was awful. I can't tell you how awful it was. I'm so afraid now."

"Why did you go see it?"

"Because everyone was talking about it."

"And so your mom gave you permission?"

She nodded.

"And is this one of the things you wish she had not done?" I asked.

"Yeah. If she loved me, she wouldn't have let me go."

"I'm sure your mother loves you very much. Parents show their love in various ways. Most parents do the best they can. Your mother probably didn't want you sneaking off to see it with some of your friends."

"That's exactly what happened. How did you know?"

I floundered. I didn't think Katherine would want Corey to know that we had spoken.

"Katherine told you—didn't she!" she shot at me.

I hesitated. "Yes."

"So that's why you're talking to me—because she asked you to."

"Yes. But that does not mean I don't care about what you're going through. That's why I'm here. I don't want you to be afraid. I know what it's like to be alone and afraid. *You're* not alone, though. I'm here for you."

"How can *you* possibly help?"

"Tell me what's making you afraid."

Cautiously, she said, "I'm afraid to go into my room. I haven't slept in it for months. I sleep on the couch in the living room. I put a chair in front of my bedroom door when I have to go in it. I'm so afraid the door will close on me, and the Devil will take over my body. I'm afraid to look in the mirror. I'm afraid my eyes will turn white. I'm afraid the Devil will throw me down on my bed and make me rape myself with something, like how that girl raped herself with a crucifix. I'm chained to this fear, and I can't break it."

The word *rape* thrust a sword into me. Corey was afraid of being raped—I actually was. But fear and reality can carry the same weight. I needed to help her. "You know, Corey, when I see an intense movie, like *The Exorcist*, I look at it pragmatically, not emotionally. I look at it through the lens of reality. Let's you and I do that. Regan's white eyes: white contact lens. The bed shaking: men behind the wall shaking it. The distorted face and lacerations: latex applications. Regan's bedroom: a sound stage. The demon's voice: the voice of an actress. The stuff of Hollywood, Corey, not reality."

"But the movie was based on true events."

"*Thinly* based."

"I can't help it. I'm scared. I don't know what to do. I even talked with a priest."

"And what did he say?"

"He said I should pray about it, ask God for help."

"Maybe you should. It certainly couldn't hurt."

"I can't."

"You don't believe in God?"

"I don't know."

"If you believe in the Devil, you have to believe in God. There can't be one without the other. But then, I understand your doubt: the Devil is easier to believe in than God. Evil has always been more prevalent than good."

"Even if God does exist, He won't hear me."

"Why not?"

"He doesn't hear people He doesn't love."

"You don't think He loves you?"

"No. There's nothing to love. People don't love me, so why should He?"

"Why don't you let God speak for Himself? I think you'll be surprised at His answer."

"Do you think God loves you?"

Her question took me by surprise. "Let's keep the conversation about you, shall we?"

"Why won't you answer me?"

"Because this discussion is not about me; it's about you."

Truth was: I didn't think God loved me either. Except in my case, I *knew* He didn't. But He *did* love her, for she was sweet and innocent. I was not. There was evil in my heart, in my past, and God cannot look upon evil.

"Corey, I want you to do something for me," I said.

"What?"

"Tonight, when you're at home, I want you to pray, and then I want you to do something else. Do you have a telephone in your bedroom?"

"No. But there's one in the hallway on a table."

"Does it reach into your room?"

"Yes."

"Good. After you have prayed, I want you to take the telephone into your bedroom, get into bed and then call me at home. I'm going to stay on the phone with you all night. Even after you fall asleep, I will not leave you. I will still be there in the morning. You can do this, Corey. You really can. All you need is one night to break the chain. Just one.

You won't be alone. I'll be there with you, and I'll be there for you—I promise. You can't sleep on that couch forever."

Her lips were dry, cracked almost. She was terrified to the core.

"What if something happens to me?" she asked, her voice quavering.

"Trust me, it won't. Believe me, it won't. Not to minimize what you are going through, but I have been in far worse places than you are right now. And look at me—are *my* eyes white?"

She smiled nervously. I took that as acquiescence; she would do as I asked.

Taking her *Pee Chee*, I wrote my phone number on the back of it.

I took a sip of Pepsi and smiled encouragingly at her.

"Sorry I took so long," Katherine said, sitting down next to Corey. "Things didn't come out as smoothly as I thought they would." She giggled.

I had the bottle of Pepsi on my lips again but withdrew it at her comment. I set the bottle down and pushed it away from me.

Standing, I said to Corey, "I'll be expecting your call."

At 9:30 that night, my telephone rang. It was Corey. She was crying. "Owen, I can't stay in here. I can't. I'm too scared."

"Where are you in your room?"

"I'm on my bed. I have the chair in front of my door."

"Did you pray?"

"Yes."

"Good. Now I want you to get into bed and close your eyes. Keep the phone close to your ear. I'm going to read to you. Keep your eyes closed and just listen to the words. Concentrate on them alone."

"I can't stay in here."

"Yes, you can!" I countered with more anger than I had intended.

There was silence on the other end for a few moments. "Can I keep the light on?" she asked meekly.

"Of course you can."

I began reading poetry by Helen Steiner Rice. After each poem, I asked Corey how she was doing. She said she was okay. After a half hour, I noticed Corey's voice had calmed considerably. The spaces between her words were longer, and her enunciations were elongated. Somnolence was taking over, which is exactly what I wanted. I continued reading. Soon, I heard deep, gentle breathing from the phone. She was asleep.

I didn't hang up. I kept the phone close to my ear in the event Corey awoke and was frightened. I continued to read, silently. Helen Steiner Rice was my favorite poet; she had a way of soothing and refreshing a troubled and heavy heart like no other author.

I heard Corey's alarm clock go off at six the next morning. I was still awake and still reading.

Groggily, Corey came back on the line. "Owen, are you there?"

"I am. How are you feeling?"

"Did you stay on the phone all night?"

"How are you doing?"

"Nothing happened."

"No, nothing happened."

"I can't believe it!"

"I can. You better get ready for school."

"You were there for me…just like you said you would be. I don't know what to say."

"You needn't say anything. However, I would take a moment and give thanks to God. He was there too."

"I will."

"I told you you would be okay. I'll see you at school, Corey."

"Thank you, Owen."

"You're quite welcome."

We both hung up.

I was at my locker, retrieving my molecular biology book, when someone tapped me on the shoulder. Mr. Taggart was standing behind me.

A medium-height man, Mr. Taggart had curly, raven-black hair. His dusky skin indicated Italian descent, but his name pointed to Scottish ancestry.

"Good morning, Mr. Taggart," I said.

"Owen, I would like you to come to my office later," he said rigidly.

His choice of words and the tone with which he said them instantly put me on the defensive. "Is that a request or an order?"

From my responses, both facially and verbally, he could tell he should have chosen better words and a better tone. "I'm sorry, I should have put that in a nicer way. Do you think you could come by my office later? I would like to discuss something with you. Actually, I have kind of a favor to ask."

"A favor?" I was no longer defensive. Now I was suspicious.

"Yes, a favor. I'd prefer not to discuss it here in the hallway. If you have time later today, would you drop by my office?"

"All right. I will be there at two-thirty."

"Thank you," he concluded and then turned and left.

Baffled, I watched him walk away. I closed my locker and turned to go to my next class.

I saw Roxanne coming toward me. Her face was sober and somber. Something was wrong.

Without saying a word, she took my hand and led me to an empty classroom. Once inside, she closed the door, removed the books from my hands and set them on the floor by our feet. She slid her arms around my waist and laid her head on my shoulder.

Something had happened. Something bad.

"Honey, what is it?" I asked.

She didn't reply or move. Then she pulled away from me and cradled my face in her hands.

"Has something happened to you father?" I asked.

She shook her head.

"Walter? Kenny?"

She smiled faintly. "No. None of those things."

"What is it then?"

Her eyes swabbed my face. It was as if she was seeing it for the very first time and wanted to know every part of it.

What was going on? Her inspection was making me nervous.

"You know," she started, "each time I see you, I fall deeper in love with you. Do you know that?"

I shook my head.

"I do," she went on. "But right now, I don't feel love."

"You don't?"

"Maybe that's the wrong way to say it," she clarified. "Right now, I feel something...*beyond* love."

"Roxanne, I'm trying, but I'm not quite following you."

"If there was a feeling above *love*, that would be what I'm feeling for you right now."

"I'm sorry, but I'm still lost."

"Do you know what makes you so lovable, so perfect?"

I blushed. "*Oh, please!* Mark Spitz is perfect. Burt Reynolds is perfect. Not me."

"But you *are* perfect. To me. Your humility makes you perfect. You weren't going to tell me, were you?"

"Tell you what?"

I was trying not to show it, but her cryptic comments were becoming irritating. Why didn't she just come out and say what she wanted to say?

"Katherine told me what you did for Corey."

"Oh, that. Is that what this is about? Believe me, it was nothing."

"Yes, it was. It was something to Corey. It was *everything* to her. Do you have any idea how much you helped her? *Nobody* would have done what you did. *Nobody*."

"I simply stayed on the phone with her. No big deal. *She's* the one who had to face her demons...so to speak." I grinned at my unintentional equivoque.

"You were there for her—not her friends, not her mother, no one. But *you* were. Because of you, she's sleeping in her bedroom again. Do you know the weight that's been lifted from her life?"

"I'm not the only one who would have helped her."

"Who else would have?"

"*You* would have, had you known."

"I wouldn't have known what to do. Besides, I'm not strong like you. I don't have your character. That's why I love you. That's why so many girls in this school have a crush on you. That and because you're so handsome!"

"You overrate me, Roxanne."

"No, I don't, Owen. Not at all."

Mr. Taggart's office door was open. I took that as an invitation to enter.

The guidance counselor was sitting behind a massive, brown-metal desk. The desk was the size of a tank and probably weighed as much. Two metal folding chairs were in front of it.

"Owen, thank you for coming," Mr. Taggart said and extended his hand to the chairs. He walked over to the door and closed it.

Suddenly, I found myself back in my first grade classroom, held captive by two closed doors and held in terror by a briary, leaden-haired termagant who didn't care how much she frightened me. Panic seized my mind. Instantaneously, I felt the urge to run from Mr. Taggart's office. But I couldn't and wouldn't kneel to the urge. I had to restore my equanimity, and I had to do it quickly. I took some discreet, deep breaths to return my body to homeostasis.

My errant equilibrium quickly recovered.

"Owen," he said, "in my many years here I have never asked a student to do what I'm about to ask you. But I have a hunch, and I'm going to go with it."

I hated it when people went the long way around the house just to get in the front door. "Mr. Taggart, why don't you dispense with the exordium and just come out with it."

His eyes narrowed. "You don't like authority, do you?"

"Is that what you see yourself as—an authority?"

"I mean, you don't like authority in general."

"I don't *respect* authority."

"Why is that?"

"Respect is earned, and most people in positions of authority have not earned it. Yet they expect it."

"You have a point there."

"What is it you want of me, Mr. Taggart?"

"Do you know that you have a reputation around school?"

"*Everyone* has a reputation. Some have a reputation that is more pronounced than others."

"Yours is very pronounced. You are able to reach people that no one else can. Corey, for instance."

I sighed. "Why is everyone making such a big deal of this? All I did was talk with her on the telephone. I didn't pull her out of a burning car!"

"Why are you getting so upset?"

"Because I don't like being the center of attention."

"Since when?"

I gave him a deliberative stare. "Is this guidance counseling in action, or is this just you being an ass?"

"I simply meant that if you don't like being in the spotlight, why do you put yourself there?"

"I don't. I merely speak up or make my opinions known when there is cause. I take no delight in gratuitous vainglory. Now, please, would you stop digressing and just ask me what you want to ask me?"

"Your maturity intrigues me, Owen."

"Does it now?"

"Yes, it does. Over the years, I've met every type of student imaginable: genius students, gifted students, precocious students, happy students, angry students, reclusive students, depressed students, chronically ill students, even a few sociopathic students, but I have never met a student like you. You're a forty-year-old man inside a fourteen-year-old body. You're an old teenager. You don't need to have a Ph.D. in psychology to know that you have experienced unusual distress in your life. As a result, you can empathize with others in emotional distress. Corey, Lyle, Joshua, Morgan are just a few. And Mr. Zigich told me what you did in his Phys-Ed class earlier in the year. All of this has led me to the idea that you might be a great help to those students who are struggling, both academically and personally. What would you think about being my aide?"

"Your what?"

"My aide, an assistant. I need someone who is a good listener, who has good intuition, and who has good insight. I think a child is more willing to open up to someone his own age than to someone older. The component of threat is diminished if a troubled child is talking to another child."

"Unless the troubled child feels the helping child is above him. Hence the many cliques and camarillas in high school. *And* in the world."

"Very true. But you don't give off the vibes of superiority that such children do."

"Mr. Taggart, I'm very flattered that you have such faith in me, but *I am* just a student, not a trained counselor."

"And I'm not asking you to be. I simply want you to lend your ear to students who want it, and if need be, offer a perspective that only you are able to give. I've spoken with Mr. Heald, and we both agree that you would be a perfect fit for this responsibility."

"Why do I get the feeling I'm being asked to be like Lucy sitting at her psychiatry booth, portioning out one-liner panaceas like lollipops?"

"Far from it. I want you to use your best judgment. If you feel you have advice that will better a student's life, I want you to offer it. But for matters beyond your experience, I want you to refer them back to me. Is that understood?"

"You're talking like I've already agreed to go along with this crazy idea of yours."

"First of all, Owen, this is not crazy. Endeavoring to help people is *never* crazy. And second, if I didn't think you could do this, I wouldn't ask it of you. During my years here, I've spoken at four memorials for students who chose suicide over life. I know that every one of them would be alive today if they had had someone to talk to."

"They had you."

"I wasn't enough. I was an adult. I was someone who they thought couldn't understand them, didn't know where they were coming from, didn't know what they were going through. Teenagers think adults can't possibly know what they're feeling. They think they're the only ones who have ever felt the way they do. They think adults were born adults and don't know the first thing about being a teenager. But we do. We still do. You don't know this now, Owen, because you're still young, but living inside every adult is the teenager they once were, a former self who has all the same longings and desires and wishes that you do."

"You're probably right."

"Not probably. I am right. So...are you interested?"

"Am I going to be the only one, or will there be others?"

"I'm not sure. I want to see if it's effective. However, I am going to be asking some of the advanced students to tutor those students who are having difficulties with their classes. They do it in college—why not in high school? I'd like you to be one of the tutors as well."

"And when do I make time for all of this?"

"You make the time."

"And who said no one-liner panaceas?"

"I know I'm asking a great deal of you, Owen, but, as I said, I wouldn't if I didn't believe you were capable. You have a feel for people. More than that, you can reach them. I think you should utilize that ability. But, of course, the decision is yours. If you choose not to participate, nothing further will be said, and I will close the subject for good."

"And where will these *tête-à-têts* take place?"

"Here, in my office, just you and the student. I will ask those students who are having difficulties opening up with me if they would rather speak with another student, someone with whom they might feel more comfortable. If they say they would, I will recommend you. If they are interested, we will proceed."

"And *when* will they take place?"

"I will arrange times that are agreeable with all schedules. So are you game?"

"It all sounds a little off-the-wall to me, but...why not?"

When I told Roxanne what Mr. Taggart had asked me to do, she seemed cool to the idea. When I asked her what her reservations were, she wouldn't answer. She simply cautioned me not to get too close. When I asked her what she meant by that, again she did not respond. I wanted to push the matter, but decided against it. When people are pushed, they usually push back.

Her name was Dana. She was a freshman. She was a fawn-haired girl with a slender build and cream-textured skin. On the surface, she appeared to be a normal girl living a normal life. But normalcy, oftentimes, is merely a mask.

I thought Mr. Taggart's office was too small and confining in which to communicate effectually with someone. I remembered how I felt when I had been there—like I was under a microscope. Open space, in my view, was a must for trust. Mr. Taggart's office was also too bright. No one wants to feel like they're on a stage when they're laying bare their feelings. I asked Dana if she would mind talking somewhere other than in Mr. Taggart's office. She said that would be fine. I chose the balcony of the auditorium.

I found her to be quite shy, like Corey at first.

"If it is any consolation, Dana," I said, "I think we are two goldfish out of the same bowl: you are a student who is asking for guidance, and I am a student who has been asked to give it. For some reason, Mr. Taggart seems to think I am capable of that."

"You don't sound too confident."

"I'm skeptical. But I should at least try, right?"

"But you really don't want to be here, do you?"

"I'm not sure yet."

"Not sure with me, or not sure period?"

"Both."

"Do you want me to leave?"

"Do you *want* to leave?"

"I'm here, aren't I?"

"But do you *want* to be here?"

"I must—at least partly—or else I wouldn't be sitting here now, would I?"

"Tell me something, Dana. Why do you want to talk with me rather than with Mr. Taggart? Do you not feel comfortable with him?"

"He's okay."

"*But?*"

"He doesn't seem very interested."

"Have you given him a chance? Have you told him what's bothering you?"

"No. A person knows when someone's interested and when they're not. He's not."

"Would you feel comfortable telling me what's going on?"

She studied me for a moment. "If I did tell, you couldn't fix it. No one can. It's just something I have to learn to accept."

"You are right, Dana—it is unlikely that I will be able to fix your problem. But I can listen. Sometimes that helps."

She looked down at her hands. "You can't tell anybody."

"I won't. You have my word."

She searched herself for the courage to tell me. "My mom murdered my dad."

Her answer—and the terseness with which she gave it—were like two hard blows.

"How...how did she do it?"

"My dad was in Vietnam. While he was over there, my mom started sleeping with his best friend. She wrote my dad and told him she wanted a divorce, but she didn't tell him why. It destroyed him. I read the letters he sent to her. He begged her not to leave him. He pleaded with her to reconsider. When he wouldn't give up, she finally told him she was having an affair with Glenn—that was his best friend. Some best friend. After she told him, his letters stopped coming. A few months later, we were told he had been killed."

"I don't mean to minimize what you're saying, Dana, but that's not murder—that's war."

"It *was* murder, plain and simple, cut and dried. Because of my mom, my dad gave up. Because of her, he let himself be killed. That's murder. I can see it in my mind: he walked out into an area where he knew the enemy would see him and then they shot him. If only my mom had been the faithful wife she vowed to be, my dad would be alive today.

"And if all that wasn't bad enough, she didn't shed a tear when she got the news. I couldn't believe it. She didn't care. She still doesn't. She doesn't talk about him or have any pictures of him. She doesn't even have any mementos of him. I don't know why she kept the letters. She probably doesn't know she's still got them."

"Why didn't your father just kill himself by his own hand?"

"Probably because my mom wouldn't have gotten any death benefits. If a serviceman kills himself, his family gets nothing."

"Wouldn't that have been a just punishment for your mother?"

"Then *I* wouldn't have gotten any death benefits either."

"But you don't know for sure that he let himself be shot. You will never know."

"You ever have a feeling in your gut about something, even if you can't prove it?"

I nodded.

"I know in my gut, in my heart of hearts, that my father let himself be killed. I can't explain it—I just know it."

"Have you ever talked with your mother about your feelings?"

"I just told you—she won't talk about him!"

"Maybe you should force the issue. Maybe she's not as indurated as you think. Maybe she feels remorseful for what she did, and she just needs someone to pull it out of her, like I'm doing with you right now. Don't mistake placidity for apathy."

"She's as apathetic as they come! I hate her for what she did! I hate her for what she is!"

"People often give a manufactured pose for the world, Dana. Things are rarely as they appear. The whole truth is seldom found on the surface. I'll tell you about a similar situation that happened to me. Many years ago, I discovered that my adoptive mother had lied to me about who she really was. I had thought she was just a stranger who happened to love me. The truth was much different. She was, in fact, my mother's sister. My young mind fashioned its own reasons why she kept the truth from me. Last summer, I learned the *real* reasons. Your own mother, Dana, I'm sure, has a much different version of what you think is the truth. That is why you should ask her. I think she is as eager to tell you the truth as you are to hear it."

"And what if I'm right?"

"Well, then, like you said, you will just have to learn to accept it."

"I don't know if I can. I wish I was strong and sure like you."

"If wishes were horses, beggars would ride. Nothing good happens on its own, Dana. You have to work at everything. You need to go to your mother and hear her side. Parents aren't perfect…even if we think they should be."

Suddenly—and unexpectedly—my heart filled with longing for Mrs. Crowley. She wasn't perfect…but neither was I. She did what she did because she felt she had to. I might very well have done the same thing had I been in her shoes.

Dana stood up. "I got some friends I gotta meet."

I nodded.

She turned and began walking away.

"Dana?" I called.

She turned around.

"Ask her."

"Maybe."

His name was Nick. He hated the name, but everyone called him that anyway. He preferred the more formal sound of Nicholas, but it simply didn't stick. Sometimes his friends would go farther with his name and cobble it together with what they saw as playful rhymes: *"Nicky wants a hickey"* or *"Nicky wants a little nookie."* What they saw as appellative cuteness I saw as unnecessary uncouthness.

Nicholas didn't want us to meet in the balcony of the auditorium as Dana and I had. He was afraid someone might see us and think we were gay and wanted to be alone to *do things*. We met instead on the bleachers above the football field.

He was a tall boy with milk-chocolate hair. He was a senior, but he looked like a September freshman. Over niveous skin, he had a slight curse of acne. Beyond that, he was an attractive young man.

"So how many kids have you talked to so far?" he asked after we sat down on the paint-chipped slats.

"A few."

"And are their lives all sparkly now?"

"You will have to ask them. I told them what I thought they should do. But it is ultimately up to them to follow through."

"What makes *you* such an expert on life? You're only a freshman."

"It is not a matter of being an expert, or a freshman—it is a matter of logic. Some people cannot see the logical answer to a problem because they are so close to it. Sometimes talking a problem through helps them to see the answers they are seeking. If the answers are still not obvious to them, I point them out."

"I hear you're a genius. You've got an IQ of, like, two hundred. Mr. Taggard says you've got something called an eatictic memory."

"Eidetic," I corrected him. Then I realized I shouldn't have. "I'm sorry—that was rude. You should never correct someone unless they need it. Listen, Nick—sorry, *Nicholas*, I understand you are more partial to that name—why don't we talk about *you*. That is why you are here, is it not?"

He looked out at the lifeless, empty gridiron.

"You're lucky," he embarked. "You've got a girlfriend you're proud of. Roxanne's beautiful."

"I take it by your comment that you have a girlfriend who is not."

"You ever hear the expression, *pretty in the cradle, ugly at the table*?"

"It's a little out of the ark, but I've heard it."

"Well, this girl I'm dating is that expression dead-on. She was a darling baby; a cute little girl. She showed me some pictures of her. But now, she's..." he stopped.

"Say it."

"I can't."

"Why?"

"Because she's a great girl—attentive, sweet, kind, giving, caring, but she's..."

"*Ugly?*"

He swallowed and looked at me.

"The word *ugly* is not a slap," I pointed out, "it is a summary. It is a simple fact that there are things and people in this world who are ill-featured. Just as there are things and people who are *not*. Not every flower belongs in a vase."

"When we're together in public, I walk ahead of her so no one will know we're together."

"Has she pointed this out to you?"

"Yes."

"What's your response?"

"I lie. I tell her I just walk fast."

"What is this girl's name?"

"Carolyn. She doesn't go here. She goes to Larchmont. She's a senior too."

"Why are you with her if you find her so unattractive?"

"I've always had guy friends, but never girlfriends. I don't know, girls don't look my way. They never have. Until last August. One of my friends had this end-of-summer party. Carolyn was there. She was kind of a wallflower. I felt sorry for her. I went over to her, we started to talk, and we really hit it off. I even drove her home and kissed her good night. She looked pretty nice at the party, but the next day when I saw her in the daylight, I couldn't get over how...awful she looked. If she was a plain Jane, I could handle it, but she's..."

"A car accident?"

His eyebrows arched at my words.

"Call it what it is," I said. "Don't dance around your feelings. Don't gloss them over."

"But she's really a sweet girl."

"You haven't answered my question: why are you with her?"

He stared at me. "Something tells me you already know the answer to that—don't you?"

"I have a hunch. But I want you to tell me."

"I can't. I can't bring myself to say it out loud."

"Then allow me. You're settling. You think no one else will ever have you, want you or love you, so you settle for Carolyn. You think she is the best you are ever going to get. And yet, in the private islands of your mind, you think you deserve better. And you are right. Don't settle, Nicholas. It will establish a pattern for everything else you do in your life, and at the end of it, you will ask yourself, why did I do that?"

He shook his head. "Nick the prick—that's me. Superficial as a guy can get."

"You're not even close. Have you had sex with her?"

He shied. "Yes," he admitted. "My mom asked me that too. I told her I had. Big mistake. I told her I really wasn't attracted to Carolyn. Second big mistake. She called me *'plastic.'* She says I'm nothing but a *'depthless, salivating tail-wagger with only one thing on his mind.'* I guess in her day that meant I'm a shallow, horny dog."

"Hardly. You are neither plastic nor superficial. Human males, by nature, are visual. As are women, though not to the degree that men are. There is nothing wrong with wanting an attractive mate."

"But looks are only skin-deep, right? That's what they say, right? Isn't that what counts the most—what's beneath the surface?"

"Yes, but for emotional fusion to occur between two people, like it or not, good or bad, right or wrong, there must be true attraction between those two people."

"It sounds right—so why don't I feel right?"

"Tell me something—why didn't you go to Mr. Taggart with this?"

"Because he'd lecture me like my mom and tell me I'm being shallow and to stop looking only on the surface."

"It is always easy for others to expect—if not demand—nobility in us. But when our shoes are on *their* feet, that nobility is strangely absent. Tell me something else—why did you have sex with Carolyn if she is so hideous?"

"Because in the dark, she's nice. Got a killer body! Great-looking house, ugly roof." He smiled wryly. "You wanted me to be honest, right?"

His analogy was tasteless but truthful.

"She's really good in bed," he annotated. "And she's really something out of bed too. She's kind and caring. She's attentive too. She really listens to me. She touches my face like it was gold."

This was the second time he remarked on her non corporeal qualities. It was obvious he cared for this girl more than he wanted to admit.

"Has she told you she loves you?" I inquired.

"Yeah."

"Have you told her the same?"

He demurred. "Yes...but I don't mean it."

"Then why say it?"

"The first time I said it we were having sex."

"That's fairly common, I hear. And not unexpected. It was your oxytocin talking—not love. Love isn't a feeling, Nicholas—it's an action. It's a commitment." I shook my head again in self-anger. "Sorry, I tend to preach. Please, finish."

"I feel that since I said it once, I'm obligated to keep saying it. I feel sorry for her. Even if I wasn't settling for her, I couldn't break up with her—it would break her heart. What if she killed herself? I couldn't live with myself. How could I do that to her? She's such a sweet and genuine girl. And she's perceptive too. She's not like any girl I've ever met. I've got two sides pulling at me. I don't know what to do. I want to be with her and I don't."

"I would say don't. Yes, she will be hurt, and, yes, she will be injured. But that's the way it is. Both my mother and father rejected me the day I was born. Everyone gets rejected, in one way or another, at some time or another. You deal with it...or you die. That's the way it is. That's life. If she kills herself, she kills herself. That's her choice. If she doesn't, she will go on. That's her choice too. She will meet someone else and fall in love again, even if right now she says she won't. You don't *have* to stay with her, Nicholas. You two are not married; you're not engaged; you're not even going steady...as they used to say. You're just dating. Dating and mating. '*A kiss is not a contract,*' as the poet said. Life goes on after people break up. It always has. It always will.

"Why don't you do this? The next stomp is this Friday night in the gymnasium. Go to it and ask a girl to dance. I think your auditory cortex will receive input that your temporal lobe will define as a *yes.*"

He looked out into the desolate field and rested his elbows on his knees. Deep thoughts had overtaken him.

"What's the matter?" I asked, even though I knew already. He was right where I wanted him.

He delayed answering. "It's funny. Before talking to you, I thought I was in a prison. I thought I was stuck with Carolyn. But after talking with you, I realize I'm *not* stuck. I can leave her. But I don't want to. She loves me. She loves everything about me. She calls me handsome and gorgeous and beautiful. She says she loves my lips and my arms and my legs and my hair...even when it's messy. She even loves my hands; she says they're masculine works of art. She adores me. Where am I going to find pure love like that?"

I smiled coyly. "Where indeed?"

He looked at me, smiling too. "You knew all along I'd have a change of heart—didn't you?"

"No, not at first. Some of the things you said later in our conversation made me think that maybe you cared for Carolyn more than you realized. I tried to get you to separate yourself for a moment from her so you could see how much value she has in your life. Sometimes when we don't feel trapped, that's when we want to stay. That's when we realize what we've really got."

"Roxanne's damn lucky to have you," he said. "I hope *she* realizes what she's got."

"Just make sure I get a wedding invitation," I said, steering the conversation away from me.

"You got it," he said and chuckled.

He stood up and held out his hand.

I took his hand and we shook.

"Thanks," he said and left the bleachers.

Her name was Nouveau. Her mother, the dominant force in her home, named her that after the art form Art Nouveau. The mother was a pushy, sniffy woman, swollen with ego and pride; the type who, regardless of circumstances, downed a nightly preprandial cocktail of sherry and bitters; the type who thought the poor and working class were a blight on America; the type who would invent gossip if none were readily available. Mr. Taggart shared this with me early on. Nouveau was a sad, sepulchral girl. She never once smiled. Tall and lean, she could have done well athletically, but she chose to stay to herself. I was surprised she wanted us to meet.

"What made you want to talk with me?" I asked.

"I don't know," the senior answered, pulling a lappet of light-brown hair over her ear.

"Someone once told me I was the most morose child they'd ever met," I said. "I think I have met my match. But a morose heart is not that way by accident, is it, Nouveau? What happened to *your* heart?"

"What happened to *yours*?" she flicked back, shimmying her head.

"You'll show me yours if I show you mine? Is that it? Fair enough. I was born—that's what happened. Some people shouldn't be born. I was one of them. The naked mole-rat—one of the ugliest creatures on the face of the Earth. Makes you wonder if God was having a bad day when He made it. That's how I think about me, if truth be told."

"That's an awful thing to say about yourself. I thought you were supposed to be this know-it-all, no-problems golden boy everybody loves."

I stared at her. "Not quite." I stared at her again. "Now—show me yours."

She hesitated. "Do you think God loves people?"

"Not as we define love."

"I think God has as much love for people as people have for cancer. If He loved people, He wouldn't have created people like my mother. He wouldn't have created pain. He wouldn't have created death."

"It'd be a pretty crowded world if He hadn't...not to side with that unkindly *Fourth Horseman* mentioned in *Revelation*. You have a rather severe view of God, don't you?"

"Call it a smart view. He's not going to get the last laugh with me, though."

"The last laugh?"

"You ever go to a dance and watch people? They flit and fly around with their hands waving and their hips bumping. They all act like they're masters of the world, invincible, indestructible. They have no idea how controlled and breakable they are—not the other way around. Gravity keeps them on the ground and air keeps them alive. Take away both and they're floating corpses. God watches from above and laughs at their arrogance, for in the end, He knows their dance will cease. People live their lives, laughing, eating, playing, having a good time, completely oblivious or consciously ignorant of a God who, in the end, will wipe away their smiles and laugh while He's doing it. He knows how everyone will die, and He waits for that day when He can see it. He relishes the terror of death in their eyes. He hates people, and He hates it when they enjoy life. He wants them joyless because He is joyless. He wants them miserable and dark, like Him, and if they aren't, He boils. But in the end, He will have the last laugh as they die in regret or agony. But He won't get the last laugh with me. I won't give Him that satisfaction. It infuriates Him that I won't."

I had heard many odd things from students, but this was the oddest. She spoke of death and had used the expression "in the end" more than once. Had there been an "ending" in her life, a death that she had not been able to accept and was laying the blame for that death on God?

"Your thesis has some holes in it, Nouveau," I pointed out. "How can God have the last laugh if He never even smiles? Moreover, shouldn't your deliberate glumness make Him happy rather than mad? If He wants everyone's mood in the toilet, shouldn't yours make His day?"

"No, because He knows I'm on to Him. He knows He can't gloat in the end with me. I won't let Him."

"And those not on to Him, those who are truly suffering, that puts a smile on His face?"

"Big smile."

"I thought you said He was never happy."

Her eyes sparked anger.

"Let's get back to God being miserable," I said. "You think He made us just so we could be as miserable as He? Why would He do that?"

"Misery loves company."

"Why is God miserable?"

"How should I know."

"Okay. Let's focus in on what you do know—you. Why are *you* miserable? What made you that way? I believe you sincerely think God lacks any kind of joy, but that doesn't explain *your* lack of it.

Remember—a morose heart isn't that way by accident. So...what happened to you?"

She said nothing.

"When I was young," I said, "I discovered one of the most effective ways of punishing someone was to shut them out. Pushing them away, letting them see they had absolutely no effect on me was a great penalizer. Worked wonders. For a while. But then I got tired of it. I think you wanted to talk with me today because you're tired of being sad. You're tired of being alone. You're tired of punishing God. He took something from you—or someone—and you're trying to get back at Him. What did He take—dog, cat, grandmother, grandfather, friend? Which was it?"

"What are you being so flippant?"

"I'm sorry, I don't mean to be. I think God loves you, Nouveau, and I think He wants to help you, but He can't until you stop punishing Him. You have to let Him love you in *His* way, not yours. You're angry with Him for removing something from your life, so tell Him that. Let Him show you His love. Stop believing He hates you. Stop believing He hates the thought of anyone—including you—being happy."

She eyes were fixed on the floor. "You think everything is going to be fine now because you've handed me your amazing pearls of wisdom? You think I'm going to hug you now and thank you for saving me from myself? You think you saved another soul? You think I'm glad we spoke?" She raised her eyes and looked at me. "Think again. I'm not glad we spoke. You wasted my time. You're just like everyone else—a full-of-himself phony. You don't care about me, you only care about being clever and being right about everything. You're just a patronizing narcissist who only wants to talk. Hearing your own voice is what gets you off."

She slung the long strap of her purse over her shoulder, stood, and walked away.

Was that how I came across to people—a high-and-mighty maven, a full-of-himself fake? Was I full of myself? Did I only care about being right and being heard? I didn't mean to. My intention had only been to help. Sometimes, though, good intentions produce an offspring of not-so-good endings.

His name was Alex. He was a sophomore. He was a short, soft-spoken youth with obsidian-colored hair. Under certain lights, his hair almost had the color of sloe. His soft, brown eyes were continually sad.

We met in the balcony of the auditorium, just as Dana and I had. He evidently didn't care if we were seen there together.

"So…what's it like, hearing everybody's secrets?" he asked.

"Illuminating. Most people's secrets are bitter. Some are sweet, some are bittersweet, but most are bitter. Secrets are like rocks: some are light, some heavy, but they all weigh people down. Everyone has them. I think deep down we all want to share our secrets with someone, if only to say them out loud. That in itself can be very healing and liberating."

"I've never told anybody what I want to tell you."

"To coin an old idiom: *Your secret is safe with me.*"

"Do you ever think about killing yourself, Owen?" he asked flatly.

His words instantly sounded an alarm in me. I remembered what Mr. Taggart had said: *"For matters beyond your experience, I want you to refer them to me."* Suicide, though it had crossed my mind when I was younger, was not a staple in my current mental diet. I needed to proceed cautiously. I didn't want to frighten him away, lest he leave and carry out his desire.

"To be honest," I started, "I have considered it. But that was a long time ago. Are *you* thinking about killing yourself?"

"To borrow your words, '*I have considered it.*'"

"Why?"

"You'll probably think it's silly."

"Nothing in this world is silly, even if it looks it."

He swallowed. "I blush at everything."

"Everybody blushes, Alex."

"I blush at *everything.*"

"Why do you think that is?"

"I hate people looking at me. When they do, I get embarrassed."

"Why do you hate people looking at you?"

"Because I don't like myself. I think people are judging me when they're looking at me. I'm weird. I always have been."

Self-image always starts at home. I needed to know how he was treated there.

"What is your homelife like? How do your parents treat you?"

"Like I'm a bug they can't get rid of. My mom rarely talks to me, and when my dad does, he just makes fun of me."

"Why?"

"Because I'm not the son he wanted. I'm a disappointment to him. I'm not the boy he'd hoped for. I don't like sports; I don't like watching sports; I don't like cars; I don't like camping; I don't like fishing; I don't like hunting. And, *no*, I'm not gay, if that's what you're thinking."

"I was not. Your sexual gravitation is unimportant to me. What interests me is you."

"But isn't a person's sexual gravitation a part of that person?"

"Yes, but that is not why you are here, is it?"

"Why is everybody always so obsessed with sex?"

"That's an unusual question for a teenager to ask. Teenagers are typically obsessed with the subject."

"I'm not your typical teenager."

"That you are not. I would say that coital interest is normal since we are all wired for reproduction. Our preoccupation with it, however, comes from a lack of restraint and the saturation of the matter in books and magazines and films. Where there is no societal control and individual self-control, there is moral apostasy and existential nihilism. When you worship before the altar of carnality, what you reap in the end is sorrow. Plain and simple. But enough of sermonizing. Let's get back to you. What sorts of things do you like to do?"

"Pottery. I love making pottery. My dad says I'm as weird as a three-dollar bill because I do. He says I'm a faggot. He calls me a *'gay who plays with clay.'* A *'pansy who will one day marry a petunia.'* He once asked me if I'd ever made a pot in the shape of a penis."

I rubbed my eyes in disgust. "I'm sorry," I offered. "Does your father also make fun of you for your blushing?"

"All the time."

"Are there times when you *don't* blush?"

"No."

"You are not blushing now. You haven't blushed once since we have been together."

"I don't know. Maybe it's because I don't feel intimidated by you. But with everyone else, forget it. If the teacher calls on me in class, I turn ten shades of purple. Even in a small group, if someone asks me something, my face goes the color of a bowl of cherries. If a pretty girl talks to me, which is rare, forget it—my face turns into a fire truck. People are always asking me why I get so embarrassed. Their questions only make it worse.

"Sometimes I wish I was a girl; then it wouldn't matter. Girls blush all the time. It's normal for them. People even expect it. But when a boy blushes, he looks like a girl. He looks weak and afraid and weird. He even looks suspicious, like he's hiding something. I'm not hiding anything except who I am."

"And who are you?"

"Invisible. No one ever sees the real me. All they ever see is a red face. No one wants to get to know me. Not even my parents. I guess I can't blame them. Why would anyone want to get to know me? I'm nothing to know, and I'm nothing to look at. Have you ever felt utter hatred for yourself, Owen?"

"Yes."

"I hate everything about me. I hate my face, my smile, my voice, my body, my thoughts, my feelings, my very life. Maybe if I liked myself, I wouldn't turn red all the time. But I don't, so I do. If I wasn't such a coward, I'd kill myself. I'd be happier; I know my parents would, especially my dad."

"Alex, I need to ask you something: has your father ever hit you?"

He didn't answer right away. "Sometimes."

"Sometimes, or *all the time*?"

"A lot."

I chewed on his answer for a moment. "I had a father once. He died when I was very young. He never hit me. He was good to me. He was an architect. What does *your* father do?"

"He works in a bank. He's a loan officer."

"My father always came home early just so he could be with me. I imagine your father gets home early too. Or are banker's hours just a myth?"

"It's no myth at my dad's bank. He's home every day at four-fifteen."

"Do you live far from here?"

"Yeah. Quite a ways."

"How do you get to school? Do you take the bus? Or does your mother bring you?"

"You kiddin'? My mother doesn't even make me dinner. I make my own. No, I walk to school. Why do you want to know?"

"No reason. Tell me, have you told Mr. Taggart about the treatment you get at home?"

"No. I can't even approach him. I get all embarrassed when I go up to people."

"Then how did this meeting get arranged?"

"*He* came up to me."

"I see. Alex, before you say no to what I'm about to suggest, hear me out. You have some problems that need attention. Quick attention. Here are a couple of cold facts. Suicide is the third leading cause of death in teenagers. Girls consider suicide more than boys, yet more boys than girls actually carry it out. You have forces in your life that are bearing down on you that you can't control. That makes you feel trapped. When we feel trapped, we fight to get free. We want out. I would like your permission to go to Mr. Taggart and tell him what we discussed today. He can assist you in getting some counseling for your blushing and your self-image. You don't have to live like this, Alex. Your erythema—your blushing—is complicated, but it is also simple. When you blush, your sympathetic nervous system is being stimulated with negative emotion and ideation; in turn, it causes the blood vessels in your face to dilate. If you can eradicate that stimulus, your blushing, for the most part, will cease. There are even medications that can help you."

"My parents will never pay for counseling. Or medication."

"Don't worry about your parents."

"How'd a kid like you get to be so smart?"

"Do I have your permission to go to Mr. Taggart?"

"Will Mr. Taggart call my parents?"

"No, he won't. I'll see to that. So can I go to him?"

"I guess so. What have I got to lose?"

After Alex and I parted, I went to Mr. Taggart's office.

The guidance counselor was sitting at his desk. Brahms was playing softly in the background.

Mr. Taggart smiled when he saw me.

"Do you have a minute?" I asked.

He removed the 8-track of Brahms from the player, and the room instantly went quiet. "Certainly."

I entered the room and closed the door.

Without sitting, I immediately began. "Alex Boyd needs help immediately. He is considering suicide."

He stood up. "I sensed something was wrong. That's why I went to him."

"He is agreeable to the idea of counseling. No offense to your skills, Mr. Taggart, but I think this situation is beyond your abilities. I would bring in a trained professional, a child psychologist, or even a child psychiatrist. And I would do it soon."

"Could he hurt himself now?"

"No, but he's close."

"I need to contact his parents."

"I would advise against that. They are part of his problem. For now, just get him into counseling. He has major difficulty approaching people, so *you* need to go to him, preferably today, and assure him that you are in his corner and that you are going to do everything you can to help him."

"I will. I will speak with him after his next class. Thank you, Owen."

"For what?"

"For making time for him."

"The credit should go to you for making the first move."

"He's a good kid—I'd hate to see anything happen to him."

"It already has. I need to ask a favor of you."

"Just name it."

"I need you to meet with Alex this Friday after school. Keep him here until five. Can you do that?"

"Not a problem. But why?"

"I can't discuss it. Just do as I ask."

He looked perplexed. "All right."

"Thank you," I said and left his office.

I followed Alex home that afternoon. I stayed back a good distance from him. He never sensed he was being followed, for he never glanced back.

He lived fifteen blocks northwest of the school. I lived in the opposite direction. This explained why I never saw him walking home.

Alex's home was modest but well-tended. How tragic that his parents didn't give their son the same affection and attention.

Perhaps that would change after my visit.

The weather that Friday was abnormally mild. Christmas was only two weeks away and the ground should have been shrouded in snow, yet it wasn't. Instead, it was a passionless sepia.

Immediately after my last class, I dashed to my locker, retrieved my coat and the books I would need for that weekend and went straight to the lavatory. Thankfully, it was unoccupied. I could put on my tie and sport coat (which had been in a plastic bag under my winter coat) without questions from any inquisitive boys. I always wore dress slacks and leather shoes to school, so my bottom half was all ready for that evening's business. Serendipity was holding my hand after I exited the bathroom, for no one stopped me to talk. I slipped out the rear entrance, serpentined through the cars in the parking lot and made my way to the street via a seldom-used back alley.

My watch said 4:03 when I reached Alex's home. It took twenty-five minutes to reach it. I hadn't rushed to get there. His father would not be home until four-fifteen.

I walked around his neighborhood for the quarter hour. When I returned, a car was parked in the driveway that had not been parked there before: a 1963 Studebaker Avanti. It was one of the most bizarre cars to come off an assembly line. How could Alex's father label his son as weird as a three-dollar bill when he drove an acid-trip vehicle like that?

Before going over to the house, I stashed my books under a bush. Alex's parents couldn't know that I was a student straight away.

The door chime hadn't finished its tune before the door opened. A gray-haired, featherweight woman was now standing in front of me.

"Mrs. Boyd?" I inquired.

"Yes," she answered reservedly.

"My name is—"

A tall galleon of a man with salt-and-pepper hair suddenly appeared at the door and pushed his wife out of the way. Mr. Boyd, I presumed.

"Who are you?" he asked bluntly.

"My name is Owen Crowley. I am from Alex's school. I was wondering if I could speak with the two of you."

"What's that little faggot done now?" Mr. Boyd spat.

"I would rather not discuss it here on the porch. May I come in?"

Mr. Boyd sniffed. "Yeah, come on in. But wipe your feet first."

I did as he asked and then entered the house. The temperature in the house was only slightly higher than the outside. The air smelled of Clorox. No pictures were hanging on any of the walls, which were all stark white.

Without being asked, I sat in one of the living room chairs: a stiff, floral-printed, Baroque-styled piece of furniture that was covered in clear plastic.

*You never heard of antimacassars?* I asked them silently.

Alex's parents sat on a yellow-brocade couch also covered in clear plastic. The slightest move made the plastic crackle and snap. These people were from another world. They were like their furnishings: cold and unnatural.

"So what's that queen son of mine done now that one of the faculty has to come over here on a Friday night?" Mr. Boyd huffed.

I stared at them. Mrs. Boyd was strangely silent and kept her eyes forward, away from her husband; it was as if she were afraid to even look at him.

"Do you know where your son is?" I asked them.

"I can only imagine," Mr. Boyd returned belligerently. "He's probably behind some building with another boy giving him a hand job."

His crudeness made my body tighten. "You know, Mr. Boyd, there is an old, crusty saying: *Those who condemn the loudest are those who have the most to hide.*"

"Meaning *what*?" Mr. Boyd asked splenetically.

"Are you one of Alex's teachers?" Mrs. Boyd asked sheepishly.

"Shut up, Doreen!" Mr. Boyd bulldozed his wife out of the conversation. "Now just what did you mean by that?" he asked threateningly.

I knew right then that Mrs. Boyd was not the disinterested mother Alex thought she was. She was bullied into being that by her husband. She cared about her son but was terrified to show it. She went along with her husband to keep herself from getting hit too. But what kind of mother puts herself first and her child second?

"To answer your question, Mrs. Boyd, no, I am not one of your son's teachers. And to answer yours, Mr. Boyd, I think you are hiding something."

He stood up. "Get out of my house!"

"Sit down, Mr. Boyd."

"Do your ears need cleaning? I said, *get out of my house!*"

"Sit down, Mr. Boyd, or you will spend the weekend in jail, if not longer."

He started to move toward me.

"Touch me and it will be the last thing you ever do as a free man. Sexual assault on a minor is, shall we say, frowned upon."

He stopped. "What the hell are you talking about!"

"That is what I will report to the police if you touch me. And they will believe me too. First because it has been done to me before, and second because I am underage. Why would a minor lie about molestation if it did not actually occur?"

"What do you mean you're underage?" Mrs. Boyd spoke up. "We thought you were one of Alex's teachers, what with the tie and good shoes and all."

"Not quite. I am fourteen."

"Like hell you are!" Mr. Boyd bellowed back.

"I am fourteen. I am also pressed for time—so sit down, Mr. Boyd! I will be brief, and then I will be gone."

Snarling, he lowered himself onto the couch.

"I want you both to listen," I commanded, "and listen well. I know firsthand what lousy parents are, and both of you fit the definition to a T. You are a sadist, Mr. Boyd, and you, Mrs. Boyd, are a coward. You, Mr. Boyd, I think are either homosexual or bisexual and hate it, or you were abused by someone who was, and you don't know how to deal with it. Either way, you take it out on your son. Because of the two of you, Alex is scattered wreckage. With help, he may someday put his life together and be able to love himself. But he will never be your son. He will just be someone you made. You had the chance to know an intelligent and gifted boy, but you both threw it away. When you die off, he will not weep because you are gone, he will weep because you were never there.

"Here is what is happening and what is *going* to happen. Thanks to the both of you, Alex is in counseling at school for social anxiety and suicidal cerebration. If, Mr. Boyd, the physical abuse you executed on Alex comes out in that counseling, you will have some serious explaining to do, if not some serious time. Child abuse is not taken lightly these days. If the abuse is not brought to the fore, but continues, I will take you down—both of you. I will go to your work, Mr. Boyd, stand in the middle of the bank floor and scream out that you raped and molested me. While it will be a lie, of course, and will subsequently be proven as such, your reputation and your job will be gone. All it takes to ruin somebody is a claim. It doesn't have to be true. Once an idea is in people's minds, that's all people will ever see. An idea is more destructive than reality. Untruth destroys more than truth. Just look at your son. The truth is, your son is not gay. But because he doesn't partake in the tree-sloth pastimes you do, you brand him a queer...or, to use your words, *'a gay who plays with clay.'* As for you, Mrs. Boyd, I will make it known to every one of your neighbors that you knew your husband was a pedophile and did nothing about it. I don't think you will want to remain in this neighborhood long after that."

I stood up. "Keep your distance from Alex, Mr. Boyd," I ordered. "Make one wrong move, just one, and life as you know it will come to an end, for good."

I looked around the room. "Odd. How is it that the two of you lean toward white so much when your souls are so black?"

The two adults sat still as stones as I walked out of their home.

Christmas was less than a week away. It was Thursday; a light day for me classwise. Only two days remained before Christmas vacation began. I was desperately looking forward to the break. It wasn't the break from the schoolwork I was anticipating; it was the escape from the endless tales of loss and rejection and regret and loneliness and self-loathing and guilt and emptiness and pointlessness I had to listen to almost daily. It seemed everyone had some story of grief they were towing. It wasn't that I didn't care, I did; I just couldn't listen to any more of it. I became more dispirited than the students with whom I met. I didn't know how social workers and counselors and psychologists and psychiatrists listened to the misery day after day. The time I spent with the students was not entirely without reward, however. I discovered that teenagers, in spite of their outward narcissism, were acutely deep-feeling and deep-thinking creatures, capable of intense compassion, profound empathy, and remarkable understanding.

My first class on Thursdays was World History. We were currently examining the Carthaginian Wars. The teacher was a thin, athletic-looking woman in her early thirties who was blessed with exceptional beauty. She was neither tall nor short, heavy nor thin. Hers was the kind of face cameras loved. Her hair was long and lush and wavy. Streams of white and russet and chestnut flowed over her shoulders and down her back. I had never seen hair like it before, not even on a department-store mannequin. At first sight, I thought it was an elaborate performance of dyes. But on the second day of class, a girl in the back row stood and asked the teacher if her hair color was real or fake. Calmly and with a gracious smile, the teacher said it was all hers; not one strand came from a bottle.

The teacher's name was Jillian Gavin, but she requested that all her students call her Jillian. (While the other students gladly accepted this invitation, I could not. It was wrong and disrespectful in my eyes for a junior to call a senior by their first name.)

Ms. Gavin was the happiest person I had ever met; she always greeted everyone with a smile and a hello. She was the most well-liked and well-respected teacher in the school. She loved children, and children loved her.

Right after Halloween, there was a climatic change in her. She stopped smiling and stopped talking. She only spoke when she had to instruct. The warm woman had become an icy statue.

I wanted to ask her what was troubling her, but I felt she would consider my concern an invasion. Added to that, I felt she would view me as only a teenager—what did I know of adult problems and troubles?

That Thursday she gave us an essay exam. She said we could leave if we finished the test early. It was a difficult exam, so no one left early; in fact, all kept writing until the bell sounded. At that point, she asked everyone to put their exams on her desk as they left.

As I was laying my exam on her desk, she asked me to remain. I nodded and stood off to one side and waited for the room to empty.

When we were alone, I went back to her desk. I waited for her to initiate the conversation.

Many moments passed before she did. "Owen...I don't know how to ask this."

"Sometimes when we don't try at something, Ms. Gavin, that's when we succeed," I said. "Just ask me, straight out."

She regarded me earnestly. "You're an exceptional young man, Owen. I'm sure you've been told that."

I detested compliments. I believed they were sincere—I just didn't believe they were true. "What's on your mind, Ms. Gavin?"

"I'm told that you have helped a number of students with personal difficulties," she said next.

"I merely listen, nothing more."

"You do more than listen. You give insight and direction. Good insight and good direction. Dana Fenton, a girl whom you *merely listened to*, has a much better relationship with her mother now. And Claire Terashima? After talking with you, she seems at peace with her little sister's death. And Marie Simon? She's okay that she'll never be a cheerleader. And Alex Boyd? Out of the blue, all of a sudden, he seems happier, less introverted. You're someone people feel secure with, someone they want to confide in."

"Everyone needs someone they can talk to. I just happen to be that someone. Nothing more."

"You truly believe that?"

"I do."

"I don't. I think you have a remarkable gift of understanding. I need someone who will understand, someone who won't pass judgment. I..." she stopped and pressed her lips together to keep from crying. "I'm sorry."

"It's all right. Just tell me."

"I can't discuss it here on school grounds. I could lose my job if someone overheard. There's a park a couple blocks from here. Would you be willing to meet me there today after school? Just for a half hour or so."

"Of course."

The park was empty of people. Outside, it was overcast and cold, but no snow was falling. The little snow that had fallen was jagged and stained with dirt.

Ms. Gavin was already at the park when I arrived. She was standing next to a tree, smoking a cigarette. I found that disappointing. Surely, she must have known that she was not only polluting her body but the air as well.

She smiled weakly when she saw me, dropped her cigarette on the ground and crushed it with her shoe.

"I didn't know you smoked," I said after I joined her.

"I don't usually, except when I'm nervous."

"Why are you nervous?"

"I don't know, being here in the park with a student seems almost indecent."

"Then don't think of me as a student. Think of me as a friend."

"How did you get to be so grown up?"

"I'd prefer not to talk about me, Ms. Gavin. Let's talk about you. Something bad has happened in your life. What is it?"

"Can we sit?"

"Of course."

She started to walk toward a metal bench by the swings. I bent over and picked up her cigarette butt. Most smokers, I found, viewed their cigarette butts as acceptable litter. I didn't see a waste can, so I slipped the butt into my pocket to discard it later.

She brushed off the seat of the bench with some tissue she had in her purse. We both sat at the same time.

I waited for her to begin.

Her eyes were cast upward when she did so. "Have you ever flown, Owen?"

"I have not."

"I have. Many times. If you don't get a cabin full of noisy children, it's very peaceful. Very soothing. At least I think so. I love to fly. Michelle didn't. Flying terrified her."

"Michelle?"

She lowered her eyes and cleared her throat. "She was my... girlfriend."

"Are you talking one word or two?"

She looked at me, puzzled.

"Two words mean she is a girl who was a friend," I explained. "One word means she is a girl who was more than a friend."

She hesitated. "One word." Her face was already pink from the cold, but it became more so.

"Okay. Why do you use the word *was*? Is she no longer in your life?"

"She was killed."

"I'm sorry. May I ask how?"

"She was decapitated," she answered categorically. "Her legs were cut off too. And one arm. If that hadn't killed her, the fire would have. Every part of her was burned." Her gaze was fixed on the swings.

I couldn't help but swallow at her words. My body went numb.

"How did it happen?" I managed to ask.

"Remember the plane that went down in Pennsylvania the first part of last month?"

"I do. Something to do with the rudder. The plane nosedived into a hillside."

"Michelle was on that plane."

"Who in his right mind would tell you how she died?"

"I wanted to know. I forgot who it was I asked to find out for me. I wanted to know if she suffered. She didn't, physically. She was torn apart on impact. Everyone was. But for the thirty seconds the plane was falling, she was in terror. They all were. It's those thirty seconds I can't get out of my head. Oh, Owen, she must have been so scared." She started to weep. "I'm sorry for getting so emotional."

"Don't apologize," I said, resting my hand on her arm.

She wiped her eyes with the back of her hand. "They say bad things come in threes. Whoever said that sure knew what they were talking about. Michelle and I had just broken up; then her brother passed away from cancer—that's why she was on that plane; she was flying back for the funeral—and then Michelle herself died."

"Why did the two of you break up?"

"Why aren't you asking me why I was romantically involved with a woman? That's what anyone else would ask."

"Because it is not relevant to the conversation. Only your feelings are."

"And if it was relevant, what would your feelings be?"

"On homosexual inclinations or homosexual acts?"

"Inclinations. The second can't occur without the first."

"I am learning, and am inclined to believe, that our sexual direction—like all our other traits, be they good or bad—is formed in utero. What we *are* is out of our control. It is only in what we *do* that we have choices."

"So you think people are born homosexual?"

"I do."

"That must mean you don't think it's wrong."

"Yes and no. I think that homosexual predilection occurs because of flawed genetics, like extreme aggression or warrior behavior. The partiality to one's own sex forms during gestation and therefore cannot be defined as wrong. It is not a choice. It is there from the beginning. I've read too many testimonials from homosexuals who state that the nascence of their affinity for their own sex was early on. Their appetition for and their bias toward their own sex is a part of their nature; it is natural for them to have those feelings. However, putting action to those feelings is *not* natural. The reproductive organs on men and women are designed to interface; it is natural for them to join. A male inside another male is *not* natural. Believe me."

"So in your eyes, I'm unnatural?" There was a thin skin of anger on her words.

"Your actions are—you and your feelings are not. Your feelings are very natural, regardless of the situation that produced them. You are in great distress because you have lost someone you cared about, and *that* is what is important. And that's *all* that's important."

"I think you would have liked Michelle. I know she would have liked you."

"Why did you two break up?"

"I broke up with her."

"Why?"

"I'm not gay all the way."

"You are bisexual?"

"Yes. I like men...but Michelle gave me what men can't."

"And what is that?"

"The only word that I can think of is...freedom. When I'm with a man, I feel I have to perform, like an animal. I feel I have to look a certain way, behave a certain way, think a certain way, feel a certain way. I can't be emotional around men because men hate that. They don't know how to handle it. They think if I start to cry, I won't stop. They think I'll crumble and fall apart. Men think they have to immediately fix everything. They don't understand that sometimes things can't be fixed, and all you can do is cry. When I was with Michelle, I could weep, and she'd let me because she understood that sometimes you've just got to let it out."

"Yes, men do tend to dash to their mental tool belts as soon as they discover a problem."

"She was such an amazing woman. I used to love to lay my head between her breasts. She'd stroke my hair and hum softly. I'd feel absolute peace then. She made me feel secure, like my mother used to. I'd lie in my mother's arms with my head against her chest, and she'd caress my hair. I'd always fall asleep when she did that.

"When Michelle and I were intimate, it was always gentle and kind. Men don't want that. They like sex rough, and I don't." Her face suddenly turned deep red. "I'm so sorry. I should not be talking like this, especially to a student. It's inappropriate and wrong. Please forgive me." She got up to leave.

I gently took hold of her arm. "It's all right, Ms. Gavin. Really. Remember, this is the seventies—teenagers know more about sex than most adults. Kids my age talk about sex the way chefs talk about cooking."

She sat back down.

I removed my hand.

Her eyes turned glassy. "I don't know how I'm going to live without her."

"You obviously thought you could at one time since you dissolved the relationship. Why is now any different?"

"Because she's gone, forever. Even if you know you shouldn't be with someone, there's a part of you that still wants to. There's always that hope that maybe things will work out, whatever they are, and you'll get back together. If the other person dies, that hope dies too."

"Why did you feel you shouldn't be with Michelle?"

"You ever have two opposing things going on inside you at the same time?"

"Constantly."

"I guess I'm both a daughter of Sappho and a niece of tradition. It angered me when you said that homosexual acts are unnatural. I felt anger because you were right, and you called me on it. People don't like it when their wrongs are pointed out to them. I know that living a homosexual lifestyle is unnatural. I know the school board thinks so too. That's why I wanted us to meet here. If they ever found out I was involved with another woman, I'd be terminated immediately."

"So you ended the relationship with Michelle because of fear and guilt."

"Yes. The whole time we were together I knew we shouldn't be doing what we were doing."

"Did you tell her your feelings?"

"Yes."

"How did she respond?"

"She was very kind, very sympathetic. She understood exactly what I was feeling." She sighed heavily, as if she were trying to exhale her pain along with her breath. "I miss her so much, Owen. When she held me, I felt she was holding *me* and not just holding my body so she could feel my breasts. That's what men do."

"Not *all* men do that, Ms. Gavin."

"Yeah, they do."

"So why do you say you like men when you *obviously* don't?"

"I like their bodies. I just don't like the rest of them. Men only think of themselves and nothing else. How's that for being open?"

"It's honest. It's wrong, but it's honest. Men can be very tender and compassionate and selfless. Men can give with no hidden motives or selfishness attached whatsoever."

"Maybe you're right. I mean, look at you—you're here talking with me and you have nothing to gain from it. But then, you're not a man yet either, even if you have the maturity and intelligence of one. It just seems that goodness comes more naturally to women than it does to men."

"I suppose we all look at people through the lens of our past."

"I know what Michelle and I were doing was wrong, but I wish I hadn't let her go. I wish I could have just one more hour with her. Just one. She was so good to me. Her face would light up every time she saw me. I mean, she would glow. No man ever smiled at me the way she did. She would give me this look when I was talking, and I knew she was truly listening. She loved me so deeply and completely, and I threw it all away. Maybe if I hadn't, she'd be alive today."

"She didn't board that plane because of *you*."

"Did I tell you she had a daughter?"

"No."

"Her name is Jacinta. She prefers to be called JC. She stayed with us for a week last summer. She lives with her father in Oregon. She was fourteen at the time; she just turned fifteen in October. Like you, she's very grown up. She's an amazing child, and incredibly sweet. And artistic! She can draw anything. She's especially adept at drawing animals. She gives them these adorable faces. She was terribly shy when we first met, but she warmed up to me very quickly. The week she was there was one of the happiest in my life. Every day the three of us would take a long drive somewhere, usually in the mountains. At night, we'd have candlelit dinners in the dining room. Afterward, we'd take long, leisurely walks around the neighborhood. Her last day with us she gave me a present. It was a drawing she had done for me. It was a Chihuahua. She knew how much I love Chihuahuas. I bawled like a baby when she gave it to me. It was the first time in my whole life

I felt like I had a complete family." She put her hands over her face and started to cry.

I found myself becoming emotional as well. I knew all too well what it was like to want a family; and I knew all too well what it was like to lose one.

Her sobs subsided, and she wiped her eyes with the tissue she had wiped off the bench with. She looked around. "It's getting late. Your mother must be wondering where you are." She stood up.

"No, she is not," I corrected, standing too. "Ms. Gavin, I know you don't think that this will ever happen, but there will come a time, perhaps soon, when this loss of yours will cease to be your enemy. The memory of Sus—I'm sorry—Michelle will, in time, lose its villainy. Pleasant reminisces will replace unpleasant ones; new memories will take the place of old. Your memory of Michelle will still be there, but its dark eyes will not stare down at you anymore. Just hold on, Ms. Gavin. Remember, sadness is always homeless: it never stays in one place for very long."

She took my hands. "Thank you for that, Owen. And thank you for listening to me. Just being able to tell somebody has helped me tremendously. I mean that. Will you do me a favor?"

"What's that?"

"Please don't ever change. Grow into the man you are right now. The world needs them. It really does."

She put her arms out and embraced me. She withdrew her arms, smiled and walked back toward the school.

I awoke the next morning feeling more saturnine than I already was. I felt I had fallen through a narrow cavern and was lying on a mound of hard rock, surrounded by pitch blackness. The time spent with Ms. Gavin made me feel alone and cut off and burdened with the darkness of her loss.

There was electricity in the air at school. Christmas day was only five days away, and Christmas vacation was due to begin in only one. Spirits were high, and moods were good.

Each morning, I was greeted with a note from Roxanne. She always arrived at school before me and she would leave some friendly—and romantic—message in my locker. She had my combination, and I had hers. With the notes, she would leave some kind of treat: usually fruit, but occasionally she would surprise me with a candy bar or bottle of Pepsi. On this morning, however, there was nothing. I wondered if she was out sick. I asked a couple of passersby if they had seen her; one said he had. Very peculiar. I didn't have time to search for her; I had to get to homeroom. I would find her later.

After homeroom, I began my search for Roxanne. She was like a missing person who wasn't missing. She was somewhere within the school—I just couldn't find her. I told myself not to worry: our paths had to cross eventually.

Around ten, I went to the cafeteria. Mark and Christopher were there. They were laughing and playfully hitting each other. On the table in front of them was a Nikon SLR. Christopher had joined the yearbook club and was their best lensman. He and his camera went everywhere together. Since joining the club, his shyness and smoldering choler had completely vanished. His camera gave him self-confidence and a measure of authority and worth.

I went over to them and asked if they had seen Roxanne.

"I haven't seen Roxanne since yesterday," Mark answered.

"M-M-Me neither," Christopher contributed.

"Hey, Owen, guess what I found in my locker this morning?" Mark asked excitedly.

"What's that?"

"Two hundred bucks! Can you believe it! I know it was for me 'cause it was stuffed in a tiny envelope with my name on it."

"I-I-I think s-s-some r-rich girl's g-g-got the hots for him," Christopher speculated. "I th-th-think it's the s-s-same chick that keeps p-p-putting tw-tw-tw-tw-twenty bucks in his locker every Monday for lunches. Wish I could g-g-g-get a girlfriend like that."

"Just grow some good looks like me and you will," Mark laughed. He then turned serious. "Hey, Owen, do you think maybe some girl really likes me?" There was almost an urgency in his voice.

Mark was desperate for a girl, any girl, to like him. He was so starved for love I felt genuine pity for him.

"I think whoever gave you the money, Mark, truly cares about you," I said. "I know you want it to be a girl, but maybe it's just someone who is looking out for you."

He appeared crestfallen at my words.

"You're only fourteen, Mark," I consoled, "there will be many girls in your life. Trust me."

He smiled.

"Until then, what are you going to do with your holiday windfall?" I asked.

"I don't know. It's a lot of money. What do ya think? Got any ideas?"

"A few," I said.

"Well, let's run 'em up the flagpole and see if anyone salutes 'em."

Christopher laughed heartily at Marks's folksy saw. "I got t-t-t-to remember that one!"

"My dad used to say it," Mark shared.

"S-S-S-So wh-wh-wh-wh-what do you think he should do with it, Owen?" Christopher asked.

Looking at Mark, I said, "It is only a suggestion, but I think you should share your bounty. Maybe you should spend fifty on you, fifty on your brother, and the rest on your mother. Something tells me few packages will bear her name this year.

"And let us not forget Christopher. He is your best friend. I think you should buy him lunch today as a Christmas present."

"Hey, yeah!" the next Ansel Adams agreed eagerly.

"Why not?" Mark approved, smiling. "No wonder everyone goes to you with their problems."

"Hey, Owen," Christopher cut in, "there's Roxanne." He was looking toward the north entrance.

I darted my head in that direction. I smiled.

Roxanne saw me…but she did not return the smile. In fact, she did just the reverse: her lips tightened, and she turned around and went out the doors she had just come through.

"Uh-oh!" Mark said. *"Someone's in the doghouse."*

I raced after Roxanne.

I caught up with her just as she was transecting the stairwell landing between the basement and ground floor. She wouldn't stop walking. I tried to stop her by reaching for her hand. She jerked her hand away and continued up the stairs.

"Roxanne, what is the matter?" I asked desperately.

She stopped abruptly in the foyer and swung around. "I don't want to date you anymore, Owen. I don't want to talk to you anymore. I don't want to see you anymore. We're through!"

Stunned and shocked, I asked, "Why?"

"I was up all night because of you! I knew something like this would happen. I just knew it! I knew when you started that counseling thing something bad would happen. I knew it! Why did you have to do this to us!"

Suddenly, I was in a cyclone of confusion and terror. "What are you talking about?"

"Oh, stop playing stupid! You don't do it well!"

"Roxanne, what did I do?" I was on the verge of tears.

"If you're going to cry, don't look to me to comfort you. Why don't you go to Ms. Gavin—I'm sure she'll be more than happy to blot your tears away."

"Is that what this is about? You saw me talking with Ms. Gavin and now you think something's going on between us? You can't be serious!"

"You weren't just talking with her—you were *holding* her! Shannon saw you and her in the park yesterday, holding hands and then holding each other. She's a teacher, Owen! She's old enough to be your mother! That's twisted and sick! And what kind of teacher goes after a fourteen-year-old boy! That's perverted! You're *both* perverted! Who knows how many other boys she's gone after! I've already talked to Mr. Heald. He says he's going to do something about it."

In an instant, the cyclone of terror was blown away by a sirocco of anger. "You did what?"

"You heard me. I hope she gets fired! She *should* get fired!"

At that moment, I didn't know Roxanne, and I didn't want to know her. This was a side I never knew she possessed. Not only was she perniciously jealous, she was poisonously vindictive.

I stepped closer to Roxanne. She drew back slightly. She knew I was furious.

"Yes, Roxanne, we *are* through," I uttered calmly. "I don't want, need or desire someone like *you* in my life. For your information—"

Just then, the doors to the foyer opened. Ms. Gavin walked through them. Her coat was over her shoulders, and her purse was in her hand. Her eyes were red, and her face was wet. She had been crying.

I went over to her. "What happened?" I asked.

"I've been let go," she answered, her voice breaking. "I guess we should have met in the school after all. I'll see you around, Owen." She walked out of the school, out into nothing. She had no one, absolutely no one.

I spun around toward Roxanne.

Her face showed a smile of triumph.

I walked over to her. "Nice going."

"She goes after kids! She *should* be gone!"

"Not everyone is like your damn neighbor, Roxanne! Not every adult who touches a child is a pedophile! For your information—not that it's any of your or Shannon's business—Ms. Gavin and I were at the park yesterday because she wanted to talk with me about a death in her life. Someone she was very close to was killed in a plane crash last month. The person she was close to was cut into pieces in that crash. She didn't know who else to talk to about it. The hand-holding and embracing Shannon witnessed was friendly appreciation—not romantic delectation!"

Roxanne's face fell. The triumphant pink in her countenance drained away. Tears swelled in her eyes. "I..."

"Save it! You are some piece of work, Roxanne! I can't believe I ever got close to a person like you. I'm going to Mr. Heald now to see if I can unscramble this rotten egg you've thrown into the frying pan!

"I meant what I said, Roxanne—we are through. Heaven help the next boy you get involved with. I'll be sure to go to him and tell him what kind of girl you are, just like you went to Mr. Heald today and told him what kind of woman Ms. Gavin is.

"*You* are the twisted one, Roxanne—no one else."

As I walked away, I heard her start to cry.

# CHAPTER 9

## *Rain and Rainbows*

*"The first breath is the beginning of death."*

THOMAS FULLER

Her scream was like that of two cars colliding: piercing, jarring, frightening.

I jolted with fright and fled back into the hallway. I heard running. From around a corner, two nurses—one young, one old—appeared and ran in my direction.

The younger nurse raced into Mrs. Crowley's room while the older stopped outside it, in front of me.

"Who are you?" the mature nurse asked me bitingly. She was a rangy, leathery-skinned woman with cold, stygian eyes. The image of a cracked, sinister-faced doll entered my mind as I looked at her.

"I'm Owen, her son."

"Mrs. Crowley has no son. She has no family."

"I'm her adopted son."

"What do you want with her?"

"Nothing. I just wanted to visit."

"Why have I never seen you before?"

"Mrs. Crowley and I have not been close for some time."

"*Mrs. Crowley?* Why do you call her that if she's your mother?"

"What's wrong with her? Why doesn't she recognize me?"

"She has dementia. The only people she recognizes are the staff, and sometimes not even them. You scared her. Do you know what dementia is?"

"Of course I know. How long has she had it?"

"For some time. Occasionally, she has a clear day, but most are murky and foggy. Why are you here all of a sudden?"

"It's Christmas Eve—I thought I'd stop by."

"Well, you're too late. The woman you knew is gone."

"Does she have long to live?"

"Hard to say. It's different for everyone. She may have a couple more years; she may have many. Like I said, it's hard to say." Her eyes narrowed. "You don't seem too shook up about it."

I gifted her a hard glare. "What I feel or don't feel for Mrs. Crowley is my own affair, not yours!"

Her rawhide face reddened. "I want you to leave, sir. *Now!*"

"I've got every right to be here!"

"Not if you're upsetting our patients, you don't!"

"I'm not—"

"Don't make me call Security."

The younger nurse came out into the hall. "Sir, I think she's right. Your mother doesn't recognize you, and your presence is only frightening her. Why don't you wait a couple of days and then call us and let us know when you would like to visit again. We can talk to your mother and let her know she will be receiving a visitor. That way, she'll be prepared, and she won't be afraid when she sees you."

She was right.

I nodded and, without an adieu, headed back to the elevator.

Late afternoon was upon me when I walked out of Hill Haven Care Center. Though the air was cold, and the distance great, I decided to walk home. I wanted to be alone. The company of anyone, particularly a detached and unfriendly cab driver, I knew, would only impel my spirit deeper into desolation.

I passed hundreds of houses and crossed innumerable streets during my walk. My eyes saw them all, but my mind saw none of them. It was manacled to another time. I was a young boy again, wrapped in the love of Mrs. Crowley. How I wished to go back to that time. I should have forgiven her secrecy. Since my talk with Dana, I realized how wrong I had been wrong to reject Mrs. Crowley. I should have gone to her years ago when I discovered the truth; I should have let her present *her* side of the situation. I should have believed she tried to do her best. I should have embraced her like she so desperately wanted to embrace me. So many shoulds. My chance for a second life with her was gone. I willingly let it fly away. I watched it disappear over the horizon without regret or apology. "*Chances are not limitless, Robin—once they are gone, they are gone forever.*" I had said those words months earlier. Why was I so quick to give advice, but so indisposed to take it?

I thought my days of loneliness and separateness were far behind me. They were not. They had returned…like an unholy habit thought to be dead, buried, and long forgotten.

Not until I reached my own neighborhood, many hours later, did my mind actually see the houses. Most were bejeweled with vibrantly colored Christmas lights. Some had plastic Santa Clauses and plastic snowmen and plastic lampposts and plastic candles on their front lawns. Not a house was dark. All were occupied with, no doubt, happy and merry families. I wondered what Roxanne and her family were doing that Christmas Eve night. Were they in high spirits, or were they in low despair? Were their hearts heavy that Mrs. Solleveld was not there with them? Probably the latter, for holidays are usually more of a boil than a blessing for those who have suffered loss.

Sitting on the top shelf of my bedroom closet were my Christmas gifts to Roxanne and her family. Lying in a white, velveteen box was a Figaro-styled silver necklace mated to a hexagonal pendant of sapphires and diamonds. Roxanne loved sapphires. Keeping company with the necklace was a thin, rectangular box. In it lay a pink satin tie with a gold-plated tie bar. Mr. Solleveld had a passion for pink, and I understood why: it accentuated his already abundant share of masculinity. Abreast of the tie box was a Lite-Brite and Spirograph, both still in their shopping bags. Walter adored drawing. In front of them all was a bag of Milk-Bones and some small stuffed animals for Kenny. I didn't know what to do with the gifts. I didn't have the heart to return them, nor did I have the heart to give them to Roxanne and her family. At some point, I would probably just take them into the basement and hide them in a dark corner.

Much as I wanted her to, Roxanne would not vacate my mind. Wherever I went, she went. In my waking hours, she was there; in my sleeping hours, she was there. I missed her, and I hated missing her. I loved her, and I hated loving her. If character could be seen, like bands of stratum below the Earth's soil, Roxanne's would show many Samaritan layers, but it would show numerous Cimmerian layers as well, dark laminas of odious jealousy and appalling cruelty. I still loved Roxanne, but I wanted—and needed—to let the love die. Once she had been a flame that ravished my heart; now she was a fire that only ravaged it.

Though very tired, I didn't want to go home. I simply wanted to sit somewhere and close my eyes. I decided to walk to the park that was close to my school. There, I could rest on one of its swings.

Once at the park, I noticed something that had not been with me during my walk home: quiet. Undeniably, it was one of the most hectic nights of the year, and yet, I heard nothing: no cars, no sirens, no parties, no dogs, no passersby. Just quiet. If I had not been in such a deep trench of depression, the serenity would have been magical.

Sitting on one of the rubber, U-shaped swings in the park, I tilted my head back and remembered the gentle way Mr. Crowley used to push me on the swing in our backyard. He gave me such priceless and peerless memories. And how did I repay him for those memories? I repaid him by rejecting the only woman he ever loved. I believed that life went beyond death, but I did not side with the idea that a soul can see the deeds and doings of those he knew in his former existence. For this, I was immensely grateful. It would have crushed Mr. Crowley to see how callously I had treated his cherished wife.

I started to cry for all that I had let go and for all that I would never have again.

Then something dissevered me from my torment. A sound. A strange sound, out of place, frail. I wiped my eyes to clear them and looked around the park.

The sound, intermittent and weak, came from a congregation of pines a few yards from me. Cautiously and carefully, I stepped over to the trees. Only faint spears of light from nearby street lights aided me in finding the source of the noise. What I saw made my dilated pupils fill with tears once more. A gray kitten, small and shivering, was crouched next to the trunk of one of the trees. It looked up at me with frightened eyes and gave me a weak and fragile cry. A cry of my own left my lips. I knew its terror, its hope for mercy, its want for safety, and its need for warmth. I knew its little body could not hold out much longer in the penetrating cold. So as not to scare the little animal away, I slowly went to my knees and held out my hand. It folded itself into a ball. Was that its way of protecting itself, or was it telling me that it wanted me to take it away from that scary place?

I carefully slid my hand under its cold body and picked it up. Immediately, it pawed to get inside my coat. Once it was inside, I petted it to make it feel warm and safe. Soon, its shivering gave way to purring.

I wasn't fond of cats, but I did like kittens. Cats couldn't be trusted: they could lick a person's hand one minute and then draw blood from it the next. They were truly bipolar and psychopathic creatures. Kittens, on the other hand, at least from what I had seen, were not. They were truly linear animals: if not injured or scared, they were always playful, always friendly.

While petting the kitten, I felt a fabric collar around its neck. Then I felt a flat, metal disk hanging from the bottom of the collar: an ID tag. I walked over to one of the sodium arc lights by the street and stood under it. Without removing the kitten from inside my coat, I looked closely at the tag. The animal's name was Mittens. Doubtless, it was named that for his front paws, which were bright white. Thankfully, but not surprisingly, the kitten's owner lived only a few blocks from the park.

It took only minutes to reach the owner's home. I was grateful for the proximity, for it had started to snow.

The home was a wide, two-story, Mission-styled structure with salmon stucco that occupied a corner lot of a cul-de-sac. Behind every window there was light. I had the sad feeling that everyone in the home was still searching for their lost, little feline.

I rang the bell. The door sprang open, almost angrily. A moderately overweight, older woman with a worry-laden face was now standing in front of me.

"I believe this little one belongs to you," I said, handing the kitten to her.

The woman didn't take the kitten; instead, she put her face in her hands and began to weep.

A man came to the door. Seeing the cat, he, too, became emotional.

A boy of about twelve or thirteen joined the group. "Hey, look at that!" he exclaimed. "Cats really do have nine lives!" He took the kitten from my hands and kissed it. "Hey, Megan!" the boy shouted. "Come here! We got a surprise for you!"

Quick to join the crowd at the door was a girl of about seven or eight with a pageboy haircut. I presumed this was Megan. Her eyes widened, and her mouth flew open when she saw her little animal. She carefully took the kitten from her brother, buried her face into its side and began to cry. The man, presumably the father, took the kitten and the girl fell into the woman's arms and continued to weep.

"What's going on?" an older girl asked from behind the gathering at the door.

The man stood back so the girl could join the reunion.

I knew the girl; I didn't know her name, but I knew her face. She went to Moran. She was an upperclassman.

"Kylie, this kind gentleman found Mittens," the woman said.

The girl briefly glanced at the kitten, smiled, and then turned her attention to me.

"Where did you find him?" the woman asked.

"He was under a tree in the park by the school," I said.

"Lucky for all of us you were there," she returned.

"He apparently has an adventuresome spirit," I noted. "I'd keep a close watch on him so he doesn't end up there again." I smiled and reached out and petted the kitten good-bye. "I'll leave you to your evening. Enjoy your holiday."

"Can we pay you for bringing him back?" the man offered.

"Of course not," I answered.

"Maybe Owen would like to come in and have some eggnog before he goes home," the older girl proposed.

All eyes turned to her.

"Do you know this man, angel?" the father asked haltingly, suspiciously.

"Relax, Dad, he goes to my school," she said with exasperation. "His name is Owen Crowley."

None of them was as shocked as I. How did she know my name?

Now all eyes turned to me.

"*You're* a student?" the father asked.

"I am, sir."

"What grade?"

"Ninth."

His eyebrows rose. "I've heard of kids looking older than their age, but you take home the trophy, kid! Were you, ah…"

"Held back?"

He nodded awkwardly.

"Dad!" the older girl cried. "Stop it! Owen just saved our Christmas, and you're interrogating him like he's a criminal! Just so you know, Owen is a genius! He's got an IQ higher than our mortgage payment. I think you owe him an apology."

"I'm sorry, son. I'm sorry, angel—I was just curious."

"It's quite all right," I assuaged, giving them all a smile. "I get it frequently. I do look much older than I am. It's a curse, really. And I'm afraid it's a curse that will keep on giving. When I'm twenty, I'll probably look eighty."

The family laughed.

"Would you like to join us for some eggnog?" the woman solicited. "We'd love to have you, if you have the time. It's the least we can do."

"That would be nice," I told her.

It was like stepping into a Viggo Johansen painting. The living room and dining room were radiant with candlelight. The air appeared almost misty, diffused. Scalloped ponderosa pine boughs climbed the wrought-iron railing leading to the second floor; red miniature lights were nesting within the boughs. Red garlands, red table runners, red stockings, red poinsettias, red nutcrackers, red spiral candles—all things holiday red—abounded in the two rooms. The Christmas tree, a nearly perfect conical Douglas fir, stood next to the fireplace. The tree was the kind found only in the imagination. Hanging in its perfect branches were countless antique glass ornaments, each brought to life by hundreds of multicolored miniature lights. A length of glimmering tinsel hung from each needle. It must have taken as many hours as there were pieces of tinsel to hang them all. Seen from afar, they gave the tree a starry coat of magic.

The warmth of the room, the amazing display of lights, the aroma from the tree, the grand spray of pine branches on the mantle above the ember-filled fireplace, and the kindness of the family made me realize how much I never had in life. It made me angry for all that I had been denied, and all that I had let slip away.

Someone touched my arm as I was gazing at the tree.

I turned.

Kylie was standing next to my side. "Are you all right?"

Delicate art. That was the vignette that came to my mind when I looked into her eyes. Effortlessly, her face could have been the oils on a George Romney canvas. It was a countenance that was graceful and subtle, much like her body. Her voice was neither daring nor dainty; it was at once confident and modest.

"I'm fine," I answered her. "Thank you for asking."

"I heard about you and Roxanne," she said. "I'm sorry."

Stunned at her words, I said, "News travels quickly."

"It depends on the news."

"Yes, I dare say you're right. Who told you?"

"I heard some girls talking about it in the lunchroom."

"Did they say why we broke up?"

"No, they just briefly mentioned it. They were more interested in talking about Ms. Gavin. She was let go. But nobody knows why. I feel bad for her. She was a great teacher."

"You needn't worry. I was able to get Mr. Heald to rescind the termination."

"Really?"

"Here's your eggnog," Kylie's mother said from behind me.

In her hands was an engraved silver platter. On it were six gold-rimmed brandy glasses, each generous with eggnog and dusted with cinnamon. She held out the platter, and I carefully took one of the glasses. She extended the salver to the others in the family.

The father held up his glass. "To Mittens and the good Samaritan who found him."

"I second that," Kylie echoed.

Each took a drink from his glass.

"Tell me, Owen, why were you in the park on Christmas Eve?" the father asked innocently. "I would think you'd want to be at home with your family."

I took another swallow of eggnog and looked at the tree. "Your home is magnificent. Everyone should have this. Or at least a taste of it anyway."

Returning my attention to them, I said, "I should be going. Thank you for your hospitality. I'll see myself out."

Amid thick quietness, I placed the glass back on the freshly polished silver tray and left the home.

I was crossing the sidewalk when I heard my name called.

Kylie was by my side before I even started to turn.

"Did we hurt your feelings?" she asked, almost beside herself.

"Not at all. I'm just feeling a little melancholy today."

"I'm sorry. Is there anything I can do?"

"No, but thank you for asking."

"Owen...before you go, can we talk for a second?"

"What about?"

She faltered for a moment, questioning herself if she should go any further. "You're probably going to think I'm crazy."

"I'm sure I won't."

"I don't think tonight was a coincidence. I think Mittens getting out and then getting lost and then getting found by you didn't happen by chance. I think it was meant to be."

"I don't doubt your sincerity, Kylie, but I doubt it was fate. All I did was find your cat."

"It's not Mittens I'm talking about." She bit her lower lip, as if deliberating again if she should speak. "I mean, I think—" she stopped abruptly. Then she continued. "Do you remember Claire Terashima?"

"The girl who lost her sister?"

"Right. She's my best friend. When her little sister was accidentally run over, I felt like it was my little sister who had been run over. Do you remember what you said to Claire?"

"I don't recall saying much."

"And that was the beauty of it. You said very little. You just let her talk. You didn't say stupid stuff like, '*She's in a better place*,' or '*She's been spared the pain of growing old*,' or any of the other asinine things people say when someone dies. I hate it when people say things like that when somebody dies. It's cruel."

"How is it cruel?"

"Because it only makes things worse. It tells the person who's grieving that they can't grieve because there's a higher purpose. People think they can heal a broken heart with mere words. Words *never* heal a broken heart."

"It depends on the situation, Kylie. Sometimes words *do* heal a broken heart."

"But many times they don't. And you knew that with Claire. She was so impressed with your willingness to listen. She said just being able to cry and talk to someone helped her tremendously. Since then, I have been kind of...watching you. You're not like any of the other kids at school."

"Yes, so I've been informed."

"I didn't mean that as a put-down. I meant that you're an exception. An exceptional exception." She smiled. "You have it all. You even have the prettiest girl in school."

"*Had* the prettiest girl."

"I'm sorry, *had*. What I'm trying to say is...I think you're one incredible boy. It's no wonder I feel the way I do."

"*Feel?*"

She wavered for many seconds. "I'm in love with you."

Her electric-blue eyes did not leave mine; they stayed fixed, as if she were forcing them not to move.

I was suddenly aboard the *SS Poseidon*, sans the sea. I wasn't expecting the declaration; it threw me upside down, emotionally and mentally. I didn't know what to say or do. Beyond Roxanne, no girl had ever told me she loved me.

"I was never going to tell you," she admitted. "This coming spring when I graduated, I was going to go on to college, and you never would have known. But then you broke up with Roxanne, we lost Mittens, you found Mittens, and then you show up at my door with him. I mean, if that's not fate, what is? I know you're grieving for Roxanne. Who wouldn't be? But I want you to know that I'm here. If you want someone in your life somewhere down the road, I'd love to be that someone."

"I don't know what to say, Kylie. I'm very confused at the moment. I loved Roxanne; I still do. But I know it's over. She has a side I can't abide."

"Owen, what happened to you that made you the way you are?"

"What do you mean?"

"I mean, how did you skip boyhood and go directly to manhood?"

"I don't know, luck maybe, or bad luck, depending on how you look at it."

"Good luck for others, but sad luck for you, I'll bet."

I marveled at her sensitivity. "Maturity seems to have smiled upon you as well."

"Well, I am almost eighteen."

"I'm not speaking of chronological age. You're mature emotionally, psychologically. You are self-assurance sewn onto innocence. Very rare. And yet...there are those who would consider your interest in me *far* from innocent. An eighteen-year-old girl pursuing a fourteen-year-old boy. Not quite conduct becoming an *angel*."

"I won't be eighteen for another three months."

"There are none your age who bring your passions to a boil?"

"If by that you mean, are there any boys in my class whom I'm attracted to?—no, there aren't. Owen, I don't want this to be uncomfortable for either of us. I don't want either of us to write a check we can't pay for. I only wanted you to know how I feel. I don't want to pressure you. It's completely up to you if you want to go any further. If you don't, I'll understand. We'll say good-bye tonight, and we'll just be two people who pass each other in the hallways at school."

I contemplated her. Her genuine sweetness was very pulling.

"Rather than good-bye," I said, "how about *good night*?"

She smiled.

My holiday vacation was like prison time: long and unforgiving. I didn't know how much I needed and depended on the people in my school until I was forced to be away from them. I actually missed them, a feeling I never thought I would have.

Amid the faces I missed was one that I should not have missed at all, for it was one nearly foreign to me, yet it was there...quiet, distant, like a safe nightlight in a dark room. Kylie.

I felt drawn to her. But just as keenly, I felt guilty for that attraction. A fortnight had not passed, and I was already roused by another girl. Could it be that I was never really in love with Roxanne? Perhaps I was incapable of feeling love. Or perhaps I was just superficial. Nick told me he was shallow. I told him he wasn't. Maybe the real shallow one was *me*.

The mother answered the door. Her face brightened at the sight of me.

"Well, hello!" she said, smiling largely. "We were hoping we'd see you again."

"Your pardon for coming unannounced," I said. "Shamefully, I do not know your last name, so I was not able to consult the telephone directory for your number."

"Please, don't apologize. We're delighted to have you. By the way, it's Ulrich. That's our last name. I'm Eleanor." She held out her hand.

"It's a pleasure to meet you, Mrs. Ulrich," I came back, taking her hand.

"Who's that at the door, mother?" Mr. Ulrich asked from the living room.

"Mitten's guardian angel," she responded zestfully.

"Well, bless our souls!" he exclaimed. "What a surprise!" He appeared at the door wearing a wide smile. "Come on in, son! Come on in! Get in out of the cold."

Once I was inside, he asked, "Can I take your coat?"

"Thank you, sir," I said, handing him my jacket.

"You know, Kylie can't stop raving about you," he let me know happily. "She thinks you're the cat's pajamas...and then some!"

"Given my chance encounter with Mittens, the expression is aptly appropriate."

Kylie's parents looked at each other and chuckled.

The two were so homespun and natural they could easily have been ice-skating villagers on a Currier and Ives Christmas card.

Both had silver hair and were somewhat on the short and portly side. They looked more like grandparents than parents. Plainly, they started their family late in life.

"Owen!" someone cried out. Megan, the young girl who wept at Mittens' return, ran to me and put her arms around my waist. "Thank you again for saving my Mittens! He's in my room right now. I'll go get him!" She dashed off up the stairs.

"Boy, is it cold out there!" Kylie broadcasted spiritedly from the kitchen doorway, unwrapping a peach muffler from around her neck.

"Angel, you have a visitor," Mr. Ulrich told his daughter.

Kylie cast her eyes to the front door. Like her sister's on Christmas Eve night when she saw Mittens in her brother's arms, Kylie's eyes ballooned when she saw me, and her lips plumed into a huge smile.

"Owen!" she said joyfully and ran over to me. She embraced me and kissed my cheek.

The affection brought color to my face.

"We were just about ready to have brunch," Mrs. Ulrich said. "Will you join us?"

"I'm not sure that would be proper," I posited. "I am empty-handed— it is a shameful solecism in manners to come to a table without a contribution to the meal."

"Applesauce!" Mr. Ulrich benched my argument. "We don't stand on ceremony around here."

"Enough said," Mrs. Ulrich concluded. "Kylie, take your young man into the kitchen so he can wash his hands."

Kylie took me by the hand and led me into the kitchen.

Ceramic roosters, copper chickens, decorative crockery, red-brick wallpaper, needlepoint Scriptures, hardwood flooring, simmering cinnamon sticks, and ruffled curtains charmed and gladdened the hearts of all who entered the room. It was like stepping into a world people only wished for but never actually saw.

The meal began with everyone at the table saying a prayer. Mr. Ulrich opened with a prayer of gratitude. He gave thanks for the health of his body, the warmth of his home, the goodness of his meals, and the love of his family. Mrs. Ulrich said a prayer of supplication. She asked that all the cold, the hungry, and the sick in the world be shown mercy and kindness, just as she and her family had been shown kindness and mercy. Collin, the boy, asked that all the homeless animals in the world find warmth and care and love, for there were as many of them as there were discarded and unloved people. (This was a phenomenally mature prayer for a youth, I thought.) Megan, while holding her treasured pet in her lap, gave a short prayer of thanks that Mittens was found. Kylie also offered words of appreciation. She said she was grateful that I was with them at their table.

Mr. Ulrich asked if I would like to say a prayer. I declined. Though I had attended many Catholic Masses, I had never actually said a prayer of my own. If Kylie and her family knew this, I was certain they would have quickly shown me the door. Only birds of the same feather perch together.

Mr. Ulrich did not press the issue, nor did he make one at my declination. He simply smiled understandingly and told everyone to, "Dig in!"

Overlaid on a Colonial dining room table was a relucent red tablecloth edged with glittery, argent reindeer and vivid green holly. Laid out on this jubilant covering were serving platters stacked with scones, French toast, scrambled eggs, ham, and cinnamon rolls. Cut glass pitchers held orange juice, apple juice, and milk. A small teepee of candy canes was the centerpiece of the table. It was apparent that Kylie's parents had done some entertaining in their time.

"Daddy, why do candy canes have red stripes?" Megan asked, looking at the spire of candy canes in the middle of the table.

"That's a good question, honey," her father commended. "But unfortunately, I don't know the answer. I'll ask around, though. I'm sure someone at the office knows. If they don't know, I'll call the public library."

"I'll bet Owen knows," Kylie gushed proudly.

"Kylie, that's not nice," Mrs. Ulrich lightly rebuffed her daughter. "You're putting Owen on the spot."

Kylie blushed at her mother's discipline.

I smiled warmly at Kylie and winked at her. "Actually, Kylie is correct. I do know."

"*You do?*" Mrs. Ulrich asked, truly surprised.

"Well, there are various accounts of its genesis, and your spiritual tenets, I believe, will determine which one you embrace. I myself subscribe to the Christian version. It seems to be the most logical.

"You see, Megan," I said, turning to the young girl, "a long time ago, there was this confectioner, or candymaker, who wanted to share his faith in God, so he made a curled piece of candy called the candy cane. Turned right side up, the cane represents the staffs of the shepherds in the field who saw the star of Bethlehem. Turned upside down, it takes the shape of a J, which is representative of the J in Jesus. The white in the cane is symbolic of Jesus' virgin birth and His absolute sinlessness. The red stripes represent His scourging and shed blood. The candy is hard rather than soft to symbolize the firmness of God's promises and the solid foundation of His church. The peppermint refers to hyssop, which is an herb in the mint family. Hyssop, in the Old Testament, was used for ceremonial cleansing. And that, Megan, is why candy canes have red stripes. All in all, quite a candy, wouldn't you say?"

"Wow!" she marveled. "Where'd you learn all that stuff?"

"Different books."

"Told you he was a genius," Kylie proclaimed, smiling broadly.

"Your parents must be so proud," Mr. Ulrich inserted.

"Dad!" Kylie cried out. "I told you, Owen's parents passed away!"

Mr. Ulrich blushed. "Oh, please forgive me, Owen," he implored. "I completely forgot."

"It's all right," I mitigated. "They've been gone a long time."

How did she know my parents had died?

"May I ask you something personal, Owen?" Mrs. Ulrich said.

"Of course."

"Since you have no parents, who are you living with? Are you in foster care?"

"No, presently I am living in my adoptive mother's home."

"Oh, then you do have some family?"

"Not quite. My biological parents died when I was a small boy. My adoptive father passed away from cancer, and my adoptive mother is currently in a care facility."

"What kind of cancer did he have?"

"Lung. Tobacco people don't care who they kill or how many."

"No, they don't. Sadly, probity and profit have never been close bedfellows," Mr. Ulrich added.

"If your parents are gone, who's taking care of you?" Mrs. Ulrich asked. "You aren't living on your own, are you?"

"No, sadly, I am under the peppery aegis of our housekeeper."

"The two of you don't get along?"

"That's a gentle way of putting it."

"When did your adoptive father pass away?"

"Halloween, 1966."

"How long has your mother been away from home?"

"She went away shortly after my father died."

"So you've been without parents all these years? It's just been you and your housekeeper?"

"Yes, ma'am."

"It must be difficult living with someone you don't get along with."

"We've learned to keep a smart distance from one another."

"If she doesn't like you, who gives you Christmas presents?" Megan asked.

"The last time I was given a Christmas present, I believe I was about your age."

She looked heartbroken. "You mean, you wake up every Christmas morning and you don't have anything to open?"

"It sounds much worse than it is."

She got out of her chair and came over to me. She put her arms around me and hugged me tightly. She looked at me and kissed me on the cheek.

Her act of kindness took me by complete surprise. I couldn't talk.

I reached up and lightly touched her forehead and brushed a wisp of golden hair off her eyebrow. In my fourteen years, I thought I had felt every emotion imaginable. At that moment, looking into the eyes of that young girl, an utterly new emotion hung its hat in my heart: fatherly love. Since when does a fourteen-year-old boy have paternal feelings? Many teen boys had confided in me, but not one had revealed having had such feelings yet. I knew I was abnormal, but this seemed to be teetering on the cliff of bizarre.

"You seem to have made quite an impression on *both* of our daughters," Mrs. Ulrich commented amiably as Megan was walking back to her seat.

Clearing my throat, I said, "Yours is a truly gracious family. You remind me of my parents...my adoptive parents, that is."

"Owen, may I ask what your father did?" Mr. Ulrich asked. "Your adoptive father, I mean."

"He was an architect. He designed commercial buildings. He was exceptional at it too. He even won some awards. Commercial buildings, by nature, are not supposed to be artful, only functional. My father didn't see it that way. He patterned his style after William L. Pereira. William Pereira designed the Transamerica Pyramid in San Francisco. He even designed a high-rise here in Salt Lake: the Prudential Federal Savings tower in downtown. My father was a remarkable man. I knew it when he was alive, and the passing of years has made me realize it even more. You would have liked him."

"If he was anything like you, I'm sure we would have," Mr. Ulrich said.

"Actually, he is the impetus that brings me here today."

"Oh?"

"Last evening, I saw a trailer on television for a movie I know he would have wanted to see: *The Towering Inferno*. He loved skyscrapers—he even had his own designs. Since my father can't be here to see it, I think he'd want me to go. Kylie has been swimming in my mind since Christmas Eve, and I have wanted to come back, but I couldn't think of a good reason to without looking too eager. Then I saw the advertisement. I thought Kylie would like to go with me to the movie today. With your permission, of course."

"I'd love to go!" Kylie sounded. "Mom, Dad, is that okay?"

"It's okay with me if it's okay with your mother," Mr. Ulrich granted.

Mrs. Ulrich nodded without hesitation.

"You know, Owen," Mr. Ulrich went further, "we're kind of watchful over Kylie. I guess you could call us old-fashioned. We don't let her go out with just anyone. Kids these days move too fast and with the wrong people and then they get hurt. We don't want Kylie to be hurt. But you're different. You not only look well beyond your years, you act it. Kylie was right—you're a very unique young man."

"Kinsy Larramie, a little-known philosopher and poet, once wrote: *A window of stained glass is but a montage of bits of melted sand; nothing; it is only when the sun nuzzles it does it become a work of wonder.* I am but bits of melted sand, Mr. Ulrich—it is your daughter who is the sun."

I was right: my father would have loved the skyscraper in *The Towering Inferno*. The 138-story aurulent minaret was the star of the show—not Steve McQueen and Paul Newman, who were said to be the real stars. It was a mile-high menhir of gilded curtain walls and au courant interiors. More than its height, its design was its glory. It was geometry and asymmetry at its finest. Both inside and out, it was a banquet of oblique angles and obtuse pitches. Yet for all its gradients and inclines, it was still a remarkably simple and unembroidered structure. That alone would have earned my father's praise. I would never know if he would have liked the movie itself, but he most definitely would have loved its tower.

Kylie's head never moved during the film. Her eyes were immersed in the images on the screen, as were the eyes of everyone else in the theater. During one scene, she grabbed my hand and clutched it so tightly I winced in pain. Twelve unfortunates were trapped in a scenic elevator after a series of explosions ripped it from its track. The elevator did not fall, but one of its passengers did. An ancient by the name of Lisolette fell to her death after one of the windows in the car easily popped out. At this point, Kylie's hand compressed mine like a vise and the pain pirated my breath. Kylie was a petite girl, but at that moment, she had the grip of a timberman.

She couldn't stop talking about the film after we left the movie house. I noticed numerous flaws in the film, but I kept the inventory of errors and demerits to myself. Had I shared them, it would have ruined the movie for her and the afternoon for us.

In the same block as the theater, there was a decades-old, badly weathered restaurant. It had been hours since we ate, so I took us there for a late lunch. I would have liked to have taken her someplace fashionable, but there was no other restaurant in the area. I couldn't wait for my sixteenth year when I could drive and no longer be at the mercy of cabs, buses, and parents.

Something had been gnawing at me most of the day. It wasn't until we were seated in the restaurant that I decided to address the matter.

"Kylie, I need to ask you something."

"Anything."

"Earlier today, you told your father my parents had passed away. How did you know that?"

Kylie blushed.

"I'm not mad," I assured her. "I just want to know."

"I...I called Mark, your friend. I thought he might know."

"Know what?"

"On Christmas Eve, my dad asked you why you were in the park and not at home with your family. You didn't answer him. It got me wondering why. So I called Mark. All he told me was that you once mentioned your parents had died. That's all he said. He told me you rarely talk about yourself, so he didn't know much more than that. I wasn't prying, Owen, I really wasn't. I just wanted to know. You aren't mad, are you?"

"Of course not. I couldn't be mad at you if I were paid."

Mark was right—I rarely talked about myself: I didn't see the need. Added to that, I didn't feel comfortable doing so; I felt more at home listening.

Satisfied, I diverted the conversation back to Kylie.

Without any coaxing, Kylie easily opened up about herself. Many of the students I talked with needed to be maneuvered to open up, and often it was frustrating. Kylie—unlike the other teenagers at Moran— was not carrying any emotional baggage openly or sub-rosa. She was refreshingly free of inner turmoil and personal conflict. If she were bound by something, I would have sensed it. I knew when someone was warring with themselves or someone else. Kylie was at peace with herself...and her world.

A person's self-image always starts at home. Kylie's view of herself was healthy because her home life was healthy. Her parents kept a tight but painless check on their eldest child. They made her feel important but not favored. They showed concern for her but did not make her feel smothered. They loved her, and she embraced that love.

Comparing two people is never right. Yet it is reality. It is also inescapable.

I couldn't help but compare Roxanne and Kylie. Both were blond-haired, but Kylie's was fine and diaphanous, like gossamer wings; Roxanne's was thick and rolling, like a plush prairie. Kylie's face was petite and subtle, like the music of a violin; Roxanne's was statuesque and strong, like the music of an oboe. Kylie's body was lithe and airy, like a ballet; Roxanne's was formal and flowing, like a waltz. And Kylie's personality was breezy, like a lullaby, while Roxanne's was potent, like an opera. I was attracted to both, yet there was something about Kylie's pastoral and peaceful nature that I found magnetic, drawing. I loved the sound of her voice; it was almost a caress.

Again, I found myself immersed in guilt for responding to Kylie. But I couldn't stop myself. *"The heart writes the rules for romance, not the head,"* I had whimsically said to Roxanne after we first met. As it came to pass, it wasn't whimsy after all—it was truth. I didn't seek out Kylie at first, but after I had been with her, she was all I could think about.

Returning to a place and finding change there is never easy, even when it is for the best.

Reflexively, when I opened my locker the first day after Christmas vacation, I expected to find a missive and morning gift from Roxanne. There was nothing. Only my books and a bottle of Elsha cologne lay on the shelf above my coat hook. My heart sank. Reality was clutching my face with cold hands: Roxanne was gone from my life. There would be no more love notes, or shared lunches, or telephone conversations, or smiles, or kisses. Change is a part of life. Some changes are necessary. This change in my life—however unpleasant—was one of them.

My first class of the day was World History. I was anxious to see Ms. Gavin. I hoped she had had a nice holiday. I was certain she had, since her termination had been lifted.

Ms. Gavin was not in the room when I entered it. I found that strange, for she was always there long before any of her students.

Mr. Heald came into the room shortly after I did. He had a visitor with him: a middle-aged man, about fifty-five. He had an uncanny likeness to the actor Ralph Meeker. Instantly, something tugged at my instincts about this guest; a quiet cue told me he was hiding something. Something dark.

"Good morning, everyone," Mr. Heald said. "I hope you all had a nice Christmas liberty. I am happy to announce that we have a new teacher on our staff. This is—"

"We heard you fired Ms. Gavin," Natalie Wingreen interrupted from the back of the room. "Why did you fire her? She was a great teacher!"

Mr. Heald's face stiffened at Natalie's blunt disclosure. "Ms. Gavin's termination was a misunderstanding and it was withdrawn," he said tautly. "However, she decided to let the termination stand, and her employment at this school has been closed."

"Why did she want to quit?" again Natalie. "She loved it here."

"She requested that I keep her reasons private, and I am obligated to honor that request. She did ask me to pass along to all of her students a fond good-bye. She enjoyed teaching here, and she hopes that her next school will be as warm and as friendly as this one. Now, without any further delay, this is Benjamin Carey. He will be teaching World History from this day forward. His credentials are nothing short of superlative. Please make him feel welcome."

Mr. Heald gave Ms. Gavin's replacement a quick pat on the back and hastily left the room.

Stonily, the teacher surveyed his new pupils.

"First things first," he started. "I understand that your previous instructor, Ms. Gavin, allowed you to call her by her given name. You will exercise no such abandon and irreverent hardihood with me. It is *Mr. Carey* today, tomorrow, and always. Are we clear on that?" His eyes panned the room for a response. None came. "I *said*—are we clear on that?"

Everyone nodded.

"Secondly," he proceeded, "I do not grade on a curve. There are no free rides in my classroom. You will pass this course on your own, or you will repeat it.

"Thirdly, anyone caught cheating will automatically fail.

"Fourthly, plagiarism will not be tolerated in your written or oral reports. Plagiarism is theft, and a thief has all the value of a pair of soiled underwear. If I discover that you have appropriated another's work, you will automatically fail.

"Fifthly, tardiness is inexcusable. If you are late more than twice, you will automatically fail.

"Sixthly, *everyone* will participate in this class. The shy among you had best shed your thin skins posthaste."

I glanced over at Christopher, who was sitting next to me. While he was clothed with confidence now, I knew it was a fragile confidence.

He was still terribly frightened to speak in front of people. His face was pale now, and his hands were fidgeting with the strap on his camera. Inside, he was being chewed up by terror.

"And lastly," Mr. Carey wrapped up, "there will be order in this classroom. No one will talk out of turn, and no one will talk unless I first give him permission.

"Now, I want each of you to stand and give me your first and last name *only*. Nothing else. Share your hobbies, your aspirations, your pet ideas with those who are interested. I am not. I am salaried to instruct, not *connect*. Now—let's begin." He pointed to Marie Nettleton, who was sitting by the window in the front row.

I had been taught by some eccentric, eldritch teachers in my life, but never one like this. This man was not right. He was unsound. His *superlative* credentials were his pass into the classroom. This man wanted in the classroom for a purpose—but it wasn't to teach; it was to do something else.

Mr. Carey was less interested in each student's first name and more in their last. He wanted to know each student's surname lineage. None of my classmates knew. This seemed to agitate him. When he first entered the room, his face was stone-cold; now it was tense with frustration.

His discomposure dissolved when he came to Noelle Dresdner. After she stated her name, he stared at her. Then his visage seemed to brighten—though not with happiness, but satisfaction. It was as though he had been on a hunt, and he had finally found his target.

"*Dresdner*," he repeated the name aloud, almost to himself. "Do you know the extraction of Dresdner?" he asked Noelle, his tone sandy.

She shook her head.

"It means one who is from Dresden. *Dresden, Germany.*"

"Okay," she uttered hesitantly. She was obviously confused at his interest. We all were.

"It is far from *okay*, my fair-haired *Fraulein*," he corrected her, "as you will learn in time. Odd that your first name should be Noelle. It is the feminine of Noel, which means Christmas. Christmas is a Christian holiday."

"So?" Noelle asked defensively.

"So it means that you have Deutschland dirt in your blood, *Ms. Dresdner.* Need I say more?" He flashed a celebratory smile. "Deutschland. More like *Douche*land...wouldn't you say?" He smiled again. "Let us move on." He set his eyes on Jeff Cromwell, who was sitting next to Noelle.

I was sitting in the center of the room. When it came my time to introduce myself, I stayed in my seat. I neither stood nor spoke. This man was a tyrant, and tyrants, all tyrants, must be opposed.

"Is there some reason you are still sitting?" he asked me coldly. "Are you a cripple? I see no crutches."

"Well, I'll tell you, Benjamin...or would you prefer Ben?"

He anchored his eyes to mine. "You will exit my classroom now, young man."

"I have a better idea—why don't *you* exit? I think you'd be a lot happier. I know *we* would."

Sounds came from the class.

"Remove yourself from my class," he ordered.

"I don't think so." I got to my feet and walked to the front of the room. I hopped up on the edge of his desk and folded my arms across my chest.

Louder sounds came from the class this time.

"Get off my desk and get out of this room!" he demanded and started to move toward me.

"Tut-tut. Freeze those Florsheims, Ben."

He kept coming.

"Stay your course, my friend, or I will bid the police an expeditious hello," I warned. "Assaulting a student is not a star that shines very brightly on a résumé."

He braked.

"I'm curious, Ben, does the KKK know you're available? I'm sure they'd love to have you on their team."

The class laughed.

"You know, Ben, I've known good people in my life, and I've known bad. *Lots* of bad people. You're one of them. But both good people and bad people have one thing in common: they all have a reason for what they do. Your behavior today has a reason. You have an agenda. I don't know what it is yet, but it's there. You're an autocrat. A dictatorial fascist. But you know, something tells me the very tools you use, intimidation and fear, are the very tools you hate. Whatever is going on in that tangled mind of yours, get control of it because, believe me," I jumped off the desk and walked over to him, "if you don't, I'll blacken you so fast it'll make your head swim. I've come up against far worse than you, and I always came out ahead. Just instruct the class like a *normal* teacher and leave your arrogance and agenda out in your car. *Are we clear on that?*"

"I will teach the way I think is best!"

"If your best is through browbeating, you shouldn't be teaching."

"If you think I am going to submit to some juvenile miscreant who thinks he is smarter than I am, you are sadly mistaken."

"Smarter than *I*—the *am* is implied, and therefore superfluous. And if you think we are your cattle that you can do with as you please, it is *you* who is sadly mistaken."

I walked up close to him and got close to his ear. "Back off, Mr. Carey," I levered, "or I will bury you with one word. Can you guess what that word is? Let me help you. It has nine letters and begins with a *p.*" I gave him a quick wink and went back to my seat.

Everyone in the room was staring at me. Truly, I didn't like being the center of attention, but I had to say something. This man thought he had the right to dominate and strong-arm his students. I couldn't let him do that. I *wouldn't* let him do that.

"Man, that was somethin' else!" Christopher whispered to me. The color in his face had returned.

After I was back in my seat, the train carrying Mr. Carey's interest in his pupils' ancestry came to an abrupt stop. Inexplicably, he quickly boarded a new train: one bound for the grisly depot called *The Holocaust*. It was centuries from where Ms. Gavin had us. Why would he leap from the Carthaginian Wars to the Second World War? Shouldn't he have continued where Ms. Gavin left off?

Mr. Carey's acute militarism...his preoccupation with our names... his interest in Noelle...his allusion to Germany...his absorption with The Holocaust—they all had a common thread running through them. This man was on a mission, a recondite mission of his own creation. Dana asked me if I ever had a feeling in my gut about something, even if I couldn't prove it. I did, and this was one such time. Mr. Carey was out to do harm. I sensed it. I knew it.

After I left Mr. Carey's class, I went to my locker, put on my coat and left. Though I had many classes that day, I cut them all without concern. I couldn't concentrate. I needed to be alone.

I walked to the park by the school.

An old man was there, throwing a frayed tennis ball to his dog.

I sat down on the very bench Ms. Gavin and I had occupied two weeks before. My mind was a vortex of thoughts. Ms. Gavin, Roxanne, Kylie, Mr. Carey, even Mrs. Crowley were swirling out of control in my head. With all the medications in the world, why wasn't there a pill that could turn off one's thoughts, if only for a short while?

"You look like you could use a friend." A female voice.

I swung my head to my left.

Standing next to me in a pink parka was one of the prettiest girls at Moran High School.

"*Kylie.*" I immediately got to my feet.

"Mind if I sit with you?" she asked.

I shook my head.

We sat down at the same time.

"Claire said she saw you leave school. I had a hunch you'd come here."

"It's a nice park, a very quiet, perfect place to think and be alone."

"Would you like me to leave?"

"I'm sorry, I didn't mean it like that."

"This is where you found Mittens, huh?"

"Yes, over there." I nodded to a huddle of trees by the parking lot.

"I heard you had quite the morning."

"*Our Town*—that's our school...everyone knows everyone else's business."

"I wish I could have been there. I heard you really let him have it."

"People think I'm full of myself. They think I carry a soapbox along with my books, ready to jump on it at the first opportunity. They're wrong. Some people believe they have the right to run over others without regard for the suffering it might cause. And they *will* run over people if you let them. *I* won't. Mr. Carey is a bald tire with a rusty nail in it. He's dangerous. He's a bridge ready to collapse. I'm afraid kids are going to be on that bridge when it does."

"That's not the only reason you walked out of school today, is it?"

Her intuitiveness surprised me.

"What's wrong?" she asked.

I didn't like talking about myself, but perhaps if I did—at least on this occasion—I might find some peace.

"Ms. Gavin is gone because of me," I said. "I should have known someone would see us here. We weren't doing anything wrong, but Sod's Law always prevails: if it can go wrong, it will, and with the worst possible consequences."

I looked at the man with his dog. I wished I were him. He seemed so happy, so free. It was as if he were insulated from the whole world and all its suffering, untroubled by the past, untouched by the present, undisturbed by the future.

Tears started to fall from my eyes. The droplets of sadness weren't only for Ms. Gavin...they were for my broken relationship with Roxanne, my lost relationship with Mrs. Crowley, my nonexistent relationship with my biological parents, my Christmases spent alone, my birthdays never celebrated, and the normal life I would never have.

Kylie took hold of my hands. "I want to tell you something that might make you feel better. A few years ago, my dad lost his job. It was a difficult time for him, for all of us. Not so much financially but emotionally. Our pastor told us something I never forgot. He told us that losing something, anything, is like getting burned accidentally—it's a pain that consumes you at the time and stops your life for the moment. You don't think the discomfort will come to an end, but it does. After the pain passes, you begin to think clearly again, and you're wiser for the experience. Life once again moves forward. Ms. Gavin *will* move forward again. Life doesn't come to an end just because a job does."

I looked with amazement at this astute and insightful young girl.

"I see why your father calls you '*angel*.' I shall never be granted that appellation. An angel I am not. With all the indescribable horrors in the world—the starvation, the disease, the torture, the abuse, the killing—here I sit crying over my own burdens. By comparison, they're more stubbed toes than woes. You know, there was a time when I refused to cry. Of course, I was stronger then. Look at me now."

"Suffering is suffering, Owen. Just because your suffering might be less than someone else's doesn't make it less important."

Her hands left mine, came to my face and cradled it. Then she leaned in and kissed me.

I returned her kiss.

It seemed neither of us wanted the kiss to end.

When it did, I found Kylie gazing at me, smiling. "Wow!" she lauded. "You really know your way around a girl's lips!"

"You too," I bestowed back. "I imagine, though, if your parents caught me here with you, they would not think too kindly of me."

"My parents *adore* you. You're better than sliced bread in their eyes. No lie. In fact, my dad wishes you were my age so that next year we could marry and start having babies."

"You might want to tell your dad to hold off on that wish—I doubt I would be much of a father. If the apple doesn't fall too far from the tree, then I best never reproduce. History has an ugly way of repeating itself."

"You wouldn't be *anything* like your real father."

"I wouldn't be too sure of that."

"I am sure of it. *Very* sure." She took my hand and led me back to school.

I expected to see a more respectful and restrained Mr. Carey the next time I saw him. But expectations and actualizations are rarely conjoined. The former is what a man wants; the latter is what he typically gets.

When I saw Mr. Carey again—in my next World History class two days later—he was wearing a hint of a grin. The cat that swallowed the helpless canary. He was a cat all right—unpredictable, untrustworthy, unsafe.

After we all had sat and silenced ourselves, Mr. Carey directed his attention to me.

"Mr. Crowley," he said, "I have some pleasant and unpleasant news for you. Which would you prefer first?"

His tone, more than his invitation, was mocking. I would not allow him to think he could intimidate me. "You decide," was all I said.

"Excellent choice," he taunted. "Let's begin with the bad news. Regarding your whispered blackmail to me Monday last, I discussed it with Mr. Heald, and he wanted me to pass along a hardy caution to you: put forth another inflammatory windage like that one and you will be expelled with meteoric haste. Moreover, disturb and/or disrupt my class again, and you will be sitting at home under suspension. I understand that you have romped with such discipline in the past. Open your mouth once more in my class without permission, and you will romp with it once again.

"As for the good news, *that* is the good news. You talk, you walk. Are we clear on that, Mr. Crowley?" His face was painted with phosphorescent victory.

"Perfectly," I answered.

*For now*, I wanted to add, but didn't.

Something was suspect about his using Mr. Heald as leverage to obtain my silence and cooperation. Mr. Heald knew me, and he knew I would not have gone in the direction I did without good reason. Why hadn't Mr. Heald come to me to discuss the matter? Why hadn't he himself made the warnings of expulsion and suspension? Is that not the purview of a principal?

"Like the Earth," Mr. Carey went straight into the class, "the axis of human history revolves around a single line. *Unlike* the Earth, the axis of human history is *not* invisible. It is as solid as cement. That line has a name. It is called motivation. And what creates motivation? Does anyone know? You, Ms. Dresdner, are you at all curious?"

Noelle seemed bemused that he would call on her.

"Not really," she replied candidly but not rudely.

"Why does that not surprise me? Your kind never have been, nor will they ever be."

What did he mean by that? Whatever it was, it was clear it wasn't flattery.

"A man's motivations," Mr. Carey explained further, "are the flora that spring from his genetic seeds. If a man's motivations are evil, it is because his genetic makeup is evil. It is said that the *world* creates an evil man. I disagree. An evil man meets his beginning when his father's sperm unites with his mother's egg. It logically follows that his parents are evil as well, which then proceeds to and concludes at the obvious terminus that entire races are evil. These races are to be opposed, even destroyed."

"So you're saying there are certain people who are evil right from the start, and we should just wipe them out?" Terence Daniels questioned from the back row.

I thought Terence's unprocedural interrogatory would earn him a verbal beating from Mr. Carey, but it didn't. Instead, our Stalin-in-residence simply replied, "Correct, Mr. Daniels."

"And how do you tell which races are evil and which aren't?"

I couldn't tell if Terence was truly interested, or if he was just challenging Mr. Carey.

"A simple though thoughtful question, Mr. Daniels. Color and facial structure are direct signposts—or meters if you will—of genetic turpitude. For example, and this may sound harsh, but truth is rarely soft: Asians are robotic; Native Americans are intransigent; Negros are entitlement-minded; Muslims are extremists; Soviets are jingoistic, and the list goes on. They all have a blemished badge. But the worst, the absolute worst, though difficult to ascertain at first because of their light skin, is the Suebi tribe...or what we now call the Germanic people."

I couldn't believe what I was hearing. Standing before us was a proud—though rambling—white-collar racist, a bigoted ideologue. He was retching out his prejudices with near joy. And he had the crust to call what I said inflammatory windage.

Terence didn't ask anything further.

For the remainder of the period, we sat and listened to the history of present-day Germany: its diverse tribal origins and parentage, its pivotal people, its seminal events, and its deep ideologies. Each sentence, without exception, was pimpled with amaroidal remarks. Because of this, I had the feeling that what we were hearing was coming more from emotion than factual data.

After class, I wanted to go to Mr. Heald and inform him that the credentials of his newest faculty member might have been nothing less than superlative, but his ethics were nothing more than putrescent. I decided not to go to Mr. Heald, for if Mr. Carey had indeed spoken with him, Mr. Heald would think I was muddying the waters even more and would dismiss what I had to say as mere denigration.

Later that day, I had Basic Spanish with Roxanne. Not once did she look my way. Her face was neither sad nor animated; it was neutral, like a wall with no pictures. Roxanne's closest friend, Shannon Manchester, was sitting next to her. Shannon did not hesitate to look at me. Her face was *not* devoid of pictures: the images on hers were of knives, hatchets, and bayonets.

I took lunch with Christopher and Mark that afternoon. They told me of their holidays. Both had a plentiful and joyful Christmas. Mark, knowing his mother would never spend any of his anonymous bounty on herself, went out and bought her a coat, scarf, boots, and gloves. Then, on Christmas night, with help of a neighbor, he made a lavish dinner with dessert for her and his brother. To cap the evening, he poured her a hot bubble bath.

I was very proud of my friend. He had grown much since I first met him. Mark, the callow teenager, had become Mark, the mature son.

"Hey, Owen, Christopher has something he wants to ask you," Mark said.

Christopher did not speak; his face turned pink, and he turned away.

Smiling, Mark spoke for his friend. "What Christopher wants to know—but is too chicken to ask—is if he can ask Roxanne out on a date. He's always had a thing for her. Is that okay with you since you don't have anything going on with her anymore?"

The request stung. My breakup with Roxanne was not a casual disassociation. Roxanne was not a car I no longer wanted. She had been a part of my blood, a part of my self. It was not easy for me to love, and I loved Roxanne. Ours was not an ordinary high school romance; it was deep and measurable and pure. Did Christopher not see that? Perhaps he didn't. Can anyone ever know how another person truly feels? Can he ever step inside him and feel his loss?

Christopher didn't wait for my answer. He quietly rose from the table and left.

"I guess I shouldn't have said anything," Mark considered.

"Don't worry about it," I diluted. "I'll go talk to him. I'll be right back."

I caught up with Christopher in the west stairwell.

"Hey, Christopher, wait up," I called.

He stopped but did not look at me.

"If you want to ask Roxanne out, it's okay with me," I told him.

He turned to me. His eyes were wet.

Christopher had more than just a thing for Roxanne—he really liked her. Maybe even loved.

"Christopher, I'm okay with it. Really."

He stared down at the floor. "You know next month I'll be fifteen," he gave away. "*Fifteen*. Not once in all that time has a girl ever looked at me. Not once. Until Roxanne. Y-Y-You don't know wh-wh-what it's like to go through life unnoticed. You think M-Mark sounds d-d-desperate—he c-c-c-can't hold a c-candle to me. A-A-All I've ever wanted is for a girl to love me. I'd give anything if Roxanne would. I'd n-never ask for anything ever again if she would just look at me the way she used to look at you. M-M-Maybe you didn't see it, but I sure did. I r-r-remember the first time she said hello to me. She cared about me when nobody else cared at all. Then she asked me to come sit by her in English class so I wouldn't have to sit alone. I know she did it out of pity, but it was still special to me. And when she p-p-p-paid for my lunch that first day of school, I couldn't believe that someone like her would do that for someone like me. You can't know what it's like to go through life a stut-t-t-tering weirdo. You and Mark are my only friends. Sometimes M-M-Mark comes over to my house and we listen to albums and t-t-talk about *Lost in Space* or *Star Trek* or *Space 1999*. It's fun and all that, but Mark isn't a girl. He isn't Roxanne. You're going to think this is k-k-k-kind of weird, but I've been to her house. Mark's got this friend who drives, and I asked him if he would take me there. I got her address from the school office. D-D-D-December thirteenth— that was the first day we went to it. I'll never forget that day as long as I live. I'll never forget pulling up in front of her home and seeing where she lived. Man, I couldn't believe I was just a few feet away from where ate and slept and watched TV. I know it all sounds s-s-s-sounds k-kind of strange, but it was the only way I could be close to her. Mark's friend ran up to her front door and stole the doormat, but the next day we t-t-t-took it back. As he was r-r-running back to the car, he grabbed a small r-r-rock from her rose garden. I keep it on my dr-dr-dresser at home. I call it my Roxy Rock. I k-kiss it before I go to b-b-bed every night. I know everyone has a pet rock these days, but I'm the only one in the whole world who has one from Roxanne's house.

"A couple months ago I started k-k-keeping a journal. It's k-kind of like a diary, but I call it a journal because boys aren't supposed to keep d-d-d-diaries. Anyway, I write in it every day. Every day has something about Roxanne: what she wore, who she t-t-t-talked to, what mood she was in, how she wore her hair, if she was happy, if she was sad. Those are my worst days.

"You ever hear the song 'Aubrey' by Bread?" he asked but didn't wait for me to answer. "It came out a couple years ago. It's my f-f-favorite song in the whole world. If I could write music, that would be my song to Roxanne. So many songs on the radio right now remind me of her. Do you know what *her* favorite song is?"

I should have known but didn't. In all of our talks, somehow it never came up. We did have *our* song, though: 'When Will I See You Again?' by The Three Degrees. Along with its pleasing melody and engaging harmony, we found its opening lyrics sublimely reflective of our relationship; the ending verses had no such application. It wasn't until after our relationship had ended that the final lyrics took on meaning.

"It's 'If' by Bread," he told me. "That's her favorite song. I know when and where she was born too. July sixteenth in Las Cruces, New Mexico. Her favorite color is blue; her b-b-best friend is Shannon; and her dog's n-n-n-name is K-K-K-Kenny. Remember last month when Mr. Wh-Wh-Wheatly made us all wr-wr-write a play for English? I got an A-plus on mine. Want to know what it was about?" This time, he waited for me to respond. I nodded.

"It was about Roxanne. I-I-I called it *Alone for a Time*. It was about this angel named Harry that helps this lonely boy win the heart of the girl he loves. M-M-Mark read it and he loved it. Mark's friend, the one who drives, he read it and he thought I should give it to her.

"I can't tell you how many pictures I've taken of her. A yearbook ph-ph-ph-photographer can take all the p-p-p-pictures he wants, you know. You probably think I'm pretty creepy now, huh?"

"No, not creepy. Slightly obsessive, but not creepy. You're just a boy who spends a lot of time alone. Unfortunately, Christopher, that can be very dangerous. Being alone too much prevents us from seeing reality. When we're chronically isolated, we tend to see only what's in our mind and not what's in the world."

"I-I-I know the score, Owen. I know Roxanne doesn't see me as anything."

"Then why do you want to ask her out?"

"I don't know. Call it w-w-w-wishful thinking. Maybe if she gave me a chance, sh-sh-sh-she would see something she liked, and I would win her heart like you did. Anything's possible, Owen. You said that to me about us being friends when we first met. Remember?"

"I remember. Christopher, it is possible that you could win her heart...but it's not very probable. I'm not sure Roxanne is for you, or you for her."

"I-I-I'll never know unless I try."

"Are you emotionally up to it if she says no?"

"I think so. I don't know until I actually hear her say it. She's the only girl I care about, Owen."

"All this just because she asked you to sit next to her and paid for your lunch one time?"

"When you say it like that, it sounds pr-pr-pretty pathetic. But I can't help how I feel. She's s-s-so sweet and pretty. I know you're mad at her for what she did to Ms. Gavin, b-b-b-but I don't have your anger. She's not like other girls. She might give me a chance. I know no other girl would. I'll never have what you have, Owen. Girls will never tr-tr-trip over themselves trying to get to me l-l-l-like they do to you. I'll never be strong and normal like you, and that's what most girls want."

"If your idea of normal is me, then your idea of normal is terribly flawed. I am the embodiment of *ab*normal. My abnormalities could fill a plane."

"Name one."

"I'll name you several. Just look at the way I talk. I talk like a textbook. Why don't I just speak like everyone else? I desire to…but I can't. I force myself to be superior so that I will never again be considered *in*ferior. I force myself to know wisdom so that I will never again be considered the fool. Injudiciousness will drive you into a ditch every time. I pan adolescent banality and frivolity, and yet inwardly, I stargaze at them. If that isn't screwed up, Christopher, I don't know what is."

"You're not screwed up, Owen. You're the strongest, smartest, most *un*screwed-up person I know."

Christopher wasn't listening to me. His mind was locked. In it was Roxanne and Roxanne alone. All that was left to give him was advice.

"Christopher, if you are determined to ask Roxanne out, do yourself one favor: wait a while. Roxanne is mending right now. Breakups leave dents. Give her time to repair herself. If you go to her now, I'm afraid you will receive an answer you do not want to hear."

"How long should I wait?"

"I don't know. Everybody is different. Maybe a couple of months. Pay attention to her moods, her face. When she begins to show signs that she is herself again, that is when I would approach her. But, Christopher, be prepared to receive the opposite of what you expect."

"I'll be prepared. Th-Th-Thanks, Owen, for understanding."

"You're welcome. Come on, let's get back downstairs before Mark thinks he's been deserted."

Strontium 90 is a radioactive isotope of strontium, an alkaline earth metal. Strontium 90 is formed by nuclear fission and is found in the fallout from nuclear detonations. If it enters the body, it is absorbed like calcium and congresses in the bones. It is radioactive waste matter that, over time, can precipitate cancer. This we learned in my Geology class.

Mr. Carey made Strontium 90 look like Bisquick. He was obsessed with twentieth-century Germany and its many flagitious sides: its knavish and savage authorities, its hardline dogmas, its verboten annexations, its audacities, its atrocities, its crimes. Yet, the most infamous twentieth-century Germans—Adolph Hitler and his confederates—were not the worst in his eyes; rather, he bundled them with the entire nation, as if the German populace and the German Nazi Party were one and the same. As he put it, "The Nazis did not invade the Fatherland—they *germinated* from it. Therefore, it can be said, unequivocally, unmistakably, that every man, woman, and child of German descent, alive or dead, is a Nazi. Everything reproduces after its own kind. Swans beget swans, and rats beget rats. Thistles can only produce thistles."

More inscrutable than Mr. Carey's mania about Germany was his omission of it in his other classes. My class was the only one who received his anti-Teutonic rantings dressed as illuminations. In his other classes, he focused on different cultures in different eras. There was something about *my* class that was causing him to bare his fangs about Germany and its sinful past. And I believed I knew what it was: Noelle. Not continually, but frequently he would eye her as he lectured. When not holding forth, he would tirelessly grill her on dates and names and motivations of enemy and Allied strategies in the European theater of World War II. Never did Noelle have an answer. This aggravated him, and he would chastise her before the class for her defiance to give replies to questions to which she, of all people, should have answers. Sometimes she would cry after class, and I would see her friends trying to comfort her.

Mr. Carey regularly spoke of motivations. What were *his* motivations? I wondered. What motivated him to despise every human who had any roots to that small European country called Germany?

Undeniably, Germany had caused incalculable suffering and loss of life, but not every German championed the *final-solution, master-race, right-of-colonization, no-détente/no-surrender* dogmas of its Nazi-era leaders. Was Mr. Carey not aware of this? Had he not been educated about Claus von Stauffenberg and his supporters? If all Germans were Xerox copies of Hitler and his abettors—as Mr. Carey espoused—why were there those in Hitler's own ranks who wanted to end his life and thus his reign? I knew Mr. Carey would never answer me as to his motivations, so I was left to surmise them. I came up with two: either he had Judaistic rhizomes and was corrosively bitter, or he lost family members in one or both world wars.

I so wanted to bring the matter of Mr. Carey's harassment of Noelle to Mr. Heald, but I decided against it. Mr. Heald would simply tell me to back off and let Mr. Carey conduct his class in his own way. He would impress on me that every teacher projects his own personality into his teaching method, and that's all Mr. Carey was doing.

Still, I felt somebody should be told. But who? As quickly as the question entered my mind, so did the answer.

"I'm sorry, Owen, I can't tell a teacher how to teach," Mr. Taggart let me know.

"He's harassing her."

"What you call harassment he might call technique. Maybe he sees potential in Noelle, and he's simply trying to challenge her. It's not uncommon."

"It's not technique and it's not a challenge. He's targeting her. She has a German name, and he hates her for it."

"Owen, no offense, but I think you're way out in left field on this. Mr. Carey is a tremendous asset to this school. I'll admit, he's a little stringent in his style of instructing, but that's simply his approach. He interacts professionally with students and staff alike. I've seen it. I don't want to risk losing him by accusing him of badgering and bullying his students."

"Not *students. One* student. Noelle."

"I'm sorry, Owen, I'm not going to get involved with this. You need to handle this on your own."

"You once told me you thought I had a good feel for people. I have a feel for Mr. Carey, and it isn't good."

"Then I suggest you go to Mr. Heald. Ultimately, *he* would have to talk with Mr. Carey anyway, not me."

I shook my head in frustration and dismay. "When something happens—and it will—it'll all be on you. Don't say I didn't tell you."

I left his office before he could give another excuse.

January shot by with the speed of sound. February was gunning down the road at an even faster pace. Valentine's Day was only a few sunrises away. I was looking forward to the day of hearts with great enthusiasm and anticipation. I had planned something unique for Kylie.

Long before Kylie came into my life, I had envisioned myself presenting flowers and candy to Roxanne at her locker so all could see how much I loved her. But that ship would never enter that port. It had sunk in the icy waters of life and reality.

I was very fond of Kylie, but I was not in love with her. I refused to let myself feel that deeply again. Kylie had no such prohibitions. She was deeply in love with me, and she told me so daily. She never made me feel guilty for not saying it to her, for she knew and understood why I couldn't. Had I never known Roxanne, my heart would have fallen immediately for Kylie, but my heart was in a cage now, where no one could get at it, not even me.

Where once Roxanne and I held hands in the hallways of the school, we now passed one another in those same halls without even exchanging glances. It wasn't supposed to be like that, but supposed-to-bes and need-to-bes are worlds apart.

It was now Thursday, February 13th, the day before Valentine's Day.

I was sitting with Mark in the library. I was studying; Mark was drawing. His love for *Star Trek* and *Lost in Space* had aroused him to create what he called *The Falcon Project*. It was a miscegeny of both series. It was an amateurish enchiridion of penciled drawings and penned exposition. The illustrations of the spacecraft, while good, were near clones of the Jupiter 2 in *Lost in Space*, and the written prong of the work, while detailed and inventive, had the unmistakable fingerprint of *Star Trek*. Although *The Falcon Project* was a mongrel at best, I had to admit it was quite the undertaking for a boy his age.

"I need to talk to you," a voice like that of closing shears interrupted us.

Both Mark and I looked up.

Standing on the opposite side of our table was Shannon Manchester, Roxanne's best friend. She was staring at me with war-ready eyes.

Crowned with long, dark-chocolate, center-parted hair that framed a fresh, silken face, Shannon could easily have been Ali MacGraw's twin.

"Go ahead," I said evenly.

Pointing to the door, she said, "*Outside.*"

She left the library.

"I'll be right back," I said to Mark, getting up.

"Owen, don't let her attack you," he admonished. "You didn't do anything wrong."

"I know."

Shannon was waiting right outside the library.

"You are such a lowlife!" she commenced immediately, her frosted lips taut and thin. "You know, if I didn't think I'd get in trouble, I'd kick you right in the stones!"

"Is this what you wanted to tell me, Shannon? You should have told me inside—you would have had an audience."

"I wish you were dead!"

"Well, that would solve your problem, wouldn't it? But then who would you have to hate?"

"You're such a smart-ass! I knew you were bad news from the start. You think you're better than everyone else with your big words and your rich clothes. You have no idea how much you hurt Roxanne! She loved you! I can't believe you chose a teacher over her!"

"Shannon, I did not choose Ms. Gavin over Roxanne. Roxanne brought about Ms. Gavin's dismissal without knowing any of the facts. She ruined a woman's life."

"And she was sorry for it."

"She never told me she was. Nor did she tell Ms. Gavin."

"You never gave her a chance!"

"She's had millions of chances."

*"Hardly millions!"*

"Shannon, fifty-five days have passed since Ms. Gavin left. That's almost five million seconds. It takes only *one* of them to say '*I am sorry.*' Roxanne never took a single one of them to say those three simple words."

"And it takes only one second to say three other words—'*I forgive you,*' which you never said to Roxanne. Forgiveness should be automatic, Owen—especially if you love someone. You should just do it. Roxanne wasn't the *only* one who didn't take a second to do the right thing."

Had it been different circumstances, I would have applauded Shannon's logic. It was flawless. Not only that, she was right. I *hadn't* forgiven Roxanne. Just because Roxanne hadn't asked for forgiveness, didn't preclude me from giving it.

"I hear you got yourself a new girlfriend," Shannon suddenly altered her flight path. "Sure didn't take you long. Kylie Ulrich, isn't it? Pretty girl. Does she know what a pile of crap you are? Have you told her what mistakes she isn't allowed to make so you won't dump her too? Does she know you change girlfriends as often as you change your underwear?"

She had drawn Kylie into her miasma of hostility and hate, and I wouldn't allow it. I could feel my face starting to redden with anger.

"Oh, are we getting mad?" she scoffed.

"You've had your say, Shannon. I'm leaving now. *Good-bye.*"

"You're not going anywhere until I'm finished!" She grabbed my arm as I was turning toward the library door. "I didn't come here just to talk about you and Roxanne—I came here to talk about Christopher and Roxanne."

"Christopher and Roxanne?"

"Yeah, your weird friend Christopher."

"He is not *weird.*"

*"He's weird!* All the girls call him '*Creepy Christopher.*'"

The cruel sobriquet seemed like a gross exaggeration, but the label *"Creepy Crowley"* had been pasted on me when I was young, so it was possible Shannon was telling the truth. But given her natural acerbity, most likely she was not.

I smiled. *"Sure they do.* Is that it for today's hyperbole?—or should I go get a chair?"

She glared at me. "Do you have any idea what he's been doing?"

"How would I know what he's been doing? I'm not his shadow."

"You should be. Someone should be. He's making a fool of himself!"

"And just what has he done that has stirred you into such a froth, Shannon?"

"He keeps giving Roxanne these creepy gifts."

"Creepy how?"

"He carries that stupid camera with him everywhere he goes. He took a picture of her without her knowing it, cut out her face and glued it to a one-dollar bill. Then he put it in a card and wrote, *I think you're number one in the whole world!"*

I had to smile. Christopher might be obsessive, but he was a clever obsessive.

"I don't think it's very funny," she seethed.

"What does Roxanne think?"

"She doesn't know what to think. She doesn't know what to do. She doesn't want to hurt his feelings. She just wants him to stop."

"It's just a dollar bill, Shannon—not a wedding ring."

"That's just the top of the mountain. He gave her all these forty-fives too. Olivia Newton-John, Elton John, John Denver. Guess what he said in *that* card? *I'll be your Johnny-on-the-spot anytime!* Then he gave her more forty-fives! All love songs. Mark told me he got her an expensive necklace for no reason at all."

"Where is he getting the money to buy all of these things?"

"How should I know? All I know is what he's doing. Somehow he found out she likes Celicas—you know, the car? He told her he was going to get her one someday. Then he asked her to come out to the parking lot one afternoon. She was terrified he had bought her one. He didn't, but it was just as bad. He put a little model of a Celica in one of the parking slots. He painted it blue because that's her favorite color, and he wrote the name *Roxy* on the roof of it."

I smiled again. "You got to admit, it's original."

"It's *weird*! He had one of those caricature drawings made of him and Roxanne. Hearts were floating all around them as he was kissing her. It was embarrassing to even look at! He's making a fool of himself!"

"No, he's just making his feelings known."

"He's making her hate him. He puts these stupid love notes in her locker all the time. He's always staring at her. He once wrote a play about her and gave it to her. She threw it away.

"He's even been to her house. Two weeks ago, he taped this mile-long paper banner to the side of the grocery store down from her house that said, *I love you, Roxanne!* Last week, he left this huge poster by her front door with all these candy bars taped to it. Each candy bar had some stupid note. Like for a Marathon bar, he wrote, *I'd run a hundred marathons for you!* For a Clark bar, he said, *I may look like Clark Kent, but you make me feel like Superman!* For an Almond Joy—"

I held up my hand. "Yes, Shannon, I get the picture. What's all this got to do with me?"

"*What's this got to do with you?* He's *your* friend! You need to talk to him, tell him to stop."

"No, I don't need to tell him anything. Roxanne needs to tell him herself. That's the only way he'll stop."

"I thought you were so big on helping people. Or is that only for people you care about?"

Before I could answer, she added, "If he was pulling this crap with your *new girlfriend*, would you tell her to talk to him herself?"

Again, she had me with her logic.

Reluctantly, I said, "I will speak with him."

I went back into the library.

Of the hundreds of lockers in Moran High School, only one was decorated that Valentine's Day morning. It was arrayed with pink balloons, white crepe paper streamers, red-foil hearts, and yellow happy faces. On the floor beneath the locker—held in a cadmium-red vase whose base was encircled with white rose petals—was a spray of red carnations, red lilies, and red Gerbera daisies. It extracted envious stares from everyone who passed it.

I watched from inside an adjacent classroom. I hoped Kylie would not be upset at the display. She was intensely private, even about us. She never sat with me at lunch or assemblies or the library or walked with me in halls. It wasn't that she was ashamed of me; she just didn't want her private life known to others. She knew how people liked to gossip, and she hated gossip. She also didn't want Roxanne to see us together and be hurt at the sight of us.

When Kylie came to her locker, her reaction was not as I had expected.

She put her face in her hands and began to cry.

Decorating her locker was obviously not the smartest show of affection.

I left the classroom and went to her.

When she saw me, she wrapped her arms around my waist and laid her head on my chest.

"I'm sorry, I didn't think this would upset you," I said.

"Are you kidding?" Kylie said. "It's a dream. It's a dream come true."

She took my hand and led me away from her locker. Before I could stop her, she opened the door to the boys' room and pulled me in.

An upperclassman was standing in front of a urinal.

"Would you excuse us?" Kylie asked him kindly.

The boy's faced reddened, and he hastily left.

I was as stunned as he was.

She politely but forcefully pushed me against the door. She brought her lips to mine and kissed me ravenously. She pressed her body firmly against mine.

My body temperature spiked. I was so aroused I became embarrassed. I tried to politely push her away.

She didn't take the hint. Instead, she pushed herself more firmly against me. Then, she took my hand and slid it beneath her shirt and then beneath her bra.

Every part of my body ignited.

I couldn't believe this was happening. I couldn't believe where I was, what I was doing, and why I was doing it. My intense pleasure was illogical. Utterly illogical. Both sexes are born with breast tissue, but only in females does that tissue develop. The female breast is simply an organization of epidermis, fatty tissue, ducts, lobules, and blood. It is simply a device to deliver nourishment. Female breasts, therefore, should bring about an asexual response, and any sensual and erotic pleasure derived from them is completely nonsensical. And yet, cupped in my hand was an incredibly soft drift that made me feel unbelievably alive and happy.

I found myself kissing Kylie with a passion I did not know existed within me. She returned my fever with equal intensity.

I could see why the Earth was overpopulated. Once a male and female began a carnal braid, copulation was inevitable.

Kylie, out of breath, stopped and gazed at me. She gently put her hand against my face. "Your face is all flushed. Did I do that to you?"

Swallowing, I said, "That...and other things."

Kylie laughed, removed my hand and straightened her shirt. "We better get to homeroom...what's left of it."

I reached out and touched her chin. "Thank you, Kylie. I didn't know it could be this nice."

"The nice part is yet to come." She winked and left the lavatory before me.

I hadn't seen Christopher the entire day. I had planned to talk to him about Roxanne before the day was out. Mark said he saw him early that morning but hadn't seen him since.

I had Art History Wednesdays and Fridays; both days at two o'clock. The Art Department occupied the north half of the fourth floor; study hall occupied the south end. For panoramic views, the floor—or 'The Nest,' as some called it—had the best in the house. From it, any part of the valley could be seen. All of its windows had been welded shut, and rightly so. In May of 1968, a student, after hearing that her brother was killed in the Battle of Khe Sanh, opened one of the windows and pushed herself out. The student, a senior, survived the fall, but later died. Since then, it was called '*The Nest*'—presumably in reference to baby birds that sometimes fall from their nests.

I was standing in front of the west windows in the Art Department, waiting for class to begin. I was happily humming Kylie's and my song: "We've Only Just Begun" by the Carpenters. We had another Carpenters song that we liked equally as much: "Only Yesterday." Most couples only have one song that is theirs—Kylie and I had two.

At one time, I never imagined myself with someone other than Roxanne. For months, I felt Roxanne and I were the perfect match; I belonged to her, and she to me. I even saw us marrying after high school. But the more time I spent with Kylie, the more I realized that *she* was my true match, and no one else. There was an almost cellular symbiosis between us. My unity with Roxanne had strength, but with Kylie, it had depth.

Looking down at the parking lot, I was reminded of a spread of Matchbox cars I had seen on a table in a Woolworths once.

Something appeared in the lot. Walking between the vehicles and heading for the bleachers was a solitary figure wearing a red-and-yellow parka. It was Christopher. His head was bowed and his step slow. Something was wrong.

I instantly left the department, went to my locker and retrieved my jacket.

When I arrived at the stands, I saw Christopher sitting in the middle of the field, staring up at the gray sky.

I quickly descended the steps.

He heard my footfalls and looked in my direction.

I hurried over to him.

I noticed that he had been crying.

Standing over someone, at least from my experience, did not foster trust, so I squatted down so my face was parallel with his.

"What happened?" I asked...although I had a fair idea what had occurred.

"You were right," he said. "Roxanne d-d-d-didn't want me. '*We don't have the right chemistry*,' she told me. '*I'm not for you, and you're not for me*'—that's what she said after she saw this." He opened his palm and in it lay a gold locket in the shape of a heart. He opened it. Seated in the left half of the heart was a petite photograph of Roxanne; in the right, a photograph of him. He turned the locket over and showed it to me. The words *Très Belle Fille* were etched across its back.

"I must confess, my French is a bit infirm. What does it mean?"

"It means *Very Beautiful Girl*."

He stood, snapped the locket closed and threw it angrily into a copse of sleeping cottonwoods at the edge of the field.

"I know as long as I live, I'll never forget her words," he foreshadowed. "Wh-Wh-Why didn't she just tell me i-i-i-n the b-b-beginning she w-w-w-wasn't interested?"

"She probably didn't want to hurt you."

"She hurt me more by not telling me. Sh-Sh-She…sh-sh-sh-should have told me she couldn't stand me."

"She doesn't hate you, she just doesn't want to date you."

"Neither does anyone else. I'm such a loser. I wish someone would just kill me. They'd be doing the world a favor. I just want to go home and go to bed and die. Do you know what it's like to feel so much pain you can't even breathe? You don't even want to breathe. You don't even want to move. I feel so worthless. I gave my all and I still wasn't good enough."

"You just gave your all to the wrong one. Most of us do. Millions have done it before us, and millions will do it after us. It's how people are. Everyone is desperate for love, but we look for it in all the wrong people."

"Why does it work for some but not others?"

"I don't think you'll like my answer to that."

"Why? Couldn't be any worse than what I'm feeling right now."

I hesitated. "It all comes down to just one simple thing, Christopher—luck. Plain, simple luck. There is a reason why everything happens, but not everything happens for a reason. I think that everything that occurs in this world occurs by chance, and chance alone. *Nothing* is fated or foreordained. You either have good luck…or bad luck. While one child is drowning, another is laughing. While one woman is weeping, another is rejoicing. While one man is being loved, another is being murdered. No meaning, no significance, no reason. It's just the way things are. You had bad luck with Roxanne. The next girl you meet might be different, and it will have nothing whatsoever to do with your value or your worth. She will like you simply because she likes what you have to offer. Roxanne doesn't. Roxanne has a list in her head of what she wants and doesn't want in a romantic partner. We all do. *Even you.* And if you happen to meet a girl whose qualities match those that are on your list and you match the ones on hers, then you are very, very lucky."

"Y-Y-Y-You're right, I don't like your answer."

"I didn't think you would. Listen, Kylie and I are going to go out to dinner tonight. I want you to come with us."

"Why, s-s-s-so I can watch you and K-Kylie kiss and cuddle? N-N-N-No, thanks."

"I promise you, you will not suffer any romantic interchanges between Kylie and me. Just consider it going out on a Friday night with a couple of friends."

"Wh-Wh-Why would you want to spend the most romantic night of the year with your girlfriend…and another boy?"

"Because I don't want you to be alone. Any night can be Valentine's Day night. It's all in the way you look at it. So…will you join us?"

"D-D-D-Don't you think you should ask Kylie first?"

"I think I know her well enough to suspect that she will not mind at all."

He thought about the offer for a minute, and then said, "All right—if you're sure you want me."

"I do. Come on, let's get back inside before we both freeze to death." I clapped him on the back.

"Hey, Owen, c-c-c-can I ask you something?"

"Anything."

"D-D-D-Do you miss Roxanne?"

I didn't even have to ponder my answer. "Yes, I do."

"Then why aren't you with her? Wh-Wh-Why don't you just forgive her?"

"Someone else asked me that recently. I don't forgive easily, Christopher. I never have. And I have a petty but bullish tendency to hold grudges. Roxanne didn't just accidentally ruin Ms. Gavin's life—she *deliberately* ruined it. I have a very hard time giving my allegiance—let alone my love—to someone who prepensely and without qualms hurts someone else."

"She hurt *me*, b-b-but *I* still care for her."

"She didn't set out to hurt you. That's the difference."

"She never would have gone for me, would she?

"No, she wouldn't. But you had to find that out on your own."

"I sure did."

As I had assumed, Kylie didn't mind in the least that Christopher would be joining us for dinner. If anything, she was happy he would be there. When I told her what had happened, she was glad he wouldn't be by himself—on a Friday night, no less—building castles in the air over the girl of his dreams and how she brought those castles down with nine simple words: *"I'm not for you and you're not for me."*

Mr. Ulrich drove the three of us to the restaurant. Christopher was dressed in a coat and tie. He was more cute than handsome in his Sunday vines. But as he matured, that cuteness would give way to handsomeness. If he gained some self-confidence independent of his camera, a thousand Roxannes would be at his feet. Good looks and unaided self-confidence were magnets that always drew the opposite sex.

The Italian Place was the restaurant's name. Though small and set back from the street, it still attracted many patrons. Reputation rather than location was what brought people to it.

Its baronial-styled double doors opened into an enchantingly dim expanse with half-moon booths that horseshoed its periphery. Diners sat on soft, carnelian-red leather seats. Subdued, Venetian-red Tiffany lamps hanging above each table showered patrons with calmative light.

In the center of every table stood an empty Lancers wine bottle, each staffed with a white, lighted candle. Streams of solidified candle wax enveloped each bottle.

The restaurant was nearly full. Only one booth was unoccupied. It was ours. I had called earlier in the week and reserved it.

A twenty-something girl came up to us, and I told her who we were. She escorted us to our table. As we were seating ourselves, we all heard, "Hi, Owen, hi, Kylie!"

Quartered at the table next to ours was a group of girls from our high school. They were a mixed bag of ages and personalities.

Kylie and I said hello back.

*So much for a quiet dinner,* my mind whispered.

One of the girls—a pretty, happy-faced teenager with spirally, blond hair—said hi to Christopher.

Christopher looked at the girl with bewilderment. I knew exactly what was in his mind, for it had been in mine not too long ago: *Since when does a girl, a pretty girl, a popular girl say hello to me?* Nervously, he said hi back.

Christopher sat closest to the booth of voluble though amiable teens.

Were there another empty table, I would have moved us to it. Not that I disliked the girls, but their laughter and talking were distracting.

A waitress came to our table, quickly gave us our menus, took our drink order and left.

"Try the Tagliatelle Bolognese," a voice suggested from behind Christopher. "It's to die for!"

We all turned to the stall of girls next to us. The girl with the curly, blond hair was facing us, her arms folded comfortably on the wide, flaring counter that separated our booth from hers.

"Thank you," I said. "We'll consider it."

"Hey, would you mind if I sat at your table for a while?" she asked. "I need a break from all these chatty chicks."

Kylie and I looked at each other. Her request took us by surprise, but we didn't want to be discourteous, so we both said, "Sure." I then asked

Christopher if it was all right with him if she sat with us. He nodded sparingly, his face skittish.

After telling her friends she would be right next door, the girl swiftly came around to our table and sat down next to Christopher.

"I'm Jill," she introduced herself to him.

"I-I-I-I'm Chr-Chr-Chr—"

"I know, you're Christopher. I've seen you around. But I haven't seen you at any of the dances. How come?"

"Um...I-I-I-I-I d-d-don't know."

"You should go. I know *one* girl who would dance with you." She smiled kittenishly.

Even in the low light, I could see that Christopher's face was as red as the Tiffany lamp above us.

My friend was drowning. I had to help him.

"So, what grade are you in, Jill?" I stepped in. "You're not a freshman, I know that."

"I'm a sophomore. I can't wait to be a senior like you, Kylie. When will you turn eighteen, or are you already?"

"Next month," she answered stiffly. "How'd you know I was a senior?"

"Word gets around."

"What word?"

"That Owen broke up with Roxanne and he's dating a senior. You're here with Owen, so...one plus one."

Christopher looked down at the table.

This night was going downhill—fast.

I had to change the trajectory of the conversation or the evening would end up a disaster. "So, Jill, is being a sophomore harder than being a freshman?"

"Sometimes. It seems the older you get the more the teachers expect from you."

"Have you got any ideas what you're going to go into after high school?" I asked, though I really didn't care.

"I think I'm going to go into engineering or something like that. I'm good at math. How about you, Kylie? What are your plans?"

"Veterinary medicine," Kylie answered tersely but politely. I wasn't sure if she was still piqued at the fact that she and I were the subject the others' private discussions.

"That's cool! I love animals too, but I could never put one to sleep. That would kill me." She turned to Christopher. "I know what *you're* going to be. A photographer. I see you working for the *National Geographic* or *Newsweek* or *Look* or some other big New York magazine."

I was tempted to tell her that *Look* went out of business in 1971, but passed on the temptation, for what good is a correction if it is exiguous and only serves to embarrass?

The waitress brought our drinks. Both Christopher and I had Pepsis, while Kylie had a Tab.

Christopher was about to unsleeve his straw when he saw that Jill didn't have anything in front of her. He handed her his straw and slid his glass of Pepsi over to her. The kindness made her freeze, as if gifts were a rarity in her life. She looked up at the waitress and asked, "Can we have another straw?" Then she turned to Christopher, "We can share."

Christopher smiled.

We yielded to Jill's suggestion and we all ordered Tagliatelle Bolognese.

The mood at our table changed the moment Christopher offered Jill his drink. Jill might have been brassy at the start, but after Christopher's gentlemanly offering, she became a pleasant addition to our threesome. She asked Christopher about himself, and he answered her with remarkable ease. Occasionally, he would get stuck on a word, but the majority of his speech was fluent and stammer-free. Clearly, he was enjoying himself, and I was glad for him, especially after what had happened earlier in the day. I had feared at the beginning of the evening that Jill might complete the words he had trouble with—as she had done when he struggled to tell her his name—but each time he spoke she remained quiet and listened to him with exceptional patience and interest. I was immensely surprised, as well as impressed, because teenagers, for all their sensitivities, are nevertheless long on themselves and short on others.

Kylie and I sat back and let Jill and Christopher get to know one another. I had to wonder why Jill waited until that evening to initiate a beginning with him. Why hadn't she done so in school? In spite of her apparent alacrity, perhaps she was innately shy and needed to be in just the right place and at just the right time to make her feelings known.

I wished Shannon had been there: she would have witnessed her exaggeration firsthand—not *all* the girls at Moran considered Christopher *weird* and *creepy*.

Perhaps I was wrong about fate and chance. Perhaps certain events *were* meant to be. The circumstances that led up to the union of Christopher and Jill was strong evidence of that. If I had not broken up with Roxanne, I would not have been in the park on Christmas Eve night, and I would not have found Megan's kitten, and I would not have met Kylie, and Christopher would not have pursued Roxanne, and she would not have rejected him, and I would not have seen him in the parking lot, and I would not have asked him to dinner, and he and Jill would never have come together.

Yes, it certainly did appear that not everything was the product of chance and accident.

When death points its finger, it never points at just one…but three.

*March 5, 1975.*
*Wednesday.*

I now had World History on Mondays and Wednesdays instead of Mondays and Thursdays. I shared the class with forty-three other students. No one enjoyed the class. Those of us in it were counting the days to the end of school when summer would begin, and Mr. Carey's class would end.

Mr. Carey was not in his room when we entered it. This was a first: he was always sitting at his desk, reading, waiting to begin his captious blustering.

Five minutes after the class bell rang, Mr. Carey entered the room and closed the door behind him. His tie was loose, his sport coat was stained, and his pants were wrinkled. The man himself was no better than his clothes: his hair was untidy, his face unshaven, and his eyes were scribed with red.

The door at the back of the room was open; he ordered that it be closed. He went to the front blackboard, turned around and fell back against it, his eyes fixed on Noelle. His body slid down the board until the metal chalk tray stopped him. He hiked himself upright and staggered forward. He wiped his mouth and spit into the metal waste can next to his desk.

"That's what I think of you and your whole rotten race," he slurred at Noelle. "No, I have not been imbibing...well...maybe just a little. Generally, it is not my custom to quaff in any measure, at any time, but I made an exception just this once." He grabbed his shirtsleeve and blew his nose.

A tear slipped from his eye.

"Herberts Cukurs," he said, looking at Noelle. "One of your *apostles*. One of your *believers*. One of your *corruptions*. Member of the Arajs Kommando. The Hangman of Riga. The Butcher of Riga. Killer of children. You shot a baby just to show you had the power to do it. You killed a crying boy who was lost and trying to find his mother. You burned three hundred Jews alive. You forced them into their synagogue, locked it, set it afire, stood back, and listened to the screams. You forced an elderly Jew to rape a twenty-year-old Jewess in front of other prisoners. You joyfully, happily, willingly ended the lives of thirty thousand innocents. You played God—when godliness was nowhere in your soul."

This man had more than a little liquor in him—he was saturated with it. He was speaking to Noelle as if she were this man Cukurs. Something must have occurred the night before to tip him over the edge.

Silence with the weight of steel fell on the room. All in it were confused; but none as confused as Noelle, I imagined.

"Reinhard Heydrich," he cited another name to Noelle. "Adolph Butcher, your Führer, called you *the man with the iron heart*.' Another of your *final-solution* men. No, I take that back: not a man—an insect. You're *all* insects. You're all locusts and lice. You always have been. You said the Jews were subhuman. It is *you* who are subhuman. Your Einsatzgruppen, one of your killing squads, shot a mother shielding her child—didn't it, Mr. Heydrich? And then you shot the child. Operation Anthropoid ended your life. But you didn't stay dead, did you? Your memory lived on in the diseased hearts of your loathsome countrymen. In retaliation for your assassination, the village of Lidice was destroyed. No male over fifteen was allowed to live. In front of a barn shielded with mattresses, you lined the boys and men up, and then lustfully filled their bodies with bullets. You even shot their pets. Those whom you didn't kill, you sent to your death camp, Ravensbrück. Then you burned the village to ashes. When the numbers were added, you had murdered nearly five thousand people in revenge for your hallowed Heydrich's assassination."

I was sickened by what he was telling us. I was also angry that he was making Noelle—and every German—equal to the Nazis. He continued to talk to her as if *she* were these men, as if *she* was Germany itself.

"Do you know what is most appalling about you Germans?" he asked Noelle. "You're cowards. You smiled arrogantly while you murdered, but after you were conquered, you ran and hid, like scared dogs. If your ideology was so right, so just, so necessary, so important, so purposeful, why did you run after the war? Why didn't you stay and stand up for what you believed in then? Where was your arrogance after your fall? Why weren't you waving your swastikas then? Because you are cockroaches, and cockroaches run when hit with the light. You were evil, and you knew it. You hid your concentration camps. You knew if the world discovered them, it would hunt you down and destroy you—and it did. You killed and killed and killed, and you kept on killing, as if you had the right! You killed children and women. You beat them; you tortured them; you experimented on them; you—"

"I've heard enough of this crap!" Terence Daniels vented aloud, his hands up in the air in disgust. "I'm leaving." He arose from his desk and headed for the rear door.

"You're not going anywhere!" Mr. Carey exploded. He pulled from his front pants pocket a Smith & Wesson .38 Special and pointed it at Terence.

Everyone screamed and scrambled to the floor, many covering their heads with their arms.

"Sit your ass back down, Mr. Daniels!" Mr. Carey demanded. "Or I'll blow it out the back of your pants!"

Terence, now cowering, made his way back to his seat.

"Get back into your chairs!" Mr. Carey screamed at the class.

Everyone fearfully obeyed.

He aimed his gun at Noelle. "Get up!" he ordered.

She began to cry.

"I said, get up!"

Trembling and crying, Noelle got to her feet. "Please don't hurt me," she begged. "Please don't kill me."

"*Please don't kill me,*" he mimicked. "Why shouldn't I? *You* killed."

"I didn't kill anybody," she whimpered, her body quaking.

"But you did. You killed children. So many children. You killed them with pleasure—didn't you, Mr. Barbie?"

He had to be referring to Klaus Barbie, also known as the Butcher of Lyon. He killed and tortured thousands of French prisoners while he was based in Lyon, France.

"How could you do it?" Mr. Carey asked, his voice cracking. "You burned children alive in front of their parents to get information. Other children you sent to Auschwitz to be gassed. '*Shot or deported— it amounts to the same thing,*' you said of the children you selected to be executed. You tortured and murdered countless souls. You broke their arms and their legs; you ripped out their fingernails; you lashed them with whips; you burned them with lit cigarettes; you electrocuted them; you bayoneted them; you cremated them alive; you kicked in their faces; you held them under ice water; you injected them with poisons; you cut them open without anesthesia; you hacked them to death with axes; you skinned them alive; you sexually abused them; you beat them until they were dead, and those you didn't beat or starve or work to death, you shot or hung. And it wasn't just Jews you slaughtered—you got rid of millions of others. Millions. Poles, Slavs, Gypsies, Americans, Soviets, Catholics, Communists, homosexuals, intellectuals, the mentally inferior, the physically inferior, anyone who resisted you or fought back, anyone you thought was undesirable or a threat, you erased. The Roman Empire, even as sadistic as it was, didn't commit the acts of barbarity you did.

"To add indignity to injury, you even claimed that the dead at Dachau were not killed in the camp, but were bodies removed from bombed buildings and taken there to be cremated.

"Isn't it interesting that many of your war crimes were tried at Dachau. But even then, you wore on your face remorselessness, even boredom and disinterest, for your monstrous inhumanity. Remember your trial for your blood purge at Malmedy? Your arrogance blazed in that courtroom like a torch. You were pleased with your slaughter. You murdered your prisoners at Malmedy like they were diseased livestock. But we had the last laugh, didn't we? After we liberated Dachau, we made *you* the prisoners. Allied soldiers and camp internees shot you, beat you, and kicked you to death.

"How did your house ever rise? How did your race ever come into being? How could you be the way you are? How do you live with the cries of the children you orphaned and brutalized and terrorized and killed? How do you live with yourself at all? You're a bestial people. Every one of you. Every last one of you. Your race is a scourge, a plague, a deadly bacteria. Every German is gangrene in the body of humanity. Every German alive should be destroyed, just as *they* destroyed. You came from the depths of Sheol. You have no remorse for what you did because you believe the world belongs to you, and you alone have the final say who lives on it. You are the—"

The door opposite Mr. Carey opened and Mrs. Millan, an English teacher—nearly antebellum and very prim; a female rendition of Cotton Mather—stormed into the room. *"Mr. Carey, what in the name of—"*

Mr. Carey stared at Mrs. Millan and then shot her in the stomach.

She grimaced horribly, her face paled, and she and collapsed to the floor—all within two or three seconds. It was chillingly and petrifyingly similar to the shooting of Lee Harvey Oswald.

In the same second Mrs. Millan hit the floor, we all heard a girl shriek outside the room and run.

The class screamed and ran for the doors.

Mr. Carey fired the gun again, this time into the ceiling. "Get back to your chairs!" he yelled.

Everyone halted and crouched down in terror.

As Mrs. Millan lay on the floor, my classmates returned to their desks. Many were crying now; some were boys.

I heard the tapping of dripping liquid. I looked around. Then I noticed a think trickle falling from the edge of the seat of the girl next to me. Her name was Jackie Bolton; she had lost control of her herself.

Minutes later, without warning, the fire alarm sounded. Immediately, we heard the rumble of students hurry out of the building.

Moments after that, we heard Mr. Heald call out from beyond the open door to our room. "Mr. Carey, this is Mr. Heald. Please listen to me. You've got to stop this. Please let the children come out. I'll come in; you can take me instead."

"It's not you I want!" Mr. Carey blared, shooting twice at the open door.

Everyone in the classroom screamed.

"I'm not going away, Mr. Carey. Neither are the police, who are on their way."

"Get over here!" Mr. Carey roared at Noelle.

The girl shrunk in her chair. She was sobbing and shaking violently.

Something had to be done or he would shoot Noelle as easily as he had shot Mrs. Millan. If his attention could be redirected until the police arrived, Noelle might survive.

"Mr. Carey," I said, getting to my feet.

All eyes shifted to me, which, for some curious reason, made me feel very uneasy.

"Sit back down, or I'll come over there and shoot you down," he flexed.

"Mr. Carey, look at what you're doing. You're inflicting the same terror that you've been condemning." I inched my way toward the windows, which were opposite Noelle. I wanted him facing me instead of her. "None of us took part in the killing during—"

"Owen," Mr. Heald called out. "Stay out of this. Let the police handle this situation."

"Be quiet, Mr. Heald," I injuncted.

"Get away from those windows," Mr. Carey insisted.

"Do you believe in God, Mr. Carey?" I put forth.

"You don't ask me questions. Now get back to your chair."

"Just answer me—yes or no."

He paused. "Yes, I do."

"Do you believe the Bible is the word of God?"

"It *is* the word of God."

"Ezekiel, chapter eighteen: *The son shall not suffer for the iniquity of the father, nor the father suffer for the iniquity of the son. The righteousness of the righteous shall be upon himself, and the wickedness of the wicked shall be upon himself.* You are making Noelle guilty for the sins of her forebears. She is not in error—*they* were…just as you are now. The Germans of that time shot innocent people. That's what you just did to Mrs. Millan. End this, Mr. Carey, before it goes any further."

A faint wail of sirens reached the room.

"Yes…I will end this—*my* way," he responded. "But before I do, here is a little something to remember me by, Mr. Crowley."

He discharged the gun.

Hollywood would have its audiences believe that a bullet to the arm is a superficial assault, like being slugged with a fist. When the bullet made contact with my right upper arm, it was like being hit with a hammer that had been sitting in a fire. The force of the bullet threw me back. My head smacked against the windows. My body had experienced many agonies over the years, but the pain from that bullet tearing my skin was the worst I had ever known. My stomach seized, and I felt like I was going to throw up. Fortunately, I had nothing in my stomach, so I didn't.

Screaming and yelling flooded the room again.

Mr. Carey yelled for everyone to shut up.

There was instant silence.

He turned to me. "Though you and I reside in different abodes of thought, Mr. Crowley, we are in accord on one matter—I *have* killed. Just like *her*." He put the sidearm to the side of his head and returned his attention to Noelle. "May you forever live with this memory…just as the survivors of the German purge had to live with the memory of their loved ones being shot."

He pulled the trigger again.

March 5, 1975 vanished instantaneously. It was now February 1, 1968. On that day, General Nguyễn Ngọc Loan delivered a bullet into the head of Nguyễn Văn Lém, a captured Viet Cong soldier, in front of two photographers, one from *NBC*, the other from the *Associated Press*. The prisoner, after being shot, fell sideways to the ground and blood jetted from his head like water spouting from a hose. Mr. Carey fell onto the tile floor, and his blood fled his body in the very same way.

As Mr. Carey's life was fountaining out of him, the students in the room screamed and ran for the doors. They trampled over Mrs. Millan and Mr. Carey; some stepping in their blood, taking it with them in their frenzied exodus.

Mr. Heald tried vainly to get into the room but was held back by the tide of students fleeing it. Once he was able to get into the classroom, he dashed over to me and wrapped his suit jacket around my arm.

I was very cold; my mouth was dry, and I was shivering.

He quickly guided me out of the room. We were met on the stairwell by two young ambulance attendants (or paramedics, as they were just starting to be called). The two attendants, one male and one female, rushed me out to a waiting ambulance. Other ambulances, response police vehicles, and fire engines were parked on both sides of the road. Students and staff were everywhere. Some of the students were laughing, though I was certain it was not because of what had happened, but because it was an exciting break in the monotony of school.

My injury felt much worse than it was. On the way to the hospital, the female attendant told me that the bullet had made a deep laceration, but nothing more than that. She said I had been incredibly lucky.

The girl impressed me tremendously. She was a female version of the male characters on the television series *Emergency*. She had a soothing voice, sympathetic touch, confident manner, and reassuring eyes. Hers was the kind of profession I wanted for myself when I became an adult.

Once at the hospital, I was examined by multiple people: two physicians, two RNs, an X-ray tech, an admitting clerk, even a chaplain. I almost felt like nobility. Not since I was a small boy had so much attention been devoted to me. Privately, I savored it. It was like a deep, warm bath.

The bath quickly cooled when I was finally treated. The wound had to be debrided and anesthetized for suturing. The cleaning stung, but it wasn't unbearable. The localizations were far more nociceptive. Each injection of lidocaine was like a branding. I had to clench my fist and teeth to keep from howling like a little child who had just fallen off his bike. I was deeply disappointed in myself at my reaction to the pain; I thought I was stronger than that. I thought I could take any kind of discomfort. I was wrong.

The ER doctor who sutured me made a bad experience worse. He was mechanical and uncommunicative, which made me feel like I was inconveniencing him. Had I been him, I would have explained to me what I was doing, assured me it would be over soon, asked me what subjects I liked in school, and told me about himself—anything to soften the situation and help me believe it wasn't as bad as it seemed. Obviously, this man went into medicine for what he could get from it, not what he could give to it.

After the doctor completed his work, he left the treatment room without a word. Almost immediately, two investigators from the police department entered it and began questioning me about the event. I told them everything I knew, although I omitted the warning I had given to Mr. Taggart about Mr. Carey. I assumed this would only bring trouble upon Mr. Taggart, and I didn't want that. Dropping him in hot water wouldn't bring back Mrs. Millan or Mr. Carey. It was over, and everyone had to move past it.

Before the men left, one of them stepped closer to my bed and patted my leg. "That was an incredible thing you did, Owen. That girl Noelle is alive because of you." He smiled, and he and his partner left.

There was a clock above the door. It read 1:55. I shouldn't have been, but I was hungry. It seemed almost indecent to be hungry after witnessing two people die.

As if my need had been telepathically transmitted to the front desk, a nurse came into my room and asked me if I wanted some lunch.

The two of us heard running, and we looked toward the door. Suddenly, Kylie and her father appeared in front of it. Kylie put her hands over her mouth. She ran over to me and laid her head on my chest.

"Of all the people to get shot, it had to be you," she said.

"It wasn't my plan, believe me," I remarked. "Are you two hungry? This nice nurse was about to order me some lunch. Would you like something?"

"No, we're fine," Kylie replied, standing up. "Just being here with you is all I want."

The nurse told me she would call down to the cafeteria and have a sandwich and milk sent up. Then she excused herself and left.

"I heard you saved a girl's life today," Mr. Ulrich said.

"I only wanted to distract him until the police came," I told him.

"You truly were a blessing to that girl. To your whole class."

"It's not over yet. They escaped the first nightmare, and now they've got the second one to deal with—the memory of it all. Memories can be harder to deal with than the actual experience."

"Well, there's our hero of the hour!" someone exclaimed from behind us.

In the doorway was Mr. Heald.

He was genuinely happy to see me. He shook hands with Mr. Ulrich and Kylie.

"Is everyone from my class all right?" I asked the principal.

"They're shook up, but I think they'll be okay. I left Noelle with her parents and a Victim Counselor from the police department. There will be other counselors on campus the rest of this week and all of next. I've canceled all classes for the day. It will give everyone time to decompress, and for us to...clean up. The room won't be used as a classroom again. I don't think anyone would ever feel comfortable in it after what happened today."

"I think that's a wise decision," Mr. Ulrich praised.

"Owen," Mr. Heald said, "I've tried calling your home to inform your housekeeper what has happened, but she doesn't answer. I'll take you home as soon as they release you."

"That won't be necessary," Mr. Ulrich put forward. "He'll be staying with us for a while. At least for a few days. His housekeeper is…not likely to tend to his needs."

Kylie squeezed my hand and smiled elatedly.

"Are you all right with that, Owen?" Mr. Heald asked.

I was so moved by the gesture I couldn't answer. It had been years since someone wanted to take care of me. All the attention I was receiving was almost overwhelming.

I nodded.

"You'll be in excellent hands," Mr. Heald extolled. "The Ulriches are fine people."

"I'm sorry about your jacket," I said, finally finding my voice.

"Don't worry about it. It was getting a bit quick on me anyway. It's time I move up to a forty-four. I definitely need to cut back on the pasta."

Then his expression turned formal and somber. "Owen, I want you to take the rest of the week off. You're going to need to relax and be away from school for a while. You're also going to need some counseling. For once, *you'll* need to talk with somebody. A counselor will be calling you, and I want you to talk to him. Understood?"

I nodded.

"Good. I have to get back to school. I'll see you on Monday. Oh, and don't worry about PE class—you're excused from it for the remainder of the year. I'm sure that won't break your heart." He smiled and walked out of the room.

Kylie kissed me on the lips and went over to her father and kissed him on his cheek. "Thanks, Dad."

Everyone in the Ulrich house, like nearly everyone in the ER, treated me like I was royalty. Mr. Ulrich was a rock-ribbed conservative and unashamed Nixon loyalist, as was I, and he loved having someone around the house who shared his views. Mrs. Ulrich was as kind as she was proper: she made sure I was never without food or drink. And she made sure I was never left alone too long. When not in school or sleeping, Megan rarely left my side. Kylie, too, was seldom far from me. Collin loved having a new chess partner under his roof. Even Mittens, who had grown considerably since December, enjoyed my company; he made my lap his new lounge. Mittens was no longer a little kitten but a young cat, and I came to the conclusion that I had been wrong about cats—not all of them were mercurial menaces.

Each night was unreal. We all sat down to dinner at the dining room table, said a prayer of gratitude, and then ate leisurely by the light from a silver candelabra, which sat in the center of the table. There was no arguing, no complaining, no fussing, no name-calling, no competing; only goodness and acceptance and love. Truly unreal.

Since Kylie and I had begun dating, we only saw each other on Saturday afternoons. Kylie wanted us to be together more, but I didn't want to come between her and what she had with her family. I had read about good children who came from good homes who got involved with someone and, unmaliciously, pushed their families aside in favor of the new relationship. I was not about to be the cause of that in Kylie's life.

The couch in the living room was where I slept. Each night, I wondered if Ms. Windom knew what had happened to me, and, if so, did she even care? How could people like Kylie and her family and people like Ms. Windom coexist in the same world?

Saturday night everyone went to bed early. The next day was Kylie's birthday. Her family had a big day planned for her: first, a large breakfast; then a party at her church; then a movie in the afternoon; and finally, a gathering of all her friends at Clair's house for cake and presents for Kylie's big eighteen!

The grandfather clock in the dining room chimed 10:00. Everyone in the home was in bed and asleep. I turned on the lamp next to the couch and sat and drank in the warmth and the peace. Though I had come a long way in my life, such things were still far from me.

I wished I was turning eighteen like Kylie. I would ask her to marry me so I would always have what I had right then. But that would be wrong and dishonest. That would be using Kylie, and that I would never do.

The Ulriches had a family album on the top shelf of a corner hutch adjacent to the front room window. I gently lifted it down and brought it over to the couch. The album, nearly the size and weight of a cinder block, was cracked along its edges and spine. Filling its first pages were black-and-whites of girls in long dresses with large bows in their hair and little boys in short pants with newsboy caps on their heads. Then color pictures began to creep in. Rarely was there one with a man smiling. Never was there one with a man in long hair. Nearly all of the women sported bold, red lipstick and short, wavy hair parted on the side, like the studio stills of Lauren Bacall and Katherine Hepburn. Later, all of the pictures were in color; that's when the first ones of Kylie started to appear. She had the face of a cherub and the heart of a seraph. No wonder her father called her 'Angel.' She was a happy little girl and a happy teenager, and the chances were very good that she would be a happy woman. There were people like that—happy head to heel, positive dawn to death.

"Hi there, handsome," a soft voice said.

I jumped and looked toward the dining room.

Standing under the archway separating the living room from the dining room was Kylie. She was wrapped in a pink robe.

"Whatcha doing?" she asked.

"I couldn't sleep," I said.

She came over and sat down next to me.

"I hope you don't mind me looking through your album," I said nervously.

"Of course not. Someday you and I are going to be in it...playing with our children."

She closed the album, lifted it from my lap and laid it next to her. She took my face in her hands and kissed me.

Then she slowly stood and removed her robe. All that clothed her now was a lacy bra and silk underwear.

As in the boys' lavatory on Valentine's Day, every nerve in my body came alive. Instantly, my breathing quickened and my mouth dried.

"I promised you on Valentine's Day that the nicest part was yet to come," Kylie reminded me. "That day is here." She held out her hands, guided me to my feet, and took me with her onto the plush Persian rug in front of the couch.

She caressed my face as I lay over her body. It would have been so easy for us to become one. It was as if we were meant to be one.

"We have each other for the next two hours," she said softly. "After that, if we make love, it will be against the law. Right now, we're both minors. At midnight, I won't be. I want us to make love so I can remember it when we can't. I want you to give me that part of you that no one else has ever had. I love you, Owen. I promise you this night I am yours forever and for always."

I looked down into her sky-blue eyes. What an incredible creation she was! She was a cool, sparkling stream winding through a field of summer flowers. She was peace and tranquility and serenity. Such perfection was bound to fly away from me. It always had.

I raised myself up and returned to the couch.

"Did I do something wrong?" Kylie asked, her tone ringed with anxiety.

Wiping my eyes, I said, "It's been so long since I felt this much love from people. Your whole family has made me feel like I finally belong someplace."

"Then why are you on the couch?"

"It's difficult to explain. It doesn't make sense to anyone but me."

"What is it?"

"I'm afraid."

"Of what?"

"Of you."

"Of *me*? Why?"

"I can't help it. It's easier to live without love than it is to live with the fear that it will be taken away. Kindness disappears; sweetness turns sour; love fades to black. Everything withers and dies. At least it does in my life."

Her eyes measured mine for many moments. "You're afraid I'm going to abandon you, aren't you? Just like everyone else."

I didn't answer her.

"That's the real reason you don't come around much, isn't it?" she said. "You stay at a distance to protect yourself. It's safer there."

"I bring out the worst in people, Kylie. I always have. Eventually, I'll bring it out in you too. There isn't a whole lot about me to love."

She got to her feet, slipped on her robe and sat down next to me. She took my hands. "Owen, there's so much about you to love I don't know where to begin. If you only knew how wonderful you are. We're going to go slow, and I'm going to prove to you that I'll never leave you. Ever. If you bring out anything in me, it's my best. I love you, Owen. I know you can't say it now, but I believe someday you will. I truly believe that someday you'll be able to say it again, and you'll say it to me. Forever and always…that will be us. Me and you and you and me; that's the way it'll always be."

We sat together as she turned eighteen. Then we kissed one last time, and she went back upstairs.

Kylie woke up glowing. I stood back and let the sun shine on her. It was *her* day, not mine, not ours, just hers. She was so happy, and I felt happy for her. People like Kylie deserved rainbows, for she herself was one… brilliant with the colors of love and promise.

Kylie and two of her friends dropped me off at my house that afternoon. She walked me to my door.

"Thank you for sharing the day with me," she said. "It was twice as special because you were there. I *love* your gift." She stroked the smooth, milky opals suspended from her ears.

"Happy Birthday, Kylie." I smiled.

"Owen, thank you for staying with us the past few days. It meant everything to me."

"I think *I'm* the one who got the better end of the deal."

"Remember that day in the park when you said you would never be called an angel?"

"Uh-huh."

"You were wrong, Owen. You *are* an angel...to me. Sent straight from Heaven."

For a reason I couldn't explain, from a place I couldn't see, a wave of sadness washed over me. I reached up and touched Kylie's face. "Thank you for coming into my life, Kylie. You've given me so much. If I hadn't met you, I don't..." I began to cry.

"Hey, you're talking like you're never going to see me again. We'll see each other in school tomorrow. Remember our song, 'We've Only Just Begun.' It's just the beginning for us. It's only going to get better from here."

She kissed me and ran back to the car.

It was snowing...just like the night we met.

When I opened the front door the next morning to leave for school, I jumped back.

Mr. Taggart was standing there.

"Mr. Taggart, what...what are you doing here?" I asked, very perplexed and annoyed at him for startling me.

"I need to talk to you, Owen," he said firmly, studying my eyes, as if he were trying to read something in them.

"Why are you looking at me like that? *Why are you even here?*"

He didn't answer straight away. "Owen, we need to talk."

"Okay...but couldn't this have waited? I mean, I'll be at school within a half hour."

"No, it can't wait. Can I come in, please?"

"Why don't you just drive me to school and you can tell me on the way."

"No. Please, can I just come inside?"

"All right," I obliged impatiently.

Once inside, I faced him disaffectedly. "Look, Mr. Taggart, I'm sure you feel bad about what happened last week, but what's done is done. You followed your judgment, and now you have to live with it."

"Yes, I do," he agreed soberly. He looked as if he had been crying. "I let everyone down. Mrs. Millan is dead because of me, and many students are traumatized because of my inaction. But…" he stopped. He pressed his lips together tightly, then licked them. "Owen, if I could take this away from you, I would. If I could take it upon myself, I would. You're the…you're the bravest, most compassionate student I've ever known. You don't deserve this. You don't."

"Mr. Taggart, I was only shot—I wasn't murdered. I will heal."

"I know you will, and I feel responsible for that too…but that's not why I'm here."

"So why are you here?"

His eyes started to tear. He opened his mouth to speak, but he couldn't begin.

"What is it?" I asked.

He licked his lips again and locked his eyes to mine. "Kylie was killed in a car accident yesterday afternoon."

# CHAPTER 10

## *Return to Yesterday*

*"Death never takes a holiday. He clocks in every day of the year. But he never complains—for he loves his job."*

TESSA STEGGO

*"Death takes more than just the life of the dead."*

SUE MALOUF

Though tens of thousands of words make up the fertile and bountiful landscape of the English language, there is still a drought of words for the enormity of death. Neither voice nor pen can adequately describe the aloneness, emptiness, and terror that overshadows a man when death darkens his door.

Mr. Taggart's words entered my ears and traveled to every nerve, every cell, every atom in my body. If they had had actual weight, they would have crushed me.

"Where?" was all I was able to say.

"Not too far from here," he said. "Seems a truck slid into the car she was riding in. If it hadn't been snowing, it probably never would have happened. The tragedy of the whole thing is that she probably would have survived if she hadn't been wearing her seat belt."

"What?"

"It seems the seat belt kept her in place, and that's what..." he stopped. "Listen, you don't need to hear this now. Owen, I think it would be best if you stayed home a few more days. I think coming back right now would be a mistake."

Speaking was impossible. Even if I wanted to argue with him, I couldn't.

"Take as much time as you need," he said. He patted my shoulder and quietly left the house.

I stood where I was, unable to move.

"So—your little princess won't be seeing any more birthdays, eh?" Ms. Windom snorted from behind me. She came around and faced me. "Pity. Pity it wasn't *you*. Seems you have cheated death twice now: first when the bullet missed your heart, and second when you weren't in the car with your now-dead girlfriend."

I could neither move nor talk.

"What's this?" she jabbed. "No smart remarks, no threats, no parading of power? How true it is: the more pompous they are, the more powerfully they fall." She chuckled and walked away.

Ms. Windom's words evanished immediately. Mr. Taggart's did not.

Numbness swirled around my body like a cold wind. Nailed to that numbness were disbelief and desolation. How could Kylie be gone? Just like that. Forever. How could she be swept away like she was nothing? She was taken away without any consideration for her family, her friends, or me. She was young, happy, and beautiful...and an instant later, she was broken, bloody, and dead.

Young people aren't supposed to die. Their parents and friends aren't supposed to attend their funerals.

I understood Mr. Taggart's words...I just couldn't internalize them. I couldn't believe I would never see Kylie again. I would never again see her smile, or look into her eyes, or feel her hands, or smell her perfume, or hear her voice. Everything she was—everything she felt, everything she thought, everything that was uniquely her—was gone, never to be seen again.

Somehow, I made my way to my room. I closed the door, pulled the curtains and sat down on the floor next to my bed. Kylie's words haunted me: *"Nothing happens by chance, Owen."* She was right. If Kylie hadn't driven me home, she would not have been killed. If only I had stayed away from her, she would have been in school that day and not a fatality stretched out in a morgue somewhere. But I didn't stay away. I came back after that Christmas Eve, and in doing so, I condemned her. There was no getting around it: she was dead, and I was responsible.

I wanted to cry, but I couldn't. All I could do was wish…wish that it had been me who was dead, and not her.

I had read that some people have a connection with their mate so strong that they know instantly when something is wrong with them, even when they are physically separated. I had no idea anything was wrong with Kylie. All night I hadn't a single feeling. While I was lying between warm sheets on a soft bed of foam, sleeping, she was covered by a cold sheet on a hard bed of stainless steel, decaying. What did that say about me? How could I not have sensed that she had passed away? I had judged others for being shallow and without substance. As it turned out, *I* was the one who lacked depth and marrow.

I didn't know how I was going to go on without Kylie. She gave me what no one else ever had. Once again, I was alone. Only this time, I didn't know how to deal with it.

For all my mental skills and abilities, I could only remember sparse areas of my relationship with Kylie. It seemed that in letting Kylie occupy only part of my heart, I unknowingly allowed her to occupy only part of my mind as well.

Hours and minutes, days and nights melded into a single span of time.

Occasionally, I left my bed and took a drink from the bathroom sink. That in itself was a considerable task. Even walking was a labor. I couldn't eat…nor did I want to. Nothing gave me life. All I wanted to do was sleep, for it was only then that there was release from the pain. When I awoke, the pain returned, for then I saw Kylie.

There was a hard knock on my door. Without my permission, the door flew open.

My eyes opened, and they drifted over to it. Ms. Windom was standing there, like a dark, demonic sculpture.

"Maybe you should go live with that wasted mother of yours!" The words discharged from her like a spit of mucoid lava. "I'm sick of answering the phone for you!" she cursed. "And now those lint-headed layabouts you call friends are coming to the door! There's some stupid memorial for that girlfriend of yours tomorrow. Do me a favor—go to it! Your constant presence in this house is oppressive." She left the room, slamming the door after her.

Slowly, I sat up and looked around the room. I had no desire to leave it, but I knew I had to. I couldn't remain on my bed forever. I had to return to the world. I had to return to school. I had to go back there—a place in which every room and hallway held a memory of Kylie.

And I needed to attend the memorial. No one knew the Kylie I knew. They needed to remember her the way I remembered her, the way she really was.

I called the school and asked when the memorial service was to be held. I was told it would begin at nine the next morning, in the auditorium.

I would be there.

Kylie died Sunday night. It was now Friday morning. I was certain that Kylie had already been buried. I was also certain that her parents were angry with me for not being at the interment. But I couldn't attend. I hadn't the strength.

When I rounded the corner and saw the school, I stopped in my steps. I wanted to go back home. Though Ms. Windom was there, it was a less ominous place than that four-story building.

Someone called to me from the street. Alighting from a silver Cadillac Seville was Mesa Sorenson, a close friend of Kylie. Children are sometimes named after seasons or places special to their parents, and such was the case with this girl.

Mesa was a natural beauty...truly a rose who needed no perfume. She was born of parents whose cotton was very high. Her father was a pediatric neurosurgeon; her mother a realtor. Yet neither she nor her parents stood in the shine of their own gold. They were mild and humble people who gave their time and benefaction to organizations that aided runaway teens and abused mothers.

Mesa ran up to me and folded me in her arms. She started to weep.

Her tears made my desire to flee intensify. I couldn't handle her grief. I couldn't even handle my own. I had lost my ability—and my desire—to connect with people on an empathetic or even sympathetic level. This incapacity made me feel cowardly and weak and hard-hearted.

Mesa released herself from me and wiped her eyes.

"I'm glad you've come for the memorial," she said.

"Yes."

"A bunch of us have called your house, but your housekeeper keeps hanging up on us."

"I'm sorry about that."

"Are you all right?"

I noticed people frequently asked that. They see someone in pain, and they ask, "Are you okay?" Of course, they're not okay. If they were okay, they wouldn't be in pain.

"How is everyone holding up?" I asked.

"Not good. None of us have ever lost anyone our own age."

"Yes, death is especially vicious when it thieves the young."

"You look a little unsteady—why don't you let me walk you to your locker."

"I'll be okay. You go on ahead. Thank you for the offer, though."

"You sure?"

"I'm sure."

Mesa left me and went into the school.

I turned around and began walking back home. Halfway there, I stopped. I had to go back. I couldn't stay away forever. And I had committed myself to speaking at Kylie's service. She deserved that.

I turned and headed back to the school.

I slipped in the rear entrance to the auditorium. I didn't want to see or talk to anyone before the service. Behind the stage were storage and changing rooms. In one of the storage rooms, surrounded by towers of dusty and water-stained boxes, I waited.

Soon, sounds of talking and walking pressed against the door of the storage room. The auditorium was filling up quickly.

My stomach felt as if it was being milled and powdered. It wasn't the idea of giving a speech that was braying my nerves; it was the fear of feeling. I didn't want to feel any more pain. I didn't want to feel anything. I wanted to be like Mr. Spock again. But I had abandoned him long ago, and now I was suffering the consequences of that desertion.

I thought about remaining in the room until the memorial was over. No one would ever know I was there; no one would ever see my pain. They would also never know about Kylie.

"Thank you all for coming," Mr. Heald began.

Quiet quickly descended on the room.

"I have been to three of these services for students in my years here as principal," Mr. Heald shared. "This is now my fourth. It is never easy...nor should it be, for when we take death lightly, we take life lightly.

"Centuries ago, the poet John Donne set down these immortal words: *No man is an island, entire of itself; every man is a piece of the continent, a part of the main. Any man's death diminishes me, because I am involved in mankind, and therefore never send to know for whom the bells tolls; it tolls for thee.*

"Less known, though equal in import, are words he penned just prior to those: *And when she buries a man, that action concerns me: all mankind is of one author, and is one volume; when one man dies, one chapter is not torn out of the book, but translated into a better language; and every chapter must be so translated; God employs several translators; some pieces are translated by age, some by sickness, some by war, some by justice; but God's hand is in every translation, and His hand shall bind up all our scattered leaves again for that library where every book shall lie open to one another. As therefore the bell that rings to a sermon calls not upon the preacher only, but upon the congregation to come, so this bell calls us all.*

"Every person dies, and God uses different ways to call His children home. And yet, when one of His children is a child, it is especially torturous, for it is too soon for them to depart. A child's death diminishes the world more than the death of someone of years, for the sweetness of that child, their talents and their gifts are gone irrevocably, never to grow, never to influence the lives of those who knew them and those who would have known them.

"I didn't know Kylie, but since her death, I have come to know about her. She was a private girl, but genuinely warm-hearted and unselfish. Her death is not only a palpable loss to all of us, but to all those she would have known. We are truly diminished by her passing.

"If anyone would like to come forward and share some thoughts or memories of Kylie, you are more than welcome to do so now."

Again, silence.

I inhaled deeply and opened the door.

I pushed aside the heavy, sage-green stage curtain and walked to the lectern.

The entire auditorium, even the balcony, was brimming with students and teachers.

When Mr. Heald first saw me, he showed surprise, then pleasure. He then stepped aside to let me have the speaker's stand.

The quiet in the tremendous room astonished me. Attaining silence from teenagers, especially when they are penned together, was tantamount to corralling a team of horses with a length of spider's silk. And yet, all were still.

Just below me, on the floor beneath the stage, was a table adorned with burning votive candles and standing photographs of Kylie. Only a few months ago, I had been in this same room for the memorial for Austin Richardson, the custodian. It was at that service that Roxanne and I shared our first kiss. So much can change so quickly.

To my amazement, Kylie's family was sitting in the front row of the auditorium. When our eyes joined, there was no anger in their faces, only delight.

Megan smiled. Then she discreetly waved at me with a couple of fingers resting in her lap.

I should have acknowledged her, but I couldn't. It was too painful to even look at her, for she was so much like her sister...gentle, pure, innocent.

My eyes panned the room. Some were blotting their eyes; others let their tears freely blanket their faces, like flags flying for a fallen friend.

"Twelve years ago this November," I commenced, "a man stepped off a plane. Many thought him youthful, but in truth, he was middle-aged. A broad, beaming smile set against a tanned and healthy visage is what the cameras captured that day. This young, vital notable was admired, loved, and adored. You might even say worshiped. From him had come words never before spoken: noble, inspiring, enkindling words. He challenged men and women, wherever they were, to rise above their innate selfishness and pettiness and be better human beings to their country and to one another.

"As this man descended the plane, he was greeted by thunderous cheers and applause from throngs of people behind a nearby fence. Another in his place might have simply waved to the crowd and disappeared into his limousine. Not so this figure. He felt he should be next to the crowd, shake their hands, acknowledge their presence. He was not a commoner, yet he lent himself to the people as though he were.

"In the crowd was a young, white-gloved woman. She, like hundreds of others there that sunny day, had her hand extended, hoping that the man would clasp it, if only for an instant. Her hope did not disappoint her. Their hands did unite, and her world, from that moment on, was altered forever. Though her contact with this man was momentary, she knew she had touched humanity at its finest. Though noise and movement were all around her, she became cocooned in quiet. All she saw and heard was their moment of connection. The woman before the touch and the woman after it were not the same. She vowed to change herself, to be like him: good, honest, charitable. She kept her vow. Who was this man who moved her so? His name was John F. Kennedy. Later that day, he would be killed.

"Kylie was only in my world for a moment, but she changed me, forever. It doesn't take years of bonding with someone to be transformed by them. It can happen in an instant. There are those in the world who are so rare and so pure and so..."

I had to stop. I didn't like where I was going. I was slipping into a pool of platitudes, and I was above that...and so was Kylie.

"I know many words," I went forth again. "I know how to mingle them and marry them, but when trying to gather them to paint a true image of Kylie, I am unfit, for she transcended all words. The majesty and light of some things simply cannot be described; their beauty is beyond the colors for the canvas, or the ink for the paper, or the words for the tongue. But still, I will try...for she deserves that.

"Kylie used to say to me, '*You are my favorite hello and my hardest good-bye.*' I never once returned the sentiment. She loved me, but I did not love her. I would not let myself. I vowed never to let the utterance '*I love you*' fall from my lips again. So foolish. I'd give my very soul if I could say those three words to her now.

"In the last speech of his life, Martin Luther King, quoting from Ralph Waldo Emerson, said: '*But I know, somehow, that only when it is dark enough can you see the stars.*' From where I am, in this space in time, in the darkness of her absence, I clearly see what Kylie meant to me. I loved her.

"I think most people who knew Kylie would say she was beyond her years. I would say she was beyond most people.

"Before I knew Kylie, I noticed something, yet it wasn't boldly distinct until she was in my life. She *asked* about me. No one else ever did. Each of you should look at your friends and examine them and then examine yourself. Examine the words you share with them, and they with you. People will always talk, usually hear, occasionally listen...but rarely ask. When was the last time any of you asked those closest to you how they really are? Not '*How was your weekend?*' or '*How was your date?*' or '*How was the movie?*' but '*How are* you—*truly?*' I venture to say that none of you have. But there was one among us who *did*. Her name was Kylie. She was the only one, in my whole life, to ever step out of herself and ask me about me: what I felt, what I feared, what I wanted.

Have you ever noticed that when people talk to one another, they open themselves up, like faucets, then close, politely, to let someone else open up? But have you also noticed that rarely does someone reach over and want to open someone else up? When was the last time you stepped out of yourselves and asked rather than talked? When was the last time you didn't consider your friends your audience? I was never Kylie's audience. And I hope she was never mine.

"Kylie was not just beautiful in skin and spirit, but in talent. Many of you are unaware of this, but she sang. Many a time she soloed for her church. She wanted me to sing for her just so she could hear my voice in song. As some of you know, I am not grass that bends at the first wind, but when it comes to singing, I demur without pause. But Kylie would not take my refusal as an answer. She kept at me until, eventually, I ceded my will to hers. Come to find out, I wasn't half bad. I'm no Dean Martin, but nor am I, as the apt playwright Emmanuel Dawson put it, *'a sinfonietta of scalded dogs'* either."

Many in the room laughed.

"It wasn't Kylie's persistence so much as her reassurance that gave me the confidence to sing," I continued. "She promised me she wouldn't laugh or even grimace if I made any nearby glass shatter. The wings, I think, of so many children never develop because they fear derision and rejection. They forever remain in their chrysalis, safe, but never seen. Kylie never ridiculed or undervalued anyone. She never built herself up by tearing someone else down. She never put herself before others. She believed in everyone. She believed in me.

"Song was but one of Kylie's passions. Writing was another. She once told me she wasn't very good at creating new ideas, but she could make old ideas better. I tried to tell her that if an old idea is made better, it is only because a new idea has been introduced into the batter. She never saw my logic. She and I went to see *The Towering Inferno* shortly after it opened. She was utterly captivated by it. She couldn't stop talking about it. Last month, she wrote her own high-rise-on-fire story. She called it *The Soaring Holocaust*. While it shared the same chassis as *The Towering Inferno*—a tall building on fire—the body of her story was completely original. Kylie was ferociously committed to honesty and truth. This commitment ran into every corner of her life, including her writing. For her high-rise fire story, she asked one of her friends, whose father is a deputy fire chief, if he would ask his father if her rather unorthodox, though inventive, solution to quell the fire was plausible, or, at the very least, possible. Her friend, in turn, asked his father. The father smiled and said, *'It's not very plausible...but it is possible.'* This was Kylie...proper and principled to the end.

"Kylie truly was a singular, unalloyed girl. So strong and unwavering. It was Kylie who first ignited our relationship. It was she who brought us together. She risked opening her heart to me...and I was forever changed for it. She showed me that people can be truly good, with no concealed motives. She let me see and feel that which I had not seen or felt before. She made me believe I was actually worth something. All of us can learn from Kylie. If there is someone you love, but they know not that you love them, clasp bravery and tell them. You may find a pleasant surprise awaiting you. But if you make known your love, and it is not welcomed, feel not the fool, for someday that person to whom you bequeathed your heart may be in a lonely place where they feel unwanted, and they will remember a time when they were not. Those three small words, *I love you*, should never be constrained. Fetter them not, even for a moment, for if you do, you may find yourself where I am now, wishing you hadn't.

"Love, however, like everything—absolutely everything—has a price. It is not costless. You pay in conflictions, contradictions, powerlessness, unappeasable hunger, dread, disquiet, death. It is said that a person's most splendid memories are made when another is by his side. This is true. It is also true that those same memories, because they include another, are also the most painful. It logically follows that to avoid the pain, one must avoid people: no people, no memories, no pain. When I was young, I lived by that principle. Unceasingly, I told myself: *If you get close, you get hurt.* It never entered my mind that the reverse was just as applicable: if you get close, you could hurt another. Kylie is dead because of me. She told me when we first met that nothing happens by chance. I did not agree with her at first. I do now. If I had not come into her life, Kylie would have that life today. The truck that struck her so close to my home would not have hit her because she would not have been near it. She is dead...and I am to blame. *A man's character is his fate.* Heraclitus authored those words. It would seem that a man's character is the fate of others as well. My weakness for Kylie brought me to her, and that same weakness took her away."

I felt tears invade my eyes. I clenched my fists to fight them off. Spock was right: emotions are carcinogenic; feelings are cancerous.

"A coward dies a thousand deaths, but the valiant taste death but once. Kylie was truly valiant. I am not. I am a coward, for I did not stay true to myself. I was weak. I gave into need. There was a time when I wouldn't cry for anybody or anything. Now it is the only path I tread. How many would cry for me if I were to die? Not many, I am inclined to believe. There was a time when I refused to feel so I would not feel what I am feeling right now. Had I not bowed to my craven side, and had I stayed loyal to myself, Kylie would be among you today, and I would not be standing up here this morning.

"'*In the end, it's not the years in your life that count. It's the life in your years.*' Abraham Lincoln spoke those words. Kylie loved Abraham Lincoln. She loved his wisdom, his judgment, his balance, but most of all she loved his knowledge: his knowledge of man and the heart of man. How fitting her admiration, for in those words, he spoke of her, and her death. Kylie's years were few, yet they counted because she made them count.

"There was another luminary who had Kylie's love: C. S. Lewis. He, too, spoke of her death. Strangely, his precise words escape me, so I will paraphrase his thought: *The treasures we leave behind cannot compare to the treasures we are sure to find.* Kylie told me the first time we spoke that she thought it cruel when people would say a deceased person is in a better place. I'm sure Kylie now knows that her censure was misplaced. I am certain she is much happier now. Sadly, we are not. Death takes more than just the life of the dead—it takes away the life of those still living. Love is a Damoclean Sword. We can lose it so quickly. It is an eccentric thing. It seems we cannot survive without it...or with it. Either way...it kills."

I turned and left the auditorium the same way I entered it.

"Finally getting a taste of your own medicine."

I turned from my open locker. Standing next to me was Shannon, smiling haughtily.

It was my first day back at school. Kylie had been gone just over a week. Time stands still for no man...living or dead.

"Payback's a bitch, isn't she? Looks like she kicked you right in the nuts."

Shannon was talking loudly. I wasn't sure if her volume was deliberate so everyone around us could hear, or if her emotions were raising it.

Had I been younger, Shannon's vulgar and insensate remark would have set me afire...but I was neither younger nor eager to set her aright. I simply did not care. Though circulation, oxygenation, and respiration were occurring in my body, I was dead. Spock had returned...though not through force of will. It simply happened. It was as though my emotions had been turned off. I was grateful for the disconnection, but I was disturbed by its autonomy and immediacy. I had wished for it, and my wish materialized. The old caveat was, once again, proven true: *Be careful what you wish for.*

"You kicked Roxanne to the curb, and now the Grim Reaper's done the same thing to your precious Kylie," Shannon stabbed. "You're getting exactly what you deserve. I hope you suffer 'til the day you die!"

I said nothing.

"Well, color me shocked!" she continued on. "Owen Crowley not talking. I wish Christopher was here—I'd have him take a picture of it! And all it took was Kylie's death to shut him up! If I'd known that, I'd have killed her myself months ago."

"*Shannon, what are you doing!*" a familiar voice barked from behind us.

Both Shannon and I turned around.

Roxanne was standing there, visibly angry.

"I'm defending you, what do you think!" Shannon retorted.

"You're not defending me," Roxanne disputed, "you're just being cruel because you don't like Owen! Why don't you just leave him alone!"

Shannon's face stiffened. "This is the last time I take up for you, bitch!" she spat and then stormed away.

"Owen, I'm sorry about that," Roxanne said.

"It's all right," I said. "Revenge is sweet…and everybody *loves* sweets."

"Not everybody."

"Yes, *everybody*. You may not like cake and candy, Roxanne, but you do like revenge."

She smiled wryly. "You're never going to forgive me for that, are you?"

"To be perfectly honest, Roxanne, I don't care anymore. I don't care about you or Ms. Gavin or anyone. I just don't care." I put my hand on my locker door to close it.

Roxanne gently took hold of my arm. "Can I ask you something?"

"What?" I replied, pulling my arm from her hand.

She didn't answer right away. "I am so sorry about Kylie. And I'm sorry you're in such pain. I wish you weren't. You don't deserve it. You're such an amazing boy. Kylie was so lucky to have you. And you didn't cause her death, Owen."

"That was a speech, Roxanne, not a question."

"Sorry. I just wanted you to know how I felt. All I want to know is… did I not ask you about you?"

"No…you didn't. You listened, Roxanne…but you rarely asked. Kylie asked. I have to get to homeroom. I'll see you around."

I closed my locker and left Roxanne standing next to it.

It was the last week of school. Everyone was excited about the approaching summer. I myself did not care. The apathy that had remanded me after Kylie's death was still my keeper. At first, I was thankful for the custody; now I was resentful of it. It was out of my control, and I hated being controlled by anyone or anything, even if that control was for my own good. This implacable and unbending warden was inside me, and yet it was as though I was inside *it*. I understood many things about life and living, but this apathy that held me down I did not understand.

When not in class, I retreated to the bleachers above the football field to be alone.

"Hi, Owen." A familiar voice.

I turned. Mark was standing at the end of the bleacher on which I was sitting. He walked over to me and sat down.

Above us, John Ford clouds were floating past, and around us, Andrew Wyeth breezes were drifting by.

"Doesn't your butt ever get sore sitting on these hard bleachers all the time?" he asked.

I couldn't tell if he was being serious or simply trying to break the ice that had formed between us since Kylie's death.

I didn't answer.

"Owen, have you ever asked yourself if this is the way Kylie would want you to be?"

I merely looked at him.

"Do you think Kylie would be sitting here if *you* were dead?"

No, I thought of saying. But I had neither the strength nor the desire to respond. I had returned to my yesterdays, when poverty of feeling was all I knew. And yet…I was not totally penniless. One feeling was still in my pocket: guilt.

"Just because Kylie died doesn't mean you have to. You know, you helped and guided so many kids, but now your own compass fails you, and it shouldn't, because you know where you should be, and it isn't here on this bench."

Again, silence was all I had to give.

"You know, after my father died," he continued, "my mom closed down, just like you. She didn't talk for months. She did the laundry and made dinner and cleaned the house, but nothing else. She slowly came out of it, but not all the way. Even to this day, a part of her is missing. But you know, I think she could have been the woman she used to be if she had put some effort into it. I think living a certain way for so long becomes a habit you can't break. It's like being negative all the time. I don't think you're born with it. I think you slowly become negative. In the beginning, pessimism is soft like dough—it can be changed. But if enough time passes, it gets hard, and you can't change. If you don't force yourself to change in the beginning, you won't be able to later on. I once heard a minister say that living a holy life is one percent inspiration and ninety-nine percent perspiration. I think that goes for everything. Nothing good happens on its own. You have to really work at it. I think if you worked at it, Owen, you could accept Kylie's death and go back to who you were. A lot of people miss you. You said at Kylie's memorial no one would miss you if you died. You were wrong, Owen."

I sat next to my friend, and I was wrapped in awe. The boy who sat with me in the cafeteria nine months before who could only talk of girls and TV was no longer that same boy. Whoever said teenagers know nothing about life knew nothing about teenagers.

"I won't be coming back next year," Mark then said.

I looked at my friend in disbelief. It was like another death had suddenly slammed into me.

"We're going to live with my uncle in Virginia. I'm really going to miss you, Owen. You were my best friend. You taught me more than all the school teachers I've ever had.

"When I was twelve, my mom made me take swimming lessons at the YMCA. She thought—and still does—that a boy should know how to swim, and if he doesn't, he's not a real boy. He's a queer. Well, I ain't a queer. It's just that water scared me. It still does sometimes, like when the toilet overflows. I panic like you wouldn't believe. My mom thought my fear of water was *unboyish*, that was her word, so she enrolled me in swimming classes at the Y during the summer. It was the worst and best summer of my life. It was my own little *Summer of '42*, you might say. Anyway, the first time I saw the pool, I panicked. I couldn't even get near it. For some reason, the other kids in the class didn't make fun of me. My instructor didn't make fun of me either, but he wasn't the nicest part of the human anatomy, if you know what I mean. He told me if I didn't get in the pool, he'd call my mother. He said if I just got in the water, I'd love it. Eventually, I did get in the water, and I didn't love it. One day, he had all of us line up on the edge of the pool and then he told us to dive in. The other kids went right in. I backed away and ran to my locker. Then I ran home. I expected him to call my mom. But he didn't. Instead, he did something totally unexpected. The next time I went to class, he introduced me to this pretty young woman. Phyllis Marie was her name. Marie was her last name. You don't find that too much, a last name that could be a first name too. Anyway, my coach told me she would be teaching me. It would just be me and her."

His eyes turned glassy, as if he were on the doorstep of tears.

"She…" he swallowed, "she treated me like I was…I don't know, like I was normal and okay…like there was nothing wrong with me for being afraid. For the rest of the summer, it was just me and her. When I came to class, it was just the two of us, no other kids. She never forced me to do things that frightened me, like get in the deep end or dive off the diving board. She let me learn at my own pace. By the end of the summer, I could get from one end of the pool to the next without sinking. I could even hold my head under water and float on my back. All because of her. No adult before her or since has ever treated me so nice."

He smiled sadly.

"On my last day…" he cleared his throat. "On my last day, she hugged me and told me what a terrific boy I was. Then she gave me this handmade certificate to show my mom what a good swimmer I was. I walked home that day feeling something I had never felt before…love. Not boy/girl love—it was the kind of love you feel for someone who really cares about you. I'd never had that before. Not even from my mom and dad. They took care of me, but they didn't care *about* me. I was only a few blocks from home on that last day, and I started to cry. I never felt so empty in all my life. They say heartache is all in your head. Not on that day. My heart actually hurt.

"I never saw her again. But I never forgot her…and I know I never will. I'll never forget you either, Owen. You're not an adult yet, but you gave to me like Ms. Marie did. You never made fun of me, you listened to me, you accepted me, you taught me, you encouraged me, and you helped me. I know it was you who gave me the Christmas money, and I know it was you who kept putting lunch money in my locker. Don't ask me who told me. I told them I wouldn't tell. There're two people I'll never forget as long as I live—Ms. Marie and you."

He stood up to leave. "You might be interested to know that the guy who was feeding me for sex is not in my life anymore. You were right—if he'd been a true friend, he'd have fed me for nothing. I think I let him have his way with me because I wanted a man to pay attention to me and make me feel like I was important and special to him. My dad never did."

"Good for you," I was able to say.

"I have to ask this before I go. I don't know why, but it's been on my mind since Kylie's memorial. How did she save the building?"

"What?" I wasn't following him. I was still trying to process his leaving and his many personal disclosures. There was still so much about him I didn't know; so much I would never know.

"You said Kylie wrote a fire story and she saved the building with some far-out plan, but you didn't say what it was."

"Um...she had helicopters hovering all over the outside of the building. While they hovered, they shot $CO_2$ inside all of the broken windows. $CO_2$ is used to kill fire."

He smiled. "She was one of a kind."

"Yes, she was."

"So are you, Owen. Don't ever forget that. Thanks for being my friend. Remember what I said—a lot of people miss you. It's not too late to go back to them."

The sun was in my eyes now. It had less than a half hour before it would disappear below the Oquirrh Mountains beyond.

I was still on the bleachers. I was unable to move. Mark's good-bye took the remaining life from my body. I couldn't believe that in a few days he would be gone, and I would never see him again. Though I hadn't spoken to him—or anyone—in weeks, I knew he was there. His presence, though he didn't know it, was a quiet constant I desperately needed. My life had changed so radically, but Mark hadn't; he was there, like a comforting picture on the wall, reminding me that some things had not gone away. But now he, too, was leaving.

I laid myself down on the bleacher, put my books under my head and closed my eyes.

Something tapped my arm. I slowly opened my eyes. Dim but new light greeted me. It was early morning.

I had fallen asleep.

"Owen, what are you doing out here?" said a gravelly female voice.

Slowly, I positioned myself upright. Standing next to me was Ms. Durham, a voluminous, white-haired ogress who wore a perpetual scowl. She was the senior cafeteria cook. She arrived each morning at six to begin her day.

Unarguably, she was an excellent culinarian, but she had all the élan of a lance. Some students used to ask how she could be such a great cook and yet such a lousy human being.

"Leave me alone," I told her.

Then she did something that staggered me. She sat down and took my hand.

"Let me take you inside, and I'll fix you some hot chocolate," she said.

Her voice, at that moment, had changed, as if she had become another person just for me. Her voice was euphonious and parental, like Mrs. Crowley's when I was a small boy.

It occurred to me, sitting there, that perhaps the reason she exhibited such a vinegary facade was to protect herself. I had done it myself when I was younger. Children, like so many adults, can be bestial, barbarous creatures. Many was the time she had been the recipient of ill-bred and ill-mannered remarks from the students. Maybe her suit of armor was simply a shield she assumed to protect her feelings.

She released her hand from mine, stood and smiled. Like metal pulled to a magnet, I was drawn to her kindness.

No one was in the school yet. I was grateful for that. I didn't want to see anyone, and I didn't want anyone to see me.

She led me to her office and told me to make myself comfortable at her desk. She then excused herself to make the hot chocolate.

I looked around the room. It was a small working box, neat and well-organized. Conspicuously absent were any pictures of family, or even a pet. Only office paraphernalia occupied the room. Maybe she did have a husband and children but was very private—like Kylie—and kept her personal life out of her professional life. Or maybe she truly had no one, and maybe that was another reason why she was so cold and curt.

She came in with a white ceramic cup heaped with marshmallows.

"Handle it gently, it's hot," she cautioned.

"Thank you, Ms. Durham," I said, gingerly taking the cup from her. I took a sip and was amazed at its taste. I didn't know hot chocolate could taste so good. It had slight hints of cinnamon and nutmeg. She indeed knew her way around her spoons and spices.

Plaintively, she smiled, sitting down in a chafed and wearied stick-back chair that was against the wall. "I can't remember the last time a student called me '*Ms. Durham*,'" she recalled. "Usually, it's '*old lady*' or '*fat ass*' or '*bitch of the backroom*.' The more intelligent ones call me '*Ilse Koch—bitch of Buchenwald*.' But what I never hear is '*thank you*.' But I suppose good manners are out-of-date, not in step with the times. Except with you, Owen. You're quite the exception. Good manners do not come naturally to people—they're taught. But in your case, Owen, I get the feeling they were forced."

I looked with astoundment at this intensely closed woman who was mocked from every corner. How did she know that about me?

"Not that you don't want to be courteous," she granted, "you do, but I think your manners were instilled with a heavy hand and not a loving one. That hard-line discipline notwithstanding, you've grown into a very sensitive boy."

"Weird's more the word."

"You are *not* weird."

"I know what I am."

"I do too. And I know what you're going to be if you don't change."

"If I don't change?"

"Yes."

"And what am I going to be?"

"Alone. You say you know what you are. I know what I am too—hated, detested, and despised. Prussic acid with dentures—that's what I am. And I have no one to blame but myself. And all because I'm alone."

"Being alone isn't a crime."

"No, being alone isn't a crime, but it can make you guilty of many things. When I was young, like you, I was in love—desperately, hopelessly, blindly in love. His name was Robert. But he favored somebody else. Someone older. Three years and seven months older, to be exact. I tried and tried to get him to love me—he didn't. I begged him to give me a chance—he wouldn't. I saw him at a dance one night, holding her hand. I actually saw it with my own eyes. Knowing something and seeing it for yourself are two different animals. I kept asking myself what did she have that I didn't? I loved him…but love wasn't enough. Never is, it seems. I made such a fool of myself over him. I vowed never to repeat that mistake again. I've kept that vow. I've been alone ever since. I was never made a fool of again. Yet that's a match that burns hot at both ends. I've never been intimate with a man, never even been kissed. I have no friends either. Being alone has made me selfish: it's made me very possessive and protective of my space and my time. I don't want to share them with anyone, except when it's convenient for me or on my terms. I'm incapable of commitment—to friend or beau. My aloneness has made me that way. Many years ago, my sister, whom I rarely see, told me I couldn't commit to a goldfish. She was trying to be funny, but she was right. Being alone has also made me sinfully critical. I've always pushed people away because they never lived up to my expectations. That's because I wasn't around them enough to know that people are imperfect and always will be. Still and all, I've learned about relationships. I've learned that the vital ingredient to a good relationship is overlooking. Like life, relationships are made up of moments—you overlook the bad ones and wait for the good ones. Those are the moments that keep you going. They're the ones that keep you committed. I said I've never been with a man. That doesn't mean I didn't have my chances. I did. Many. But I always pushed them away.

None of them was ever good enough. We get rid of people so easily when we're young. I was just like Robert: I didn't want to give any of them a chance. Didn't want to risk getting hurt again, didn't want to trust, didn't want to do this, didn't want to do that. I'm a mean, judgmental, selfish, self-centered woman, and I only have myself to blame."

"I guess I'm in error—I thought your meanness was a defense against the kids in this place."

"I was mean long before I got here, because I was alone long before I got here. Don't you see, Owen, if I hadn't been alone, if I had let people in, if I hadn't shut everybody out, I wouldn't be the way I am. I was so foolish to do what I did. But I was young and thought I knew best. I think it was George Bernard Shaw who said, '*Youth is wasted on the young.*' Young people think opportunities will always be there waiting for them. They think they will always have their youth. I long to tell them that the pretty faces they see in the mirror today will be gone tomorrow. They need to appreciate their beauty while they can still hold it. The world is more willing to help the pretty than the plain, and it is more willing to love the young than the old. People your age take so much for granted. You make such poor choices. I certainly did. I so wish I hadn't closed myself off. I look at all the young boys around here and wish I'd done differently. But my chances are long gone, never to come back again. I look at all the pretty girls who line up for lunch every day and then go sit with their boyfriends or other pretty girls, and I wish I'd gone in a different direction. Should be me out there, sitting with a boyfriend, laughing, kissing, enjoying my youth. But, no, here I am, an old woman clogged up with bitterness and jealousy. I don't like being jealous. It eats you up inside. Funny thing about jealousy—it comes out as hate, but what it really is is hurt.

"I miss my youth before Robert. I was happy then. Truly happy. If I was fifteen again, I'd get on a different bus. I wouldn't put all my love in one basket. I'd care less about the past and more about the present. I missed out on everything, Owen. Before Robert, I so wanted children. After him, I couldn't stand to look at them. But age and distance make you look at life through different eyes. I'd give anything to have children now. People think I'm this quill-covered mossback whose only use is cooking and who wouldn't know a warm feeling if it ran over her. But I hear things. And I see them too. There aren't many, but there are a few kids in this place who actually love their parents. A couple of months back, there was this girl here who lost her mother and father to a drunk driver on the freeway. She had to go live with her grandmother. That poor child cried and cried over her mom and dad. I didn't know a child could love so deeply, leastways not her parents. I felt terrible for the girl and sad for me because I would never have a child who would love me the way she did hers.

"There's this show called *Star Trek*, maybe you've heard of it. I'm not an avid watcher, but I happened to catch it one afternoon. This doctor was telling this pointed-eared alien that he pitied him. He said he felt sorry for him because he'd never know all the things that love pushes a man to do—the heartaches, the joys, the defeats, the triumphs—all because he was forbidden from embracing love. Very insightful for a fantasy show, I thought. After Robert, I never tasted the agony and the ecstasy of falling in love. I never felt anything again. I banished love from my house and slammed the door.

"My point in all this is, don't do what I did. Don't close down just because you lost someone. Don't miss out on life just because you lost a life. Sounds awful, I know, but it's the truth. Just last week I read that there're over four billion people on the Earth right now, and over a hundred thousand of them die every single day around the world, most of them tragically. Leaving out Enoch and Elijah, nobody makes it out of this life alive, not the sweetest child or the cruelest adult. Everybody dies, Owen: grandparents, parents, wives, husbands, brothers, sisters, babies, toddlers, teenagers. Couples break up, friendships break apart. Nothing lasts. All we have is now—the past is gone, and the future isn't here yet. If you make your home in either, you'll live to regret it. That I'm sure of. I'm telling you all this as a warning. If you don't change, and quickly, you're going to end up just like me. I know it. Locking yourself away is gratifying at first, because you're finally locking out the main source of pain in this world: people; but then that gratification turns into your convention—your way of life. It almost becomes an addiction, all on its own. Funny thing about addictions—if you don't squash them early on, they end up squashing *you*. Change now while you can, Owen, because when you get older, like me, everything is harder. When you're young, big obstacles are small, and when you're old, small obstacles are big."

"My heart tells me to go back," I said, "but my head tells me I can't. It tells me not to feel. It tells me what will happen if I do."

"I know. My head told me the same thing...and look where I am. You know, Owen, there's an old saying: *If you go through the motions, the emotions will follow.* That works for both good and bad. If you make a sustained effort to reach for what you used to be—friendly, warm, kind—you'll return to that. But if you wait, you never will. Follow your head, Owen, and you'll be alone. Follow your heart, and you won't."

"Easy words...but not so easy to walk behind."

"But not impossible. You're such a unique boy, Owen—so different from most of the kids around here. Don't let that boy disappear. You know, I heard your speech at the memorial for Kylie. Beautiful sentiments, but wrong in places. You said no one would cry if you were to die. I know for a fact there'd be crying if you were to die. But me, I'm the one no one would cry for. Don't let your life be a copy of mine."

She stood up. "I've got to start my day. Please consider what I've said." She smiled warmly and left her office.

After my last class on the last day of school, I slipped out of the building without saying good-bye to anyone. Mark's and Ms. Durham's words were not lost on me. They were there, in my heart, trying to get me to move back in time, to that place before Kylie, before Ms. Gavin, before I turned away from everyone. I wanted to heed their command, but my jailer's command was louder, stronger, wiser: *If you get close again, you'll get hurt again.* It told me if I did as Mark and Ms. Durham suggested, made a deliberate effort to return to who I was, it would end in my ruin. My keeper impressed on me that its handcuffs, while uncomfortable, were far less afflicting than constantly being the target in the telescope of pain. Sometimes being under arrest is for one's own good.

The first month of that summer was remedially peaceful. To Ms. Windom's pleasure and my salvation, I spent my days in the park… although not the park close to school, for it sheltered too many ghosts. This new park in which I sequestered myself was a long way from my school, its direction west. It was a much older park, considerably larger than the one by my school, and unlike that one, which catered mostly to couples and kids and an occasional pet with its owner, this one was home to joggers and birthday gatherers and picnickers. Mammoth pines, maples, ashes, boxelders, poplars, and buckeyes shaded its many grassy plains. In the pleasant months, children and teens, and even young adults, would strap on metal roller skates and breeze over tree-lined roads and sidewalks. It was in this new sanctuary that I returned to my roots and ventured back into the deep universe of the written word. I had to wonder what humans did before the salvation of books. What did they do to keep their minds from imploding when grief landed and deplaned in their lives?

I took different routes to and from my new refuge each day. Though I had lived in this mountain-flanked city my entire life, much of it I had not seen. My daily walks to this new haven led me to areas I had never come across.

One area I had seen but could not even look in the direction of was downtown. More than a few times, Kylie took me there so we could *"walk among the skyscrapers,"* as she used to say. I never had the heart to tell her that Salt Lake technically had no skyscrapers. I learned from my father that while Salt Lake's city center did have a trifle measure of high-rises, many of its structures fell into the mid-rise metric. My father once told me that Salt Lake was a Volkswagen who thought of itself as a Buick: it believed it had a climbing and impressive urban core when in fact it had nothing of the kind. I didn't share this with Kylie either. What was the harm in letting her enjoy her own beliefs? I had read once that when information serves only as a weapon, it is best to keep it holstered.

Kylie's assessment about buildings might have been slightly askew, but she was as sharp as a saw when it came to people. Though she came from an idyllic, even poetic, family, she saw people through streetwise eyes. *"People,"* she once said, *"are foul things who love foul things. Our planet is filthy because we are morally filthy. Every generation thinks theirs is better than the ones before it. No generation is better—they're all polluted. The only thing about man that has changed during his residence on the Earth is his imagination. The longer he lives, the more inventive he gets at being bad. He is, has been, and will always be dishonorable."* In one of our many talks, she predicted that the planet's population would rocket in the coming decades, and technology would become its god and king.

No one knew Kylie had this side to her. But I did, and I counted myself privileged that she trusted me with it. She was so ahead of her age, and her time. Thinking of her was unbearable. Being near or looking upon those things that pleased her was impossible.

I spent my fifteenth birthday in my new park. Few people were there when I arrived in the morning, but by mid-afternoon, it was alive with activity: children were laughing, dogs were running, briquettes were glowing, badminton shuttlecocks were parachuting, Frisbees were flying, sparklers were waving. The place was happy, the time was happy. It was the 4th of July—the perfect holiday: it's in the heart of summer, it's out of doors, it's carefree, and most importantly, it's largely unemotional—unlike Christmas, and Thanksgiving, and Memorial Day, and Valentine's Day.

I wasn't the only one in the park whose birthday fell on Independence Day. Not far from me—sitting around a red picnic table—was a little girl and her family. On the little girl's head was a conical, yellow polka dot hat. In the center of the table was a white, two-layer cake with slim, yellow candles anchored in its frosting. Encircling the cake were colorfully dressed boxes. The scene made me remember the last time I received birthday presents. I was seven years old. Seven—the number of completeness; that was my seventh birthday—complete. Less than four months later, that completeness would be gone without a footprint.

I had to turn away from the little girl.

Another scene quickly filled my vision: clusters of intrepid children were swinging and climbing and hanging upside down on the park's massive jungle gym. Other youngsters were lionheartedly chuting down tall slides. Still others were fearlessly trying to touch the sky on alpine-high, chain-link swings. I wondered if any of them would remember this gleeful day when old age had stolen the sap from their bodies.

Something odd then caught my attention. She had been obscured by the swarms of children, so I didn't see her at first. I had to keep angling my head to see her fully.

*Why is she there?* I asked myself. *She shouldn't be.*

I arose from the metal bench and walked toward her. She looked like somebody I knew...but I couldn't place who it was.

There was another metal bench next to the girl, so I availed myself of it.

The girl didn't acknowledge me. I gathered from her condition that she probably didn't even see me. She was a young woman, perhaps twenty. She was severely disabled and wheelchair-bound. Her limbs were thin from atrophy and red from the sun. Her hands and feet were stiff and gnarled, like old wood. Set in a nearly paralyzed face were eyes that did not track. Beads of perspiration were running down her forehead and cheeks from the stifling July heat. It enraged me that her family would leave her there in the merciless sun when only a few feet behind her there was shade. At the very least, they could have given her a hat for her face.

I wasn't about to sit there and watch the young woman suffer. If she wasn't cooled soon, she would lose consciousness.

I got up, unlocked the wheels to her chair and pulled her into the shade.

"Hey, what the hell do you think you're doing!" someone yelled.

A tall, fiftyish woman in a white shift came running over to me. It was an easy guess that this was the young woman's mother.

"Get your hands off my daughter!" she roared. She pushed me back and rolled her daughter back to where she had been. "I knew we shouldn't have come here," she boiled, stroking her daughter's hair. "Nothing but perverts in this park!"

Angrily, she came over to me. "The only sparks *you're* going to see tonight are the ones the other prisoners are going to give you for molesting a defenseless, handicapped girl!"

A crowd was gathering around us.

"All I was—"

"Shut up!" she commanded me. "Tell it to the cops!"

Unfailingly, no good deed goes unpunished.

Had it been another time, I would have jumped on the mother for leaving her daughter out in the hot sun, but I didn't have it in me for a fight, not anymore. If the police arrested me, they arrested me. I didn't care.

From out of nowhere, a familiar face appeared. A girl. Yet she was no ally. She wasn't even a nice acquaintance. It was Shannon Manchester. Roxanne's best friend.

*Oh, good, screaming in stereo*, I thought.

"What's happening?" Shannon asked the woman in the white shift.

"This pervert here tried to molest your sister!" the woman blustered, pointing at me. "He was pulling her back in the shadows so he could rape her!"

Shannon looked at me...and started to laugh.

The park was home to hundreds of people that day, but it seemed Shannon's laughter was the only sound that could be heard.

"What are you laughing at!" the woman raged.

"Mom—*seriously*? This is Owen—he goes to my school. He's no pervert. If anything, he's just the opposite. He's probably the most decent person you'll ever meet."

I was unconcerned...until her last words. This wasn't the Shannon I knew. The Shannon I knew would have unfalteringly sided with her mother. What was she up to?

"What's your idea of decent—Charles Manson!" the woman gainsaid.

Shannon rolled her eyes. "Oh, Mom, please. Did you even ask him?"

"What's there to ask? It was obvious what he was going to do."

"I doubt that." Shannon looked at me. "Owen, why were you—"

"She was in distress," I answered...though not for me, but for the girl. "Look at her—she's perspiring terribly; her face is all red, and her legs and arms are burned from the sun. She's not enjoying herself like *you* are. She should be in the shade—not out there."

"Who are *you* to tell me what I should do with my daughter!" the woman hurled.

"Mom, he's right," Shannon conceded. Shannon walked over to her sister and wheeled her back into the shade. She removed the red-checkered scarf from around her hair and wiped her sister's face.

Shannon came back to me. "You were right, Owen—we shouldn't have left her there. We should have known better. I'm glad you came by."

"I'm not!" the woman punctuated. "Let him tell his lame story to the cops. I'm going to have him thrown in jail. It's where he belongs!"

"No, it isn't, and, no, you're not," Shannon deadpanned, then took me by the hand and led me away from the crowd and her mother.

When we reached the jogging trail, which circled the park, she stopped.

"None of that should have happened, Owen," Shannon said. "I apologize for my mother."

I wasn't raised in the wilds with no exposure to people. I knew them, and I knew that no one goes from black to white just like that. Shannon was up to something.

"You can cease the show, Shannon," I checked her. "You can't stand me. You know it, and I know it. You're up to something. What is it?"

Without looking away and without bashfulness, she said, "I'm a Christian now. I got baptized last month. I asked Jesus to come into my heart, and He did. I'm not the same person you knew. He changed me. I had a dirty mouth and a dirty mind. I was angry and jealous and envious. I don't feel those things anymore. You can believe me or not believe me—I don't care. It doesn't matter what *you* think of me anyway. All that matters is what God thinks of me. When I die, I'm not going to stand before you or any other man—I'm going to stand before

God. So if you think I'm up to something or whatever, go ahead. Jesus knows I'm not." There was a faint smile on her face.

The smile could have been taken for smugness, but something told me it wasn't. Shannon had *truly* changed. She *had* gone from black to white.

"I believe you, Shannon," I said. "I'm happy for you. I'm happy that you have found a new direction in your life. I wish you success." I turned and began for the street.

"You could have that direction too, Owen," she freelanced loudly from behind me. Then suddenly she was walking next to me again.

"I don't think so," I answered.

"Why?"

"I never paid God much mind before, Shannon—I doubt He'd hear me now."

"He hears everyone, even those who don't believe in Him. As long as you have life in your body, His ears hear you. *Now is the accepted time*, He says."

"I'm not an atheist, nor am I an agnostic. I believe in God. But I also believe there are those who are simply unworthy of Him."

"No one is worthy of Him. But *God don't make no junk*, Owen. I'm sure you've heard that expression before. It's true."

"Not in my case."

"In *everyone's* case. Everyone has sin in their life, and everyone falls short of His glory...but still He counts us as valuable. He loves us all."

"Try *pities* us all, for how can you love someone who you feel is unworthy of you? I don't want to be the beneficiary of anyone's pity. I've sat down to that meal before, and I don't like the aftertaste."

"What aftertaste is that?"

"Inferiority. Good-bye, Shannon. I have to go."

She took my hand as I was about to leave. "Owen, I don't know how it is for other Christians, but after I accepted Jesus, I felt the need to apologize to the people I treated badly. You're one of them. I said some awful things to you in the past, and I'm very sorry."

"If you are referring to your words regarding Roxanne, don't apologize. You were only looking out for your friend."

"Not totally. I was also jealous of her."

"You have nothing to be jealous of. You're as intelligent, pretty, and popular as Roxanne is. You have everything she has."

"Not everything. She had you." Her face pinked. "When you two were together, I was so jealous of her. She had the smartest, cutest, sweetest boy in school, and all I could get were the horndogs. Sorry... that was crude. I still have a ways to go with my mouth." She smiled crookedly. "Anyway, after you and Roxanne broke up, you still didn't even notice me. That made me angry, so I lashed out at you whenever I could."

The words of Ms. Durham sped across my mind: *Funny thing about jealousy—it comes out as hate, but what it really is is hurt.*

"Not that I didn't care about the pain Roxanne was feeling over her breakup with you, I did," Shannon went on. "I was just dealing with my own pain too, which she never knew about. I really am sorry for all the rotten things I said to you."

"Don't dwell on it, Shannon. I don't, so why should you?"

"Maybe I shouldn't say this, but I care about you, Owen. I know that sounds weird after all the terrible things I said to you last year, but I truly do care. If you need someone to talk to, or you just don't want to be alone, I'm here."

"Thank you, Shannon, but you can do better than me. You're a Christian now—you need to give your heart to a Christian boy. God commanded the priest of Israel if he still found mildew in the home to remove the contaminated stones and take them to an unclean place outside the city. That is what I am, Shannon: mildew, unclean. You no longer are. You are newly fallen snow now. God doesn't want His people yoked together with those who are outside His fold."

"I heard Kylie was a Christian."

I couldn't tell if she was using Kylie as leverage to pry her way into my life, or if she was simply trying to make a point. I gave her the benefit of the doubt.

"Yes, she was a Christian," I deeded. "And I shouldn't have been with her, but I was. If she had chosen a Christian boy instead of me, she would be alive today. Maybe God punished her for that choice. He might kill you too for making the same selection."

"You don't really believe that?"

"I do. I need to go now, Shannon. I hope you have a pleasant summer."

Before she could pose another question, I leaned in, kissed her cheek and started my walk home.

# CHAPTER 11

# *Yesterday's Return*

*"It's never too late to be what you might have been."*

GEORGE ELIOT

There was a large supermarket a few blocks east of the park. Taped to one of its many tall windows was a large, hand-drawn sign. It read:

BAG BOYS/STOCKBOYS NEEDED—INQUIRE WITHIN IF INTERESTED

As much as I loved to read, I needed something else to occupy my summer days. I was beginning to feel indolent and useless. I needed to feel productive in some way. I wasn't sixteen yet, so I wasn't sure if I would even be allowed to work. But perhaps I would be if I were able to obtain a work permit.

The manager of the store was a middle-aged man, short, stocky, and of Mexican origin. I sensed immediate dislike from him. But I didn't let it trouble me, for I didn't need the job—I simply wanted it—so if he told me to be on my way, I wouldn't have cared.

"It's only part-time," he told me. "And only in the afternoons and weekends. It pays a buck ninety-five an hour. Plus, you have to wear a nice tie, nice shirt, and nice slacks. Nice shoes too. I want my employees to look respectable. No punks or greasers will ever work for me. You good with all that?"

"Yes, sir."

I wanted to tell him that the term *greaser* was no longer in vogue because the look was no longer in vogue. But I kept quiet: this was his show, and if I wanted to be in the cast, I had to let him be the director.

"Hours won't interfere with your school?"

His question threw me: how could it possibly interfere with school? It was summertime. Why would I be in school?

"No, sir," I said. "Not yet anyway."

"You taking the summer off?"

Of course I was taking the summer off! What was I supposed to do—go to school and teach myself?

"My school isn't open in the summer, sir."

"What kind of college isn't open in the summer?"

"College?"

"That's what I said—college. You are in college, aren't you?"

"No, sir, I'm in high school."

*"High school?"*

*"Yes, sir."* Why was he making such an issue of my schooling?

"You don't look like no high schooler. What, were you held back or something?" Enmity was tightly foiled around his tone.

Displacency excluded, this conversation reminded me of my first meeting with Mr. Solleveld.

"No—I was not *held back*," I corrected him with a scowl.

His brow chevroned. "You're pretty quick with a tone there, young man."

"So are you, *old man.*"

The man's face twitched at my words. "You may have pretty teeth, kid, but behind them you got an ugly tongue that's gonna get you in a lot of trouble someday. You better learn to keep it on a leash."

I definitely did not need this job. And I certainly didn't need to work for a pustular pimple like him. I wasn't in the mood to continue sparring with him…yet I couldn't let him think he could say whatever he wanted to me.

"Do yourself a favor," I handed him, "and tell yourself this tomorrow morning before you come to work: *Better to remain silent and be thought a fool than to speak and remove all doubt.*"

His lips tightened. "You're in for some hard times, kid, if you don't learn some manners."

I let my tongue off its leash one last time. "Though actual ascription and provenance is unknown, it is believed these words hailed from the hand of Shakespeare. I will now hand them to you: *I would challenge you to a battle of wits, but I see you are unarmed.*" I smiled. "You can take your cretinous cautions and your backwater beliefs and shove them in the first hole you can find!" I turned about and left.

I was out in the parking lot when I heard, "Hold up there, boy."

I turned and saw the manager coursing toward me.

"You're a gutsy sprat, aren't you?" he said when he reached me.

I gave him no reply.

"I like that," he asseverated. "I like your chutzpah. More boys need it. If they cared less about being silly showoffs in front of the girls and cared more about showing some moxie, this nation would be a stronger country. So how old are you, exactly?"

"Fifteen…today."

"*Fifteen?*"

"*Yes—fifteen.*"

"Sixteen's the youngest we hire…but I suppose we could get you a work permit. When could you start?"

"As soon as you need me."

"Be here tomorrow at four. Remember—nice tie, nice shirt, nice pants."

"I'll be here—with ties and bells on."

He smiled and went back into the store.

It certainly is so: working hands make the clock hands speed by. It was now the last week of August; school would be restarting in a few days.

The world called it a regathering—I called it an *anschluss*, a forced, involuntary union. But it was one that was going to occur regardless of my feelings. In the meantime, I would concentrate on my job at the store and not on school.

While bagging bananas and brooming the backroom at the store was not mentally demanding, it did as it was supposed to do: I finally felt productive and useful. Bordered to that, it put money in my pocket; it wasn't much, but it was money that came from my own hands and not Ms. Windom's.

My co-workers were a mixed bag of ages and behaviors: there was a bucketful of mid-lifers, a handful of quarter-lifers, and a thimbleful of minors, myself being one. Most of the staff was professional and friendly. The others were a little less than professional and a little more than friendly—these were the other bag boys. There were three in all. Two of them loved to flirt with the younger checkers. The third, whose name was Garrett, flirted with only one. Though the most attractive of the three, Garrett was also the most immature. He had just turned sixteen, yet he often behaved half his age. I liked him, but he was as moody as the skies of March. One day he could be chatty and happy, the next silent and surly. When corrected for the slightest mistake, he would close like a clam and say nothing for the rest of the shift. I concluded that either no one had taught him how to take criticism profitably, or he lived with criticism continually and shuttered himself in as a means of self-protection.

The checker Garrett secretly but conspicuously favored was Pam Ashland, a pretty young woman with subtly pouting lips that could charm a lion into purring. If the store was busy, every bag boy was to be up front, bagging all large orders; if an order was small, the checker could bag that purchase herself. Busy or not, large orders or small, Garrett was always at Pam's checkout stand. The other baggers complained among themselves about this, but no further than that, for Garrett continued to confer on Pam special consideration. I knew she was aware of this, for I saw concern in her eyes sometimes when he was at her counter. I suspected she didn't bring it to Garrett's attention because she didn't want to hurt his feelings, and didn't bring it to the manager's because she didn't want to cause Garrett any trouble. He was a sweet kid who was only following the whisperings of his heart. But age would teach him that listening to the heart is never a prudent course.

It was the last Sunday of the month. I was in the break-room cleaning the overhead fluorescent lights. Pam entered the room and saw me on the ladder.

"Don't you ever take a break?" she asked.

"No. I enjoy working."

"You're a switch—most kids your age only work because they have to."

"We are all different, Pam. Each of us is written by a different author."

"You're a puzzle, Owen. But I mean that in a good way."

*They all mean it in a good way*, I thought. *Just once, I wish someone would call me ordinary or common or even boring.*

She sat down at one of the round tables. I noticed something I hadn't before: she was wearing a wedding ring. Hadn't Garrett seen it? Surely he must have, for he was by her side every second he was on the clock. What did he hope to gain by privileging her with special attention? He must have known there would never be anything between them. Even if she weren't married, the age chasm alone would keep them apart.

Pam's eyes settled into a stare, as though something weighty was preying on her mind.

"Would you like me to speak with him?" I offered.

She looked up at me with a start. "I'm sorry, what did you say?"

"Would you like me to speak with Garrett about his...*yen* for you?"

"No, that's okay. But thank you anyway. Besides, it would do little good: he's mad at me right now. Won't talk to me; won't even look at me."

"Why?"

"I had to put him in his place yesterday. He was in one of his moods and was throwing the groceries in the bags, so I told him to cool it. He didn't like that, so today he's not talking to me, and he's bagging the other checkers."

"Would you like me to say something to him?"

"No. He'll snap out of it. He's just a sensitive boy with a crush, that's all. Besides, the bloom will fall off the rose soon enough. After school starts next week and he gets around all those blond, bouncy cheerleaders, he won't even remember my name."

"I doubt that. I think what happens in our high school days usually stays with us all our days. Joseph Katsaris, who lived to a hundred and three, said, '*When you are old, nothing stays, because nothing matters. When you are young, everything stays, because everything matters.*' Garrett will never forget you...or your name."

She looked at me like I was a mystery wrapped inside a riddle wrapped inside an enigma. "You *are* a puzzle, Owen."

"Is that approbation or *dis*approbation?"

"Observation." She smiled ruminatively. "You know, you remind me of my husband a little. He taught psychology at UO. He was—"

"UO?"

"Sorry, University of Oregon. He was the smartest man I ever knew. What he saw in me I never understood."

*Remind...taught...was...knew...saw*—all past tense. She had seated him in the preterite tier. Apparently, he had passed away. I didn't want to pry, but she seemed like she wanted—if not needed—to talk about him, so I decided I should ask. I dismounted the ladder, walked over to the table and sat down next to her.

"What was his name?"

"August. He was born in August, so he was named that. He also died in August."

"This must be a doubly difficult month for you then."

"You could say that. He was murdered on his birthday. Six years ago today. Two years before that we got married...on his birthday. I was twenty when we first met. I was in his class at the time. We knew we liked each other, but he refused to date me because I went to the school where he taught. He was very adamant about that. So I changed schools. He was older than I, almost twelve years older, but neither of us cared about that. I loved him, and he loved me. That's all that mattered to us."

"Did you two have any children?"

"I was pregnant when he was killed. I lost the baby shortly after that. Miscarriage." She shook her head. "Never rains but it pours." She shook her head again. "I really shouldn't be telling you these things. I mean, I don't know you that well. Besides, you're just a kid."

"Kids can know and understand a lot more than you think."

"Yeah, you're right. When I was your age, I remember adults always brushing me off because they thought I couldn't understand what they were feeling. I knew *exactly* what they were feeling."

"Why was your husband…"

"You can say it—murdered."

"Why was he…murdered?"

"One of his students, a man—much older than the other people in the class—shot him. He followed my husband out to his car after class, put a gun against his back, pulled the trigger and ran."

"Why?"

"My husband gave the man a failing grade on a test. Strange…people do the biggest things for the smallest reasons."

"What is small to one is large to another."

"Yeah."

"I'm surprised you're here at work today."

"Better than being at home, thinking about him. But I've moved forward. I'm proud of that. It's been hard, but I've done it. I'm even dating—kind of dating—this guy from my church."

"Was it your church that gave you the strength to go on?"

"No. Believe it or not, it was a novel."

"A novel?"

"It was called *Past into Tomorrow*. It was only fiction…but you know what they say: fiction is only reality wearing a mask. It was a tragic book, poignantly written, very graphic in places, but it had a very happy ending. The main character's wife and daughter are murdered, and he spends decades blaming himself for their deaths. Then, miraculously, he's sent back in time and given the chance to save them. I was really moved by the story, but I was more moved by the writer, because you could tell he had written about himself, about the loss of his own wife and child, and the guilt he felt over it. He was imprisoned by the guilt. I think that's why he wrote the book."

"Allot me forgiveness if I am wrong, but I am hearing self-recrimination in your words. Do you blame yourself for your husband's murder?"

"It was his birthday. I should have taken him somewhere for the day. But I didn't. I let him go to work."

"That student could have easily killed him another day."

"True, but if my husband hadn't been there *that* day, the guy might have had time to rethink what he was going to do. I know he acted out of impulse—that's when trouble happens, when people don't think about what they're really doing."

"People also kill *without* impulse. Some kill with great care and calculation."

"Not this man."

"How do you know?"

"Because he was dead quiet at his trial. Didn't say a word, didn't look at anybody, didn't do anything. He was just slumped in his chair, his head always down. That's why I say he did it in the heat of the moment. But I've managed to come to terms with what he did, and with what I did...or *didn't* do. For five years, I could barely look at myself. Then a friend gave me that book I told you about. Going back in time doesn't happen, I know that, but being obsessed does. That's what happened to the author, and that's what happened to me. For five years, I did nothing but obsess about my husband's death and my part in it. I didn't want to end up a fifty-year-old woman—that was the age of the author— who spent her whole life loving a dead man and blaming herself for his death. Where would be the dividend in that? What good would it produce? Just as you can't save every puppy in the pound, you can't stop every tragedy from happening. I'm gradually realizing that. I'm still young, and I want a family. I want a husband. It's slow going, but I think someday I'll get there."

"I'm sure you will."

"There was a particular part in the book I never forgot. It was toward the end. It had been years after the man had lost his family. A female friend of the man got very angry at him. She was angry because the man was still grieving over his wife and child. She told him that people lose children every day. Life goes on. Then the man said, '*Yes, but they didn't lose* my *child, and for her, life did not go on.*' People expect you to grieve in a certain way and for a certain period of time. And yet… if you're not careful, grief will devour your life. Your past will become your tomorrow. Months will turn into years, and before you know it, you've grown old, and you discover you haven't moved an inch from where you were when tragedy hit you.

"I think you should read the book, Owen. I have a feeling you could use it. Don't take this the wrong way, but you're probably the most starless person I've ever met. I've never once seen you smile or tell a joke or say anything happy. You don't even get mad. I have a feeling you've got some guilt going yourself. Am I right?"

I didn't answer her.

"Interesting thing about guilt," she noted, "a little goes a long way. If we take in more than we're supposed to, we defeat its purpose. If we take it in when we're not supposed to at all, we defeat ourselves. We end up drowning, but not dying. We're held under water, unable to grab onto anything firm, just flailing our arms in pitiless blackness, our whole body flooded with senseless remorse. Bad things happen, Owen. That's just the way it is. We have to move on."

I swallowed, though I tried not to.

"So would you like me to bring you that book?"

"Yes."

Pam was correct: the book was tragic. While it was indeed beautifully written and peopled with unique if peculiar principals and walk-ons, it was freighted with anger, sadness, and guilt. It had moments—like life itself—where all was not bleak, but those moments were scarce.

While I read fictional works routinely, rarely was I moved by one, for their characters frequently seemed plastic or predictable or both. Rarely were they leavened with hard realism and depth of heart. I read fiction nonetheless, for it tendered me perspectives and word pictures not seen in the pages of nonfiction. Pam's book was one of those rare narratives that moved me, grabbed me, and held me. And, like Pam had been, I was moved by the writer. I knew the author had kneaded himself deep into the character. It was as though he had made the book his confessional and the reader his priest. Though the author called his book a *work of fiction*, I had to agree with Pam that he must have lost his real wife and child and, for some reason, blamed himself for their deaths. His story was his guilt impressed on paper. Yet he was not guilty. Thus, his self-condemnation was wrong, profitless. He had ruled himself blameworthy, just as I had done. This gave birth to the obvious questions: would the author's doom be mine if I did not absolve myself? Would I enter the last years of my life still feruling myself for Kylie's death? Yes. *"History doesn't repeat itself, but it rhymes,"* Mark Twain is credited as saying. Whether they were his words or the property of another, they were true nonetheless. The history that occurred in the author's life would not occur in mine, but its rhyme would doubtless visit me if I didn't stop charging myself with Kylie's death. Its rhyme would be the closing words in the last chapter of my life. Flemming Sutton—an eighteenth-century librettist whose family had perished in a fire—at the close of his life, said, *"I held the guilt all my days; 'twas my lot to bear for all my thoughtless ways."* I didn't want those words to be the summation of my existence too. And loath as I was to admit it, the guilt and depression that tailgated me dawn to dusk were fatiguing. I felt it was my lot to feel responsible for Kylie's death, and yet I had to ask, as Pam had, where was the dividend in the guilt? What beneficial harvest could I possibly reap in the end? And the harvest from siloing myself off from people, what would that yield in the end?

Nothing.

*"Bad things happen, Owen. And that's just the way it is,"* Pam had said.

She was right.

The necessity of shedding my self-recriminations and rejoining humanity was as a clear as a summer morning.

What was not so clear was how I would accomplish that. Ms. Durham had been right: the longer I remained cloistered from others, the harder it would be to rejoin them. I had been disconnected from people for so long, I didn't know how to reunite with them.

The opportunity to father that reunion would soon present itself.

Two weeks into the new school year a poster appeared in the cafeteria. On a large, rectangular sheet of white paper with candy-apple red lettering was an invitation:

> *Christmas will be here before we know it! We need your ideas for a totally new kind of Christmas dance—one that will say good-bye to 1975 in style and usher in the Bicentennial year of 1976 with a bang! The Activities Committee will be meeting this Friday afternoon at 4:00 in the Art Department—so come and share your ideas! Remember, be there or be square!*

I had come to believe in fate for bad but not for good. Until now. Now I was beginning to believe that fate was without prejudice, for within the book Pam had loaned me there was a chapter on a Christmas dance. Not only did the protagonist play a prominent role in the dance, he made it one his school had never seen before and would never see again.

This was my open door to finding my way back to the boy I used to be, for I had—for quite some time—been courting a chimera of my own kind of dance. The dance I had in mind for my school would be a hybrid of what took place in the book and what took place in my fantasy. As in the novel, the dance I visualized would be something *my* high school had never seen before and would never see again. Yet...it would finish as mere draff if this committee thought my idea ludicrous.

I entered the Art Department just shy of four o'clock.

Seated around an oblong table at the north end of the department were the members of the committee. Filling in the suit of the Activities Board were two students from each grade, one male parent, one female parent, and Ms. Harriett Longmire, a mauve-haired soon-to-be-pensioner who always had a ready smile and an open ear. She lessoned junior and senior social studies and proctored study hall on Friday afternoons. I guessed the presence of the three adults was more for decency than balance.

All eleven heads turned to me when they saw Ms. Longmire look in my direction. All but the two parents smiled when they saw me. It was obvious these parents were curious about this boy who extracted such an affirmative reaction.

"You here for the meeting?" Tara Connally asked me excitedly. Tara was also a sophomore.

"I am," I answered, feeling like a prospective juror who had just entered a courtroom whose *voir dire* proceedings were already under way.

"You have an idea?" she inquired eagerly.

"I do."

"Well, by all means, let's hear it," Ms. Longmire encouraged. "Don't be shy. Come on over."

I was shy indeed. It had been months since my emotions had seen freedom. This would be their first parole since the winter of that year. Apathy was still making a strong effort to keep me immured. But I had had enough numbness and dispassion—I needed to take back control and become my own keeper again.

"Have a seat," Cassidy Hollister invited. Though sightly and shapely, Cassidy was a thoroughly unpretentious girl. A rare thing, for the three traits rarely ride in the same car together.

"So what's your idea?" Josh Rafferty asked after I had come to a stop at the table. He was a tall boy, a senior, and a rising star in the debate club.

I wondered, as I stood there, if Kylie would have liked my idea. I would never know.

I pulled out a chair, and instantly Kylie came to mind again. I scolded myself for being there. How could I do such a thing? How could I reach out to enjoy life again when Kylie's life was gone forever? What kind of boy was I?

I pushed back in the chair. I had to leave. "I'm sorry," I said. "I shouldn't be here. This is wrong. I have to go."

"Owen, do you mind if I tell you a quick story?" Cassidy solicited.

I sighed. "If you feel you must," I gave her, even though I wanted to give her: *Yes, I do mind*. I knew she was going to try to talk me out of leaving.

"Last May, my cat, which I'd had since I was a little girl, was killed. She was run over. I blamed myself for it the whole summer. I should have watched her more closely, but I didn't. I got careless. Last month, my mom got me a new cat without asking me. I hated it. It finally ran away. It knew it wasn't loved. I wish I'd given it a chance because now I think I would have loved it. Chances aren't endless, Owen. Sometimes we only get one. Maybe this is yours."

I had said the same thing to Robin the previous September. And then I said to myself: *Life goes on. It has to.*

I pulled out the chair again and sat down.

"I don't know if this is even possible," I got underway, "but I think if it could be done—and done correctly—it will be something we will affectionately remember all our lives."

"You got me interested," Brandy Alexander slipped in.

*What a thoughtless name to give a child*, I mused.

"Most dances follow a formula," I proceeded further. "Dapperly dressed, everyone shows up with a date in hand. They dance to sounds that are more related to screeching bats than music; they make out at every turn; they drink without pause; they laugh at everything, and they talk about nothing. I want to reverse all that. I want everyone to show up without dates. I want—"

"We already have that," Josh interrupted. "They're called stomps."

"Almost, Josh…not quite," I returned. "True, while stomps lack the formality of dances, they are traditionally stag or drag affairs. I don't want that."

"*Stag or drag?*" Camille Mann inquired, visibly puzzled.

"I'm impressed," the male parent extolled with a smile. "I thought only *my* generation knew that expression."

"What's it mean?" Again, Camille.

"Stag means you come alone and drag means you bring someone," I answered. "Everyone has a secret love in high school, yes? So why not go a step farther and bring the one who is loved and the one who is *in love* together?"

"How would you do that?" Tara asked.

"Well, here's where it gets a bit sticky. If done incorrectly, it will be farcical at best and embarrassing at worst."

"What if the one who is loved doesn't want the one who is *in love*?" Josh explored with an almost adversarial tone. "What if they're already going with someone?"

"Good queries, Josh. Those students already a couple will meet at the dance. Those to be paired will be paired at the dance. This will give them the confidence to come, since everyone is already coming alone."

"And how will they be *paired*, to use your word?" Ms. Longmire asked with more distaste than interest.

"We will find out who likes whom, and then we *sing* them together."

"We *sing* them together?" Josh delivered. "You're kidding."

"I am not," I delivered back.

"How did you come up with such an idea?" Ms. Longmire questioned me viperously.

"It was in a book I read recently," I related. "It went very well in the book, and I think it will here too if only we believe in it."

"When you say *we* sing them together, you mean the kids here at school?" Josh again.

"Yes," I affirmed, trying to be patient.

Josh broke out in loud laughter. He then quickly tented his mouth with his hand to mute his amusement. "I'm sorry, but that is...the stupidest idea I ever heard of."

"There's no call for rudeness," the female parent reprehended Josh.

"Even if it's done *correctly*," Josh carried on, undeterred, "as you say, it'll be embarrassing. Most of my friends can't even carry a C-average, let alone a tune."

"Your friends don't make up the whole school, Josh," Brandy wrangled hotly. "I want to hear more. Go on, Owen."

"This school has hundreds of students," I forged on. "Everyone has gifts and talents...even you, Josh. I think if we delved a little, we'd find *many* here who can sing and play and even write music and verse. We just don't know who they are yet. The songs should be originals... or most of them anyway. The musicians and singers should be us, the students of this school."

"This is supposed to be a dance, Owen, not a concert," Josh impressed.

"It will be both. It will give those who sing in the shadows a chance to sing in the light, and those who love in the shadows a chance to love in the light."

"How do we find out who sings and plays?" Ally Sheehan inquired. Ally was her nickname; her given name was Alifair. It was rumored— through Alifair herself—that she was distant blood to Randolph McCoy (the head of the McCoy family who feuded with the Hatfield family in the latter 1800s) and was named after Randolph's daughter who was murdered in the New Year's Day Massacre in 1888.

"We will ask," I answered her. "We will put up posters around the school asking if anyone would like to lend us their talents for a night. Of course, there will have to be plenty of practice beforehand, as with any performance."

"Let me see if I'm getting this straight," Ms. Longmire sifted. "You want to bring kids with crushes together with kids who don't know they have crushes, and you want to accomplish this through singing from kids who have never sung before? Is that your plan?"

What happened to the sweet lady who only moments ago was so athirst to hear my idea?

"You're mocking it, and me," I said angrily.

"No, I'm just trying to understand it."

The vision I had of the dance was crystal clear, at least to me, but maybe it was foggy to those around the table.

"It would seem I am faulty in my explanation," I acknowledged. "This is all I want to do: I want to have a dance in which the singing and the music come from our own, the students of this school. I want to bring together the students who are in love with—"

"Teenagers are *incapable* of feeling love," Ms. Longmire barged in. "All they feel is lust. People your age don't even know what love is. You're too young."

"That must mean then that what children feel for their parents and siblings is actually lasciviousness," I leveled at her.

"I didn't say that, and you know it!" she barked back. "I was referring to romantic love, not familial. Teenagers, because of their age, are simply incapable of having true romantic feelings."

"Is that a fact?" I asked.

"Yes, it is."

"You were a teenager once—*eons ago*—were *you* ever in love?"

"Whether I *was* or *was not* has no relevance to this discussion!"

"I think it does. If you were in love, then you should understand. If you weren't, then you should keep quiet, since you know nothing about it."

Cassidy and Camille tittered, but then quickly covered their mouths.

"As I was saying," I pressed ahead, "I want to bring together those boys and girls who are in love with someone but can't bring themselves to unveil that love. We will bring them together through music. We will find them in the crowd and join them as one. I am usually very good at elucidation, but with this, I seem to be found lacking. I think this is one instance in which a picture has the value of a thousand words. Once I start showing everyone what I mean, it will make sense."

"You want to captain the dance *too*?" Josh asked with more than a dash of salt on his words.

"My idea, my show."

"May I ask you something, Owen?" the female parent broke in.

"Yes," I said.

"Why this idea? Why is it so important? I'm not putting it down... I'm just really curious."

Mrs. Crowley's face appeared in my mind, then Kylie's. "I think this time of life, the adolescent years, the years when boys and girls become who they are, feelings often go unsaid, and later in life those boys and girls—now old men and women—wish they'd spoken those feelings, if only once, so the ones who held their hearts would know how dear they had been. But by then it's too late. Cassidy's right: chances aren't endless. Sometimes we only get one. Maybe this is the only chance that some of the kids here will ever have to be heard. I'm not onward in years yet, but I can't help but believe that in every older adult there lies under the hard stones of age at least one grain of regret for not having reached out for a dream or reached out for someone they loved when time was on their side." I arose from the table. "You know where to find me if you like my idea." I nodded to the female parent. "Ma'am," I said to her respectfully and then left the room.

Early Monday morning Cassidy came up to me while I was at my locker. She was smiling. She was like Kylie in many ways: sweet, authentic, undauntable. She even had the chiffon, blond hair that Kylie had. She was a born-again Christian, just like Kylie.

"You made quite an impression on the group last Friday," she said, "especially on the parents. Except for Ms. Longmire and Josh, who thought your idea was..."

"Stupid, I believe was his word."

"What do they know? Everyone else loved it, and the majority rules. Besides, compared to the other suggestions, yours was the prettiest apple on the tree."

"What were some of the others?"

"There weren't from this world, I can tell you that. One girl wanted to have a July-in-December dance—kind of the reverse of Christmas in July. She wanted the girls to come in bikinis and the boys in Speedos."

"That's different."

"Smutty too. Another girl wanted us to have a ballroom dance, with waltzes and stuff. Another suggested we have a square dance. What that has to do with Christmas or the country's two-hundredth anniversary she never said. One boy said we should have a traditional Country music dance. *'Classic Country for a classy country'* was his push. One guy said we should all dress up in red-white-and-blue outfits for the Bicentennial. There were others just as bizarre. But yours was the only one with heart."

"It doesn't hitch to the Bicentennial theme, though."

"No, but it has dimension and soul, and that's important too. So, it looks like the ball's in your hands. There's just *one* condition, though." She grinned.

"And what might that be?"

"You have to sing...at least one song."

"Sing?"

"At the dance."

"I don't sing."

"You do now."

"Not *now*, not *ever*."

"At Kylie's memorial, you said you did, and as I recall, you said even though you're no Dean Martin, you aren't half bad."

"This is beneath you, Cassidy."

"No, this is blackmail," she converted, still grinning. "I think Kylie would want you to sing. I know we do."

"I don't—"

"That's the condition, *Dean*," she said with a wink, then flashed a glance at her watch. "Oh, look at the time. I gotta put an egg in my shoe and beat it." She dashed away, giggling.

As I suspected, there were as many students in the school who had high singing amplitude as there were who had high musical aptitude. I didn't know how to create music, but I knew what was aurally pleasing and what was not, and I knew what I wanted and what I didn't for this dance.

There were so many students talented in voice and instrument I couldn't use them all. I knew there had to be a few who were gifted musically, but not as many as there were.

There was one girl I knew who could sing, and sing magnificently. She was one of the students Mr. Taggart had sent my way the year before. Then a junior, she told me her only escape was singing. She would go deep into the cemetery by her house and give freedom to her voice.

Jodi Payton was her name. She was a fair-complexioned girl with hair the color of rich whiskey. Her sweetness was equaled only by her shyness. Born on a small farm in Wyoming, she grew up with few friends. That solitary life followed her to Moran. She told me she hated being alone, but she accepted it as a fact of her life.

The bus took her to and from school. One afternoon, I walked over to her while she was waiting for the bus. When she saw me approach, her eyes widened with pleasure.

"Hi, Owen!" she greeted me sunnily.

"Hello, Jodi," I returned the greeting.

"What brings you to this side of the road? You always head that way after school," she said, nodding to her left.

"I'm on an errand of sorts. I came to talk to you."

"About what?"

"I came to ask you something."

"Is it good or bad?"

"Good, if you ask me...which you did."

She laughed. "I never met anyone who talks like you."

"Is that good or bad?"

"Good, if you ask me, which you did."

This time we both laughed.

"What did you want to ask me?" she asked, still smiling.

"I submitted an idea to the Activities Committee for the Christmas dance, and they accepted it."

"Was that your idea? I saw the posters around school."

"Yes, it was mine."

"It's a great idea. Having our own do the singing, rather than some lousy band full of potheads who only know how to play acid rock, will make for a terrific evening."

"I think so. Which is what brings me to this side of the road."

"Oh?" A thread of suspicion was sewn into her tone.

"Now don't say no until you've heard me out."

Her smile melted into a frown. "You're not going to ask me to sing, are you?"

"I am, yes."

"Then here's your answer—no."

"Come on now, what's the worst that can happen?"

"Other than looking like a fool, not a thing in the world."

"If you couldn't sing, you wouldn't do it at all—not in the cemetery, not anywhere."

"Thanks but, no, thanks. I'm sure there are lots of other kids who would love to be in front of the microphone."

"There *are* lots of others, and there will be, but I want you there too."

"Well, you know what they say: you don't always get what you want in this world."

"How about I make a deal with you: if you'll sing, I'll sing."

"*You'll* sing?"

"I will."

"Can you sing?"

"Kylie thought so."

Jodi gazed at me thoughtfully. "Is that why you're doing this...for her?"

"Partly maybe. I know she would have enjoyed this, seeing all the invisible kids for once not be invisible...if only for a night. I know what it's like to be invisible. You do too."

She studied me closely. "Would I have to talk?"

"Only if you want to. But, no, you will not have to talk."

"And you're going to sing too?"

"Like I said, if you will, I will."

She eyed me closely again. "This I can't miss."

In Pam's book, there was a character kindred to Jodi. Her name was Basha. Though proportionate in talent to her real-life counterpart, Basha was not nearly as bendable as Jodi. In the book, the main protagonist endured considerable resistance from Basha before she finally acquiesced and agreed to add her talent to his dance. While not always exactly, life does indeed imitate art.

Though there were some contrasts between my dance and the one in the book, there were far more similarities. It was amazing to me that there were any similarities at all, for how was it even possible? It was as though the lightning in the book's world was striking my world in the very same place. And yet it really wasn't lightning at all—it was life. Ecclesiastes spoke of it centuries ere: *What has been will be again, what has been done will be done again; there is nothing new under the sun.*

While I was immersed in the preparation for the dance, I was not unaware of the world around me. Over the summer, Roxanne had found a new boyfriend. Barry Fidel was his name. A senior from another school, he was a well-heeled, titian-haired, surefooted drama student whose hands helmed a Corvette Stingray around town. Roxanne was happy again, and I was happy for her. But under the table, where life is never seen, I was jealous of him. I missed her. I never thought I would feel anything for Roxanne ever again. Yet I did. And I felt hideous for it. Kylie hadn't been in the ground a year, and my heart had already returned to a girl who I once called *"twisted,"* a girl who I once believed to be the keeper of *dark laminas of odious jealousy and appalling cruelty.* How could that be? How was it possible? I hadn't any answers. All I knew was how I felt.

The final rehearsal for the dance had arrived and concluded. Four more days would have to pass before the dance itself took place. In that time, the gymnasium would be decorated and appointed for the event.

After the last bar had been played in the last rehearsal, I thanked everyone for their belief in me and my admittedly far-from-center concept for a dance. Their commitment—not to mention their considerable gifts—was far from what I had expected. Because of these students, my romantic fantasy would become a romantic reality.

I had made a gentleman's agreement to deliver at least one song at the dance. I had hoped, over the course of the months, that that agreement had been forgotten. But hope is not solid…it is a vapor. Who can stand on it with any confidence?

Right before we left for home that last night of practice, Jodi asked me to sing. She reminded me it was part of our deal. I then reminded her that the deal was for me to sing the night of the dance—*not before.* "You don't sing now, we don't sing then," she promised. The group, a large ensemble, agreed with her. I couldn't tell if they were toying with me or if they were actually serious. I had put too much into this to call their bluff. I stared at Jodi in controlled anger. I wondered what had become of the shy, reserved girl who would only sing in the cemetery. Jodi the lamb had become Jodi the ram.

Most of the songs to be sung at the dance were originals, written by students, but some came from the radio. A familiar voice on the AM and FM dials at the time was Lobo; a well-loved, soft-rock soloist whose birth name was Roland LaVoie. His voice, more than his lyrics, drew me to his music. One of his first radio ballads, "I'd Love You to Want Me," found a wide and loyal audience. I was a part of that audience. So was Roxanne. Shawn Bartlett wanted to sing it the night of the Christmas dance. When he sang it in rehearsal, I discreetly left the room until he finished. It simply was too painful to listen to. And yet, on that wintry December evening, four nights before the dance, it was the only song I wanted to sing. Surrendering to Jodi's wishes, I told the musicians what song I wanted them to play. I brought over a backless barstool, sat down and began "I'd Love You to Want Me."

Memories of Roxanne filled my mind as the melody flowed from my lips. At times, I closed my eyes so I could see only Roxanne.

After I had finished, I gave my attention back to Jodi. "Satisfied?" I asked her.

She looked at the others in the group, who seemed stunned. She walked over to me and wrapped her arms around me.

"I've never heard anything so beautiful in my life," she said. "Why didn't you tell us you could sing like that?"

"Because I didn't really give it much thought. Besides, this isn't about me."

"If it weren't for you, none of this would even be happening."

"This is happening because *you're* making it happen, not me."

She stared at me for a long moment. "You don't like praise, do you?"

I didn't answer her.

"Would you get mad if I asked you another favor?" she asked.

"It depends."

"Would you sing another song? For me?"

"Why?"

"Why for me, or why do I want another song?"

"Why do you want another song?"

"Because I want to hear your voice again. Is that so terrible?"

"Why don't you ask—"

"Please."

*Please*...one of the mightiest words in all the world. Who can resist it?

"What song do you want to hear?" I relented.

"It's another Lobo song, 'How Can I Tell Her.' Shawn was going to sing it after 'I'd Love You to Want Me.'"

"I know. Why that particular song, Jodi? I mean, it doesn't really suit you, if you don't mind me saying so."

The song spoke of unfaithfulness and desertion of commitment; it was not the breed of musical poesy that someone like Jodi, a girl who hadn't even one love, let alone two, would want to hear. Then again, maybe that was no longer the footing.

She looked away from me for a moment, then brought her eyes back to mine. "Would you sing it?"

She obviously didn't want to answer, so I didn't push the matter.

"If it will make you happy," I said.

"It will."

Jodi left me and rejoined the group and told them I was going to sing a second time.

As I sang, I became aware I was being watched. At the back of the gymnasium, I saw a figure in the shadows by the locker rooms. I couldn't tell if it was a boy or girl, man or woman. The person disappeared when they saw I had become aware of them.

After I completed the song, the group stood and applauded impassionedly.

Uncharacteristically, I blushed. Profitably, the lights were low, so I was certain they could not see the change of color in my face.

"Hey, look at that, he's blushing," Louisa Gail pointed out playfully.

Apparently, the lights had not been low enough.

"Okay, okay, leave him alone," Jodi stepped in. "Thanks, Owen...that was beautiful."

"All right, everyone, let's pack it up," Kevin Braga quarterbacked.

Kevin, a short, stocky, moon-faced boy who played the electric guitar, was disposed to give orders to all, even to me. More than once, I had to remind him he was there to play, not conduct.

Soon, everyone had their instruments cased and their coats donned. They all bid me good night, and, in a tick, were gone. I was now alone inside the enormous, two-story building.

*Life is a smile whose teeth don't always show at first,* I ruminated, still sitting on the barstool. *But eventually, it bites. It goes in cruel circles, life does. A baby is born needing care, and if his years are many, he will need care once more. A man and a woman begin apart, then they wed, and if their years are many, they will be apart once more. A boy begins life alone, then his aloneness leaves him, then it finds him again, and he is alone once more. Yes, life is a smile...for a while.*

"You never cease to amaze me, Mr. Crowley," a voice said from a distance.

The shadowy figure from before reappeared. This time it emerged rather than receded.

It was Ms. Longmire.

She was dressed in an abundant, ruby-red coat with white leather gloves. A cerise handbag was snug in the nook of her right arm and a turquoise-paisley scarf was mantled over her lavender hair. All dressed up with nowhere to go.

"Tell me," she inquired, "is there anything you *can't* do?"

As in our first meeting together, her tone was radioactive.

"What is it you want, Ms. Longmire?"

"Just wondering how your...*dance* was faring."

"You saw for yourself. Answer for yourself."

"Do you always answer your betters with such disrespect?"

"Is that what you think you are, better? If so, *think again.*"

"You know, in my day, children who backchatted like you would get their mouths slapped."

"This is not your day, Ms. Longmire. That day is gone. Respect is earned—it is not just handed over like an allowance simply because of age or title."

She said nothing in return.

"Tell me, what is it about this dance that galls you so?" I asked.

"If I could work my will, this dance of yours would be snuffed out like a bad cigarette."

"First, Ms. Longmire, there is no such thing as a *good* cigarette. And second, I'll ignore your conspicuous cribbing of Dickens in an attempt to be cleverly rude and I'll ask you again—why does this dance offend you so?"

"*You* offend me."

"No, I don't. This dance is what is pricking you. I only represent it."

"Not only are you offensive, you are arrogant!"

"I'm sure I am, but that's not why you're here tonight, is it?"

"Your cheekiness must tax your parents greatly."

"I'm sure it would if I had parents, but I don't."

Her face, in an instant, reversed in mood: it went from antipathetical to maternal. "What do you mean, you have no parents?"

"Just what I said, I have no parents. They died when I was young. I'd prefer not to talk about me. What I would like to talk about is *you*, or, more particularly, your abrupt change in attitude. At the start of last September's Activities meeting, you were wide open to all suggestions for a Christmas dance, but then when I gave you mine, you closed right up. You rejected it. Why was that? Why are you so hostile to this dance?"

"Be sure all the doors are locked before you leave tonight." She turned and headed for the rear entrance of the building.

I jumped off the stool and ran to her side.

"What are you running from?" I put to her.

"Add pertinacity to your rather lengthy inventory of rebarbative characteristics," she hissed, still walking.

"You can play hawkshaw, but I can't?"

She stopped and stared at me. "Where in Heaven's name did you come from?"

"Not from Heaven, I assure you. But then, you didn't mean Heaven, did you? You meant somewhere else, somewhere where there's... *weeping and gnashing of teeth.*"

"I didn't say that!"

"No, but you meant it. But repine not, Ms. Longmire, I have developed a very thick skin. I've had to. I am different, and I know it. But then, we are all different, aren't we? No two people are alike. Genomes in our bodies and mileage in our lives make us that way. When I was a boy, a very sapient and compassionate custodian told me something, and I never forgot it. He told me that people act the way they do for a reason, and that reason is usually linked to their past. You're here tonight bearing gifts of enmity and scurrility for a reason, and that reason is tied to the life that was yours long ago. Am I right?"

"What you *are* is egotistical."

"You are confusing conceitedness with curiosity. It's how I am, Ms. Longmire—I desire to know. It's how I've always been. It's how I'll always be. I'm afraid I've never been much good at anything else. I apologize if I came across as arrogant. It's acetose comportment, and I know it. It's a defense I developed when I was a boy. That's *my* reason for acting the way I do. What's yours?" I smiled, hoping that would lift the heavy air between us.

Her face warmed.

"How did your parents die?" she asked.

I truly did not want to discuss my life, but if I expected her to open up to me, then I had to open up to her.

"My real parents killed themselves," I gave away, "and my adoptive parents are gone as well. He died of cancer, and she has...well, mentally decamped."

"I'm sorry."

"Life keeps on walking. I've learned that over and over. What about you—what have *you* learned about life?"

Melancholy dripped down her face. "You can't go back," she let go. "That's what I've learned. When you reach my years, you realize you've passed the age of falling in love again, even if you desperately want to. You wouldn't understand that because you're still very young. I've never told a soul this, but in my heart and in my mind, I remain a teenager. I just don't look it anymore. When I was in my salad days, like you, I used to have such hope for love. But as I grew up, I ran from it. Oh, how I long to be young again when I didn't run, when I believed love was for everyone…even me."

"Why did you run?"

"Immaturity partly, insecurity mainly. I just didn't have what it took to make love work. I was too afraid of being discarded. So I ran. Over and over."

"That doesn't make any sense. You found love—more than once—but then you would run from it, even though you wanted it."

"What may make no sense to you, Owen, may make perfect sense to someone else. My shoes may not fit you, but they do fit me."

"Okay, so if you knew you were going to run, why did you keep trying?"

"I guess I hoped I wouldn't run. I didn't want to be alone."

"But you *are* alone, are you not?"

"Yes, I am."

"You must have been hurt pretty badly to have chosen aloneness over closeness."

"No more than anyone else. I've just never been good at good-byes. Endings are difficult for me…so I always made tracks before the one I loved did."

*Security starts at home,* psychologist Christopher Masterson scribed. *If a child grows up not knowing it, he grows old not having it.*

"Who left, your mother or your father?"

Offense flashed across her eyes. "What makes you think one of them left?"

"Am I wrong?"

Her irritation abated. "My mother. She ran out on us when I was about eight. We never saw her again. Maybe you're right, maybe the mileage in our lives makes us who we are. She ran so I ran."

"Was there ever anyone in your life you wouldn't have run from?"

"There was one. A boy. A long time ago."

"He must have been very special."

"Only to me. We were in the same class in high school. We were both juniors. He was very popular and outgoing. I wasn't. But I was the only one who loved him the way I did. Most faces in your life come and go...but some faces *never* go. His never left mine. Strange how one person can stay in your heart forever. When you're my age, very few things stick, but when you're sixteen, everything sticks. "

"What was the boy's name?"

"Rex. He and I never actually went together. We just went out just one time, just one evening. He was always so sweet to me. He never called me what the other kids did."

"What was that?"

"I was born at home, not in a hospital. Somehow the kids at school found out about it. *'Hatched-at-Home-Harriett'* they used to call me. Not Rex. He may not have liked me romantically, but he showed me kindness and dignity."

"It's hard to be the class outcast."

"It was for me. I was the girl who lived on a street without lights and in a home that had sheets for curtains. I was the class joke whose father who worked in a warehouse and whose mother walked out because of it. My grandparents offered to help us out, but he refused the help. Too poor to paint and too proud to whitewash."

"I'm sorry."

She gave me a dolent smile. "Life never allowed me to kiss Rex...but death allowed me to touch him."

I squinted at her words. I didn't understand her.

"A few years ago, I saw his obituary in the paper. I must have sat at my kitchen table for an hour just staring at it. I couldn't believe he was gone, the only boy I ever truly loved; the only boy who made my soul swell. I wasn't able to go to his funeral, but I went to his viewing. He had an open casket. I went up to it, and I couldn't take my eyes off of his face. Lying in front of me was the boy who stole my heart and ran away with it. I reached down and touched his hand. I wish I hadn't. It was cold and hard. It was all so pathetic. The only time I was allowed to touch him was in death."

"I wouldn't call it pathetic. I'd call it life. I'm sure you're not the first whose only time they were allowed to touch a lost love was in their casket."

"I'll tell you something, odd as it sounds, I miss my girlhood. I miss feeling what I used to feel. I miss loving what I used to love. I miss being young and unknowing. I miss feeling alive. I miss feeling hope. When you're young, everything is new and electric. When you're young, you never think you're going to miss your youth. And then when you're old, you do. You ask yourself, why didn't I savor my youth while I was living it? This hasn't happened to you yet, but when you get older, the past has a power it never had before. Memories have more meaning; places have more importance. Even smells. They have a force all their own. You can be outside under the sun or inside under the lights and all of a sudden, a smell you hadn't known in years breezes past you, and instantly you're taken back to a time long forgotten. You desperately long to go back to that time…but you know you can't. Don't saw sawdust, they say. Do not dwell in the past, the Bible exhorts. It's hard not to when you're my age and you feel so little."

Her words, in many ways, paralleled Ms. Durham's. It was tragic to me that these two women—fine women—chose paths that led them to such emptiness.

"If you don't mind me asking," I said, "why didn't you and Rex become something?"

"I wasn't running yet, but I was insecure. That'll kill a relationship faster than Raid on a roach. We were doomed the moment he picked me up. You ask me what I've learned about life. I've learned you can't go back. You can't go back to an old love, and you can't go back to your youth. That's why I was so opposed to your dance: it made me want to go back…and I can't. That's a painful reality when you're my age. When someone says something hurtful to us, our first impulse is to say something hurtful back…even if it's untrue. That's what I did to you. I said teenagers only feel lust. I didn't want to see the boys and girls here get the chance at love that I squandered. Your dance is a dance of hope, a chance for two people to find love. And, yes, people your age do feel love. But such hope does not belong to me anymore."

"So why were you at the meeting that day if you knew it was only going to upset you?"

"Because I chair the committee, so I have to be at all the meetings. I try to keep a happy mask on, but it's difficult sometimes, like when you suggested this kind of dance. But I'm glad, very glad that your dance was chosen. I've been watching all of you and listening, and I have to say you have created something quite phenomenal. I mean that. I wish we had had something like this when I was in school. This dance of yours is going to be...amazing. And the talent of these children is nothing less than remarkable. I had no idea our students had such abilities."

"Yes, they are quite remarkable. I wish I could do what they do."

"I heard you sing—you *do* do what they do."

"We'll see Saturday night. If I'm not stoned, you might be right."

"You won't be. If anything, you'll be tossed roses."

"I doubt that."

"I'll be one of the first to do so."

"You'll be there?"

"I will." She smiled blackly. It was obvious she did not want to attend. "I'm one of the chaperones."

"Perhaps it won't go as badly as you think. You know what they say: What we expect is rarely what we get."

"This is true. But somehow, I don't think that will be the case this occasion."

"I'm curious about something. If by chance love were to knock on your door again, today, what would you do? Would you run again, or would you seize the chance and make the most of it?"

"Why would you ask that? After what I just told you. Love will *never* knock on my door again."

"But if it did, hypothetically, would you run?"

"I would hope I wouldn't."

"You say you're too old for love. I've never heard of a cut-off date for it."

"There's no written law, but there is an unwritten one: there simply are things you don't do past a certain age. If a twenty-year-old wears a miniskirt, she draws looks of desire; if a fifty-year-old does, she draws looks of pity."

"So people your age are not permitted to fall in love?"

"Everything is permissible, but not everything is beneficial. Everything is permissible, but not everything is constructive."

"First Corinthians, ten twenty-three."

Her eyebrows rose. "*Very good.* Few adults know that verse, let alone adolescents."

"You're a Christian?"

"A devout one."

"Do you think God wants you to be alone?"

"I don't think getting a man to walk with me in the moonlight is on the top of His to-do list."

"God said, '*It is not good for the man to be alone.*' Genesis, two-eighteen. I don't think God wants anyone to be alone...including you."

"*You* are."

"But I haven't always been. Everyone should be coupled with someone. It's the way of the world."

"It's not the way in my world."

"Could be."

"I beg to differ."

"There isn't *one* man who tugs at your heartstrings?"

"Not really."

"Not really sometimes means really."

"Not this time."

"So truly there is not one person in this whole world who stirs your blood? Everybody has at least one. Remember now, Ms. Longmire, lying is a sin."

She said nothing. No answer is an answer.

"What is his name?" I drilled down.

She stared at me, her eyes like lancets. "You are an unusual boy— anyone ever tell you that?"

"Incessantly. If I were given a quarter every time I was told that, I could—" I clipped the rest of my answer. She was trying to circumnavigate the issue, and I wasn't going to let that happen. "Let's not wander from the subject, shall we? What is his name?"

She looked around the room. "He doesn't make it over here very often, except as a spectator."

"So he is employed here?"

"Yes."

"Do I know him?"

"Everybody knows him."

This time it was my eyebrows that rose. "Mr. Heald?"

She angled her face heavenward, as if she were about admit something very deep and difficult. "Yes."

"He's a good man. Widower, I believe. He lost her some years ago."

"Yes, acute sepsis. Started in her right hand. She died within a matter of days. Her death nearly brought about his own. Why did you bring all this up?"

"To show you that love is ageless. Just because a miniskirt isn't for you anymore, doesn't mean love isn't."

She gave me a piercing stare again. "Over and above being markedly out of the ordinary, you are extremely tactical and maneuvering. Absent all those things, you are a charming boy, very sharp and quick. I'll see you Saturday night, Owen. It should prove to be a night...not soon forgotten."

*By anybody*, I thought as she was walking away. *Including you, Ms. Longmire.*

I smiled.

The gymnasium was a riot of Christmas colors: red and green and gold and silver were taped, tacked, hanging, and standing throughout the building. Hundreds of miniature white lights, like alabaster rain, dangled from the ceiling trusses. Joining them was a plenitude of mirrored balls—or *disco balls*, as they were more commonly known. Spotlights gelled with amber, green, and red showered the gymnasium with holiday tints. Two Balsam firs—bursting with clinquant glass balls and hundreds of clear, miniature lights—stood on either side of the area where the musicians would be playing. At the back of the room, in front of the girls' locker room, bright red balloons were arched over a long, metal folding table. Over the table was a red and gold checkerboard table runner. Arrayed on the napery were wreaths of homemade Santa and snowman cookies. Neighboring them were rows and rows of clear plastic cups. Into them, a Sprite-and-pineapple punch would be ladled. To the right of the refreshments, in front of the boys' locker room, an indigo backdrop splashed with stars and spangles had been erected for photographs. The decorators were to be mightily applauded.

The musicians were already in place and practicing when I arrived. The girls in the assemblage were attired in form-fitting but tasteful dresses, while the boys were in patterned shirts and checkered double knit or solid-color Angels Flight pants. Music from an eclectic variety of instruments would fill the air that evening. Camden Mathews would be on the drums, Kevin Braga on the electric guitar, Justin Conti on the acoustic guitar, Walton Montgomery on the bass guitar, Susan Overstreet on the piano, Cory Jenna on the violin, Sindie Barr on the cello, Kerri Porter on the oboe, Kathryn Sullivan on the flute, and Michelle Ambrose on the clarinet. And sentinelled in front of them all were amps, power cords, booms, microphones, and microphone stands.

The vocalists had not yet arrived, or if they had, they were elsewhere in the gymnasium or school.

I went over to the band. Kathryn, Sindie, and Michelle told me they were very nervous. I told them they needn't be. When buttoned up, the evening would be a memory everyone would forever hold in their hearts like one holds a newborn puppy in their hands.

The room was rapidly filling with students. I wished the group well and disappeared into the shadows far behind them.

I happened to catch sight of Mr. Heald at the back of the room by the refreshments. He was still in his trilby hat and herringbone overcoat...as if he were letting everyone know that his presence was only temporary. Initially, he was not going to attend the dance. "There's no reason in the world for me to be there," he said to me. In response, I told him that his appearing might add an element of class to the affair.

After all, it was the last school function before the country began its Bicentennial birthday. He told me it was a weak argument, but he agreed to come nevertheless.

Looking around at the throngs of buoyant and lively students, it suddenly occurred to me that the dance was no longer a destination but an arrival. After four long and anxious months, and after so much practice and preparation, the night was here. While I was outwardly sanguine and positive that it would be a hands-down success, inwardly I was seriously doubtful. The night could easily turn into a terrible joke, an embarrassing bungle in which everyone would leave shaking their heads in disbelief that such an absurd and preposterous dance had been allowed to go forth. The dance in Pam's book was beautiful and magical, but that didn't mean this one would be.

*What was I thinking?* I chastised myself.

While standing there, surrounded by burgeoning loudness, I heard the quiet questions again, the same questions I had been hearing since I first proposed the dance: *Why are you really doing this? Why are you so bent on this idea?* And as before, I had no complete answers. Yes, I did want the shy to be seen and heard, for I had been where there were—a ghost, a life unseen—but there was more to it than that. Far more. I just didn't know what it was.

Then I spotted Roxanne. She was fantastically beautiful. She wasn't on anyone's arm, yet she was smiling and conversational with everyone around her.

In that instant, as clear as the moon on a cloudless night, the answers to my long-unanswered questions came to me: more than for anyone else, the dance was for *me*. I so wanted to be in the arms of Roxanne again…to feel her love, her desire, her security…but she belonged to another now, never to be mine again. So, from afar, I would watch her—and all the others as they fell in love—and imagine that it was me.

Britannya Russett, one of the vocalists, appeared and stepped forward to the microphone.

Britannya was in a class by herself. Softhearted to a fault and conscientious to a T, she always made sure that no one upstaged or took a backseat to someone else. A senior and plentifully well-proportioned, though not zaftig by any stretch, she had the eye and attention of many a boy. But most captivating was her name. It was an aggregate of Nadya and Britannic: Nadya from a grandaunt on her father's side—a survivor of the 1906 San Francisco earthquake, and Britannic from a granduncle on her mother's—a musician who perished on the HMHS Britannic in 1916. The HMHS Britannic was the sister ship to the RMS Titanic.

"Good evening, everyone," Britannya welcomed the multitude lustily, scooping back long, lustrous flèches of red hair behind her ears.

The crowd quieted almost immediately.

"This is going to be a night we know you're never going to forget! We have planned some great stuff for you! So what do you say we get started!"

Everyone cheered and clapped.

My stomach felt like it was going to collapse in on itself. Josh was right—this was a stupid idea! The night was going to be nothing less than a disaster. I wanted to slip out the back, go home and never come back. But that wasn't my way. This was *my* ship…and I had to go down with it.

Susan began immediately with an allegro tempo, then Camden came in with the same meter, then Justin and Walton followed. Kerri, Kathryn, Michelle, and Sindie rose and began clapping in unison. Jennings Reindel—a boy who was a near carbon copy of Danny Bonaduce of *The Partridge Family*—joined Britannya in front of the mic. The song was called "Good Time," a fast-paced, fast-moving, heavy-on-riffs, dense-with-refrains number that had no meaning or message—it was just a fun piece to start the evening off.

Jennings and Britannya kept their intro strong but not overpowering, just the way I suggested; then, a few measures into the song, per my suggestion, they incremented the tempo and volume. Then they did what months before they had been reluctant and wary to do: enter the crowd. When I first proposed the idea, they were worried they would look preposterous: no one sings *within* a group, they sing *in front of* it. I asked them to try it anyway. They did. And the more they did it, the more they liked it.

Many in the room looked surprised, then mystified when Jennings and Britannya began walking into the middle of the room and singing at the same time.

I closed my eyes in dread and turned away. Just like the vessel after which Britannya was named, this ship would sink quickly and disastrously.

Then I heard something I had hoped for but didn't expect after what I had just witnessed: more clapping and more singing.

I turned and allowed the room to reclaim my eyes.

Not only were all the students dancing, but so were Jennings and Britannya. Around them, everyone was clapping and dancing and singing.

I couldn't believe it—it was happening just as it had in the book. *Fiction is only reality wearing a mask. What has been will be again, what has been done will be done again; there is nothing new under the sun.*

As the song was approaching its windup, Jennings went in one direction and Britannya in the other.

Nervously, I chewed on the inside of my lip in anticipation over what was about to happen and if it would actually work. This was the cotter pin that would hold the evening and success together...or at least my idea of success.

Jennings took hold of Jacqueline McGregor's hand and began walking her toward the center of the room. While Jacqueline was making plain her utter bafflement, so, too, was Peter Yarbrough, a boy Britannya was guiding to the center of the floor. Jennings and Britannya came together and joined the hands they had been escorting, and then brought the song to a crescendoed wrap-up.

The hands that came together did not part once the song was over. Jacqueline and Peter bashfully glanced at each other, then smiled.

Peter had a crush on Jacqueline but was too unassured to let her know. Though she knew already of his shine, she was waiting for him to make the first move. We in the band knew he wouldn't, so we made the move for him.

The crowd whistled, cheered, and clapped.

I found myself clapping with them.

Finding out who had crushes on whom was as easy as peeling a ripe banana. All we had to do was a little furtive investigating. In no time, we had dozens of names. Everyone has someone they love. Of course, we made sure—through a few more artful inquiries—that the ones we brought together would want to be together.

Smiling, Jennings and Brityanna handed their mics to Belinda Welch and Jodi Payton. The two girls began a song that was apace with the one before it. And like Jennings and Britannya, Belinda and Jodi sang amid the crowd.

As if reborn, Jodi was now fearless. Once the fainthearted farm girl, she was now the stouthearted city dweller. After she let her singing voice be heard, she became the darling of the group. She became outgoing and assertive, proffering proposals and ideas on what would make the dance better. Everyone, me included, was glad the demure wallflower had bloomed into a daring sunflower. All she needed was for others to take notice of her.

The evening unfolded just as I had hoped it would. Whenever the singers started to move, the dancing, be it slow or fast, would stop, and everyone would watch to see which boy and girl would be united. Song after song entwined the shy with the shy and the shy with the unshy. We were even able to seam back together two couples who had been fighting. Both couples resisted at first, but persistence from the singers and cheering from the crowd broke down their obduracy, and the two couples came back together. The night was a fantasy come to life. Hands that had never been held were held. Souls that had never been embraced were embraced. And lips that had never been kissed were kissed.

There was one splice that had not yet taken place. Bringing two teenagers together was calm sailing compared to entwining two adults. Adults are more walled and demanding than their junior counterparts. Where teenagers simply want unconditional love, adults will not give it without conditions. So stitching together the two adults I had in mind would be a toss of rounded dice. If the joining went badly, everyone would leave with a sour taste. If it went as planned, it would be the glory of the dance, which is what I wanted. The outro of a show will make or break the show. The walk-away feeling will determine how that show will be judged and remembered.

Jennings and Britannya would close the night just as they had opened it. The two would give new life to *The Sound of Music*'s dated but euphonic love song "Something Good."

With all the other songs, I had the singers wait until the fourth, fifth or even sixth stanza before they began moving to their target boy or girl, for I wanted to give everyone time to enjoy dancing before they stopped to see which boy and girl would be united. But with this final number, I told Jennings and Britannya to start moving on the first stanza against the possibility that my two unsuspecting adults would not wish to be matched and behave contrarily. Extra time might be needed to couple them.

Right on cue, Jennings and Brittanya began moving to my two unwary adults.

I discovered that both marks adored *The Sound of Music*, so I decided the best oeuvre to commence their courtship was the song that commenced the courtship between the humorless and distant Captain von Trapp and the reflective though cheerful Maria.

Britannya reached her objective first. Mr. Heald drew back in disbelief. He smiled awkwardly as Britannya took his hands. Surrounded by cheers and howls, she playfully pulled him toward the middle of the room, singing as she went.

Meanwhile, Jennings had just reached his aim. Like Mr. Heald, Ms. Longmire was in disbelief. Queerly, she seemed to resist more than her hoped-to-be better half. A couple of girls nearby put their hands on her shoulders and gently nudged her forward.

Adults are indeed more walled than teenagers. Once Mr. Heald and Ms. Longmire were side by side, they seemed to be profoundly embarrassed. Not angry or unhappy, just very embarrassed. I did not understand it. Then it dawned on me: in their generation, courting, at least at its outset, was a private, intimate experience. I was suddenly faced with the possibility that the dance would end badly.

Then something happened that even I would not have imagined. Seeing the two grownups in a state of disconcertment, everyone in the gymnasium returned to their slow dancing as if the two chagrined adults were not even present. Brittannya walked over to Mr. Heald, took his hands and interlaced them with Ms. Longmire's. She then rejoined Jennings and the two of them returned to the stage and continued the song, hoping that Mr. Heald and Ms. Longmire would follow suit and come together like everyone else.

Seconds later, they did. Their discomfort vanished and the two finished the song smiling, still holding hands.

The room erupted in applause and whistles and cheers when the song concluded. Even the two resident seniors joined in the exuberance.

I looked up at the dangling white lights and smiled.

The night was a success.

Yet the smile was edged with sadness. From afar, I watched Roxanne dance, just as I had wanted, and I imagined it was me she was dancing with. Yet instead of feeling satisfied, all I felt was alone, lost, and empty.

It mattered not, though. What mattered was that the evening was a triumph. The shy and the invisible had their moment. I hoped it would not be their last.

I turned and headed for the back door where I had hung my coat.

Leaning against the door was Jodi. "Looking for this?" she asked, grinning, holding up my parka. "Can't have it...not quite yet." She handed my coat to Jeffry Rice, another singer, who took it with a smile and walked away.

"You know," a familiar voice filled the gymnasium air, "this whole night would never have happened without one person."

I recognized the voice: it was Cassidy, from the Activities Committee.

"Jodi, bring him back on out," Cassidy boomed enthusiastically.

Jodi crossed the entryway and looped her arm through mine. "You really didn't think you could just disappear, did you?"

People plan, God laughs.

Jodi the ram led Owen the dope back into the gymnasium. I should have stowed my coat elsewhere.

Amid rooting and applause, Jodi walked me over to Cassidy. The musicians behind her stood and added their applause to the crowd's.

I sighed quietly.

*Just let me go home*, I pleaded inside my head.

"The Christmas dance was the school's idea," Cassidy addressed everyone, "but what we had here tonight was Owen's. I know he hates any fuss and feathers made over him, but if it hadn't been for him, the magic we all shared this night would never have come about. He had a vision, and he believed in it and followed it. If he hadn't, this dance would have been like any other...but it wasn't. It was a fairy tale, a wonderful dream. Good dreams usually end all too quickly...but not this one. We let Owen do the dance his way on one condition: that he sing at least one song tonight. He agreed."

The room burst out in a thunderous ovation.

Jodi leaned close to me. "Remember what you said—'*if you sing, I sing*.'"

Cassidy turned and handed me the mic.

Both girls stepped away. Just when I thought the evening had been a success....

I cleared my throat. "Well...I'd tell you to put in earplugs," I said, "but then you'd miss out on a truly beautiful song. It came from the hand of Shari Bavaro. Many of you know her. She's a senior, who, unfortunately, could not be here tonight. Or, *fortunately*, if I ruin her song."

Many laughed.

"She has called the song 'Silhouette,'" I told them.

The piece was dulcet and slow, so the crowd congealed into intimate twos. As heads lay on shoulders and arms enringed waists, I began.

The song was entrancingly sad; probably not the most felicitous piece to sing at a dance, but it was my favorite of all those sung and unsung. It spoke of the pain of mistakes, how the memories of those mistakes make one feel alone, empty, and apart...like a silhouette.

I would never know for certain, for I never asked Shari, but I suspected the song was a musical journal of sorrow...sorrow she carried for an abortion she had had the year before.

Though the words in the song came from Shari, they were everyone's, for everyone has in his life at least one mistake that follows him unrelentingly. I know I did. And more than just one.

There were two of me on the stage right then: one lost in the song and the other lost in the past. In that span of fabric that was my life, there were many threads that had been broken because of me. There were my real mother and father...both gone because of me. There was Susan...gone because of me. There was my first Yogidog...gone because of me. There was Ms. Dobson...sent away because of me. There were Elizabeth and Rebecca...separated because of me. There was Ms. Windom...more hateful because of me. There was Mrs. Crowley...alone in the world because of me. There was Ms. Gavin...let go because of me. There was Kylie...killed because of me. And there was Roxanne... gone forever because of me.

The song came to an end, but my memories didn't. They played endlessly before my eyes.

Someone tapped me on the shoulder. Instantly, I returned to the present. All eyes were fixed on me, wondering where I had been.

"Forgive me," I said, blushing at my mental absence.

The room broke out in roaring applause. I didn't know if it was because I was good or because I was done.

Cassidy came around to my side, gently took the mic from my hand and said, "Like I said, good dreams usually end all too quickly. But not this one. We have one last song, Owen...and it's for you."

Jodi came alongside me and took my hand. From behind me, there came an ariose cooing. Immediately, I knew those notes were kin to only one song: 'When Will I See You Again,' originally done by The Three Degrees.

It was my and Roxanne's song.

Jodi started the song, and then she started to walk, holding my hand in hers.

*What is this? What is she up to?*

I didn't see her coming. As if out of nowhere, there she was. Jennings was holding her hand and guiding her toward me.

Jennings led Roxanne to me, and Jodi led me to Roxanne. The two united our hands together and then stepped away.

Roxanne had always been an auroral jewel, but on this night, she was a dazzling diamond. A cerulean-blue gown flowed over her body like liquid following a path. Shimmering hair cascaded over her shoulders like a wave lapping over sand. And a sparkle adorned her lips like a twinkle floating on an autumn stream.

Her eyes did not leave mine, and mine did not leave hers.

My head was swimming. I couldn't believe this was happening.

She stepped near and wrapped her arms around my waist.

"I'm sorry for everything I did," she whispered to me.

"I'm sorry I let you go," I whispered back, tears filling my eyes.

"I love you, Owen," she said.

"I love you too, Roxanne."

Slowly and nervously, it happened. Like two drops of water coming together on a summer leaf, our lips met.

Jodi finished the song, but I barely noticed. And I only faintly noticed the clapping, cheering, whistling, and crying.

# CHAPTER 12

## 2 + 2 = 5

*"Be not deceived with the first appearance of things, for show is not substance."*

ENGLISH PROVERB

"It sure has been a year to forget, hasn't it?" Roxanne said quietly. "I'll buy a ticket to that," I agreed.

The two of us were lying together on a tan, pleather couch in the teachers' lounge. Only the faint light from a horizontal window on a wall beyond illuminated the room.

Roxanne had arrived at the dance with Shannon. She had planned to go out to dinner with Shannon and her new boyfriend after the dance, but when our reunion happened, Roxanne told Shannon to go on without her. Shannon understood completely, and she and her older but clean-cut swain went off to dinner by themselves. Roxanne called her father and asked him if she could spend some quiet time with me at school. Without reservation or worry, he said yes and would pick her up at midnight.

Though obviously now a non-issue, I still had to ask: "Roxanne, do you mind if I ask about you and Barry?"

"Owen, you can ask me anything you want. I don't want to keep anything from you ever again, and I don't want you to keep anything from me. I didn't live up to what I said that first night we went to the park by my house. Our relationship died because I didn't trust you. I trusted my own feelings rather than the truth. I said that night we have to be open and honest with each other about everything, even if it's painful or embarrassing. So I want you to ask me whatever's on your mind."

"Why aren't you and Barry together?"

"He wanted more of me than I wanted to give."

"You mean sex?"

"Yes."

"You don't want sex?"

"I didn't want it with him."

"Why?"

"You know me; I'm an old-fashioned girl—I'm not going to give myself to someone until I'm married."

"Why didn't you and Barry just plan to get married after high school?"

"Because I didn't love him, and he didn't love me. We liked each other, but nothing more."

"So you and Barry never..."

"No. You're the only boy I want to do that with. You're the only boy I want to marry. Did you and Kylie ever..."

"No."

"Why?"

"She wanted to, but I stopped us."

"How come?"

"It's difficult to explain. It's..."

"We don't have to talk about it if it's too difficult."

"It's not that. I'm just...I'm just a spilled box of toothpicks, Roxanne."

"What do you mean?"

"I'm a mess. My mind is a mess."

"Isn't everyone's, just a little?"

"Not like mine."

"Why do you say that?"

"I feel so unnatural, unnormal, if that's even a word. I'm Pinocchio. I just want to be a normal boy."

"Sweetheart, you're as normal as they come. You have the same needs and wants as anyone else."

"But I don't think and act like everyone else."

"What's so great about acting like everyone else? Barry was like everyone else, except that he came from money and could remember every *hath* and *doth* from *King Lear*, but he didn't have any depth. You do. After a while, he was actually kind of boring."

"Why were you with him then?"

"He was like a new car at first: fun, exciting, different. But the newness quickly wore off because there was nothing new or meaningful beyond the ride. He was like most people: all he did was talk about himself. I got tired of it. I got tired of hearing about all the Broadway shows he was going to do, all the places he was going to visit, all the rooms his house was going to have. It was always about him...and his best friend Corry. He wouldn't shut up about him. When we weren't talking about Barry, we weren't talking. He never once asked me about me. I remember you asking everyone at Kylie's memorial when was the last time we didn't consider our friends our audience. That's all I was to Barry—his audience. At Kylie's memorial, you said she stepped out of herself and asked you about you. Barry never once did that for me. But *you* always did. You know what you remind me of? You remind me of a good movie you don't want to see end. You're a great leading character with lots of unexpected twists. Take tonight. I had no idea this dance was your idea. You made so many kids happy tonight...me, especially. Who would have come up with a dance like we had tonight but you? Yeah, you don't act like everyone else, and you don't talk and think like everyone else, but those aren't bad things, Owen—they're *good* things. They're what made me fall in love with you."

"That may be, Roxanne, but I am still abnormal."

"In what way?" she asked tenderly.

"Girls don't want boys who are afraid. Girls want boys who possess unbendable bravery, who are unswervingly fearless."

"Where'd you hear that?"

"Ask any girl."

"I'm a girl, and I've never said it. Besides, what's that got to do with you feeling abnormal?"

"I have many fears, Roxanne."

"And that makes you abnormal?"

"Yes. Girls want security. They want someone they can believe in and depend on and feel safe with. They want someone who can shelter them from the world. A boy who holds fears cannot offer that."

"Whoever you've been listening to is way up past their bedtime. *They're up in the night,*' as my mom used to say."

"Are they? Boys aren't supposed to fear. Fearful boys are unwanted boys."

The two of us were lying side by side. Roxanne shifted herself sideways so she could see me directly. "Are you afraid I'll leave you because you're afraid? Is that what this is about, me leaving you?"

"Everything goes in circles, Roxanne," I answered her, remaining on my back.

"You really think I'd abandon you just because you're afraid of things?"

"Yes."

"So if a boy has fears, he's less of a boy and no girl would want him?"

"Girls don't want fearful boys. And they don't want boys who bring out the worst in people either…which is what I do. People fly away from me. I shouldn't even get involved, you know. Better to be alone in the beginning than forced to be alone in the end."

My words reminded me of Ms. Longmire's.

"Are you saying you don't want to be with me?" Roxanne's voice tremored.

"It's not *me* wanting to be with *you*—it's will *you* want to be with *me*?"

"I'm here, aren't I?"

"Future tense, Roxanne—*will* you want to?"

She stroked my face with her finger. "That's why you and Kylie didn't make love, isn't it? That's why you didn't let yourself love her—because you didn't want to get too close. You were afraid she'd leave you. You think I'm going to do the same."

"I told you my mind is a mess."

"Your mind is not a mess. You're just…multilayered. Heck, everyone is when you stop to think about it. You've been through a lot in your life, and it's hard for you to trust. As for me leaving you because you're afraid, I'll tell you something my grandmother used to say: '*That's two slices of baloney slapped between two slices of baloney.*' You don't know this about my dad, but he's terrified of flying. He's never been on a plane in his life, and he never will. He's deathly afraid of bugs too. All of 'em. If he finds a spider or earwig or something in the house, he won't touch it. He'll find one of us to get rid of it. My mom knew these things. She didn't think less of him or love him less because of it. You know, for such a smart boy, Owen, you aren't very bright. I'm not going to leave you just because you're afraid."

"Fear is repulsive to me. I just assume it is to everyone else as well."

"It isn't. If you really want to know what repulses me, it's lying and self-confidence."

"What's wrong with self-confidence?"

"I'm sorry, that's not what I meant to say. What I should have said was that too much self-confidence or too little is what I don't like. Too much will destroy a relationship. Barry had too much. It dripped off him like sweat. I felt intimidated around him because of it. I felt like I always had to measure up to him. And then there were times when I felt totally invisible around him because he was so into himself. He has everything going for him, and he knows it. I was nothing more than an armpiece, a pretty face for him to show off. When I wasn't his audience, I was his jewelry.

"Too little self-confidence will kill a relationship too. You can feel just as alone and insecure with someone like that. You don't feel protected by them, and you don't respect them either because you're more like their parent than their partner. You have to hold them up and build them up all the time. You're alone in a two-person relationship.

Two people should be there to build and hold each other up, not one supporting both. You don't lack self-confidence, Owen, but it doesn't drip off you like sweat either. You have fears—but so what. You may think that's a terrible thing, but to me, it's a beautiful thing. I can be myself with you because I have fears too."

"What fears could you possibly have?"

"That my dad will die, for one. I don't know what would happen to Walter and me if he did. I'm afraid of tests. All tests. I'm scared to death I'll make a mistake in cheerleader practice. I'm afraid of getting sick when I'm young and dying. When I was a little girl, I had this voice in my head that told me I would pass away when I was twenty-three."

"Why didn't you ever tell me these things?"

"I didn't want you to think I was weak...or weird."

"I'm sorry I made you feel like that."

"You didn't. I was just afraid you'd think less of me if I told you. No one wants to admit their fears...do they?"

"No."

"Are you going to leave me now because I've got things I'm afraid of?"

"Of course not."

"So why would I do it to you?"

"You would have made a fair Mr. Spock."

"Those aren't my only fears, Owen. I have other fears too. Do you want to know the biggest one?"

I nodded.

"That I'll lose you like you lost Kylie."

I shook my head. "I think that's a tad unlikely, Roxanne. I've been shot, beaten, kicked, raped, starved. I think if I were supposed to be in a coffin, I'd be in one by now."

Her eyes moistened. "Do you know how much I love you?"

I raised my arm to touch her face. My navigation was afield, and my hand accidentally glanced against her breast.

I quickly dropped my arm, and I felt my face flush. "I'm sorry. I didn't mean for that to happen."

She giggled. "I think you're about the only boy in the whole world who would apologize for that. Others would have had their hands all over me by now. Barry certainly would have."

"There are some things better than sex, Roxanne. Just talking and looking at you are choice delights to me. Just being with you has no peer. And knowing you trust me to be with you—here like this—is one of the greatest feelings I've ever had."

"Me too. Did you ever think we'd get back together?"

"No. You were with Barry, and I assumed that's the way it was going to stay. Yet I longed for us to come back together. I felt bad wanting you after Kylie died, but she was gone and was never coming back. I didn't plan for you to rejoin my heart; you just did."

"Don't take this the wrong way...but are you with me because you can't be with Kylie? I mean, am I her replacement?"

"Those are fair questions. I'd probably ask them too if I were in your place. But no...you're not. After Kylie died, it was like I died too. I never saw myself with anyone again. Then, for some reason, you came back into my heart. I didn't will it or even want it at the time. It just happened. I think my spirit was lost without you. You and I were so comfortable together. We fit so well together in so many ways. I felt safe with you...and loved. I missed you terribly. Did *you* ever think we'd get back together?"

"Uh-huh. After I broke up with Barry, I knew it would happen. I didn't know when, but I knew it would. It's like we were made for each other, and we were made to be together."

"It certainly seems that way, doesn't it?"

She smiled impishly at me. "Tell me something, if you've never had sex, how do you know there are things better than it?"

My face turned mercurochrome red.

"*Yes?*" she asked glidingly.

I cleared my throat. "Well...let's just say that I know the sensation... if you know what I mean."

She smiled reflectively. "I know what you mean. I do it too."

She leaned over and kissed me passionately. She took hold of my hand and placed it on her breast.

"I love your cologne," she murmured. "No one else wears it. It's such a turn on."

"It's Elsha," I said abstractedly, folding my body over hers.

She was now beneath me. My lips hungrily roamed her mouth, her face, her neck. Not far below, my hands greedily toured her firm but unbelievably soft breasts.

Whirlwinds of carnal chemicals were flying wildly within our young bodies.

I felt her hand reach up and begin to pull down the top of her gown. If I didn't stop us then, we wouldn't be able to stop later.

I intercepted her hand and stilled it.

"What's the matter?" she asked, confusion and anxiety tinting her words. "Don't you want to?"

I lifted myself onto my hands so I could see her face more clearly. "I want you more than anything, Roxanne. But actions father consequences. I don't want either of us to face those consequences. I want us to be married if we do these things. I want it to be right. If we did things tonight, we'd feel guilty and weak tomorrow. I want us to feel good about touching each other. I want there to be more than love between us when we come together. I want there to be a vow of commitment, a vow of dedication, a vow of faithfulness."

She canted her head slightly. "What are you saying?"

"What do you think I'm saying?"

"It sounds like you're...are you...are you proposing to me?"

Without hesitation, I said, "Yes."

Her eyes teared. "I would love to be your wife," she said, smiling happily. "Wow! I started out the night single, and I end up engaged! Boy, is everyone going to be surprised!"

I felt tears gather in my own eyes. I laid my face against her neck and the tears rushed out of me. It had been years since I wept so freely.

"Hey, what's the matter?" Roxanne asked softly, stoking my hair.

"I hate needing people," I struggled, "but I need you. I need you so much, Roxanne. I love you so much. I really hate feeling. I'm not good at it. I've never been good at it. I don't know how to handle emotions.

If I were normal, maybe I could. I don't want to feel, but I do. So many thoughts and emotions are clashing inside my head. I just want things to make sense and go in a straight line. But they don't."

"And they never will. Nothing ever goes in a straight line when people are involved. Bad people aren't bad all the time, and good people aren't good all the time. They're not going to make sense sometimes. I'm not going to make sense, you're not going to make sense. It's just the way it is. Stop trying to be a machine, Owen. Stop fighting being human. You told me yourself once that the less you fight something, the more success you'll have with it. It's a good prescription. I think you should have a bottle filled for yourself."

"Dispensing advice and taking it are two different kinds of pills."

"You know, when you and I broke up, it was one of the hardest times in my life. It was almost as hard as when I lost my mother. I hated you and loved you at the same time. I wanted the best for you, and I wanted the worst. When you lost Kylie, I felt ashamed for wishing you tragedy. I got what I wanted, and I hated it. People simply don't make sense sometimes."

"You make it all sound so normal."

"It is normal."

"Then why do I—"

"Why is being normal suddenly so important to you? I mean, you were so comfortable in your own skin before."

"I've never been comfortable in my own skin, Roxanne. Sometimes I really hate who I am. I've been called odd all of my life, and it's true. What kind of boy plans a big dance just so he can watch his ex-girlfriend dance and pretend he's dancing with her? What kind of boy talks like a textbook? What kind of boy dresses like he's always on his way to an interview? What kind of boy wishes to be normal but disdains those who are? What kind of boy longs to feel but hates it when he does? I feel weird and empty so much of the time, but when I'm with you, I don't feel those things. I feel complete and right. When I'm with you, I feel at peace, safe. I don't know what I would do if I lost you again. And yet, I'm afraid that's exactly what's going to happen. What did you say about a lack of self-confidence killing a relationship?

This is who I am, Roxanne: a peculiar, illogical, abnormal, chronically fearful boy who wishes he could be anyone other than himself. What do you say now?"

"I don't say anything, except this—you're not going to lose me...ever again."

The new year of 1976 was twelve days old. It was nearly a spring-like day: the air was warm and the sky Hawaiian blue.

I was walking home from school.

Someone tapped their horn. I turned to my left and saw a solid-black Ford Elite stopped by the curb. The big-steel automobile was clearly fresh-from-the-factory new: the chrome on its bumpers danced; the onyx skin below its sable landau roof sparkled; the glass enclosing its cabin shimmered, and its split opera windows (which were a unique departure from the single, vertical portholes found in the C-pillars of other luxury coupes on the road) glinted.

The driver of the Elite was Shawn Bartlett, a mulatto-haired, fair-skinned, well-framed, sharp-witted senior at my school. He had sung two songs at the Christmas dance. Shawn was a superior student and masterful tenor.

Shawn was also gay...and he made it known to everyone. More than a few adolescent trolls would verbally job him in the halls or cafeteria, but he would simply ignore them. He hated the remarks, but he wasn't going to hide what he was.

"Would you like a ride home?" Shawn asked me, craning his neck toward the passenger side window.

Suspicion instantly befriended me. Why was he suddenly offering me a ride when I had seen his car pass me many times before while I was walking home?

Seeing my hesitancy, Shawn said, "Don't worry, I'm not going to make a pass at you, if that's what you're thinking."

"I'm not," I assured him.

"Then hop in."

I transected the front lawn of the house where I had stopped.

Shawn opened the passenger door from the inside, and I reservedly took the seat. The cloth bench seat was smooth and inviting. The cabin was open and uncluttered, and the air was filled with the nonpareil aroma of new-car materials.

"Quite the carriage you have here," I extolled.

"Thanks. It's a combination birthday and Christmas present."

"Really? Your parents must do well for themselves."

"They do. My dad's the vice president of a hospital, and my mom's a head nurse. How about yours—what do your parents do?"

"At present, they're lying in the ground."

I had no tangible proof, but I was distrustful of Shawn. That he would suddenly offer me a ride after passing me so many times before made me leery of his intentions.

Shawn's face took on the mien of pain, as if he had just barked his shin. "I'm sorry, I didn't know."

"How could you?" I said.

"When did they die?"

"Fortunately, when I was very young."

"*Fortunately?*"

"*Yes, fortunately.* They're where they should be. But enough of them. I've seen you drive by many times. Did you not see me?"

He didn't answer immediately. "Sorry, can't say as I did."

"But you did today?"

"Yeah, I guess I did."

"Why do you think that is?"

"I get the feeling you think I'm up to something."

"Are you?"

"What would I be up to?" he volleyed back edgily. "Look, I was just trying to be nice and offer you a ride home. If you don't want it, you can walk."

Perhaps my mistrust was misplaced, and Shawn was actually telling me the truth.

"It's a nice day, but a ride home might make it nicer," I said.

We rode with the windows down and the radio playing loudly. I couldn't understand it, but it seemed Shawn and I had been friends for years, and that afternoon was just one of many we had shared. How can two people feel close when they barely know one another?

We pulled up to my house. John Denver was singing "I'm Sorry." Shawn closed his eyes as John was humming the closing bars of the song.

He opened his eyes and looked over at me. "I love that song, especially the ending."

"Remind you of somebody?"

He surveyed me thoughtfully, almost regretfully.

"Something the matter?" I asked him.

"No. So this is where you live, huh?" he queried, eyeing my home. "You're not exactly deep in the glue yourself, are ya?"

"Not at present."

"Nice home."

"Only on the outside. Behind the fashionable front door, it's a cemetery, a charnel house with chandeliers."

"I know what you mean. My dad only bought me this car if I agreed to start dating girls."

"Pretty pricey bribe."

"He thinks money can buy anything. He thinks that if I just start dating girls, I'll turn straight."

"And have you started dating them?"

"A couple. I didn't feel anything. My dad just doesn't get it—I go for boys. Period. It makes sense, you know—only boys know what boys like. Girls can't. Besides, girls always fake it when they make it. They pretend they're enjoying sex when they're really not. Boys don't do that. I mean, you can't fake a hard-on. People think gay men only want to make it with little boys. Nothing could be further from the truth. There are more straight perverts out there than queer perverts."

"You may be right."

"It ever cross your mind—making it with another boy? And, no, I'm not asking for me. I'm just curious."

"You don't have any trouble expressing yourself, do you?"

"Not really. Why not say what you're thinking? People will always know where you stand then."

"Pretty bold for someone your age. Young people like you typically want to fit in, at any cost."

"You talk like you're above me."

"Not at all. I say it only in passing."

"I hear you hate gays," he stated flatly.

His revelation slapped me. "Where did you hear that?"

"It's around."

"It's also wrong. I don't hate gays. As long as they don't force themselves on me, I wish them no misfortune or adversity."

"So if I were to reach over and kiss you, you'd wish me dead?"

"No, but I would hope you wouldn't."

"Don't worry, I know you're straight. But what if I asked you if you wanted to be friends—would you?"

"I don't know, I've never had a boyfriend before."

His eyebrows arched.

"I meant a friend who is a boy."

"What about Christopher and Mark?"

His second revelation was as disturbing as the first. "How do you know about Mark and Christopher?"

"I was told."

The atomity of his answer was perplexing.

"Why would somebody tell you about them?" I said in return.

"You're nothing like I expected."

His evasiveness was getting on my nerves.

"Why would you be expecting something?" I cornered him sharply.

"When we were doing the practices for the Christmas dance, you were always so tense and serious. Like an old man in a boy's body. But now that I get to know you, you're not at all like that. You're nothing like what people say you are."

"Gossip and reality are seldom twins. Come on, Shawn, why did you offer me a ride home today? You've seen me walk home before—why did you stop now?"

He averted his eyes.

"You might as well tell me—I'll find out eventually."

"I was asked to," again a flat tone.

"By whom?"

"An old friend of yours. William Farnsworth."

His answer jarred me. "That's one I didn't see coming. I thought he had finally evolved into a non-necrotic bacteria. Evidently not. He wanted us to become friends and then what?"

"His plan was that I start hanging around you and then everyone would think that you're gay like me. You'd lose Roxanne and be branded a fag...just like me. Chargeable by association."

"I see."

"William's gay too, you know."

"He surrendered that to you?"

"No, but I can tell. You don't have that kind of hatred unless you have something to hide. He likes boys, but he hates himself for it. He hates you too."

"No kidding."

"I think he's jealous of you. I think you're what he wants to be, but will never be able to be."

"If true, it's tragic. He used to hate me because we were alike—now it seems he hates me because we are not."

"He's a dangerous boy, Owen. Really over the edge. He could make a lot of trouble for you."

"Yes, I know. I've been witness to his black side."

"Be careful—you may just witness his backside too one of these days."

"I'm sure I will. Why would you be a part of this? I never did anything to you. We never even really talked before today."

"William told me you hated gays."

"And you just believed him without question?"

"I had no reason to doubt him. Why would he make up something like that?"

"Because he's a sociopath."

"He didn't come across as that at the time."

"So when he told you I'm *anti-gay*, you simply swallowed it, spoon and all, no questions asked, and decided to go out and ruin me?"

"Yes. I'm sick of being hated for what I am."

"I see. So instead of doing unto others as you would have them do unto you, you want to do to others what's been *done* to you. Is that the idea?"

"That was the plan. But now that I've talked to you, I realize it wasn't such a good one. My uncle once told me that if you get to know somebody you dislike, your dislike will probably disappear because you'll see them through different eyes. You won't see them as a rumor, or an image, or even a belief anymore—you'll see them as a person. He was right. I'm sorry, Owen, I never should have listened to William."

"No, you shouldn't have. But...no harm, no foul."

"You got a ride home out of it, at least."

"And in a nice car, no less."

"You can thank my homophobic dad for that."

"Would you mind if I did something?"

He looked at me aslant. "Depends."

"May I sit in the driver's seat?"

He blinked. "*Why?*"

"There is something I would like to find out."

"In the driver's seat?"

"Yes."

His face froze for a moment. Then his face loosened, and he said, "Sure, why not. But don't even *think* about driving."

"I won't."

We both exited the car at the same time and reentered it at the same time.

Upon closing the door, I instantly found myself enfolded in a stirring, new world. A sense of freedom, maturity, and control came over me. I ran my eyes over the gauges, buttons, and dials. It occurred to me only then that he who sat in that seat was in command of them all; indeed, every millimeter of a car was under the authority of the one who guided it; it was like being the captain of a ship. With two fingers, I clasped the right spoke of the steering wheel and gently turned it. It moved almost on its own. A surge of excitement and electricity shot through me.

"Fascinating," came from my lips.

Though Mark had explained to me his obsession with driving his friend's Grand Prix, I always thought the infatuation inane. Until that moment. Though I was not actually driving, I felt a marked measure of importance, significance, and power. Just like Mark.

I opened the door and let myself out of the car. Shawn met me in front of it.

"Thank you for letting me do that," I said.

"Find out what you wanted?"

"I did."

He studied me for a moment. "So do you want to try?"

"Try what?"

"Being friends. I'm willing if you are."

"Why would you want to be my friend?"

"You make it sound like something terrible."

"I'm sorry...I've just never had people eager to get close to me."

"Maybe they sense you don't want to get close to *them*, so they don't even try. But I am. You're a bit on the intense side, and you don't—"

"Spare me the old joke if that's what you were about to say."

"What old joke is that?"

"That the only humorous bones I have in my body are the two in my arms."

Shawn looked at me with confusion in his eyes. "I don't get it."

I sighed. "The bone in the upper arm is called the *humerus*. Get it? It's a joke usually reserved for people like me who have no sense of humor. That's what you were about to tell me, wasn't it?"

He dithered momentarily. "Yes...but not in those words."

"So why would you want to be my friend if I have no sense of humor and I'm not gay?"

"I have straight friends too. And two of them never even crack a smile. Why don't you let me pick you up for school tomorrow? What have you got to lose?"

I considered his offer. "Why not?"

"Great! It's a date."

"*So to speak*," I made clear.

"So to speak," he reaffirmed with a nod and a smile.

The next day, I met Roxanne after homeroom so I could walk with her to her first class.

"Wow! That's a nice jacket!" she commented gamely upon seeing me.

Over me was a rust-toned sport coat made of brushed suede.

"I got it half-off at Auerbach's. End-of-the-season sale. I don't get it. The season won't be over for another three months, but they already have their spring lineup out."

"I don't think it was on sale at all," she protested jokingly. "Was it a man or woman who sold you it?"

"Man."

"Well, there you have it. He was probably gay, and he couldn't resist giving a bargain to such a cute boy." She winked.

"Then I'll bet *you* get tons of bargains."

"Very funny."

"As long as we are on the subject of gay, I need to ask you something."

"Ask away."

"Do you know—"

"Wait a minute—you're not going to tell me you're a closet queer, are you?" she laughed.

"No, I'm not a *'closet queer,'* as you put it. Why would you even ask that?"

She appeared embarrassed. "I'm sorry, it was just a joke."

"If that was a joke, I'd hate to imagine what you'd say if you *weren't* joking."

"I'm sorry, I didn't mean to make you mad."

"It's all right. What I wanted to ask is if you know Shawn Bartlett?"

"Isn't he the senior who lets everyone know he's gay?"

"Yes. He and I have become friends. Are you okay with that?"

"Sure, of course I am. Why wouldn't I be? Everyone needs friends. It shouldn't matter if they're gay or not."

"What if people started thinking *I'm* gay? Would that bother you? Would *you* start thinking it?"

"No, of course not. People are going to think what they're going to think. You can't stop them. I want you to be friends with whoever you want to be friends with. I lost you once because I thought the wrong thing—I'm not going to lose you again for the same reason."

There was a comma of silence between us.

"What's the matter?" she asked.

"Nothing."

"Sweetheart, are you okay? You don't seem yourself lately."

"I'm fine."

"Hey, you two lovebirds better get to class before you're late," Mr. Taggart cautioned us as he breezed by.

"See you around twelve-thirty?" Roxanne confirmed as she entered her classroom.

"See you then."

I walked away from Roxanne feeling something I had been feeling more and more: unease. I couldn't put my finger on it, but I felt something was going to happen between us. Something unexpected. Something far worse than before.

Later that day, Shawn came up to me while I was at my locker.

"Why don't we get married?" he asked with a toyful grin.

I knew he was only playing with me, so I played back. "Let's don't and say we did." I smiled.

"Let's do and say we didn't."

We both laughed.

"You doing anything Friday night?" he asked.

"Why, you have something in mind?"

"I thought we could go and watch the planes rotate."

"*What?*"

"It's an aeronautical term. They say it in the flight deck when a plane is at takeoff speed and they raise the nose gear. The rotation is complete when the aft of the plane is airborne. My dad's a weekend pilot."

"You just couldn't have said '*watch the planes take off*'?"

He blushed slightly. "Okay, so I was showing off. Sue me."

"How much would I get?" I teased.

He smiled ludically. "I thought after the airport we could get some hamburgers and take them up to the high Aves and look at the city for a while. Then I thought we'd go downtown and drag State. My car will cream every other car on the road."

"Shawn's black panther—stately on the outside, vicious on the in."

"So do you want to go?"

Planes and hamburgers sounded a little strange, yet they appealed to me nonetheless. I had never been out with another teenage boy, in a teenage car, doing teenage things. It was a chance to taste a normal life for once.

"Sure...why not?" I said.

Shawn drove me home that Friday afternoon and waited in my room while I quickly showered and redressed.

Ms. Windom always eyed me disdainfully, but when I entered the house with Shawn and then left with him shortly thereafter, she gave me a harder stare than usual.

"What charm school did she graduate from?" Shawn asked as we were walking out to his car.

"All of them. And with honors."

"Valedictorian, no doubt."

"Of course."

"She must fit right in at Halloween."

I laughed.

Laughter was not a staple in my behavioral diet, but when I was with Shawn, it was always the main course. His sense of humor was sometimes light, sometimes dry, sometimes sardonic, sometimes satiric, but always fresh. I was envious of his wit and wished that I had one, but I didn't. I was, as he so accurately pointed out in the beginning, a bit on the intense side.

Shawn headed north rather than west toward the airport.

"I thought you said you wanted to go to the airport," I refreshed his memory.

"I do. We are. There's a little something I want to do first."

Anxiety sidled up next to me. The memory of my first ride with the Wilsons crept out from beneath the layers of my mind and slithered through my body like a tapeworm. At every stop, I was tempted to run from the car, but something held me back. Maybe Shawn only wanted to drop by a friend's house first or pick up something from the store before heading over to the airport.

We entered an area of town known as the Avenues. It was an older section of the city on a hillside landscaped with turn-of-the-century homes and geriatric apartment houses. We climbed the steep hill until we came to 11th Avenue, at which point we finally turned west.

I had never been to this part of the city, even though I knew it existed. As we passed through the intersections, I saw the valley below and was mesmerized by the enormity of it. After the sun set, it must look even more amazing, like a clear, moonless night deep in the mountains. No wonder Shawn wanted to revisit it later when it was dark.

Shawn pulled the car over at the end of the avenue and put it in park. Before us now was a trisection: one road went south, the other north, and the one we had just traveled returned east.

"I thought you might enjoy this," he said.

"Yeah, it's nice up here."

"No, not that. Let me see your hand."

"*Why?*" Loud alarms went off in my head.

"Trust me."

The calmness of his voice silenced the alarms. I held out my hand. He took it and placed it on the steering wheel. He then shifted the car back into drive, and we started to slowly move.

"You better turn or we're going to go over that cliff," he advised playfully.

I didn't want to be on a residential street, so I turned the wheel to the right. The street going north was a narrow, two-lane road that led into wooded territory. Shawn told me that it was a road that looped around the mouth of a gorge called City Creek Canyon. On the other side was the State Capitol Building.

At first, Shawn kept our speed slow. Then, gradually, he gave the accelerator more pressure.

I couldn't believe how something so simple—turning a steering wheel—could make me so stupidly happy. I definitely saw why Mark was so obsessed with it.

Shawn suggested I sit closer to him so I could better "*feel the wheel*," as he put it. At that moment, it all became clear: him letting me steer was a setup. By giving me the wheel, he was able to get near to me. Though he had avowed he only wanted friendship, it was now evident he wanted more. The situation suddenly struck me as tragically ironic: I was beginning to replicate Mark's former life, a life I had reproved him for living. Yet there was a marked difference between Mark's world and mine: Mark needed his friend in ways I didn't need Shawn. Mark needed an older male to give him attention and affirmation of value. I needed neither of those. Still, I enjoyed Shawn's company immensely—he was bright, funny, perceptive, and sensitive. I wanted his friendship, but I had to set a boundary between us. If he opposed it, we couldn't be friends.

When we reached the other end of the loop, Shawn retook the wheel and said, "The other day, you looked so enthralled with playing with the wheel, I thought you might like to play with it on the road."

"That was very thoughtful. But a touch self-serving, don't you think?"

"What do you mean?"

I cocked my head in impatience. "Come on, Shawn, I'm not as naive as you would have me. You let me steer just so I would move close to you. Thigh to thigh...boy to boy...pretty titillating."

His eyes narrowed. "We now know who Carly Simon was singing about, don't we? Talk about vain!"

"No, let's talk about *us*. I want to be your friend, but that's as far as it goes."

"You must *really* think you're hot stuff, don't you?"

"No, I just don't want there to be any misunderstanding."

"You're cute, Owen, but you're not that cute."

I sighed. "There's an old Irish proverb, Shawn: *There are good ships and wood ships, ships that sail the sea, but the best ships are friendships, may they always be.* I want us to be friends, Shawn, always, but that can't happen if you aren't honest with me. Are you honestly going to sit there and tell me you have no sexual predilection for me?"

His face reddened slightly. "Okay, so I'm attracted to you—is that such a crime?"

"No. I just don't want you thinking you can do something about it. I want us to have fun together and do things together, but I don't want us to come together, if you know what I mean. You think you can do that?"

He smiled. "I think I can do that."

"Good. Now let's go watch some planes rotate."

We watched the planes do their thing until it became too dark to see them; then we left. Shawn spotted a Red Barn close to the airport and pulled into its parking lot. I wanted to pay for the meal since Shawn's contribution to the evening had been his car, but Shawn refused my money. We took our high-calorie/low-nutrient fare to the top of the Avenues and parked. We ate and watched the city lights below. The heat from the busy city made them twinkle. The radio played unobtrusively in the background.

"Something tells me you've been up here before," I guessed. "And not alone. With another boy, I'll lay odds."

"Your tall IQ is showing."

"I'll also lay odds that this boy was someone you loved…but who did not love you. Am I correct?"

Shawn stared at me, his eyes on the precipice of tears. "They were right about you: you are as sharp as a barbed-wire fence."

"And are you and I reliving some of those times you had with him?"

"*Sharper* than a barbed-wire fence."

"What was his name, this boy you brought up here?"

He hesitated at first. "Preston," he answered, wiping the inside of his eyes. "He went to my other school. He was a year behind me. He liked girls too…just like you."

"What is it with you and straight boys?"

"The heart wants what the heart wants."

"And why does yours want boys and not girls?"

"You won't like my answer."

"I don't have to like it. I just want to know it."

"They destroy everything they touch."

"Boys?"

"Girls. They destroyed Preston. They destroyed *us*."

"Us?"

"Me and Preston, our friendship. Despite my feelings for him, we were really good friends, but thanks to a girl, our friendship died. We had some great times together, me and Preston. We used to play tennis in the cemetery a few blocks from here…or our idea of tennis, which was nothing more than hitting a tennis ball back and forth on one of the streets. We'd go to drive-in movies, and then we'd go for hamburgers and critique the films. We'd go for walks and look at the houses and wonder when they'd been built and who lived in them and who used to live in them. We'd go out to the airport and watch the planes take off and wonder where they were going. We'd go to my house and eat Fritos and drink Shasta and listen to Elton John and John Denver and The Eagles and America. We'd come up here and look at the lights and share our dreams of the future and our fears of the present…and our dreams of the present and our fears of the future. We'd sing together and laugh together and talk on the phone for hours. He was the best friend I ever had. And we helped each other too. He was really shy and not very good at school. One of his crummy English teachers told him he couldn't even write a sentence after she read a paper he did on a Woody Allen movie. And yet he was smart about the things he liked. He was a terrific artist. Could draw anything. Me, I can't draw a straight line with a ruler, but Preston could draw the ceiling of the Sistine Chapel with his eyes closed. He would do my art assignments, and I would do his reading assignments. He didn't like books, and I didn't like art. I helped him, and he helped me. We made each other's lives easier…and happier.

"He liked girls, but he didn't have any self-confidence, so they all treated him like he was invisible. There was this one girl, Ann. Man, was he heels over head for her. We used to drive out to her house and park in the dark, eat dinner there, and he would just gaze at her home. Before we left, he'd sneak up to the Econoline van her mom took her to school in and kiss the handle of the sliding door. Every time we came up here, he would gaze at that part of the city where she lived. He knew he wasn't in her league, but he loved her anyway. We went to this stomp one Friday night last year. We saw her there, and he really wanted to ask her to dance. I encouraged him, but I shouldn't have: I knew she'd turn him down. And sure enough, she did. I never saw anyone so brokenhearted. It took every molecule of courage he had to ask her. You'd think she'd have had the decency to give him at least one dance. But not her. She looked at him like he was something she just stepped in, said no and went on talking to her friends. He already had a lousy self-image, and after that night, he just kind of folded up. That's when our friendship melted away. I tried to get him interested in other things, even other girls, but he wouldn't. He wouldn't do anything. That one rejection, that one girl destroyed him. I'm no psychologist, but I think that night will stay with him the rest of his life, and it'll always hold him back. I never understood what he saw in her. She was easy on the eyes, but beyond that, she was nothing but a shark with blond hair. I don't get it. Why do we want things that only hurt us? I wanted Preston, and Preston wanted Ann. It doesn't make sense."

"I need to ask—did you ever force yourself on him?"

"No. I asked him once if I could kiss him. He let me. But he didn't kiss back. I think he did it because he felt obligated to. I was his only friend, and I think he felt he owed it to me."

"Did you make him feel like he owed it to you?"

"I hope not. I really loved him."

"Why? Why'd you fall for him? Why didn't you fall for one of your own?"

"I've asked myself that a thousand times. I think I loved him because he was never fake. What you saw is what you got. He never hid anything. He never played games. He was vulnerable, and he knew it. You asked me why I don't like girls. Girls are phony, teeth to toes. They're masters at lying and deceiving. They're always playing with your head...*both* of them. They're never consistent—one minute they're sweet, the next they're sour. They treat you whatever way they want. They use you and then throw you away like a dirty paper towel. They never admit they're wrong, but they shout it to the world when a guy is. They're always the victim, never the villain. They're always the offended, but never the offender. They're professional victims. They're nothing but moody, narcissistic, mean-spirited, self-absorbed, cold-hearted, cold-blooded rats!"

"That's quite a list."

"It's all true."

"Uh-huh. Tell me, how can you label them all those things if you've never even been with one?"

"Because I have. Girls are always saying boys treat them like objects. Girls do the same thing. Worse, in fact. Girls are always vaunting themselves as angels, dehumanized and persecuted saints, Joans of Arc all. *Jonesing to get laid* is more like it. Girls think boys are nothing but lusting, sweating pigs. Let me tell ya, girls are far more raunchy and barnyard than boys. And a boy dare not show imperfection or emotion around a girl. He better not show weakness or fear either. He better be self-confident all the time and able to perform anytime. If he can't, she's gone. The only way a boy can keep a girl is if he can always keep her satisfied."

"You don't paint with a big brush, do you?"

"I tell it like it is."

"That may be, but that's not the way it *really* is. When I was a young boy, I was…abused by an older man. More than once. But I don't hate all men because of it. I don't think all men are evil. There are millions of fine men in the world. Just as there are millions of fine women and girls."

"I know what you're trying to say, but you're not going to change my mind—so don't even try. I like boys. I know what pleases them, and they know what pleases me. The only thing girls care about is pleasing themselves. Boys don't expect you to spoon-feed them twenty-four hours a day. That's all girls want. Boys don't play judge, and they don't play jury. They take you for what you are. Simple as that. No fuss, no muss, no pus."

"I'm sorry you feel that way."

"Sorry that I like boys or sorry that I don't like girls?"

"Both."

"I'm not sorry at all. I like boys, and I like liking them. I like what's between their legs. I like their chests; I like their arms; I like their necks; I like their—"

I held up my hand. "Enough." His talk was starting to sicken me.

"You asked."

"I asked why your heart wanted boys—I didn't ask for an itemized list."

"Sorry, didn't mean to upset you. I thought you wanted honesty."

"Honesty, yes, X-rated particulars, no."

"You're...you're kind of a prude, aren't you?"

"Better a prude than crude. You know, sex would hold the honor it's supposed to have if people like you didn't reduce it to some animalistic amusement. You reduce the human body to parts for fun. Sex loses its grandness, its glory, its mystery when it's thought of as nothing but entertainment; something to be laughed at and made fun of, to be satirized rather than respected."

"This is just my opinion, Owen, but I think you'd get more out of life if you weren't so uptight."

"I, too, have an opinion. May I share it?"

"Isn't that what you just did?"

"Only partly. You're as guilty of objectifying boys as girls are. Your erogenous itemization is evidence of that. Seems to me, *you're* the one who is playing judge and jury."

He pursed his lips in thought. "You should go into politics when you get older."

His remark confused me. "What's that got to do with anything?"

"Isn't that what politicians do—filibuster? Talk something to death?"

"Is that what I'm doing? Or does it only seem that way because you're uncomfortable hearing the truth?"

"So you're after truth, huh? Okay. Tell the truth: you've *never* objectified girls? You've never passed a pretty one in school or at the mall and wondered what she looks like naked and imagined yourself on top of her? Or, closer to home, you've never looked at Roxanne's boobs and butt and imagined yourself playing with them?"

I felt my face flush. He was absolutely right. I was immensely thankful it was dark in the car.

"Touché," I handed him.

He smiled. "I think we've had enough sex-talk for one night. I think it's time we get down to State Street."

He turned up the radio and Pilot's "It's Magic" was now the object of our attention.

Roxanne was behaving strangely. She was irritable and short-tempered, even mean. I tried to discuss the matter, but she wouldn't talk. Something had happened…but I had no idea what it was. I only hoped it wasn't me.

Roxanne and I were walking in the park by her house. We had just been to Sunday Mass, and she said we needed to talk.

I reached for her hand when we came to our favorite bench, but she pulled her hand away. Not far from us, Kenny was happily leaping around a patch of mid-March snow.

Without preamble, she said, "We need to talk about Shawn, Owen."

"What about him?" I heard defensiveness in my tone.

"True or false—you'd rather be with him than me?"

"False, of course."

"You're lying!"

"No, I'm not."

"Yes, you are!"

"Is this what's been eating at you—my friendship with Shawn?"

"Don't change the subject!"

"I'm not. I'm just trying to understand what's gotten into you."

"Admit it—you like *him* more than me!"

"No, I don't," I protested sternly. "Roxanne, Shawn is the first close boyfriend I've ever had."

She shot me a cold look.

I rolled my eyes. "I meant he's the first close friend I've ever had who's a boy! What is it with that word? Why do people automatically think it's a synonym for lover? You have girlfriends, but you don't see me assuming you're romantically inclined toward *them*."

Her eyes thawed. "It's just that you're always with him, even at school. We used to have lunch together every day and spend every Saturday together. Now we rarely have lunch together, and maybe it's every *other* Saturday we see each other. You even brought him with us to our Valentine's Day dinner at The Old Salt City Jail. I wanted that to be *our* place—not yours, mine, and Shawn's."

"It's a nice restaurant, and he doesn't go out to nice places much anymore. Besides, he was alone. It's a hard night to be alone."

"Yeah, I know—I was more or less alone myself that night. The two of you laughed and giggled and talked amongst yourselves all night, leaving me out, making me feel like I was in the way."

"Oh, we did not!" My tone was more oppugnant than I wanted it to be, but I felt she was attacking me.

She gave me a wounded look. "I know you took Christopher with you last year when you and Kylie went out on Valentine's. Why'd you do that?"

"For the same reason I invited Shawn. I didn't want them to be alone."

She gave me an auger-eyed stare.

"You're suspecting something," I conjectured. "I've seen that look before."

"What look is that?"

"Distrust."

A tinge of fear appeared on her face. "What can he give you that I can't?"

"You make it sound like I need him."

"Do you?"

"I like him—I *don't* need him. I enjoy his company, and he enjoys mine. We have a good time together. We have a lot in common. I like the way I feel when I'm with him. I like the way I feel about myself when I'm with him. I like driving down the road, just the two of us, listening to the radio, just being teenage boys, doing teenage things. I like the freedom I feel when we're together. He makes me feel good. He makes me laugh. No one makes me laugh the way he does. He's smart and clever and funny. He's my friend. Is that a *felony*?"

Roxanne looked at me blankly. "No. It's not a felony. You can be friends with whoever you want."

"*Thank you!*" I came back angrily.

She smiled. But it wasn't a smile of happiness—it was one of resignation and surrender.

"You're right," she finally said, "you don't need him. You're in love with him."

My whole body froze.

I couldn't believe what I had just heard!

Just because I had a close friend who was gay meant *I* was gay? Just because I enjoyed being with him meant I was in love with him? After all the intimate talks she and I had shared, after all the intimate kissing, she actually believed I was homosexual? How could she believe such an untruth?

"Roxanne, can we back up, please," I pleaded.

"No, we can't. It's all over school about you and Shawn, but I ignored the gossip. I gave you—"

"What do you mean, it's all over school? I haven't heard anything."

"That's because you've been too wrapped up in your new *boyfriend*."

My face tightened at her use of the word.

"Yes, *boyfriend*," she repeated. "You're all alike."

"What is that supposed to mean? Who are you grouping me with?"

"You're nothing but a liar and a queer!"

"Are you listening to yourself! *Me*—with another boy? Have a brain, Roxanne!"

"I am...finally. It all makes sense now. Why else would you defend Ms. Gavin, a lesbian, if you weren't on her side of the room? Why else would you have as your best friend a boy who is openly gay if you weren't bent that way yourself? I mean, there're hundreds of boys in our school you could be friends with who *aren't* gay, but you choose to be with one who is. And why else would you want us to wait to have sex if there wasn't something you liked better?"

"Wait a minute—we *both* decided to wait until we got married to have sex."

"But you never even *tried*. A straight boy would have at least tried."

"What did you want me to do, *rape you*?"

"I just want a normal boyfriend who doesn't get off on other boys."

"I don't!"

"Owen, stop, okay! Just stop! Boys are your bag—I get it, and so does everyone else."

"Boys are *not* my—" I shook my head in disbelief. "I can't believe we're having this conversation! Look, I'm sorry if I made you feel slighted and left out. I would never do that intentionally. It's just that having a close friend is a new thing for me. I've never had one. Can't you try to understand that?"

"I understand. I understand perfectly. You're in love with Shawn... plain and simple. You're gay. I think you've just hid it from yourself all your life because you never wanted to admit it. I think you admire Shawn because he has the guts to admit it and you don't. I think the reason that old man molested you when you were young is that you wanted him to. You gave him hints you wanted to have sex with him."

I couldn't believe what I was hearing.

"That's disgusting, Roxanne!" I charged. "Little boys *do not* want to have sex! Why would you say such a thing!"

"Why would you *do* such a thing? Because you're a pervert, that's why! Little boys should want to play in the dirt—not with dirty old men!" Her eyes became matches on fire. "I can see *you* wanting to play with little boys too when you're old. Maybe even now. Isn't that's what all fags do?"

"What is with you!"

She shook her head. "Why did you have to do this to us?" she begged. "Why did you have to do it to me?"

"I haven't *done* anything—*you're* doing it! I asked you last January if it would bother you if Shawn and I were friends. You said no. I asked you if you would start thinking *I* was gay. You said no. You said everyone needs friends, and it shouldn't matter if they're gay or not. You said people are going to think what they're going to think. You said you wanted me to be friends with whomever I wanted to be friends with, and you didn't want to lose me again for thinking the wrong thing. That's exactly what you're doing again—thinking the wrong thing!"

"Things have changed since then. My eyes were closed when I said those things. Now they're open. I don't want to see you anymore, Owen. I don't want to talk to you; I don't want to be around you; I don't even want to know you. I just want to forget you."

She hunkered down and called out Kenny's name. He came running over to her. She scooped him up, turned around and headed out of the park.

There was a young tree next to me. My hand reached out and took hold of it. My legs lost their strength, and I collapsed onto the ground. My hand slid down the tree as I fell. My brain suddenly registered an odd warmth in the hand that had been holding the tree. I looked down. A streak of blood was widening in my palm. The bark on the tree, or something in the bark, had cut me. I hadn't even felt it. The sight of the blood didn't frighten me. All I could see was Roxanne walking out of the park.

The ground below the tree was cold and muddy. The wet earth was quickly penetrating the knees of my pants.

I watched Roxanne disappear from the park. I didn't understand it. I had done nothing wrong. How could this be happening? How could she say what she did?

I closed my eyes, hoping I was caught in a terrible dream, and it all would vanish when I reopened them. When I did, seconds later, the snow-mottled park was still beneath me, the barren trees were still around me, and the warm blood was still dripping from me.

Numbness had enveloped my body. But it wasn't from the cold, it was from disbelief. Tears abandoned me; movement escaped me. My body was frozen. Simultaneously, my chest felt empty and chokingly heavy. The world I knew was gone. The one person I trusted with my heart twisted it into pieces and threw the pieces into the wind. The one person I trusted with my secrets twisted them into a weapon and then used that weapon against me. The one person I trusted never to attack me did precisely that. The one person I trusted with my future had thrown that future away.

I wanted to leave the park, but I didn't know where to go or what to do once I got there.

Shawn. He would know what to do. He would help me.

"Oh, my heavens, Owen, what happened to you?" Mrs. Bartlett asked fearfully after she answered the door.

"I-Is Shawn home?" I asked unsteadily.

"He's in his room."

The petite, middle-aged, blond-haired woman stood back, and I entered the French Provincial-decorated home and made my way to Shawn's room, which was in the basement.

I knocked on Shawn's door. On the other side, the Eagles were spinning a trebled tale about lying eyes.

"It's unlocked," Shawn answered from behind the Spanish-style door.

Shawn's eyes widened when he saw me. He shut off his radio, sprang up from his desk and rushed over to me.

"Wh-What happened?" he stammered, his wide eyes panning my soiled and bloody clothes.

"She broke up with me."

"Who?"

"Roxanne."

*"Roxanne? Why?"*

"She thinks I'm gay."

Shawn stood motionless for a moment. *"You?"*

"She thinks I'm a pedophile and a pervert...a *gay* pervert."

Shawn shook his head in shock. "Wait, wait, wait—back up. Why would she think that?"

"She thinks I'm gay because we're friends. She says it's all over school too. She thinks all gays are perverts and child molesters. What am I going to do, Shawn?"

"Let's cross one broken bridge at a time. We need to get you cleaned up first. How'd you cut your hand?"

"On a tree."

In bewilderment, he shimmied his head again. "Let's go upstairs and my mom will take care of it."

Mrs. Bartlett was the kind of mother every gay child should have: accepting, loving, unjudging; the total opposite of her husband. She accepted Shawn steadfastly for what he preferred and who he liked. Her staunch and resolute nod to her son's homosexuality had caused more than a few stentorian arguments between her and Mr. Bartlett. Shawn himself had, on occasion, jumped into the disputes. Each time, he paid for his interference with dark bruises.

Being a nurse, Mrs. Bartlett had both the supplies and skills to dress deep cuts. She told me the laceration in my hand really needed stitches, but she knew my situation at home, so she cleaned and sealed the cut with a thong of cyanoacrylate so it wouldn't need them. Then she wrapped it with gauze and secured it with waterproof surgical tape. She had such a delicate, soothing touch I almost wished I had more injuries for her to treat.

After the cut was wrapped, she pulled a loose-fitting surgical glove over my hand and slipped a tight rubber band around my wrist. She then told Shawn to go get a pair of his pants, some underwear, a shirt and some socks. While he was gone, she told me to go upstairs to the master bathroom and take a shower. Shawn would leave his clothes outside the door. While I was showering, she would drop my clothes in the washer and start preparing dinner for Shawn and me. I tried to argue with her, for I felt I was putting them both out, but she held up her hand with a smile and told me the best patients were *silent* patients.

I did as she said.

After my shower, Shawn and I went to his room. Upstairs, Mrs. Bartlett was fixing dinner. Mr. Bartlett, to my good fortune, was up in his plane.

"How'd you get here?" Shawn started. "The buses don't run on Sundays. You didn't walk, did you?"

"I walked to a gas station and called a cab."

"*A cab?* That must have cost you a fortune."

"I was lucky I had the money on me, or I'd still be walking. Shawn, what am I going to do? She knew you were gay; she knew we were friends. It never bothered her before. Why did it all of a sudden?"

"I'm sure it wasn't all of a sudden. It's probably been bothering her all along—she just never let it out until now."

"Why? Why didn't she say something in the beginning?"

"She probably thought she could handle it. I don't mean to play Devil's advocate here, but I think you had this coming...except *I'm* the one who's to blame."

"What?"

"Roxanne's jealous of me, and she has every right to be. You and I have been spending a lot of time together, more than we should have. I really like you, and I like being with you. I should have reminded you that you have a girlfriend who wants to be with you too. But I didn't. She sees you now palling around with me, an unabashed gay boy, and she begins to wonder if you're gay too. Two plus two equals four. But in this case, our case, it's two plus two equals five. Everyone's doing the math wrong. On top of being your friend, people now think I'm *on top* of you as well."

"You knew about the talk around school?"

He appeared shamefaced. "Yeah."

"Why didn't you tell me?"

"I didn't want to lose you. I was afraid you wouldn't want to be friends anymore. It's not easy being the destination of smears and swipes."

"I don't understand—why haven't I heard about any of this before now?"

"People genuinely respect you and like you, and I think that's why they held their tongues when you were around. But after what happened today, I'm afraid those tongues are going to start to wag right in front of you. Roxanne isn't on your side of the aisle anymore, and she's going to start badmouthing you something wicked. That'll be the green light for everyone else to do the same. Owen, I don't want to lose you, but if you don't want to be friends now, I'll understand."

"No, I want us to be friends. I like you. Besides, it would be wrong to let this come between us. I'm not going to let people tell me who I can associate with and who I can't. If we stop being friends, that'll mean they've won. That'll mean William has achieved his goal."

"He *has* achieved his goal. Roxanne is your enemy now. She believes you'd rather be with another boy than her. In her eyes, you've chosen someone else—another guy, no less—and Hell hath no fury like a schoolgirl scorned. Roxanne is going to be on you like stink on scat. Mark my words."

"How could all this be happening?"

"You haven't seen anything yet. If it was just our friendship she was mad about, it might blow over, but her mother and brother are in the mix now too. She's also going to come after you because of them."

"I had nothing to do with their deaths."

"You do now. In her eyes, you're gay, and she's angry with you because of me, so all gays are like the pedophile fag who took their lives."

I was confused. "What?"

"Anger can make a bad situation worse. It can make untruths true. It can make a mound into a mountain. Jealousy in and of itself is bad enough, but when it's combined with the acid from bad memories, it's explosive. Very few gay men go after kids, but in her mind now, they *all* do. From what you told me, she never got the opportunity to confront the man who killed her mother and brother. You're going to become that opportunity. You're going to become that man. She's going to make life very difficult for us, you especially. We're both in for a very rocky ride at school."

"I can't believe this is happening. I don't deserve any of this."

"I know you don't. But you're going to get it. And excuse the crudeness, but you better grow an extra pair, because you're going to need 'em. The worst is yet to come."

Just then, Mrs. Bartlett called down the stairs and told us that dinner was ready.

Shawn gave me a low-wattage smile. "Last supper."

The next morning, Roxanne came up to me while I was at my locker. In her hand was a large box, its top flaps folded over one another. She unfolded the flaps, turned the box upside down and let its contents fall onto the floor in front of me. At my feet were all the presents I had given her since the beginning of our relationship. Sweaters, shirts, figurines, jewelry, books, cards, letters now lay on the tile floor, some even on my shoes.

"You can give the clothes and jewelry to your new *boyfriend*—I'm sure he'll *love* them," she smirked. Then she dropped the box on top of the castoff gifts.

Christopher, whose locker was not far from mine, came over to me, knelt down and started putting the discarded items back into the box.

"Be careful, Christopher," Roxanne said. "He may want you to do something else for him while you're on your knees." She laughed and jutted her middle fingers at me before she walked away.

I watched her leave. I was numb once again. How could she say such a foul thing? She, of all people. If she had been harmed by homosexuality so deeply, why was she now making lewd jokes about it? It was like making light of a suicide. I couldn't believe she had gone from love to loathing in practically the blink of an eye.

"And t-t-to th-think I actually had a th-thing for her once," Christopher remarked. "What a hypocrite."

"She's certainly not the Roxanne I fell in love with," I sighed.

Shawn caught up with me later that day between classes.

"I hear the rocky ride has begun," he relayed.

"You sure were right," I conceded. "I never would have thought it of her. I wish I knew what to do."

"There's nothing you can do. She wouldn't think differently even if *I* talked to her, so what's going to happen is going to happen."

"I don't know if I can take this."

"Today was just the start. You ever read any of *The Gathering Storm* by Winston Churchill?"

"Yes. Quite a bit."

"You and I are in for a storm ourselves, and it's just beginning to gather. Remember when you told me you used to wear an invisible shield to school when you were young so no one would hurt you?"

I nodded.

"You better pull that shield out of the closet, 'cause you're gonna need it. Roxanne's going to come at you until your intestines are lying on the ground. I've seen it before. I've been where you are, and people like her don't want anything but blood. Even after they get it, they want more. That's why I changed schools. I'm not going to hide what I am, but I'm not going to hang around and continue to get beaten up for it either."

"You were beaten up?"

"Between my dad and the homophobic shrikes at school, I had more colors on my body than a basket of Easter eggs. And in the background were their girlfriends spurring them on. Haven't you asked yourself why only *girls* are cheerleaders? Because they're natural fomenters."

Someone touched the back of my arm.

I turned around.

Shannon was standing there. The last time we spoke was on my birthday, in the park.

"Do you have a moment, Owen?" she asked.

"I'll catch up with you later," Shawn said tightly.

"Actually, I'd like to talk with both of you," she modified. "Let's go around the corner where it's a little less noisy." She immediately began walking.

Shawn sighed and shook his head, but he joined my side and we followed her.

"I heard about what Roxanne did today, Owen," she related once we joined up with her. "I'm sorry. It was very callous."

"Thank you," I said.

"But...you brought it on yourself."

I paused. "I beg your pardon."

"I think what Roxanne did was right—I just think she went about it in the wrong way."

"Do you now?" Shawn entered in.

"Yes," she maintained. "Homosexuality is a sin, a vile abomination in the sight of God. The relationship you two have is unnatural, unclean, and unholy."

"You know for a fact that Owen and I are *penis pals*?" Shawn dished out.

"I don't appreciate your vulgarity, Shawn," she dished back. "And, yes, I do know it for a fact. Everyone's saying so."

"And that, of course, makes it true."

"Why would they say it if it *wasn't* true?"

"Because lies are tastier than the truth. *The words of a gossip are like choice morsels; they go down to the innermost parts.* Proverbs eight-eighteen."

"I know the passage," she told him tartly.

"*I'm sure you do.* Here's another one: *Do not judge, and you will not be judged.* Luke six thirty-seven. I'm certain you've run across *that one* a time or two as well."

"I have," she came back stiffly.

Shawn smiled smugly at her. "Is that irritation I'm hearing in your voice, *Johnboy*?"

Confusion appeared on Shannon's face, and on mine.

"Johnboy?" Shannon queried, shaking her head.

"Yes, that's who you've become, isn't it: John Bunyan? The great sermonizer, the great condemner. *Pilgrim's Progress* was your most famous work. Tell us, which of its characters are you today—Mr. Worldly Wiseman or Mr. Legality? Unless I miss my guess, I'd say you're *both*."

Shannon was about to speak when Shawn cut her off. "I was raised Baptist, Shannon. Standpat Baptist. I know all the verses you sanctimonious blackcoats love to use so you can make yourselves feel big and blameless while making others feel small and dirty. I also know the verses you hate because then you can't play judge. Like John eight: *Let him who is without sin among you be the first to cast a stone at her.* You've heard that passage, I'm sure. Everyone has. But like everyone, that's all you've done—*heard it.* You haven't *lived it.* I'm gay, Shannon. It's who I am and what I am. If that's a sin, it'll be God who judges me, not *you*."

"It's my duty as a Christian to point out sin when I see it."

"Then point your finger at yourself before you point it at us. Clean your own house first before you try to clean ours. You don't have your angel wings yet, little girl. What about all the boys you used to put out for and go down on? What about that abortion you had last year?"

Shannon face turned igneous red. "That's a lie!"

"That's not what I heard. Ask anybody. You were quite the dirty-mouthed little slut before you got religion."

"I never had an abortion!" Her eyes moistened.

"But you did spread your legs whenever you got the chance."

"You're a filthy—" Her eyes were now glassy with tears.

"And you're a self-righteous, self-satisfied, stuck-on-yourself plaster saint who thinks she's higher than God! So you didn't have an abortion. *Prove it*. And while you're proving that, prove for a fact that Owen and I are *bed buddies*!"

The tears that had been pooling in Shannon's eyes slipped from them and they dripped down her cheeks.

I felt sorry for her. It hurt me to see anyone cry, especially a girl.

I expected Shawn to crow over his victory. He didn't. Instead, he went in the opposite direction.

"I know you're only doing what you think is right," he consoled her. "But what is right isn't always best. I lost my older brother because of what was right. He got into drugs, bad drugs, hard drugs, but instead of trying to help him, all my parents did was tell him he was going to Hell. My parents pushed him away with all their preaching. They thought they were doing the right thing. He eventually overdosed. They found him in his closet, dead. My mom came to admit her failure. It was too late, but she admitted it. My dad never did. Christians are more interested in being heard than hearing. They're more interested in making a point than making someone feel loved. They'd rather be right than be understanding. What seems like the perfect case for condemnation is sometimes the perfect case for compassion. There is a time for everything, Shannon. Everything. Read Ecclesiastes: *There's a time to kill, and a time to heal; a time to tear down, and a time to build up.* The whole Bible isn't a hammer, Shannon." He shook his head in disgust. "Come on, Owen, let's get going."

Shawn and I walked away. Before we rounded the corner, I looked back. Shannon was gone.

As Shawn had warned, the remarks once said behind my back were now said to my face. The kindness once shown me by the other students had been replaced by taunts and dirty digs. A storm was indeed gathering, and at its nexus was Roxanne. Without reservation, she would fling denigrating labels at me in the cafeteria, in the hallways, in class, even in assemblies. Routinely, she taped freehand sketches to my locker, each sketch an obscene image with an even more obscene legend limned below. As Roxanne had wanted, her base drawings, her profane hand gestures, her coarse words—spoken and written—all slashed deeply. And yet, what was most painful was the memory of what she used to be. The Roxanne I once knew would no more have engaged in such immoral invective than encouraged someone else to do it. Shawn was right: I had become the pedophile fag who had killed her mother and brother, and she was finally able to assail him.

Bright velvety flowers, eager young leaves, strong chromatic grass greeted the first day of May. It was the month when every living thing came alive. Every living thing but me. Not since grade school had I felt so isolated and dead. Shawn was the only one left in my corner. Christopher and I would talk here and there, but his heart and his life belonged to Jill. I didn't fault him for that, for mine had once belonged to Roxanne. Loyalties shift, priorities change. I couldn't wait for summer to begin so I could escape the desolation and repulsion everyone gladly showed me.

The first Monday of May was cloudless and warm. After school was over for the day, Shawn and I met and began our walk home. (Shawn didn't bring his car to school anymore. A few weeks into our friendship, he came out to the parking lot and found his driver's-side window in pieces.)

A block away from school, a 1965, aureolin-yellow Corvair pulled up alongside Shawn and me. Its cabin was teeming with teenagers, like fat pickles in a small jar. The car had no more come to a stop when all of the pickles poured out. I counted eight after the car was empty: all boys, all from my school, all mountainous. Leading the platoon of beefy blooms was William. Three of the eight walled off the sidewalk leading south to my home; four others made a wall on the sidewalk leading north back to the school. One of the boys, I noticed, was holding a Polaroid camera.

"Why aren't you two holding hands?" William sneered. "Isn't that what lovers do when they take a walk?"

"I don't know, William," Shawn pulled a face of innocence. "What do you do with *your* boyfriend when you go for a walk?"

"Shawn, don't," I enjoined.

We were powerfully outnumbered. If we weren't calm and sagacious, we would find ourselves on the ground, bloody and humiliated. William wanted a fight, but he wanted *us* to trigger it; he wanted *us* to give him a reason to strike. But if we kept our cool, or even just kept quiet, he wouldn't have that reason. A fire isn't extinguished with gasoline.

William stepped in front of me.

"What would you do if I made a pass at your boyfriend here?" William asked, looking at Shawn.

"I wouldn't care—he's not *my* boyfriend," Shawn shrugged nonchalantly. "But I think yours would."

William's face turned rigid with anger. Then he turned back to me.

"We're not going to fight you, William," I laid out. "We'd be foolish to even try. Two against eight, come on. If it's a fight you want, why don't you confront your father? He's the one who's really at the core of this. Isn't he?"

William's lips thinned. "No—*you* are. And we're not here for a fight—we're here for a kiss."

"I'd kiss you like I'd kiss a cactus."

"It's not *me* you're going to kiss—you're going to kiss Shawn."

"Oh, really?"

"Really. Because if you don't, I'm going to cut your little baby-maker off. But from what I hear, it's not that little, is it?" He smirked at Shawn.

From his front pocket, he lifted out a cracked and seemingly effete Boker pocketknife. With dirty fingernails, William pulled out one of its blades. The pocketknife appeared small with the blade retracted; now, with it extended, it was long and menacing. He put the tip of the rusty blade against my crotch. Shawn moved to interfere, but two of the boys, James Brinkley and Dan Bergman, both varsity football players, took hold of his arms and kept him in place. The boy holding the camera, Garrick Chancellor, walked over to William and me.

I wished Shawn and I had taken a main thoroughfare that day, for then William and his pack of monosyllabic mandrills would have kept driving. Instead, we were on a quiet side street. Shawn and I always took them when we walked home so we wouldn't have to talk over the noise of passing cars.

"Now, go over to Shawn and kiss him," William instructed me.

"No," I refused.

Two other boys came up behind me and took hold of my arms and pulled them behind my back. I winced in pain. Despite my struggling, William unzipped my pants and slipped the knife inside them until it made contact with my white briefs. I stopped cold.

"I can go farther, or you can go over and kiss Shawn," William grinned.

"Why are you doing this, William?" I asked. "Don't you ever get tired of hating? Haven't you ever heard of living and let live?"

"I'll live when you die. All fags should be wiped off the face of the Earth! I hate queers!"

"Then you must really hate yourself."

The hand holding the knife thrust forward.

I jerked in pain—the point of the blade was now pressing against flesh.

"Get over there, or I *will* cut it off," he vowed. "And then I'll go over and cut the weenie off your fag-faced queeny."

"I can't very well walk with your porcine primates holding me back, can I?"

The two condors behind me unlatched their talons. I walked over to Shawn. He smiled wanly at me.

"On the lips," William specified.

The two deadhead dirigibles restraining Shawn kept a hold of him but stepped back.

"I'm sorry this is happening," Shawn said.

Saying nothing in return, I leaned in and gave him a quick kiss. The instant our lips came together, I saw a flash go off beside us.

"Now take one of Owen from the front kissing him," William directed Garrick.

Calmly but decisively, I turned to William and said, "Wrong. You'll get no more pictures, William. You can stab me or beat me or even kill me, but you'll get nothing more out of us."

William came over to me. "I'm not going to stab you or kill you...but I am going to beat you."

Faster than a hummingbird in flight, William's fist flew into my face. I reeled backward. As I was falling, William caught my shirt collar and then rammed his fist into me again—only this time he plunged it into my stomach.

I collapsed to my knees in agony.

"You son of a whore!" Shawn wailed.

The two pilose pythons holding Shawn threw him to the ground. Then they sprang over to him and clamped his hands and feet to the grass. Though swearing and thrashing, Shawn was like a frog pinned to a dissection tray.

William grabbed my hair and yanked my head back.

"I don't forget anything, queerboy!" he informed me. "Remember that day in class two years ago when you got me on the ground and ripped out my hair? And then you gave a ballsy speech about how you don't *scare anymore.*' Where's your balls now, femboy? Why aren't you braggin' today? Maybe because you're saving all your mouthwork for your pretty-faced peter-eater over there."

I so wanted to kill William; I actually wanted to end his life as violently as I could. But I could barely move.

"Get away from them!" a gruff voice yelled.

All eyes turned toward the voice.

On the front porch of the house in front of which we were all stopped was a sparse-haired, elderly man. A long, thin rifle was berthed in his arms.

"You kiddin', old man?" William heaved at the gentleman. "You goin' to take us all down with your Civil War BB gun?"

"No—but I can take out some a yer eyes. Yer on my property! Now get off it!"

None of the eight rhinos moved. Instead, they simply smiled mockingly at the man.

Just then, there was a loud pop.

Everyone flinched.

The man had fired his rifle.

"Next time, yer gonna be pickin' yer eye outta the gutter," the man guaranteed, giving William a hard stare. "Or what's left of it."

"You're crazy, old man!" William shouted, releasing my hair. "Why don't you go back inside and shove that gun up your saggy ass. Then take your—"

"Come on," Garrick cut him off, "let's beat it. We got the picture. That's all we wanted."

The eight pachyderms returned to their cage and quickly sped off.

Shawn lifted himself off the grass, came over to me and helped me up. While Shawn was dusting himself off, I massaged my eye and stomach.

"You scouts okay?" the man asked.

Shawn and I nodded to him.

The man laid his gun down on his porch swing and came over to us.

"Yer gonna have some bright, autumn colors on that eye tomorra, boy," he predicted, looking me over. "Put a bag a frozen vegetables on it when ya get home. Don't use ice cubes. They don't mold so good. That sock ya took to yer belly is nothin' ta sneeze at neither. Don't eat nothin' 'til later on tonight. Give your insides a chance to settle. If it's still painin' ya come mornin', I'd have it looked into."

"Thank you, sir," I said. "For everything."

"Yer plenty welcome. Why was them hostiles all over ya?"

Shawn and I looked at one another.

"Because they hate gays," Shawn said, almost proudly.

The man nodded. "Yeah, people have always hated things that are diffrnt. We had a couple fellas in my unit that had that stripe. We gave 'em a hard time. But I'll tell ya, when the hard stuff started flyin', they sure saved our bacon...more'n once. Shouldn't judge another man. Shouldn't compare him neither. I seen a lot a senseless hatred and death in my days. Heard more foul language than I care ta remember. All of it, every smidgen of it, comes down ta one a two things: people not gettin' their own way, or people wantin' somethin' that ain't theirs. Just like little kids. 'Cept that little kids only throw fits. Big kids throw fists... and grenades. Don't add ta the hatred of the world, boys. Don't talk its talk. And don't walk its walk. Don't ever act like your enemies...'cause then you'll be just like 'em. Can I offer you scouts a lift somewheres?"

"No, thank you," I told him. "We could use the walk."

"Okay. You boys take care now."

The man went back to his house, and Shawn and I went on our way.

During the night, the colors of red, yellow, black, and maroon had set up camp around my eye, just as the man had said they would. There was some edema, but not as much as I thought there would be. Still, there was some, and it added to an already grotesque collage. I didn't want to go to school. I was already the recipient of more jokes than I could count. But I couldn't stay away. That would be cowardly. I couldn't let William and his league of lesions rule my life; and I couldn't let the rest of the school rule it either. Besides, the school year was nearly over. If I could hold out until then, all would be fine. Summer would be in place and life could only get better.

When I appeared on the school grounds that morning, I immediately noticed I was the object of inordinate attention. I expected people to give me looks because of my eye, but I didn't expect them to stare. And I noticed something else: the looks I received were more opprobrious than usual. I couldn't help but wonder why?

I entered the school, and in the foyer was my answer.

Taped to the foyer doors leading into the school was an 8 x 10 black-and-white photograph of the duressed kiss between Shawn and me. Written at the bottom of the enlargement was the caption: TRUE LOVE.

That's why the Polaroid picture. Neither Shawn nor I had been able to figure out why William wanted it.

In disgust, I grabbed the photograph, wadded it into a ball and threw it to the ground.

I soon discovered that was not the only copy.

Beyond the doors, the photograph was everywhere: on lockers, on classroom doors, on walls, on bulletin boards. My first thought was not how was I going to get them all down, but why would the faculty allow them to remain up? Why would they let this happen? Unless… they approved.

How did William do it? How did he get so many copies made in the space of just a few hours? And how did he get them up so quickly? It was only early morning. He must have had substantial help. The dusty adage certainly was true: *Hate, like love, can make people move mountains.*

Instead of removing the photos, I simply made my way to my locker. It would have been pointless to take them down, for—like ants that have found food—they would have been replaced just as quickly.

While on my way to my locker, I ran into Shawn coming out of the boys' restroom. His eyes were red. It was clear he had been crying.

I nudged him back into the lavatory.

"I'm so sorry about all this," his lips quivered. "If I had just kept driving that day in January, none of this would be happening now."

"*Hardship defines character,*'" I quoted. "Alex Larrabee uttered those words before his execution. I'm glad this has happened, Shawn. Roxanne's character has been defined by the hardship of the rumors about us. She is weak and readily swayed by the notions of others. I'm glad this has happened now and not after our marriage. If she could abandon me in the face of something false, like this, I can only imagine how quickly she would have deserted me in the face of something real, like cancer. I fell in love with her because of her strength and her character…but she has neither. She would rather embrace rumors and hearsay than embrace me. Some would argue it is simply her young mind that is guiding her. They'd be right, but only partly: her mind *alone* is skippering her, not her age. She is congenitally barren of virtue and fairness. So don't apologize, Shawn. Because of you, I have been spared a miserable future. The only decent girl I ever knew was Kylie… but she is long gone. She never would have treated me like this. She would have stood by me, no matter the hardship."

"I wish I could have met her."

"Even though you think all girls should be buried alive, I think you would have liked her."

"I'm sure I would have."

"You know, as I was walking to school today, I was thinking about our situation. It came to me that this whole thing is actually *my* doing. If only *I* had told you to keep driving that day, our picture would not be the school's new wallpaper. Granted, you have been teased and harassed for who you are, but you weren't, at least in this school, attacked physically. I think people are disappointed in me, and they're taking it out on both of us. They think I lied to them about who I am."

"Who you are?"

"They thought I was a through-and-through heterosexual…but now it seems I am not. It's not being gay they're in high dudgeon over, it's the lie, the greasy duplicity they can't stand. Roxanne once told me that people marveled at me, that I was someone they admired and wanted to be like. Disappointment is much greater when you are forced to look down on someone you used to look up to."

"But we haven't lied, neither of us. We haven't done anything wrong. We're just friends. Why can't they just believe that? Why can't they just leave us alone?"

"When you stop and think about all of this, we really shouldn't care. We're fertilizing dead ground."

"What do you mean?"

"*All of man's plots to reap to rend will fall to the Earth come the end.* Raymond Boone."

"What does that mean?"

"In the end, all of this, all that we're going through, will fail. Evil never wins; it just puts up a good fight. *Truth will out.* William Shakespeare. Gandhi put it even better: *Even if you are a minority of one, the truth is the truth.* It always prevails."

"Until then, what do we do?"

"If you are in a hurricane and can't run, you ride it out."

He flipped up his eyebrows. "I guess we'd better get in our rain slickers and get out there then."

We smiled at one another and left the restroom.

Amid stares and glares from nearly everyone, Shawn and I went to our respective lockers.

Mike Radin, a toothy, clear-faced sophomore with waterfall hair, was waiting for me at mine.

Mike had never held me in high esteem. Like William, he had openly displayed his distaste for me. But unlike William, I never knew the reason why. On this day, however, I knew the exact reason.

I went to my locker, opened it and began searching for the books I needed.

"*Owen and Shawny sittin' in a tree,*" Mike opened up immediately, "*k-i-s-s-i-n-g, first comes love, then comes marriage, then comes Sammy-from-sodomy in a baby carriage.*"

Many in the hallway laughed freely.

I met his eyes. "Cute, Mike. Juvenile, but cute."

"You think I'm *cute*, huh?" he kept going. "You want to kiss me too?"

"No, thanks, you're not my type. I like to kiss other humans."

Angela Bailey, whose locker was next to mine, chuckled.

"Where'd you get your pretty shiner?" Mike continued. "You and Shawny have a lovers' spat? Or was it just some rough sex?"

Angela leaned over to me and whispered, "If you don't want the pigeons to come around, don't feed 'em."

Not understanding her meaning, I looked at her.

"Ignore them and they'll go away," she advised.

"The dyke and the queer—what a pair," Mike chortled. "Hey, Owen, maybe Angela can teach you how to like girls, and you can teach her how to like boys."

"*Pigeons,*" Angela whispered.

Taking Angela's counsel, I closed my locker and headed for my homeroom.

"Owen, watch out!" Angela shrieked.

Something slammed into my lower back.

I screamed in agony as the force of the impact threw me face-first to the ground.

My nose hit the tile floor. Immediately, needles of hot pain punctured my face. An instant later, I felt blood drip from it.

Then something struck the side of my ribs. Then again. And again.

As I was being kicked, Ms. Windom entered my head. If spectator tickets were sold for this, she would have bought them all.

I tried to crawl away.

"Stop it!" Angela cried. "You're going to kill him!" From the tensity in her voice, I could tell she was being physically restrained.

Erik Reynolds, one of the school's few black students, grabbed my hair and threw me onto my back and, with his other hand, gripped my neck. I tried to emancipate myself from his hold, but I couldn't. His hand was like an iron vise.

Mike joined him and resumed his siege. My legs, my thighs, my abdomen—anywhere Mike's foot could make contact without hurting Erik at the same time—were his objectives.

"What the hell are you doing!" cried an adult voice.

Then I heard running and a sharp whishing sound, like papers falling.

Almost simultaneously, Erik and Mike were thrown against a bank of lockers. The two of them hitting the metal sounded like one car hitting another.

Mr. Taggart bent over me, gently purchased my arm and helped me to my feet. He removed the dress handkerchief from his blazer and handed it to me to wipe the blood from my face.

From experience, I knew I had more than a few fractured ribs. Within hours, I would resemble, as Shawn had so suitably described it once, a basket of Easter eggs. *Broken* Easter eggs.

"You won't be coming back to this school next year if I have anything to say about it!" Mr. Taggart fulminated, pointing a pencil-straight finger at Erik and Mike.

They looked at the floor. On it were the photographs of Shawn and me. Apparently, he had ripped them off the walls and then dropped them when he saw Erik and Mike attacking me.

Mr. Taggart shook his head at the large crowd. "I don't believe you people! Who do you think you are! You think you can just do something like this and believe it's okay! *It isn't!* It isn't tolerated here or anywhere else! You think you can just maul someone without consequences? Try doing this when you're eighteen. You'll find yourself in a room with a hard bed, a stained toilet and a life with a whole lotta nothin' in front of it! You think you can just wipe out anyone you don't like? What if someone didn't like *you* and wanted to wipe *you* out? But that would never happen, would it? You're all too pure and perfect. Not from where I'm standing. To me, you're nothing but a pack of predatory alley cats! And let me tell you, the world likes alley cats about as well as it likes rotting fish!"

"I'd rather sit next to a rotting fish than a rotten faggot!" Erik disgorged. "He deserves everything he gets! The world doesn't want his kind!"

"Not too long ago, Mr. Reynolds, the world didn't want *your kind* either," Mr. Taggart recalled for Erik. "In some places, it still doesn't."

Erik's face was now a brew of hurt and rage.

*"How does it feel?"* Mr. Taggart threw at him. "It's a different story when the claws are scratching at *you*, isn't it?"

"He's nothin' but a crotch-watching crap-crammer!" Mike echoed his friend.

Mr. Taggert stared at Mike, obviously wondering how something so filthy could come from someone so young.

I wasn't so wounded that I didn't notice Mike's semantic error. I wanted to tell him that his vulgarism, while punchy, was incorrect. He had the right idea but the wrong word. A crammer is not one who pushes but memorizes—he is a student, not a sodomite. Odd the things that go through one's head when he is in an extreme situation.

"Can you prove that?" Mr. Taggart asked Mike.

"Look at the floor, stupid! What's in those pictures—two *cows* kissing?"

Mr. Taggart stared at the brazen-lipped teen again. "Don't forget who you're talking to, Mr. Radin. I'm not one of your stupid, yardbird friends. And as for those pictures, *you* take a look. They're staged. Any *idiot* can see that."

Mike scowled at Mr. Taggart. "I can't call you stupid, but you can call me an idiot?"

"That's right. But in your case, *stupid* idiot. Look at the right edge of the photograph—there are fingertips on the front of Shawn's arm. They can't be Owen's, because he's facing Shawn, so they must belong to someone else...say, someone very strong who's holding Shawn in place. And look at their lips and their eyes. Their lips are tight, and their eyes are open. I'll admit it's been a while for me, but I seem to recall that romantic kisses are a tad less *constrained*. And if that isn't enough to prevail upon your meager common sense, ask yourself this: *why* would Shawn and Owen allow themselves to be photographed kissing in the first place?"

"Because they're proud that they're faggots!"

"Like I said—*stupid idiot.*"

"You can call me whatever you want, you're not going to change my mind."

"W-W-W-Would the truth ch-ch-change it?" a stammering voice came from the crowd.

Dozens of eyes turned.

Christopher stepped out from inside the assembly of students. His face was turning deep red. He walked over to Mike.

"I s-s-s-saw Sh-Sh-Shawn and O-Owen l-l-l-leave yesterday," Christopher recounted, his voice trembling. "And I s-saw W-W-William and a b-b-b-bunch of guys f-f-follow them. I f-f-followed them too. I knew s-s-s-something was going to happen. A c-c-c-couple bl-bl-blocks from here, they st-t-t-topped Owen and Sh-Shawn and they forced them to kiss."

"Sure they did," Mike controverted, his eyebrows trenched in doubt.

"T-T-Two guys held Shawn while W-W-William p-p-put a knife to Owen and t-t-told him if he didn't k-k-kiss Shawn, he'd c-c-cut him. So Owen kissed him. That's wh-when they took the picture. W-W-William wanted Owen to k-k-kiss Shawn again, b-b-b-but Owen refused, s-s-s-so William slugged him, twice. Then this old guy c-c-came out with a gun and st-t-t-topped it all. W-W-William and his fr-friends g-g-g-got in their car and t-t-took off."

Christopher turned from Mike and focused his attention on the large body of youthful onlookers. "I-I d-don't understand any of you. Wh-What's Owen done to all of you? Nothing. He never once turned on any of *you*—but now, all of a sudden, you're all turning on *him*! Just because he likes somebody you don't. You'd rather believe a lie than the truth. Owen isn't gay. He's as queer as me— *and I'm not a queer.*" He shook his head and sighed. "What he saw in all of you I'll never know. And I don't *want* to know. You're not worth it."

Christopher looked over at me, smiled sorrowfully and went on his way.

Mr. Taggart pointed his finger again at Mike and Erik. "Get to Mr. Heald's office—right now!"

After the two firebrands had left, Mr. Taggart ordered everyone to get to their homerooms. The crowd quickly broke up...but not before giving me daggers and dirty looks.

Christopher's and Mr. Taggart's words had fallen on deaf ears. In their hearts, I was gay, and that's all there was to it. Their minds were made up because their hearts were made up. Though bromidic and musty, the long-in-the-tooth expression was still true: *Change is a matter of the heart...not the head.*

After Mr. Taggart had made sure Mike and Erik were in Mr. Heald's hands, he drove me to the emergency room. As I suspected, I had broken ribs—but only two. The ER doctor gave me a codeine prescription for the pain and told me to apply ice and take aspirin for the inflammation. A couple days rest was advisable too.

The ER doctor was not the only one to give me advice that day. Mr. Taggart suggested, during the drive home, that I keep a low profile at school. While the cafeteria was for all, it was a place I should steer clear of for the remainder of the year. I should also avoid lingering in any of the hallways or stairwells. Because of my injuries, I would be excused from the last few PE classes. Hopefully, he said, the summer would diffuse the tensions and I could return in the fall to a less hostile building. He didn't come right out and say I should end my friendship with Shawn, but he said I should reevaluate it and weigh its benefits against its liabilities and detriments. I still had two more years of high school, and it could be a long two years if I continued my friendship with him. He had nothing against Shawn; he just didn't want to see me go through any more days like that one, or the one before. The world did not accept homosexuals, he said; one day it might, but that day was a long way off.

I returned to school the next day. It seemed there wasn't a part of me that wasn't sore. I walked like an old man: haltingly, guardedly. No matter where I went, I drew stares; no words, just stares. Eyes followed me as I walked to my classes, out of my classes, and into my classes. Shawn kept his distance. I wasn't about to seek him out to find out why, although I knew it could only be one of two reasons: either Mr. Taggart had asked him to for my sake, or Shawn had decided to on his own for the same reason. Shawn wouldn't stay away because he had been threatened and was afraid; that wasn't his way. He ignored threats and was afraid of no one.

Throughout the morning, I looked for Christopher to thank him for the stand he took the day before. The one who had been the most frightened had come forward. To me, he was a true friend. Apart from Angela, no one else, not one person, came to my defense. They all believed I was some kind of human aberration who was simply sitting at a table he had prepared for himself.

Around noontime, I found Christopher. He was sitting alone on a narrow stretch of grass by the east entrance (which was also considered the back entrance) to the gymnasium. No one else was around. I was grateful for that: I didn't want him to catch any more fire for being seen with me. I was certain he had taken some bitter needling for defending me.

Christopher appeared very sad. I walked over to him. He looked up at me, then away. The last time I saw him that low-spirited Roxanne had just rejected him.

"Thank you for doing what you did yesterday," I said, lowering myself to the grass.

"Y-Y-You're welcome," he told me pensively after a few moments. "Y-Y-You would have d-done the same for me."

"Yes, I would have. What's the matter, Christopher?"

Again, he did answer immediately. "Jill broke up with me this morning."

I shut my eyes in distress. "I'm sorry."

"It's all right."

I looked straight at him. "Because of me?"

"She thinks I'm a queer b-b-because I defended you."

"I'm really sorry, Christopher."

"It's j-just as well. We'd have had to br-br-break up anyway."

"No, you wouldn't."

"Yeah, we would. My f-f-f-family's moving next month. Idaho. Bl-Blackfoot. C-C-Couldn't be California...or even W-Washington or Oregon where the ocean is. No, it's g-g-gotta be Potatoland, USA. N-No D-D-Disneyland for me, it looks like."

My body froze—I couldn't breathe; I couldn't move; I couldn't speak. It was Mark's departure all over again. As with Mark, there was so much about Christopher I didn't know. So much I would never know. Another person was leaving my life. The water in my glass was vanishing quickly.

As death comes in threes, loss comes in waves. Roxanne was gone, my good reputation was gone, and Christopher would soon be gone. How many more waves would crash into me? How many more surges were yet to come?

"Y-Y-You b-b-b-b-better be careful, Owen," Christopher warned. "You got a b-b-boatload of enemies. I-I don't understand why. I kn-know they don't like Sh-Sh-Shawn, but I don't g-get why they hate you so much. I-I-It's like th-they hate you m-m-m-more than him, and h-h-he's the one who's gay. I don't understand it. I w-w-wish I—"

"Beat it, retard!" a voice from above us bellowed.

Both Christopher and I looked up.

Standing in front of us was William. Not a second later, Erik, Mike and two other boys joined him.

William held out his hand. At first, I thought he was making a gesture of friendship, but then he opened his fingers and in his palm was a Colt snub-nosed revolver, its short barrel glinting ominously in the high-noon sunlight.

I heard the breath leave Christopher's body.

"I said, get lost, retard," William repeated, his eyes glued to Christopher.

Christopher tried to get to his feet, then lost his balance and fell onto the grass.

"You're a joke," William gibed. "You tell anyone about this, stutterboy, and we'll do to you what we're going to do to your fag-friend here. You got that *Chr-Chr-Chr-Chrisy?*"

Trembling, Christopher raised himself from the ground. He and I shared glances. Then, reluctantly, he walked away. He looked back once before he disappeared inside the school.

"Get up, piglet," he commanded me. "You got some squealing to do."

William could only be referring to the scene in the film *Deliverance* in which one of the male characters was forced to squeal like a pig while being raped.

"If that detritus-laden mind of yours thinks I'm going to calmly let you rape me, you've got a big surprise on the way," I said.

"Oh, you won't be calm—you'll be screaming, crying, bleeding... *and* squealing."

Flight-or-fight adrenaline flared through my body. Memories of Mr. Wilson instantly flooded my mind. I was a small boy again, terrified, alone. I wanted to run. But I wouldn't run. I wouldn't let William see my terror. And I wouldn't let him defile my body like Mr. Wilson had, even if I had to die in the effort.

Pinning my eyes to his, I said, "The only way you're going to rape me is if I'm unconscious, or dead."

He grinned. "Have it your way."

Before I could react, he slammed the revolver into the side of my head.

The shaking brought me back to consciousness.

At first, they were distorted, like images seen through a prism. Then they cleared. But I was registering them through only one eye, my right eye; my left eye was dark, as if zippered shut. I saw two people above me: Mr. Taggart and Christopher. Surrounding the three of us were ceramic-tiled walls with metal pipes projecting out of them every few feet. Christopher and Mr. Taggart helped me off the floor. But for my socks, I was naked. Blood trickled down the inside of my legs. Higher up, I was burning, inside and out.

The identity of my environs finally came to me: I was inside the shower room of the gymnasium. I looked around the room. I noticed smears of blood on the floor. I also noticed my black-gray-and-ash argyle socks had taken on a new color—red.

My hand inspected my visionless eye. Thankfully, it wasn't blind: the tissue around it was simply distended from edema and was preventing the eyelid from opening. Below my eye, my upper and lower jaws throbbed. I slipped a finger through swollen lips and into my mouth: two of my teeth, one maxillary bicuspid and one mandibular molar, were loose. If I pulled hard enough, I could have removed them.

Mr. Taggart told Christopher to run and get some towels.

Christopher returned a minute later with a stack of folded, white towels. Mr. Taggart wrapped one around my middle, and Christopher draped two over my shoulders.

Taking my arms, Mr. Taggart and Christopher led me out of the shower room and over to a locker bench.

Mr. Taggart instructed Christopher to run to the main office and tell them to call an ambulance and the police.

"Who did this to you, Owen?" Mr. Taggart asked, his voice both angry and heartbroken. "Christopher told me William was carrying a gun. He said Erik and Mike and two other boys were with him."

I didn't answer.

"Come on, Owen, this has gone far enough. They could have killed you. They might succeed next time if you don't speak up."

"I don't want to speak up. I just want to go home."

"You're not going home, Owen. You're going to the hospital. Look, they can't be charged if you don't name them."

"No," I said flatly. "I'm done getting involved with people. I just want to leave."

"Christopher wanted to leave too, but he didn't. He came and found me, even though he was scared to do so. You need to be like your friend and do the right thing. If you don't name these boys, they'll get away with it."

"They've already gotten away with it."

"They could do it to somebody else."

"I'm the only one they wanted to do it to."

"All the more reason for you to speak up so they can't do it again."

"No," I repeated, trying to straighten my hair, for I knew I must have looked a terrible sight. "Mr. Taggart, I want you to do something for me."

"What?"

"I want you to arrange a transfer for me to another school. I know that a student has to go to the school that is closest to his home, but you could get that changed for me."

"You can't let them win, Owen."

"They've already won. I'm not wanted here anymore. It would be to everyone's benefit if I were gone from this place."

"What if this kind of thing comes up again in your life—are you going to let those people win too?"

"More than likely. It's what the craven do. It's what we do best."

"Wait a minute. You don't—"

"Where are my clothes?"

"You don't really think you could have stopped William and those other boys, do you?"

"Had I been brave and strong, I could have."

"You can only stop them now. You *couldn't* have stopped them then."

"I failed to stop them at the time—and that's all that counts."

"There were *five* of them. And you were unconscious."

"Not the whole time. I was out at the start of it and the end of it… but during it, I was fully awake, fully aware."

"And I'm sure you tried to stop them."

"Trying is but a sugar-coated metonym for failure. I tried...and failed. Failure is weakness. And weakness is cowardice."

"You weren't weak, Owen."

"If a little boy is being raped, that's just the way it is. It's going to happen until it's over. He is powerless to stop it. He has an excuse. If a man is being raped, he has no excuse, for he is a man. He is weak for letting it happen. His offense of weakness is fouler than the offense done to his body."

"First of all, Owen, you're *not* a man, you're a boy...a very intelligent, mature boy—but *still* a boy.

"Secondly, rape is not just a crime committed against children and women. Strong and able men get raped, and for different reasons. Rape is a dirty house with many rooms, and in each room, there is a reason. In this room, your room, I think it was about power and anger. William's power and anger. He meant to inflict dominance and humiliation. For once, *he* was the one in control, *he* was the one doing the humiliating.

"And thirdly—"

"Mr. Taggart—"

"And thirdly, Owen, your perspective on weakness is—"

"Mr. Taggart—stop. Please stop. I know you're only trying to help, but you weren't there. You weren't in that room. You weren't made to feel weak and enslaved and gutless. You weren't treated like a...a girl. Please, just help me get into another school. If you won't, I'll drop out."

He was momentarily speechless. "I don't want you to do that. I don't want you to leave Moran, but I don't want you to drop out either. I'll arrange a transfer for next year. You can finish your schoolwork at home, and then you can take your finals in my office. Will that work for you?"

"It will."

Mr. Taggart put his hand on my shoulder.

The kindness of his touch, the reality of the end of my days at Moran, and the enormity of the day itself fell in on me. I dropped my face to my knees and began to cry. Everything I had grown close to, everything I had adapted to was about to come to an end. I had always explored the new, but what I held onto was the familiar. Now the rock on which I had secured myself had slipped under the water.

There were so many students and teachers I would miss...yet I knew of only three who would miss me: Shawn, Christopher, and Mr. Taggart. They believed me, and they believed *in* me. But no relationship is forever. *Friendships are but meals*, Graham Utley believed. *You enjoy them, glean from them, gain strength from them...and then you begin again.*

Sitting there, I remembered the first time I saw the shower room nearly two years before. I feared Mr. Wilson and Ms. Windom were hiding somewhere within it, waiting to attack me again. I came to see it was an irrational fear. In the end, though, it wasn't irrational. I *was* raped in it...just not by them.

I heard hasty footsteps. Through the doorless entrance, Christopher, Mrs. Jarriel from the office and two police officers hurried into the locker room.

One of the officers, a balding quadragenarian, came over to me. He squatted down so we would be eye to eye.

"What happened here, son?" he asked softly.

"Nothing," I answered coldly.

"Nothing? It sure looks like something."

"I slipped in the shower."

"It looks like you were thrown around in the shower. Who assaulted you?"

"No one. Look, officer, I don't mean to be discourteous, but what happened to me *stays* with me. So go back to your car, write it up, call it in, or do whatever you are obligated to do, and then be on your way."

"Owen, he's only trying to help," Mr. Taggart inserted.

I sighed at the officer. "You want to help me? Drive me home—that will help me."

"Son, you were attacked. That just can't be dismissed. Now your friend here said that a group of five boys surrounded you. He said one of the boys, William Farnsworth, a sophomore, had a gun. That's a felony. As is what happened to you today."

"It's only a felony if I say it is. If I don't name names, if I don't pursue charges, you have nothing. Never happened."

The officer raised his eyebrows.

"It *did* happen, Owen," Mr. Taggart adjusted. "You were sodomized and assaulted."

"Both my business—no one else's."

"Owen?" the officer advanced again. "May I call you Owen?"

"No, but I'll tell you what you can call me—*a cab.* I want to go home!"

"The school can't do that—it's legally bound to make sure you're treated medically before you can be released."

Just then, two paramedics, an older male and a younger male, almost a boy, entered the room. The junior paramedic stopped when he saw me. His eyes widened in disbelief.

"Owen—" the officer stopped himself. "*Sorry,*" he rectified. "Are you afraid they'll come after you if you talk to us?"

Mr. Taggart coughed deliberately. He was trying to tell the policeman to tread lightly in this area.

"They won't come after me again," I reassured the officer. "Trust me. They got what they wanted."

"What if they go after your friend here?" the officer pursued. "He identified them. Don't you think you owe it to him to say something?"

"All the more reason *not* to say something. I can tell you who they are, and this will go forward, or I can say nothing, and it will go nowhere. I choose nowhere. It all stops here."

"No, it doesn't. William was carrying a weapon. He will be taken into custody for that."

"On whose word was he carrying a weapon?"

"On the word of your friend."

"And William will have *four* of his friends who will say otherwise. Five nays against one yea. As I see it, unless another Abraham Zapruder was here, or unless you can produce the alleged gun *with* William's prints, or produce more witnesses, your grasshopper will not jump. You have *one* witness, and one witness *only*, and that's *all* you have. So I say again, go back to your car, call it in, write it up, or do whatever your protocol demands you do, and be on your way."

The officer studied me, and then stood up. "You're a smart boy, young man. But you know something? Even smart people can be very foolish."

As I had wanted, the two officers went on their way.

Sleep evaded me that night. Holding my Yogidog against my chest, I hid in my closet like a hunted animal. I wrapped my discolored body in blankets and towels and sweaters and coats and bathrobes...anything heavy I could find. The heat of the clothing, the nearness of the walls, the softness of my Yogidog, and the cover of the darkness made me feel safe, secure, protected. They kept the memories of that afternoon from ripping me apart.

I didn't understand any of it. Why would they force sex on me—another boy—if they hated both homosexuality and me? Was it because William—as well as his friends—were indeed driven by power and anger, as Mr. Taggart had surmised? If so, why didn't they just break my limbs, or cut my flesh, or simply take my life if it were only about that? Or did they derive some diseased guilty pleasure in having intercourse with another boy? Forbidden fruit? If so, why didn't they just pick one of their parents' basements and indulge in their own private, perverted orgy? Why did they have to descend to rape, and why me? Only one answer came to my door: raping me was a much sweeter piece of forbidden fruit.

What further escaped my understanding were the smiles on many of the faces of those who saw me leave the school by ambulance. Why would anyone take satisfaction in the suffering of another? There were those I disliked, but if I saw them hurting, I wouldn't derive gratification from witnessing it.

Rare was the day I didn't see the face of Mr. Wilson somewhere in my mind. Six more faces would now join his. The sixth had no features, but it would be the hardest to look at and the most difficult to live with: weakness. I could not have stopped Mr. Wilson, for I was only a boy, but I should have stopped William and his carnivores because I wasn't. I tried to fight them in the shower room…yet I had failed. Failure is weakness. And weakness is cowardice.

I returned to school that Friday, but not until the afternoon. I wanted to come back the day before, but I was in too much pain.

With gym bag in hand, I entered the school through the south rear entrance. The final bell of the day was a half hour away from ringing. My plan was to gather my things from my locker and leave while everyone was still in class. I didn't want to come back after the final bell to empty my locker, for many teachers remained on campus long after the students had left, and I didn't want to risk running into any of them.

As I had expected, the corridors were empty. I quickly made my way to my locker, opened it and hurriedly put into the bag my pens, notebooks, binders, anything I could later use. I left all the textbooks, even though I had paid for them. I wouldn't need them…nor did I want them.

Staying with luck, I took the same route exiting the building as entering it. If success availed itself once, it should do the same again.

I entered the south stairwell and immediately heard ascending footsteps. Panic grabbed me, and I retreated back into the hallway. As the door was closing, I heard an angry voice below: "N-Not so fast, Roxanne!"

It was Christopher!

"What do you want?" Roxanne asked, sighing impatiently.

Odd that they were not in class.

Odder still was the timing: the three of us uniting in the same stairwell at the same time. Truth was indeed stranger than fiction.

"Just a moment of your pr-precious time," Christopher answered.

"If this is about Owen, I don't want to hear it. I don't care about him, and I don't want to know about him."

"D-D-Did you know he was beaten up and raped?"

"Everyone knows about it. He got what he deserved."

"Did he? Wh-What if *you* were raped? Would *you* deserve it?"

"If I was messing around with another girl, yeah."

"A-And what if Walter turns out to be gay? Would it be okay if *he* was raped?"

"Did Owen tell you about my family? That son of a bitch!"

"Owen didn't tell me anything—*Shannon* did. Sh-She told me lots of things. She said she was pretty hard on Owen and Shawn at first. Th-Then she realized how wr-wrong she was. Sh-She realized she was playing jury and judge. Just like you're doing now. Like you've been doing for weeks."

"Shannon's a pansy since she got God. She used to be a—"

"*Weed*, like you? Y-You used to have God yourself. Y-You used to be a pr-pr-pretty devout Catholic, if I remember. You give God the boot too? Or did you just give Him the finger like you did Owen?"

Roxanne laughed. "Man, you're weird! No wonder Jill broke up with you." She began climbing the steps.

I backed up.

"I wouldn't go any higher if I were you," he warned.

"Oh? Why not? You going to tackle me and spit me to death while you s-s-s-stutter?"

It was Christopher who laughed this time. The Christopher of two years ago would have crumbled at such a remark.

"Not bad, Roxanne," he commended. "Not bad. I give it an eight on the insult scale."

I could tell from his voice he was smiling.

"No, I won't spit you to death while I s-s-stutter," he ensured, "I'll do worse. I'll ruin you. So get your ass back down here!"

"You can *wipe* my ass!" She began climbing again.

"I don't think so. You got enough people doing that already. I've got something to say to you, Roxanne, and you're going to listen, or you're going to find your picture all over this school tomorrow morning. A picture of you kissing another girl. You may even find the picture *away* from school."

She stopped rising. "You can't do that," she came back, her tone smug.

"No? *JUST—YOU—WATCH—ME!*" he almost shouted. "I know a lot about photography, Roxanne. And I have a lot of pictures of you and your friends. Combine a couple of you and Michele or you and Ann Marie and you have one ruined reputation. What William did with force, I will do with ease. What William did with a knife, I will do with a darkroom."

I noticed Christopher wasn't stuttering. He once told me he wished he could be angry all the time, because when he was angry, he didn't stutter. He was rarely roused to that point. He was at that point now.

"What the hell do you want!" she execrated, her legs returning her to the lower landing.

"Like I said in the beginning, just a moment of your *precious* time. Shannon told me you're acting this way because of what happened to your mom and little brother. I don't—"

"That lousy—"

"Don't get mad at Shannon for caring about you."

"I never should have told her anything."

Christopher sighed deeply. "They say nothing stays the same—you're sure proof of that. You used to have the mouth of a saint, now you've got the mouth of a—" he stopped. "No, I'll leave the profanity to you. Comes more naturally out of your mouth than mine."

"Since when did you get so saintly? I hear you laid your pipe in Jill every chance you got."

There was a long pause.

"What happened to you?" Christopher asked sadly.

"Stay in your own yard, Christopher."

"I don't talk so good, Roxanne, but I see quite a bit. I sense even more. I know something's happened to you. I don't know what it is, but I know something has. Shannon says it's got something to do with your mom and brother. I think that's only part of it. I think somebody really hurt you, somebody you really cared about, not Owen, but Owen's the one you're taking it out on."

"Go screw yourself, Christopher! Scurry off to your darkroom and make your little dyke pictures. No one will believe them."

"Really? They believed the one about Owen."

"That's because it was true."

"No, it wasn't. I was there, Roxanne. I saw it all. Owen and Shawn were *forced* to kiss."

"Yeah, I heard about your little speech. The Lone Ranger comes to Owen's rescue in front of everyone. If you were such a good friend, why didn't you come to his rescue when it was actually happening?"

There was silence.

"Can't answer, can ya?" Roxanne jabbed. "That's because it *never* happened!"

More silence.

"I-I was afraid," Christopher owned. "Th-That's why I d-d-didn't help him on the s-s-street. I-I-I'm afraid of nearly everything. For the longest time, I-I was even afraid of *you*. I loved you so much. I s-s-so wanted us to get t-t-together. But I look at you now, and I'm so grateful we didn't. You've turned into this crawling, g-g-g-gutter-talking, v-v-vengeful-hearted, unfeeling, uncaring bitch. Owen told you he wasn't gay, but you wouldn't believe him. Just because he had a gay friend. Owen likes boys about as much as I like giving speeches. But you'd rather listen to gossip than him. Did he ever lie to you before? No. So why would he lie to you about being gay? And if he *was* gay, why would he want to be with you? Appearances? He doesn't care what people think of him. He's strong that way. But you, you're as weak and as shallow as they come. Personally, I'm glad this all happened, because he's better off without you. You're a spineless, disloyal, backstabbing snake! You're ruled by your past and your narrow-minded friends! You had the best boyfriend a girl could have, and you threw him away like trash. But *you're* the one who's trash, Roxanne!

"You don't know it now, but all this is going to come back on you someday soon, and it's gonna haunt you for the rest of your life. But for now, you're getting your wish: Owen is gone, and he won't be back. He's going to another school next year, and he's finishing out this one at home. Congratulations, Roxanne, you wanted him out of your life, and that's exactly what you got."

Roxanne said nothing back. Then I heard their landing door squeal open. I didn't know who was leaving, Roxanne or Christopher.

"Owen t-t-told me something r-r-right a-after we became friends, a-and I've always remembered it," Christopher supplemented. "I-I-It was a qu-quote from Ralph W-W-Waldo Emerson. He said, '*What lies behind us and what lies before us are tiny matters compared to what lies within us.'* He was right, because when it c-c-comes right down to it, it doesn't matter what's in back of us, in front of us, or even on top of us—it only matters what's *inside* us. That's where our goodness lies, where our changeless virtue is. I believe most people are truly good at their core; I never used to, but I do now. I think good people sometimes just choose the wrong answers on the tests they get in life. When good people do bad things, they're still good underneath, because none of us really ever change. Time makes us change how we dress and how we act and how much we trust and what we say and what we believe, but what we are underneath all that stays the same. I think deep down, Roxanne, you're still the same girl who bought me lunch that first day of school two years ago, and then invited me to sit with her the next day so I wouldn't be alone. I think that Roxanne is still there. She's just covered over with scales right now. I hope, I really hope, they fall off someday."

I was right about Christopher. If pushed far enough, he would shove back with a force that would stun and astound. Beware the quiet man.

The door below squealed once more. One of the two had just left. I had a feeling it wasn't Roxanne.

I wasn't about to stay and find out, so I reversed my path and left the school through the south front entrance.

No one stopped me.

I took an unexpected detour home. I stopped off at the park by the school. It would be the last time I would see the park. The other schools in the city were miles from it.

The swings were unoccupied, so I took rest in one. My swing stayed still; I simply stared at the bench on which Kylie and I had sat so long ago. I missed her so. I was completely alone in the world now. I used to love being alone. Now I hated it.

I wished I could return to the days when I preferred detachment to attachments, when separateness rather than togetherness was my drink of choice. I should have been strong. I should have been true to myself. I should have remained alone.

"This swing taken?"

My head spun to my right.

Standing in front of the adjacent swing was Lyle, the boy who two years earlier suffered an erection in the showers after gym class.

Outside of an occasional nod when we passed one another in the halls, we never interacted.

"I saw you leave school," he planted himself on the u-shaped leather seat next to mine.

"You sure you want to do that?" I precautioned. "I'm the gay plague, or haven't you heard?"

"I've heard. I don't believe it, though."

"That makes you a minority of one."

"A minority of many. A lot of kids don't believe you're gay. They really feel bad about what's happened to you."

"They have an unusual way of showing it. So far, everyone seems quite pleased with William's work."

"You're wrong, Owen. A couple girls were even crying about it today."

"Tears of joy, no doubt."

"Hardly. Just because people don't show a feeling doesn't mean they don't have it. I think many of them were afraid of what others would think of them if they spoke up for you. Try putting yourself in their place."

"Forgive me, but I've been a bit busy being in *my* place."

"I know, but try cutting them some slack."

"Of course. We mustn't be too hard on them." My tone was bushy with sarcasm.

"There's a rumor going around you're not coming back next year. Is it true?"

"Typically, rumors are bad inventions from good intentions, but in this case, it is not a rumor."

"I didn't think it was. A bunch of the kids are really upset about it."

"I'm sure they are. Please send them my sympathies."

I was being rude and mordant, and I felt guilty for it. Lyle was there just trying to be a friend.

"Remember what you told me two years ago?" he asked. "We were sitting on these very swings."

"I remember."

"You told me not to run."

"Yes, I did tell you that, but it's not the same with me."

"Isn't it? Running is running."

"I'm not running. I'm leaving. When you're no longer welcome at a party, you leave. There's no place for me at that school anymore."

"I'm sorry you feel that way. You'll be missed."

"No, I won't."

"Yes, you will. You gave me some good advice that day while we were sitting here. You told me don't react, don't show fear. I didn't. You told me to weather the storm. I did. You told me if I ran away to another school, I'd be remembered as the queer boy who turned tail and ran. I wasn't."

"I still hold to those words. But you weren't raped. I was. There comes a time when you have to say enough is enough. Sometimes leaving is the wrong thing to do, but sometimes it is the *only* thing to do."

Looking down the road on which both of us had just walked, I said, "I'm going to miss our school. I met many incredible people there. I experienced many incredible moments. Some of the best memories in my life happened in that place. And some of the worst. Thank you for coming to sit with me, Lyle. I'm sorry we never got to know one another."

Lyle smiled sadly. "Me too." He stood up. "One of the last things you said to me that day two years ago was that life is a trade-off: when you let go of something bad, something good will always take its place. You were right about that. You're letting go of something bad now, so something good has to take its place, and if anyone deserves good, it's you."

"No, I don't, but it is kind of you to say. The one who truly deserves good is *you*. I hope life treats you well, Lyle, and may the wind be cool and always at your back."

"I hope the same for you, Owen," he reciprocated and then made his way out of the park.

I looked over at the bench again.

The wind ahead of me would neither be cool nor caring.

It would, in fact, be hot and cold and cruel.

# CHAPTER 13

# Moving Forward...Going Back

*"Some people are going to leave a mark on this world,
while others will leave a stain."*

ELEANOR ROOSEVELT

"You never struck me as a sausage-and-eggs kind of boy," Ms. Windom said to me while I was reaching for a can of Pepsi inside the refrigerator.

I had just arrived home after ten hours at the store. I was tired and in no mood for riddles, let alone *her* riddles.

"Go away," I told her, closing the refrigerator and opening the can. "Go away and do whatever rodents do."

"First, you're hot for that Virgin Mary Kylie, then you're all aflame for that jelly-wristed Shawn. You really are a bi-guy, aren't you? A regular sausage-and-eggs boy."

I squinted at her. What was she talking about?

"Don't give me those questioning eyes. You know what I mean."

"No, I don't—as usual."

"That's funny. I would think your kind would know that expression like you know the size of your penis."

"*My* kind?"

"Yeah, *your* kind. The kind whose sexual sails are angled right down the middle. One day your eyes are down on the bulges, the next day they're up on the boobs. Sausage-and-eggs boy."

I stared at her, still bemused.

"I don't know why people say you're so smart. You're actually quite stupid. Girls have *eggs*, boys have *sausages*. *Link* sausages. Get it?"

Had it been another day, she would have had my opinion, but right then I had neither the will nor the energy to give it.

"Aren't you interested in what was left for you at the door today?" she called as I was walking away.

I turned around.

"You're like a scourge," she compared. "You kill everything you touch: your family, your teachers, your girlfriend, and now your *boyfriend*."

"What?"

"Death notices are always so bland, don't you think? Most of them have the potential to be so exciting, but they aren't. They rarely give the gruesome details. I like it when they do. What they never say, unfortunately, is when the dead die by their own hands. This one does." She picked up an envelope lying on the counter next to the sink and held it up in front of her. My name was written on its front. "This one also gives an editorial. And a pithy one at that."

I walked over to her and grabbed the envelope out of her hand.

She smiled as I read what was inside it.

### Shawn Robert Bartlett

Shawn Andy Bartlett, my dear son, hanged himself on his birthday, Friday, June 4, 1976. He came into the world on that day, and he left it on that day. Shawn was a soft-hearted boy with a big-hearted spirit. Shawn was gay, but he wasn't ashamed of it. There were those who thought he should be. Closed-minded and manikin-brained people will always think their way is the only way. Shawn took his life because of them. His death was called a suicide—but to me it will always be a murder. A memorial for Shawn will be held Friday, June 18th, from 6PM to 8PM at Serling Family Mortuary. May my son find peace—may those who hated him never find it.

I stood in silence.

After Kylie, I thought I would never feel the sting of death again. I was wrong.

Ms. Windom was dead-on about me: I *was* like a plague.

I put Shawn's obituary back in the envelope, folded it, slipped it into my back pocket and headed for my room.

"It looks like you won't be eating your boyfriend's sausage anymore," Ms. Windom laughed. "Or he yours."

The can of Pepsi in my hand was open, but I had not yet taken from it. It was still full, and very heavy. The can was propelled not just with the force of muscle, but also with the force of hate. It struck Ms. Windom with the energy of a falling brick. It shoved her sideways, then—like a branch being released after being pulled back—her body whipped forward. She fell to the hardwood kitchen floor with a loud thud. Her hands flew to her forehead to cover a long, deep gash.

Walking over a thin trail of Pepsi, I returned to Ms. Windom. I opened the long, narrow utensil drawer next to the stove and pulled from it a wood-handled, two-tine carving fork. I squatted down next to her and pressed the fork into the underside of her chin.

"If you ever talk to me again, Ms. Windom," I said, "I'll kill you in your sleep. I'll take this fork and I'll shove it into your brain. And then I'll take the first knife I can find and open you up crotch to crown. I've had it with your filthy mouth! You've said your last disgusting word to me!"

I ran the piercing end of the fork up her chin, scratching but not cutting the skin.

I arose and left the kitchen.

Once in my room, I shed my clothing and laid down on my bed. Normally, I wouldn't even imagine touching my bed unshowered, yet this was not a normal day. It was a dark day; a day whose edges were as splintery sharp as the fork I had pressed against Ms. Windom's chin.

I sat up and looked around my room. Throughout it were all kinds of plants. Shawn had bought them for me. My favorites were the rubber plants and red Coleuses. Sitting on my nightstand was a small fish tank he had given me for Valentine's Day. "Where's it written that friends can't give gifts on Valentine's Day?" he said to me. Swimming in the tank were two goldfish and three neon tetras.

Why did they wait? Why did the person (or persons) who left Shawn's obituary wait until after he was in the ground to tell me he had died? Were they trying to hurt me or save me? Were they saying, *We hope you enjoy this*, or were they saying, *We're sorry to tell you this*? I would never know for certain, but I suspected it was the former. The obituary was the cross, the delay was the nails.

There was one thing of which I was certain: Shawn didn't kill himself because of hate; he killed himself because of guilt. Guilt over me. One of Shawn's most virtuous qualities was also one of his most destructive: his sensitivity. He knew what had happened to me in the boys' shower room—as did everyone—and he felt responsible for it. In his mind, if he had not befriended me, I would not have been stamped a homosexual, and I would not have been attacked because of it.

Another life was gone because of me. It should have been my obituary in Shawn's pocket, not Shawn's in mine. It should have been him reading about me rather than me reading about him. He gave far more to us than I ever did.

So why did I continue to stay? I certainly had no reason to. I stayed for the same reason I was attacked: I was weak. I hadn't the bravery or the courage or the strength to end my life. Everything Ms. Windom ever said about me was true.

Months earlier, Ms. Longmire told me she anguished over not savoring her youth while she was living it. Now I was doing the same. Only I wasn't lamenting a lost appreciation of former years, but a lost appreciation of my time spent with Shawn. I wished I had savored it more when he was alive.

I never told Shawn how I felt about him and what he meant to me. It was time I did that.

I slid off my bed, walked to the small, cherry wood desk I had had since I was a boy and removed from the bottom drawer a steno pad. I went to my closet, slipped inside, and sat down on the floor, keeping the door slightly ajar for light.

My hand instantly began to move.

*June 20, 1976*

*Dear Shawn,*

*I should have spoken these words to you while you were alive instead of giving them to you now. But I didn't do that. One of the many selfish mistakes I made in our friendship.*

*It is no exaggeration to say I will never again come across another like you in my lifetime. You saw things in me I never saw in myself. Even though I was conceived in violence and born without welcome, you made me feel like the world was a better place because I was in it. You showed me a level of loyalty and acceptance I didn't think mere friends could give. You let me taste a life I thought only the advantaged lived. You gave more to me than I ever gave to you. You were my friend—my best friend. The last friend I will ever know.*

*I will never forget all the priceless experiences we shared together.*

*I didn't know so many visual and performing arts existed in our mountain-flanked, religion-ringed city. It seemed you and I saw the lights dim on them all: the ballets, the symphonies, the operas. Of the three, I enjoyed the symphonies the most. You did too, I think. You loved it when the strings and woodwinds took center stage; I came alive when the brass and percussions took over. And let's not forget the art galleries. The many art galleries. The things we did! There we were, two underaged high schoolers, strolling among the canvases and sculptures, dressed in suits and ties and polished shoes, drinking wine and eating crackers and cheese and critiquing the pieces like we were a couple of New York art critics.*

*And let's not forget the live play we saw at Arrow Press Square. Neither of us had ever seen a professional play before. Remember how we couldn't get over how loudly the actors spoke. We laughed more at their volume than their lines. (Speaking of plays, you tried out for one at school. Remember that? Dames at Sea was its name. You lost to Tom Wilks, a kid so putridly full of himself we both wanted to shoot him. When he wasn't flashing his steroid smile, he was flashing his overrated talents. He thought he was the coolest thing to ever hit the stage; I thought he was the loudest narcissist to ever hit the planet. He was such a bad actor he couldn't play dead even if he were. You could act circles around him! You had such courage, Shawn. You were never afraid to walk into a dark room or down an untraveled road. I never had such strength.)*

*Remember all the movies we saw? I was partial to studio celluloids, while you were a partisan of indie efforts. My favorite was Harry and Tonto; yours was Easy Rider. But we both loved Jaws and One Flew Over the Cuckoo's Nest and The Reincarnation of Peter Proud. Laughter came easier to you than to me. I never would have paid a penny to see a comedy on my own, but because of you, I saw many, and I was better for the experiences. There were two we especially appreciated: Blazing Saddles and The Return of the Pink Panther. Remember what you wrote about them in your nostalgia film class? You had to select two significant comedies of the 1970s and explain why the Production Code of the 1930s would have rendered them insignificant. Your paper earned you an A+, and rightly so. It read just like a review in one of those film magazines. Of Blazing Saddles, you said: "Underneath the tongue-in-cheek racism, Blazing Saddles was actually brutishly and unapologetically bigoted and misanthropic towards blacks. But this was its purpose: to make us sit down at the table and eat our own prejudices. In short, it was Mel Brooks' widescreen treatment of All in the Family*. When not dining on xenophobic tags, the audience was served dogged and unexpected anachronisms, which made this 8500-foot stretch of anamorphic images a brilliant and skillful piece of humor and commentary. Had it been saddled—pun intended—with the Hays Code, it would not have been called *Blazing Saddles* but *Grazing Saddles*—slow, lifeless, and lame." And for *The Return of the Pink Panther*, you wrote: "Truly a slapstick gem. Had it a production code, it still would have been priceless. Most modern films are soaked with sex. Not so with this film. It tickled without teasing. It was a ball without balling. And it was adult entertainment without being adult entertainment."

We were oceans apart in many regards, you and I; we had many differences, but we always fished in the same pond when it came to respecting those differences, and one another.

When we weren't taking in productions on stages or representations on walls, we were enjoying the road. Remember those times? I was probably the only student in our whole school who drove without a license. Doing it illegally made it that much more exhilarating. I had always been the good boy who went by the book. But when I drove, when I was with you, the book went under the bed, and I was glad I put it there. There's something secretly thrilling about blatantly choosing wrong over right.

Before you entered my life, I rarely laughed. I rarely found anything funny. But the way you saw people and life and tragedy and coincidence really made me laugh. You were funny because you didn't try to be. Remember the Pizza Hut we always went to, even on school nights? We were always seated at the same table...as if the staff knew we were coming and they had it reserved just for us. We laughed more than we ate when we went there. I never felt more alive than when I was with you.

Sambo's—a popular restaurant, though not a notable one. Yet you were their most notable waiter; the best they *ever had. Except for me. Ha ha! Remember when you let me help you wait tables that one Thursday night because you were so busy? I got better tips than you! After your shift, we went to the Hilton and bought dinner with the tips we made. Remember what we did while we ate? We started planning what we'd do for your eighteenth birthday. We decided to go to California for a week.*

*A road never taken. A time never seen.*

*Most couples have a song, but not most friends. We did. The theme to <u>Laverne and Shirley</u> was our song. We broke rules, we took chances, and we ignored the word "impossible." We did it our way.*

*Remember the last weekend we shared together? It was just last month. Seems like a lifetime ago. We went to a book signing of that local author, Richard B. Shipler. <u>Illusions</u> was the title he gave his book. The title seems tragically prophetic now. The few months you and I had together now seem like an illusion, a dreamlike trompe l'oeil, a space of time too precious to be real.*

*I am an abnormal boy, Shawn; this is without doubt. It is also without doubt I am quite normal...at least in one respect: I took for granted the good things in my life. One of them was you.*

*Thank you for teaching me honesty in thought and purity in speech. Good-bye, my friend. May peace be your new companion.*

*Love,*
*Owen*

I was asleep when it happened. At twelve midnight, two weeks later, I turned sixteen. No one knew it was my birthday. I had always heard that a person's sixteenth birthday is a turning point in his life, a time in which the child in him says good-bye and the adult says hello. It is a time to laugh, a time to celebrate, a time to fly. Laughter and celebrations were gone from my life, but I could still fly...and fly I did.

For my sixteenth birthday, I bought a car. One of the cashiers at the store was retiring and was selling her son's. He was in prison for drowning his girlfriend. She wanted it out of her sight and out of her life. But she didn't want to just give it away. Because she was fond of me, she let me have it for three hundred dollars. Truly a steal, for the car was cherry and had been garaged most of its life. It was a 1971, two-door Chevrolet Chevelle. Without question, its exterior color was sunset gold, but GM's designation was *Sunflower Yellow*. It had all the comforts of a covered wagon. The windows, brakes, and steering were all powered by muscle, and the air was conditioned by the wind. However, unlike a covered wagon, it did sport the amenities of a heater and push-button AM radio. It mattered little to me that it lacked the luxuries of air conditioning, power windows, and power brakes, yet it did matter that it didn't have power steering. I had to have it...not because it would make driving easier, but because it would be a remembrance of Shawn, of our friendship, of the most wonderful time of my life.

I paid a garage just slightly less than what I paid for the whole car to have a power steering unit installed.

That previous spring, Shawn and I saw a trailer for a movie we both wanted to see: *Ode to Billy Joe*. It had the look of a studio film but the soul of an independent work. Shawn wanted to see it for its mystery value: why did the boy, Billy Joe McAllister, jump from the bridge? I wanted to see it for its vintage value. It was a period piece set in the 1950s, an era I desperately wished I could have lived in. People were different then, better. They saw and treated the world differently than my generation did. Reading, writing, and arithmetic were taught at school, while restraint, respect, and rules were taught at home. In my era—the *Me Generation*—restraint was rarely seen, respect was rarely extended, and rules were rarely enforced. It was the age of *anything goes* and *everything is okay to say*.

The cinema was packed with teenagers the night I went to see *Ode to Billy Joe*. More girls than boys were in the seats. The few boys who were there were with their girlfriends. I was the only boy in the entire theater who was alone.

What expectation promises, surprise usually delivers. What I thought would instantly seize my attention in the film—its 1950s backdrop—didn't. Instead, I was grabbed by something else, something unanticipated: Bobbie Lee Hartley, a fifteen-year-old farm girl who was deeply in love with Billy Joe McAllister. She was played by actress Glynnis O'Connor. I had seen her in a low-budget, arthouse-style film called *Jeremy* three years before. Neither the film nor her performance moved me in any breadth, but in *Ode to Billy Joe*, she was different—more mature, more intense, more honest. She was naturally beautiful, a girl who needed no makeup or expressive lighting.

Self-recrimination took the seat next to mine while I was watching the film. I was mesmerized by the character Bobbie Lee, and I shouldn't have been, for I had vowed to closet that part of me away forever. But I couldn't help but watch her and fantasize about her...about us. I wondered what it would be like to be near her, to touch her, to kiss her, to have her look at me the way she looked at Billy Joe. The way Kylie and Roxanne used to look at me.

The third act of the film was tasteless. The audience was delivered the reason Billy Joe drowned himself in the Tallahatchie River: he had had sex with an older man. I sighed with dismay. I thought the suicide should have had another cause. It reduced the film to something low-end and trashy, and the film was far from that. I was glad Shawn had not been there to see it, for he would have felt the same disappointment I did.

As the closing credits scrolled up the screen, some tragic reflections lighted on my mind: the film was released June 4th; Shawn killed himself June 4th. Shawn killed himself because of homosexuality; Billy Joe killed himself because of homosexuality. Shawn had just turned eighteen; Billy Joe was no more than eighteen himself. Common sense told me the similarities were only coincidental, yet it seemed they were beyond that. It seemed Shawn and the movie were somehow linked together, as if the film was not only an ode to Billy Joe, but Shawn as well.

I saw the film four more times. The fourth occasion was under the stars, at the Woodland Drive-In. As in the show house, I was the only boy in the entire lot who was alone. I took a cassette recorder with me so I could record the film. I couldn't have done that had I been in an enclosed building with other people close by.

During the following weeks, I listened to the movie over and over. No matter what I was doing—cleaning the car, mowing the yard, driving to work—I had the tape playing; although I really didn't need to play it at all, for I had every gerund, transitive, contraction, predicate, and syllable memorized. Sometimes I would walk my neighborhood and recite the movie aloud, not caring if outsiders heard me. And they did. More than once I captured the attention of people out in their yards and on their porches.

If I had been close to anyone, they would have called me obsessed, and they would have been correct—I *was* obsessed...but I didn't mind, for the film was taking me back to a time when life was my friend, to a time when my heart was my guide. It made me long for romance once more. It made me think of all the people who had once meant so much to me. Roxanne, especially. It made me wonder how she was and how her summer had been. It made me miss her. It made me want to see her again, or, at the very least, her home. I had a car now, so getting there would be very easy. But that would mean I would be stepping into the desperate shoes of Preston and Christopher. Preston, under the cover of night, had parked himself next to Ann's house and imagined her inside it; and Christopher, also hidden behind a drapery of darkness, had secretly spied on Roxanne's and then stole from it, twice. It would now be *me* performing those pathetic rituals instead of them. Yet it would be different for me. I would visit Roxanne's house only once. And what harm could come from it? Christopher and Preston probably said the same things.

Lying next to me on the front seat of the Chevelle was my Lafayette radio/cassette recorder. A shirtless Billy Joe McAllister was introducing himself to Bobbie Lee's father on the Tallahatchie Bridge as I was turning the corner onto Roxanne's street.

Her house was in the middle of the block, so there was no street light to identify me if she or anyone in her family was outside.

Thankfully, no one was immediately visible when I pulled up in front of it. Her front porch light was on and lamplight was pressing against the living room curtains. Her father's 1971 Riviera was gone from the driveway. A white-over-red, newly minted Monte Carlo was in its place. A temporary registration sticker was affixed to the inside of the rear window. He must have traded in the Buick for the Chevrolet. I wondered if he changed out of boredom or breed. Breed probably. The Monte was a sophisticated and aristocratic automobile, whereas the Riviera was baffling at best.

Without looking, I reached over and tapped the OFF button on the cassette player. I was now surrounded by darkness and quiet. It had only been a few months since Roxanne and I had split up, yet it seemed much longer.

I mused over what she was doing that night. It was the last Friday of summer vacation. Was she in? Was she out? Was she looking forward to school? Was she ever moved to think of me?

Looking at the house made me remember her father, her brother, and little Kenny. I missed them too. I missed being a part of their lives. They always made me feel so welcome and wanted. I hoped Roxanne didn't tell them the truth about us, for it wasn't the truth. I hoped she told them we simply grew apart...which, in a way, was the truth.

I wanted to drive up to the park near her house, but the painful memories it held were darker than the brightest ones we ever made there.

Pulling away from her house, I knew I would never return.

A few blocks away I passed an ice cream parlor. It wasn't there when Roxanne and I were together, so it must have just opened. I loved ice cream, and I needed some food that would lift my spirits.

I turned my car around and went back to the parlor.

Roofed in pastel pink and sided with brilliant white, the budding confectionery was called Sugar Tree. From the outside, it appeared small, but on the inside, it was airy and spacious. It was appointed with bright-pink walls and numerous low-backed dining booths. Along the north and east sides, glass displays teased patrons with a medley of candies and ice cream. The south and west sides were partnered with booths that chummed panoramic windows. An island of six booths was stationed in the center of the room.

Only four booths in the restaurant were occupied; three with teenage couples, the fourth with a solitary boy, about sixteen or seventeen. Seeing him made me feel better: for once, I wasn't the only boy in the city who was alone.

I took a booth with a window. From it, I saw the parking lot, a Pizza Hut, two gas stations, and a Kmart. Not a stellar perspective, but who goes to an ice cream shop to look out the window?

While waiting for the waitress, I enjoyed the warm and lifting aromas of chocolate and mint and other sweet flavorings.

A young woman in her early twenties came up to my table. Thick, blond hair framed an angelic face. The ends of her hair lay on plentiful breasts.

"What's a handsome boy like you doing all alone on a Friday night?" she asked, removing a pad and pen from her waitress smock.

I was in no mood for a personal conversation. The best way to kill one is to return the scrutiny. "Why is an attractive woman like you *working* on a Friday night? We each have our reasons, don't we?"

She pulled her face back and a tinge of red burgeoned on her cheeks. "I'm sorry, I didn't mean to pry. I was just trying to be friendly."

"To procure a better tip, no doubt."

Anger crossed her face. "Would you like another waitress?"

"What is your best ice cream?"

The sudden change of subject made her pause. "I don't know. I like Neapolitan myself. But that's me."

"Neapolitan it is then."

"In a cone or dish?"

"May I have it in a dish with bananas and some—"

My peripheral vision saw the solitary boy on the opposite side of the room stand. Then it registered another teenager…a teenager whose features my peripheral vision recognized. I turned. Now filling my central vision was a girl whose arresting beauty Helen of Troy would have coveted, a girl whose face would also have launched a thousand ships.

*Roxanne.*

She was walking toward the boy.

The boy reached out to her and the two embraced, then kissed. After their tenderness, she handed him a white paper bag. He smiled at her sweetly, then led her to the entrance. He smiled once more, kissed her once more, then left.

As the glass door was closing, Roxanne glanced up, then closed her eyes for a moment. It was obvious she was distressed. Was she distressed because he had left, or because she really hadn't wanted him there?

She looked down at her smock, smoothed it, then returned to the front of the store. She wrote something on the wall by the cash register, then disappeared into the back.

It wasn't numbness, or anger, or disbelief I felt—it was foolishness. I had been foolish to let her back into my mind, foolish to let myself start feeling again. I should have known better.

Seeing my redirected attention, the waitress asked, "You know Roxanne? Would you like me to get her?"

"No, thank you," I said, sliding out of the booth. "I'm sorry to have bothered you."

I left the parlor, reunited with my car and rejoined the road. I had nowhere to go but home...but home was not where I wanted to go. I wanted to drive. I found it calming. It made me decisive and resolute.

*Ode to Billy Joe* had become a part of me, an important part, but one that had become lethal. It made me open my heart again. If I hadn't let it into my life, I wouldn't have traveled to Roxanne's house, and I wouldn't have later seen her. The movie made me want to reach out again. It made me want to feel again. But feelings are malignancies... and malignancies will kill if not removed.

Every excision must start with an incision. There was an entrance to a freeway a few blocks away from the ice cream parlor. I immediately drove to it. When I reached an area on the highway where there were no other cars close to me, I rolled down my window. I ejected the cassette from the player, took it, glanced at it briefly, and then pitched it into the wind.

I wanted it in a place where I could never go back and retrieve it.

I rolled the window back up.

"Good-bye, Roxanne."

As I was exiting the expressway, I turned on the radio. Just beginning was a song from Lobo: "There Ain't No Way." The smooth ballad spoke of the futility of trying to bring back yesterday—there ain't no way.

There sure wasn't.

What's done is done. What's undone can't be redone. What's over can't be done over. Roxanne was in the past—that was where she belonged, and that was where she would stay.

Always.

The black-handled steak knife was pressed against the boy's bare skin, just below the xiphoid process.

"I told you before to stay away from her," the boy holding the knife said.

The knife-holder was a muscle-bound boy with luxuriant, blond hair that lay over the collar of his shirt.

The boy about to be knifed was a medium-sized youth dressed in a flowered shirt, crisp, olive-green slacks, and dark-brown patent leather shoes. More bizarre than as his clothes was his haircut. It looked as if he had cut his hair himself with a pair of dull scissors and a dirty mirror. I couldn't decide which was worse: his pinguid, uneven mane or his pimple-ridden face. I had many curses, but fortunately acne was not one of them.

The acned boy was flat against the wall, staring at the boy with the knife. His face showed no fear. James Dallek was certainly right when he observed: *A lack of looks doesn't always equate to a lack of nerve.*

Standing only feet from them was a thickset boy with ten pounds of riotous, frizzy, brown hair and a face as pocked as the surface of an orange. He reminded me of a charcoal rendering of a brujo I had seen once in a folklore magazine.

All three boys were standing on the south stairwell landing between the basement and ground floor of my new school. It was a three-story, sandy-bricked building housing as many students as Moran. On its facade, on its north corner, was its name: Hillside High School.

The brujo noticed me. He raked his eyes over my body; then, like a good, little sycophant, lightly tapped the knife-holder on the shoulder. The knife-holder turned his attention away from the acned boy and directed it to me.

"Get lost," the knife-holder told me, pointing the knife in my direction.

His kinesics didn't frighten me. Very little stirred my emotions anymore. Apathy does have its blessings.

"And if I don't?" I asked.

"After I cut *his* guts out, I'll cut out *yours*."

"And then what—go to your next class? Probably not. Your life as you know it will be over. Felonies have a way of doing that. But go ahead, do it. Rive and rend us both. Your vacancy will be worth it. Your breed belongs in a barred room anyway."

I descended the steps and went over to the knife-holder. Without any resistance from him, I took hold of the blade of the knife, and guided it through the placket of my white, Oxford shirt. Its sharp vertex was now pressing against *my* bare skin.

"Do it," I repeated.

The knife-holder simply stared at me, almost palsied.

"Do it!" I screamed for effect.

All three boys flinched.

The knife-holder jerked the knife back, and he and the brujo dashed up the stairwell, each taking two stairs at a time.

"Faggot freak!" the knife-holder salvoed before he disappeared.

"Your hand is bleeding," the acned boy noticed.

I looked down at my hand. A deep cut ran along the underside of my index finger. Neither the blood nor the cut impressed me. It would mend. My body had been the conferee of far worse, and it had always healed.

I stuck my hand into my pants pocket and resumed my course.

"Thanks," the boy called down to me.

I neither responded nor looked back at him.

*Valentine's Day.*
*1977.*

Mr. Vincenzo came into my biology class. Mr. Vincenzo was the principal of the school. He was a short man with an old-man's skullet. Without excusing his intrusion, he walked over to the marble-top table at which I was sitting and bent down to my ear.

"Owen, we have a situation in the basement, and I need your help," he whispered.

He should have been a pensioner rather than a principal. Easily, he was seventy years in age and four times that in weight. The stitching in his brown leisure suit must have been snapping as he spoke.

"What's the matter?" I asked.

"I'd rather discuss it on the way."

"What could—"

"Owen, every second we waste here leads us closer to a disastrous outcome."

I arose from my stool and the two of us calmly left the room. Once outside, however, he rushed to the basement level. I took my time following him.

Once I reached the basement, he told me there was a boy holding a gun on another boy and his girlfriend in a storage room. The couple was returning from a nearby 7-Eleven when a boy waylaid them as they reentered the school grounds. The boy surprised the couple, pointed a gun at them and then guided them into the school. He led them into a storage room in the basement. All of this had been seen by many students.

"So what is it you want of me?" I asked him once we were outside the room in which the couple was being held.

More and more students were filling the hallway as news of what was happening spread. Mr. Vincenzo told them to leave the area.

"The boy holding them wants to talk to you," Mr. Vincenzo released, "and only you."

"Me? Why me?"

"He said you came to his aid last month; something about you stopping the boy he's holding from hurting him. He said you're the only one he trusts."

"What does he expect me to do?"

"I don't know exactly. I think he just wants someone to listen to him."

I looked down the empty hallway. There were no police. When it became known that Mr. Carey had a gun, law enforcement was almost immediately on site.

"Where are the police?" I asked. "Shouldn't they be here?"

"I don't want them here yet."

"*What?*"

"I don't want them here yet, I said."

"When *do* you want them here—after he's gunned everybody down?"

"He won't. Look, I want to diffuse this situation before it gets ugly."

"It's *already* ugly—he has a gun!"

"And there will be more guns if the police get involved."

"Are you *ever* planning to call them?"

"After he's out of that room."

"And what if he doesn't come out?"

"He will. But I don't want him coming out dead. If we call the police at this point, that's precisely what will happen."

"You don't know that."

"Yes, I do. I was up against this same thing some years ago. I called the police. They came. Tempers got loose. Guns were fired. Kids were killed. I'm not going to let that happen here. This kind of thing is rare. People don't know how to react, so they overreact. That's when people get hurt. I just want to give this boy a chance to—"

"Mr. Vincenzo?" the boy holding the gun called out from inside the room.

"I'm right here, Richard," Mr. Vincenzo answered loudly. "And so is Owen."

"I told you I don't like that name!"

"I'm sorry."

"Tell Owen to come in. If anyone else comes with him, pretty-boy in here won't be in any cap and gown in three months—he'll be in a coat and tie and lying in a box."

"It's just talk," Mr. Vincenzo whispered to me.

"Sure it is," I disputed. "Just so you know, Mr. Vincenzo, I've had some experience with guns too. People who wave them usually shoot them. I thought I was finished with all this crap!"

I pushed him aside and entered the storage room. The temperature in it was like the inside of an oven set on broil.

Sitting in a corner was the thimble-headed knife-holder. A girl, also a blond, was sitting next to him. She was clutching his arm and crying. The knife-holder's hands were pressed against the side of his shirt. Peninsulas of blood lay over them. His face was pink and alert, which said to me his wound or wounds were superficial.

All three faces were beaded with perspiration.

I sighed in annoyance. Another crazy. Another mental with a gun.

The boy holding the gun was also holding a steak knife; one almost identical to the one the *pretty-boy* almost used on him.

I sighed in exasperation. "Richard, what the hell is this all about? What do you hope to accomplish by all this?"

"Don't call me that!" he shouted.

"Call you what?" I asked angrily.

"Richard!"

*"It's your name!"*

"No, it isn't!"

"It isn't, huh? What is it then? Richie, Rick, Dick, what?"

*"Dick's* a good one," the knife-holder offered.

"Shut up!" I threw at him. "This whole mess is because of you, you moron! If you had just left him alone, none of us would be here!"

The girl's sobbing was starting to wear on my nerves.

"Give it a rest, will you!" I hurled at her. "You're not dead, and neither's your bovine-brained boyfriend, so shut up! If he was going to kill you, he would have done it by now. Act your age! You're not four!"

"Don't talk to her like that!" Richard roared, pointing the gun at me.

"If you're so damned concerned about her, why don't you let her go?" I fired back.

"Because there're things I want to tell her."

"Then tell her! I don't have all day!"

"I want her to calm down first."

"Then put down the damn gun!"

"No."

"The more you prolong this, Richard—"

"I told you, don't call me that!"

"Oh, for the love of— All right, you don't want to be called Richard— what the hell do you want to be called?"

"John."

"John? That's original."

"You never heard of John the Baptist?"

"Is that who you are?"

"No, but he had a message. So do I."

"And what message is that?"

"I love her."

"Oh, please!" I let out with a sigh. "I got a news bulletin for you, pal— you may love *her*, but she ain't *never* going to love *you*. And after this stupid stunt, you'll be lucky if she doesn't throw up when she thinks about you. She will never, ever, ever be yours! *Ever!* Get it through that psychotic head of yours and move on!"

"But I love her."

"Who the hell cares! *She* doesn't. The only one who gives a crap is you and that macho mouth-breather over there with a wasteland for a mind who doesn't know up from down or left to right. Richard, what'd you—"

"The name's John!"

"*Whatever!* What'd you call me down here for?"

He didn't answer.

"*Well?*" I prodded angrily.

"You helped me once," he said cautiously. "I want you to help me again."

"*You're* not the one being threatened this time—*they* are?" I pointed to the couple.

"You saved my life once; now save my heart. Talk to her. Convince her I'm worth it. I know she'd love me if she just got to know me."

"You mean talk her into loving you?"

"Yeah. You can do it. I know you can."

I closed my eyes and shook my head again. I sat down on the floor and stared at this boy who was incontestably delusional; truly *non compos mentis.*

"I know I sound crazy," he admitted, "but I'm not."

"You ever watch *Star Trek*, Richard? Sorry...*John.*"

"Never."

"Pity. There's an episode called *Charlie X*. The boy in the episode is like you: he loves someone who doesn't love him back. What Captain Kirk told him I'm going to tell you: there's a mountain of things in this life you *can* have and there's a mountain of things you *can't* have! It's a painful pill to swallow, but that's the way it is. Never being able to bed blondie over there is one of the painful pills. You can't have her."

"I don't believe that."

"It doesn't matter if you believe it—it's the truth. An atheist's disbelief in God doesn't make God any less real. The truth is the truth. What brought on all this anyway? Why is she so special?"

"Because she's the only girl who doesn't mess her pants when he looks at her," the knife-holder answered for his assailant. "He's like that chick in that movie *Carrie* no one could stand."

"Shut up, you half-baked halfwit!" I blasted at him. "No one cares what you've got to say. Just sit there and concentrate on that hole in your side! Better yet, why don't take your hand away from it and maybe you'll bleed to death and we can all leave!"

I turned back to John. "Okay, so why her, John? Of all the girls in this school—why'd you choose her?"

"Because...she was nice to me," John said calmly.

"That's it? All this because she was nice to you?"

"She said hi to me when no one else would even look at me."

"Heaven help the girl who ever starts up a conversation with you."

"Stop making me sound like I'm weird! I'm not weird!"

"You're certainly *something*—John! Look around you! You've stabbed a kid; you've kidnapped his girlfriend; you're holed up in a hot, dirty storage room, and you're waving that damn gun around like you're flipping a yo-yo!"

"You're not nice like I thought you'd be."

"The approximate words of Charlie X. No, John, I'm not nice, and I don't want to be. Nice guys end up desperate...like you. And me. Besides, true niceness doesn't even exist. Every act of kindness is merely a pretty skin over an ugly skeleton. How did Isaiah put it: *And all our righteous deeds are as filthy rags.*"

"So that day in the stairwell...it had nothing to do with me?"

I stood up. "Of course not. I did it because I hate punks like that teratoid idiot over there with the slit in his side. Thugs like him think they can control the world and everyone in it. He's nothing more than a chamber pot with arms, legs, and hair. Give me the gun, John, so we all can get outta here. And if you're not going to give it to me, then use it on yourself." I pointed at the couple again. "You can't make her love you, so don't even try. If you go after things you can never have, you're useless. You should end it. You're just using up oxygen and taking up space."

"Who do you think you are talking to him like that?" the girl interjected, no longer crying.

"Shut up!" I came back. "Just tend to that bedpan you call a boyfriend!"

"No, I will not *shut up*! John's a human being. He has value. Everyone has value, and it's not up to you to say they don't!"

"A man who wastes his love wastes his life. He has no value. He should be dead."

"*You're* the one who should be dead!" she whipped at me.

"I love you, Rochelle," John proclaimed to the girl.

I couldn't help but roll my eyes.

"Every place I go reminds me of you," John expanded. "Every place in the city I see your face."

"Why?" she asked, rising and walking over to him.

"Because you're all I think about. You're all I care for. I carry you with me wherever I go. When I'm studying, you're there. When I'm at my job, you're there. When I'm in the car, you're there. When I'm in the shower, you're there."

"*I'll bet she is,*" the punk added with a smirk, despite the pain from his wound.

"If you say one more word," I pledged to the knife-holder, "I'll shoot you myself."

The smirk morphed into a grimace.

"Every song on the radio," John continued, "every one, reminds me of you...'Dancing Queen'...'Don't Stop Believing'...'Torn Between Two Lovers'...'The Princess and the Punk'...'You've Got Me Running'..."

I had to put my oar in. "John, are you going to enumerate every song ever recorded?"

"I want to hear," Rochelle broke my oar. "If you don't want to, *leave.*"

"No one gives a damn what songs remind him of you!" I said.

"I do," she countered. "Go on, John."

"He's right—no one cares."

"*I* care. I want to know what they are."

"'Aubrey'—that's my favorite."

"Are there any others?" she asked.

"Why don't you just have him sing them for you while you're at it," I put in.

Glaring at me, she said, "No one's stopping you from leaving."

"A few," he answered her. "'Don't Give Up on Us'...'Lost Without Your Love'...'This One's for You'...'Hooked on You'...'Secrets'...'I'm All Strung Out on You'..."

"Why don't I just go get you a chalkboard, and you can write them all down for her," I submitted.

"What is your problem!" she flung at me.

"You're kidding, right?"

"Your beautiful face is in every song I hear," John said. "You're always in my head, Rochelle, and everything I see gets married to your image. But I guess that's the closest I'll ever come to marrying you...isn't it?"

Rochelle inhaled deeply, smiled sympathetically and shook her head.

"I'm sorry, John, it's just not there," she labored. "You're very sweet and thoughtful, but…I'm not for you, and you're not for me. We just don't have the right chemistry."

Are those the lines *all* blonds use when they kick a boy to the curb? Roxanne said the exact thing to Christopher. But then, John was nearly a traced copy of Christopher.

I had to add my say. "Seriously, Rochelle? That's the best you can do? *'I'm not for you, and you're not for me. We don't have the right chemistry.'* Please! If you're going to broom him, at least be genuine about it!"

"Stay out of this!" Rochelle demanded.

"Just tell him he nauseates you and to get lost."

"Will you shut your stupid mouth!"

"He's a loser—he knows it, and we know it. Not only that, he's a *sore* loser. He can't have you, so he throws a tantrum and drags you into this room. If he were any kind of a man, he'd be mature and accept the fact that you two are never going to be together. He'd move on and find someone else. But no, he can't have you, so he steals you. He's nothing but a childish, selfish, useless, lifeless carcass! You're already dead, John, so put a bullet in your head and get it over with!"

Rochelle vaulted over to me and pushed me with the force of a moving car. My legs stuttered back, and I collided with a student's desk that was against the wall. It tipped, and I fell onto the floor. The desk followed, and the edge of the wooden seat smashed against my ulnar nerve. My body spasmed from the pain and a scream left my mouth.

"Now lay there and shut the hell up!" Rochelle squalled.

"You two lovebirds are gonna miss the best part," Rochelle's footling pinhead nodded to John.

Rochelle turned around and gasped.

John had the gun pointed at his own temple.

"John, please don't do this!" Rochelle implored.

I got up from the floor and walked over to Rochelle. I grabbed her arm and put my face close to hers. In a low voice, I said, "Go back over to your lobotomized boyfriend, sit your ass down and let me handle this! If you don't, I'll kick it over there!"

Fear dripped down her face along with her sweat. She returned to her boyfriend.

Turning back to John, I said, "You're doing good, John. You're almost there. But I just have one last question to ask you before you go. Think hard before you answer. So what if Rochelle doesn't love you? So what? Hell, no one loves me—I don't give a damn. Rochelle's not the only tulip in the patch, you know. She certainly isn't the prettiest. And she certainly isn't the smartest: just look at the Philistine clown she has for a darling. Trust me, you can do better than her. You don't have to be a useless, lifeless carcass. You don't have to be taking up space and using up oxygen. You could still find someone else to love, someone who won't reject you. But if you pull that trigger, you'll never find her. Remember what H. R. Haldeman said to John Dean during Watergate: *'Once the toothpaste is out of the tube, it's hard to get it back in.'* If you pull that trigger, it will be *impossible* to get it back in. You'll never find love then.

"You'll never get Rochelle, John, which leaves you with two choices: be done with your life or get on with it. End it or get over it. Make up your mind. Not getting someone you love—or losing them, for that matter—isn't the end of the world. Life goes on. Trust me."

John slowly let the gun and knife drop from his hands. He fell onto the floor and began to weep.

I took hold of the weapons, went to the door and walked out.

Mr. Vincenzo was waiting outside.

"Here, choke on them!" I said to him and dropped the gun and knife into his hands. "Don't ever bother me again."

She ran over to me as I was walking to my car.

"I didn't get a chance to thank you for what you did this morning," Rochelle said, gently taking my hand to stop me from walking.

"I didn't do it for you."

She looked visibly hurt at my answer. "Why'd you do it then?"

"It is mine to keep the answer close to the vest, and it is yours to keep away from it."

"Was that whole thing an act this morning?" she asked. "Or are you really that pissed off at the world?"

"What do you care? You came out of it with your skin intact."

"It wasn't an act, was it?"

"You don't hear very well, do you?"

Her hurt turned into sadness. "I don't understand how anyone can be so angry at the world."

"You're young yet. Wait a few years. Life will lose its luster. Now, if you will excuse me."

"That was a pretty risky gamble you took, baiting him like that."

"If a car's stuck in the snow, you push it."

"Your pushing could have pushed him over the edge. He could have shot us all."

"He wouldn't have shot anybody—not you, or me, or your boyfriend from central casting. Like Mr. Vincenzo said, he just wanted someone to listen to him, you primarily. Incidentally, that was a very percipient move on your part, taking an interest in him like you did, especially when he got diarrheic about the songs. Softened him. Making him think you truly cared put the pin back in the grenade. Kudos to your performance. There truly is a brilliant thespian within all of us."

"I wasn't acting. I do care about John, and I care about his feelings—I just don't share them. Just because I don't want to be his girlfriend doesn't mean he's unimportant to me. I've never had anyone who feels as deeply for me as he does. I wish I could feel for him like he feels for me, but…"

"*It's just not there*,' I believe were your words. Tell me, if he were clear-skinned and good-looking and self-assured and outgoing, would you feel differently about him?"

A spark of anger sparked across her face. "Maybe."

"*Definitely*. Tell me, are all blonds small-minded, or is it just a coincidence?"

"Just because I have preferences doesn't mean I'm small-minded. You don't go for every girl who likes you, do you?"

"No girl is the holder of any such partiality."

"I wouldn't be too sure about that."

"I'm positive about that."

"You may be positive, but that doesn't make you right."

"Opinionated little thing, aren't you?"

"Isn't everybody?"

"No, not everybody."

"*Yes*, everybody."

"You should join the debate team. You certainly have the mouth for it."

She stared at me. "Do you coat *every* word you say with sarcasm?"

"You *are* on the debate team, aren't you?"

She paused. "Yes."

"*Surprise, surprise.* And is your *nom de guerre* among your fellow argufiers *The Blond Blitz*?"

This time, it was she who stared at me. "Some girl must have really kicked you hard. Someone *blond*."

I glared at her.

"You like to dish it, but you hate to eat it," she cornered me. "You can call me out, but I can't call you out, is that it?"

"I believe we're finished here." I began moving again. She took my hand once more to stop me.

"Is it true what you said today…about no one loving you?" she asked.

"What if it is…what's it to you?"

"I just care. Is that okay?"

My throat tightened. "I have to be going." I pulled away from her and resumed walking.

"I'm sorry I pushed you," she said from behind me.

"You did what you had to do."

"You're wrong, you know."

"About what?"

"You *are* loved."

Seven boys came over to my lunch table and sat down. Rochelle's brainless beloved, whose name I had learned was Danny, was one of them. He sat directly opposite me. Next to him was the brujo. I had learned that his name was David. Unoriginal names for unoriginal boys. They, along with the five others, were all seniors.

"Do you know what Rochelle did today?" Danny asked, his eyes staring piercingly at me.

"Pinched you lovingly because it's Saint Patrick's Day?" I answered. "Or did she go one better and spit in your face?"

"She dumped me."

"Even sweeter."

"You think this is a joke?"

"No, I think *you're* a joke."

"Do you know the reason she gave me?"

"You're not the brightest bulb in the chandelier, are you? If I didn't know that she *had* dismissed you, how could I know *why* she dismissed you?"

"You talk weird."

"It's a wonder *you* can talk at all with that calcified, atrophied, dystrophic brain sitting inside your head."

"I'm going to pound your face into the ground."

"Ground meaning dirt, or ground meaning flooring?"

"Dirt."

"Right now, or would you prefer later in the season when the earth is more malleable?"

"Now."

"Are you sure you're up to the effort? The ground outside is bound to be on the hard side."

"Just beat the crap out of him right here," a boy standing behind Danny urged.

I knew this boy; his name was Miles.

I smiled up at him. "Do you know what an anagram is, Miles? What am I saying?—of course you don't. You probably don't even know what year it is. An anagram is a word formed from the letters of another word. Take the word *Miles*, for example. Move it around a little bit and it becomes...*slime*." I winked at him.

"Let's go," Danny stood up, staring at me.

"Just for clarification, this will be between you and me, yes? One against seven could scarcely be considered fair."

"That's *you and I*, Mr. English!" he corrected, gimbaling his head back and forth.

"No, it is *you and me*, Mr. Mensa reject. A pronoun that follows a preposition is an objective pronoun. *Me* is an objective pronoun. I am the object in the sentence, not the subject; therefore, it is *me*. Again, this will be between just you and *me*—yes?"

"Just us—*wiseass*! And remember, once we get started, there's no crapping out."

I stared at him. "That's *copping* out! The malcontent strutting his malapropisms. And you wonder why Rochelle *dismissed* you."

"Get outside."

"Lead the way."

In almost single file, the seven left the large cafeteria. I followed them. As I was walking out, I noticed many eyes following us.

The sky was gunmetal gray, but the football field was dry.

Danny stood an arm's length from me.

"Don't you want to know *why* you're about to die?" he asked, grinning.

"Leave it to a buffoon to blazon histrionics. But do tell—I would *love* to know before I *die*."

"She used the same lines on me she used on that retard Richard, '*I'm not for you, you're not for me. Bad chemistry*.' We were good before *you* came along. She won't shut up about you. You ruined us."

"Perhaps it is not me, but you. Perhaps she realized—like others possessed by someone obsessed—that he who sups with the Devil should have a *long* spoon."

Danny smiled and looked behind him at his anencephalic, knuckle-dragging friends.

A sudden change in demeanor—like Danny's just then—a head turn, a sudden smile, is often a prelude to a strike. It is a calculated distraction, a move intended to derail an opponent's concentration. This tip—and an argosy of others about street fighting—Anthony Simms shared with me. Anthony was the assistant manager at the grocery store at which I worked. As a boy and teenager, he lived in

Brooklyn, New York. He spoke with a delightful diphthonged and dentalized Brooklynese accent. He had been in many fights as a youth. Anthony saw me a few days after my locker room experience at Moran and asked me outright if I had been beaten up. Reluctantly, I told him I had. He told me to meet him after work and he would give me some tips on street fighting.

The tips Anthony gave me were simple but crucial. "Regulation fighting is different from street fighting," he said, "one has rules, the other doesn't; one's about sport, the other survival. A fight will always start out with both guys on their feet, so keep your legs far apart with your knees bent; keep your dominant leg out front with the other directly behind it. Look at your entire opponent for movement—not just one part of his body. Never tuck your thumbs inside your fists. Keep your teeth clenched. Keep your stomach muscles tight. Keep your fists in front of your face. And above all, don't show fear—your body will heal from a punch, but your self-respect will never recover from cowardice. If your fight regresses to the ground, make sure the other guy doesn't get on top of you: roll, use leverage, do anything it takes to get out from under him; then get on top of *him* and let him have it. Don't be afraid to fight dirty: kick, claw, gouge, do anything you have to do to take out your enemy before he takes *you* out. And never, ever throw the first punch: you can't land in jail for defending yourself."

It happened in seconds, but it seemed like it took place in slow motion. Danny's body swiveled back around toward me. As it was moving, his right arm ascended and it flew toward my face. I jerked my head back, and his fist shot past me. Seeing an opening, I thrust my right fist in the direction of his head. My knuckles made contact with his left cheekbone. He staggered back and fell onto the hard soil below. I, too, staggered, though not as much; hitting him had been like hitting a brick. My fist was pulsating with pain. I wasn't expecting that. Anthony had left that part out.

Danny was quickly on his feet again. He lunged for me like a linebacker. He tackled me and began pummeling my face with punches. Using my legs as leverage, I was able to roll my body over.

This unexpected move threw Danny off balance, and he fell onto the brown grass. The sudden advantage took my mind off my throbbing face, and I sprang up and threw myself onto Danny's torso. It was now my turn. Though I was right-handed, I gave his face both my fists. The first few punches were for Danny, but the succeeding strikes were for others—William, Mike, Erik, Mr. Wilson, Mrs. Wilson, Ms. Windom, all the kids in grade school who wanted to see me intimidated, all the kids in high school who wanted to see me gone.

Danny was no longer moving. His eyes were only half-open and his face, along with my fists, were smeared with blood. Undoubtedly, some of it was mine, for I'm sure the thin skin on my knuckles could not have escaped the pounding without splitting.

My arms were grabbed, and I was pulled from Danny and thrown back.

"Enough!" the brujo shouted at me.

"I'll say when it's enough!" I shouted back. "This is between him and me!"

"Not anymore. Hit him again and it'll be between you and all of us."

Anthony didn't tell me what to do if there was more than one opponent, but I'm sure he would have told me not to back away. Disparity should never be a reason to stand down.

"No," I refused.

The brujo came over to me. Easily, he was six inches taller than me, and he outweighed me by at least thirty pounds.

"Do what you have to do," I said to him. "And I'll do the same."

"Hey, what's going on over there?" a deep, male voice boomed to the east of us.

Everyone turned.

One of the school's coaches was walking toward us. He, along with his flattop haircut, reminded me of a deep-dyed, hippie-hating, kill-all-invaders Marine.

He saw the blood on my hands and face. "You start this?"

"No," I replied, "but I was in the process of finishing it."

"This true?" he attempted to verify from the group.

No one would answer.

Danny was moving again and making sounds. One of the boys bent over and helped him up. Danny was unsteady on his feet, so the boy kept hold of his arm.

The coach went over to Danny. "You draw first blood?"

Danny hesitated, then nodded.

"A candy-ass runs from his wrongs. A real man owns up to them. You're no candy-ass. Good for you. Now the two of you shake hands and be done with it."

No hands left their sides.

"Shake, or get suspended for fighting," the coach threatened.

I walked over to Danny and lifted my hand. He took it and we shook.

"Good," he commended us. "Now get to the showers and clean up."

I didn't go to the showers as ordered. I went to my locker and then went home.

Danny treated me differently after that day on the field. He wasn't friendly to me, but he wasn't unfriendly either. He was both warm and cool at the same time.

On the last day of school, everyone was signing yearbooks. On all the floors, in all the hallways, there was laughter and merriment, even tears. I was one of the few—if not the only one—in the school who didn't purchase a yearbook. I hadn't any from Moran either, which is the way I wanted it: I had enough bad memories in my head—I didn't need any photographs of them.

Rochelle came up to me as I was cleaning out my locker.

"I came by to ask if you'd sign my yearbook," she said.

"You don't want to tarnish the silver, Rochelle."

She gave me a face of irritation. Then she took my hand. "Come with me."

Into an empty classroom we went. She released my hand, closed the door, walked over to the windows, dropped their blinds and returned to me. She cupped my face in her hands and put her lips to mine. I forced myself to resist the pleasure of her touch. I kept my eyes open and my hands at my sides. This resistance didn't douse her fire. She pressed her body closer to mine. The feel of her young breasts against my chest, the feel of her warm lips on mine, the feel of her hands in my hair excited and weakened me at the same time. I had to cut the sexual rope between us. If I didn't, I would start enjoying her, and I couldn't let that happen. Not with her, not with anyone. Not ever again.

I gently pushed her away.

Hurt did not replace her passion. Contrastingly, she smiled. "I knew you'd do that."

"Then why did you do it?"

"Because I've wanted to for months. I knew today would be my last chance. High school's behind me now. I graduated."

"Yes, I know."

"I'll never see you again."

"And you'll be better for the absence, believe me."

"No, I won't. You're a very strange boy, Owen. More a man than a boy, really. In some ways, an old man. A bitter old man; one clinging to the past, but also hating it. You're also a hypocrite. You told John to end his life or get on with it. You told him he should kick the pail over that holds his life because he was already dead. But look at you. You're dead too, but you're still alive. You won't move on because someone hurt you really bad. You've closed off your heart. How'd you say it? *'Losing someone isn't the end of the world. Life goes on.'* Why haven't *you* moved on? And don't tell me it's none of my business."

"I told John that anyone who wastes his love is wasting his life. I'm not giving my love to someone who doesn't want it."

"Yes, you are. You just won't admit it. You only want one girl, but she doesn't want you, so, like John throwing a tantrum on the outside, you're throwing one on the inside—by turning yourself off. You used to do that as a kid to protect yourself, didn't you? Now you're doing it again. I know you wanted to do more than just kiss me a minute ago, but you stopped yourself. You told John that guys like him end up desperate...just like you. You'd rather be dead on the inside than desperate on the outside again.

"You know, I don't think you hate people as much as you let on. I think you really care about them—you just don't want them to know it.

That's why you helped John in the stairwell, and that's why you helped Danny and me in the storeroom. I think the person you really hate is *you*. You gave your heart, and it was thrown back at you, in pieces, and now you feel foolish and weak. And you hate yourself for all your mistakes. You feel like a stain rather than a person. That's why you made that remark about tarnishing my yearbook. You push people away so weakness and foolishness won't stand next to you ever again."

"You think you know it all, don't you?"

"Not all. But about this I do. I know about it because I was the same way. I'm not that way anymore, though. I forced myself to change. Self-hatred never accomplished anything. Neither does closing yourself off. Life's hard enough without going through it alone.

"You better learn to forgive and forget, or you're going to spend the rest of your life alone. You may think being cold as ice is a good move now, but when you get to be an old man, you're going to think differently."

"I thought you said I already was an old man."

"You know what I meant. You told John so what if I didn't love him. Life goes on. Good words. Your words. This girl who hurt you...so what? It's not the end of the world. There are others to love, and others who want to return the love. Stop living in the past, Owen...or you're going to die in it."

She wrapped her arms around me, kissed me one last time, and left the room.

# CHAPTER 14

# *A New Spring,*
# *A Lasting Autumn*

*"So we beat on, boats against the current, borne
back ceaselessly into the past."*

F. SCOTT FITZGERALD, *THE GREAT GATSBY*

Hillside High School selected its valedictorian through voting. Mr. Vincenzo told me I had been chosen to be valedictorian at my graduation. I told him to tell those who elected me to elect another. He told me he wouldn't. I told him he'd better. He told me it was an honor. I told him it wasn't. He told me he was confused. I told him he needn't be. He told me to at least show up. I told him I wouldn't. He told me I had to. I told him I didn't. He told me it was necessary. I told him it wasn't. He told me there was every reason to be there. I told him there was no reason to be there. He told me he did not understand. I told him he didn't need to understand. He told me that wasn't good enough. I told him that was as good as he was going to get. He told me he wanted an explanation. I told him he wasn't going to get one. He told me I needed to act like an adult. I told him he needed to mind his own business. He told me he wouldn't. I told him he would…and walked away.

What goes around comes around. What one gives is what one gets. Do good and good will follow you; do bad and bad will accompany you. Karma is plugged into every life. No one is left out. I had cut John off when he was telling Rochelle of the songs that reminded him of her. I didn't want to listen to him. He was pathetic. In my eighteenth year—in my last year of high school—there were many songs on the radio that reminded me of Roxanne. I longed to share them with her... but I was cut off from Roxanne, so she would never know them. Life had cut me off, just as I had cut John off. What goes around comes around.

Many songs heard in teenage cars and in teenage bedrooms that year were on the sorrowful side. It seemed there were more joyless melodies than joyful ones. Or maybe not. Maybe I was just more tuned in to the sad ones.

The records spun that year not only spoke of broken love, but lost love, momentary love, hopeful love...

"Please Tell Him That I Said Hello"..."We'll Never Have to Say Goodbye Again"..."Before My Heart Finds Out"..."Falling"..."Sandy"... "Goodbye Girl"..."We're All Alone"..."If I Can't Have You"..."Dust in the Wind"..."Aubrey." All of these songs made my heart yearn for Roxanne, but two of them made it ache—"Dust in the Wind" and "Aubrey."

Kansas, a popular art rock band, was Roxanne's favorite group. "Dust in the Wind," one of their most admired songs, spoke about us. It spoke of the impermanence of everything; it warned against holding onto anything. If my union with Roxanne had not died before, it would have died eventually. How ironic that the group Roxanne loved the most would sing of the death of our relationship.

Had I been able to compose music and write verse, "Aubrey," a first-person love song from Bread, would have been the song I would have written about Roxanne and me. Near its end, David Gates crooned a sorrowful couplet about being different from all the rest, and that if he could not win the one he loved, he wanted no one at all. This coda was the tragic summary of my time with Roxanne. Christopher and John also loved the song. I had to wonder if those two lines were as rending to them as they were to me. Most likely.

On May 24, 1978, a movie came to the theaters. Not a month later, it was gone. It was a simple story, a tender tale about a man who reunites with a woman who left him many years earlier. *If Ever I See You Again* was its name. Before its departure, I saw it thirteen times. Not an auspicious number. The movie's soundtrack was made into an album, and I was certain I was the first to own it. Every night, while lying in bed, I listened to the film's music. While the turntable played its melodies, my mind played her memory. And a single question: What would I do if I ever saw Roxanne again?

An addiction is not always a dependency on something external; it can also be an enslavement to something within. Addictions are never conquered—they are kept at bay, held at a governable distance. An addict must be ever-watchful of his addiction, for if he isn't, his enemy will slip back over the wall and invade anew, with the same intensity as before, sometimes greater. I let the memory of Roxanne slip back over the wall, and it overtook me…again. Had I any friends, they would have asked me why I let it happen…twice? Why did I relight the torch for Roxanne when she had been so cold and hateful toward me? Why did I listen to music and look at things that reminded me of her? The answer was simple: they made me feel the way I used to feel—alive. Ms. Longmire confessed to having had the same feeling. But hers was not an addiction; mine was. My addiction had once more slipped over the wall. To beat back an addiction, one must be smarter than it; one must have in his mind the wisdom that it is more gainful to say no to something eternally bad than yes to something temporarily good. One must have unflinching determination to say no to something he desperately wants to say yes to. Epictetus philosophized: *It is the nature of the wise to resist pleasures, but the foolish to be a slave to them.* I might have been a peculiarity, but I was not a foolish one. I was intelligent, and I would deploy that intelligence to drive Roxanne out of my mind, once and for all. I would not be subjugated a third time. As the saw says: *If once is enough, and twice is too much, then thrice is stupidity.* I was the holder of many sad things, but stupidity was not, nor would it ever be, one of them.

I took a hammer to the album, and I vowed to move on. Barring any chance encounter with Roxanne, I would never let myself think of her again. This time, her memory would remain behind the wall.

I was offered a scholarship to the University of Utah. I declined it. I wanted no handouts or free rides. I didn't desire them; I didn't grow up with them, and I didn't respect them. So many teenagers, I noticed, had their lives, their pleasures, and their futures handed to them. I was not going to be a part of their *do-for-me, provide-for-me, pay-for-me* fold. I wanted to say I paid and made my own way.

I decided to wait until the fall to start college. Roxanne filled the adolescent years of my life; nursing, I decided, would fill the adult years. I wanted to help afflicted and suffering children the same way I had been helped by the young paramedics after Mr. Carey had gifted me with the penultimate bullet in his Smith & Wesson. Yet there was no such thing as a paramedic who helped children exclusively. The only way I could minister to children every day is if I were a nurse. I knew it shouldn't have mattered who I was helping, that anyone in pain has importance, but children were the only people I wanted to comfort. If I could help those children—or even one child—who were in a place I used to be, my life, for once, would have meaning and value.

I had little doubt I could climb the academic peak of nursing school, but I was not so confident I could scale the mountain next to it: the clinicals. The sight of terminal children, sick children, vulnerable children, burned children, deformed children, abandoned children, scarred children, scared children, abused children could cause my endeavor to miscarry. I didn't know if I was up to it. But I needed to try.

### July 4, 1978.

I walked into the liquor store without anxiety. An adult could not buy alcohol in the state of Utah until he turned twenty-one. Three years would have to pass before I turned that age, but I already looked well beyond that, so I was confident I could walk out with whatever I wanted. It was my eighteenth birthday—legally, I was now an adult, allowed to cast a ballot or join the military if I pleased; if I could vote to elect and shoot to kill, I could drink.

The young woman behind the counter at the package store didn't card me or even give me a second look when I slid the bottle of Bacardi Gold over to her. Rum and Coke, I had heard, is a good beginner's drink; unlike other alcohols—like vodka, which I had read was fiery, and wine, which I had been told was bitter—it is genial and mellow.

I left the store, went to my car, opened the trunk and laid the bottle next to a six-pack of Coke. Next to the Coke was a small, Styrofoam ice chest. Inside the chest was a short, crystal tumbler buried in ice.

Having a strong memory is a mixed blessing. It is highly profitable for exams and arguing a point, but it can be a crown of thorns if one has a past best forgotten. Though it had been thirteen years, I remembered the exact spot on which Susan had been kneeling before the earth collapsed and the water stole her away. The height of the trees and the ambit of the verdure had expanded, but not much else had changed since I was there as a boy. Even the granite promontory on which I hit my knee was still there. But then, why shouldn't it be? Where would it go?

The site, like everywhere else in the country, should have been alive with picnicking, frolicking, and laughing, yet it was silent and lifeless, dead as a cemetery, which, in a way, it was, for it was there that Susan lost her life.

The creek was high, but not nearly as high as that spring day in 1965. I stepped into the cold water, onto the spot where Susan's death began. The limpid water instantly turned turbid from the disruption of the streambed sediment made by my shoes, but then it quickly cleared. I got down on my hands and knees and submerged my head in the water. Some would say I was dancing with danger. I wasn't. I was simply trying to touch my sister in the only way I knew how. I lowered my face onto the streambed and pressed my lips onto a smooth, round rock and kissed it. An ocean of memories filled my head as I knelt there.

The memories stopped abruptly as my body was pulled away. Something was clutching my arms, and my body was being dragged from the water. Only seconds before, I was staring at shimmering and rippling rocks; now the faces of two girls replaced them.

"*What are you doing!*" I roared at the girls, wiping the water from my face with the front of my shirt.

"We thought you were—" one of the girls tried to explain. "Wait a minute, I know you. Do I know you?"

After my vision had cleared, I stared at her. I recognized her too.

"Yes, you know me, and I know *you*. Robin Jordison...from grade school. And the first year of high school. Dropped out, if memory serves."

"*Transferred*," Robin corrected defensively.

I turned to the second girl. "And you—Aasha Arapaho, I believe. You disappeared as well after that freshman year. But look at this, here you are again. Bad pennies do roll back, don't they?"

Both girls squinted at me.

"What was that for?" Robin gave me a face of indignation. "We just saved your life!"

"You saved nothing! It was no accident I was in there."

"What, you were in the river on purpose? Were you trying to off yourself or something?"

Angry at her idiotic assumption, I came back, "No, I was not trying to *off myself*. I had my reasons for being there."

"*What* reasons? No one would do nothin' like that. Not even you."

"Still in grand command of our language, I see."

She glared at me. "And I see you're still in grand command at being a royal prick. Still talkin' like you're above everyone else. Why have you always been such an ass?"

"Because I have always been surrounded by *asses*. I'm looking at two right now."

"What'd we ever do to you?"

"You can't be serious. You don't remember that December day in eighth grade when you tried—*unsuccessfully*—to get me to go to the Sadie Hawkins dance with you? You were given five dollars for your effort. But then you had to give the money back because I wouldn't go. Poor Robin—no money, no victory. You tried to humiliate me, but you failed."

"That was…*five* years ago!"

"I don't care if it was five *centuries* ago. You tried to humiliate me. Yet your pathetic effort ran aground."

"Boy, when you hold a grudge, you really hold it."

"You said I'm an ass too," Aasha subsumed. "What grave infraction am I guilty of?"

"Certainly not a poor vocabulary. You told me to *shut up*— remember?"

The two girls looked at each other, then began to laugh.

"The two of you have me at a disadvantage," I bristled. "What is tickling those microscopic minds of yours?"

They continued to laugh

Their laughter pushed me back to grade school; back to a time when being laughed at was all I knew.

I gave the two girls an iron stare. *"One who does not laugh is one who thinks; one who laughs is one who cannot think.* Ward Unsworth. How many times have the two of you stood in the breadline for brains…and were turned away?"

Aasha stopped laughing and shook her head. "You're such an ass."

"Yes, your simple-minded friend said that already."

"Has anyone ever told you you wear ugliness well?"

I feigned pain. "Ouch! Harpooned by the trenchant tongue of Aasha Arapaho. Will I ever recover?"

She smiled and shook her head. "You're not only an ass, you're an idiot. You step over dollars to pick up pennies."

"You're pitching a misplaced metaphor, Aasha. Try again."

"And you're pitching a misplaced sense of self-importance. The metaphor's right. You think by collecting your petty, little grudges that you're accomplishing more than letting them go. You see them lying there on the ground and you stockpile them, thinking you're gaining more than you had, but all the while you're losing, not profiting. You don't know how foolish and ridiculous you sound. No adult—no *mature* adult—carries around a grudge from *grade school.* It's pettiness at its worst. You think we care that you've got a chip on your shoulder about us? We don't. No one else does either. You're not the center of the damn universe, Owen. You're nothing. No—I take that back—you *are* something: you're a little boy who's crying because he got made fun of at recess. Tough! Everyone gets made fun of. Get over it. You have the brains of a genius, Owen, but you have the behavior of a child. You were the smartest kid in our class, but the dumbest when it came to people. I remember you always had a book in your hand...but you didn't read everything."

"As opposed to you."

"I read more than you knew. You ever read Medgar Evers? Of course not. He was a lover of people—the complete opposite of you. He said: *'When you hate, the only person that suffers is you, because most of the people you hate don't know it, and the rest don't care.'* You're in for a sad life, Owen. And a short one too. All that negative emotion charging through your veins like an army is going to put you into an early grave. Stop living in the past and grow up!"

Aasha took hold of Robin's hand and the two girls went on their way.

Then Robin turned around and smiled, "You can go back to playing in the water now, little boy."

They wanted me to genuflect to their indictments. But I would not. If I did, it would mean I accepted their words, that their words were acceptable. I didn't, and they weren't.

Though wet, I was not cold. The air, despite the high elevation, was tonically warm. A motherly breeze was wafting through the trees and bushes.

I retrieved the Coke and rum and ice chest from the trunk and went back to the creek. Serendipitously, there was an accommodating clearing on the south bank of the stream. I forded the creek at one of its few shallow spots and sat down on a leaf-covered glade I had seen from the other side.

After mixing the drink, I raised my glass and made a silent tribute to Susan. The liquor burned slightly as it traveled over my tongue and down my throat. It had been my first taste of alcohol. I wasn't impressed.

Almost immediately, my head began to float and teeter. I didn't like anything controlling me, but the numbness filling my brain was a welcome guest. For once, the constant barrage and bombardment of memories and regrets were muted.

I mixed another drink. This time, I didn't notice any burn, just a warmth that took over my body. A third drink passed my lips, then a fourth, then a fifth. Time left my world, and all I saw was the vegetation darken and the shadows lengthen. The temperate air had cooled, but I wasn't uncomfortable. Just the opposite: I was relaxed and content and untroubled.

I laid down on my back and gazed at the sky. It was evening but not yet night. It was that magical vesper hour at which the sun bids good night with a wave of candescent yellow. I closed my eyes and absorbed the opiate sounds around me: the rolling water, the brushing leaves, the trilling insects.

When I opened my eyes again, the sky was fruitful with glistering stars. The air was cold now, unpleasantly cold. My neck was sore and my head thick. Unsteadily, I got to my feet. I collected the empty Coke cans, the tumbler—now chipped—and the empty rum bottle and dropped them all into the ice chest. The darkness prevented me from seeing where I had originally crossed the stream. I decided to take my chances and just walk across it. Its frigid temperature made me gasp. I wobbled and staggered, but I made the short journey without going down.

I put the ice chest in the trunk and climbed into the back seat. Immediately, my eyes closed, and I was asleep.

The sounds of singing birds awakened me.

My eyes opened, and sunlight stabbed my optic nerves. Every inch of me was my enemy: my head throbbed, my stomach churned, my mouth thirsted, and my neck, back, and legs ached. Was this a hangover? If so, why would anybody want to even touch alcohol, let alone drink it? I should never have bought the rum. I should have come to the stream with flowers, not liquor. But I didn't do that. I made my own pain. If one plays with lions, he gets eaten.

From the backseat, I saw my reflection in the rearview mirror. Frightful would have been a polite appraisal. My hair looked as if it had been torpedoed, and my face looked as if it had been coated with a thick film of Elmer's Glue.

After climbing into the front seat, I quickly tried to mat down my hair with saliva. A few strands obeyed, but the rest remained defiant. Maybe luck would accompany me home and gift me with green lights on the way so no one would see me.

Not only didn't luck accompany me, it wasn't even nearby. I hit every red light, and I was stalled in traffic by two accidents. I'm sure I looked as if I had been in an accident myself to those who were stopped next to me.

Ms. Windom's Cordoba was not in the driveway when I arrived home. This was odd: she never left the house until the afternoon, if then.

I parked my car in the garage and pulled down the door. Once in the house, I immediately noticed something was off. Things were missing. Ms. Windom's things. In the kitchen, the radio she kept on the counter by the sink and the notes she had taped to the refrigerator door were gone. In the living room, her many pieces of Delftware and the five white, porcelain rabbits she had sitting about had also been removed.

My mind nudged me to go upstairs.

Only carpet, furniture, and draperies occupied Ms. Window's bedroom. All of her jewelry, clothing, wigs, perfumes, medications, and toiletries were among the ranks of the missing.

I heard walking downstairs. Maybe it was the police searching for me to inform me that Ms. Windom had been murdered. Now *that* would be a nice birthday present.

From the top of the stairs, I saw a gray-haired, bathyscaphe-sized woman making her way to the kitchen. It wasn't the police. Or Ms. Windom.

"Are you lost?" I asked loudly. "Or are you just browsing?"

The nor'easter of a woman shrieked and shot her head upward. Her old face reminded me of a weathered walnut shell.

"Are you Owen?" she inquired with a tottering voice.

"No, I'm the gardener. Of course I'm Owen! Who else would I be! Who are you?"

"I'm Elsie Clemenson, Hilda's best friend."

"*Hilda?* Ah, yes, Ms. Windom's Christian name. Although she could scarcely be called a Christian. How about *Hilda the Hateful Harrier*, or *Abaddon, Angel of the Abyss*? What are you doing here? You've never visited here before."

"I don't live in Salt Lake. I live in Anaheim, California."

"You've answered the second part of the question—now what about the first?"

"There are some items in the basement that Hilda forgot. I've come to get them."

"Why?" I started making my way down the stairs.

The woman backed away.

"I'm not going to hurt you," I snapped defensively.

"Hilda is leaving," the woman informed me. "She's moving to California. She'll be staying with me for a time."

"Why are *you* collecting her things and not her?"

"She is saying her good-byes to your mother as we speak. After that, we will be leaving for California."

"And why is she saying good-bye?"

"You don't know?"

"Obviously not, since I'm asking."

"You told her she must be out of this house when you turned eighteen. She's just respecting your wishes."

"*Respecting my wishes.* Hmm. She never respected them before. I'm curious—if this is all so innocent, why were you so startled to see me?"

She didn't answer.

"Could it be you weren't expecting to see me at all?" I lassoed her.

"As it happens, I wasn't. You were supposed to be at work this morning."

"I changed my shift yesterday. I'm working this evening."

"May I go and get her things?"

"Knock yourself out."

She turned around and hurried into the kitchen. Minutes later, she was back in the living room with a large box clutched in her short-fingered hands.

I didn't know what was in the box, and I didn't care.

"Would like to inspect it before I go?" she held out the box.

"No, thank you. People don't ordinarily inspect garbage."

"Good-bye, Owen. It was a pleasure meeting you."

"No, it wasn't. Let me ask you something before you head off to Disneyland. Why are you friends with her? I would think it would be like having a jackal for a pet."

"She's not a jackal."

"No? How about the Devil's spawn?"

"Don't be so quick to judge. She's not a monster."

"Yes, I'm sure under her slick horns there glows a radiant halo."

"She told me about your relationship, all the things she did to you."

"Why would she share that? Are you actually a priest under those muliebris civvies?"

"I'm her friend. We've known one another since we were young women."

"*You* I can see as a young woman. *Her*, on the other hand, I can only see as a tumor in the body of humanity."

"Why don't you try being a little less sarcastic and a little more understanding?"

"Understanding? You're kidding. The woman berated me, insulted me and disrespected me at every turn. And not only me, but the girl I loved and the friend I cared about. She locked me up, kicked me, hit me, did everything but rape me, and you want me to understand that?"

"There's no excuse for what she did, but there are reasons."

"Don't tell me—her father molested her, so she got back at him by trying to molest *me*. I was an easy mark, just like her. Is that the story?"

"Her father didn't molest her; he wasn't even around. Neither was her mother. They left Hilda with her uncle, her mother's brother, when she was an infant."

"So her uncle molested her—so what? People get raped every day—they don't turn into rapists themselves."

"He didn't molest her. He did far worse. Hilda was a young teenager at the start of the Depression. She was a beautiful girl. Truly beautiful. She was also poor. Very poor. Poverty-stricken, actually. Millions were. She had this pet rabbit, pure white, like snow. She named him Charlie, after Charlie Chaplin. She adored that little thing. She loved it like you and I would love a dog or a cat. It even behaved like a dog or a cat. It would follow her everywhere. It would sleep with her, cuddle with her, lick her. It truly was her only friend. Most of the time, she and her uncle had no food, certainly no food to feed a rabbit, so every night Hilda would go into the alley behind their tenement and go through the garbage cans to find anything for Charlie. One night, very late, Hilda's uncle snuck into Hilda's room while she was asleep, took Charlie, killed him and ate him. Her uncle was a...well, *he* was the Devil's spawn. Her uncle used her niece's beauty to get them out of their horrible poverty. During the Depression, not everyone in the country was destitute; there were a few who had coins in their pockets. Somehow, Hilda's uncle made contact with them and...well, offered her niece to the men and their sons. That's how they survived. Some would call her uncle an enterprising ponce, a savvy opportunist. I call him a sickening, detestable, disgusting pimp."

"Why did she stay?"

"Where could she go? The only place was the streets. At least with her uncle, she was warm and fed. Hilda's sexual development was permanently deformed when she was young. Her sexual imprinting during adolescence was corrupted. Because of her uncle—her weak, degenerate uncle—Hilda never matured sexually. She became sexually ungrounded and unstable. She's damaged mentally and stunted emotionally. What she went through made her distrustful, resentful, perverse, and violent."

"Did she ever express remorse to you for what she did to me?"

"No—because she wasn't remorseful. You represented everything she hated. You were the sons of the men who, in her eyes, took her innocence, even though she consented to have intercourse with them. You were the rich boys who had everything when she had nothing."

"My mother told me she's a widow. How's that possible? What man would ever want her?"

"He was a wealthy man, and very sweet. His name was Shamus. Hilda hated him. She married him only for his silver. His kindness she took for weakness, and his money...well, she just took. She made him feel so small he left her two years into their marriage. Before their divorce was finalized, he died of a heart attack."

"Why would you be friends with someone like that?"

"I felt sorry for her. I still do."

"Pity? That's why you're her friend?"

"Love is not at the center of every relationship, Owen. We all have our own secret reasons why we welcome someone into our lives. None of us are angels. Hilda was alone when we met. She still is. She needs somebody. Everyone needs at least one person who is on their side. Hilda is not a nice human being—I know it, and she knows it. But I don't blame her. I blame her mother, I blame her father, I blame her uncle, and I blame the men and their sons for taking advantage of her just because they could.

"Hilda would be a different person today if she hadn't had the life she did. You'd be different too if it weren't for your past. From what I hear, you have a pretty violent streak yourself: threatening Hilda with Drano and forks and screwdrivers, causing her to fall down the stairs, throwing cans of soda at her and putting gashes in her head."

"Correction—*one* fork, *one* screwdriver, *one* can of soda, *one* gash. *Singular*, not plural. But it would have been nice if it had been plural."

"Whether it was plural or not, there's no excuse for what you did… but there were reasons, weren't there?" She ended her case with a proud stare.

I returned the stare. Her arguments for and backstory on Ms. Windom held no currency with me. Ms. Windom was a grizzly who loved the taste of blood.

"I wish you a good life, Owen," she finished. "Try to remember something throughout that life: there are *always* two sides to every situation—the side you see and the side you don't."

She left the house without closing the door.

I went over to the door and closed it. I walked over to my father's red leather armchair in the living room and gently, almost reverently, sat down in it.

The house was as quiet as a mortuary. And just as lifeless. My life would have been so different had my father lived. There would have been no Ms. Windom, no ridicule, no humiliations, no beatings, no rape, no Roxanne, no walls, no emptiness, no loss. Inversely, there would have been no Christopher, no Mark, no Kylie, no Kylie's family, no Shawn. I would have been a completely different person, with a completely different past. It was, after a fashion, the butterfly effect. My father's death was by no means small, but it permanently altered my life.

Rewinding even further, if Susan had lived, my parents would have lived, and I would have known a far worse life than the one I eventually experienced. Tragically, but thankfully, Susan died.

Throughout the rest of the summer, I cleaned and rearranged every room in the house. I threw away everything Ms. Windom considered hers or I knew made her happy. Her television, her phonograph, her magazines, her plants, her food, her towels, her sheets all went into the garbage. I wanted no physical reminders of her.

I left the basement until last. Just thinking about it made me anxious and caused my pulse to race. I remembered vividly my fall down its stairs when I was a boy and the subsequent two-week imprisonment within its walls. Even though the imprisonment turned into something positive, the memory of it had become black and gangrenous. Time, someone once said, has a funny way of turning bad memories into good ones and good memories into bad. The boy in me expected Ms. Windom to return any minute and imprison me once again. Only this time, she wouldn't let me go—she would jail me until I died. Before venturing into the basement, I removed its door and took an electric saw to it.

Once in the basement, however, with the peaceful quiet all around me, I relaxed and realized I had overreacted.

The first box I opened, which was snug under the stairs, made my body go numb. In it were the gifts I had bought for Roxanne and her family in 1974, nearly four years before. I had completely forgotten about them. I had taken them down into the basement a few weeks after Roxanne and I split up, and I never went back. They were the first items to go into the garbage bag I brought with me.

On the top shelf of a dusty, shadow-dressed bookcase lay a long, shallow box cocooned in a dingy-white pillow case. Yellowed and edge-torn newsprint—the front page of *The Dallas Morning News*, dated November 23, 1963, the day after the Kennedy assassination—was wrapped around three high school yearbooks. They belonged to Mr. and Mrs. Crowley. I had never seen them before. I didn't even know they existed. Only black-and-white photographs filled the pages of the crimson-bound annuals.

My adoptive parents were the *It Couple* of Ventana High School. Either arm-in-arm or hand-in-hand, they were featured on many pages throughout the three books. Their faces were always happy, their bodies always in crisp apparel. Their given names were never annotated below the photographs, only their nickname: *Here's JJ at the dance...Here's JJ taking a break between classes...Here's JJ studying in the library.* Tragedy awaits every man in the end. Did Mr. and Mrs. Crowley know this when they were beaming in every snapshot? Or if they did, did they care? Would he have been so jaunty if he knew cancer would one day destroy his body? And would she have been so happy and effervescent if she knew her mind would one day leave her? Most likely not. Does anyone really care about death when it's decades away? No. But I did. In the back of my mind, I always knew death would have the final say, the last word. It was, in part, why I hated to smile. I didn't want to feel a fool in the end for being happy. Sadness could not gloat if you made it to the finish line first.

Holding the yearbooks made me feel guilty for abandoning Mrs. Crowley. I couldn't bring myself to call her *"mother,"* but I did feel bad for not being there with her and for her. I had had my chance—*many* chances—to be in her life, but I let them all slip away. I had been a terrible excuse for a son.

Ms. Windom wasn't the only spawn of the Devil.

While their grounds are home to lively juvenescence—with its boundless belief that all is possible—high school and college are worlds apart in maturity. As I began my college years, it seemed to me that students in college took life and learning more seriously than their registrants in high school. Because of that, I actually respected those who sat in class with me.

Tertiary education came easy for me, just as primary and secondary education had. What would not be so easy, I feared, is what would follow it: life.

While doing the colorless but compulsory general education classes (English, Mathematics, History, Science, etc.), I began laying the pavement toward nursing school. In addition to the basic core classes, I took anatomy, microbiology, chemistry, medical terminology, and nutrition. Listing these courses on my nursing school application would offer witness of intent and commitment, which I indeed had. But more importantly, the more courses I took, the more knowledgeable I would be, and the more knowledgeable I was, the more I could bring to my patients and their families.

My chemistry professor suggested I volunteer at a hospital. She said the experience would have a twofold profitability: first, it would give me exposure to what I would be facing in the future; and second, it would help me decide if nursing was the career I truly wanted. She said some students go into nursing because the pay is good and the need perdurable, which, while both true, were, in her estimation, the wrong reasons to become a caregiver. When someone is a patient, they are at their weakest and most vulnerable, and they need a caregiver who will see them as a hurting human being, not a means to a healthy paycheck.

She said being a volunteer would also let me experience the rigors of nursing. Many do not have the physical mettle to do the job.

Volunteering would draw the curtains even more and let me see the many faces of human suffering. Some people don't have the emotional constitution to take the sight of disease and wounds and the pain that comes from both. She said the sufferings of children were the hardest to see, and given that I wanted to be a pediatric nurse, I definitely should be a volunteer. She suggested that I offer my time to St. Bernadette's Hospital, a long-standing care center that had a Level 1 ER, multiple ORs, Psych, Rehab, Orthopedic, Hospice, Med/Surg, Maternity, and Pediatric units. If I could brave what I would see there, I could brave anything.

I asked her why she was not a nurse herself since she obviously had her finger on the pulse of the profession. Her answer was sorrowfully short: "I don't have what it takes."

Though decades old, St. Bernadette's was considered the finest hospital in the city. The Volunteers director was a sweet, thin, quinquagenarian with a Marlo Thomas hairdo. Incredibly, her first name was Marlo; her last Jefferies. I was upfront with her about why I was there: I needed to be a free observer rather than a free laborer. I particularly wanted to observe the pediatric unit. She appreciated my honesty and told me that the children's unit was a secured area, and for that reason, only certain staff were allowed access to it. I would have to wait to be cleared to be given that access. In the meantime, she would introduce me to the other department heads and ask that I be allowed to watch and learn and perhaps even assist.

Everyone but the ER director was agreeable and willing to let me observe and lend a hand. More crowbait than human, the ossified ER director was less than elastic to the idea of a spectator in his department, let alone a spectator who wasn't even in nursing school yet. Mrs. Jefferies took her colleague aside and spoke to him out of my hearing. Soon, they came back, and the ER director told me if I got in anyone's way, I'd be out the door faster than a Concorde. Mrs. Jefferies left me with a smile. Just as quickly, the ER director left me in the hands of one of his nurses: an older woman who I immediately sensed was as annoyed at my presence as her superior. Tersely, the older nurse—a reedy woman with a drinker's rosacea and whose name was Judy Corbin—showed me the various devices used in her department. As she was telling me about the three types of patients they saw (the *"Chronic Criers"*—the kind who rush in for every scrape and scratch; the *"Chronic Cadavers"*—the kind who are always in extremis; and the *"True Emergencies"*), a loud and discordant alarm came from the nurses' station. We both went out to the station. Another nurse was listening intently to a speaker mounted on a wall. Paramedics were coming in with a twenty-year-old male in cardiac arrest with an accidental amputation. High on heroin, the young man drove his motorcycle into a tree. Next to the tree was a stop sign. His body was thrown from the bike, and his left arm hit the edge of the pole supporting the sign. The metal stave cut his arm off just above the elbow. The arm had been placed in a plastic bag with ice and was being transported with the man.

Immediately, a Code Blue was called overhead for the ER.

My tour guide told me to stand back and not get in the way.

Within minutes, the ambulance arrived, and the arrested amputee was rushed in. Blood was everywhere: on the gurney, on the man, on the paramedics. It made me swallow, even though my mouth was completely dry.

Multiple people were racing into the department. Doctors, nurses, technicians, therapists, supply and pharmacy staff, security people, even a priest from Pastoral Care now filled the once-quiet hallways of the unit. The clinical staff rushed into the trauma room where the man had been taken. I stood back in awe. Each person knew his function. Even though they were all darting around like ants, they were precise and calm. Not one of them appeared stressed or strained. Though it was all happening on a landscape of an incomprehensible tragedy, their precision and professionalism were undeniably impressive. One man—I presumed he was the ER doctor—was calling out orders and demanding information. The trauma room floor was fast becoming a landfill of blood, bloody bandages, bloody gauze, bloody bags, bloody pouches, bloody sheets, bloody tubing, and bloody towels.

A young woman ran into the unit. She was crying convulsively. The priest immediately went over to her, and they spoke for a minute. The priest walked her over to the trauma room door so she could see what was happening. She must have been the wife or girlfriend of the man. I thought it was inappropriate of the priest to let her watch. He should have taken her out of the department and stayed with her until the situation was in hand. Instead, he let her watch her partner be pounded with unmerciful CPR and invaded with unpitying instruments. What if he died on the table? She would *never* be able to get that out of her head.

After about ten minutes, the ER doctor called the code, and everything in the room ceased; even the resuscitation bag came to a stop. An unearthly quiet permeated the room.

The woman with the priest collapsed to the floor. She began to shrill and beat the sides of her thighs with her fists. Two women in shamrock-green scrubs went over to her, helped her up and took her out of the department.

I was certainly no expert, but I felt the ER doctor should have continued. It had only been ten minutes. I sensed he called the code because he didn't care. What was the point in trying to save the life of a fruitless, fainéant addict? The heroin would have probably killed him someday anyway.

With an almost smug smile, the ER doctor went around the room and asked each person if they agreed that the code be stopped. Each said yes. The doctor looked directly at me and asked me my opinion. Why was he asking *me*? What did *I* know? I wasn't even a nursing student yet. I surmised he was aggrandizing himself at my expense.

"Yes, I think you should continue," I said, glaring at him. "That's someone's son on the table. What if he were *your* son?"

He—along with everyone else in the room—stared at me in surprise. Who was I to speak up? But if he didn't want an answer, he shouldn't have asked.

The ER doctor smirked. "I don't have a son."

I gave him an unblinking stare. "Thank goodness for that."

He sniffed indignantly, plucked off his bloody gloves, tossed them into the already-full kick bucket and walked out of the room.

Gradually, indifferently, everyone left the room, leaving the dead man all alone.

Slowly, I walked over to him. He looked like he had been in a war—bloody, still, and ripped apart. His eyes were half open; a tracheal tube was extruding from his mouth; IV lines were taped to his body, and monitor leads were draped over his chest. He was now just another number, a statistic. Just a dead addict. An anonymous, deceased junkie. But not to his parents, and not to the woman who watched him die.

I touched his face. It was already cool.

"I'm sorry," I whispered to him.

I began to cry.

Moments later, someone touched my arm.

It was the ER director.

"You're going to drown before you even get in the water, son," he passed along to me. "People die. Every age. Every day. They die at the hands of others, themselves, disease, accidents, addictions. Death is a fisher of *all* men. If you want to be a nurse, you gotta grow some calluses. You'll be no good to anyone if you don't. I think you should go home, get some rest. If you want to come back tomorrow, you're more than welcome to."

I gave the dead man one last glance and left the ER. While driving home, I took a hard look at myself. Like my chemistry professor, maybe I, too, was not strong enough to give care to others. Or maybe I was. Seeing someone die is never easy, especially when their blood is everywhere but inside their body. Maybe I just needed some rest, as the ER director suggested. I would go back the following week when I had a free day and try again.

The following week, I went back to the hospital. Only this time, I chose the OR to visit. I really didn't know what type of reception I would receive. I wasn't even staff—I was just a volunteer. Maybe the OR director—a midlifer by the name of Mrs. Eileen Finley—would be as unwelcoming as her ER analog. She hadn't been there the previous week when Mrs. Jefferies introduced me to the other directors.

In appearance, the director of Perioperative Services had unmistakable shades of Ms. Windom, but in temperament, she was just the opposite: understanding, unthreatening, likeable. She was happy to let me observe. She said I could spend as much time as I wanted in her department. Maybe one day I would be one of her nurses.

Once in my scrubs, I felt like Hawkeye Pierce in M*A*S*H, except that my mask, cap, and shoe covers were all disposable. I half expected to see Radar, Winchester, Colonel Potter, and the rest once I got back into the OR. They never showed.

I was put into an ENT room. I had never seen so much green in my life. The walls, the scrubs, the masks, the towels, even some of the equipment was green. Was it a style choice, or did it have an actual purpose? I wanted to ask, but I felt I would look benighted and ignorant if I did.

The circulating nurse, whose name was Bob, was a tall, paunchy, mustached, middle-aged man. He had a maddening habit of ending every sentence with a laugh. I didn't understand it. What would possess him to suffix every utterance with a chortle? It made no sense.

Throughout the morning, I watched, stayed out of the way and answered an endless stream of questions as to why I was there and what area of nursing I wanted to pursue.

I took a lunch break in the cafeteria about twelve thirty; actually, it was more of a Pepsi break. Without asking, a young, redheaded girl sat down next to me. Without preamble, she introduced herself. T'Ann was her name. Out of politeness, I told her who I was, even though I wanted to tell her to go away. I needed a rest from talking and listening; I just wanted to be alone. For the next twenty-five minutes, without pause, she filled the air between us with the story of her life—from her first boyfriend to her last, from her love of colored chalk to her infatuation with charcoal, from her allergy to strawberries to her belief in oatmeal. She took prating to a whole new plateau. She was in mid-sentence about her supervisor when I got up to leave. I told her I had to get back. Before I left the table, she wrote her phone number down on a napkin and handed it to me. Graciously, I took it and departed. There was an elevator just outside the cafeteria entrance. Below the call button was a trash can. In one move, I called the car and threw the napkin away.

I decided to take a brief tour of the Surgery department before I returned to the ENT room. Many of its key parts were a mélange of old and new. Half of the scrub sinks were porcelain, the others stainless steel. Half of the autoclaves were démodé, the others state of the art. Half of the cabinetry was glass and metal, the rest veneered particle board. Even the hallways were dissimilar in fashion: half were insipid, the others inexplicable. Half were painted with a gushing orange and the others wallpapered with bare-winter trees. The make-overs looked less like improvements and more like the opening credits of *The Twilight Zone*. The unit was built in the 1960s, but it was obvious it was given a fractional and funky facelift in the 1970s.

On a gurney outside the ENT room was the next patient. I guessed her to be about twenty-five. She was crying and holding the sheet tightly against her neck as she told the anesthesiologist she was terrified of needles. My heart broke for the woman, for I knew what it was like to be so scared that tears came. I expected the anesthesiologist to be blunt with her, or, at the very least, impatient: after all, what did she expect coming in for surgery—cotton candy and clowns? Instead, he was unbelievably compassionate. He touched her arm and told her very soothingly he could put her to sleep first and then start the IV. The woman sat up and hugged the doctor.

I swallowed.

Just when you think someone will act like a machine they act like a human being.

By the end of the day, I had lost interest in ENT cases. I wanted to see more invasive procedures. I wanted to watch a coronary bypass or craniotomy or total hip, anything to let me see inside the body. Of course, this would depend on the surgeons. Some do not like extraneous staff in their rooms. I would ask Mrs. Finley if I could watch some open-cavity surgeries the following week.

The last patient of the day for the ENT room was a twenty-four-year-old male from Colorado. He was there for an endonasal rhinoplasty. He was wheeled in wearing a surgical mask. I thought this peculiar since none of the patients before him wore one. Apparently, he was sick. But if this were so, why was he allowed to have surgery? Elective and cosmetic surgeries, I was told, were always postponed if the patient has any type of respiratory illness. Bob told me this at the beginning of the day. Then he laughed.

While the scrub tech—a young girl by the name of Margie—was preparing her back table, the young man slid over from the gurney to the operating table. He kept his eye on the scrub tech once he was securely on the table.

I noticed something else out of order: the plastic bottle of LR hanging next to the bed had no IV line in it. When the other patients were brought in, the bottles were spiked and ready for use.

Instead of starting the IV, or placing the ECG backpad, or drawing up his meds, or readying the laryngoscope and intubation tube, the anesthesiologist sat by the anesthesia machine with his hands in his lap. What was he waiting for? Even I, a novice, knew something was off.

Just then, eleven more people entered the room: Mrs. Finley, three surgeons, and seven women. They all gathered next to the patient. They all were facing Margie, the scrub tech.

*Okay—this is weird.*

Margie turned her Mayo stand around toward the operating table and jumped at the sight of all the people.

"What's the matter?" Margie asked nervously. "Did I do something wrong?"

"Of course not, dear," Mrs. Finley ensured. "On the contrary, you did something very right. Margie, this young man has something to ask you."

Looking at the patient, then at the group, she said, *"What?"* It was obvious she was very puzzled.

The young man sat up, then stood.

Margie drew back, frightened.

The man lowered himself to one knee and removed his mask.

Margie gasped. "Patrick!" Like fireworks, delight burst from her eyes.

The young man raised a closed hand and then opened it. In his palm was a diamond ring.

"Margie," the young man started down the runway, "the marriage ring is a symbol of two hearts united as one. It is a banner that tells the world I am one with another. Margie, my love, will you take this ring and unite your heart with mine? Will you be my mate for the rest of my life?"

Margie instantly broke out in tears. Her fiancé stood, went to her and held her.

"Yes! Yes! Yes!" Margie cried, holding her boyfriend tightly.

Everyone in the room clapped and cheered.

Quietly, I slipped out of the room. It was too much to watch. I would never know such joy and belonging.

I changed back into my street clothes and went home.

I never went back to the OR. I couldn't take seeing another marriage proposal, and given the notorious proclivity of humans for imitation, I was certain I would. But deeper than that, I didn't want to go back. I had seen all I needed to see. Perioperative care was not for me. I wanted to be in the lives of children. Children have surgeries, but their nurses are only in their lives a few hours. I wanted longer. I needed to see them heal. But first I needed to see them die. I would have young patients who would succumb in my care and in my sight. I needed to see if I could take it. I needed to see death up close. The only place to view it was in the Hospice unit. I asked Mrs. Jefferies if I might spend some time there. She was hesitant to let me, for it was not an easy floor to work on, but she agreed to talk to the Hospice supervisor about it.

The Hospice director, a white-haired woman whose name badge read Loretta Faine, was very open to the idea. Like Mrs. Jefferies, she admired my honesty and candor. She said their patients, however, were typically geriatric, not pediatric. Rarely did they administer end-of-life care to children and only occasionally to young adults. But there was one young adult currently on the unit: a nineteen-year-old girl on palliative care for metastatic liver cancer. I asked the director if I could visit the girl. She gave me permission.

The girl in the bed was ravaged. Her hair was all but gone; her skin was yellowish-brown; her face and neck were anorexic; her arms and hands were skeletal, and her eyes were only half open. An IV line was taped to a cadaverous wrist. A brown leather Bible was lying underneath her hand. A long, white bookmark was propped against the Bible. There was a lengthy sequence of letters and numbers running lengthwise across it: *KOG495.KBC512.674.1393.07221.* I wanted to ask what it all meant, but I wouldn't.

There was a woman sitting next to the girl, holding her hand. I presumed it was her mother. The woman was herself thin, although not nearly as insubstantial as her daughter. It was plain that she, like her daughter, was no longer eating.

"Hello, I'm Owen," I introduced myself. "I'm a volunteer. I just wanted to know if there is anything I can get you."

"It's kind of you to ask," the woman said. Her eyes were red and tired. "This is Cynthia."

"Hello, Cynthia," I said to the girl.

The girl's eyes opened fully.

"She loves rainbows and unicorns," the woman shared. "Rainbows remind her of the Lord, and unicorns remind her of...happier times." She paused. "I'm all she's got now. Her father hasn't been by once. All her friends stopped coming around when she got sicker. Her boyfriend used to call her his *'Cindybear'*—now he doesn't even call. Even those from our church stopped visiting. Why did they abandon her? I don't understand."

I didn't know if she was actually asking me or just simply asking. Either way, I felt I should say something.

"I'm sure it's not your daughter, ma'am. Death is the hardest good-bye. Death is more than just the end of the person, it's the end of all the things that gave us comfort and security. No more smiles...no more phone calls...no more conversations...no more meals...no more embraces...no more sharing...no more security. They didn't abandon your daughter...they're just dealing with her ending in their own way."

The hand that had been resting on the Bible slowly rose. The girl was looking at me, pleading.

"I think she wants you to take her hand," the woman said.

I took it.

It was frail and algid. There was a time, maybe not long ago, when it was strong and healthy and warm.

I believed in God, even though I did not understand Him. I believed in demons and angels, even though I did not understand them. I did not believe in telepathy, even though I understood it. It was the stuff of Ray Bradbury and Stephen King; the stuff of the imagination, not reality. The moment I touched the girl's hand, it became reality.

It wasn't a succession of words, like a sentence; it was a complete thought, a complete message, instantaneous, like a heartbeat. *I need to die*, the girl told me without speaking. *I don't want my mother to see me die. I don't want her to have that memory. Would you take her from my room? Please...*

I gave the girl a small smile.

I laid the girl's hand down over her Bible.

I excused myself and left the room. I saw a young nurse at a drinking fountain a few yards away. She was an attractive girl with an understanding face. I hoped that understanding traveled below the pretty skin.

"May I ask a favor of you?" I petitioned once I got close to her.

"Of course," she answered, daintily blotting her lips with a napkin she had retrieved from her pocket.

"Cynthia, the girl in two thirty-one—would you ask her mother to come out into the hallway?"

Her eyebrows dug in. "Why?"

I hesitated, for I knew how my answer would sound, but I needed to give the answer nevertheless. "The girl needs to die; she wants to die, but she won't if her mother is with her."

"Did the girl tell you this?"

"In a way."

"In a way? What does that mean?"

"She...conveyed it to me. The girl wants to be free from her body. Can you understand that? She doesn't want her mother to live with the memory of seeing her die."

The nurse stared at me in contemplation. "I wouldn't know how to do it. She won't leave. She hasn't left since her daughter was admitted. She won't leave to eat; she won't leave to walk around; she won't even go home to shower. She uses her daughter's restroom and leaves the door open."

"Tell her you want to speak with her out in the hall, away from her daughter."

"I wouldn't know what to say. I just can't make something up. That would be a lie. I can't do that. I won't do that."

"Does the girl sleep?"

"She should, but she doesn't. She's on morphine, which should—"

"So there's your answer. The girl needs to sleep. The mother's presence is preventing that. That's the truth."

"I don't know. It doesn't sound right."

"Neither is the disease that's killing the girl. Be very firm with the mother or she will not go."

The nurse stared at me again.

"This whole thing can be over in a matter of minutes," I pointed out.

The mother was kissing her daughter's hand when the nurse and I entered the room. The nurse went over to the mother's side of the bed. I went to the other.

"Mrs. Gillis," the nurse put her hand on the mother's shoulder. "May I speak with you out in the hallway?"

"I can't leave my daughter," the mother resisted.

"Please, Mrs. Gillis, this is important."

"My daughter needs me."

"Mrs. Gillis, I *need* to speak with you privately—*now!*" The nurse's words were less than a shout but more than a command.

The mother winced.

"I'm sorry," the nurse apologized. "Please, I really need to speak with you outside."

The mother kissed her daughter on the forehead. "I'll be right back, sweetheart," she said and left with the nurse.

I gave the girl another small smile.

She reached over and took hold of my hand.

"Thank you," the girl said, her voice frayed and weak. She brought her other hand over and laid it over mine. For some reason, her hands were warm now.

"She's still yours," she whispered to me.

The girl closed her tired eyes. Her chest tremored momentarily, then stilled. Then both of her hands relaxed and fell away from mine.

"I haven't left, sweetheart," the mother said, coming back to her daughter's bed.

Her face went blank when she looked down at her daughter.

"Cynthia?" the mother's voice trembled. "Honey? Sweetheart? Sweetheart? Oh, no. Please no. No, no, no, no, no. Please don't go. Please don't be gone." She buried her face in her daughter's hair and wept fiercely. "Please come back," she cried, clutching her daughter's dead body.

I went over to the mother and rested my hand on her back. She threw herself around and collapsed against my chest and wailed in agony.

I said nothing.

"I didn't want her to die alone," she said through her sobs.

"She wasn't alone," I told her.

After her tears abated, I sat her down on the edge of the bed.

"Some years ago," I held her hands, "my girlfriend told me she hated it when people said the dead are in a better place. She hated it because it told the ones who were grieving they can't grieve because there is a higher purpose. She was wrong, and all because of one word...*can't*. It's not *can't* but *needn't*. After my girlfriend died, I was bound in pain for a very long time...and it was all unnecessary, for she *had* gone to a better place. A far better place than being with me. Cynthia is also in a better place now, a safe place. Nothing can ever hurt her again. She's in God's care now, and nothing harmful ever gets past God. Your daughter's pain is over...and so should yours be."

I got up to leave.

"Owen," the mother took my hand. "Thank you for being here."

I squeezed her hand and walked out of the room.

The young nurse was just outside the room. She touched my arm as I walked past her. "For what it means," she said, "I think you're going to make one hell of a nurse."

I returned to St. Bernadette's the following week.

During the week, something gnawed at me, something small but at the fore, like a sliver in the hand. Before she died, Cynthia said, "She's still yours." What did she mean? Was it delirium from the morphine or fatigue from fighting her death that made her utter those words? I didn't think it was either, for she was silent before that, except to say thank you, and though fragile, she seemed lucid. I truly wanted to know what she meant...but I never would.

After I entered the Hospice unit, I went to the nurses' station and gave the nurse behind the desk my name and the purpose of my visit.

With a smile edging on coy, the nurse told me she already knew who I was. Surprised, I asked her how that was possible since we had never met. She said Mrs. Faine had mentioned I would be working on the floor from time to time.

Gratified that I was starting to be accepted in the hospital, I asked her if I could go visit the patients. She said the floor had only one admit: a fifty-three-year-old female with T4 N3 M1 breast cancer.

I asked her if the woman was up to seeing visitors. The nurse said she was.

The woman was in 231. Cynthia's room.

I never forgot a face. Though debility had appropriated the woman's strength and cachexia had stolen her body, I knew instantly who she was.

No one was in the room with her. Her eyes were open, staring up. Was she remembering her past or contemplating her future? Was she remembering those who had injured her, or was she remembering those whom *she* had injured? Had it been me, I would have been thinking about all those whom I had hurt and the terrifying judgment awaiting me.

"Well, well, well," I grinned. "Look who we have here. What an unexpected pleasure. I never thought to see your face again. What's it been, six years? You don't look like at all like you used to. But I'll bet inside that rawboned body you are still the fly larva you once were. Tell me, are you ready to meet your maker? Are you ready to meet Austin as well? I'm sure he's ready to meet *you*. They say wishes don't come true. I say they do. I was so wishing you would die a terrible death... and here you are."

Sharla neither spoke nor reacted. Her dying eyes simply looked at me.

"What, no cocky comebacks? Where's the arrogant Sharla of six years ago? Your status and hauteur don't mean much now, do, they? How ironic. I once called you a cancer, and here you are filled with it. How amazing is that? You ripped Austin apart, and now cancer is ripping *you* apart. Talk about poetic justice. You criticized every part of Austin—from his gray hair to his slow driving. Now look at you—

hardly any hair at all, and as for driving, the next ride you will take will be in the back of a mortuary van. Just goes to show—better watch what you say. You told Austin to stop living in the past and get on with the future. Would you say that to him now, knowing that the past is all you have left?

"You said he was an empty, barren man. Now look who's empty and barren. If you aren't, where are your friends and family? Why aren't they here with you? You said Austin was going nowhere. Look who has ended up there herself—on her deathbed, completely alone. You called him a failure. If you are such a success, why are you forsaken and friendless? Funny how life pays us back. Do good and good will follow you; do bad and...well...look in the mirror, Sharla. You're an evil woman who didn't care how much your ugly words hurt, just so long as they were heard. Your tongue had no kindness, only poison."

Tears slid out of the corners of her eyes.

"Do the world a favor, Sharla, and slip away. For the good of the world—let go." I smiled boastfully and turned to leave.

Standing in the doorway was the nurse I had conversed with earlier. Her lips were taut, her breathing noticeable. A rime of rage was matted to her face.

"I want you out of this hospital—now!" she ordered. "If you aren't out in five minutes, I'm calling Security. I'm calling them anyway. I'm going to have them post your name and picture on every floor. If you're seen in this facility again, they will be called, and so will the police. You have no business working with patients. Marie told me what happened last week and how amazing you were with Cynthia and her mother. I agreed with her that you would make an extraordinary nurse. After what I just witnessed, you'd be a *dangerous* nurse. A good nurse gives good care to *everyone*, not just the ones he or she likes or feels pity for. That woman lying there isn't the evil one—*you* are. Now get out."

Without words, I walked past her.

I went to my car, got inside and locked the doors. I didn't start the engine. I sat, staring at the speedometer. I couldn't believe what I had done. I attacked a dying woman. What kind of man was I? Within me had always been a vein of meanness, a silent rage, a hunger for revenge, a thirst to punish. Whenever I heard that revenge was wrong, I turned a deaf ear. To others, revenge is injustice. To me, it was the *only* justice. God had it right when He commanded the early Israelites to grant no mercy to the guilty: *"You must show no pity…eye for eye, burn for burn, wound for wound, bruise for bruise, life for life."* Then Jesus came and put forth a new command: *"But I tell you, do not resist an evil person. If a man slaps you on your right cheek, turn to him the other also."* To me, that new command slept in the same house as a broken promise, an abrogation of what was right. To me, an eye for an eye and a hand for a hand was the only way to punish. Why did I think God's new command was inferior to His first? Why couldn't I change as I was instructed? Did I, like Satan, think I was higher and wiser than God? Was crucifying a woman on her deathbed God's way? Would I want to be treated like I treated Sharla? Would I be a dangerous nurse? Was I evil?

Yes.

I *was* dangerous. I *was* evil.

The nurse was right: I had no business working with patients.

I decided to abandon my aim at nursing. I should not have the lives of others in my hands. My vindictiveness made me unsafe, unfit, unworthy.

*Flowers in the Attic. Petals on the Wind.* Two connecting novels by V. C. Andrews. By accident, I happened to see *Flowers in the Attic* in Sam Weller's Books, an independent bookseller whose shelves had held the writings of the well-known and the unknown since the 1920s. I remembered reading a review of *Flowers in the Attic.* Both the writing and the story, the reviewer said, were fresh, authentic, and gripping. I quickly bought the thick paperback and was greedy to start it

In my life, many a book had made its way into my hands, but *Flowers in the Attic* was unlike any I had ever read. Written in the first person, it was a labyrinthic *roman à clef* about four children locked in an attic by their mother and grandmother, and the desperation, neglect, abuse, predation, killing, and incest that occurred during their captivity. The writing was as evocative as it was distressing. From prologue to epilogue, the book was an agonizing crossing. From opening to closing, it both repelled the reader and seduced him.

Some people cry over what they read. I never did...until I read V. C. Andrews' inaugural novel. At the close of the book, one of the four children dies. His name was Cory. He was but eight years old. He dies at the hands of his own grandmother. Slowly, methodically, she poisons him. Though not a mother herself, V. C. Andrews knew children: she knew how they talked, how they acted, and how they felt. She knitted this knowledge into her writing. It was this inclusion of understanding and the story preceding, surrounding, and following Cory's death that sent me to a place I rarely visited: my basement. Cory had died from his imprisonment. I, too, had been imprisoned, not above, but below. With David Gates' "Clouds Suite" playing above me, I wept for hours for the little boy. The words in David Gates' pensive song seem to mirror the words in V. C. Andrews' torturous story.

In *Petals on the Wind*—the sequel to *Flowers in the Attic*—there is more anguish, more suffering, and more death.

Another review, a broad step from the first, said the concatenation was "...*a nonstop traffic accident; a downer from beginning to end.*" I didn't agree. I saw the series as liniment, a comforting balm to my restless mind. It assured me I wasn't the only one in the world with a haunting past. I read each book as slowly as I could to lengthen my stay in them.

As each person takes away a different perspective of a film, so does each reader of a book. From V. C. Andrews' gothic duology, the perspective I took away was more about V. C. Andrews the storyteller than the story from V. C. Andrews. I felt she was fixated on one thing: revenge. Untied, untamed, unrestrained revenge. If the story were true (as was implied at the beginning of the book), was the need for revenge a compulsion or a decision? If the story were a fabrication, why the fixation? Either way, I needed to know, for I, too, was obsessed with revenge. The answer lay only in V. C. Andrews herself. I needed to ask her. I had never written to anyone of consequence before. I never felt the need. But with V. C. Andrews, I did. I needed to know if the story were true or untrue. If it were true, was *she* was the protagonist, or had she written about someone else? I couldn't verify the story's veracity in any old newspapers or magazines. If the story were fictional, was the vengeful complexion of her story creational or constitutional? If it were creational, why did the aorta in her story carry only the blood of revenge and not forgiveness? If it were constitutional, how did she deal with her vengeful feelings? How did she live with them? Was it through her writing...or something else? I enjoyed the idea of revenge, and I enjoyed the act of delivering it, but in the end—as was evidenced by my reunion with Sharla—revenge was nothing but an immoral and brutal deed. I needed to know how to control it.

In a corner carrel in the University of Utah Library, I wrote my letter to V. C. Andrews. When completed, it was eleven pages in length, front and back. I was as intimate with my questions as I was with my confessions. I so hoped the bluntness of my words would not offend her. I simply wanted and needed her to know about me, and I wanted and needed to know about her. I didn't proof or reread the letter, for I didn't want to dilute its honesty and purity with an editorial eye.

Once I arrived home, I sealed it in a long envelope, and then I sealed that envelope in a larger one. Addressing it to Pocket Books, I hoped they would forward it on to her.

Every day, I rushed home to see if there was a reply. Only ads and bills lay in the mailbox. After many weeks, I accepted that my letter had either reached Pocket Books and been lost, or it had reached V. C. Andrews and been thrown away.

After returning home from work one Saturday, I walked unhurriedly to the letter box. I didn't run to it like I used to. In the box was only one envelope. It had no return address. The writing was unmistakably feminine.

V. C. Andrews!

My hands trembled as I tore open the letter.

*August 25, 1981*
*Dear Owen,*

*I hardly know how to respond to a letter like yours. Please don't mind if I avoid answering some of your questions, for I have gone to a great deal of trouble in seeking to keep the true identities of Catherine, Chris, Carrie and Cory unknown. You can give up your search, for it would be impossible for you to hunt them up in ANY newspaper, or any profile on me. Although I did let* People *magazine do a story on me last fall. A decision I now regret. They exploited a temporary injury and made me 20 years older.*

*In every "novel" there is a great deal of truth, and I'm sure a psychologist could analyze the writer and come up with a pretty good personality profile. That is the risk all writers take when they put pen to paper and begin. We lay ourselves wide open for praise or ridicule--and I'm happy you have praise instead of the latter.*

*"Flowers"* was *based on a true story, although it was not about me and was greatly exaggerated. If you cried when you read "Flowers," be assured I cried even more when I wrote it. Life can be unkind, and Fate isn't always fair, but still we have to go on and make the most of it and think the more suffering we have lived through, the stronger we become. It's like developing muscles...the more we exercise (and that can be painful), the larger our muscles become.*

*You called yourself evil. You are NOT evil. You don't even come close. I know what evil is, and you aren't it. You couldn't have written the kind of letter you did if you were. If you were evil, you wouldn't feel the guilt you do over Sharla. Good men feel shame, evil men don't. Evil is when a man should act but doesn't, and evil is when a man shouldn't act but does. While what you did to Sharla in the hospital was regrettable and sad, you should remember that your actions were in the defense of your friend Austin, and defending a friend is never wrong.*

*Don't give up on your nursing career because of what happened with Sharla. And don't let revenge eat up your life as Cathy did. Novels, I think, are more than just stories to entertain us--they are tools to help us grow. The capacity for revenge is within all of us. The secret is to not let it consume us, and it will if we let it. People, I think, are naturally bent toward darkness. We must force ourselves to turn toward the light. That's what you must do, Owen. Turn in the direction you know to be right. You have a true talent for helping others--don't throw that gift away, for not everyone has been given it. Turn back toward the bright future of nursing and turn away from the dark attic of the past.*

*Please don't feel annoyed if I address you by your first name, whereas you were very respectful in calling me "Mrs. Andrews." I am a bit older than the ages you guessed, but I do hope you go on to find that perfect blonde, blue-eyed girl to love, and the world is full of beautiful women waiting for someone to adore them faithfully.*

*You express your feelings very well. I think if you gave some serious thought to writing, you would give me some stiff competition in the bookstores, although goodness knows I have enough of that already. Your use of adjectives, allegories, portmanteaus, and alliteration is very striking. So, perhaps you can, like me, turn your unhappy background into an advantage and pour out your soul on paper.*

*You asked if there are any other stories in me beyond the "Flowers" series. There are, and I am looking forward to writing them. It will be a happy day when the "Dollanganger" series is over, for I find it traumatic. But then, that will always be the kind of book I write--the kind that makes the reader hurt, and hopefully, think.*

*With many best regards,*

*Virginia Andrews*
*(V. C. Andrews)*

I reread the letter many times. I couldn't believe she actually wrote me back, even though that had been my hope from the start.

For many days, I intently considered her words. She was right: I shouldn't let the incident with Sharla deflect me from the calling of my heart. I needed to go back. I needed to set my sights on nursing once more.

Something else V. C. Andrews told me that swirled in my mind: putting my soul on paper. I had never even considered it. Perhaps I should. Heaven knew, I certainly had plenty to put down.

# Part 3

# CHAPTER 15

# *20 Years Later*

*"It is men who raise a gallows, but it is the man who hangs
from it who drives the first nail."*

THAYER ARENTS

I was carrying Timmy back to his room. He was squeezing my nose like a toy ball. Each time he compressed it, I would quack like a duck. He would throw his head back and giggle.

Then, suddenly, he froze in my arms. He was now staring straight ahead. Fear was wedged in his young, blue eyes. His parents were walking toward us. He cinched his arms around my neck. His hold was so tight I could barely breathe. I didn't want to frighten him by repositioning him too quickly—if I did, he would think I was returning him to his parents—so I slowly raised the arm on which he was sitting and turned him a few inches to one side. This simple negotiation allowed the air to pass again.

"We did further X-rays on Timmy," I notified the parents once their acned grilles were close to mine.

Both the mother and father were no more than children themselves; late teens at most. Below a black and mangy do-rag, tattoos of spiders and flies covered the father's neck. Bannered across the mother's nearly exposed left breast were the words *Jesus Is Dead*. Below broom-textured, pink hair, a red swastika was blazoned across her forehead. They were angry human beings who vented their immature hostility and rage on their son. They had brought him into the ER a few days before and told the attending physician he fell down the basement stairs. After X-rays were taken, it was discovered the boy's right femur was fractured. The ER doctor suspected the injuries were not the result of a fall but abuse. He admitted the three-year-old boy for observation. It was discovered through subsequent X-rays that older fractures were also present.

The little boy would not look at his parents. His body was trembling.

"We want our kid!" the mother told me in a shrill voice.

"Well, you're not going to get him," I came back. "You'll have to go through me first."

"You can't keep our kid!" the father reared and reached for the boy.

With the celerity of a young man, I grabbed the father's wrist. "You're not touching him. You're never going to touch him again. Either of you. He's going into Child Protective Services. Your dirty little secret is out. Those additional X-rays we did—they showed previous breaks. Timmy didn't fall down the stairs—not this time or any other. You've been beating him. Maybe even other things. People like you should be put away and sterilized so you can never hurt another child again. If you had to have sex, why didn't you go out and get some condoms? Why did you bring a child into the world only to hurt him? He's just a little boy! A parent is supposed to stand between his child and harm—not push him in front of it! Children have enough predators in the world—their parents shouldn't be part of the pack. You had a chance to make your little boy smile and laugh and grow; instead, you beat him like a speed bag and filled his mind with terror. You're nothing but—"

"What's going on here?" a woman asked.

We all turned.

It was Desiree Neil, a stylish, sixtyish woman with burnished, auburn hair. She was the charge nurse that day. Resourceful, alert, and commanding, she could diffuse any situation. She had no children of her own, which made me wonder if that were the reason she wanted to care for them as a profession.

"This pervert here won't give me my kid!" the father stormed.

"You watch your mouth, young man!" Desiree called the boy down. "Owen is our best nurse. Your son couldn't be in better hands."

"He's in the hands of a perv! No old guy likes to work with little kids unless he likes to *touch* little kids. Especially when they're little boys."

I still had hold of the father's wrist. I gripped it tighter.

"Let go of my wrist, man!" he routed. "That hurts!"

"Let go of him, Owen," Desiree ordered. "You don't want to lose your job over the likes of him."

She reached over and yanked my hand away. I started to speak, but she pointed her finger at me and shook her head.

A small crowd of staff was beginning to gather around us.

"Young man," she turned to the father, "you could be sued for what you just said. But we won't go that far. We'll just consider the source, which happens to be a cur who doesn't have the good sense God gave a goose. You're to leave here at once. Your child is going into Protective Services. From here on, you'll be dealing with them. Now, if you don't want to spend the night in jail for endangering this child, you'll take yourself on home, along with your underaged ladylove."

"I'm Timmy's mother, you stupid bitch!" the girl retaliated.

"Owen, go call Security, please," Desiree tongued calmly.

The father lunged for Desiree. I gave Timmy to Stacey, another nurse who was standing close to me. Immediately, Timmy began to scream.

The father had Desiree pinned against the wall and was choking her. I grabbed the tails of the do-rag and threw him to the ground. He landed facedown. Before he could get up to renew his fight, I sprang onto his body and commandeered the small of his back. I grabbed his hands and wrenched them over his coccyx. He yelled in pain. Though cursing and jerking, he wasn't going anywhere. He might have been younger and sprier, but I was heavier and more experienced.

As if they had been hiding in a nearby closet, two security officers were instantly on the floor and took command of the father and mother.

Timmy was still screaming. He was squirming wildly in Stacey's arms, his own arms outstretched for me.

I went over to Stacey. He almost tumbled out of her grasp trying to get to me. Once in my arms, he stopped screaming and laid his head on my shoulder.

I took Timmy back to his room and read him Dr. Seuss until he fell asleep.

I stroked his soft, blond hair while he slept. I wondered what kind of future he would have. He would not go back to his biological parents—that much was certain. But would his new parents be any better? Mine certainly weren't. But times were different than when I was a boy. Foster and adoptive parents were screened more thoroughly than they once were. Timmy was such a sweet and loving child...he deserved sweet and loving parents.

I bent down and kissed his forehead.

Snug in his arms was a stuffed animal...a very old stuffed animal. Larry the janitor had given it to a scared little boy a long time ago. It was time that little boy gave it to another scared little boy.

"Take good care of him, Yogidog," I said, and gave Timmy one last kiss. Then I stood and turned to leave.

Desiree was standing in the doorway with her hands tucked in her pink scrub pants. "Why aren't you a father?" she asked. "You'd be Dad of the Decade."

"Quite the day, eh?" I said, changing the subject.

"Indeed it was. I think you and I could use a drink."

"I don't drink."

"Then I think we could use a banana split or something. I don't want to go home just yet."

"Won't your husband wonder where you are?"

"If I were gone for a few weeks he might, but not an evening. Come on, humor an old woman."

"You're not an old woman."

"Don't argue with your elders."

I stood silently next to Timmy's crib, not knowing how to tell her no. I had lived my life completely alone; I wanted no friendships or connections, for connections, at some point, have to be *dis*connected. People, the way I saw it, were never a hello—they were always a good-bye. I had lived through enough endings—I wasn't about to live through any more.

Seeing that I was not encouraging an evening, Desiree showed disappointment, almost hurt. I truly did not want to spend time with anyone outside of work, no matter who it was. But she had had a rough day—it wasn't going to kill me to spend a few hours with her.

"How does Italian suit you?" I proposed.

She grinned. "Right down to the ground."

Giovanni's Grill had been part of the dining landscape of the city for decades. Abutting the driveway of an aged and down-at-the-heels apartment house, the restaurant was an unusually long building that was strangely out of place. But it was a quiet restaurant and dimly lit, which is what I needed after the harsh fluorescents at the hospital.

A waiter costumed as an elf took us to our table. *Mannheim Steamroller Christmas* was playing softly in the background.

"You never answered my question," Desiree reopened the subject after we ordered. "Why aren't you a father?"

"Why aren't you a mother?"

"Don't spin this around to me. You have neither chick nor child. Why?"

"It's…" I shook my head, not knowing really how to answer.

"Complicated?"

"Something of the sort."

"You don't like talking about yourself, do you?"

"I don't see the point."

A scrim of confusion folded over her eyes. "Then why did you write a book?"

A flash fire of anger shot through me. I thought no one at the hospital knew about my book. My private and secret thoughts were for the eyes of strangers only. The eyes of those who knew me were allowed nothing.

"Yes," she unveiled, "I read it. Very poignant. Very enlightening. And *very* well written. I cried in many places. If you're wondering how

I knew about it, Kim Reams in Dietary told me. She said she was in Bakers Shoes in Valley Fair Mall and saw it lying on one of the chairs. She has a huge crush on you, by the way. So does Perry Dracos in Respiratory. Who do you think is cuter, him or her?"

"I honestly haven't given it much thought."

"But if you *were* to think about it, who's cuter?"

"If I say Kim, you'll think I'm interested. If I say Perry, you'll think I'm gay."

"Are you?"

"Would I write a straight love story if I were?"

"Maybe. Maybe you're bi."

"What is this all about, Desiree? Why are you so interested in my sexuality?"

"Are you by yourself because you're gay?"

"Just because a man chooses to live his life alone does not mean he is gay. Maybe he's just had his fill of the world, so he stays away from it."

"I don't mean to pry, I really don't. I just worry about you. I want you to be happy, whether it's with a woman or a man."

"Don't waste your feelings on me."

"That's a terrible thing to say about yourself. I truly care about you, and I want the best for you. You're an amazing man. You really are. You need someone in your life, Owen. You definitely need children. Man your age shouldn't be alone. It isn't healthy. What are you, thirty-four, thirty-five?"

"Forty-one."

"You underscore my point even more. You're closing in on middle age. You need some kids of your own before it's too late. If you have them when you're older, it's too hard on your body. And if anyone should have children, it's *you*. Today I said you were the best nurse we have—I meant it. In all my years, I have never seen a nurse—or anyone, for that matter—who has a way with children like you do. It's as if you're a guardian angel sent from Heaven and they know it."

"Hardly a guardian angel."

"No? What about today? As soon as Timmy was back in your arms, he stopped crying. Whenever one of us has to give an injection, we come to you. The children never cry when you give them shots. Never."

"The art of injection is distraction. You know that. Just like the magician: he redirects the attention of his watchers away from his endeavor. And, of course, there's speed. The faster the needle, the fewer the tears. This, too, you know."

"Yeah, I know. But it's more than technique—it's a gift. I don't have it. You do. You get kids to relax, and *that's* the secret. Injections are less painful if the person is at ease. You get kids to loosen up. You make them feel at peace, even when they're dying."

"Children are far less afraid of death than adults. It has nothing to do with me."

"You underestimate yourself. You'd be a father like no other."

"I doubt that."

"I don't. Although I have to admit that while marriage would be good for you, it would be a challenge."

"It would be impossible."

"No, not impossible—just challenging. You're literally two different people: one with adults, one with children. Remember the little boy last Christmas who was abandoned in our parking lot. All he ever said was, *'Momma go bye-bye car.'* You wept for him like he was your own. I've seen you do extraordinary things with children. I've seen you cry with a child who's in pain from cancer; I've seen you hold a child's hand and caresses his brow as he passes away; I've seen you console a child when she asks why her mommy hits her; I've seen you comfort a child who has lost her doggy; I've seen you comfort a child when he's lost a leg or an arm; I've seen you color with a child who has no friends; I've seen you listen to a child who can barely talk; I've seen you sing a child to sleep; I've seen you walk with a child all the way to Surgery, and then stay with him the whole night so when he wakes up the next morning there would be somebody there; I've seen you make tears of fear on a child vanish and tears from laughter take their place; I've seen you literally work wonders with kids. And yet, when you're with adults, you're not so...angelic."

"It depends on the adults."

"True. When that doctor yelled at that housekeeper last year, you immediately went to the housekeeper's defense. I had never seen a doctor and a nurse go at it before. I wouldn't have imagined you as a screamer. Administration called you in for that."

"Yes, doctors, not nurses, bring in the rubles."

"But they didn't fire you. The doctor wanted you gone, but the CNO went to bat for you. Funny how that worked out—it was the *doctor* who eventually went away. Someone ignited a rumor he was touching a few of his patients inappropriately. His privileges were terminated. The hospital couldn't afford to have that get out, even if it weren't proven to be true. They never found out who started the scandal. Curious it all started after the incident with the housekeeper."

"It is curious, isn't it? But not terribly heartbreaking. He had the skill of a missile in flight, but all the charm of a warhead going off. Just one less self-obsessed, self-proclaimed deity walking on our waters."

"See what I mean?—that enthusiastic scorn you have for adults. And then there was Lisa last month. When I told you someone had slashed all her tires, you smiled. Kind of like how you're smiling right now. She was very upset about it."

"Yes, she had to come to work in her Audi rather than her Lexus. Poor child."

"There it is again. If an adult—correction, if an *advantaged* adult—has a problem, you deride them."

"Most of the difficulties adults deal with come from their own hands. Not so with children."

"Lisa didn't bring that on herself."

"But she did. Lisa is a self-minded, money-minded, entitlement-minded upstart. I've seen the way she is with the senior volunteers. She acts like she's better than they are simply because she's young and they aren't. I heard her say to one of them once, '*I'll never be old like you*.' The fool says in his heart, '*There is no God*.' He also says, '*I will never grow old*.' Whatever dishes of humility Lisa is served, she deserves. Karma is simply providing her the paycheck she has earned."

"Are there *any* adults you like?"

"Not really. Some adults, like the housekeeper who was humiliated by the doctor, I feel sorry for. Others, like you, I respect. But there are none I particularly like."

"Do you *want* to like anybody? Do you ever want to love and be loved?"

"Like Perry and Kim, I truly don't give it much thought."

"I think you give it a lot of thought. If you didn't, you wouldn't have written such a beautiful love story. You can't write about love if you don't believe in it."

"Love stories sell."

"Horseradish! I think you really want love—you just don't know how to trust anyone to get it. The only people you trust are children."

"God said, '*Unless you turn and become like little children, you will never enter the kingdom of Heaven.*' We're supposed to model ourselves after little children, but instead we run from them. We run to adulthood. We all race to be grownups. Monsters."

"I'm curious about something. Why didn't the main character in your book ever have children since you adore them so much?"

I thought about it for a while. "I don't know. That's a good question. Maybe I made the characters as good as children, so none were needed."

"Interesting. You want to know what I liked most about your book?"

"While most prefer to be ruined by praise rather than saved by criticism, I prefer the reverse—but I'll make an exception just this once and join the majority. So please, praise away."

"Did you ever watch *St. Elsewhere*?"

"It was one of the best shows ever to come through an antenna."

"Your book was like that show. I mean, it flowed like it. A scene went along, then it just stopped. Then another scene went along, and then that one just stopped. Characters would come and go; relationships would flourish, then die off. No tidy endings, no fancy bows on the final sentences. Just like life."

Her observations pleased me.

"Why the smile?" she asked.

"You're the first person to ever notice that I patterned my style after *St. Elsewhere*. I had hoped it would be noticed."

"It was."

The waiter brought us our meals. Spaghetti Siracusani was mine; Fettuccine Florentine was Desiree's.

"I answered *your* question," I said, curling some spaghetti atop my spoon, "now you answer mine. Why aren't you a mother?"

"It wasn't by choice, believe me. When Harold and I were dating, he said he really wanted children. Then after we were married, he said he didn't. *Ever.* I didn't know what to do. I didn't want to divorce him, so I held onto the hope he would someday change. He didn't."

"Such resolve must have made intimacy rather tricky."

"It made it impossible. We slept together, but we never once made love. He would take care of himself and then go to sleep."

"What about you? Didn't he care about *your* needs?"

"Nope. But I adapted. Besides, as audacious as women might be about liking sex, they don't need it all the time like men. Women need love more than they need intercourse. They need tenderness and affection and security more than they need physical fulfillment. The old adage is true: Men give love to get sex, and women give sex to get love."

"You didn't have *any* craving for sex?"

"Occasionally, but not all the time."

"Why didn't you use condoms or something?"

"He didn't want to take the chance of me getting pregnant."

"He hated children that much?"

"He hated the thought of being tied down to them."

"Why did you stay? Why did *he* stay?"

"He stayed because he loved me…in his own peculiar way. Me, I stayed because, like I said, I had hoped he would eventually change. But he didn't. Before we knew it, our best years were behind us, and we were too old to start over. We're simply roommates now, two people sharing expenses."

"Albert Einstein once said, '*Men marry women with the hope they will* never *change. Women marry men with the hope they* will *change. Invariably, they both are disappointed.*' He sure pierced the bullseye on that one."

"I never figured Einstein for a psychologist."

"Still think I should go on a quest for a wife?"

"My husband and I are the rare—if not freakish—exception."

"You're not as rare as you think. Fifty percent of all marriages fail. Each divorce has its own set of causes; some of the reasons are simple, some bizarre. But people keep tying that matrimonial knot, only to have to untie it later. They just don't learn. They keep playing the same game over and over, hoping to win. I think every couple should have to watch the movie *War Games* before they are allowed to marry."

"*War Games?*"

"Remember the moral of the movie?"

"I never saw it."

"The best morals are the simplest ones. The moral of the movie was very simple. It was about games. There are certain games in this life that, no matter how intelligent and diligent you are, you can't beat, so the only way to win them is not to play them. Love is such a game. It's a game of unending competition, unnecessary secrets, unwarranted distrust, and unreasonable expectations. It's impossible to succeed at it...so the only way to win is to not play."

"That's cynical in all capital letters."

"Cynical but true. *Mass Appeal* was another movie with a profound moral about giving your heart away. Its message, though bleak and lunar, was also accurate."

"And what was that?"

"That—in the end—friends are flighty, promises are transitory, and love is untrustworthy."

"Your outlook is so astray," she said, shaking her head.

"No, it isn't. Love has a mind all its own, and it doesn't mind if you get hurt. It isn't worth it to pursue love, in any form. In the end, you just get crushed, robbed of the best parts of yourself. If you stay alone, you don't get hurt. If you get close, you do."

"You know what I think? I think you've been watching too many serious movies. You need some comedy in your life. It would do you some good. Just last week I was reading about laughing. Did you know that when you laugh, your brain releases endo—"

"Endorphins. Yes, I know. A false high. Wouldn't matter if it wasn't a false high—I hate comedies. They go for laughs at the expense of all that is good. They cheapen and trivialize and degrade everything that is decent—friendship, marriage, children, the human body, sex, even God Himself."

"Serious movies do the same thing—just without the punch lines."

"I don't agree. Dramas try to make sense of the world—they don't make fun of it. Comedies don't care about reaching people—all they care about is reaching for laughs, regardless of how offensive the humor is. Dramas aren't about that. A pity, though, that the actors who perform in them aren't half the people their characters are."

"Humor reaches out to people too, just in a different way. Remember what they say—much truth is said in jest. I think people are more open to instruction or correction when their hearts aren't weighed down with life. Comedy opens the window and forces us to look at ourselves—our imperfections, our shortcomings, even our insecurities. Take the other night. There was this Neil Simon movie on cable—*I Ought to Be in Pictures*. Walter Matthau's was in it. His character was just like you."

"Me?"

"There was this scene where Ann-Margret asked Walter Matthau what it was about attachments that he disliked so much, and Walter Matthau said, 'Un*attachments*.' That's you, through and through. Hasn't there ever been anyone special in your life?"

Roxanne appeared in my mind. "Once. A long time ago."

"Nobody since?"

"Nope."

"Not to put too fine a point on it, but what about…"

"Sex?"

She nodded.

"I have no interest in it," I took a long drink of Pepsi. "I am what you might say…*uninterested and unclaimed*."

Her face wrinkled. "Is that your way of saying…you're a virgin?"

"A *dead* virgin."

Her face froze. "Wow. I've never heard of a man your age—"

"If clergy can be celibate, why not laity? You yourself said women don't want sex. So why should men?"

"I didn't say we *never* want it."

"Well, *I* don't."

"That's not normal, Owen."

"One thing I have never been is normal."

"So you never, ever get…"

"Amorous? No, I don't. When I was teenager, I was always…*ready*. That was the only area in which I *was* normal."

"Then somebody came along and stepped on you and—"

"Can we change the subject, please?" I requested. The conversation was dragging me back to ground I had left behind long ago. I didn't want to continue.

"I'm sorry. Nosiness has always been one of my worst faults."

"It's all right. I'm meddlesome myself sometimes. My mother used to say my eagerness to learn was going to get me far, and then get me in trouble afterward."

"Are you close to your mother?"

"She's dead. They're both dead. They're all dead. My natural parents died when I was a boy; my adoptive parents when I was older. As a matter of fact, my adoptive mother died ten years ago yesterday."

"It must have been devastating to be left all alone like that."

"It didn't hurt that I was alone; it hurt that I left *her* alone. I should have been there for her, but I wasn't. I was too immersed in my own life. Misspent youth."

"We all do things when we're young that we regret later. I still feel awful for how I treated my parents when I was a teenager. If ever there was an unprincipled daughter, it was me. I was the kind of girl who made Patty Hearst look like Princess Diana. I was hateful, ungrateful, and disrespectful. So many things I wish I could take back. But I was young, and we do terribly unkind things when we're young."

"Youth is not a hall pass to err and injure."

"Are those your words or someone else's? I notice you like to use quotes."

"A quote is to speech what salt is to food—both enhance. William Lane Craig frequently cites the views of others. If he can do it, so can I."

"Who's William Lane Craig?"

"Historian, apologist, philosopher. Incredible mind. Incredible man. I bet *he* wouldn't have left his mother alone in a nursing home."

"Owen, one of the worst things you can ever do is compare yourself to someone else. Everybody's different; every situation is different. None of us can change what we did—all we can change is what we do. If you dwell on what you should have done, you'll be beating yourself up for the rest of your life."

"Just punishment for conscious mistreatment. You say the past cannot be changed. True. Since we cannot change it, we must pay for it. That is why we have prisons. Punishment for conscious mistreatment."

"And *your* prison is some self-imposed guilt? What is it accomplishing?"

"Punishment is not a choice. It's a necessity. Proper payment."

"And are you going to punish yourself forever?"

"Some punishments should never end."

"What about forgiveness?"

"What about it?"

"Do you believe in it?"

"For others, yes. For me, no."

"What makes you above mercy?"

"Because I don't deserve it."

"There is no trespass too high for absolution. What could you have done that's made you so terrible?"

"The list would take us into tomorrow."

"I doubt that. Each of us is our own worst judge. You want to know what I think? I think there are people in this world who are so hard-boiled they feel absolutely nothing. And then there are those who are so sensitive they feel absolutely everything. That's you. You're the opposite of the hard-as-nails guy who wouldn't bleed if he were cut in half. You bleed for *everything.* Okay, so you've done and said some things you regret—you're no different from anyone else. Stop wallowing in your failures. It accomplishes nothing. Do something positive with your wrongs—don't just stare at them in your self-made prison. I know you're a man who believes in God, so do what He says: '*Go and sin no more.'* He's saying leave the bad stuff behind and move forward. He's *not* saying, *'Go home and dwell on it.'*"

"He also said we are supposed to become like little children. Children are pure, humble, without malice. That's not me. Maybe that's why God loves little children more than adults. Adults are loathsome things. Children aren't. Adults don't have a conscience. Children do. Adults can hurt others with the greatest of ease. Children can't. Adults have to have big things to be satisfied. Children don't."

"I don't know about that. Adults can benefit tremendously from little things."

"Like what?"

"Like little dogs. I think a dog would be just the answer for you. It would pull you out of the deep swamp you're stuck in. You don't have a dog, do you?"

"No."

"I do. A Chihuahua. His name is Yoda, from *The Empire Strikes Back*, but most of the time I call him Yodapapoda. He's helped me through many hard times. In many ways, dogs are better than people. They stay with you no matter what; they're there at your side through thin and thick, good and bad, life and death. They're not judgmental or grudge-holding or moody. They don't care if you're bald or ugly, skinny or fat, short or tall. They don't care if you have fifteen toes or no toes. They sense when you're sad or happy or sick. They can't converse, but they're great listeners. They're there when you're on the ropes or on the edge. They're there when friends and family don't want to be."

"I can't have a dog where I live. My condominium doesn't allow them."

"Maybe you should consider getting a house. You can do anything you want when you own your own home."

"I had a home once. I sold it years ago. Too many bad memories."

"What about an apartment? There's a real classy apartment house a couple of streets down from me on Butler Ave. I have a friend who lives on the top floor. They allow pets. It's the Rigby Apartments. It's an older place that's been totally renovated. I can get you their number if you want. Or I can ask my friend if they have a vacancy.

"Come to think of it, my place has two apartments available. It's not far from here. All new. Not even a year old. They allow pets too. Could be just the ticket for you."

Why was she telling me all these things? Why did she even care? She said she wanted the best for me...but why? Was there an extra layer of something beneath her concern? I needed to end this evening as quickly as possible.

"No, thank you," I said. "But it's nice of you to offer."

"I think a dog would be just what the doctor ordered. You know what they say—*God's in dogs.*"

"I had a dog once. A Chihuahua, like yours. My natural father killed it in front of me."

"That's terrible. I'm so sorry."

"I'm not going to face another good-bye, Desiree, and pets have a bad habit of dying long before their owners."

"Good-byes are a part of the natural order of things, Owen. You know that. Look at your book: it's full of good-byes. Endings are a part of life."

"Not *my* life. Not anymore."

"Then why is your book filled with them?"

"Invented good-byes and real good-byes I keep in separate cages. One I let loose on paper; the other I never let loose. One is useful, the other is baneful."

"Okay—so if you never let real good-byes loose, why are you a nurse? Patients come and go like the tide."

"Patients are different—I don't invest in them; I just help them."

"If you didn't invest yourself, you wouldn't be such a good nurse."

"I mean, I don't invest my heart."

She laughed and shook her head. "Hogwash! You invest your heart more than anyone I know. You just don't want anyone to know it. You think every relationship is going to end badly. You've thrown away most of your life because you were afraid of getting hurt. Are you going to throw away what's left of it too? Are you going to spend your last years doing what you're doing now—coming to work and then going home and being alone?"

"I just want to help children. Short of that, I really don't care if I live or die."

Her face froze for a moment. "Owen, you shouldn't say a thing like that. It worries me."

"I say again, don't waste your feelings on me."

She pursed her lips in contemplation. "Have you ever thought about maybe getting some counseling? I go myself. The right counselor can do a world of good. You won't be the same person when you're done."

"Counselors can't change what you are."

"No, but they can help you change the way you look at yourself."

"Counselors are paid to build you up. If they weren't, they'd tear you down and throw you away, because deep down they know people are nothing more than wild animals dressed in pleated pants and polished shoes. Savagery is baked into the species."

"Children are people too—why aren't *they* wild animals?"

"I meant *adults* are ferine, not little children."

"I don't know. I've known some catty, bratty kids in my day."

"By and large, they are not."

"By and large, neither are adults. You shouldn't lump them all together."

"Point taken."

"Have you *always* been so unhappy?"

"When you think about it, happiness is truly wrong, even sinful. How can anyone allow himself to feel happiness when so many in the world aren't?"

"Seen from a draconian point of view, you're probably right, but that wasn't the question, was it? Have you always been so unhappy?"

"Not always."

"Were you ever happy?"

"Once. A lifetime ago. There was a short time when I was a teenager when—" I stopped. I was getting pulled back again. "Doesn't matter."

"You know, Owen, happiness is a lot like a cake: it doesn't make itself—*you* have to make it."

"*Please*—spare me the poster platitudes."

"Someone must have kicked you pretty hard."

"I let them kick me by letting them get close to me. My mistake. I'll never make it again."

"Don't you ever want to be happy again?"

"That is an impossibility, so the desire is pointless. Let's not talk about this anymore, okay? Let's just finish our meal and call it an evening."

I froze when I saw her. Just like Timmy froze when he saw his parents.

I couldn't breathe. I felt like I was going to collapse.

It *couldn't* be her.

She was dead.

Everyone knew it. Especially me.

She was gone...so how could she be standing there?

Speaking with Beth Lyman, a young CNA, was a girl who was ripped from my life when I was fourteen.

At 4:52 in the afternoon, on March 9, 1975, she died. At nearly five in the afternoon, on November 9, 2001, over a quarter-century after her death, she was in my eyes again.

*Kylie.*

She must have sensed eyes watching her, for she turned from Beth and looked my way.

My body went numb, as if it had been dosed with a potent narcotic.

Her eyes widened, then her lips fanned out into a joyous smile. Without any parting words to Beth, she rushed in my direction.

I had only seconds to recover. I took some quick, deep breaths.

She threw her arms around my neck and embraced me tightly. For many seconds, she enclosed me in her arms, her head against my shoulder.

My hands gently touched her back. I couldn't believe I was holding her again. I closed my eyes and then forced them open, thinking it a dream.

It was no dream; I was still there, and she was still there.

She released her arms and stared into my eyes.

"Owen," she murmured, "it's so good to see you! Look at you! Look how handsome you are! You were something when I was a kid—now you're something else!"

"*Kylie...*" was all I could say.

"Kylie?" she smiled with surprise, then sympathy. "No, no...Owen, I'm not Kylie. I'm Megan, her sister. Remember me? Remember Mittens, you found him that Christmas Eve?"

"*Megan?*" I was mortified. How could I have made such a terrible mistake? I felt my face burn. "I'm so sorry. That was unbelievably—"

"Don't worry about it. Really. I've been told it before. It's a compliment that I look like her. She was a beautiful girl."

"Why...why are you here?"

"My daughter needs surgery."

"*Your daughter?*"

"Yeah, poor thing, she's scared to death. I told her an appendectomy is nothing these days. She'll be in and out in no time. She'll be back to playing with her paints and—"

"An appendectomy? Why isn't she in surgery?"

"They said they'll get her in as soon as they can. They said they have a lot of add-ons today. She'll probably have to stay the night since it's so late."

"They know best."

"What about you? Why are you here?"

"I work here. I'm a nurse."

"No kidding. Small world. You just coming on?"

"Actually, I'm off today. I just came in for my annual review."

"How'd it go?"

"Well, I'm still employed."

"I bet they all love you here."

I smiled reflectively. "Not all. Where's your husband? Is he with your daughter?"

She cleared her throat, as if talking had suddenly become difficult. Ponds of tears formed in her eyes.

"I'm sorry, did I say something I shouldn't have?" I said.

"No. No. My husband...he...he died two years ago. He was in Desert Storm. He left as one man and came back another. He took his own life. He had really bad PTSD. He tried to fight it...but...it eventually won."

"I'm sorry."

"Yeah, he was a wonderful man. The only good thing about his death was that he wasn't here to see what happened to us two months ago. He loved this country. Seeing those planes kill so many Americans would have destroyed him."

"Yes, it was...unbelievable. I had to throw away the clothes I wore that day. The smells wouldn't come out. It's like they glued themselves to the fibers. So much dust. So much paper. So much smoke. It was one of those times in your life when you realize how infinitesimal and impermanent you are. And how breakable."

"Wait—you were there?"

I nodded. "Right place, wrong time. I was—"

"*I don't want that!*" a young girl screamed from down the hall. "*I don't like you!*"

"That's Kylie!" Megan cried and ran to her daughter's room.

I ran with her.

Together we raced into the room, past the door with the number 452 affixed to it.

Beth was standing at the foot of the little girl's bed, visibly shaken. The little girl was crying and shivering, her knees folded up to her chin.

"What happened?" Megan asked, herself shaken.

"I don't know," Beth answered, beside herself. "I just went to take her blood pressure, and she got upset. I don't understand it—I took it earlier, and she was fine."

"Sweetheart," Megan soothed, touching her daughter's hair. "It's okay now."

The child, about four or five, swatted her mother's hand away. Megan instantly stepped back. She looked at me, helpless.

"She hasn't been the same since her dad passed away," Megan elucidated. "She frightens easily."

I went to Megan's side.

"May I?" I asked Megan.

"Sure," Megan said with surprise.

Smiling, I turned to Beth and pointed to the blood pressure machine. "Why don't you roll that out into the hall, and then could you bring me a manual cuff, please?"

Beth returned a nervous smile and rolled the Dinamap monitor out of the room.

Still smiling, I turned to Megan and said, "And, mom, why don't you have a seat in that chair by the window, and we'll see if we can't get a couple smiles out of this adorable little girl here."

Beth returned with a manual blood pressure cuff.

"Thank you," I said to Beth, setting the cuff on the bedside table. "In the break room is my guitar—would you go get it for me, please? It's on the window sill. You can't miss it."

"Sure." The tall, short-haired CNA was out of the room in a heartbeat.

Just as quickly, she was back.

I thanked Beth, took the guitar and stood it up against the side of the bed.

I squatted down so I was eye level with the little girl. Her eyes were still tightly shut.

"Hello, Kylie," I said softly to the small child with corn-silk hair. "My name is Owen. My, you're as pretty as the first day of May. And what a pretty name too. You know what the name Kylie means? It means graceful and beautiful and handsome. But handsome is for boys, huh? And you don't look like a boy. Boys look like frogs. I'm a boy, and I look like a frog. You don't look like a frog. You look like a princess."

The little girl opened her eyes.

"You want to know something else?" I said. "I once knew a girl named Kylie. She was the sweetest girl I ever knew."

"What happened to her?" the little girl asked, still curled in a ball.

"She went away."

"Far away?"

"Far away."

"My mommy had a sister named Kylie. She went away too. A long time ago. My mommy and daddy gave me her name."

"*'She is little stars now, making the face of Heaven so fine that all the world is in love with night.'* Romeo and Juliet. That was Kylie...and that is you."

She smiled. Then her face turned sad again. "Why do grownups have to die?"

"That is a very good question, Kylie. And you're a smart little girl for asking it. But I don't know the answer. I wish I did. Someday when you get to Heaven, God will tell you, and you'll smile because you'll understand. But until then, you'll just have to have faith that God knows what He's doing when He lets somebody go away. Kylie, what frightened you a minute ago?"

"That black thing hurts."

"You mean that black band she put around your arm?"

She nodded.

"She won't use it again. I promise. She was just taking your blood pressure. We all have blood pressure. If we didn't, we'd all be like strings of wet spaghetti and fall onto the floor."

I let myself slowly drop to the floor.

The little girl peeked over the bedrail.

"Help me, help me," I pitched my voice high like a character in a Saturday morning cartoon. "I need some blood pressure. Little girl up there, can you give me some?"

Kylie giggled and threw down some imaginary blood pressure.

Beth and Megan laughed.

Slowly rising, I squealed again, "Oh, thank you, little girl. Now I'm not wet spaghetti no more."

Kylie giggled again.

Staying in character, I said, "But I gots to know if I really gots blood pressure. Can you help me?"

Kylie nodded with a smile.

Slowly, I reached over and unrolled the cuff and handed it to Kylie. "Can you wrap that around my arm?" I squeaked.

I told her where to wrap it and to squeeze the rubber bulb a few times. She did so. When it was inflated, I smiled euphorically. "Ahhh...I gots blood pressure. Do you want to see if your mommy gots blood pressure?"

She nodded excitedly.

Megan came over to us, and Kylie wrapped the cuff around her mother's arm. After it was inflated, she, too, smiled rapturously. Then Beth lent herself to the skit.

"Looks like everybody has blood pressure," I said in my normal voice again. "Do you want to see if *you* have blood pressure? It won't hurt. Promise. I don't see no tears in this room." I turned to Megan. "Did it hurt, momma?"

Megan shook her head with a grin.

Smiling, Beth also shook her head.

"Okay," Kylie nodded hesitantly.

"That's my girl!" I exclaimed. "Now this is called a sphygmomanometer. Can you say that?"

She shook her head.

"I couldn't either for the longest time," I sided with her. "So I just called it '*mammy*.'"

Everyone in the room laughed, Kylie the loudest.

"That's a old lady's name," Kylie educated me.

"Doesn't it look like an old lady?" I asked.

"No. It looks like a sleeve of a sweater."

"A sleeve of a sweater? Naw...it's a old lady, and she wants to see if you got blood pressure. So why don't you lie back and relax your whole body. Close your eyes and think of your most favorite thing in the whole world."

Nervously, she closed her young, trusting eyes.

Slowly and carefully, I wrapped the cuff around her upper arm, inserted the chestpiece of the stethoscope I borrowed from Beth and inflated the cuff. Less than a minute later, I was done. Her systolic and diastolic pressures were normal.

"Okay, we're all done," I told her.

She opened her eyes and smiled widely. "That didn't hurt at all."

"Sometimes those machines can pinch a bit."

I turned to Beth. "Beth, make sure when they take her vitals for the rest of the day to use the manual cuff. And tell them to be extra gentle."

Beth nodded.

"You're a brave little girl," I said to Kylie.

"You're a good doctor," she beamed. "The best!"

I bent over, took her face in my hands and kissed her forehead.

Like water rushing into a mortally wounded ship, regrets flooded into every corner of my mind. Kylie reminded me of her mother when she was a little girl. Megan was such an empathetic child; for her alone, I should have gone to her sister's funeral. I should have stayed in her life. I remembered taking breakfast with Kylie and her family and Megan getting up from her chair and walking over to me and hugging me because she felt bad that I awoke every Christmas without presents. I remembered touching her face and feeling for the very first time the kind of closeness and protectiveness only a father feels. I remembered how magnificent that was. I would never know what it is like to be a father. Desiree was right: I stayed away from love because I was too afraid it would be taken away. Kissing that little child's forehead took me back to my fourteenth year when her namesake was still alive and offering me her love without conditions and without walls. The only wall was me.

I kissed Kylie's forehead once more, hoping in some way that Kylie the little girl in the hospital bed and Kylie the young girl in Heaven were together as one, if only for a moment, and that Kylie the girl in Heaven could see my sorrow for pushing her away.

"You kiss me the way my daddy used to," Kylie imparted.

"He was a very lucky man to have you for his little girl," I told her.

Reaching up, she wrapped her arms around my neck and kissed my cheek.

I had to steel myself so she wouldn't see my emotions.

From behind me, I heard weeping.

I turned around.

"What's wrong, Mommy?" Kylie asked. "Why are you crying?"

"I'm fine, sweetheart," Megan assured her daughter. "I'm just happy."

Kylie tugged on my sleeve. I faced the little girl again. She was eyeing the Gibson's headstock resting against the edge of her bed.

"What's that for?" she wanted to know.

"Well, you were kind of frightened earlier, and I thought a song might take your fears away. But since you're not afraid anymore, I guess we don't need it now."

"Please sing for me. Please. I love singing songs. Please."

I couldn't help it…my eyes teared. Her aunt also loved to sing. "Okay, sweetheart, I'll sing for you. I'll sing you a song your mommy's sister loved. It was called 'Will You Still Love Me Tomorrow.' It was first sung a long, long time ago by a group of girls called The Shirelles. Shortly before you were born, someone else sang the song. His name was Lobo. Your mommy's sister loved Lobo as much as I did, so I'll try to make this song sound just like him."

"You loved my mommy's sister, didn't you?"

The eyes of children may be young, but they see everything.

"Yes…but not until it was too late. So never close your heart to good people who want to get close to you." I stroked her forehead. "Now lie back down and let's see if we can make some happy music with this old guitar."

I picked up the 1982 acoustic Gibson and began.

Around Kylie's bed I walked and sang. The little girl wouldn't take her eyes off me. Smiling broadly, she bobbed and bounced her head to the rhythm of the melodious but sprightly cadenced, forty-year-old earworm. Seeing her enjoy herself so and seeing her mother and Beth enjoying it too made me perform the song more charismatically.

Midway through the song, I noticed the doorway to Kylie's room was crowded with staff and children. Some of the children came into the room and sat down on the floor. Soon, they were smiling and seesawing their heads to the breezy and copiously refrained love song.

Before wrapping up the song, I leaned in and kissed Kylie on the cheek. She clapped as only a small child does, with her fingers outstretched and palms flat together. Pure praise.

My final strum was met with wild applause from all the children; even the adults were ardently clapping.

"Another! Another! Another!" Kylie nearly screamed.

"Yeah, sing us another one!" Emily, a five-year-old with asthma who was sitting on the floor Indian-style with the other children, agreed exuberantly.

"Okay," I nodded. "I guess I must not be doing too badly if I'm asked to do an encore. How about one called 'Wide Open Spaces?'"

"Yeah!" all the children roared.

"Kylie's aunt," I told the children, my hand resting on Kylie's shoulder, "whose name was also Kylie, loved being outside. She loved big buildings and pretty flowers and sweeping deserts and huge mountains. So this is for her, and for her niece. It was sung by a man who simply goes by the name Lobo."

The children laughed at the funny-sounding name.

I sat down on the edge of the bed.

Like the song preceding it, "Wide Open Spaces" was allegretto in tempo and easy on the mind: it had no abstruse meanings, no heavy messages. It was simply a chipper, 1990s pop song with a snappy melody and happy hooks.

Most of the children had probably never seen the rippling air in a desert or smelled the earth of a prairie, but they enjoyed Lobo's lyrics describing them nevertheless.

When I finished, they all shouted, "More, more!"

Interned by the many smiling faces, I said, "Okay. How about some Peter Cetera?"

"Yea!" Emily called out. "My mommy plays him in the car!"

"Kylie's aunt loved him too."

"I'm Coming Home" was the first song I sang. Though andante in pace, it still delighted all the young ears in the room. I knew it wasn't just the song that pulled them in; it was the delivery. With a degree of *de jure* immodesty, I knew I had a pleasing voice; not opera-esque by any stretch, but aurally pleasing just the same. I wished my Kylie, the Kylie of 1975, had been there with all the children—I would have sung to her into the night.

"Whatever Gets You Through," "Have A Little Faith," "Perfect World"—all Peter Cetera works—were the other tunes I and my guitar gave my junior attendees.

"Sing another! Sing Another! Sing another!" they all chanted after I had finished.

I turned to Kylie. "Do you want another? You're the guest of honor."
She nodded feverishly.

"All right. I think you'll like this one. A band named The La's—who lived way across the ocean in England—came up with it. They call it 'There She Goes.'"

To match the original song, and to entertain the children, I attached a fun falsetto to my voice. The children got up from the floor and started to dance to the lively though cryptic piece. I didn't know the meaning of the song, nor did I want to; I just liked its frolicsome beat.

I was on the last bar when a woman in teal scrubs came into the room.

"Sorry to interrupt," she said, "but I'm here for Kylie Gourde."
Kylie immediately started to cry.

Distraught now, Megan went over to her daughter. "Oh, sweetheart, it's going to be okay. You'll be—"

"Mommy, please don't let her take me," Kylie begged. "Please. I won't ever say it hurts again."

"Honey, the operation won't hurt at all," Megan's voice was breaking from distress. "I'll be—"

"Please don't let the lady take me, Owen. Please," Kylie pleaded through her tears.

I set my guitar down on the floor and climbed onto Kylie's bed and sat down next to her.

"Kylie, honey," I took Kylie's small hand, "I promise you, it won't hurt at all, just like your mommy says. You'll be fast asleep for a little while and then you'll be wide awake again and all better. You won't have that pain in your side anymore. You'll be as speedy as a Frisbee and dandy as candy. I promise."

She wiped the tears from her face. "You promise?"

"Was I wrong about mammy?"

She slowly shook her head.

"And I'm not wrong about this. Your mommy and me will walk with you all the way downstairs, and we'll be right there when you wake up.

By tomorrow, you'll be happy and smiling again, just like you were when we were singing."

Kylie threw her arms around my waist. "I wish you were my daddy."

"How do you deal with it?" Megan asked exhaustedly. "All the sick children. All their tears, all their fears. Every time Kylie falls down or gets a cold or something, I hurt more than she does. I just want to keep her home twenty-four hours a day so she'll never get hurt. But I know I can't do that. Still, I want to shelter her from everything. I don't know how you deal with hurting kids every day, all day. Doesn't it get to you? Do you ever take it home? Do you ever just go into a room and cry your eyes out?"

Megan and I were sitting at a corner table in the hospital cafeteria. We were waiting for Kylie to get out of surgery. Megan was sipping a Sprite and nibbling on some sticky rice; I was nursing a Pepsi and trying to get down a dry grilled cheese.

"Many times, a child's tears are not as big as they seem," I said. "Crying is one of their ways of communicating and coping. It's just like when adults cry: it's a release. Tears from a child, while heartrending to see, are not a sign that their world is coming to an end. Tears are not always droplets of agony. The last thing you want to do is shelter a child from everything that will make him cry. Children need bad experiences to make them strong because, as you know, the world is a pitiless place. A child needs difficult times to teach him that he'll make it through future difficult times. A child cries for the first time, but the second time he may not, because he remembers he made it through the first time. Take Kylie. This surgery will make her strong. If she has another, she'll remember she made it through this one, and she won't be as afraid. It's the fear of the unknown that frightens us all. Once we know, we aren't nearly as fearful.

"Children are remarkably tough. Tougher than many adults. Some go through Hell and come out the other side. Those are the worst ones. The abused ones. Those are the ones who get to me. The pain of an injection or an accident or a chemo treatment or a surgery—that suffering goes away; but the pain from abuse, that never goes away. Ever. The children who've been abused sexually, the children who've been deliberately starved, the children who've been locked out of their homes, the children who've been locked in their basements or sheds, the children who've been beaten so badly they're just a swollen mass of purple and black, the children who die from their abuse, those are the ones I take home. Those are the ones I weep for. I've seen children tortured with drills, belts, crowbars, lighters, pliers, scissors, broken glass, you name it. I've seen unspeakable things done to children's bodies. If I've learned one thing in my life, it's this: if adults can hurt children, they're capable of anything. But children are strong, often stronger than the attacks of their attackers."

"Why do you do it? It sounds like you're just pouring acid on yourself."

"Every abused child has a story. Every abused child is important. Every abused child needs to see that not every adult is a beast. They need to see that not every adult is out to harm them. They need to be reached before they turn into the adults who put them here. I can't reach all the battered children in the world, but if I can reach even a few, it's worth it. If I can make them feel secure and safe and happy, even for a few days, it's worth the acid."

"The kids who get you for a nurse are very blessed. Kylie and I were blessed today. I don't think we could have gotten through this if it hadn't been for you."

"Don't sell yourself so short, Megan. You would have gotten through it just fine."

"I don't think so," Megan pushed her plate away. "My sister was very smart. She used to say nothing happens by chance. I believed her then, and I believe her now. Especially now. I don't think it's coincidence that you and I came together today. You were on your way home, and I could have missed you...but I didn't."

"I'm glad I was here to help."

"You did more than help. You saved us. You turned the whole day around. Kylie and I both were very afraid, and you made that fear go away. You are an *incredible* nurse. The way you have with kids...it's unbelievable. I've never seen it before. No wonder my sister loved you so much."

"Children are like small animals: you have to show them that you're on their side, that you're someone they can trust, that you're not going to hurt them."

"That's the way I felt when I was with you when I was a young girl. You were so kind and sweet and understanding. I trusted you like I trusted my dad. You were a gentleman and an angel even then. My mom and dad thought so too."

"How are your parents?"

"They died a long time ago. They passed away within hours of each other."

"I'm sorry. They were good people. Death just has it in for some families. But you still have Collin, though."

She shook her head. "No, he's gone too. My sister's death really messed him up. He got in with the wrong kids. Started doing drugs and stuff. He died on his eighteenth birthday. Just like Kylie. He was crushed to death. He was driving through the Acoma Indian Reservation in New Mexico and rolled his car. He was high on meth. He wasn't wearing his seat belt and the car rolled over on top of him. Two years later, my parents died. First my mom, then my dad. Collin couldn't live without Kylie, my mom couldn't live without Collin, and my dad couldn't live without my mom. They all died because of a broken heart."

"No, they all died because of *me*. Nothing happens by chance."

"*You?* You didn't have anything to do with it."

"I had everything to do with it. If Kylie hadn't been in my life, she wouldn't have been anywhere near my house, and she wouldn't have been killed."

"You said that at Kylie's memorial. Have you been carrying that around all these years?"

"Some things should never be forgotten…or forgiven."

"Oh, Owen. Kylie could have died from something else."

"But she didn't die of something else; she died because of her closeness to me."

"You still love her, don't you?"

"I love her memory. She's not here to love, so all I've got left to love is her memory. She had so many textures, Megan. She loved history, and she loved modernity. She loved intricacy, and she loved simplicity. She loved humility, and she loved surety. She loved honesty, and she loved mystery. She truly was, as a friend of mine said after her death, *'one of a kind.'*"

"That she was."

"It's funny, the weirdest things can make you think of someone you've lost. Occasionally, I'll run across a photograph or see a movie or TV show from the mid-seventies, and if the scene is outside, it always dawns on me that I'm looking at the same sunshine that was shining on me when I was fourteen, when I was in your sister's arms, when our whole world was just the two of us. I wish I had told her I loved her. But I didn't. I couldn't. Just as I can't do it now. I'm still the same insecure boy I was in high school and grade school. Pathetic. My body has changed, but so much of who I really am never did."

"I think most of us stay the same throughout our lives."

"I certainly did."

"Did you ever fall in love again?"

"Regrettably, yes."

"Regrettably? You mean it turned out badly?"

"In a word."

"Her loss."

"She didn't think so."

"What about now, are you with someone?"

"The last time I was with someone I was in high school. The last time I felt the lips of a girl I was seventeen. Decades ago. Seems like only yesterday, though. Odd how some things never leave your head and others leave it seconds after they're over."

"Are you saying you've never made love to anyone?"

"Never."

"Wow."

"That seems to be the standard response."

"I'm sorry, I didn't mean for that to sound rude. I've just never heard of it before."

"Yes, it is…unusual."

"You didn't even do it with Kylie? I mean, you two were so close."

"She wanted to, but I couldn't. I was afraid. I was afraid she'd leave me. And she did…although not in the way I imagined. There isn't much that fear can't stop. People have always labored under the mistake that I am utterly intrepid. I'm not. Take my trip to New York. I was terrified to go. I don't like to travel. I travel through books. But who in the world doesn't like to step on new soil and see new places?"

"I'm sure many people. They like to be close to home, to what's familiar. It's nothing to be ashamed of. If you don't mind me asking, why did you go to New York if you didn't want to? Were you there for work or something?"

"I was there for my father. My adoptive father, that is. Fifty years ago this last September, my father won his first architectural award. My father had seen drawings of the Twin Towers, and he was fascinated with them. He thought their spareness was beautiful. He couldn't stand cloisonné-style architecture. Like Kylie, he loved simple-lined structures; no fancy facades, no Art Deco, no jabot. He wanted to see the actual towers before he died. That didn't happen. A year after they started clearing the ground for the towers he passed away. So I went for him. I figured it was the least I could do. It was kind of an anniversary-slash-proxy pilgrimage."

"Did you have a chance to go into the towers?"

"No, I didn't. I wouldn't have gone anyway. I can't stomach that kind of height. I did go onto the Austin J. Tobin plaza, though, and I got up next to the towers. Even from the ground, their height was dizzying. They were magnificent buildings. Their tight, vertical lines are what made them so powerful. My father was right: the simpler the better. In buildings, and in life.

"Later that night, I remembered being on the plaza that morning and thinking how spacious and clean it was, and then minutes after I left it, that same clean plaza was littered with pieces of burning aircraft, pieces of charred curtain wall, and pieces of blackened and bloody body parts.

"I was on the corner of Cortlandt and Broadway when the first plane hit. I was walking to see the Brooklyn Bridge. After the plane hit, I rushed back to Church Street to get a better view. That's when the South Tower was hit. There literally aren't words to describe that kind of violence. There was so much fire, so much debris. So much chaos and noise. There was as much disbelief as there was falling paper. People jumping from the towers. Hitting the ground with such force their bodies exploded like balloons filled with red water. They say around two hundred fell that day, slamming onto the ground with a terminal velocity of a hundred and twenty-five miles an hour or more. They were lost the second they hit the air. I so wanted to catch them…but I couldn't. I just watched them die. We all just watched them die.

"It was such a beautiful day; the air was clear, the sky was blue, the sun was warm. How could so much torture and ruin take place on such an exquisite day? I'm glad my father wasn't alive to see it.

"My father told me that architectonics is as much about function as it is about form. How a building will stand against the forces and stresses of wind, compression, tension, gravity, and the load of the building itself is critical to its survival. After the second plane struck, I had a feeling some kind of collapse was going to happen. The plane hit toward the corner of the South Tower, which meant that the tensile strength of the support members in that part of the building had been critically undermined. *'Don't trust the truss'*—every firefighter's maxim. Both towers were basically held together with trusses. The weight of the top third of the South Tower was still pushing down on the weakened corner trusses. I feared that top third would eventually disjoin, cant, and fall. If it did, I would be right in the path of the debris wave once it hit the ground. So I quickly headed back to Cortlandt and Broadway. I figured that was a safe distance. It wasn't. When the building came down, minutes later, the noise was deafening, like bomb after bomb going off. A pyroclastic flow of what was once Two World Trade Center surged in every direction. Everybody was running away from it as fast as they could. I knew I couldn't outrun it, so I crouched down into a ball next to the side of a building and put my head between my legs, hoping the cloud would roll over me. It didn't. It slammed into me and threw me out into the gutter. But I was lucky—I only got one bad cut out of it. A piece of glass on the sidewalk got me on the outside of my left wrist. Hundreds of others got much worse."

"Did you have nightmares about it?"

"Yes. Still do. I'm certain everyone who was there still has them."

"Do you blame God for not stopping it? I do. I can't stop blaming Him."

"I don't blame Him at all. The world has pushed God away, so what's He to do? If you're not an invited guest, you don't show up for the dinner."

"But He could have intervened. Even just a little."

"Who's to say He didn't? I was right in my speculation that the corner of the South Tower would buckle and collapse. If you look at the video footage of the failure, the top third of the building starts to fall forward, but then it rights itself and falls straight down...as if a hand took hold of it and kept it from falling over, which would have caused more death and more damage. Other people have noticed this too. Maybe the hand of God kept that building from falling over and killing more people. Read Corrie ten Boom if you believe God doesn't reach out to those in terrible situations. I think God intervenes—He just doesn't do it in the way we think He should. Many times He helps us in spite of our offenses. But He won't stop us from committing those offenses. He'll only help us to stop if we ask Him...but most of us don't ask. He's put in place boundaries He won't cross. He won't force Himself on anybody. He wants to guide every man, but He won't force that guidance on any man. He lets us choose to either go His way or our own. Most of us choose our own. He lets everybody sin...including you. God can't stop evil on principle, and He won't stop it on commitment."

"Sounds like you're very close to Him."

"I'm not."

"Sure sounds like you are. I mean, how could you have these insights if you weren't?"

"I know about God, and I know about people, but I'm close to neither."

"But you're so wonderful with people. And you're such a good man. It's usually the bad people who are distant from God."

"Exactly."

She squinted. "How could you possibly think you're bad?"

"Comes with living with the merchandise all these years."

"No offense, Owen, but I'm not understanding you."

"Don't try to get inside my head, Megan; you won't be able to find your way back out. My mind's a messy maze of contradictions and inconsistencies. It always has been. It's always been at odds with itself."

"Why?"

"It seems I've always wanted diametric things. I've always wanted someone to love me, but not being loved is safer. I've always wanted friends, but not having friends is kinder. I've always wanted to be normal, but being abnormal is truer. When I was a young teenager, I so wanted to be loved. But when I got older, I ran from it…and I'm still running. If you're having a difficult time understanding me, Megan, imagine how I feel."

"Maybe it's time you stopped running, Owen. Being alone is far worse than being left alone. At least you have the memory of the one you loved to keep you warm."

"Memories are cold companions, Megan. Being left alone is *far* worse."

"What about what Alfred Tennyson said? *'Tis better to have loved and lost than never to have loved at all.'*"

"His canon, not mine."

"So you never want to fall in love again?"

"It wouldn't matter if I did—I don't deserve love, Megan. I'm guilty of too many wrongs. Every day I wake up and wish I hadn't. Every day I wish I had never been born. So many times I wish I had been under those towers when they fell. I would have been erased, and it all would have been over. But, like always, I went in the wrong direction. And here I am."

"Why would you say such things?"

"There are so many things I wish I could take back; so many things I wish I hadn't said. So many foolish words have come from my mouth. Hurtful words. Permanent words."

"And that makes you wish you were dead? Everybody has things they wish they could do over, say over, or not say at all. You're not the first."

"You don't understand. Every word from my mouth, every action from my hands was deliberate, enjoyed. I have intelligence I don't deserve. I have used that intelligence to make others feel minimal and trivial, even disposable. So many times I strutted my vocabulary to depreciate and devalue someone, very happy to mount the steed of my intellect and trample them without mercy. In my youth, whatever was on my lung was on my tongue. I minced and tore people apart without any regard for how destroyed they might be afterward. I made people feel small, and I relished that ability. Just like a woman I once knew. But age has taken me by the hand and shown me that it's only the truly small who want to make others feel the same way."

"You're being so unfair to yourself."

"No, I'm being honest. My mouth is acid, and my life is poison. When you kill people intentionally, you're a murderer. When you do it unintentionally, you're toxic. That's what I am. Many people are lying in the Earth because I'm walking on it. Many people have headstones because I was given birth. I'm strange because I'm abnormal, I'm cruel because I'm insecure, and I'm dangerous because I'm alive."

"Owen, if you're talking about my sister's death, it *wasn't* your fault. Did you know that over three thousand people die in car crashes every day? *Every day.* I learned that in a torts class I took a few years ago. When they say it's safer to fly in a plane than it is to drive in a car—*they're right.*"

"Then your sister should have spent that day in a plane rather than with me."

Megan shook her head. "If you could only see how special you are. If you could only see you the way I see you."

The clock suddenly rewound. It wasn't 2001, it was 1975; and I wasn't sitting with Megan in a noisy, over-lit cafeteria with uninviting meals between us, I was sitting with her sister at candletime in a peaceful restaurant with just our beating hearts between us. Megan's eyes had become her sister's. There was love in her powder-blue irises.

"Owen...can I be totally honest with you?"

I nodded, even though I didn't want her to be, for I knew what she was going to say.

She took a deep breath and exhaled. "I want you in my life. I know in your eyes, I'm still Kylie's little sister, but I'm not. I mean, I am, but I'm also a grown woman now. I never thought I would want someone after Peter. But after what I saw today, I do. You are so incredibly sensitive and compassionate. My daughter already loves you, and...I'm heading there myself. You and my sister never..." She cleared her throat. "You and my sister never made love. I want to give you that kind of love. It's not my—"

"Megan..." I shook my head.

"Please, just let me finish. It's not my intention to take Kylie's place. I just want to be happy again, and I know you do too. I could make you happy. And I know you could do the same for me. I think together we could have a life we both want. Don't say no right off, okay? Just think about it."

"Megan..." I had to pause. "I've already given you the long version of why I'm not worthy of what you're offering. The short version is: I'm damaged goods. You can do better than me. Far better."

"I disagree. From where I'm sitting, there's no one better than who I'm looking at right now. Just think about it. *Please.*"

"Okay," I said, even though I already knew I wouldn't. Megan was like her sister...an angel. She was from above, where God dwells. I was from below, where the lost scream in agony.

I knew after her daughter left the hospital, I would never see Megan again.

"Where's Desiree today?" I asked Nina Lancaster, a passable LPN and inveterate saucebox on my floor.

With hair like the pelt of a sickly animal, Nina was as thin as the tine of a fork and as tall as a basketball center. She was young in years, but more often than not she had the disposition of a cross-grained old woman. A vocal vegan and proud atheist, she made her views and opinions known to everyone, whether they wanted to hear them or not. To her face, many called her "*M and M,*" after Madalyn Murray O'Hair. She took the cut as a compliment. On the back bumper of her Subaru, she had a sticker of a large ichthus with the name Darwin in its middle eating a smaller ichthus with a cross in its middle.

"She had surgery," Nina answered, a wide slick of insouciance covering her face.

"Is she okay?"

"How should I know?"

"She didn't mention to me she was going to have surgery."

"Maybe because she didn't want you to know. You ever think of that?"

"Do you know what hospital she's in?"

"What am I, her mother?"

"Do you know or not?"

"*Iron Mountain Medical Center!*" Nina came back acerbically and sibilantly.

"Do you know what kind of surgery she had?"

"Now you know perfectly well we're not supposed to discuss patient information."

"I'm not asking you to go steal her H and P—I just want to know what kind of procedure she had."

"Why don't you go to the phone, pick it up, call her up and ask her yourself. Or better yet, why don't you get in your rich man's sports car, zoom down there and find out on your own."

"A Camry is a thousand miles from being a rich man's automobile, Nina," I said. "And it's light years from being a sports car. If anything, it's just an old-man sedan."

"Whatever," she rolled her eyes and walked away.

Desiree was indeed at Iron Mountain Medical Center. Like most health-care facilities, it resembled a hotel more than a hospital.

I found Desiree's room: she was on the third floor, but there was a handwritten note on her door saying that the patient did not want to be disturbed. I went to the nurses' station and asked what would be the best time to come back. The unit clerk told me the next day. Nina was right: I should have called.

As I was leaving, my eyes, out of habit, gave the patient board a cursory glance. Patient privacy dictated that only a patient's last name and only the first initial of their first be displayed. A name on the board caught my attention. It was a name I hadn't seen since I was a boy; a name that still made my heart race with fear.

*Wilson.*

Mr. Wilson, my *I-love-to-touch-little-boys* foster father.

His first name came to mind as easily as his last: Herman. *"Herman the hermaphrodite,"* Rebecca once called him

The first initial of the patient's first name on the board was *H*.

Inside my mind, a small voice told me to walk away and leave it alone. Another voice, louder, told me to ignore the first voice. It told me I needed to go to the room. It told me I needed to see if it were him.

H. Wilson was in room 3366; Desiree was in 3427. I walked in the opposite direction of Desiree's room.

Room 3366—or, coincidentally, *666* if the two threes were added together—was a semi-private room, but on this day, only one patient occupied it. The privacy curtain was drawn, so I couldn't see from the doorway if the person in the bed was the filth who took so much pleasure in fondling me in my underwear, and out of it.

I entered the room and walked over to the occupied bed.

The eyes were closed; the face was old; the skin was creased; the ears were oversized; the nose was bulbous; the jowls were age-spotted; the neck was flabby; the body was rawboned, and the sex was male. The name was *Herman*.

My hands began to tremble, and my chest began to pound.

Most faces in a person's life come and go; some faces *never* go. Mr. Wilson's never left mine.

I was once again next to the man who, with a smirk and a smile, fouled me whenever the urge struck him. For all their brutality, my real parents never descended to the depths of this man. They may have beat and bruised my body, but they never pawed it, fondled it, and raped it.

*"Death is a fisher of all men,"* the ER director at St. Bernadette's told me many years before. It was time death drop its line into the lake of life and drag out Mr. Herman Wilson. It was time for him to part ways with his existence.

I took many deep breaths to calm myself. Looking at Mr. Wilson's IV line, I knew just what needed to be done.

There was a large supply room three doors down. Its door was open. Two items were all I needed: a large syringe and a large-gauge needle.

No one was in the supply room; no one was even in the hallway. Like a seasoned thief, I coolly pocketed a 60ml Luer-Lok syringe and a 19-gauge needle that were lying in yellow bins sitting on a wire cart.

Everything was falling into place, almost as if I were meant to be there on that day: I found Mr. Wilson; I found him alone; I found a way to dispose of him, and I encountered no impediments keeping me from doing just that.

I returned to Mr. Wilson's room. As before, no one was in it except him. I wondered where Mrs. Wilson was.

Before returning to his bedside, I plucked two medium-sized exam gloves from a box inside a cage mounted to the wall by the door and pulled them on.

Standing next to Mr. Wilson, I peeled the plastic sleeves from the syringe and needle and tucked the sleeves into my pants pocket. I couldn't leave any trace of my presence. After twisting the needle onto the syringe, I drew the plunger up to the edge of the barrel flange. I inserted the needle into one of the injection ports in his IV line. All that was left to do was push the plunger. This would send a massive air embolism into his vein, which, hopefully, would travel directly to his heart and kill him instantly. A venous air embolism is fatal only if it is massive enough. It *would be* for Mr. Wilson. I would make certain of that.

I was taking an enormous risk, though: an air embolism can be discovered in an autopsy; not easily, but it can be done. But then, why would an autopsy even be considered? Mr. Wilson was an old man now. An older death, unless it is suspicious or requested by family, is not examined. Older people typically have numerous health conditions. Everyone would simply think Mr. Wilson experienced a massive stroke or MI. But even if there were suspicions and an autopsy were performed, how could it be proved I was the one who manufactured the embolism? There were no cameras in the hallways or in the rooms, and the area surrounding Mr. Wilson's bed would have none of my fingerprints. A simple, clean, spotless homicide. Although it actually wouldn't be a homicide—it would be justice. Or would it? Any way I tried to dress it, it was still murder. If I pushed the plunger, there would be no uncrossing that line. If caught, my autonomy would be taken away and given to a prison. Mr. Wilson had already taken my life—his death would then take my freedom. Was I going to let him do that? Even if I weren't caught, could I live with what I had done? As a nurse, I was taught to honor and protect life—every life. Wouldn't I be just like Mr. Wilson if I killed him, taking something that didn't belong to me? Mr. Wilson took my body and enjoyed it. If I emptied the syringe, I would take his life, and I would enjoy it. I would be just like him.

Mr. Wilson slowly opened his eyes.

I jerked.

"Who are you?" the stubbled face asked.

I stared at him. My breathing became rapid, and my chest started to pound and throb as before.

He blinked a couple of times to clear his vision. He cocked his head, then spoke with a demonic grin, "Wait a minute, I know you. Oh, boy, do I know you! Oh, yeah, I remember you good! You were the best poke I ever had. You were such a pretty boy. You're even prettier all grown up. You had such a nice ass. Turn around and let me see if it's still pretty."

I was a little boy again. I was frozen with terror.

"Been a long time," he continued. "You miss me? Is that why you're here? I can still get it up, you know. Big and tall, like a sequoia. I'll show you my stick if you show me yours. Although I haven't seen yours in some time. Must be a lot larger now."

The demon was still grinning.

I looked down at the hands holding the syringe. They were a man's hands, not a little boy's. I wasn't a child anymore. I was an adult. He could not hurt me like he used to. He could never hurt me again. He could do nothing unless I let him. I was letting him terrorize me.

But no more.

I withdrew the needle from the injection port, recapped it and slipped the needle and syringe into my back pocket.

I couldn't explain where it came from, but peace came down like a dove and folded its wings in my hands. The fear was gone. The human aberration lying before me was just filthy wind now, nothing but flatus from waste-gorged intestines.

My days of hurting because of Mr. Wilson were over...but Mr. Wilson's days of hurting because of me were just beginning.

"Where's your *wed accomplie*?" I asked. "Or should I say *Lady Macbeth*?"

"My wife?"

"Yes, your scummy wife."

"Went the way of all the Earth," he replied blithely. "Pity. She would have liked to have seen you again. She loved it when you cried. Really turned her on."

"Then she'd be greatly disappointed since I'm not crying. How many other little boys did the two of you destroy?"

"If they didn't have a good time, it wasn't our fault. We told to 'em to relax, but they wouldn't. All they did was cry. Like little sissies."

"How many?"

"Who's to say? Could be a dozen, could be two dozen. Lots of boys dripped my baby-batter, but *you* were always my favorite."

"They say there are seven deadly sins known to man. I say there are four, and, curiously, each begins with the nineteenth letter of our alphabet...S. Interestingly, the name Satan *also* begins with an S. Care to guess what those four moral offenses are? Allow me to help you. Sloth, self, sex, and silver. Each man owns one. Some own two; some three. Rare is the man who owns all four. *You*, Mr. Wilson, are that rare man."

"Look closely at my face. Do I look like I care?"

"What made you into the paraphilic garbage heap you are? I'd really like to know. How does a grown man enjoy the blood and cries and terror of a child?"

"You should give it a try sometime—there's *nothin'* like it."

"Do you have any idea how you ruined my life? Do you know much I hate myself because of you? It's one thing to be a man who wants to ejaculate inside another man. It's quite another to be a man who wants to ejaculate inside a little boy. Do you know what that does to the little boy? Do you know how revolting and polluted it makes him feel? It never leaves him. He always feels dirty in the sight of men, unclean in the sight of God, filthy. He feels he is unworthy to be close to anyone. That's what you did to me. What you did to other little boys."

"O, well, *c'est la vie, c'est la mort.*"

"Funny that you should mention death. Was Oliver the only child you killed—or were there others?"

He didn't answer. Instead, he gave me a young-moon smile. Was he toying with me, or answering me?

The words of Larry the janitor once again came back to me: *"We all do what we do for a reason."*

Mr. Wilson wasn't born a jagged, hardened pedophile; he was fashioned into one.

"Did you like it when your own father raped you?" I put to him.

His smile faded.

"Did your mother watch while he did it?" I then asked. "Did you scream when you saw the blood for the first time? Did you cry because of the pain? Did you cry because your father was doing something other fathers didn't do? Did you cry out to God? Did you only hear silence from Him? Did you wonder where He was while you were being used like some dirty sex toy? Did you hate God for His silence and stillness? Did you hate yourself while your father's *'baby-batter'* was dripping from you? Did you wonder how life could be so normal in the houses all around you when yours was filled with so many unspeakable perversions? Did you wonder where the police were? Did you hate them because they weren't there for you like they were supposed to be? Did you feel ashamed at school? Did you fear all the other children could see in your face what was being done to you at home? Did you hate the other children because they had loving parents and you didn't? Did your mind fly away while your father was doing to you what he should have been doing with your mother? Did you feel yourself start to die inside?

Did you feel weak and powerless when your father forced himself on you? Did that feeling of weakness and powerlessness go away when you forced yourself on your first little boy? Did you like that feeling so much you continued to seek out other little boys? Did your acts ever torture you? Did remorse ever try to befriend your heart? If so, did you push it away with more acts of perversion so you would not have to look at what you had done? When you look in the mirror, do you ask yourself, *'What have I become?'* Do you say, *'Like father like son?'*

"I was all set to kill you, but death would be wrong for you. Too easy. You need to be trapped, the way you trapped me, the way you trapped other little boys. Your snare will either be a prison of bars or a prison of social condemnation. You escaped punishment once—you won't do it again."

"Good luck with that. It'll be your word against mine."

"Your word isn't a matter of record—*mine* is. So are Rebecca's and Elizabeth's. After you fled decades ago—like the coward you were, and I assume still are—all our stories were recorded by the police and the State. So when I call them shortly, they will believe me."

"Tell them all you want—the sand in that statute of limitations has long run out."

"Yes, for me it has, but not for others. Once I put you in the light, your current crimes—which I am sure are many—will be excavated, and the local law will be your new best friend. But if by some unfortunate turn of events the police are unable to bury you, the newspapers will. I will make certain of that. I will make sure they know about you. *All* about you. So either way, your train is fast approaching the stopblock.

"I've always wondered what I would do if we ever reunited. Each time the thought terrified me. I don't fear you now. I feel sorry for you. I think you were scathed as a child, which turned you to anger. But you chose to hold onto that anger. You could have chosen peace, but, as Judge Edward Cowart said to Ted Bundy after he sentenced him to death, *'You went another way, partner.'*

"A corrupt man constructs his own end, Mr. Wilson. It is men who raise a gallows, but it is the man who hangs from it who drives the first nail."

I pulled off the gloves and dropped them into a plastic waste can by the bed and walked to the door.

"Don't go away now," I said to him from the doorway. "I have a couple of phone calls to make...and then we're going to have a *very* interesting afternoon."

For the first time ever, I saw fear in his eyes.

For the first time ever, I was in control, and he wasn't.

# CHAPTER 16

# The End,
# The Beginning

*"To the last, I grapple with thee; from Hell's heart, I stab at thee; for hate's sake, I spit my last breath at thee."*

HERMAN MELVILLE

*"Always give your best. Never get discouraged. Never be petty. Always remember, others may hate you, but those who hate you don't win unless you hate them, and then you destroy yourself."*

RICHARD M. NIXON

*"If you prick us, do we not bleed? If you tickle us, do we not laugh? If you poison us, do we not die? And if you wrong us, shall we not revenge?"*

WILLIAM SHAKESPEARE

*"Step not on him who is beneath you, for in the end, he may step on you."*

KAREN DORAN

*"The choices we embrace in the future are decided by the moments that embraced us in the past."*

P. W. WALTERS

M r. Wilson shot himself in the bathtub of room 105 of the Sandman Inn. He had been living in a squalid, pay-by-the-week apartment house called The Stewart. He had been alone for almost twenty years. Mrs. Wilson died on August 21, 1982, of coronary artery disease. If there ever had been a logical death, it was hers: Mrs. Wilson's emotional heart was, from end to end, corner to corner, rotted and diseased, so it only followed that it would eventually corrupt and destroy the one encaged in her chest. I believed that somewhere in her past, somewhere in her youth, she, like her husband, like all fell human beings, had been tooled into a deviant. A part of me didn't want to bow to this belief, for I wanted to keep hold of my hatred for her, for she deserved it. But I had to let the hatred go, for I knew it would make living with her memory easier. A reason is not an excuse, but it is an explanation, and from that, peace can finally begin.

As was his wont, Mr. Wilson fled The Stewart after investigators once again entered his life. I was certain he felt alone, isolated, and trapped. With no home to hide him and no wife to aid him, he must have decided his only escape was his Colt 45. (I wondered if it was the same Colt 45 he repeatedly said he would use on me if I let slip to anyone what we were doing.)

I wasn't happy he was dead. I was, of all things, sad. I didn't forgive him, but I felt bad for him. Though he lived much of his life in depravity and profligacy, I'm sure when he was a boy he would not have elected such a life. When young, he probably never imagined he would emerge as his father, a violent molester of children. No one desires to be such a creature—they are molded into one. And once the mold is set, it is unshatterable.

My attitude toward Mr. Wilson changed with my reunion with him. I came to believe that beyond his bandwidth of mephitic thinking and debauched practices, there was a man who knew right from wrong, acceptable from unacceptable, good from evil. I believed he both enjoyed and detested what he let his hands do. But years of dissolute behavior had become so deep-rooted, he could not stay himself. He knew what he was doing was wrong but doing what was right was impossible.

It is difficult to separate what a man is from what he does. Is not a man's actions a link to his character, his value?

No.

I believed Mr. Wilson, like his wife, was born with good character and great value, but, like his wife, had both stolen.

My cell phone moved in my pocket. I had set it on vibrate because I was at work.

It was Desiree on the calling end. She was crying. I asked her what was wrong. She wouldn't tell me. She simply asked that I come to her apartment as soon as I was finished at the hospital. I told her I would. After I hung up, it came to me why she had been crying: Yoda, her Chihuahua, had either passed away or was beginning to.

The Candlewood Court Apartments, Desiree's roost, was a three-story, ranch-style affair with dark timber trim, speckled brick, and primrose-yellow stucco. The bricks ran the length of the ground floor, while the stucco adorned the second and third floors. Above immaculate grass, finely trimmed scrubs, bright annuals and perennials ringed a three-tier, Botticino marble fountain that stood outside the main entrance. Flowered balconies and cozy Georgian windows graced all sides of the building. Clearly, only those with means could live there.

There was a telephone next to the main entrance. Visitors had to call the tenant they wished to see before they were allowed into the building. I called Desiree's number. She picked up but would not talk; she simply buzzed me in.

I had never been to Desiree's home before, even though she had invited me numerous times. Though I had never set foot in her house, I was well-acquainted with her homelife. In 2002, six years earlier, she and her husband finally divorced, and he moved away to another state. After he left, she took up oil painting, a talent she never knew she had until she was alone. Outside of work, her whole life was her canvases and her little Yoda.

She answered her door almost immediately. Her face was tired from fatigue and wet with tears. Cradled in her arms was her sweet, white-haired companion. Chihuahuas are small by genetics, and Yoda was no exception, but he looked even smaller right then. His abdomen, however, was grossly distended. He had a secretive, though aggressive, cancer found typically in older and larger dogs: hemangiosarcoma. But cancer, be it in those with two legs or four, shows no partisanship. When eventually discovered, hemangiosarcoma has usually progressed beyond treatment. Both Desiree and I knew the disease would eventually take the life of her precious friend. While at work, Desiree left him with her neighbor.

"I don't know what to do," she wept, holding Yoda like he was a newborn again. "I know I should take him in so he can be free from his suffering, but I can't bring myself to do it. I can't let him go. He's everything to me. He's all I've got."

The little animal's eyes were only partly open. They had no want, no shimmer. His breathing was slow and shallow. He wasn't whimpering, and his thin, little body was lax. He didn't appear to be in any discomfort.

She walked back into her apartment. She entered an ultra-modern living room, the walls of which were nearly floor to ceiling with oil seascapes, desertscapes, and mountainscapes. She had a particular fondness for aspens in autumn. I assumed they all came from her own hand.

She sat down on the couch and stared down at Yoda.

"What should I do?" she asked, crying.

"I don't think you need to take him in," I counseled. "I think his time is close."

She swallowed. "I know what you mean now. You told me you don't get close to anyone because you don't want the hurt of saying good-bye. I understand now. I shouldn't have been so glib with you about it. I've never had this kind of pain before. I don't know how I'm going to get through this."

"You will. At first, you don't think you will, but you will get through it. Time will pass, and the hurt will recede, like the waters after a storm. More than you do now, you will feel grateful, even favored, that yours was the life Yoda entered and not the life of someone who would have thought of him as just a dog, or worse still, neglected and abused him."

"Most of the people around here think he's just a yapping little mutt, but he isn't. He's an angel with a tail and four paws. He's the best friend I've ever had. He loves me, and I love him. I love everything about him...his ears, his eyes, his walk, his bark, his smell. He's lost many of his teeth, so his little tongue slips out of his mouth when he goes to sleep. He has...*had* almost human ways. At night, before we'd go to sleep, he'd stretch out on my chest and lay his head close to my neck. It was our bonding time, like when two people hold each other and the only communication between them is their bodies. I'd come through the door after work, and he'd run as fast as he could to me. He'd stand up on his little back legs and plead with me with his big, beautiful eyes to pick him up. When he knew he was going to get a treat, he'd get so happy. He'd spring around from place to place and bark excitedly, his little tail going faster than the wind. I used to sing to him right on this couch. I'd put on a record or CD and sing to him very softly. He'd always close his eyes, stretch out his little legs and go to sleep. Whenever I was in the shower, he'd lie on the bath mat and wait so patiently for me to get out. When I would have dinner, he would lie quietly on my lap. He wouldn't beg or fuss or anything. Whenever we'd take a walk, he'd always look back to make sure I was there. He always slept with me, even as a puppy. He loved curling up next to my stomach. He loved it when I kissed his chest and his tummy. For every kiss I gave him, he gave me ten. How am I going to live without that?"

Her tears fell onto Yoda's dying body.

I had seen enough death over the years to know there was nothing I could say that would ease her pain. Tragically, she would simply have to go through it. All I could do was listen and perhaps take her mind off of it for a few minutes.

I noticed something propped up on the triangular glass-and-chrome coffee table in front of us. It appeared to be a newsletter. A grainy, black-and-white photo filled the front of the letter. Desiree was in the photograph—a *very young* Desiree.

"What's that?" I asked, nodding to the piece of paper.

Desiree wiped her eyes. "Oh, that's from my high school. I get them once a year. That one's letting me know that my class reunion is in a couple of weeks. The big Five-O. I was going to ask if you'd go with me. I don't want to go alone."

"Of course I'll go."

"You ever been to any of your reunions?"

"Never been invited."

"Not even one?"

"Nope. My senior class had a graduation party at the Tri-Arc TraveLodge downtown. Wasn't asked to that either. I was never the peach people wanted to pick." I leaned forward and clasped the newsletter.

"I was seventeen in that photo," Desiree shared. "Prom night. You ever go to any proms?"

"Nope. No reunions, no proms, no parties."

"I'm sorry."

"Oh, well, you know what they say—life's a bitch and we're her puppies. You look very happy in this picture."

"I was. It was a happy night. It was a happy life. I enjoyed my high school years. I was at the top of my game back then."

"And at the top of your class too, I'll wager."

"I was. I was voted the most popular girl in the school. I was Class President, head cheerleader, head of the Science Club, Cooking Club, Arts and Crafts Club, always made the honor roll, never missed a dance, never was without a date on a Saturday night." She shook her head. "Now look at me—all I care about is this little dog."

"Everybody changes, Desiree. The things we used to hold dear we wind up not holding at all."

"Yeah. I guess that's a good thing. Keeps us moving forward. Can't live in the past. But I do miss that time in my life. It will be good to see everyone again. Talk about the old times and, for a few hours, feel the way I used to feel."

"That's what reunions are all about—or so I'm told."

"If you were asked to a reunion, would you go?"

"If I did, I'd probably end up killing everyone there."

Desiree's eyebrows arched. "Because they didn't invite you to some silly graduation booze party?"

"I'm talking about my first high school."

"You were in two?"

"Yes."

"The first one treated you badly?"

"In a manner of speaking."

"Many people have unpleasant high school days."

"Went a shade beyond unpleasant. But it's all suppositional. Since I didn't graduate from that first high school, I will not be on the list of invitees."

"Well, if you are, let me know and I'll go with you. Can't have you blowing everyone away. But you know, Owen, if you were invited and decided to go, you'd find everyone there different. Anyone with half a heart regrets the mistakes and miscues of their youth."

"You have to have hearts to begin with, and they didn't." I looked down at Yoda. "May I hold him?"

She gave him a look of farewell, kissed him on the forehead and gently handed him to me.

Suddenly, I was five years old again and holding the limp, lifeless body of my Yogidog. My father had broken his neck as easily as one steps on a crawling bug. If only I hadn't brought him into our apartment that day. If only I had left him alone, he wouldn't have been killed. Someone else would have found him and taken him in. His death was on me.

Tears left my eyes. They, like Desiree's, fell onto Yoda's delicate body. I bent forward and kissed his face.

Though Desiree was within inches of me, I cried as though I were alone. I think I heard Desiree's voice, but I wasn't sure.

Yoda slowly turned his head toward me, and his eyes met mine. They were glassy now. He slowly turned his head again and licked my finger.

"Sleep well, little one," I whispered. "Dream happy and fly free. Thank you for being born and coming into the life of my friend."

His eyelids fluttered briefly, then his chest went still.

I heard Desiree start to weep. Then I heard weeping coming from me. Desiree was crying for her lost friend...and I was crying for mine.

I was thankful that I was holding Yoda when he passed instead of Desiree. I was more accustomed to loss than she. Desiree already had the memory of seeing him die, she didn't need the memory of feeling it too.

I stroked Yoda's soft, delicate face and then gave him one last kiss. Then I carefully handed him back to Desiree. She put her face to his and kissed him too.

I reached over and tenderly clasped his paw. "Please tell Yogidog I love him," I said. "Please tell him I'm sorry."

Desiree graduated from Edison Memorial High School on May 30, 1958. Her reunion took place on the same day, only fifty years later. I accompanied her, as I said I would. The gathering was held in a taper-lit, semi-formal, basement-level restaurant at the Hilton. Including Desiree, seventeen invitees showed. We both were surprised at that number: we expected far fewer, for only thirty students were in her entire class.

Many of her classmates thought I was Desiree's grandson. I took it as a compliment; Desiree did not. She was intensely self-conscious about her age, and to have it assumed she was a grandmother, even though women of her maturity typically are, made her feel even more ill at ease.

With the exception of Desiree, everyone who came was gray-haired, overweight, dentured, and slow-moving. They all were delighted to be together again. They had shared a short but seminal part of their lives together, and they were happy to be there to commemorate it. They were cordial and polite and gracious to one another; but then, such civility was instinctive to them. They came from an era when respect was the standard, when obeisance was second nature, when raping a fellow classmate and approving of it would never have happened. It would never have entered their minds.

While watching Desiree's class, that day in May in 1976—the day William and his *band of brothers* took me into the showers—once again came back to me. By the time the evening with Desiree came to a close, I was water in a hot pot—steaming with rage and anger. I had, for over thirty years, been in a fight with myself over the rape and everyone's acceptance of it. I wanted to both forget the memory and never let it go. Each time it stepped in front of me, I shoved it to the ground, for I didn't like the choler and hatred it stirred. But afterward, I would always turn, grab its hand and pull it to its feet. Exiling it from my life was wrong. Forcing it away meant I sided with those who created it.

Summer, Desiree informed me, is the time classes traditionally reunite. Moran's Class of 1978 would come together again sometime that summer. I could see it as clearly as my reflection in a mirror: my class would laugh and joke and drink and have a fine time, not paying a penny of regret for what they did that spring day in 1976, not caring in the least how their actions had destroyed the trust it took me so long to welcome. They would reminisce about my rape and smiles would abound. They would believe, as they believed thirty years earlier, that I had it coming. Because I had a gay friend meant that I was gay, and all things homosexual should be felled and set afire like a diseased forest.

In school, they fouled me and my friendship with Shawn. They would do it again in their reunion, as they undoubtedly had done in reunions past. Shawn and I would again be the feather that tickled them, the joyride that amused them, the tale that entertained them. I couldn't let it happen again. They had to see how vile they were. They had to feel what I felt that spring day, what I felt for the next thirty years: alone, trapped, weak, and ashamed. I had to let them know—as I had let Mr. Wilson know—that I had not forgotten. But unlike Mr. Wilson, my class had no excuse for what they did. They hadn't been pushed by their past—as Mr. Wilson had—they had been pushed solely by their prejudice.

The memory of Sharla came back to me as I drove Desiree home. I felt despicable for what I did to Sharla. Did I really want to feel that way again? Was I going to let myself go down that road again? Was I going to hold revenge in my hands one more time?

Yes.

For this time was different.

Sharla hadn't wronged me; my class had. Sharla was dying; my class wasn't. Sharla couldn't defend herself; my class could. Sharla didn't deserve my vengeance; my class did.

Desiree noticed my mood during the ride home and asked me what was wrong. I told her I was tired. I would never tell her the truth. I would never tell her what was in my heart, what was in my head. I would never tell her that all I could think about was an event that forced its way into every house, every public place, every school, and every life nine years earlier: the Columbine shootings. I would never tell her that the next day I was going to buy a gun, and along with it, multiple boxes of ammunition.

But before I did that, I would go home, get on the computer and see exactly where and when Moran's Class of 1978 was going to come together for its reunion.

Its *final* reunion.

The Internet has made the world a small place, an exposed place, a vulnerable place. Little is secret, little is unknowable.

Saturday, August 9, 2008, was the day my class was going to reconnect. They would come together at 7:00 P.M. in the same gymnasium in which they played basketball as teenagers. I was certain that many of them—if not all—would attend, if only to be regaled by William about my rape. I was certain I would headline the invitation:

*COME TO OUR 30<sup>TH</sup> AND BE ENTHRALLED AS*
*WILLIAM FARNSWORTH AGAIN SERVES US A FEAST OF*
*MEMORIES OF OWEN'S ORGY!*

I had never lounged in the lap of delusion or paranoia. I was as plugged into reality as anyone else. I didn't suspect I would be the cardinal source of amusement at my class' reunion—I *knew* I would be. I would not and could not let it happen again. They had had enough entertainment at my expense; first in 1976, then at every reunion since their graduation. It was time *I* be entertained for a change. It was time *I* held the rapture, and they held the terror.

A black, dull-finished Glock 17 semi-automatic with three extra magazines accompanied me out to my car. It would be the first time ever my wages as a nurse went toward the purchase of something that would do harm to another.

Even after 9/11, it was fairly uncomplicated to acquire a firearm. It was all too easy. Even my plan to square accounts seemed too easy. There should have been at least a few potholes in my plan, but there weren't. Not one.

After Moran's Class of 1978 reunion was underway, I would silently chain together the exterior push bars of the east entrance of the gymnasium; the same entrance William and his water boys dragged me through after I had been struck by William's gun. The only other entrance was on the south side of the building; this was the main entrance. After I entered the gymnasium, everyone in the building would see my gun and their gaiety over my gayness would come to an abrupt stop. Amid screaming, I would herd everyone toward the west wall and have each throw his cell phone into a box I would bring with me. I couldn't very well have them calling for help and accomplish my goal at the same time. Memories of the Christmas dance of 1975 would return to me, and regret would take my hand and prod me to leave before it was too late, but I would push the memories away. After my class was cut off and defenseless, I would take them back in time and make them feel the same terror I felt that day in 1976. They would be at the hands of someone who would show no mercy, no compassion, no sympathy, and no pity. I would conscript Erik Reynolds and Mike Radin—who, like parched dogs, would undoubtedly be at William's side lapping up his every word—and order them to pull William to the center of the room. Before ending his life, I would say, "William, remember what Mrs. Dobson said to you years ago? It was right before you lied about her so that she would be fired? She said, '*Choices have consequences, Mr. Farnsworth.*'" Before he could answer, I would implant two 9 mm rounds into his head, one for good reason, a second for good measure. As Erik and Mike ran, like the cowardly dogs they were, I would then shoot them down. Others would start running, and I would drop them as well. After I felt a proper number had fallen, I would call it paid. I would return to my car, lock the doors, press the gun against my temple—just as Dylan Klebold had done after killing his schoolmates at Columbine High—pull the trigger and join my murdered classmates in Hell.

If Roxanne were there, I would let her live. I would want her—as well as the others I let live—to be afraid for the rest of her years. She and my surviving classmates would never again feel safe away from their homes. They would feel, as I felt all of my adult life, trapped by unutterable memories.

More than once, I considered taking the Glock into the mountains and throwing it into a deep lake where it could never be touched again. But I always put the car keys back on the wall, for the Class of 1978 needed to pay. They had to make recompense for what they did, for what they took. If they didn't pay, it would mean that what they did was right...and it wasn't.

*August 9, 2008.*
*9:30 P.M.*

It might have been Providence, but I suspected it was simple luck that met me at Moran when I arrived. Directly across the street from its south entrance was a span of naked curb for one car. My car. All the available curb spaces near and around the school were occupied by cars belonging to my former classmates...or rather, my soon-to-be-dead or traumatized former classmates.

I came late because I needed the cover of night to mask me. Had I been seen before I entered the gymnasium, I might have been stopped and asked why I was there: after all, I hadn't graduated from Moran, so what was I doing on the property?

Not a brick or window or door to the school was different from when I walked away from them thirty years before. It seemed even the shrubs, flowers, and lawn had not been touched by the passing decades.

It had been thirty-two years since I had been this close to the building. If necessity brought me near the school, I would detour around it. I was an utter paradox. People with few years notice that people with many years live in the past. I was no exception; and yet, when it came to embracing the past, I turned my face away: I refused to look at photographs of my youth; I refused to collect mementos of my youth, and I refused to step near the places of my youth. And yet, in my mind, it was always there.

I gripped the steering wheel to still my trembling hands. I was not so clouded by my rage that I could not see the graveness of what I was about to do. There would be no turning back once I started. It was a rubicon without an escape. If I began the journey, I had to finish it.

Lights shone from Moran's many classrooms. Why was the building kindled when the reunion was taking place in the gymnasium? And why was it occurring in the gymnasium and not the auditorium? For the first question, I had no answer. For the second, there was only one: since I was the highlight of the evening, what better venue for a reunion than the place of my disgrace. If he hadn't done so already, I was certain William would give everyone a guided tour of the shower room with a second-by-second ledger of my much-deserved assault.

I took many deep breaths, turned off the engine and opened the door. The gun, chain, padlock, and box were in the trunk.

Not locking the door, I walked around to the trunk and keyed it open. Like seeing a dead animal in the center of the road, the sight of the box with the gun, chain, and padlock inside it stunned me. The enormity of what I was about to do came at me again. I stared at the cardboard container. It was a 15 x 15 bandage box I had retrieved from the hospital's Materials department. The coldness of my plan locked its hands around my throat. My eyes remained on the box while its fingers tightened.

Who was I kidding? I had never fired a gun in my life...and I never would. Be it a lack of nerve or strength or courage, I didn't have what it took to kill. I could kill about as easily as I could turn copper into gold. I would have made a disgraceful soldier. I couldn't even view violent segments in movies; I would always fast-forward through them. When I found a bug lost in my home, I would capture it and take it outside where it could continue to live. I wanted to make my class pay, but there was no way to make it happen. I had lived with what they had done for thirty years; what was a few more? I was nearly fifty. Many men die in their fifties. Hopefully, I would be one of them.

I closed the trunk.

My car was facing north. Ahead of me was the way to Kylie's house.

Dear, sweet Kylie.

I turned around and gazed at the street that led to the small park two blocks away. Kylie found me there one day many years ago and comforted me. So did Lyle. And there was the day that I found him. Dark days for both of us. Ms. Gavin and I shared an afternoon there. Dark times were on the horizon for her as well.

Turning back around, I caught sight of the sidewalks that took Shawn and me home.

Shawn. What an incredible boy.

Just as Desiree had been blessed to have had Yoda in her life, I had been blessed to have had Shawn. Everyone should have such a friend, if only for a while.

I turned my eyes toward the school. So much happened in the two years I spent there. So many things that forever changed my life. I had been told that a child's first years are his formative years. I didn't agree. The first years are just the beginning. The determinative years don't end until high school is in the rearview mirror.

My legs began moving. A part of my head commanded them to take me to the front doors of the school.

Out of habit or instinct, or maybe even hope, I tried the door.

It opened. My heart skipped.

Why the lights were on became clear: the school was open for the reunion. Everyone could walk the halls and go back to a time when life was quizzes and crushes, first dates and first kisses. A time when all things were new. A time when any future, any wish, any dream was possible.

Not a soul was in the main corridor when I entered it. Every place, small or large, has its own perfume. Moran, too, had its own. In its air was the redolence of old books, old wood, old paint, old walls. In its atmosphere was also the scent of generations past, of lives come and gone.

Other than the addition of multiple security cameras, inside and out, nothing had changed at Moran. If those same cameras had been present when I was a student, William would not have had the nerve to plaster the photograph of Shawn and me kissing everywhere he could. I wasn't the only coward.

I wasn't ready to look at the locker I used as a sophomore, so I returned to the foyer and climbed the stairs to the second floor. On those same stairs, my blood dropped after Mr. Carey had shot me. Once on the second floor, I opened the stairwell doors. Directly opposite the doors was Mr. Carey's room. A shroud of black paint had been applied to its window. Below the window was a gray nameplate that read: *Storage 2A*. I couldn't help but think of Mr. Heald and Mr. Taggart. I wondered if they were still alive. Mr. Taggart probably; Mr. Heald probably not. Both were extraordinary, exemplary men. If they had passed, I hoped death had been kind to them.

Down the hallway was the boys' lavatory. Kylie took me into it and delighted my young body with hers. Near the lavatory was Kylie's locker. 2377 was its number. I walked over to it and looked down at the hasp. I touched it lightly. How many students had used that locker since she died? None of them would ever know they shared a place with the loveliest, sweetest girl Moran ever knew.

Returning the way I came, I walked down the corridor where the freshmen had their lockers. Each grade had a specific floor designated for them. The juniors had the third floor; the seniors and freshmen had the second, and the sophomores had the main. Why they did not go in order I had no idea. High school, like adolescence, was full of unsolvable mysteries.

I came to the locker I had as a freshman. Its number was 2241. All the lockers in the school were fallow brown. Mine was in the center of the corridor. It, like most of the other lockers, was scratched and scuffed. Some of the lockers were even gouged and dented. After thirty years, they should have been replaced, or, at the very least, repainted. Each student was responsible for providing their own lock, so all of the lockers were free to open. I lifted the hasp and opened mine. A small, thin strip of red cloth lay on its floor and a thin film of dust lay on its shelf. There on that shelf my books waited for my young hands to retrieve them. There on that shelf presents from Roxanne awaited me every morning. It seemed like only yesterday I was fourteen, standing on that very floor, with decades of life and possibility ahead of me. Now, thirty-two years later, most of that life was behind me, gone swiftly and spent unhappily.

The fragrance of Elsha cologne always greeted me when I opened my locker, for I kept a bottle of it on the shelf. I leaned in and inhaled. The scent was long gone. Why is it that good things go away and bad things endure? I closed the locker.

Far down from my locker was Roxanne's. I walked to it and stood in front of it. Why do good things have to go away? Roxanne was probably in the gymnasium at that moment, happily enjoying William's ribald account of my rape, and no doubt cheering him on. How little distance I had traveled in all the years. How little I had grown, for there I was, still standing in front of a girl's locker who once wished I were dead and, in all likelihood, still did. Why did I still keep a candle burning in the window for her? Why did I still love her? Why did I still care? I often wondered what I would do if I ever saw her again. Would I ignore her or acknowledge her? Would I speak to her or remain silent? Would I be civil...or be cruel?

Another part of me, a secret part, wondered if Roxanne ever regretted, even for an instant, what she did to me as a person, or to us as a couple. Did she ever once feel remorse for the words she threw or the feelings she crushed? Not likely.

Useless speculation. I would never know what she felt. She could be dead for all I knew. Many of them could. Inexplicably, the thought saddened me.

I continued walking.

I came to Mark's locker. There was a true triumph. At only twenty-three, he saw his first novel in print. That first work, *Menlow*, was a science fiction supernova. It was an ingenious tale and masterfully told. I came across it by accident while browsing the shelves in Waldenbooks. He dedicated it to his wife, Holly. The love he always wanted he finally found. Saguaro Press published his second book just three years later. He had christened it *Gone*. And gone from the bookshelves as well, for it was always sold out. Mark had come a long way since his *Falcon Project*. I was proud of him. And happy. He started out low and ended up high. I started out high and ended up low. He became what I didn't—a success.

I left his locker and continued on.

My feet took me to the auditorium.

As in the hallways, no one was in the auditorium. It was lit with the same dim, inverted lights, and the walls were still clothed in the same bland white.

Immediately, I was taken back to the first time I saw Roxanne. It was in that same room. What a day that was. I saw Austin for the first time, too, that day. A sad beginning, a sad ending. I looked up the stage. I saw myself speaking at Kylie's memorial. Another sad ending. Little did I know how many more were to come.

I turned and glanced up at the balcony. It was 1975 again. Kylie had been gone two months. I was sitting up there, alone and invisible. I left my seat, climbed to the highest tier of chairs, which were against the back wall, slid the ceiling panel forward, wrote my name and the date on the wall above the panel and slid it back in place. Why did I do that? Was it because I felt like I didn't exist, and that was my way of feeling like I did? I needed to climb the balcony stairs once more and see that inscription. I needed to touch it; I needed to feel like I still existed.

"Owen, is that you?" A woman's voice.

Like a startled bird, my eyes flew from the balcony.

"It is you!" A silver-haired woman ran over to me. She wrapped her arms around me and hugged me tightly.

She released herself and looked at me heartfully. My brain quickly scanned the pages of my past to place her. At first, her face did not register. Then it did. She was Audrey Ann Conti, a former student at Moran. When a tenderfoot within its walls, she was a shy, anonymous girl with lustrous, wavy, black hair who frequently smiled at me; a smile that always made me feel favored and important.

She wasn't in my class…so why was she at my class' reunion?

"You look so young!" she extolled. "You've hardly aged! What's your secret?"

I hadn't expected to see anyone, so my conversation engine wasn't warmed up. "Just lucky, I guess. You were a freshman when I was sophomore, I'm sure I remember, so…"

"Why am I here?"

I nodded.

"I married Gregory Schmythe. He was in your class. He's over in the gym. I thought I'd take a walk around. It hasn't changed much, has it?"

"But for the cameras every three feet, it's the land that time forgot."

She giggled.

Then her face turned thoughtful. "I'm really sorry about what William and the other boys did to you. I never got the chance to tell you that. You didn't deserve it."

"Oh, well." I had other things to say…but what would be the point in saying them?

"It was a happy day for everyone when William got expelled. He was nothing but a troublemaker and a thug. He got what he deserved."

Either she misspoke or I misheard. "Expelled?"

"Well, yeah. You don't think he was allowed back in school after what he did to you? He and Mike and Erik and the other two boys were expelled too."

"I thought he'd be over in the gymnasium, serving everyone a delicious account of…*the event*."

Creases of confusion formed on her face. "Owen, William is dead."

"What?" The air left my lungs, and none took its place.

"He was murdered. Back in the early eighties. Eighty-four, I think it was. Knifed about ten times. Last I heard, Mike was in prison for shooting his girlfriend, and Erik just disappeared. Probably wound up dead like William. So many of us felt awful about what they did to you. So many of us wished you'd stayed after what happened. You had such an amazing influence on so many kids. So many people liked you."

"That's not what my eyes saw."

"What people wear on their sleeves and what they have in their hearts are miles apart sometimes."

"True."

"Something else I never told you," her cheeks flowered red. "I had a huge crush on you. Every time I saw you in the halls, the butterflies in my stomach went wild. Over the years, a bunch of us tried to locate you, but we never had any luck. We thought for sure we'd find you on Facebook, but you weren't there either."

"I don't do Facebook. It's shallow and unprincipled. It panders to the conceit in people. Its whole bent is *self*: *look at me, look at what I did, look at what I'm doing, look at what I have, look at what I own, look at what I drive, look at where I live, look at where I've been, look at who I'm with, look at me.* You can *friend* someone or *unfriend* someone. Childish. It makes people more thoughtless and cruel than they already are."

She smiled appreciatively. "I wish Greg was like you—passionate."

"I remember Gregory. Sports fanatic, if memory serves."

"Sports fanatic is right. I wish he paid half as much attention to me as he does to his ballgames."

"I take it the gloss has faded from the table?"

"Something like that. He loves me...he's just not *in love* with me. Not anymore."

"Are you *in love* with him?"

She didn't answer right away. "No. We just have a marriage of convenience now. Don't get me wrong; he's a great provider and a great father. We have two wonderful daughters. We hardly ever fight, and we live in a nice home."

"But he lacks what you need...passion."

"He has passion about things shaped like a ball, but when it comes to me, he's in a coma."

"He wasn't always like that, was he?"

"No. He used to treat me like a queen. That's what hurts so much. But I suppose nobody stays the same, do they?" She shook her head. "I can't believe I'm sharing all this with you."

"I don't mind."

"People always did open up to you. Your wife is one lucky lady."

"I never married."

"That's a crime. Some woman is truly missing out."

"The same could be said of Gregory—he is missing out on an extraordinary wife."

"So many times I wish I hadn't married him. But I did, and I can't unring that bell." She sighed. "You mind if I tell you something personal?"

"Not at all."

"I wish I had chosen you. I wish you and I had gotten together. Is that terrible of me to say?"

"No. But if we had, you wouldn't have your daughters."

She laughed. "My friends used to say you had the most level head of any kid they knew. You've still got that level head. It's nice to see some things don't change."

Our conversation fell silent, and she gazed at me. Then she forced her eyes away.

"I better get going," she said, "or Greg's going to think I got lost. He thinks I called in sick the day they passed out brains."

"Sounds like *he's* the one who called in sick."

She smiled. "It was really good to see you, Owen."

"It was good to see you too, Audrey Ann. Don't give Gregory's words too much weight: he never was the sharpest knife in the drawer."

She hugged me again and kissed my cheek. Then she walked out of the auditorium.

My chest felt strangely heavy. Was it because my own reunion with Moran had been so sad? Or was it because I might have killed Audrey Ann had I gone through with the attack? Or was it because I wished, as Audrey Ann had wished, that the two of us had come together? Maybe it was all three.

It was time to go. It was time to leave Moran and say good-bye to it forever.

I stopped as I was leaving the auditorium and looked back. I thought of William. The idea that he was dead did not gratify me. Rather, I felt for him what I felt for Mr. Wilson: sad. Neither would have had a tragic ending if they hadn't had a tragic beginning. They were monsters by design, not choice.

There was one last place I had to see before I gave the front doors my back: the locker I used as a sophomore. Physical objects are much like photographs: they represent a time in life, a way of mind, a path of the soul, a course of the heart. My locker represented the best and worst of my sixteenth year. Bound to it were my first memories of Shawn and my last memories of Roxanne. After we became friends, Shawn would stop at that locker every morning and say hi and wish me a happy day. Soon afterward, that same locker became a signboard of abhorrence from Roxanne; the same locker in which she once placed gifts of love she later used as a billboard of hate.

The evening had been sad, but not without fruit. By coming to the school, I found that I had been wrong. Audrey Ann had shown me how mistaken I had been about my classmates. I assumed they all had been against me and were unquestioning allies of William. My rush to judgment had come from apocryphal feelings, not actual facts. A man's perception is his reality, and my perception had been wrong. It nearly cost many lives. The malice I had arrived with at Moran would not be accompanying me home. The rage was gone. Even the hurt and malignant anger I felt for Roxanne, so long a part of me, had surrendered. The past was the past, and that's where it would stay.

I saw an analogue clock after I reentered the school: its needles told me I been there slightly over an hour.

My locker was located on the south arm of the school, close to the stairwell.

I turned the last corner and stopped in my steps. Sitting on the floor with her back against my old locker door was a woman. Lying on the shoulders of a slender body was feathery, blond hair. Though the distance appreciable, I knew instantly who it was.

*Roxanne.*

When Audrey Ann told me that William was dead, my breath left me. When I saw Roxanne sitting there, it fled again. My mouth dried, and my legs went weak. The last time I saw her was the summer of 1976. I was just a boy then. After I saw her in the ice cream shop, I left and vowed to remove her from my pocket and pin her to the past. And yet, she always found her way back into my pocket. What would a psychologist say of a man who, for all of his adult life, loved a girl, now a woman, who didn't love him?

Roxanne was appareled in a long, Brandeis-blue dress. If it hadn't been so long ago, I might have thought it was the same dress she wore to Austin's memorial. It was at his memorial that Roxanne, so young and kind, accepted my first kiss.

Even though it was thirty-two years later, Roxanne didn't look much different than when I saw her in the summer of 1976. But then, maybe it was my heart seeing her and not my eyes.

She was sitting with her knees elbowed close to her chest. She looked like a cast-aside child: small, alone, and frightened. She was staring straight ahead, occasionally wiping her eyes. She must have sensed she was the object of attention, for she looked in my direction, just as she had done the first time I saw her when I was a young teenager.

Both of us remained still, as if locked inside a photograph.

Roxanne wetted her lips, then said, *"Owen?"* Joy...disbelief... apprehension...fear were marbled together in her tone.

"Hello, Roxanne," was all I said. Though I had had time to gather many words, those two were the only ones that came to me.

She slowly stood.

Though I made no move, she asked, "Please don't...don't go."

I said nothing.

She carefully walked over to me.

It is said everyone has a double—or at least a near one—somewhere on the Earth. Roxanne had more than one...Susan Olsen and Tina Yothers from television; and Lisa Hartman and Diana Scarwid from films. Whenever I saw them, I was instantly taken back to a time when I was young, a time when Roxanne was my whole life. Like Roxanne, they all had satiny, blond hair, exquisitely feminine faces, and soft, melodic voices. Mark once said Roxanne reminded him of Farrah Fawcett. He was right. Both had windswept hair and radiant smiles. And yet, I never thought the two were in the same class together. To me, Roxanne was rich honey; Farrah Fawcett was guilty chocolate.

But there was one woman who, in my eyes, was Roxanne simply clothed with another name. This woman, a trace younger than Roxanne, possessed a sultry shyness that was both sensual and childlike. She wore her hair short and feathered, which gave her an air of freshness and purity. She gave the public a smile that was sometimes free-spirited, sometimes secretive, sometimes seductive. But she was never afraid to let the world see her heart. She was Princess Diana.

Standing there in the hallway we both walked as teenagers, Roxanne was still a masterpiece. Her hair gleamed, her lips sparkled, and her face glowed. The air about her was fragrant with Opium perfume.

"You look...*incredible*," she said. "You've hardly aged a day."

"I've aged many days. But you are the one that time has been kind to."

"Thank you. That was sweet of you to say."

"It is true."

"How come you're here?"

I didn't know what to say. A lie would be wrong, and the truth would be too painful to share. "It's a very long story."

"You really do look wonderful. But then, you always were a handsome one."

"And you are still a poet's inspiration. I'm sure eyes escort you wherever you go."

She smiled sadly. "Maybe at one time. How have you been?"

"That's a question that would take a pocketful of hours to answer. And you, how have *you* been?"

"That's a question that would take a pocketful of hours to answer," she smiled nervously.

"Yes, I suppose a quick, neat reply would be difficult at our age."

"I read your book," she said almost proudly. "You still word yourself beautifully."

The definition of *overstatement* is to state too strongly, to exaggerate. Shock would not have been an overstatement at Roxanne's words. How could she have known about my book? It had had no press, minimal marketing, and very limited exposure. It had sold, since its release in August of 1993, less than one hundred copies. It was an inconsequential novel written by an inconsequential author living in an inconsequential city.

"How did you find out about it?" I asked her.

"Remember Mark, your friend from here?"

"I do."

"He came across a copy and mailed it to me. Somehow, he got my address. I don't know how; I was unlisted at the time, and it was long before the Internet. He thought I should have it. He told me the book was about me."

My mind jumped from shock to unsettled. Years ago, I told Desiree I didn't want anyone, other than strangers, knowing my feelings. Outsiders, in my mind, were safe; insiders, those who knew me, were not. Knowing they knew what was in my heart and in my mind made me feel vulnerable and exposed. I feared they would use my thoughts and feelings as armament against me.

"Is it about me?" Roxanne asked searchingly.

"Mark was always very perceptive."

She smiled briefly. "Your writing reminded me of John Steinbeck."

I blushed. "Thank you, but John Steinbeck I'm not."

"You still feel uncomfortable taking compliments, don't you?"

"Yes."

"It was one of your most endearing qualities."

She turned her face away and began to cry.

Seeing her heart break broke mine. Apprehensively, I reached out and took her hands and pulled her close to me.

She held me tightly and wept.

I said nothing.

"I'm so sorry for what I did to you, Owen," she said through her tears. "I let you go...*twice*. I can't believe I did that. I can't believe the things I said to you, the things I did. They were so awful and filthy. I'd give my life to take them all back. I should have been there for you. I should have stood by your side, but instead, I let you stand alone. I hurt you more than anyone. After your attack, I ran into Christopher in a stairwell. It was in the stairwell just behind us, in fact. We argued, and I said some horrible things to him too. Awful, awful things. He defended you like a true friend. He told me a couple of things that, had I been a decent human being, I should have seen myself. But because I wasn't decent, I didn't. He said that all the things I did to you would one day come back to me, and when they did, they would haunt me for the rest of my life. He was absolutely right. They haunt me every day. And every night. That's the hardest time of all. That's when the demons come close. They lie down next to me and remind me of all my cruelties, all my faults.

"Christopher told me something else that day. He told me somebody hurt me, somebody close, and you were the one I took it out on. He was right about that too. He was right about everything."

She stepped away from me, wiped her eyes and folded her arms over her chest. "Remember me telling you about Barry, the boy I dated after you and I broke up the first time?"

I nodded.

She cleared her throat. "Turned out, while he was dating me, he was dating another boy."

"How did you discover this?"

She cleared her throat a second time. "One of my girlfriends started dating him after he and I broke up. She went to his house one Friday after school. His mom told her she could just let herself in whenever she came over. His car was there, so she went inside. She went up to his room. He wasn't in it. She heard moaning coming from the bathroom. She thought he was in trouble, so she went in. He wasn't alone. Corry, his best friend, was in there with him. They were...in the shower together. She went over to the toilet, sat and waited for them to finish. They opened the curtain and there she was. Barry and Corry both screamed. She told Barry she wasn't going to leave until he told her why. He did. The guy in the shower was his boyfriend. They'd been seeing each other for a couple of years."

"So why was he with her...or you?"

"He swung both ways, but I think he swung more toward boys. He liked getting in girls' pants, but I think he liked getting in boys' more. Besides, his mom and dad were die-hard, dyed-in-the-wool, die-to-the-end Mormons. He said he had to keep up appearances or he would have been thrown out of the house. So...while he was kissing me, he was also kissing another guy. The same lips I let kiss me had also been on every inch of another boy. Do you know how disgusting I felt? How used? How foolish? How inadequate?"

"Why would you feel inadequate?"

"How would you feel if you were in a relationship with a woman and you found out she'd rather be with another female?"

"Sounds to me like you weren't in a relationship at all. Sounds to me like you were more of a prop than a part of his life. It's been my experience that homosexuality is not a choice. The lifestyle may be, but not the feelings."

"It's kind of you to try to make me feel better about it," she said, trying to smile, "but I don't, and I never will. I never should have gotten involved with him. It was terrible judgment on my part. That judgment hurt you the most. When I saw you and Shawn getting closer, I feared you and he were more than friends. I thought it was Barry all over again. I judged you on what was on the stage, not what was behind it. That's where the truth is. By the time I realized that, you were long gone."

The words of Elsie Clemenson—Ms. Windom's only friend—came back to me: "*There are always two sides to every situation—the side you see and the side you don't.*" She was right.

And once again, so was Larry the custodian: "*We all do what we do for a reason.*"

"I'm so sorry, Roxanne."

"What have *you* got to be sorry for? You didn't do anything."

"I didn't look behind the curtain either. I didn't ask you what was wrong. I only looked at me—my needs and my wants."

"I wouldn't have told you anyway. I was too ashamed. To be the pawn of a straight guy is one thing; to be the pawn of a gay guy is another. Just thinking about it still makes me sick. I mean, one day he's giving his boyfriend oral sex and the next he's kissing me on the lips. How disgusting is that? Why couldn't he have just been honest with me? How could he have used me like that? For the longest time, I feared I had some venereal disease. Eventually, I got over it, and him."

"Did you ever fall in love again?"

She considered her answer. "No. I fell in lust, but not love. I think people too often think they're one and the same. I know I did. I got married when I was twenty-six. His name was Robb. He spelled it with two b's. I didn't love him, but I needed him. I didn't want to be alone, and he was right there. He was killed seven months after we were married. He was hiking with some friends, and he slipped. Fell forty feet. Died in one of his friend's arms. When I got the news, all I felt was guilt. He should have been married to someone else, someone who loved him. If only I had been honest with him, he would have had another life with another woman and wouldn't have been on that mountain that morning. I was no better than Barry. He wasn't honest with me, and I wasn't honest with Robb."

"Death plays mean head games with us, doesn't it? I still feel guilty for Kylie's death, and you still feel guilty for your husband's. It's not *that* people die—it's *how* and *when* they die that beats us up."

"Isn't that the truth," she agreed.

"Do you have any children?"

"No. I put my heart into my career after Robb passed away, and that's where it's been ever since."

"And what career is that?"

"Attorney. I have my own practice. It's small, but it keeps me busy."

"What made you choose that?"

"You and Robb."

"Me and Robb?"

"At first, I wanted to work for the DA, someone who went after those who do harm. But then I realized we *all* do harm. I willingly brought pain into your life and death into Robb's. If I were put on trial for those choices, I'd want someone who would be on my side, someone who would try to understand my reasons for making those choices."

"I think it's a bit much to say you willingly caused Robb's death."

"Do you think it's a bit much to say you caused Kylie's?"

Her edgy comeback surprised me.

"The blond barrister at work," I lauded her. "You return very well."

"So do you. But then you always did. You should have gone into law—you would have been excellent at it. What did you finally go into?"

"Nursing."

She smiled. "Making people feel better—that was always one of your strong suits. One of many."

"Why didn't you remarry?"

"The only man I wanted to marry was out of my life forever. His name was Owen."

"The Owen you knew is not the same one you see standing here. He doesn't talk the way he used to; he doesn't care the way he used to, and he doesn't feel the way he used to. His heart moved out of the house a long time ago."

She touched my cheek. "Does his heart still love me?"

I took hold of her hand and kissed it. "It never stopped."

A smile blossomed on her face. "Then the Owen of yesterday isn't completely gone, is he? One of the best parts is still here. Although I always loved the way he talked. It was like listening to Charles Dickens."

"Charlie Brown perhaps, but not Charles Dickens."

She laughed. "Remember the song 'You Needed Me' by Anne Murray? They played it back in our day. *Back in our day*. Sounds funny to say that. I guess that makes us the older generation now."

"Older, but not gone. And, yes, I do remember it."

"It was my song to you. Over the years, I played it over and over. I never got tired of listening to it."

"I, too, had a song," I let out. "I wore down many a needle listening to it. God bless the man who invented CDs."

"What song was it?"

"'Even Now.' One of Barry Manilow's best. Many a night I played that song in the dark, with nothing but you on my mind."

"I never should have left you," she said.

"Maybe there was a purpose in us breaking up. If our split caused bad things, like Robb and Kylie's death, then maybe the reverse could be true. Maybe we accomplished some good things by not remaining a couple."

"Maybe. Maybe we wouldn't have lasted as a couple if we stayed together when we were young. Maybe we needed to be apart then so we could be together now."

"Lots of maybes. But there usually are at our age."

"Yeah. You know, there's something you and I never did when we were together."

"What is that?"

"Made love."

I touched her hair. "Perhaps there's something we can do about that."

She canted her head alluringly, gave me a whisper of a smile and pressed herself against me. Lips that I never expected to feel again were touching mine once more. A fire I thought had gone out long ago came surging back.